SHADOWS

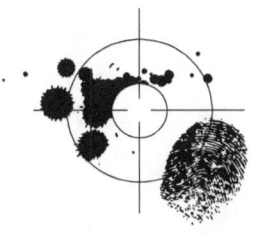

R. A. PUNDT

SHADOWS

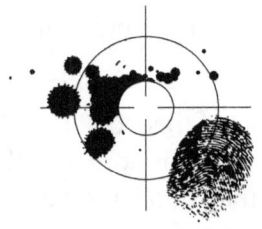

A NOVEL BASED UPON ACTUAL EVENTS

R. A. PUNDT

PRESENTED BY:
THREE TREE RIDGE PUBLISHING LIMITED
and
Fox and Hounds Publishing & Distribution
Cedar Rapids, Iowa

SHADOWS

Fox and Hounds Publishing & Distribution

Copyright © 2013 R. A. Pundt

Three Tree Ridge Publishing Limited

Library of Congress Cataloging-in-Publication Data is available.

Copyright Registration Number: TXu 1-847-231

ISBN-13:978-0989249300
ISBN-10: 0989249301
LCCN:2013944799
ISBN (electronic version): 978-0-9892493-0-0
ISBN (paperback version): 978-0-9892493-1-7
ISBN (hardcover version): 978-0-9892493-2-4

Cover design by Clayton Chambers
www.claytonchambers.com

Printed in the United States of America
Distributed by Fox and Hounds Distribution Co.

DEDICATION:

In the first instance, I wish to dedicate this work to my wife, Joyce, and to my family, Vince, Jennifer and Heather, for the grace, dignity, and stability that they have demonstrated through their unceasing support and understanding during what has been an unbelievable and life-altering experience.

Secondly, to those innocent individuals who have been wrongfully indicted by overzealous prosecutors who have lost their moral compass and who have ignored their oath of office as they take pride in indicting and attempting to convict the innocent.

OF SPECIAL THANKS:

Let me express my deep appreciation and thanks for the excellent and detailed editing that was done on this novel by Joyce Pundt, Marty Berry, and Bette Tropek Miller. I also wish to acknowledge and thank my friend, Joseph Trento, for his good counsel and review of this novel. Additionally, there are so many individuals to whom I owe debts of gratitude, I have made special mention of them in the Acknowledgments section directly following the novel's Epilogue.

CONTENTS

INTRODUCTION

May 4, 2013

When I first spoke with Richard Pundt, it was because he had contacted me regarding one of the books I had written about the United States intelligence community. During our conversation, Mr. Pundt shared the fact that he was working on a novel. I knew after our first discussion that this sober and methodical man had a personal story that was extraordinary. What happened to him was the metaphor to explain how the Republican Party marginalized itself by using its power to manipulate and to ruin the lives of those in the party who did not go along with their new extreme vision of America.

Richard Pundt had been a moderate Midwest party supporter and activist for most of his life. He is what most of us thought of as a "middle-of-the-road" Republican: A family man who was reliable, calm, fair and decent. Like most moderate Republicans, Mr. Pundt noticed the change in the party. But he had no idea that the special interests the new GOP represented would toss aside the Constitution to pursue its own ends. What happened to Mr. Pundt stemmed from his ignoring a political request from a Bush White House loyalist. What he had no way of knowing was how far his party would go to punish someone who did not closely tow and accept the new GOP line. He never thought his party would place operatives throughout the government – particularly in the Justice Department – who used these positions to destroy the lives of those who would not go along.

After Mr. Pundt was arrested on trumped-up charges that would eventually be completely discredited, he began digging. What he found is fictionalized in **Shadows**. What Mr. Pundt discovered is that the new conservatism is not about ideology but about corporate control of a political party for its own financial interests. The temptation for money interests to try and influence and manipulate our democracy has never been subtle. In 1934 the giants of Wall Street hatched a conspiracy that would have destroyed our country had it not been for a friendship between a Quaker General and a patrician President. Though Franklin Roosevelt had vanquished a plot that included elements of the US Army, these forces were always out there. President Eisenhower had personally worried about these same forces in the Republican Party and was uncomfortable because these were the supporters of his own Vice-President.

Under President Nixon, the extreme elements were used but kept under Nixon's own control. Nixon's enemies list, the use of the CIA, FBI and IRS for political purposes was a preview of how big money supporters wanted their party to play hardball but on a larger scale. I personally ran into it as a young reporter for Jack Anderson as I learned how organizations like Liberty Lobby worked secretly with right-wing Republicans in Congress. As big money played a larger and larger role, the Republican Party political apparatus grew - especially in the oil, mining, and gas industries. During Ronald Reagan's Presidency, powerful Republican televangelists took over mining concessions in the Congo and other African nations under the guise of missionary work as the Reagan Administration ran a religious war in Angola. By the time George W. Bush was elected, The GOP was controlled by the religious right, big money interests, and other factions. The GOP had become a collection of racial, religious and ethnic resentments - often at complete odds with each other - that could be shaped and used by a coalition of big money corporate interests. But the biggest influence on the party was the Wall Street banks. They had succeeded in privatizing local and community hospitals and had made huge profits by getting governments from Greece to Orange County to float bond issues that would drive taxpayers into poverty.

Shadows is the story of how Lincoln's Grand Old Party was turned upside down: how Nixon's Environmental Protection Agency became the GOP enemy and how race-baiting individuals and groups acquired a voice in The Party. The goal was to feed the hate and anger by distracting the masses while the greatest transfer of wealth in history – from the American middle class to Wall Street - took place. **Shadows** is a book of big secrets and the means that are used to keep those secrets.

Joseph Trento
Washington, D.C.

Books by Joseph Trento that relate to the
U.S. intelligence community include:
Prelude to Terror, 2005 First Carroll & Graft.
The Secret History of the CIA, 2001 Prima Publishing.

PROLOGUE
S. A. COFFEE

It was back!

For days A.T. had been bothered by the recurrence of the same black SUV that kept lingering in the area of his house. From a vantage point at a window in the upper level of his home, he watched as the large vehicle slowly proceeded down the street. While it moved, he noticed a discoloration on the front tire that gave the impression that the wheel was like a cat's paw deliberately stepping forward as if the car were following and assessing some unseen prey. At the oddest times, the car would appear and then disappear into the shadows of the large leafless, snow-laden trees that lined the street.

Before he left for work on this particular morning, A.T. noticed that the same vehicle was again creeping by his home. However, when he left his house, the vehicle was nowhere in sight, so he decided to put it out of his mind. After all, Summit was a historic street with A.T.'s home only a short distance from a number of famous residences, including those of writer, F. Scott Fitzgerald; James Hill, the railroad tycoon of the Great Northern Railway; and Nobel Peace Prize recipient, Frank B. Kellogg, who had been a former United States Senator and Secretary of State. There were always tourists, and the time of year didn't matter.

With the week winding down, this particular Thursday had not been a very good one, and the car incident was just one of many annoyances. Once at the office, there was the unnervingly rapid pace of phone calls, video conferences, and appointments, along with a late-in-the-day unscheduled court appearance called by an overworked and frazzled judge.

Upon leaving the courtroom, A.T. noticed several prisoners in orange jump suits rounding the upcoming corner as they were being escorted by two deputies. For a moment he felt something was wrong as he thought he observed a black shadow floating behind the prisoners and the deputies as they turned the corner and approached him. The shadow reminded him of what had often been portrayed as the "Grim Reaper." He stopped in his tracks but soon realized that what had appeared as a black shadow was nothing more than a bailiff carrying high over his head a black judge's robe that hung loosely from a wooden hanger. No doubt one of the judges had either forgotten a robe or the bailiff was returning it from the laundry.

After he returned to his office, he decided to access his computer one final time. When he did, he noticed another late email communication from an old "political friend" who had been in the George W. Bush White House from day one. Without a doubt, she was making it an unforgettable day since this was the last of several emails she had sent within days of each other on a subject that made A.T. very uneasy. He was purposely trying to avoid her. Noticing the last email from her, he thought: *That's it! I've tried and now I've seen enough of the law practice for today. I'm out of here.*

Since he was one of the partners in a law firm he had helped establish nearly twenty years ago, he had attained a point in his career where he felt he could call it a day whenever he determined it was time to leave. In addition to having been a practicing lawyer in the community for many years, A.T. had been active in local service clubs, school programs, sports clubs, and non-profit organizations, as well as being quite active in the Republican Party in the state of Minnesota, where he had lived most of his life.

His only real absence from the state occurred when he served as a Special Agent with the FBI. After leaving the Bureau, he returned to the Twin City area and worked several years as a local prosecutor. It was while in the office of the local prosecutor, that he had been offered a position with a well-established law firm in St. Paul. The offer came from an older attorney who had become a bit of a mentor after the two of them had met at a meeting of the "Society of Former Special Agents of the Federal Bureau of Investigation." After several years with his mentor's firm and upon encountering several former law school classmates, he and the former classmates decided to start their own law firm.

Although the hectic schedule of the day had irritated him, it was the receipt of the last email from the former political friend at the White House that caused him grief. It had been years since he had last been active in the political arena, and he was happy that he had gotten out of the political fray. His old political friend, Julian Tilson-Gould, had remained active in Republican politics and had been a strong activist for both George H. W. Bush and George W. Bush. A.T. had worked in the campaigns of the first President Bush but called off any further personal involvement when W. decided to run for president. From that point forward the relationship between A.T. and Julian, which had been a bit of a strained political accommodation, chilled even further as he tried to avoid her at every opportunity.

For months Julian had been calling and emailing A.T. She wanted to see if it was possible for him to join the "President's National Businessman's Forum" for small businesses. At that time, he was also receiving calls from former Congressman Tom Delay, who was also trying to get A.T. to join the "President's National Businessman's Forum." Although A.T. had called and told the congressman, who later had gotten into serious trouble, that he was not interested in joining the "Forum," he totally ignored Julian's calls and emails. He now realized that was probably a mistake.

Since he had decided to leave the office for home, he thought that once there he would change clothes and recheck his emails from an old computer he kept in his study. Perhaps in the more relaxed atmosphere of his home, he could bring himself to finally answer Julian's persistent emails. As he neared his home, he again observed the large black Suburban he had seen earlier in the day and for days before. This time he noticed that the car was sitting several houses away from his. He shrugged the matter off and proceeded home.

Due to the advances in technology, the old laptop was limited in its function to some online research that he did using his personal Wi-Fi. He reread Julian's email and carefully composed a response to her. He decided it was best to look it over. The people at the other end were politically powerful and did not take refusal lightly. He wanted to be sure the response was worded appropriately. Once finished, he noticed a dark shadow pass by the window. He hit "save," minimized the email, and went to the window.

In front of his house, he again observed the large black Suburban. Since his neighbors were in the process of selling their house, he decided to go out to tell the occupants of the Suburban that it was the house next door that was for sale. When he opened the door, he noticed both men had exited the vehicle and were approaching him.

He called out to tell them it was the house next door that was for sale. They both turned in the direction that he had pointed; then they turned back as they approached the front door. While walking out from under the late afternoon wintery shadow of a large oak tree, one of the men reached into the coat pocket of his dark blue suit. He verbally identified himself and, in turn, asked A.T., "Are you Albert Thomas Van Doren?"

"Yes, that's my name. I live here. What can I do for you gentlemen?"

"We have a warrant for your arrest," said the individual presenting FBI credentials that identified the holder as Special Agent Mark Coffee, who was of medium build and stood a few inches short of six feet tall.

"You can't be serious! What's this all about?"

"You've been identified as a defendant in a federal case," stated the second agent as he presented his credentials that identified him as Special Agent William Stern, a burly man who stood at least two inches above A.T., who himself was just over six feet in height.

"That's not possible. You have the wrong person," said A.T as his legs nearly gave out beneath him. "I haven't done anything wrong. This can't be happening."

"We'll need to take you into custody," asserted S. A. Coffee.

"What?" asked A.T.

"That's right, and we will need to cuff you," ordered S. A. Coffee while reaching for a pair of handcuffs.

"This can't be. I've never committed anything close to a criminal act in my life. I have had a few speeding tickets, but that's it."

"This doesn't relate to a minor matter like that. Sorry, but you need to hold out your hands. I will need to cuff both hands in front of you."

"Wait! I have a computer running in the house, and I need to shut it off," said A.T. who turned and went back to his house. The two agents followed him.

When the newly accused A.T. turned off the computer with his hands shaking, he noticed that his dog, Remington, had taken up a position in the elevated living room above and behind the agents. He knew the dog was silently preparing to attack, as the dog sensed something unusual. The dog, that weighed as much as a small man, would always get very silent and position himself behind his prey with his head lowered when he was about to pounce. The dog was fully capable. A.T. raised his hand for the dog to halt, and the dog complied. The two agents did not see the dog and apparently missed the hand gesture. Fortunately, the dog had responded to the silent command. A.T. was fearful that if the agents had seen the dog and had turned, an incident would have resulted with either the agents being attacked or Remington being shot or both. At that point, he led the agents back to the outside of the house and locked the door behind him.

"We'll need to cuff you and pat you down for any weapons," repeated S.A. Stern taking the cuffs from S.A. Coffee. At that moment S.A. Coffee began to pat down A.T. while S.A. Stern placed the first cuff on the accused.

"Is this really necessary?" asked A.T. "To begin with, this has to be a mistake. Somebody has apparently gotten me mixed up with someone else. The two of you probably know I am a former agent myself, and I'm not going to cause any trouble. Of course, I would like to see the warrant."

"You will need to be cuffed. If you are a former agent, you should know that it's policy," commented S.A. Stern.

"He is a former agent. I already know that, but we need to proceed," said S.A. Coffee as he clipped the second cuff on A.T.'s other wrist.

"Look, you guys," urged A.T., "please don't do this in front of the neighbors. If you know I'm a former agent, you know I will cooperate in whatever way possible. But where is the warrant?"

"When we get into the car, we'll show it to you. So please duck your head…" ordered S.A. Stern while opening the door and pushing A.T.'s head down to miss the top of the car. The door was closed with the accused in the back directly behind the front passenger seat. At this point he still had absolutely no idea what the charges were or what was happening. With S.A. Coffee sitting in front of A.T., S.A. Stern got behind the wheel. He started the car, and the three of them drove off with A.T. sitting uncomfortably in the back with his hands cuffed. He strained to turn only to see his home disappear. He had no idea when he would see his family or home again.

Once his home disappeared behind them, A.T. tried to make himself comfortable and asked, "What the hell is this all about? I deserve answers, and so far all I have seen is a glimpse of a document that you have kept in your hands. Presumably, that's the arrest warrant for God knows what-"

"It is the warrant for your arrest," said S.A. Coffee holding it up so A.T. could see his own name on the sheet. "All we know is that you have been accused of several counts of fraud and conspiracy."

"That's absurd! In what regard?" asked the accused.

"You will get a copy of the charges and the indictment at your arraignment. For now all I know is basically what I've told you. The arrest warrant doesn't have much on it in terms of details. Apparently, you and others were involved in some sort of investment program."

"I've never been involved in any type of investment program in my life. There has to be a mistake of some kind. May I see the document?"

"No," answered S.A. Coffee. "I'm not permitted to give you this document. It's the arrest warrant, with some other paperwork that is for us. It just mentions the charges and does not go into detail."

"I would like to know something about the charges. You mention an investment of some sort, yet you have me completely baffled. I have never been involved in any investment program of any kind. Ever!" pleaded A.T.

"According to this warrant you have," responded the agent. "Do you know George Lipke?"

"No, I've never heard of him."

"Well, he is apparently one of your partners in the alleged enterprise," commented the agent. "What about Pat Merrick?"

"I don't know him either. Who's he supposed to be?"

"One of your co-conspirators..."

"Well, I don't know him, I've never heard of anyone by that name."

"What about W. J. Perry? Do you know him?"

"No, I don't know him either."

"Another name on here is Darrel Simpson. What about him? Surely you know him."

"No, I don't know him either. I don't know any of these people. Once again, what is this all about?"

"It's about an investment group of some sort. What about Lester Gee? Surely you've heard of him," prompted the agent.

"No. I have never heard of him either. This is ridiculous."

"What about Albert Cherry?" laughed S.A. Coffee. "I suppose you don't know him either."

"Well, I don't know him, but I have heard of his name. I believe his name was on some documents I was to review for a client. I told the client that it would not be advisable to proceed, and the client took my advice and refused to follow through with the matter," stated the accused.

"Now we're getting somewhere," said S.A. Coffee. "There's one final name. What about Ralph Nester? Do you know him?"

"I do know him. He works for the Federal Reserve, if I'm not mistaken," said the accused.

"I doubt he's with the Federal Reserve," said Agent Coffee. "In any event, all of the people whom I have mentioned, along with you, are accused of having been involved in a type of investment scheme of some sort. That's about all I can tell you from the information I have. You will simply have to wait until your arraignment to learn more."

"Where are we going? Is it okay for me to make a call?" asked. A.T.

"We've been instructed to take you to one of the county jail facilities that processes our suspects until we can get them in front of the magistrate for arraignment. Based on the recommendations of Milford Dunreath, our newly appointed United States Attorney here in the Twin Cities, Judge Rice instructed us to pick you up and arrest you today. Since it is after six in the evening, you will need to stay overnight at the jail facility until we come to pick you up in the morning," said Agent Coffee.

"You're kidding! You're telling me that I will need to stay overnight in a county jail until morning?" asked the accused realizing he would be spending the night in the very jail that housed the prisoners that he observed earlier in the day while leaving the judge's chambers.

"That's correct since the judge and the local United States Attorney thought that it would be a good idea for you to spend the night. We could have picked you up earlier or even tomorrow, but the judge didn't want to arraign you today and wanted you in custody."

"That's insane! What possible objective could that serve? This is totally out of hand. Do you mind if I make a call?"

"Who do you intend to call?"

"To start with, I need to call my family. None of them were home. Then I would like to call one of my attorney friends, if I may."

"Sure. Do you still have your cell phone?"

"Yes."

"May I see it?" At this point A.T. strained to retrieve his cell phone from his front pocket and hand it to the agent. The agent examined the phone and looked to the accused. He said, "That's a nice iPhone. Give me the number for your family, and I will dial it for you.....I see that you need a code to access it. First, give me the access code. Then give me the number, and I'll call it for you."

The process of attempting to reach family members was frustrating since no one was available, and A.T. did not want to leave the type of message that would alarm them. Finally, he reached his son, Adam, also an attorney and explained the situation. A.T. then called his wife, Jacci, who couldn't believe what he was telling her. He told her that he had contacted Adam, but she would need to call their two daughters, Rachael and Renée, in order to fully advise them. Finally, A.T. was able to reach one of his associates, and asked if the attorney would try to reach a magistrate for a possible release. Upon learning that the magistrate could not be reached, it was apparent A.T. would be spending at least the upcoming night in jail.

Although the ordeal he was experiencing was difficult to fathom and worse to bear, A.T. knew that the news was going to have a devastating effect upon his wife and family. Not only had Jacci been his best friend and confidante in all matters of life, but she had been his most trusted sounding board for every significant event in his life. Although she was a very strong person, he knew this unexpected event was going to be nearly as hard for her as it was for him. The two of them had prided themselves on the fact they had always walked straight and narrow paths in their efforts to be model citizens and good examples for their children. Jacci had the good fortune of always maintaining a youthful appearance of a person half her age. When she was younger, she wore her blonde hair at shoulder length, but now and as her hair had darkened, she sported a shorter cut which she explained felt more comfortable when she wore her riding helmet while engaged in her favorite hobby of dressage and stadium jumping. At a very trim 5' 6" in height, she looked as athletic as she was.

It was impossible for A.T. to explain to Jacci what was happening to him since he was unaware of whatever it was that had led to his arrest. Trying to tell her what had transpired was a heartbreaking task. He searched his mind in order to try to determine what possible event from his past could have created the situation in which he now found himself. He could not think of anything out of his past that could have generated the type of circumstances he now faced.

Then he imagined how difficult his dilemma would be for his children. He and Jacci had three children. Their oldest, Adam, like A.T., was an inventor who had developed several high tech items being marketed by a company that he, A.T., and several others had founded. The company had struggled to find its niche in the marketplace, but it was finally starting to experience success. Adam devoted most of his time to the company instead of the practice of law since the company needed his day-to-day guidance. A.T. and Jacci's second child, Rachael, also worked for the company where she wore various hats that included research for updating the websites the company maintained. Their youngest child, Renée, had just finished her master's degree in an ancient history/archeology program. Although she had done some design work for the company, she was now working as a research assistant.

For the sake of Jacci and the children, A.T. needed to get to the bottom of this unfolding chain of events. Various pleas were made to the two agents as A.T. continued to ask for more information about the allegations against him. He was told little more, other than the fact that an undercover task force operating in Southern California had been set up by the Department of Justice and the FBI in order to locate individuals who were believed to have been involved in a form of a "trade or investment program." A.T. searched his memory and explained to the agents that he had filed a complaint with the FBI on behalf of a client who had been defrauded out of funds the client had paid out to a number of venture funds.

Continuing, he said that the FBI had determined that he and the client had been identified as victims. In fact, he had written communications from the FBI, and the Department of Justice that referred to A.T. and the company as victims. The FBI and the DOJ had even recovered part of the funds A.T. and the company had paid to the people who were the subject of the official complaint he had filed. He also noted that although he had been invited to meetings in California at least five different times on behalf of his client, all invitations but one had been turned down. That was all he could recall.

From what A.T. could determine, the single meeting in California was the apparent connection to the task force. He explained that nothing had come of the meeting, and he had to wait most of the time in a coffee shop while others participated in the meetings that seemed to be ongoing. While A.T. was attempting to guess whether that experience was relevant to the charges against him, S.A. Coffee stated that he felt it necessary to advise the accused of his rights. A.T.'s pleas fell on deaf ears. There was no point in saying anything more.

Upon delivery to a county jail, he was processed through the booking procedures, fingerprinted, photographed, and ultimately taken to a holding cell. Before going to the holding cell, A.T. was told to place all of the personal property that he had on his person into a tray that he was handed at the processing counter. After he complied, the officer behind the counter started to inventory the items; he looked at A.T. and asked several questions.

"Is this your full name, 'Albert Thomas Van Doren?'"

"It is," answered A.T.

"This license states that you are 72.5 inches tall with brown hair and blue eyes. Look at me. Yeah, that looks right. I see you have a 'B' restriction. That means you have a need for corrective lenses. Are you wearing contacts?"

"Yes, I am."

"Do you need to remove them?"

"No, they're extended wear soft bifocal lenses. I can wear them for fairly long periods, if necessary."

"Let's see…in addition to your license, you've got $102.43 in change, three credit cards, a family picture, some membership cards and a couple of blank checks in your wallet. You also have a ring of keys, a key for a car with automatic lock system, a USB flash drive and a pair of sunglasses along with this iPhone. Is that everything from your pockets?"

"It is."

"Now, let me ask you if you have any medication needs and if you have taken any prescription or non-prescription drugs of any kind within the last 24 hours?"

"No…why…is there a requirement for you to search me?" asked A.T.

"Not at this time," laughed the processing clerk. "You are going to be placed in a holding cell with some of our other less-than-notorious criminals. So, your body will not be searched, and you will not need to change into one of our 'flashy' inmate uniforms. However, I will need to have you remove your shoes. I will look them over and then you can put them back on."

A.T. complied and asked, "Do I get a phone call?"

The processing officer looked at Special Agent Coffee and asked, "Did he get to make a call?"

"We let him make several calls. He's had more than his quota," answered S.A. Coffee, who then looked at A.T. and said, "We'll try to be back for you before 9:30 in the morning, so we can transport you to the U.S. Magistrate for your arraignment. We'll see you then; have a good night." With that Agent Coffee turned, walked to the door, and left when the door buzzer sounded.

A.T.'s shoes were returned to him, but his personal property was taken and placed in an envelope. The processing clerk then handed A.T. a copy of the signed receipt for his possessions. Another deputy escorted A.T. to a holding cell that had four other individuals waiting. They were watching a program on a television set that was mounted on the far wall, opposite a restroom. The deputy unlocked the cell door and motioned for A.T. to enter.

A.T. decided to keep to himself. He was asked why he was incarcerated, and he honestly responded that he had no idea. The other prisoners laughed and volunteered the reasons for their incarceration. Two of the prisoners had been arrested for domestic abuse; one had been arrested for a controlled substance violation; the last prisoner was being held on a warrant for his failure to appear in regard to a "no contact" order.

Although several of the other prisoners tried to get A.T. to talk, he was not in the mood for discussion. He sat by himself with his eyes closed, except to occasionally watch the news on the T.V. monitor on the far wall. To add to his discomfort, he had to listen to a brief television news broadcast pertaining to his being arrested on a federal warrant. During the broadcast, the anchorman reported that A.T., an attorney, former prosecutor, and former FBI agent, had been arrested on federal charges that involved an investment scheme and a conspiracy to defraud others. The other prisoners heard the broadcast and turned to look at him, while he shook his head.

He thought to himself: *Where do I begin? What have I done to deserve this? I've never been involved in anything that could possibly be considered a crime. For my entire life I have been on the law enforcement side of the aisle. After serving as an FBI Agent and as a prosecutor for a combined seven years, I worked in the private practice of law on civil matters only. My record with both the FBI and the prosecutor's office were not just good but outstanding; at least that's what I thought, and I believe that's what my records show. The only issue I can remember from my days at the Bureau involved an instance where another young agent and I referred a situation that involved an older agent to the Special Agent in Charge of the Field Office where I was assigned at the time. The older agent, about whom we complained, had been fabricating security files in order to have enough of a case load to open a Special Desk as a Supervisor. Sometime later and after I had left the Bureau, I was told that a secretary in that office had tried to set up both the other young agent and me. But that ended with her being prosecuted when a search warrant of her home revealed that she had been removing and hiding files from the Field Office at her house in order to try to frame the other young agent and me.*

Although that incident from so long ago could have been behind this chain of events, it seemed doubtful that the older agent and secretary would even be alive, and if they were, it seemed a long time to carry a grudge.

A.T.'s thought process continued with his racking his brain to determine what was behind his situation. Again he drifted off into the recesses of his mind and thought to himself: *As a prosecutor I tried many people who were found guilty of serious crimes including murder, rape, extortion, burglary, delivery of controlled substances and an array of other felonies. It doesn't seem likely that those felons would be in a position to do this to me.*

In addition to his professional career as a former agent, prosecutor, and attorney, he thought about his work with the corporate clients that he had represented: *For the past few years I have been actively involved in a high tech company where I have invested heavily as a principal. All of the company activities have been well above board. In fact I have performed investigative due diligence for the company on many occasions. Since most of the company's clients were from the legal community, including court systems, lawyers, experts, court reporters, law schools and government entities, it wasn't likely that any of those company customers would be involved in something like this. They had to be ruled out.*

Then A.T. remembered: *Wait, there were those individuals who were able to extract about half a million dollars from the company that I had helped start. Those individuals misrepresented themselves to the company and the due diligence failed to disclose their false intentions. But in that case, they were the ones who defrauded the company by creating false documents which included a multitude* *of letters that indicated that they were working with the Federal Reserve. Plus, I had filed an official complaint with one FBI Field Office to report the fact that the main individual and his company were receiving funds under false pretenses. Although the company received a judgment against those parties, the case never worked out since the individuals who had received the $450,000, and who the company sued, ended up filing for bankruptcy. They were granted a discharge, despite a claim against them for fraud. Perhaps those people were upset enough to make a false claim against me.* Then he also remembered that those individuals were referred to another party who claimed to also be working through the Federal Reserve.

What was really troubling was the fact that I had called the Federal Reserve several times to try to verify a connection between the individuals in question and the FED. Unfortunately, I constantly got the runaround and no one at the FED would either confirm or deny any relationship between the FED and the individuals who received funds from A.T.'s client. Perhaps they were the ones behind this since one of the individuals in the indictment was a party who claimed to be working for a FED Trader who was supposedly under credentials with the FED. I remembered asking for credentials and warning others to do so as well.

At this point there was another television broadcast about him on the local news that came across the monitor on the far wall. As the broadcast ended, one of the other individuals in the holding cell said, "Hey man. Why don't you tell us what you did? We don't often see lawyers in here or former FBI agents. You must have really pissed off somebody. I'll bet your story is a good one. Why don't you tell us? We're not going anywhere."

"Frankly," said A.T. "I have absolutely no idea why this is happening. While I've been sitting here, I have been trying to figure it out."

"Come on, man," urged the young prisoner who had been arrested for violating a 'no contact' order. "We would really be interested in your story."

"I don't have a story to tell, or at least I don't know what to say," answered A.T. "I've been trying to think about what type of event it was that could have brought this about, and I can't recall what it might be."

"A loss of memory is a good ploy," said the older and disheveled prisoner who looked as though he had been far too long engaged in some form of drug habit. "I think I'm going to try that next time and see if it works as a defense. If I remember correctly, it worked for Reagan in the Iran-Contra affair. I don't know why my attorney hasn't thought of using it. He's pretty good at coming up with new defenses for me."

"The T.V. guy said you're an attorney. Is that right?" asked the more vocal of the prisoners who was incarcerated for domestic abuse. "Tell me this…if I didn't hit anyone, and, in fact, if it was my mother-in-law who did the pushing, shouldn't the charges against me be dismissed?"

"That's something you will need to discuss with your attorney," answered A.T. "I really haven't been involved in the criminal defense practice of law, but if you didn't engage in any physical contact yourself, then it would seem to me that you would have a pretty good defense."

"Naw, he's guilty, man," inserted the youngest prisoner. "He's been in here before, and he's probably going to get the book." The youngest prisoner then looked at the prisoner who had asked the question and said, "You're going to get some time, man. Your wife's old lady knows the sheriff, and she's got a real problem with you. You weren't supposed to be at her house anyhow from what I hear."

"You're full of it, Howie," said the prisoner who had asked A.T. about his situation. "When we're out of here, you and I are going to have a talk."

"Why not now?" baited Howie.

"Because of the camera and the guy behind the desk over there," answered the prisoner who presented the question to A.T.

"Say, Mr. Lawyer man," interrupted the last prisoner who had remained quiet throughout the previous discussion and who seemed to have been sleeping with his head against the wall. "I'm psychic, you know."

The other prisoners all laughed, but he disregarded their laughter and continued saying, "I had a vision, and you're here because you ticked off someone. You probably said something you shouldn't have, or did something to someone powerful. That's what I'm getting from the thoughts coming to me. You have got a real problem, and the people who are mad at you have some real power. You're in trouble way over your head."

"I didn't piss off anyone," insisted A.T. "Now if you don't mind, please let me rest a bit."

What was said could have been true, but it seemed so unlikely. A.T. kept wondering over and over if his dilemma could have had something to do with his refusal to be a part of the "Business Forum." It was an uncomfortable thought, but whatever the case, he resolved to use the limits of his investigative abilities, and contacts to find out whom and what were behind this horrible and misplaced set of events. It was a long and uncomfortable night. Sitting in a jail cell with a number of admitted criminals was never something that A.T. envisioned as a part of his life.

"Obviously, he doesn't want to talk. So why don't you just leave him alone," insisted the young prisoner named Howie.

SHADOWS

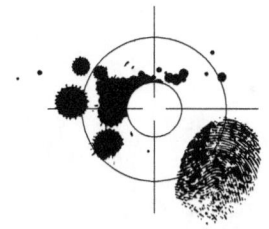

A NOVEL BASED UPON ACTUAL EVENTS

R. A. PUNDT

CHAPTER 1
FOUR YEARS LATER

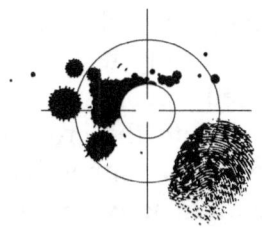

What a nightmare! None of that was real; was it? Wake up! It happened.

It now seemed as though a lifetime rather than four years had passed since A.T. had been arrested on charges for a crime he did not commit. As he now often thought: *I've learned the hard way that there is no such thing as the 'presumption of innocence.'* In the process of attempting to prove his innocence, he had forsaken much of what he had spent a lifetime accomplishing. His reputation had suffered greatly. His law practice had nearly evaporated with some clients departing for other law firms and others minimizing the use of his services. The relationship with his wife and family was not the same. How could it be?

The arrest, the incarceration, and his connection with the American system of justice overshadowed every bit of his new lifetime activities. Nothing was the same and nothing would ever be as it once was. Nearly every day during a long four years, A.T. found himself engaged in a daily ritual of pacing the floor and thinking through the entire scenario of events. He organized everything into notebooks and would review and rewrite or supplement the contents on a weekly basis. The world around him no longer seemed to be the free and open place he had enjoyed up to the point of the arrest. He felt confined, and in his mind he seemed restricted to the events that still puzzled him greatly.

For two out of the last four years, A.T. found himself preoccupied with the task of clearing his name and attempting to get to the bottom of what was behind the wrongful charges against him. He had no recourse other than to turn around the investigation, and, in the process, he found it necessary to investigate what the FBI and the DOJ had been doing with the task force that they had set up. He did know how to investigate.

What he was finding shocked him. Soon after he commenced his counter-investigation, he found case after case where his old employer, the FBI, and the Department of Justice deliberately hid exculpatory evidence; intimidated witnesses; purposely targeted innocent individuals; engaged in suborning perjury by attempting to force certain people to falsely testify against others; falsified records; illegally accessed records; and attempted to target individuals who had come into the cross hairs of people within those agencies who seemed to either have their own political agendas or close ties to certain active politicians.

Through his investigation, he learned that several federal district court judges had dismissed numerous cases because of the misconduct of the DOJ and the FBI. Government attorneys were fired or asked to leave the DOJ, and FBI agents who were found to go beyond their oath of office had been fired and prosecuted, including the agent who headed the task force that wrongfully implicated and indicted A.T. He found from his investigation that certain individuals at the DOJ and in the FBI developed the philosophy that they could do anything to anyone: all without consequence to themselves.

He realized that his fear of being under constant surveillance was based on a political reality. Reflecting on the past four years, what came to mind were some of the literary works of post-World War II that described the atrocities of Nazi Germany and the removal of people from their homes without justification or purpose. No doubt those accounts were far worse than what had happened to him, but his experience had been bad enough. The reality of what he had experienced over the past few years was that of being accused without basis or reason. Those feelings prompted him to believe that he had become an unwitting participant in the events of an imagined time. Here, he had been placed onto an unfolding "Kafkian" stage, coupled with the actions of people who left the same indelible mark as was presented in *'Der Process,'* the unfinished and well-known novel, *The Trial*.

What A.T. had been through diminished the enthusiasm he had always carried as he went from one life challenge to another. Before his arrest, he had been able to enjoy tackling any and every new hurdle that came his way. He believed that he had the fortitude to rise to each occasion no matter how difficult or problematic. Now, his former optimism had been replaced with a compelling need to focus on a single and begrudging task. It was that compulsion that drove him now. He was dedicated to finding out the who, why, and what it was that caused the negative changes in him. He didn't want to be this way, but something darker kept forcing the issue.

These were the sorts of things that happened to other people, and when A.T. had previously heard such stories before his experience, he thought they were made up fantasies. Now he knew better. Never in a million years would something like this have been expected in America. But to his shock and out of the blue, he became "the accused." It was apparent that what had happened to him could happen to anyone no matter how careful he was and no matter what his background was. He now believed that if "they" want you, "they'll" try to get you. Innocence had nothing to do with the unrestrained abuse of the criminal process. The judicial system, if used as a political tool, was dangerous in the hands of people who wanted to flaunt their authority and did so.

* *

Reflecting back upon that terrible time, it was troubling to recall the events that followed his arrest and incarceration of four years ago. He remembered that he ended up waiting until midmorning before the two FBI agents came to retrieve him from the jail cell where he had spent the night. After a long drive, he was taken to the U.S. Marshall's office where he again went through a complete booking process. He was then placed in leg irons, handcuffs that were attached to the leg irons, ordered into a van, and taken to the courthouse for the arraignment. It was the same courthouse where A.T. had handled cases for clients on numerous occasions.

The humiliation of walking to the courtroom in chains and seeing his wife, Jacci, his children, Adam, Rachael, and Renée, who had flown back from the West Coast, and his attorney friends waiting for him was overwhelming. Jacci's hug was comforting.

The charges that were read made no sense. The statements contained in the indictment were totally false. He had not done a single one of the acts attributed to him. As an accused, he stood baffled at what was being said. It was embarrassing to hear such accusations. He wondered how a grand jury could ever approve such an indictment, unless false information had been provided. Then he realized that, as in every case where a federal indictment is presented, it is the prosecutor who drafts the document which is then presented for a perfunctory signature by the foreperson of the grand jury. The prosecutor was free to indict anyone he pleased for any reason. He also recalled the popular saying among federal prosecutors that, "…anyone can prosecute a guilty person, but it takes a very skilled prosecutor to indict and convict an innocent person."

After the magistrate read the indictment, A.T. heard arguments about bond and release. The magistrate decided to release A.T. without bail due to his ties in the community and the fact that he had no criminal record. It shocked A.T. that he would be required to report to a probation officer who had the option, without advance notice, to stop at A.T.'s home or office at any time. He was also required to turn over any and all firearms, ammunition and his passport.

The magistrate then read the other conditions of probation to A.T. and advised him that at some point in the future he would be arraigned again in federal court in California. The magistrate stated he did not know when that would be. After that A.T. never did hear from anyone in the court system as to when he would need to appear in California.

Ultimately, A.T. and his local counsel contacted and interviewed numerous attorneys in the Southern California area to locate capable legal counsel. It seemed that no matter which attorney was contacted, a minimum retainer of one hundred thousand dollars was the standard retainer to be paid in advance. Fortunately for A.T., he was able to find a former Assistant United States Attorney whose specialty was white collar crime. As it turned out, A.T. could not have made a better choice. A.T. and one of his local attorneys traveled to California to discuss the case with the newly hired attorney and to appear at the arraignment of the other defendants, just in case A.T. needed to be there as well. When A.T. showed up, he learned that his presence was required, and if he hadn't shown up, there would have been an arrest warrant issued for him, and his release conditions would have been revoked. He wondered if he was purposely not informed so that he would have been arrested and incarcerated.

Out of the other seven defendants, A.T. did not know six of them. Of the one he did know, it turned out that this individual was introduced to him by the party against whom A.T. had filed an official complaint with the FBI on behalf of a client.

The indictment, in addition to stating that A.T. had been a conspirator with people whom he had never heard of, stated that he had initiated contact with an undercover task force; that he had encouraged the undercover task force to engage in acts that A.T. had warned them against; that A.T. had engaged in acts that he would never contemplate doing; and that there was a type of investment program that A.T. had neither heard of nor agreed to be a part of. Also, of significant interest to A.T. was the signature on the indictment of an Assistant United States Attorney who had the unique last name of a person whom A.T. had encountered many years earlier when A.T. had still been active in Republican politics. If the person whose name on the indictment was the same person A.T. had encountered earlier in politics under an internal political disagreement within the Republican Party, it would seem that the individual who signed the indictment was going out of his way to target A.T.

What happened to A.T. was just as the former chief of the New York Superior Court had once said, "The grand jury system is so unregulated that a prosecutor, if he wanted, could indict a ham sandwich." Nevertheless, the hard and cold reality of the situation was that once a person had been indicted, regardless of innocence, the damage was done, and that damage included being tainted for life. As Jacci had told A.T., "…being indicted is analogous to that of a broken fine piece of china; one can attempt to glue it back together, but no matter how skillful the job, it will always remain a broken piece of china." The damage had been done, and A.T. had done nothing to deserve such a fate.

At the end of the day, who knows what the average person would have done. In A.T.'s case, he had one thing going for him that few other people had. He had Jacci. Once everyone else had gone, A.T. knew he would be able to face the barrier in front of him because of the warm and devoted support he received from her. Because of her reassurances, it didn't matter what had happened or what others thought or what others were led to believe from what had been said in the charges or otherwise. Jacci told him that she knew he couldn't have even contemplated doing anything close to what had been alleged. She knew him like no one else. As she told him when they drew close, "I know you, and I know that you would never in a million years do anything wrong to anyone."

At the time of the second arraignment, A.T. was reassured when he encountered Ralph Nester, the defendant he had been investigating, and while in the presence of his attorneys was asked by Nester, "A.T. what are you doing here? You don't belong here with the rest of us. I have no idea why you were included in this, and, as I told you before, I thought that I had the authority to act as I did on behalf of the Federal Reserve. I'm sorry you got included in this matter. You definitely don't belong here. For my part, I apologize." Ultimately Nester was acquitted.

Then, weeks later when some of the government's evidence was produced, it became more and more apparent that A.T. had nothing to do with whatever enterprise was taking place. There was nothing in the evidence that implicated A.T. in any way, and based upon what was produced, there was a serious question as to whether a crime of any kind had been committed. There was absolutely no evidence of a criminal act relative to A.T. What was even more troubling was the fact that the audio tapes the government obtained from recorded conversations were missing blocks of actual discussions where there were simply blank spaces and clicks. When A.T.'s legal counsel demanded the complete tapes, it was obvious the tapes had been altered and that exculpatory information and discussions had been deleted or conveniently lost by the government. Once the missing parts were provided, additional exculpatory evidence was apparent.

For two of the last four years A.T. devoted most of his days and nights to reviewing and re-examining the emails, audio tapes, videotapes, the research, and the law. He was not able to accomplish much else. What had happened to him totally preoccupied his mind and time. Plus, it was expensive. The amount of attorney fees for the lawyers involved totaled just below two hundred thousand dollars, exclusive of other costs and expenses, before the case was finally dismissed. He wondered what people did when they were unable to raise such funds. A.T. was fortunate that he was able to hire the excellent attorneys that he had.

Even after the case was dismissed, the events that had played out continued to plague A.T. and consume his life. He vowed that he would do whatever he could to make certain this sort of thing did not happen to others. In his research, he was appalled to find a plethora of cases in which innocent people had not only been indicted but had been convicted, only to later be exonerated when the evidence withheld by prosecutors was revealed. He soon learned that prosecutorial misconduct and FBI misconduct were commonplace. He also learned that the task force that had been set up in this instance had repeatedly tainted itself with improper acts, witness intimidation, fabrication of statements, and the withholding of exculpatory evidence. His case was not the only one that was dismissed.

His view of prosecutors and of the FBI changed markedly as a result of what had happened. In his research he found that one of the prosecutors had the audacity to author a law review article in which the prosecutor stated that he would include the victims of crimes as defendants in a case. That prosecutor stated that once the victims faced the power and might of the federal government, those victims would attempt to work out some kind of "deal" with the government. For a prosecutor to think of such a thing was unbelievable, yet to place it into practice was unfathomable. It was that article more than anything that set A.T. in the direction of his own investigation after the case against him was dismissed. He was surprised at the extent of unofficial "help" he received.

For years now, the arrest and the entire ordeal haunted him daily as the experience had become a part of his every moment and every breath. Even his attempts to sleep were disrupted with bouts of a frantic realization that his relationship with his wife, family, and friends, along with all he stood for could have been completely lost. His freedom, dignity, and life, as he knew it, had nearly been taken from him. He had come so close to losing everything that took a lifetime to accomplish, including that of a good reputation.

It was as if the carafe of life had been emptied before him. Finally, the four year anniversary of the date of his arrest was about to occur, and it was time to rest. He got up from the desk in his study and looked through the stack of phone messages, including one marked "urgent." It was from a political acquaintance that had been on the Republican Central Committee when A.T. had been Party Chairman. This was not a good time. A.T. needed rest. He did not need a meeting. He just wanted to sleep, so he tossed aside the message and decided to go to bed.

* *

AN OLD LAPTOP

And then there was the dream. It was the same sweat-inducing dream that he seemed to have every night. It always began with his being chased. Although his oppressors were a considerable distance away, he could see into the dark and soulless eyes of the one closest to him. He kept trying to break free, yet it seemed as though something was pulling at him. Finally, he broke the restraint and began to run. While they continued to pursue him, he knew he had to make a turn; however, when he slowed for the turn, his movements again became so labored that it felt as if his left arm were being pulled out of its socket.

They were still coming after him, and there were so many of them. He felt that if he didn't get turned and turned quickly, he would be overcome by the mysterious figures following him. He had to act with precision, and it had to be "post haste." Although he was strong, his body didn't seem to respond normally. He wondered if they had done something to him or if he had been drugged. There was no time to think about it. Once past the upcoming barrier, he knew that any mistake would cause a loss of balance. If he slipped, he was sure to careen down the steep slope of an embankment that now appeared on each side of the path.

There was another reason for him to be careful. The laptop that he was carrying had important information. He could not remember what it was, just that it was important. The dream presented such an overpowering threat of immediate danger; he had to act quickly. He needed to find a safe place to work with the computer. He had to free the arm. Something had to give, so he pulled hard. That's the moment he awakened with no answers and no real memory of the details of the dream.

A.T. rationalized that the dream was being stimulated by the new evidence he continued to uncover. To be sure, the evidence served to exonerate him, but it did far more. From the initial evidence, he was learning far more about what was transpiring behind the scenes, and he was beginning to get a picture of who was involved.

In addition to the "discovery evidence," there was more information including the names, dates, places, and agendas of various government employees who had been involved in the task force that had been set up by the Justice Department and the FBI. What the evidence demonstrated was nothing short of outrageous.

The task force had apparently been set up with the stated purpose of ferreting out white collar crime; however, the new evidence that had developed over the past four years exposed the task force as essentially a front or device for a particular agenda by individuals within the Justice Department. It was their apparent plan to target individuals who had somehow come into the "cross hairs" of a certain group of political operatives within the Department and try to couple them with likely criminals who the DOJ and FBI were either unable to catch or who had been a part of the FBI informant program that went bad.

There was also a pattern that demonstrated connections to individuals within the George W. Bush campaign committee and to other political action committees. Some of the evidence was leading to a particular group of lawyers who had positioned themselves within both the Attorney General's Office and the FBI in such a way that would allow them to exert their political agenda. In nearly every example of new evidence, direct ties could be made to certain employees within the DOJ who had gained their positions under the tenure of two former Attorneys General, namely John Ashcroft and Alberto Gonzales. In regard to the FBI, the investigation was revealing that there was a close-knit group of agents at the street level, all the way up the ladder to the position of an Assistant Director, who had a set political agenda.

A.T. needed to determine just how and why it was that he had become targeted. He was compelled to investigate those who had investigated him and those who had charged him without basis. Having to begin such an investigation was especially painful because of his background and because he had always been dedicated and supportive of the Bureau. Therefore, investigating FBI agents and prosecutors was not his idea of a good time. Plus, A.T. had been an active member and onetime state level officer of the Republican Party. Before long, and as a result of his investigation of the government, he suspected that certain individuals within the Republican Party had become upset with A.T. due to the fact that he would not agree to work with them on specific and undisclosed matters. He felt that the presence of the long-forgotten laptop in the dream might offer a clue.

It was apparent from his investigation that the Republican Party was being used by specific individuals as a springboard to power. He had learned that their plan was to infiltrate the DOJ purposely in order to mold it into a political instrumentality that could be used to accomplish defined political objectives through the court system and the Department. The people behind the operation relished the power that positions within the DOJ and the Bureau would offer them.

To these political operatives, the equitable and fair administration of justice was only an important matter in terms of their distorted view of controlling the Department of Justice. The apparent intention was to position themselves within the DOJ and the FBI through both political appointment and through the civil service system in such a manner that over time they would be able to control or influence judicial nominations, elections, investigations, the grand jury process, and those to be prosecuted. The counter-investigation also revealed that several decades had passed while this unbelievable plan to control the Department was underway. Although A.T. had some proof, he needed more. He needed witnesses who would come forward to publically testify since there was so much involved. There was no way he could let it go, for he was on a mission.

As his investigation progressed, he found that he was not alone in his concern about the Department of Justice being used as a political tool by certain politicians and egocentric attorneys who craved recognition, position, and power. After a matter of months into his investigation, he found himself visiting about his findings with a trusted friend, Bud Hawthorne, who had graduated from the world of politics into the intriguing realm of investigative reporting. Soon after the discussion with Bud, he received a private call from another mutual friend, a United States senator, whom he had met many years earlier during a separate investigation of another matter. The earlier investigation had been performed at the direction of A.T.'s boss, who at that time had been the local prosecutor. This prosecutor had been given confidential information by the local media who were trying to break a story about corruption within law enforcement. That investigation had involved a volatile situation where a number of prominent political figures were named.

Ultimately, and as a result of that earlier investigation, some members of law enforcement agencies were forced to resign and others were prosecuted. Unfortunately, one FBI agent had suffered a nervous breakdown, and another ex-agent had taken his own life. It was during that earlier investigation that A.T. and the Senator developed a significant level of regard for each other. Although they were from different party affiliations, a mutual friendship had developed to the point of joining each other's families in social activities, as well.

While A.T. had chosen the quiet life of a practicing attorney once the earlier investigation was over, the Senator continued his political career. Over time the Senator became quite prominent. Their friendship cut through their political differences as they were, during earlier times, idealists in two different political parties who believed that people in government positions could work together with integrity in order to solve problems.

Because of his discussion with Bud, A.T. had taken a personal call from the Senator, who offered belated congratulations on the dismissal of the bogus charges. Additionally, the Senator told him that he wanted to collaborate on A.T.'s investigation relative to the Justice Department. From Bud, the Senator had heard that A.T. had taken up an investigation of his own and had developed some critical information. Because the Senator was interested in working with A.T. on the endeavor, A.T. found himself reenergized about moving the investigation to a new level.

On this fourth anniversary of his arrest, A.T.'s mind was churning as he turned in that night. The dream had repeated itself, but this time the dream was different. When he freed his arm to turn, he awakened and found himself completely cloaked with sweat. He was gasping for air and sat up abruptly. He noticed that the pillow and sheet beneath him were soaked. Next to him, Jacci was still sleeping. At least he hadn't disturbed her. He was thankful that the experience had only been a nightmare, but for the first time he realized that there was a purpose to the nightmare. It was too vivid and too time-consuming to have been a random dream. What had been happening to him over the past four years had been real.

A.T. got up, showered, shaved and dressed. With all that had occurred, he had forgotten all about the laptop until the nightmare urged him to find it. He saw the email in his dream. Now awake, in his mind's eye, he could remember the bizarre series of emails from Julian. Had he sent a response? He thought about it while he was looking for the laptop, and then he remembered that the long-forgotten email response had remained for nearly four years in the "unsent" portion of the *Outlook Express*.

He looked and looked. It just had to be there. Finally, he found the antiquated computer. There had been far too many major events that had intervened from the day of the obsolete laptop's placement on the shelf between several stacks of research material and the present. Critical and urgent life-saving and career-saving tasks needed to be performed during the passage of time. In the process, the forgotten laptop failed to serve any functional purpose other than to hold down some old research papers.

When he picked it up and blew the dust from it, the laptop seemed to take on the persona of a lost friend. Memories came rushing back. A.T. suddenly felt reinvigorated. The connective tissue to the investigation was the ominous emails from his old political colleague. A.T. had spent his career living on facts derived from hard, definable and verifiable information. But now his mind was reeling. The convergence of the emails and the abuses of power he had since discovered came together in A.T.'s mind as being somehow connected for the first time since the nightmare had begun.

Remington's soft bark interrupted A.T.'s thoughts when the dog demanded his attention. A.T., while stroking the dog's ear, realized that the laptop needed to be recharged. He made way for the kitchen to put on some coffee and try to find the ancient computer power supply. Jacci found him sitting at the kitchen table absentmindedly rubbing Remington's head as he tried to piece together events in his mind.

"You're up awfully early," Jacci said leaning over to kiss him.

A.T. smiled at her and she smiled back.

"I think I have good news and bad news, honey. The good news is I think the nightmares will stop now. The bad news is I think we are in the middle of a vast political conspiracy that reaches into every important institution in American life."

Jacci smiled, refilled his coffee, and bent over and kissed A.T. He got up to give her a great hug and went back to the study to find the computer.

He felt that, most likely, it had been the call from the Senator that had prompted the laptop dream. He found the old power supply and plugged in the machine. It took forever to boot up after downloading an endless array of Microsoft updates. He finally got Outlook Express to open and began reading the unsent email response, along with the initial email he had received four years ago.

The email was helpful in jogging his memory as to what had been happening during that earlier and turbulent time. He needed to carefully examine each of the emails in order to see if there were any clues about the situation that led to his arrest and the charges against him. He recalled a series of emails from Julian that he had ignored, and there was just one email response that he had written. Finally, he found them. After examining the emails, he was happy he had not sent his draft. First, he read his unsent response to the White House staff member:

From: atv@it.law
Sent: Thur. 8/23/2008 6:43 PM
To: jl.til.gol@wh.gov
Subject: Bus. Leader Forum

Dear Julian,

It is with deep regret that I must again decline your invitation to be a part of the Business Leadership Group. As you know, I have repeatedly declined to serve on the Committee and really do not have either the time or the interest to be a part of the Business Policy Forum. I have purposely tried to stay out of politics these past years.

Frankly, I am concerned about the direction that the economy has taken under W. I don't believe I am alone in this regard. What is troubling is that promises are being made in exchange for the funding of businesses. Both seem to be tied directly to those who are willing to blindly support certain PACs. With all due respect, that is very dangerous territory. Does President Bush know this is being done? I can't imagine he would agree if all of the facts were known to him.

Recently the President stated that there was plenty of money in Washington. What on earth is he saying? The country is in a hole that is expanding by the minute. What has become known as the "Bush Era Tax Cuts," along with the wars in Iraq and Afghanistan, are burying the economy. Surely, I can't be the only Republican who finds fault with the direction of this philosophy. How can you expect me to be a part of the Business Policy Forum and support an economic plan that I find unworkable? Forgive me for saying it, but it sounds and looks like you are attempting to sell "Cowboy Economics," or what Pres. Bush Senior termed "Voo-Doo Economics."

I do not wish to be a part of the Business Policy Forum. For the Forum to guarantee funds to my clients and to any company for which I am responsible in exchange for having a political commitment from me is unacceptable. Therefore, I must once again decline your invitation to participate in and/or to endorse the Business Policy Forum. I don't like the ties to the PACs. In my view that is not appropriate. The whole thing, especially as to the banking aspects, sounds misguided. I don't want to be involved.

Count me out and don't try to threaten me by implying that I might be on the wrong end of some task force. We've known each other for a long time, and I can't believe you would say or imply that. It's senseless, and you should know better than to think it, let alone say it. Please don't contact me again about this!

Very truly,
A.T.

One of A.T.'s faults was in being too direct, along with the capacity to unintentionally insult people in the process. While considering his "unsent" response, he recognized that it might have been taken as an insult and could have provoked anger from his old political friend, Julian. He wondered since the email was not sent, how could it have had anything to do with what happened to him? There had to be something more. Maybe there was a clue in Julian's earlier email of the same day. As her email indicated, it was apparently not her first effort to get him to join the Business Leadership Forum. It read:

From: jl.til.gol@wh.gov
Sent: Thur. 8/23/2008 10:53 AM
To: atv@it.law
Subject: Bus. Leader Forum

Dear A.T.:

This is the fourth time I have tried to contact you regarding the Business Leadership Forum. It is very disappointing that you have chosen not to respond; however, granting you the benefit of the doubt, I presume you have been detained by an emergency. I fully trust you understand and appreciate the honor it is to be asked to serve on this committee. Both the known and the unknown benefits of being a member of the committee should be obvious to you as many doors could be opened to both you and your clients. You are expected to participate. I would imagine you would want to be a part of the "New Order." I've told the powers to be that we could count on you.

It is most urgent you <u>call</u> me immediately. Do not wait another minute! You will not be asked again. Unfortunately the wheels are in motion that might well prove quite uncomfortable for those who choose not to respond and participate. Obviously we can help you. It is for our mutual benefit. You should agree to step up. For at least the next few days or so, I can act in a very beneficial way for you. I am certain you will want to speak with me.

By now, you must know that we are looking for particular business leaders who have been active in the Party in the past. We feel most leaders, such as you, are best suited for our objectives in moving forward. It goes without saying that those who participate will be well rewarded simply by being a part of the Forum. You would benefit, and your clients would benefit. Presumably, you and those clients would be eager to contribute in many ways.

Those who do not participate could be regarded as being opposed to the purpose of the Committee. Today it is important for all of us to lock down our allies and know who we can count on. Changes are taking place, particularly in the world of finance (including the use of bank instruments that can be traded or held for the benefit of participants and their companies), and you will want to be a part of those changes. I know you would not want to be at the wrong end of any task force enterprise.

Call me ASAP!
Julian

The email was revealing. Julian was not really asking him to participate; she was ordering him to participate. He had completely forgotten that she had mentioned a "task force." How could he have missed that point? There was a direct threat in her email, and he had missed it. Ironically, the email came the same day that he was arrested. Was there a connection? What if he had responded favorably to her invitation? Was she implying that she had the power to stop the arrest? Were the wheels already in motion to punish him for his earlier refusals to act? He needed to find Julian. He had to see if she would agree to talk with him.

More than ever, he wondered if his refusal to serve on the committee had something to do with what had happened to him. If the refusal to serve on the business forum was the basis for the action of the task force, then it was apparent that certain people who were working in the White House in August of 2008 were willing to carry their vindictive nature too far. He was going to have to get proof.

It was important to locate Julian. He was pleased he had acquired some of the information available under the Freedom of Information Act (FOIA). He suspected he had not received everything from those files, regardless of certain legal mandates.

A.T.'s old political friends had even expressed concern that the making of a shadow government was being formulated over a period of time and that timeline could be traced as far back as the late 1960s and early 1970s. The people orchestrating those efforts were far too clever than to reveal their plans to any of the presidents whom they served. Most of those presidents would have been too busy to notice.

A growing concern had developed that the Party machinery had been hijacked by various individuals of a particular political philosophy that was anything but mainstream. It was also the belief of most mainstream Republicans that W. had allowed the changes to occur. That possibility was near the surface of the thinking of those who felt they were being disenfranchised little by little over the past several decades.

He pulled out the material he had received under FOIA. Reviewing those items in tandem with the documents developed from the investigation, A. T. was convinced his hunch was right. The information he had received pointed to an inquiry made of the FBI task force from an unidentified party at the White House in the spring of 2008, approximately five months before the indictment against him was rendered. He also found that the first effort to indict had resulted in a "no bill" which meant that whoever sat on the

Grand Jury at the time didn't think there was a case. Someone had gone out of his way and had taken the matter back to the grand jury a second time. He had contacted the Justice Department after receiving the information under FOIA and was advised that there was nothing more in the record in regard to any contact to or from the White House. There was no particular individual who was identified in the file regarding contact with the FBI task force. He needed to find Julian. If it wasn't her, she would know who it was. He was sure of it.

In attempting to locate her, A.T. scoured his databases and noted that all of the contact information he had for Julian was at least four years old and obsolete. He thought about the past and the time when he had been active in the Republican Party. He recalled the initial introduction to Julian by Blaine Jeffers. Jeffers was quite active within the Republican Party in California and had been on the Central Committee in Orange County, California, many years ago. He would have to wait until later in the day to call Blaine as it was now just reaching eight o'clock in the Midwest. Since it would only be six on the West Coast, it was too early to make the call.

While sorting through the contact information at his desk with the computer running, A.T. sensed he was being watched. He looked up to see Jacci, standing before him with her coffee cup in hand. Before he could say anything, she smiled and asked, "Apparently your repeated trouble with sleeping prompted something new."

"It has," commented A.T. "I had a dream about this old laptop. It had an old email I had forgotten about."

"If you were dreaming about it, there's a good chance it might be important. What was it?"

"Actually there were two emails. There was one from Julian Tilson-Gould and a reply from me that I never sent."

"I thought you promised that you were finished with politics. Are you planning to get back into that messy arena?" Then she laughed and said, "Remember, you told me to be sure to have you committed if you ever got involved again. Should I make some calls?"

Finally, he got up to stretch his legs, smiled, and said, "You're right! I did say that, and no, I'm not going to get involved in any political activity. No calls are necessary. These emails go back about four years when I was asked to be a part of the Business Leadership Forum sponsored by the White House in 2008. I think there might be a connection to my investigation."

"But that sounds political."

"It was, and as you should remember, I decided not to be involved. So I've kept my promise. I was just curious as to whether that request to join the leadership group had anything to do with the indictment. From an earlier request I made under FOIA, there was an indication that contact had been made between the White House and the task force that indicted me. However, there were no names since there was a claim that the names could be redacted from the documents. Now I want to conduct some follow-up investigation to see who was behind the calls to the task force."

"Were the emails helpful?"

"I think so. Do you remember Julian?"

"How could I forget? Wasn't she that superficial blonde who kept flirting with everyone?"

"I guess that's the one," laughed A.T. "In any event, she's the one who sent the email from the White House back in August of 2008, and her email seems to have contained an implied threat. It also mentions a task force."

"So, how is that important? The Bush White House was always threatening someone, weren't they?"

"Well, the FOIA material I received revealed that there was a call from the White House to one of the attorneys who was involved in the task force a few months before Julian sent her various emails to me. I now think there may be some connection. I need to track her down to find out."

"Well, why don't you call Blaine? I thought they were kind of involved."

"I'm sure their spouses would love to hear you say that."

"All I remember is that they were together an awful lot, and they seemed to have a bit of 'give-away' expression when they looked at each other. Who knows? Besides, it was their business. I'm sorry I mentioned it."

"You are right about one thing. The two of them were good friends, and I was thinking about calling Blaine to see if he knew how to reach her."

"I'm sure he does. Give him a call, but don't make it too late. We're scheduled to be at the symphony later tonight. You haven't forgotten, have you?"

"No, I haven't forgotten. In fact, I'm looking forward to a relaxing evening. Since I have to fly out tomorrow, a pleasant evening is just the right prescription."

With that comment, A.T. went back to his desk to once again take up a position in front of the computer in order to search his archives for the contact information that he had for Blaine. Before he was able to sit down, he noticed that Jacci set her coffee cup on the edge of the desk, stepped behind him, and gave him a hug. It was a gratifying sensation which made him feel better about what he was about to do in contacting Blaine. Once he contacted Blaine, he would stop thinking about the investigation and would focus on the forthcoming events of the day. He was looking forward to the evening.

A couple hours later, A.T. called his friend, Blaine, and learned that Blaine had maintained contact information for Julian. However, since Blaine was in his car, he would have to call back with the information. When Blaine called back later in the day, A.T. was preparing to go to the symphony with Jacci. The two of them exchanged pleasantries. They had been good friends and hadn't seen each other for several years. Blaine said he would set up a meeting between Julian and A.T. He then stated that any meeting would have to wait until after the first of the year as Julian was out of the country with her family until after New Year's. Tentative arrangements were made for A.T. to meet with Blaine and Julian in early January at Blaine's home in La Jolla, California.

Given A.T.'s schedule, he was glad the meeting with Blaine and Julian would take place after the first of the year. A.T. was not in a position to change the convoluted travel plans he was facing. It had taken months to set up the various meetings in Kentucky, Texas, and Washington D.C. that were to advance his investigation. After all, the travel plans had been made weeks ago when A.T.'s investigation took him to the nation's capital.

After A.T. returned to the Twin Cities to digest the material he received while in Washington D.C., he decided to act on the new material. Tomorrow he would be boarding a plane to fulfill his commitment to a United States Senator and to continue his investigation. The schedule for the upcoming travels had been set. Plus, soon it would be the holiday season. A.T. decided to put the matter of the investigation on hold, if he could, since it was time for him to prepare for the evening concert.

While he started up the stairs to change, the doorbell rang. Since the arrest of four years earlier, A.T. had become uneasy and a bit agitated every time the bell rang or there was a knock at the door. When A.T. opened the door, he immediately was shocked to see a short man in his mid-fifties.

The balding man combed his fine and stringy blondish-gray hair over his head in an attempt to cover the absence of growth on the top of his head. The man sported close-fitting glasses with frames that were little more than wire rims. A perpetual sneer appeared on the man's face whenever he displayed his toothy and open mouth smile. His rumpled dark brown suit had a "sleep-in' appearance. The tie he wore was of an odd green color, and he held a rather old-fashioned hat in his left hand. When he wiped his nose across his right sleeve, he gave A.T. a perplexed look and demanded, "Why didn't you call me back? I left a message to let you know it was urgent."

After A.T. squinted to assess the man, he recalled him to be one of the so-called Republican Party reformers who twenty years earlier had headed a neo-conservative faction of activists that had started to make their presence known in Party circles. It had been that long ago when A.T. had last seen or spoken to Leslie Winthrop. Perhaps if he had called him, Leslie would have left him alone and not bothered to come to the house. As A.T. continued to study the man in the doorway, he remembered that he shouldn't call him Les. The man hated this nickname, yet it was the name used behind his back. Finally, A. T. said, "Sorry, Leslie, but it was late by the time I got the message, and I thought that I might try to call you sometime after I returned from an upcoming trip I have planned."

"Didn't my message say it was urgent for us to talk?" asked Leslie.

"I guess it did," answered A.T. "Since the two of us have not seen each other or spoken for nearly twenty years, I thought it couldn't be too urgent."

"When I said urgent, I meant urgent," said Leslie with his face reddening from his obvious frustration. "Do you mind if I come in? It is a bit chilly out here, and I do have something important to discuss. I believe you will find it to be a crucial matter."

Although A.T. wanted this man of past bad memories to disappear, he relented. He opened the door wide and motioned toward the foyer and said, "By all means, please come it. However, I must tell you that my wife has made some plans for us to be with friends this evening, so I won't be able to visit long."

"Don't worry," insisted Leslie, "I won't take long. I won't even bother you for a chair. I hope you realize that I don't have to be here, and I don't have to do this. I know the two of us never got along well and that you resented the fact that I replaced you on the Central

Committee, but those days are long gone, and I certainly carry no grudges, and I hope that you don't."

"I have no grudge against you, Leslie. None at all! My time was up on the Committee, and I was more than happy to step down. If you will recall, after I left that post I kept my political involvement to the support of selective candidates. And frankly, for the past few years, I haven't even allowed myself to get involved in individual campaigns. Now what is so urgent that you decided to brave the weather to see me?" asked A.T.

"You've got to back off what you are doing," insisted Leslie. "It was unfortunate what happened to you, and I am sorry for that. Regardless of the fact that we have never been friends, mostly due to your liberal political views, I knew you couldn't have been involved in what the newspapers were reporting. Nevertheless –"

"I like to consider my views to be moderate views, and I believe that is what quite a number of Republicans and former Republicans believe. I really have no interest in discussing politics right now, so if there is a reason for us to be discussing something urgent, do you mind telling me what it is?" asked A.T.

"Bluntly, you are in danger," Leslie warned. "Apparently you are conducting an investigation, and from what I understand, that investigation involves some very powerful people. Those people have means beyond what you realize. I happen to know from discussions I have heard that if you don't drop what you are investigating, you will only bring more trouble to yourself, and that trouble could be in the form of physical harm."

"Who told you this?" demanded A.T.

"You know I can't tell you that," said Leslie. "I shouldn't be here in the first place, and obviously the two of us do not run in the same social circles. However, you don't deserve what they will do to you if you don't back off. Now I need to go. Consider yourself warned, and if you tell anyone I gave you this warning, I will deny it."

"That might be a little hard, especially since it is more than likely that someone might have seen you 'drop by' the house like you just did. If I'm in some sort of danger, then the people to whom you make reference probably have seen you here. Besides, how will your friends know if I have stopped with my investigation or not? I presume the people you are referring to are your friends."

"They are acquaintances of sorts, and they will know whether you have stopped or continued with your investigation. I will just say that 'my friends,' as you call them, have people in certain positions who will know. That's all I will tell you," answered Leslie while he lifted a small box he was carrying and removed a wooden object. "Oh, by the way, the official reason I am here is to deliver this wall plaque to you. It is supposed to acknowledge your service to the Party for your work on the Central Committee."

"Oh, thanks so much," said A.T. accepting the plaque from Leslie. "Since my service on the Committee was over twenty years ago, it is so nice to receive something of timely recognition. I will forever treasure it. In fact, I'll want to be sure I find a special place for it in memory of this moment…oh, and of my past service."

"Do with it what you want. Actually it was made up years ago, but since you never came to any more meetings, and since none of the new people felt the urge to deliver it, it has been in the Party office for a long time. Now, be a reasonable person and take heed to what I've told you," said Leslie backing out of the door and turning.

"Perhaps we could do this again…possibly in another twenty years," A.T. commented as he watched Leslie pull his hat down and walk away.

"Who was that?" said the voice behind A.T. It was Jacci who had already dressed for the concert and night out. Standing near the doorway, she looked stunning in her formal attire. She inquired, "You aren't going like that, are you?"

"No, I'm about to change," answered A.T. "It won't take me long. Let me run upstairs to change now. I'll be back down in less than ten minutes. Oh, here. Perhaps we should find a place on the wall for this, or better yet, perhaps you might have a special place for it like file thirteen."

"What is it?"

"It's a wall plaque that commemorates my service on the Republican Central Committee of twenty years ago. Isn't it nice! By the way, that was Leslie Winthrop. You know an old 'political ally,'" said A.T.

"'Political ally, indeed," noted Jacci. "Wasn't it more like a political Judas? What did he want?"

"Nothing, I guess. He just wanted me to have the plaque and reflect on the past."

In short order A.T. was ready, and the two of them left for the concert. The concert that Jacci had booked was the holiday concert they had been attending for several years. It was a major event for them and for a number of their close friends. There was no way he could miss this event. In the morning, he would have to fly out for Lexington. He could think about the investigation while on the plane. With that in mind, he was hoping he could put it out of his thoughts and enjoy the upcoming evening.

CHAPTER 2
SETTING A PLACE

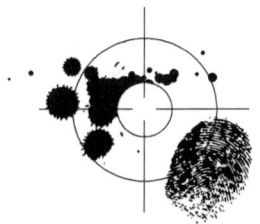

Leslie Winthrop never did care for A.T. To Leslie it seemed as though everything came easily for A.T. while he, on the other hand, had to work extra hard for whatever minor roles he received in the Republican Party. Leslie wasn't sure why he disliked A.T. so much. Whenever A.T. came into a room, people would notice him and talk to him. That was not the case for Leslie who people never seemed to notice or care about. Sometimes people would totally ignore him. Those days were over!

To Leslie the world of politics was the most important aspect of life. It was all that mattered. Although he did enjoy his family, a nice wife and two children, political life brought the power, prestige, and prominence that he so much admired. All of the diligent work behind the scenes and the volunteering for the most demeaning of tasks was now starting to pay off. Things were changing and changing rapidly, especially in the realm of Republican politics. If ever there was a person who felt he had dearly paid his dues over years of hard work and long hours in the world of Party politics, it was Leslie.

Walking away from A.T.'s home, Leslie smiled while thinking: *The days of people like A.T. having their way with the world are over. There is a new "world order" taking over the entire body of politics. Now, everyone will start to take notice of those of us who have had to work doing the little menial jobs. It's going to be different for you now, A.T. You've had to fight your way out of a criminal indictment, and neither you nor your name is anything special to anyone anymore. As I see it, you are finished, and you will never stand with the proud and accomplished ever again.*

This had been a mission for Leslie. It was a mission that he relished as he constantly remembered the political differences between A.T. and himself. While A.T. had been sought out for political office by some of the wealthiest and most powerful people in the state to seek a position on the Central Committee and then emerge as the selected Chairman over twenty-six other candidates, Leslie had to claw his way to the top through constant diligence and volunteer work. Since both A.T. and Leslie had come into active political life at about the same time, it seemed natural to Leslie that he would compare himself to A.T. Now with A.T. at the bottom of the world and Leslie Winthrop at the top, well, almost at the top, he felt like skipping the rest of the way to his car that was parked just a block or so up the street from A.T.'s house.

If Leslie wasn't at the top, he was close, and he could see the top from where he stood. After all, he had been sought out this time, and the people who sought him out were very powerful. Powerful, indeed! The people he was now working with were significantly involved in the new Republican Party and had held various positions of power in the government including spots at the Department of Justice, the Federal Bureau of Investigation, various Congressional committees and offices at the highest levels within the Party itself. He had even been invited into their strategy meetings in Washington D.C., as well as to private meetings at some of their homes. There were also some obscenely rich people involved and even a person who had been more than instrumental in getting George W. Bush elected as President. He knew they were using him, but it was a fair and equitable arrangement because he was using them as well. He felt that finally he was a part of the team. It was almost the "A" team. He was their man in Minnesota.

At that point in his reminiscing and as he reached his car, he remembered that he needed to place a call to some of his new benefactors who were waiting for him to report on his meeting with A.T. He wanted to make the call on his cell while heading back to his home but realized that he would need to take notes and be fully attentive, so he decided to wait until he could access the land line at his house. He had worked hard to get where he was, and he wasn't about to jeopardize his new position or his new friendship with the power elite.

On his drive home, Leslie thought about the call he would be making to Washington D.C. He wasn't sure if he would be speaking to the head of the 'ad hoc' committee that had been formed over the past couple years by some former government employees or if he would be speaking only to a committee member. It didn't matter. He was instructed to make the call regardless of whether or not he had been successful in tracking down A.T. This time he was told to call the private office number of the committee's attorney who was situated with one of the largest law firms in the United States. The committee's attorney always acted as the chairperson every time Leslie had been present for meetings.

This attorney was a former DOJ lawyer who had been given a position with one of the country's largest law firms. Apparently the firm had about a dozen offices worldwide and at least a thousand lawyers. This particular lawyer had been involved in politics for a long time and knew the ropes, especially having served at the DOJ during the George W. Bush administration.

At least eleven people were present during most of the previous five sessions of the ad hoc committee when Leslie was present. The other participants at each of the meetings included a guy named "Big John," who was the personal representative of a very wealthy businessman, a small guy referred to as "Squeaky," an unnamed person who was either a current or former FBI agent who sat next to Leslie, a large man who worked for a well-funded political action committee, a political lobbyist of some sort and a younger person who had recently graduated from Georgetown Law School and who was currently clerking for a member of the United States Supreme Court. Leslie noted that the young law clerk always sat along the wall in a second tier of chairs along with a male secretary who took notes and a large bald man who never said anything.

It wasn't until Leslie had been to at least three meetings when he was told that he was being invited back repeatedly because of his general philosophical outlook in regard to politics and due to his many years in being instrumental in organizing conservative causes within the Republican Party in the upper Midwest. During the fourth meeting of the Committee, he learned that the group was a part of a solid movement in the United States that involved selected factions from conservative politicians. It also included people who shared very conservative religious views and individuals of great wealth who wanted to see a strong paramilitary aspect of private citizens prepared to protect the American way of life as it was meant to be.

At the fourth meeting, when Leslie was officially invited to become a permanent member, he learned that he would be handling certain special assignments. At that meeting he was informed that the committee members regarded themselves as what they termed the "Neo-Con-versionists" which developed from a philosophy that the committee internally termed the "Neo-Convergence." They were all well-known neoconservatives or as they were commonly called by the media: "Neo-cons." It was a varied group of individuals who believed in political, economic, and social conservatism. The committee was an assembly of people with a very conservative financial outlook supporting the "trickle down" economics, coupled with conservative religious beliefs that found unity with certain paramilitary groups, along with some very well-to-do businessmen and most importantly, certain people who had become very powerful in the past when they worked within the ranks of government. The group's goal was to end what they believed was a trend by government toward moderate and liberal thinking of any kind. The group's official name was "Legislative Enterprise and Study To End Restrictions"; it went by the acronym: LESTER.

When he got home, Leslie couldn't wait to make the prearranged call to the committee in order to report on the recent task assigned to him. Once at home, he said hello to his wife who was waiting for him. He felt he had married well. His wife came from a very conservative "Born Again" Christian family who owned several florist shops throughout a three state area that included Minnesota. She was short, thin and a reasonably attractive brunette. The fact that Dorothy, who everyone called Dotty, was considerably younger than Leslie worked out well, especially since he felt that a younger woman was "easier to train." Best of all, she knew a "woman's place" and went along with Leslie's complete control of the household finances and general direction. She always kept their home very tidy and made sure the children wore the properly branded clothes and attended a good parochial school where the children, a boy of thirteen and a girl of ten, participated in proper activities including the annual Easter pageant at the school. Dotty was supportive of

Leslie's political activities and made sure the room Leslie used as his study was always in perfect condition.

After speaking briefly with Dotty, Leslie went to his study. The walls were lined with pictures of him taken with some well-known neo-conservatives of the past three decades. Additionally, and along one wall, he had obtained pictures of some of the people whom he considered the most important people of the time. The pictures, including some with autographs, were photos of Pat Robertson, Supreme Court Justice Anthony Scalia, Karl Rove, Eric Prince, Grover Norquist, David Koch and Dick Cheney. None of those pictures included him, but that was okay since he knew those people were too busy to pose for pictures. Also, on a shelf near the pictures, Leslie displayed some of the awards and plaques of recognition he had received. After he closed the door, he unlocked his desk and removed a notebook used particularly for the work he had been performing for LESTER.

The notebook was already half-filled with notes from the meetings and his outlines for voter organizational work he had completed along with pages of contact names and phone numbers with the individual interests and organizational ties of each contact. He also kept a record of who on the list needed funds and who on the list provided funds. He was very good at organizing. The notebook for LESTER made that point very clear.

Once he was situated, he placed the call to his new and powerful lawyer friend. After just the first ring, his friend answered.

"What have you got for me, Leslie?" asked the heavy and deliberate voice on the other end.

"I went to A.T.'s house under the excuse of delivering an old plaque for his membership on the central committee; I followed your instructions," answered Leslie.

The deep voice on the other end that still had traces of a southern drawl replied, "I'm going to put you on the speaker phone, if that's all right."

"Sure," said Leslie.

"Here with me are a few other committee members including Big John and Squeaky, who you've met, along with Victor, who I believe you have seen at a couple of the earlier meetings. He is the big balding fellow who usually sits in the back of the room with the Supreme Court law clerk, whom you have also met. Since it is getting late out here on the East Coast and since the week is winding down, these are the only members I've been able to bring together," said Osborne Leeds, the attorney.

"That's fine," said Leslie. "I'm not sure I remember a guy named Victor."

"You've met Victor but probably don't remember him since he would always remain fairly quiet during our meetings," commented Osborne.

"Oh, now I recall," responded Leslie. "Hello to all of you. Sorry I am getting back to you so late, but I was just able to track A.T. down. He had been ignoring my calls and messages-"

"Did you tell him that your need to speak to him was urgent?" asked Osborne.

"I did in every message, but as I said, he ignored all of those messages, so I drove over to his home to see him personally," said Leslie.

"That's great. Good initiative," noted Osborne.

"Were you able to find his home and gain entrance easily enough?" asked Victor who up until that moment in time, Leslie had never heard him speak.

"Sure. It was quite easy. I just looked up his address in the phone book and drove over," said Leslie.

"Did you have any trouble or note any security?" asked Victor.

"No, why?" questioned Leslie.

"It's not important," interrupted Osborne who scowled at Victor, but fortunately, Leslie could not see Osborne's obvious displeasure with Victor. "Victor is always interested in details and how people live. Don't give it another thought. Now, what did you tell A.T.?"

"Just as you instructed, I told him that he could be in danger if he continued his investigation. I played up the fact that we knew each other years ago and told him as an old acquaintance I didn't want to see him get himself involved in something well over his head."

"Are you friends with A.T.?" asked 'Big John.'

"Not at all," answered Leslie. "For me it has always been difficult to talk to A.T. He and I are worlds apart when it comes to Republican Party politics, and years ago we were involved in Party politics at the same time. But we are definitely not friends. Why do you ask?"

"You knew we indicted him a few years back, didn't you?" asked Osborne.

"Yes. Everyone knew about that since it was in all the papers up here. As much as I don't like A.T., I couldn't imagine that he would have been involved in something that would result in a criminal indictment. He always seemed like such a straight arrow," noted Leslie.

"It's too bad the case was dismissed," commented Osborne. "We were using him as a guinea pig in order to see how far we could take certain matters. We felt if we could prosecute some of our own Republicans who had gotten too liberal for our tastes, the Democrats would look the other way. We wanted to see how far we could go, so we made a test case out of A.T. If A.T. hadn't been an attorney and hadn't been a former prosecutor, we don't think he would have been able to fight the charges.

"We were pretty sure we would be able to get away with it," continued Osborne. "We didn't think he would have the resources to fight us. We threw a lot at him and originally we thought we were going to pull it off. We had already been successful in a number of other instances in using the power and financial strength of the United States government when we had similar issues with other political individuals who insisted on giving us problems. We stretched matters a bit; however, we felt there was nothing he could do since there was no oversight to the grand jury process. Hell, we even started out by deleting some of the statements he made on the audio tapes thinking he wouldn't catch the missing parts, plus we held back a couple matters including a conversation where he volunteered to call the FBI while our task force guys were on the phone with him. Ultimately, we produced that stuff since we didn't want to jeopardize the rest of the case against some others. Obviously, he was able to dig deeper than a number of actual office holders we were able to destroy with indictments."

"Wow!" commented Leslie. "I didn't know our committee was involved, and I didn't realize we had that kind of power."

"Remember, Leslie, it's who you know in office and whether those whom you know have the ability and the guts to use the power of their office," bragged Osborne.

"Let me just say that I'm glad it is our committee that has the connections and knows how to use the power of the government," beamed Leslie.

"That's what government is for, son," noted Osborne.

"Why did I need to warn A.T.?" asked Leslie. "As a practical matter, isn't he really finished? What could he possibly do?"

"He won't give up," said Osborne. "He is stirring up a lot of issues. He's beginning to hit a few nerves, and people are starting to ask questions. We have been trying to join an international concern that has been around for a very long time. It is our belief that some of our interest in molding the government of this country is similar to theirs. We also believe if we are granted membership in that particular international group, we can wield even more power and prestige. Plus, if it came up, he might recognize my name from years earlier, and I don't need that. Bottom line is that we don't want your friend, A.T., digging up things that are long over or not his concern. Did you tell him he was getting in over his head?"

"I did," answered Leslie. "But what international group are you talking about? Sorry to ask, but, as you know, I am new to the committee, and I don't want to make any mistakes. Also, as I've said before, A.T. is definitely no friend of mine. I have never liked him."

"Then you're in good company," interjected 'Big John.' "He has been a pain in the side for a long time, and believe me, the experience some of us had with him many years ago caused us to be derailed on a matter we thought we had pretty well resolved until he, his boss at the time, the local prosecutor, and a guy who is now a U.S. Senator got in the way."

"Enough," exclaimed Osborne. "For your information, Leslie, the international group is not known in public circles. But so you know it exists, let's just call them the GGG or 'Good Government Group.' You might just as well know this since we will be expecting to have you do some additional work relative to A.T. in the event he continues his investigation. We really don't need to have him doing any more nosing around."

"What type of work?" asked Leslie.

"Nothing too special," answered Osborne. "We will want to keep the channels of communication open with him, and I believe you are the best one for that task since 'Big John' and 'Squeaky' here may not be able to speak with A.T. without his getting suspicious. But let me caution you not to mention anything about the GGG, or, knowing A.T, he may try to add them to his already misguided investigation."

"What would you have me do at this stage?" asked Leslie.

"There might be an occasion or two for you to either photograph or film A.T. in the presence of others if we find out that he is continuing with his silly investigation," instructed Osborne. "If we find out that he is continuing, we will need to discreetly learn just who he is speaking with and when. Don't plan to do anything until we have a chance to instruct you as to how to proceed."

"One thing I can do is be discreet," boasted Leslie. "Do you know if there will be any need on the immediate horizon? The reason I am asking is due to the fact that we are about to enter the Christmas holiday season."

"Not at this point unless you've heard anything about A.T. traveling or visiting with particular people," said Osborne.

"Come to think of it," answered Leslie, "he did say he was going somewhere, but there were no details. I don't know if it was out for the evening or a trip somewhere."

"See if you can find out," instructed Osborne.

"I'll do what I can in a discreet manner. Perhaps I might run into A.T. at a restaurant or public place like that and use a chance meeting as an excuse," suggested Leslie.

"Great idea," said Osborne. "Why don't you try to do that and get back to me. Now, don't make it too obvious, okay?"

"Right, I'll be very discreet," said Leslie.

"That's it for now, Leslie. We'll talk later. Good-bye," responded Osborne hanging up the phone in his usual manner which was an abrupt hang up whenever Osborne decided the conversation was over.

With the phone call over, Osborne made sure the speaker phone was off when he turned to the four others at the table. He looked at Victor and admonished him about his off-the-cuff question to Leslie about security at A.T.'s home.

Victor, who was a former Marine, had been hardened and battle-scarred from a significant amount of front line action in Vietnam and subsequent "special assignments" for the Central Intelligence Agency. He guarded a number of secrets that few people, except Osborne, knew. Unfortunately for Victor, he had been expelled from the Marine Corps for what was termed the "physical and mental abuse" of some new recruits assigned to him. To Victor that was simply a badge of honor rather than a problem. Apparently, the "Survival, Evasion, Resistance and Escape" program, mostly known as SERE, agreed with Victor in that his questionable behavior as an active marine was a badge of honor. As a result, he became an invited member of SERE, a program started by the Air Force at the end of the Korean War.

After being trained by SERE, Victor was once again contacted by his old friends at the CIA and introduced to several mid-level operatives at the Agency. They liked what they had heard about Victor, and soon he was once again busy with one "high-risk" assignment after another. In each case, he performed beyond expectations. Later, he was given a position at the Air Force Academy by an instructor who shared the same strict religious beliefs as did Victor. Once again, however, Victor ran into trouble when he went beyond the normal agenda and began to impose some of his own disciplinary measures upon a number of cadets. His record at the Academy was tainted with numerous allegations of his singling out particular male cadets for "after hours" religious training and personal relationships. It had taken a lot of courage for several cadets to come forward especially due to Victor's position, the embarrassment of the situations, the fear of personal reprisals from Victor, and the likelihood of dismissal of the cadets from the Academy. However, after the changes to the "Don't Ask, Don't Tell" policy, the matter of coming forward by the cadets was made easier.

Upon being forced to resign from the Academy, Victor planned to go back to the CIA where he knew he would always be welcome for additional assignments. However, when his "deeply religious" mentor at the Academy found out about Victor's situation and dismissal, the mentor recommended that Victor contact a former DOJ attorney who shared their religious beliefs and who had been asked to leave the DOJ when the Obama administration took over. That was when Victor was invited into Osborne's Washington, D.C. law office which was where Osborne landed upon his departure from the DOJ. Despite their common interests, Victor and Osborne had some personality issues due mostly to the significant egos that each man possessed. Victor hated to take orders from anyone. He worked best as a "free-lance" contractor, and as a part of his agreement to work with Osborne, he was given an extremely wide range of latitude in completing the tasks assigned.

The tasks assigned to Victor by Osborne were best termed to be too "dirty" and too "involved and sticky" for Osborne to soil his hands. Victor had always completed his tasks with great ease, and in virtually every case, there was no trace of his involvement or the committee's involvement when Victor was done. It hadn't mattered whether the task involved a break in, surveillance, the administration of a physical punishment, or the elimination of life itself. In fact, Victor was quite proud of one particular incident where a potential witness who was scheduled to appear before a

Congressional committee regarding missing e-mails and voter machine irregularities simply disappeared in an airplane accident that Victor had skillfully arranged. He realized that his efforts in that regard were appreciated by the real power brokers behind the committee, the people above Osborne. For that endeavor he received significant praise and an unexpected monetary bonus from the LESTER committee.

Victor was feeling good about himself and believed he was the only member of the committee who had the balls to challenge Osborne. When Osborne chastised him in front of the others, Victor felt it was time for a showdown. After Osborne's comment, Victor turned in his chair to directly face Osborne and said, "Bull Shit! I'll ask that question if and when I believe it to be necessary."

"Oh, no you won't," responded Osborne whose large flock of grey hair seemed to hop up and down as he spoke. Getting up from his chair, he removed his glasses and deliberately placed them on the table in front of him. "I'm running this operation, and the rest of you take orders from me. I've spent too much of my life working my way into this position, and I'm not going to have anyone screw it up - not A.T., not you, and not anyone else. There is far too much at stake. Let me remind each and every one of you here that none of you would have the positions you have or receive the funds you do for your assignments if it were not for me. I wasn't made one of the partners of this law firm for nothing. I was begged to come here after I was asked to leave the DOJ, and the reason I was begged to come was not just because of who I knew and what I know but because of my ability to think strategically and place the right people into the right positions."

Victor, who was still a fine example of marine training at a very well developed six-foot-five frame, moved to stand up. Osborne, who was quite a bit older, but at least an inch taller and still in good condition for a man nearing seventy, calmly walked to Victor's chair. He stopped short of the chair and said, "Why don't you get up, Victor? Go ahead and test this old man. Why don't you try to see what I'm made of? I'm confident enough to know that one way or another you will lose this confrontation. However, in the event you believe that someone has died and left you in charge, let's determine that right here and now."

It was more than obvious that Osborne was seriously irritated at Victor's comment about security at A.T.'s home. Victor knew he could have ended Osborne's harangue and even his life in an instant. Instead and while half way up from his chair, Victor, who had been regarded by everyone on the committee as dangerous and capable of virtually anything at anytime due to his size and demeanor, slowly sat back down, and in an attempt at laughter said, "It's not worth it, old man. This is your turf, and I work for you, so I will take my place, but don't ever challenge me in front of others again unless you really do want to see what I'm made of. Keep in mind, what you've hired me to do. Those tasks are performed by specialists. I am a specialist in every respect. When you reflect on what I do and can do, please also remember that I have a very good success rate at what I do."

Osborne stood tall above Victor's chair, and in his southern drawl which he seemed to accentuate responded, "Son, don't threaten me. If you ever do again, let me suggest you hire a very good attorney since I have enough on you to get you indicted on matters that will set you up for a couple lifetimes in some very dark and damp places. Don't ever think that I am joking. I hold the reins of power, and I know how to use them. I also hold your questionable future in my hands. I won't have discord, especially on this committee. Plus, you are paid very well for what you are asked to do from time to time. Everyone here has been chosen by me personally; I am quite familiar with everyone's past."

Osborne began to walk back to his chair, and at that point the law clerk started to cough and nervously reach for a glass of water in front of him. He cleared his throat and in almost a whisper started to say something. Victor laughed and said, "Speak up there, little man."

A glance from Osborne back to Victor stopped the laughter. Osborne calmly sat back down and placed his glasses back on his face and looked intently at the law clerk. In a sing-song and belittling tone, he stared at the law clerk and asked, "I'm sorry, did you have a question? I wasn't able to quite hear what you were trying to say."

The room fell silent as the law clerk, who was a scholarly-looking man in his early thirties, adjusted his wire-rimmed glasses and again cleared his throat to speak. He took another sip of water and finally said, "I really don't th-think I should be here, nor do I think I should be seeing or hearing this conversation. I need to keep myself free from this sort of thing. With my position and all -"

"Your position and all," drawled Osborne. "Why, do you now believe yourself to be an esteemed member of the Supreme Court?

Are you suddenly a member of the judiciary? Have you suddenly taken some form of medication that has reformed you? Have you forgotten who you are or how you were able to gain the position you now have? Perhaps you have also forgotten some of our many discussions on an array of subjects including the one about how important it was for this committee to have both a quiet voice and big ears at the most esteemed bench in town? In fact, didn't you come to me with that idea while you were clerking at the DOJ? No, don't try to attempt to answer any of those questions because you and I both know the answers only too well. You will sit here and you will follow my instructions to the letter. If not, who knows, you and Victor might end up cell mates. Of course, that would depend upon the indictment."

"I'm sorry, but… wait, I haven't done anything wrong. Why would I have to worry about any kind of indictment?" asked the perplexed law clerk.

"You forget," responded Osborne. "Consider the things that you have done both while you were at DOJ and with this committee. Remember what we were able to accomplish relative to certain regulatory matters. Don't you remember what 'we' were able to accomplish in that regard? What about some of the extraneous research you were a part of? Do you remember how that information found its way into the discussions of the Supreme Court? And don't forget about the files you helped create regarding both federal and some state members of the judiciary. As you well know, there are tidbits in over one hundred dossiers on judges that would even cause the late J. Edgar Hoover to blush. And don't you ever forget that you were a part of the planning when we hatched the scheme to end most of the civil litigation in federal court by encouraging defense counsels across the country to file motions for summary judgment in virtually every civil case that came along because we needed the federal court system to be devoted to the criminal cases we were creating while we were at DOJ.

"Apparently you have forgotten exactly how we have been able to control the judiciary, as well as the federal court system, to a significant degree. Wasn't all of that part of the planning that was done while both of us were still at DOJ? And here I thought you were the bright and shining star that I had taken under my wing. Plus, need I remind you that you can be indicted for anything and at any time we decide? As you should know by now, I could have that bookshelf behind you indicted if I so chose, so long as our people at DOJ are not hindered by the current Attorney General and his top people. Don't forget that the power of LESTER is real, and you are a very small part of the picture. Am I clear on this point?"

"Y-yes," stammered the clerk who meekly sat back with his hands folded in front of his chest while he lowered his head.

Then Osborne looked around the room and saw 'Big John" and "Squeaky" taking it all in. He smiled and looked at the two of them and asked, "Any comments from the two of you?"

"Not at all," answered 'Big John.' "But in getting back to Leslie and the fact that he said he would check on A.T.'s activities. Do you think we can really trust that little weasel? Leslie seems to be such a -"

"Weasel," Osborne calmly repeated. He then sat back, folded his hands in a "church-steeple" formation in front of his chest and looked at 'Big John' and then at 'Squeaky,' who was affirmatively shaking his head. At that moment, Osborne leaned forward with his hands placed on the table in front of him and said, "Let me say this. You're all weasels. Without me or this committee not a single one of you has a future worth snot."

The room drew silent with no one daring to say a word. Finally Osborne sat back in his chair with a satisfied smile on his face and said, "Sorry if I am a bit testy today, but this A.T. thing has become a bit of an annoyance I didn't anticipate. It was too bad I had to leave the DOJ when I did. If I had still been there, I would have fought the dismissal. The top guys at the DOJ today don't have the balls to use the power of the office, and they don't even realize the political power that they could generate from that office. Actually that's probably good since the top people at the DOJ today are of the wrong party affiliation. In any event, we have a situation with A.T., and I will have Leslie continue to work on that matter. I have some other tasks for you 'Big John' and you 'Squeaky.' The two of you will need to make an additional contact with a person who works for the GGG. I have her name and phone number. I am hoping that she can help us with our application to the GGG. Victor, you will privately receive instructions from me regarding a matter that has come up at the DOJ and one of their former young attorneys. You need to see me after we adjourn."

Then Osborne turned his chair to the law clerk and said, "Aaron, here's what I want you to do. I will need some details regarding the Court's calendar and docket. I will need to know the details of the docket and calendar since some of our major financial contributors want to place a significant amount of capital at our disposal so we can hire and schedule a number of demonstrations before the Supreme Court. Our financial benefactors want to be sure there is a public outcry relative to a couple of major matters that are soon to be argued before the Court. Can you do that for me?"

"Yes. That should not be a problem," answered Aaron Farmer, who had spent his abbreviated legal career since graduation from law school working as a clerk for both the DOJ and the Supreme Court.

Then Osborne rose from his chair as an indication that the meeting was over. He turned to walk back to his adjacent office while the others rose from their places at the conference table. They all stopped short when Osborne abruptly turned with his finger pointed in the air and said to Aaron, "One more thing, Aaron. Do you remember another young attorney at the DOJ by the name of Felthaus?"

"Yes, as a matter of fact, I do," said Aaron. "Why do you ask?"

"No particular reason," answered Osborne. "Will you provide me with a memo detailing everything you can find out about this Felthaus fellow? I'll need it before the day is over. Okay?"

"I'll get right to it and have it emailed to you later today," said Aaron.

"Good," commented Osborne while he motioned for Victor to follow him back to his office adjoining the conference room through two massive double doors.

* *

Back in Minneapolis and well after the call with Osborne and the LESTER Committee, Leslie was still wiping the sweat from his forehead and straightening the few strands of the thin, straight and blondish-grey hair that had fallen over his glasses during the conference. He had tried to produce a plan to reopen the door to A.T., and in the process came up with the idea of calling A.T. to tell him there was a certificate that went with the plaque he had delivered earlier. That, Leslie thought, was a brilliant idea. All he had to do was use his computer to come up with an official-looking certificate and print it out on some heavy stock paper he kept handy.

This ruse would give him an excuse to call A.T. so he could learn of A.T.'s plans and report back to Osborne. With that idea in mind, he finished writing up his meticulous notes from the meeting when his wife knocked on the door. Dotty had been waiting for him to join the family for dinner, and when he didn't come to the dining room as expected, she thought she would check on him to see if he would be able to finally join the family. After she knocked on the door, she cautiously opened it and found Leslie smiling and placing his LESTER notebook back into the desk which he always kept locked. She asked, "Are you ready to join us for dinner? That was a long call, wasn't it? Is everything okay?"

"Yes and yes," answered Leslie. "It was a very good call. The Committee and especially its chairman really seem to like me, and they have indicated that they want me to continue to work with them. That is very gratifying. I believe we have finally made our mark."

"That's great, dear," said Dotty as she walked over to him to straighten the few strands of hair that had once again slipped down over his forehead. "Now, why don't we go downstairs and join the children for dinner?"

"Okay," answered Leslie. "However, let me make a quick call to A.T. It will just take a second."

"A.T.?" asked Dotty. "Is that the A.T. who used to be so involved in the Republican Party then just abruptly dropped out?"

"Yes, that's the guy," responded Leslie who never suspected, and neither did A.T. for that matter, that Dotty had a personal liking for A.T. That was one of the reasons she had been active in Party politics so many years earlier. She enjoyed the excitement of politics and being around people like A.T. who always seemed to know what to do. Back then she had been a young campaign worker and got to know both A.T. and Leslie around the same time. But A.T. was married and Leslie was not, so she spent time with Leslie, often to be close to A.T. and all of the political activity.

Being active in local politics had been good for both Leslie and Dotty. Dotty had been able to date not only Leslie but a number of other older and politically ambitious men beyond her age group. She had a natural affinity for older men. Plus, the political arena was a better place for meeting people. It was better than bars since so many of the men in that environment seemed too sleazy for her. Meeting people at church was about as bad but in a different way; the guys she met there were boring and dull.

For Leslie, especially when he became Chairman, political activity always meant that there were a lot of young and attractive girls around. The late night campaign meetings were especially fun for him since he was in a position to assign the young ladies to different tasks and then watch them work. He got to date a number of the lady workers but almost got into some serious trouble that would have ended any hope of a political career. Someone had discovered a video camera that Leslie had set up in the women's restroom. He was told about it, and the ladies asked if he would call the police. Acting as if he were outraged, Leslie told the complaining ladies he would personally get to the bottom of it and he would call the police.

Later that night and before contacting the police, Leslie went to the office. He made every effort to wipe the camera device clean of any possible fingerprints, burn the video tapes, and smash the recording device set up in a locked file cabinet that had one key that he kept in his pocket. After burning the tapes and smashing the recording device, he placed the destroyed material in the trunk of his car and took the items to a dumpster in a nearby community. Fortunately, nothing came of the matter even after the police had "supposedly" conducted a complete investigation which included impounding the camera. With Leslie's help the police concluded that someone on the floor below was the likely suspect since there was an advertising agency directly below the Republican Office.

After that incident, Leslie decided he would need to get serious about one person. He chose Dotty for a number of reasons which included her looks, her family wealth, and her willingness to date him on a routine basis. As it turned out, the two of them had similar religious views. Over time Dotty fell in love with Leslie, and they married. She had lost complete track of A.T. and didn't recall hearing Leslie mention his name for years.

"Why do you need to call him after all this time?" asked Dotty.

"Late this afternoon I delivered a plaque to him for his service on the Central Committee, and I forgot to give him the certificate that goes with it," answered Leslie. "So I'll just call and see what his schedule might be. Go on downstairs to the dining room; I'll be there in a couple of minutes."

While Dotty was walking to the stairway, she could hear Leslie start a phone conversation. "Hello, A.T.," said Leslie. "Sorry to bother you again, but I forgot to deliver a certificate to you that goes with the plaque. Is it possible for me to drop it off yet this evening?"

"Sorry, but no," responded A.T. "We are going to the symphony tonight, so it won't work. In fact, we are about to leave."

"Okay then," noted Leslie. "What about tomorrow?"

"That won't work either, I'm going out of town," said A.T. "I'll be back in a few days. We could meet then, or better yet why don't you just mail it?"

"I wouldn't want to mail it," insisted Leslie. "It might get ruined in the mail. By the way, where are you going? Any place exotic?"

"No," said A.T. "Just a business trip out East. I'll be back in a few days. Perhaps we could meet for a coffee; however, I still think you should just mail it. Now, if you don't mind I need to go. Have a nice evening. Bye."

Before Leslie could say anything more, the call was over. He thought, *That's okay. A.T. is just going to a concert and then out East for some business. Maybe when he returns, I can take him up on the coffee invitation and find out more about his schedule. When that happens, I'll be able to report back to Osborne.* With that thought in mind, Leslie started down the stairs to the dining room.

Prior to having a pleasant dinner with Dotty and his children, Leslie decided perhaps he should give Osborne a quick call to let him know he had at least talked to A.T. and found out A.T.'s travel plans. If Leslie didn't call Osborne, he knew he would have trouble sleeping. So he doubled back from the stairway and went back to his study and placed a call to Osborne.

"Hello Leslie," said Osborne. "What do you need?"

"Oh, you knew it was me?" asked Leslie.

"Of course, I've got you programmed into the phone. What do you need?" asked Osborne again.

"Sorry to call so late, but I wanted you to know I found out that A.T. will be at a concert this evening and in the morning he is flying out East somewhere," answered Leslie.

"Did you find out where he is flying?" asked Osborne.

"No. He hung up the phone before I could ask. He said he had to go," said Leslie. "Do you want me to pursue it?"

"Not at this time," answered Osborne. "I'll have 'Squeaky' check out the flights. He has some contacts within the industry, and he will be able to find out exactly where A.T. is headed. Once we know that, I may give you a call and have you do some traveling in case we need you to be a bit of a tail on A. T. Do you think you are up to that task?"

Although Leslie wanted to tell Osborne he didn't want to since he and the family had a rather busy holiday schedule, he knew that if he refused, it might just ruin what he had worked so hard to accomplish, so he said, "Sure, I can do that. Just let me know what I need to do. Will my expenses be paid?"

"Sure, we will pay for your time and your expenses. That's a good man, Leslie. I'll get back to you when I know more and if travel is required; we will take care of the tickets at this end. How does that sound?"

"That's okay with me," answered Leslie. "What do you think--" Before Leslie could ask another question, the call with Osborne was over.

Finally, Leslie was able to join his family for dinner and a relaxing evening at home where he could hear about all that was happening in the lives of Dotty and the children. He particularly made it a point to find at least one night each week when he could spend some quality time with each of his family members and catch up on their activities. Because of his desire to move up the ladder in the Republican Party, Leslie had a tendency to allow politics to overshadow and cloud everything else in his life. To some degree his family life suffered when it came to the daily activities of Dotty and the children since he never seemed to find the time to participate in those activities. Even his job as a county employee suffered since others would often be promoted above him due to the fact that his attention was diverted to Party politics. He didn't really mind, especially now that his star was rising within the Party. He felt he had finally arrived at the point in his life where he was an important "player."

As Leslie and Dotty were about to retire for the evening, the phone rang. According to the caller ID, it was an unknown number. The voice on the answering machine was loud enough for him to hear the message. It was Osborne. He scrambled to catch the call before Osborne hung up.

"Hello," said Leslie as he interrupted the message being left by Osborne. "Sorry I didn't pick up sooner, but I didn't know it was you."

"That's okay," responded Osborne. "I'm working late as I often do. I'm happy I caught you. 'Squeaky' was able to find out about A.T.'s travels. Well, at least he found out part of the itinerary. It appears as though A.T. will be travelling to Lexington, Kentucky, early tomorrow morning. Later he will be taking an evening flight down to Houston. Apparently he will be there for two days and then will be flying back to the Twin Cities."

"So do you want me to book a flight for Lexington if I can?" asked Leslie.

"No," answered Osborne. "At this point I plan to send 'Big John' and 'Squeaky' to Lexington. Instead, I had my secretary book you on a flight to Houston. You can pick up your ticket at the terminal in the morning. The committee has been able to learn from a source within a Senator's office that A.T. will be meeting a self-fashioned investigative reporter of sorts in Houston. We don't know where this supposed reporter and A.T. will be staying, but we do know where they plan to be for part of the day after tomorrow."

"Really," exclaimed Leslie. "What do you want me to do?"

"Pick up your ticket sometime late in the morning," instructed Osborne. "Your flight is scheduled to depart from Bloomington for Houston in the early afternoon. My secretary will email your flight, hotel, and auto confirmation numbers yet this evening. The email will also provide the contact information you will need when you arrive in Houston. Follow the instructions in the email to the letter, including your need to meet with our person in Houston early in the morning, day after tomorrow. The instructions that you will receive will be detailed. By the way, do you have an unobtrusive video camera?"

"I do have a small and very good one. It can record digitally, and I can transfer the video images via computer," answered Leslie. "Why do you ask?"

"Take it with you and be sure to get to the designated location," said Osborne. "Make contact with the individual who is identified in the email from my secretary. Take the email with you so he knows you are working with me. Have him set you up in a strategic spot on location so you can video record A.T. without being noticed. It is very important that you not be noticed, for if you are, your cover will be blown, and you will not be of much assistance to the committee. Is that clear?"

"Very," answered Leslie. "I will be very discrete. He will never know I am there so long as our contact assures me of a hidden location. I trust once I take the video, I should transfer it back to you?"

"That's correct,"

"Do you want me to follow him to any other locations in the event he moves from the location that your secretary and source indicate?"

"No. Just follow the instructions in the email and get a digital image of whatever you video back to me when you return to the Twin Cities. Do we have an understanding?"

"We do," answered Leslie, and before he could ask or say more, Osborne had hung up the phone.

After the call, it was difficult for Leslie to explain to Dotty exactly why, on short notice, he had to travel to Houston the next day. He simply told her that it was a matter of important Party business and he would be back in the evening a day later. Leslie wanted to assure Dotty that he would be around for the school play scheduled for later in the week. She knew better than to ask for more information. She realized the less she knew about Leslie's political activities the better.

CHAPTER 3
START THE ROASTER

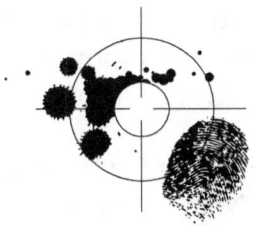

Memories of the events of the past evening, along with the smell of the newly roasted coffee and the aroma of freshly baked cinnamon rolls permeating the crowded corridors of the Minneapolis airport, were enough to keep A.T. in a good mood. As a bit of an annoyance, inadvertently, his mind kept replaying portions of the allegro of J.S. Bach's Brandenburg Concerto that he had just heard the night before at the Minneapolis Symphony. The unexpected repetition of the sounds of the imagined music kept him in a pleasant frame of mind.

To him, it seemed as though the airport patrons were all moving to the quick pace of the music. The lady stirring her coffee seemed to be doing it at the same quick measure of the music, the guy munching his breakfast appeared to be following the music, the janitor seemed to be moving his mop to the music, the young girl sitting on the windowsill seemed to be texting to the music, and the general movement of the entire place seemed to take on the very beat that kept repeating itself in his head.

As he was processed through the airport, his mood was constantly being elevated by the memory of the imagined musical sounds. By the time he boarded the plane, he felt positive about the trip and looked forward to the new information he was promised. While the plane taxied toward the runway and waited an unusually long period of time for its turn and untimely departure, he noticed the Minnesota sky was displaying its usual dark and disgruntled attitude for this time of year. However, the dark November sky was not going to be enough to change his mellow mood. Finally, as the plane rose upward during the takeoff, he sensed what he believed was a good omen. When the plane traveled on its southeastward path, the sky evolved from a heavy dark gray to a softer shade of gray.

The gray turned into a deep blue and, ultimately, became a beautiful powder blue with large white clouds that seemed to venture slowly eastward while the plane moved smoothly forward. Unexpectedly, music again began playing over and over in his head. This time the music was Bach's "Air on a 'G' String." This particular music once again seemed to match the events unfolding before him as the mellow strains appeared to flow as smoothly as the plane's movement forward. If this kept up, he was going to be "Bached-out" before the trip was over.

With so much Bach in his mind, he began to think of a certain politician who had just been in the news and whose name was Bachman. It was that "Bach" thing again. To him the congresswoman epitomized the unnerving changes that were occurring in the political world. Whenever she would speak, her dialogue was downright puzzling. To him she made no sense and always seemed to make up whatever struck her fancy whenever she opened her mouth. He thought about his rendition of the famous saying attributed to Mark Twain, "It is better to keep your mouth shut and appear stupid than to open it and remove all doubt."

He marveled at how certain people could ever become elected officials. Even though Congresswoman Bachman was well outside the mainstream of normal political thinking and was what A.T. considered an embarrassment to the State of Minnesota, she didn't seem as unhinged as a congressman named Steve King from the neighboring state, Iowa. Congressman King had repeatedly made himself appear foolish before Congress. As one would watch him on C-SPAN, he would make rash statements. In order to make matters worse for Iowa, it was recalled that Congresswoman Bachman was born in the Waterloo, Iowa, area. With ties to Iowa by both King and Bachman, those poor people in Iowa had reason to be embarrassed. The embarrassment had to be especially painful for Iowans because the people of Iowa had always been regarded as being particularly level-headed.

From years earlier when A.T. had been active in the Republican Party, he had witnessed the major transition of the party as it evolved into a closed club of fringe interests. Those with moderate political views, the one-time strength of the party, were being forced out. Fortunately, by thinking of other music and of matters of a non-political nature, he was able to recapture his earlier good mood. By the time the plane was nearing Lexington, the sky had become an effervescent whitish-blue. He just knew this was about to be a good day.

In Lexington, A.T. would be meeting an individual whom he hardly knew. However, and to somewhat ease his mind, A.T. had learned that this new acquaintance, Robert, had fulfilled several tours with the Navy. It was because of Robert's military background, and how and where the introduction was made, that A.T. felt reassured about trusting this new participant in the ever-expanding investigation he was conducting. The introduction had come through Bud Hawthorne. Since A.T. had known and trusted Bud for many years, he felt good about the fact that the trip to Lexington was the right thing. The whole idea of the trip came about during A.T.'s recent travel to the nation's capital. His introduction to Robert had taken place in the office of A.T.'s friend, the United States Senator, just weeks ago.

Until that meeting, A.T. had not been in Washington D.C. for some time. It was during his recent trip there that he and his friend, Bud, had met with the Senator. While in the Senator's office, the three of them had discussed some common issues relative to A.T.'s investigation before they broke for coffee, allowing the Senator to fulfill some meeting commitments. It was during the break that Bud introduced A.T. to Robert, who happened to be delivering a box of materials for the Senator's staff. After the introductions, while waiting for the Senator to return, the three of them had begun a casual conversation that led to a realization they were each involved in a common cause on behalf of the Senator.

The three men had an engaging conversation for a couple of hours before the Senator returned. As a result of their discussion, Bud insisted that Robert and A.T. meet again in Lexington, in order for Robert to show him something he didn't believe existed. The Senator confirmed its existence, and A.T. grew intrigued with what Bud and Robert described. Although he thought a trip to Lexington would be a total waste of time, particularly in regard to what he had been compiling, it was the Senator who insisted that A.T. take the time and allow Robert to show him first-hand what was difficult to believe without some proof. Since he was not about to turn down the Senator or Bud, he was fulfilling that commitment.

After disembarking from his plane at the Blue Grass Airport, and as agreed, A.T. met Robert at the appropriate baggage carousel. Robert, who had flown directly from Washington D.C., was ready to go. Following the appropriate greetings, the two of them grabbed their bags and headed toward the main entrance of the terminal. Robert asked about A.T.'s flight from Minneapolis and appeared to be in a very chipper mood. Robert told A.T. that he had made some transportation arrangements for the two of them and that a young friend of Robert's was going to pick them up and drive them to the location.

They continued to visit while they walked to the exit. When the two of them stepped out of the terminal, they couldn't help but notice a commotion of sorts taking place along the vehicle access area not far from the main entrance. A black SUV-type vehicle with an open engine hood was parked directly in front of the main entrance. A young man with his head partly under the hood of the vehicle was arguing with a nearby security guard. Two other security guards were purposefully moving toward the vehicle. Nearing the vehicle's location, part of an ongoing conversation near the doorway seemed to grow more and more animated by the moment.

"You need to move the vehicle, sir! You should know from all the signs that you're not permitted to park here. This area has to remain open for emergencies and ground transportation."

"I won't be long. As you can see, I've got the hood up on my car and -"

"That doesn't matter. You need to move the vehicle."

"Please give me a few minutes, and I should be able to fix it. I'll get it out of the way as soon as I can."

"I can't let you stay here under any circumstances. It's a security violation for you to have a car parked in this area."

"Look, it won't run until I get it adjusted. It will only take a minute."

"It will have to be removed if it doesn't run."

"Only a few minutes…okay?"

"I'm sorry. I can't allow that. I have to call additional security. Sorry!" At this point, the guard used his shoulder microphone to contact additional security that had already sensed a problem and were well on their way.

The driver of the vehicle continued to work under the hood, while keeping an eye on the security guard. The two new guards came at him at a quick pace and looked serious. Both looked well-trained and probably no older than thirty, which was about the same age as the driver. The first one to arrive spoke immediately.

"Sir, that vehicle needs to move right now."

"Gee, I'm sorry, but I think I might be able to get it started if one of you could give me a hand. Here hold this, if you would--"

"No sir, we are not permitted to assist. Ray, call for the tow truck immediately...Brent, there's another one down there trying to park. Tell them to move." It was obvious this guard was not afraid to take command and was apparently in charge. The driver thought of one more plea.

"Hold on, I think it will start now." The driver got behind the steering wheel, and sure enough the vehicle started. With the car running, the driver stepped back out to pick up his tools. At that moment, a booming voice came from the direction of the passenger exit area of the terminal.

"James, is that you?" The man behind the voice was Robert, who stood just over six-two and was about the same height as the remaining security guard. Robert was in his mid-forties and obviously very fit. His military green t-shirt was tight at the shoulders and revealed an upper torso that had a serious relationship with the weight room. He moved at a smooth, deliberate pace and came to the vehicle carrying a duffel bag that looked like a military issue. Following him was A.T., who at a couple inches shorter was also fit but not as chiseled as Robert. A.T. was dressed casually with a dark blue polo shirt. He was carrying a soft case, large enough for a laptop, and a small leather suitcase. The security guard, who had been talking to James by the vehicle, and his backup, who was walking along the curb toward the other vehicle, turned in the direction of the two approaching men. Suddenly, James slammed the hood of the car. The two remaining security guards jumped, with the one on the curb reaching for his firearm.

James raised his hands and said, "Sorry, I didn't mean for it to come down so hard." He diverted his attention to the two men who were approaching and greeted them. "Hello, Robert. How was your flight?"

"Fine, fine," said Robert as he stretched out his hand to shake with James. "James, this is A.T. Van Doren. A.T., this is James Robbins, a friend of mine. A.T. and I just arrived and had hoped we would find you near the terminal." He looked at the security guards and asked, "Is there a problem of some sort?"

The security guard, who had been speaking with James, said, "Your friend here has his vehicle parked in a secure zone, and we were about to have it towed to-"

James interrupted and protested, "Look, I said I was sorry. I was having some difficulty, and I had to make some adjustments in order to get my car running the way I needed. I haven't even been here that long."

"It doesn't matter. You need to get it out of here and now. I presume the opened hood was just a ruse to park here in order to pick up your friends. If you do this again and I catch you, I will give you a citation, and I will have your vehicle impounded. I hope I have made myself clear on this."

"Yes, sir," said James. "I won't let it happen again." James looked in the direction of Robert's associate and protested, "Please don't touch the car. I will get the door for you and help you with your luggage."

"No need for that," commented A.T. "I'll keep my case with me if it's all right with you?" He looked to Robert and nodded for Robert to take the front seat on the passenger side, while he opened the rear passenger door to get in. James quickly came around to the passenger side of the car and held the door while A.T. got in. Robert got into the front passenger seat and handed his duffel bag over the back of the seat to A.T. James crossed over in front of the car and apologized once more to the security guard before getting behind the wheel to drive off.

As they drove off, the tow truck was coming down the access road behind them. James accelerated, and the three of them were finally departing the airport without further incident.

"Thanks for picking us up," said Robert. "Sorry about your incident back there with airport security. That was quite a trick with the hood up and all, but I imagine they see that all the time."

"I'm happy to pick you guys up," said James, "especially since I will be doing some work in the area, as well. By the way, I was actually doing some adjustments under the hood, just in case we need some additional horsepower over the next day or so."

"Hopefully, we won't need that. Why? Do you expect problems? No one except the three of us should be aware of why we are here," said A.T. "And, by the way, I wasn't going to scratch your car when I got in. Perhaps, you thought I was going to put my bag on the roof or -"

"No. It wasn't that. I didn't think you were going to scratch the vehicle…but you see… black is not its actual color. I've got a coating over the color areas, and I didn't want any of it to rub off. That would have made it rather tense for us with the guards. We are really lucky we have a clear day. In fact, the next several days are supposed to be clear and crisp. Late autumn down here is absolutely gorgeous. You'll need something warmer to wear before the day is over. If we had rain or an early snow, I would have had to rent a car, and I wouldn't have been able to use this. I call it the 'Roaster.' I know it is a bit novel to name your car, but a lot of folks down here have names for their vehicles. Many of us do it as a bit of backward humor directed toward the local habit."

"So, why have you painted the car, and why were you making some 'adjustments' under the hood? We have jackets for later," commented A.T.

"Well, in regard to the car…actually, it's probably a misnomer to call this a car. It is an Avalanche, so it's really part car and part truck, although it is classified and licensed as a truck. It's built on a Chevrolet 1500 truck frame. I bought it because of its versatility. It has the comfort of a passenger vehicle but the power and usefulness of a truck. Mine has a V-8 8100 VORTEC engine, so I sometimes tune it a bit for maximum horsepower. Today we may or may not need it, so I was under the hood to be sure we were ready for anything that came along. Plus, this is a well-balanced off-road vehicle. It will be handy if we need to travel on some remote roads."

"When you grow up down here like James, you talk a lot about your car. Also, you need to be able to tune your own car and that sort of thing," said Robert. "Did you know that the forerunner of NASCAR-type racing started in a region nearby? It was really a bunch of rumrunners who started it because they were always modifying their cars in order to outrun the law enforcement officials. A competition developed between the competitive moonshiners over in Wilkes County, North Carolina, and car racing grew into what it is today."

"You've got to be kidding!" exclaimed A.T.

"It's true! There were moonshiners, and quite a few of them, in this region of the country...North Carolina, eastern Kentucky, West Virginia, Virginia, Tennessee, Alabama, South Carolina, and Florida," said James. "But, Robert knows better; I didn't grow up down here. My mother was originally from an area southeast of Lexington, so we had relatives in this area. I would visit my cousins at least once or twice a year. I learned a lot about the culture, including how to work on my own vehicle."

"So, you learned to change the color of the car, as well?" asked A.T.

"No. That's my own idea and formula. I use a water-based paint like the material used in 'paintball' guns. It washes off, and quite readily, so I use some of the very fine clay from Georgia to give it body. Plus, I have a few other 'secret' ingredients."

"What's the real color of your truck?"

"It's red. But the nice thing about this Avalanche is that a good share of it, about half of the body, is grey plastic molding. So, as you can imagine, the color disguise will get us by as long as there is no precipitation."

"But if you were trying to elude someone, couldn't they just get your license plate and have you tracked, or are you going to tell me that you stole someone else's plates for your truck?"

"No, no! I didn't steal anyone's plates. My license plate has a couple of threes that I have temporarily altered to look like eights; a 'C' has been changed to an 'O' and an 'L' to an 'I.' Those alterations will wash off, as well."

"It seems that you are going to a lot of trouble for what I thought was a routine and easy task," observed A.T.

"It should be routine, but with what we are up against, we need to be prepared. We will proceed down Interstate 75 and pick up the Tollway around London and then head east for a ways...then, I'll drop the two of you off near the Goose Rock area. From there I am heading over to Hazard, which is near the area where my mother's family originally settled. Some of my cousins and friends have been providing information to me. In fact, that's how we came to know about the area where the two of you are going. Robert has been there before several times and once with me," said James.

"The truth is that James has a few lady friends in the area who are not his cousins, as far as I know; I really suspect he is making a social call," commented Robert.

"No, Robert. This is strictly a matter of business."

"So, is she charging you now?"

"No, no. She sent me an email and indicated she had more information for me."

After hearing James's explanation, Robert turned to A.T. who was seated directly behind him on the passenger side and said, "You know, A.T., a few years ago James's lady friend decided to leave Hazard and head up to the big city, Cincinnati. Her grandmother told her to be careful and to behave while she was up in that den of iniquity. Well, anyway…what's your lady friend's name, Rosey?"

"No, it's Ruth."

"In any event, Rosey, or excuse me, Ruth, came back to Hazard with her new Cadillac, her mink stole, and her high heels. She decided to go up the mountain to see her grandmother in order to show off a little bit. Well, when she arrived and her grandmother saw the car, the mink stole, and the high heels, she commented that she didn't think her little Rosey had been a very good girl while she was up in Cincinnati. As the story goes, Rosey looked her grandmother in the eye and said, 'You know, Grandma, you've got to be good in order to have the fine things that I have.'"

At this point, James looked at A.T. and said, "Robert is so full of it. He's always telling that same old story. If we weren't such old friends, I'd probably take him out to one of the more risky 'still' areas and just drop him off. My friend, Ruth, is a grade school teacher, and she has a boyfriend who could be the source of some of the information we are getting."

"So, the two of you…you and Robert, are old friends? How did that come about?" asked A.T.

"My father had his medical practice in Cincinnati. That's where I still live. Robert is originally from Cincinnati, and he was a patient and a friend of my dad. When my father died, Robert was there to help me get through a very troubled time."

"Death of a parent can be pretty traumatic, no matter what age you might be. How did your father die, if I may ask?"

"He was gunned down in cold blood, simply by being in the wrong place at the wrong time."

"Boy, I really am sorry. He was a doctor, and he was gunned down? Did they find out who did it?"

"No, but I think I'm on the right track in finding out. That's one of the reasons why I'm involved with this entire enterprise. My father was also a friend of the Senator and…"

"Wait a minute!" said A.T. "Did you say a friend of the Senator… which senator?"

"Don't worry; it's not one of the Kentucky senators, especially not the one who looks like a chicken. That would be one of the last people who we could confide in. The Senator I work with is the same one who is working with you. He's the one who arranged for me to assist the two of you today and tomorrow, if necessary. After that, I need to get back to my regular job in Cincinnati. When I'm not pretending to be a redneck, I'm an engineer for a firm that does municipal planning for cities throughout the Midwest."

"I didn't know you knew the Senator with whom we are working, so I just thought it might be a senator from Kentucky and…How do you know the Senator?"

"He and my father were very close friends in undergraduate school many years ago. When my father died, the Senator and Robert helped to get me focused, get my degree from Virginia Tech, get the right connections when I went into the Navy, and later they helped me channel some of my energy into this sideline."

"So, your father was he –"

Robert interrupted the conversation, saying, "His father was a urologist in Cincinnati. That's how I met him. I was a patient. Not only was James's father a very good friend of the Senator, he was also a good friend of a gynecologist, who had allegedly performed abortions in a Cincinnati suburb. This doctor friend of James's father was being threatened by a couple of people. A patient of James's father reported during an exam that the gynecologist was in grave danger. On the day of the warning, some protestors surrounded the clinic of the gynecologist. James's father, after hearing about the threats on the life of his doctor friend, went over to the clinic to warn him. While he was attempting to get into the clinic, one of the protestors shot James's father. The police presumed he had been mistaken for the gynecologist. He died on the spot, and to date, the authorities have not been able to determine who did it."

James added, "The police have a rather complete file, and there are some very good leads and a solid indication as to who actually did it. However, witnesses are hard to come by. It seems that although a good number of people actually saw the shooting, no one will come forward to identify the guy. I am certain I know who it is, but I need more proof. As I said, that's how and why I got involved in this investigation. It's related to what you are doing, and the guy who did it is a part of the group that Robert is tracking. I hope to pick up new information while I'm in Hazard."

"Isn't it a bit implausible that the people who shot your father would be a part of the group we are investigating for the Senator?"

"Not at all; most of the people down here are dirt poor. They are also very prejudiced. They start out poor, they come from poor families, and the education is not the best; they can't find a way out, and they become rather calloused in their thinking. A lot of them want to blame someone else for their plight. Some become violent and are just looking for a way to channel their frustration. It is easy for the group that you are investigating to recruit these folks, and it's not just happening in this area of the country but elsewhere, as well. I am certain I already know who killed my father, and he is definitely a part of the group you are investigating. I've wanted to handle it myself, but both Robert and the Senator have convinced me their way is better."

"This must all be very difficult for you," said A.T.

"It has been more than difficult. Initially, I wanted to personally avenge the death of my father. He and I were close, and I was really hit hard emotionally at the time. I still have days where I want to take the entire matter into my own hands. However, Robert has been a really good friend. He has kept me on the straight and narrow by channeling my rage into a more calculated investigation," observed James.

"It was really the work James has done that has led us to what I'll be showing you. I trust you realize the Senator wants the lid kept on this until everything is in place, and he is ready for a presentation to the appropriate Senate subcommittee in Congress."

"I understand that completely, Robert," said A.T. "The Senator has asked me to do this on my own time because he does not have a budget for me or my part of the investigation. That will soon need to change since I will request funding. By the way, from what the Senator said on the phone this morning, one of you is supposed to have some new information for me."

"Oh, I have it," answered James as he reached under his seat to retrieve a large envelope. "I was also instructed to take a bit of a detour before I dropped the two of you at the location. It is my understanding that you are to meet a gentleman in Mt. Vernon in the parking lot of the Daniel Boone Inn. He is supposed to have an additional package to the one I'm handing you. From what was explained to me by the

Senator, the package that I just gave you and the material that the man in Mt. Vernon is going to give you will match up and only make sense when you see the materials side by side. Also, no cell phones from here on. Just to be safe, it would be a good idea to turn them off now."

"We have to meet someone else?" asked A.T. as he and Robert turned off their cell phones. "Who is he, and what is his connection? Also, did you say Mt. Vernon?"

"I don't know his name, but I was told that he is an accountant of some kind," answered James. "I have no idea how he fits into this mess, but Mt. Vernon is on our way. It's a bit over halfway to the toll road, and it's right off the interstate. I found the Daniel Boone Inn through MapQuest, so I am pretty sure I can get you to the hotel. However, I'm not sure how to identify the guy we're supposed to meet. I have no idea what he looks like or exactly where to meet him in the hotel."

"I may be able to help in that regard," said Robert. "When I got my instructions to take A. T. out through part of the Daniel Boone National Forest, I was told there would be another man. I was concerned because the more people I had to watch, the more difficult the task. At that point, I protested. I was then told that the other individual, the man we are to meet in Mt. Vernon, would not be going with us. He is simply to deliver a package personally to A.T. When I asked about the contents of the package, I was told that it did not involve me, so that was it."

"So, Robert, were you told how to identify this guy in Mt. Vernon?"

"Well, I was told he left Washington D.C. a couple days ago and was taking a convoluted path to a location that was to remain confidential. All I know is that after he talks with you, he will be going to New Orleans, where he will be boarding a plane for the West Coast. Today he is supposed to be driving a rental car, a black Malibu. He apparently has a neatly trimmed beard and will be wearing brown slacks with a tan sweater. I understand he was an economics or finance professor at one of the colleges on the East Coast. He is to answer to 'Professor' when we locate him. We are to ask if he has the 'test scores', and he will answer, 'They're in the envelope.'"

"The 'test scores?" asked A. T. "I wonder what that means."

"Maybe it's nothing. It could just be the code word for the package he is to deliver to you."

"How will he know us?" asked A. T. "How will he know whether he is to deliver the package to me or to one of you?"

"He probably has a description of you, and I would imagine he has been told that there would be three of us. Anyway, we don't want to spend too much time with him because we have tracks to make after we meet him. We have some serious hiking to do, and we must get what we need and get back out," said Robert. "You're still going to pick us up, right, James?"

"As long as everything goes as planned," answered James. "No one knows I'm going into Hazard except Ruth and the two of you. She will meet me at the schoolhouse during her lunch break, so I have to watch the time. As soon as I have the new information from her, I will visit my aunt in order to catch up on family matters. I'll plan my departure from Hazard so I am not waiting around the pickup point for you too long. I don't want to be sitting along the toll road for very long. It will look suspicious; they check on all parked vehicles. So if I'm not there right away, stay patient and concealed until you see me pull up along the agreed-to road marker. Be assured I will be there, unless something totally unforeseen happens. If that becomes the case, you're on your own."

"Well, let's hope nothing out of the ordinary happens."

"Better yet, let's just say that nothing happens since this entire matter is anything but ordinary. So, let's all be careful," cautioned A.T.

* *

The trip south to Mt. Vernon, Kentucky, was relaxing and uneventful. The quiet time allowed A.T. to organize his briefcase and the documents that he received from James. Robert and James visited about past times together and caught up on current events that involved family and friends. Once in Mt. Vernon, James navigated his way to the Daniel Boone Lodge. Robert then spotted the black Malibu.

While approaching the Malibu, Robert observed, "Don't look now, but a green car just pulled up directly across the lot. The two people inside seem to be watching our professor friend."

"I think you're getting paranoid," said A.T. "No one is supposed to know he is meeting us or even that he is here in Mt. Vernon. My guess is that it is just some other hotel guests."

"Perhaps, but it is a little odd that the two people in the green car were intently watching the professor, and now they are watching us," commented Robert.

At that point they neared the Malibu, where the professor had the back door open and was rifling through a stack of papers he began stuffing into an envelope as they approached.

A.T. asked, "Professor, is that you?" At that point the man with the grey beard turned while he was closing and sealing the envelope.

"Excuse me," answered the man.

"Do you have the test scores, Professor?" asked A. T.

"I do have the test scores, but do I know you?"

"I'm A. T. I thought you would have the test scores for me to review."

"Oh, okay. A.T., I guess you do look like the right guy, but I thought you would be alone."

"It's okay. This is Robert, and he is an associate of mine."

"I was told there would be a single person from the education committee who would review the test scores, and I was instructed to only provide the test results to a gentleman named A. T., who fits your description. Do you have some form of identification?"

A.T. presented his driver's license and said, "There are three of us. As I mentioned, this is Robert, and the third member of our party is James."

"Who are your friends, Professor?" asked Robert.

"What? What do you mean? I'm here alone. I'd better be-"

"I thought the two people in that green car were watching you."

"What green car?"

Robert nodded in the direction where he had seen the car. It was gone. James said, "We really should be moving on if we're going to try to remain on schedule. What are you looking for?"

"Robert thought he saw a green car parked over there," A.T. said nodding in the direction where the car had been located.

"There's nothing there now," observed the Professor.

"Let me take a minute with the Professor," said A.T. as he waved the other two off to a distance away from the Malibu. He asked the Professor, "What do you have for me, and do I call you Professor?"

"What I have will take some explanation, so we need to sit down at a table somewhere. My name is Charles Brougham, and I was an adjunct professor with the Economics Department at Yale for some time. During the last few years, I have been an economics and accounting consultant for an organization that has various interests across the globe. Their activities seemed quite understandable, as well as altruistic initially, and I agreed completely with the basic philosophies at first. I had been placed on some of their more strategic committees, and after a few years, I began to change my views on the overall concept. At that point, I asked to be dropped from the committees. They wouldn't let me step down without certain conditions I cannot accept. Look, we need to take some time here -"

"Time is not what we have to offer," said A.T. "I need to get to another location. It will take a while to get there and back, so we need to get along."

"Not with my documents. Not unless I have time to explain them," said Professor Brougham. "There's a restaurant in the lodge, so why don't ..."

"The lodge is not going to be a good place for us to discuss anything of a sensitive nature," noted A.T. "We need to find a place that has a lot of public traffic and is noisy and difficult for anyone else to eavesdrop."

"After getting gas for my car, I noticed a hamburger place not far from here. Would that work?" asked the Professor.

"Well," began A.T., while motioning for Robert and James to join them, "that would assure our getting through the material a bit more quickly since they probably won't let us stay there very long." A. T. told Robert and James that they were going to make a quick stop at a hamburger place nearby.

"I know where to find the hamburger place, so why don't you hop in your car and follow us. We're in the black Avalanche over there," commented James, pointing in the direction of his vehicle.

The Professor got into his car and followed the other three to the nearby hamburger "drive-through" that fortunately had indoor seating. After the short drive and after getting situated at a table for their order of coffee and soft drinks, Robert noticed a familiar green Ford Taurus drive to the order window. He pointed out the vehicle to both James and A. T. Robert suggested that he and James locate themselves near the main entrance just to be extra cautious while the Professor and A.T. took another table in order to discuss the materials the Professor was intending to deliver to A. T. After they were seated, the Professor placed his envelope with the documents on the table. He removed a selected group of papers.

"These documents are the ones I've been instructed by the Senator to present to you and only you. That's why I needed to see your identification back at the hotel. I have been advised that you have a special commission from a United States Senator in regard to an investigation, and that these documents will tie together some of the information you have been seeking. What I have are copies of certain ledgers, as well as particular bank accounts, which belong to the group I have been with since my retirement. As you will see, the corporations, LLCs, the hedge funds, the partnerships, and the nonprofits are all identified, along with the various account numbers. These are samples from what you will find on the enclosed "thumb drives" and disks. The accounts and entities are real, and some have been in existence for decades. In fact, quite a few of the account holders have been around for nearly a century. All of these groups that you see identified in these materials are tied together in some way or other."

"What's the point of all of these accounts, and how are they supposed to relate to what I'm doing?" asked A.T.

"From what I believe," said the Professor, "these documents will demonstrate that a significant number of our laws have been violated in terms of outside financial interests attempting to undermine the republic as we have come to know it. Money talks and you will see that these documents will lead you to the names of various parties, here in the U.S. and across the globe, that are attempting to buy the operations of government."

"That would be a surprise to me," stated A.T. "I cannot believe any sum of money could be significant enough to do what you say. No one group could be that well financed. It may be suitable for the world of academia, and theoretically, something you might tell your class. I'm sure that articles have been written about such matters, and I applaud your efforts to bring this to the Senator's attention. However, I fail to see how your research and theories would have any application to my investigation or the reasons behind my investigation," noted A.T.

"You're wrong," interrupted the Professor. "Just so you know, I was specifically referred to you by a mutual friend, who is also a friend of the Senator."

"I am really and truly not the right man for this sort of thing," protested A.T.

"Well," said the Professor, "you are involved whether you like it or not. As you read the material...You will see just how well financed these people are. You will also see where some of the funds originate, and I assure you that you will be surprised. You will see that funding has come from different parts of the globe. There are interests or concerns outside the borders of the United States. Once you get into the detail, I am certain you will be as shocked as I was. Keep in mind that I am giving you my only remaining copy. The other copy has been given to a former student/current colleague who's been instructed to hold the materials for up to four years. He will then have them delivered anonymously to the House Banking Committee. By that time, you will have either succeeded or failed in your investigation. If you have succeeded, it may be presumed that certain people will have been brought to justice and particular reform and oversight will have occurred. If you have failed, the consequences for American Democracy, as we know it, will be forever changed, and I might add, not for the good."

"Well, thanks for dropping such a burden on my shoulders."

"Look, I'm not dropping any burden on your shoulders. It's part of what you do, and it's just in a day's work for you. That's not the case for me. I am a marked man, and I have no choice but to disappear. The information I am turning over to you is about as damning to these people as you can imagine. I was a part of the inside regarding certain secret operations. I sat on some committees. I know too much. My conscience would not allow me to continue. I needed to do the right thing, and now it's up to you. Here are the materials you need. Thank you, sir, for allowing me to hand you the baton." The Professor placed the papers that he had shown A.T. back into the envelope and slid the envelope across the table.

A.T. took the envelope and asked, "What will you do now, Charles?"

"Immediately, I will drive to New Orleans where I will board a plane for San Diego. Then I will drive down to Mexico. There is a place in Mazatlan that belongs to a dear, personal friend of mine. I will be able to stay there until I decide where to live on a more permanent basis. I expect to receive a new identity and papers that go with it. I've learned much from the committees, so I should be able to transfer enough of my funds to a place where I should be able to live comfortably. I may even tend bar just to have something to do. But I have a plan that should work."

"What about family?"

"I have no family. Not anymore. I haven't spoken to any relatives for many years and haven't even kept track of their activities or their lives. The committee members know that. With what I have planned and with a new identity, I intend to disappear from the face of the earth. However, the reason we are meeting here is due to the fact that I was just down in Tampa meeting with a lawyer in order to set up a trust for my two children whom I haven't seen for many years. One is in Atlanta, and the other is in Tampa. I wanted to be sure they had something to remember me by, even though they said they never wanted to see me again. They never forgave me for divorcing their mother, and that has been nearly twenty years ago. Under the circumstances, it's better this way."

After they were finished, the two of them walked near the door where Robert and James were sitting. A.T. asked, "Did you see the green car again?"

"Just once," said Robert. "It drove through the fast order line and disappeared down the street, and we haven't seen it return."

"That's good," said A.T. as he turned to bid farewell to the Professor, who walked out of the restaurant with the three of them. The Professor almost skipped to his car, hopped in, and drove off, apparently as a happy man who seemed as if he had dropped the burdens of the world on the unsuspecting lap of someone else.

Robert motioned for A.T. to sit in the front passenger side of the vehicle while Robert climbed into the backseat behind James who had started the Avalanche as he was ready to go. The three of them headed south on old Highway 150 toward Pine Hill, where they would pick up Interstate 75.

A. T. began to think about how this entire investigation had come into existence. First there was the bogus indictment that took years to overcome after the dismissal. Then the losses to reputation, relationships, health, and the law practice that were incalculable. Next there were the sleepless nights and the constant paranoia of being constantly under surveillance. Worst of all was the strain that exerted itself upon a wonderful marriage. All of those agonies led to this intense investigation which revealed a sinister plot formulated by former political enemies. The investigation had stolen precious time from A.T. and Jacci along with the plans they had once made for travel. Now, the Senator wanted more to be added to the investigation. A.T. wondered: *Should I do the Senator's bidding just so I can push for the reform I want to see at the DOJ and the FBI? Is it worth spending so much time away from Jacci? Should I allow this investigation, along with all of the new twists, consume my life? Is it worth the danger? You damn right it is! Those bastards started it, and I'm going to finish it. Reform must take place, and if it means placating the Senator on some investigative twists, I'll do it. Hell yes!*

While A.T. was thinking through the investigation and a couple of miles from Pine Hill on 150, James noticed a green Ford Taurus a short distance behind them. James decided to let Robert and A.T. in on the fact that it appeared they were being tailed. "When the two of you have a chance, take a look behind us. You will see a familiar green Taurus. I think that I will stay on 150 and skip the interstate."

"What do you mean?"

"I'm going to head down 150 toward Livingston, and if they are still with us, I'll head up 89 toward McKee. Be prepared! The road is not a super highway by any means, and it will be a bit of a nail biter. I do know the road, and we'll see if they do."

As to be expected, the green vehicle took the bait and began to follow James up 89 where he had some familiarity. James nurtured the vehicle through Lamer before he decided to see what kind of driver was following him in the Taurus. The road was tricky and displayed its share of twists and turns. James was able to demonstrate his driving skills that seemed considerable to A. T., who had a ringside seat in the front. From this position, he felt on more than one occasion they would soon be airborne and meeting their creator. But, to his surprise, James was able to either slow or speed the vehicle at the right moment taking one challenging turn after another. At a point where the roadway ran nearly parallel with the middle fork of the Rockcastle River, the challenges grew greater and greater. Due to James's driving, A. T. had to swallow hard a couple times in order to stave off car sickness. Then, without warning, James hit the brakes and came to a complete stop. Fortunately, there were no other vehicles in either direction. While A.T. was attempting to recover his bearings, Robert asked, "What the hell! What are you doing?"

James turned toward the back seat and said, "They just went off the road behind us! It didn't look pretty. We had better see what happened. With what I saw, someone could have gotten hurt."

"How far back?" asked Robert.

"Not far…maybe a quarter mile or so. Stay here; I'll go check on them."

"No! No!" said Robert. "I'll go. You stay behind the wheel in case we need to get back to it." Robert opened his door to the seat directly behind James and reached down and grabbed the socket wrench James had been using at the airport. With that, Robert bailed out of the car and headed back down Highway 89. James began to slowly back the Avalanche toward the location where he had seen the Ford Taurus slip over the edge.

Once James was able to back around the last curve he had taken, he saw Robert running toward an area of the ditch where either steam or smoke rose from below the roadway. James continued the backward motion until the Avalanche was about twenty yards from the location where it appeared the Taurus had gone over and where the cloud of steam or smoke was rising. When James placed the Avalanche in park, another car, a red sports car, slowly came up the road directly behind them and in the vicinity of the ditching of the Taurus. The vehicle stopped as Robert came up from the road embankment. Robert went straight to the stopped vehicle and talked to the passengers. Robert pointed to the ditch, and then there was a loud bang.

"I'm telling you that there are two people down there, and I think they are going to need some help. The three of you will need to help me get them out of their car before it gets serious," Robert said to the three young men in the newly arrived red Dodge Challenger.

"What was that loud bang?" asked the driver of the Challenger.

"Don't worry about the loud bang. Just give me some help in getting those people out," said Robert. "Does anyone have a cell phone? We need to call the authorities."

"That's not going to be a good idea," commented the passenger in the back seat.

"Shut up," ordered the young guy in the front passenger seat turning to chastise the kid in the back.

"Have you boys been drinking? Isn't it a bit early in the day?" questioned Robert?

"None of your business!" said the driver.

"Look!" Robert ordered. "You three need to get out now and help with these people. They could be injured. If you were down there, you would want someone to help whether the people helping had been drinking or not. Now what about that cell phone?"

The three got out of the car, and the guy getting out of the back said, "Just don't tell Billy's uncle. He's a deputy sheriff here in Jackson County -"

"Didn't I tell you to shut up," said the passenger in the front seat as he started to get out of the car.

"It isn't going to matter if you've been drinking. Someone's life may be at stake, and the least thing the three of you can do is get down in that ditch and see if you can offer some help. Whoever has a cell phone better call for assistance. By the time help arrives, your alcohol levels will probably be significantly reduced, and no one will notice because they will be concerned about the people in the car off the road. Now make that emergency call and get some help out here," urged Robert.

The passenger from the back seat pulled out his cell phone and made the emergency call while the other two went down into the ditch to see if they could help. After the one young man made the call, he reached into the back seat and grabbed an armful of empty beer cans and tossed them into the opposite ditch. He then reached for some pocket mints. Robert was amused but wanted to keep the young guy on his toes, so he said, "You better get down there too. They are going to need all the help they can get."

After the third young man headed into the ditch, Robert ran to the nearby Avalanche and hopped into the backseat. He told James to get going and that the three young guys would be help enough.

"What about our helping?" asked A.T.

"No one was hurt, but they were shaken up. The driver was trying to get out, so he could help the lady on the passenger side."

"The one was a woman? How do you know? Did they see you? What did you tell them? Should we go back?"

"I know a woman when I see one. Her baseball cap had come off, and I could tell from her hair, her shape, and size that the passenger was a lady. Things were happening too fast for them to pay much attention to me. I told them that I was going to bring help. The car was upright, and no one looked injured. And no, we shouldn't go back but get out of here ASAP."

"What was that loud bang that we heard, Robert?"

"Oh, I used your socket wrench to hit the side of the kid's car. I needed to get their undivided attention. It needed to be done because those kids in the sports car were all about half-sauced. I needed to sober them up and get them out of their car. From what one said, another apparently has an uncle who's a deputy sheriff down here, so they were a little concerned about calling to report the accident. They'll probably see the damage to their car after they get back on the roadway. I imagine at least one of them will be a bit pissed. By then, we should be well on our way and out of here."

"If we can get out of here," said A.T. while pointing to the temperature gauge on the dash of the Avalanche.

James said reassuringly, "Don't worry! It does that when I tune it for extra power. It's nothing serious; the over-heating will stop as soon as I get it back on the road and start moving. It is just the way the vehicle behaves with my adjustments. That's why I call it the 'Roaster.'"

"Well, 'Roaster' is appropriate since it seems to me that it is hot enough right now to roast coffee beans on the hood."

CHAPTER 4
COUNTING BEANS

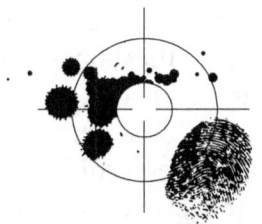

After attempting to put the incident along the Middle Fork of the Rockcastle behind them, the three adventurers continued northeasterly on Highway 89, until it intersected with 421. James's plan was to pull off the Tollway at the interchange at Thousandsticks, then proceed through Hyden and back toward the Tollway before dropping Robert and A. T. at a predetermined point south of Dryhill.

Once Robert and A.T. were on their way through the Daniel Boone National Forest, James would reenter the D.B. Parkway and head east toward Hazard. After his meeting at Hazard, James planned to double back and pick up Robert and A. T. at a specific road marker along the Parkway. A.T. was sorting through the paperwork from the Professor when A.T. observed, "This is interesting country. I have never spent much time in Kentucky. I just drove through a couple times on my way from the Midwest down to Florida."

"It's definitely interesting country," commented James. "It was not far from here back in September 2009 that the authorities were called in to an old cemetery near Arnett's Fork in Clay County. They were called to view a body of a U.S. Census worker who had allegedly been hanged because he worked for the federal government. The people in this part of the country are poor, and many of them raise marijuana for a living. They don't like and don't believe in the authority of the federal government. In addition, they use public land, including the Daniel Boone National Forest, as if it were their own private property. However, it is questionable as to whether the census worker was murdered or committed suicide. An investigation subsequent to the death apparently determined it was a suicide, even though his mouth, hands, and glasses were taped. The rumor was that there was a large insurance policy, so there would have been a suicide motive, at least."

"Well! You've got a lot going on down in this area. It almost sounds like they are on the brink of anarchy. It must be a real problem for law enforcement," said A.T.

"Law enforcement in this area has its hands full when you're talking about the serious and the honest officials; however, there is also the other side of the coin that involves the 'good ole boy' network in which some law enforcement officials just look the other way when certain 'things' happen. You've got to remember to walk and talk very carefully in this part of the country," warned James.

"Thanks for those reassuring comments," noted A.T.

"What's in the batch of documents our friendly Professor handed you?" asked Robert.

Reluctantly, A.T. decided to provide some general information. He said, "You've got to remember Mr. Brougham is a bean counter, so the information that he provided is a matter of accounting. There are a series of spreadsheets that reflect a number of bank accounts, both here in the U.S. and all over Europe. In fact, I see accounts at Bank of America, J.P. Morgan Chase, Wachovia-Wells, UBS, Lloyds, Royal Bank of Scotland, Deutsche Bank, HSBC, and a couple of others. Most of the accounts involve companies I do not recognize, and the deposits, transfers and bank balances, for the most part, reflect very sizable sums. There does appear to be a rather large balance of just over two hundred and thirty million Euros at UBS in Zurich."

"Aren't all foreign bank accounts supposed to be disclosed to the Internal Revenue Service? I thought Congress passed some legislation a while back requiring a full disclosure of foreign bank accounts due to both corporations and individuals parking money offshore in order to avoid paying taxes on certain earnings," stated Robert.

"You are partially correct. I don't think Congress passed any new legislation. However, during a period of time between 2000 and 2008, many U. S. businesses and businessmen were setting up offshore accounts to hide and park money. Many of them didn't pay taxes on the money in those accounts, and there really wasn't any serious enforcement during that time. I believe it was back in October of 2009, after Bush's presidency, when the U.S. government set a deadline for possible tax leniency for individuals with foreign bank accounts. When the smoke cleared, UBS ended up turning over the names of about 4,500 wealthy American clients. Other foreign banks then followed suit instead of facing criminal charges or being fined. I believe UBS ended up paying about three-quarters of a billion dollars as a settlement," noted A.T.

"Any other interesting tidbits from what the Professor handed to you earlier?" asked James.

"I'm really not sure how this will impact what I've been investigating. Although, I see there is a U.S. account at Bank of America that is in the name of CRPC. I've seen that name, CRPC, before but not for quite a while. If it's the same non-profit 351, it was a fragmented group of operatives within the Republican Party. I thought they had disbanded long ago."

"So, what was the CRPC?"

"If I'm correct, it was an abbreviation for the Committee to Re-Elect the President Corporation. It was a nonprofit that developed out of the CREEP Committee back in the early 1970s."

"Was it really called the CREEP Committee?"

"It was indeed. That's what they called themselves. Just so you know, the CREEP Committee was the 'Committee to Re-Elect the President' established to re-elect President Nixon. It was quite active in the early seventies and included some of the more notorious Republicans in modern history. You've probably heard of some of the more infamous, most of whom were indicted, convicted, or pled guilty. There was John Mitchell, the former Attorney General; the president's legal counsel, John Dean; Jeb Magruder; Maurice Stans; Kenneth Dahlberg; James McCord; G. Gordon Liddy; E. Howard Hunt; Don Segretti; Fred LaRue; Chuck Colson; and Roger Stone," commented A.T.

"Well then, CREEP was an appropriate name. Although my folks were Republicans, they never really cared for Nixon," said Robert.

"I have you beat there," said A.T. "Of course, I'm a lot older than you. I was actually invited through our state's National

Committeeman and our National Committeewoman at the time to attend some of the meetings the CREEP Committee held in Washington D.C. in 1971. When I went to Washington D.C. to attend some of the meetings, I was so disillusioned that I skipped out of the meetings and just ended up touring the D.C. area with my young family, who had come along for the trip. I had been stationed in D.C. a few years earlier, so I took the opportunity to see some old friends."

"So, did you go back to any of the meetings?"

"No. However, I decided to remain a Republican because of some of my basic philosophies that I thought were common Republican principles. You know... balancing the budget, no deficit spending, small central government, strong individual state governments, diplomacy, promotion of small business, oversight of private enterprise, regulatory systems for banking, insurance, and other major industries, etc., - a lot of Teddy Roosevelt-type things. But not many, if any, of those principles, remain as part of the Republican Party's agenda today. Today it is exclusively a political party that is only friendly to the very wealthy, certain religious people, and some disgruntled party members."

"Wasn't it our Republican Party who also pioneered civil rights?"

"That's true. It should also be remembered that the issue of civil rights was first credited to the early Republicans as they became a truly functioning political party by the time of Abe Lincoln. In fact, two of the foundation principles of the Republican Party in Lincoln's time were the promotion of small business and anti-slavery. It was much later that the Republican Party embraced the early child labor laws, civil service, regulated work hours, minimum wage, and such. Those principles were mostly promoted by another Republican, namely a New York governor, Theodore Roosevelt, either as governor of New York or as president."

"The issues you outlined as Republican sound more like the Democrats of today."

"Certainly that can be said. Today the Democrats seem to own each of the issues I mentioned, while the Republicans of present appear to be content in limiting their party's interest to only those who agree with the current party operatives on matters of wealth, religion, and certain social issues. Personally, I believe issues of religion and social reform are just diversions to get support from certain fringe interests," said A.T.

"Even I am having trouble being comfortable with today's Republican Party," commented Robert. "What's especially troubling is that I am very conservative and a former military officer."

"I too was a Republican until my father was murdered," interjected James. "The guy whom I believe actually set up the murder is a part of the Republican movement here in Kentucky. That fat little son-of-a-bitch doesn't realize I have just about enough evidence on him already, and I am hoping Ruth has some final items that will help me put him away."

"As I said, you can't blame the Republicans for what happened to your dad, James. We have been over that many times, and I thought that you understood. You've got to control your anger in order to be effective in bringing these guys to justice," warned Robert.

"I don't think party officials care. I'm not trying to pat myself on the back, but I'm the one who's been collecting the evidence on that little worm. Down here it seems that the Republican Party has been hijacked by what mainstream America is calling the 'lunatic fringe,'" said James.

"Since we are dissatisfied Republicans, perhaps the three of us should start our own Republican Party. By the way, isn't the term 'lunatic fringe' something the Democrats have used as a label for a certain segment of the Republican Party? Perhaps you're becoming one of those radical Democrats and just don't realize it," joked Robert.

"No. No. Not at all! I'm an independent more than anything. Well, at least I don't think I've become a Democrat. In any case, if I have, it can't be all bad; I don't want to be bunched together with the 'lunatic fringe'," said James.

"Actually," interjected A.T., "the term 'lunatic fringe' was coined by one of our more popular Republican presidents, Teddy Roosevelt, who called a portion of the activists of his time the 'lunatic fringe.' They were anarchists and separatists. There is still a faction within the Republican Party who believes that today. So, is it a fair understatement to say that your father was a Republican?"

"In a big way," said James. "He was active in party politics and was on the Republican Central Committee in Ohio. I got to meet a lot of the party leaders of the Republicans back when I was a kid. They would come over to the house quite a bit, and because my dad was a doctor and a party official, we were always being invited to all kinds of political events. Ohio boasts that it has elected more presidents than any other state. I think that all, if not most, were Republicans, so the Republican Party there is very active. Today's Republicans are mostly regarded as emotional and single-dimensional ideologues, and -"

"Let's stay objective, if we can," interrupted A.T. "It is my firm belief the reason the Senator has us, or at least me, working on this matter is that he wanted the investigation to remain as non-partisan as possible and to demonstrate that it is not the Republican Party, but a faction of the party, that is engaged in the illegal acts I'm investigating. I believe the Senator feels that if the investigation is done objectively, he can demonstrate to the more rational Republicans in Congress that they are being sidetracked into an area of limited good or benefit, in addition to the fact that these 'behind the scenes groups' have been violating the federal laws and the Constitution. Although the Senator is not a Republican, he is a strong believer in a two party system. Can you imagine how many others are out there like us who have been driven out of the party?"

"Well, you need to talk to the Senator about the matter instead of me. I doubt he will listen to me on the issue because he knows where I'm coming from," said James.

"You know guys, asserted A.T.," I never expected my investigation to demonstrate just how certain interest groups would be imposing such an influence within the U.S. government as they have moved to control the Republican Party. I was surprised to find that the investigation took such a turn; however, it has. It has not been from just a contribution perspective; however, it looks like our friend, Professor Brougham, is providing information that would send the investigation in a new direction in regard to political contributions.

"So, if the Professor's war is with the groups that you don't have under investigation, why all the information about the Republican Party and their contributors?" asked Robert.

"I'm not sure," said A.T. "He must think there is some tie between some of the big contributors to the Republican Party and the group for whom he was working. I don't know why our friend, the Senator, thought it was important for me to have these documents and what relationship there might be to my investigation. At this point, I just don't know, and I personally don't plan to go there."

"It seems apparent the Professor was upset with someone, and he clearly felt that there were ties to the Republican Party," said Robert.

"That seems to be the case, and I don't even know for whom he was working. But I will tell you this…he hit some kind of nerve in order for those two people back there to be tailing him."

"Tailing him? Maybe they are tailing one of us. Don't forget they were following us and not the Professor."

"That's a good point, but which one of us would they be tailing?" asked James.

"Your guess is as good as any," said A.T. "I doubt it is me because I have really kept the lid on my investigation; plus, we didn't encounter them until we were meeting with the Professor. My guess is they were following the paperwork and the money."

"I'm not so sure," commented Robert. "You seem to be the one with the most significant political connections, and it would seem that James's current dislike of the Republican operations, along with his investigation into his father's death, would make either one of you a reason for a tail on us."

"What about you, Robert? Perhaps those two people back there were following you," commented A.T.

"I can tell you about me, but before I get into that, tell me more about what you've seen in the documents the Professor gave you back at the hamburger place," urged Robert.

"There are accounts in the name of the 'CRPC,' or what I believe is an off-shot of the CREEP Committee, as I mentioned. There are also accounts for a number of other interesting groups. For example, there are accounts in the name of 'U977 A. G.;' 'Poor Knights, Inc.;' 'Bunch of Grapes, Inc.;' 'SIS A. G.;' 'CFR, Ltd.;' 'OCB, A. G.;' 'COR, A. G.;' 'Paraguay Partners, Corp.;' 'Asuncion A. G.;' the P2 Lodge;' and quite a few others I don't recognize."

"You recognize some of these names?"

"If they are the ones I think they are, yes. But I can't be sure if they are the same names I'm familiar with or some other groups. Plus, I don't have any idea just how they would tie into the investigation I have been conducting. Unless I receive more information, there is no way that I could be sure, so it would be just conjecture on my part. I don't even know if the name 'CRPC' is the old 'CREEP' Committee or not."

"Give us some idea what these other names represent."

"As I said, I have no way of knowing for sure, but I could give you an educated guess as to what I think each of them might be."

"Go ahead, I'm interested," said Robert.

"So am I," added James.

"The 'U977 A.G.' could possibly be named after the World War II German U-boat that was a submarine commissioned late in the war, if my memory serves me correctly. It was stationed in Norway about the time the war was coming to an end. It is alleged that this particular sub transported some high-ranking German officials to Argentina as the war ended. Ultimately, the Argentineans turned the boat and crew over to U. S. officials, and the ship was towed to Boston, as I recall. The U-boat was then sunk in the Atlantic off the Boston coast. It was alleged that Hitler was on the ship when it arrived in Argentina. However, that story was dispelled by the crew when they were interviewed by U.S. intelligence and when the Russians later came up with Hitler's teeth, which they found at Hitler's bunker. Those two factors ended the speculation that Hitler was on board the U-977. However, it has otherwise been speculated that certain German officials who were trying to avoid the Nuremberg Trials were released in Argentina before U. S. authorities could take the crew into custody and question them. I don't know why there would be an account in such a name 'U977 A.G.'"

"What about the 'Poor Knights?'"

"The only recollection I have of such a name would relate to an Order of French Knights called the 'Order of the Poor Knights of Christ' that were a part of the early Crusades to Jerusalem. They were supposedly the forerunners to the 'Knights Templar,' and like the 'Knights Templar,' were considered a secret society of sorts. They had close ties to the Cistercian Monks. I believe some British engineers found some evidence of them in the area of Solomon's Temple when they did some excavating in the late 1800s. I have no idea if there would be any connection, or more accurately, any imagined connection, to some modern group that would in any way tie itself to the investigation I have been asked to conduct for the Senator. My guess is that someone liked the name and just began to use it."

"There was one called the 'Batch of Grapes.'"

"No. It is listed as 'Bunch of Grapes, Inc.' There was a group called the 'Bunch of Grapes Tavern' that I believe was the first officially chartered Masonic Group in the United States. This group originated from a duly-constituted Masonic lodge of England that involved the first township laid out in Marietta, Ohio, but was later reconstituted in Boston. It is my guess someone has used that name to set up an organization that has some accounts listed. Someone may have felt it had some historical significance, so they simply used its name. I don't know."

"What about some of the lettered names that you mentioned?"

"Let's see...there is the 'SIS A. G.' There is, of course, the British Secret Service that is often abbreviated as 'SIS.' However, I cannot imagine their being tied to this material. Really, I don't know what this 'SIS A.G.' would be. Some of the old conspiracy theorists believed the British 'SIS' has always been involved in orchestrating a way to control the world's wealth. There is also listed a 'CFR, Ltd.' account. That again gives me some pause for doubting a connection to the groups under investigation, if it is the same entity that comes to my mind. The 'CFR' that I am familiar with is the 'Counsel on Foreign Relations' started by President Woodrow Wilson's administration. It has been an active group of advisors to the State Department, the CIA, and virtually every president of the United States since it was formed. I doubt the 'CFR, Ltd.' on these accounts is the same group or entity. Of course, who knows –"

"And the others?" questioned Robert.

"The 'OCB, A. G. could be a foreign corporation that might be an outgrowth of the 'OCB' or 'Operations Coordination Board' President Eisenhower modified from the 'CFR' or 'Counsel On Foreign Relations.' It was disbanded by President Kennedy but seems to continue as an 'ad hoc' committee of sorts that is probably run by some CFR members. The 'COR, A. G.' could be an off-shot of the old Counsel of Rome, which is supposedly a worldwide think tank based out of Hamburg. It is a globalist organization said to be involved with global economy and world politics. Its website promotes a fairly altruistic cause as a catalyst of change," said A.T.

"What about the Paraguay SS Partners you said was listed –"

"The Paraguay SS Partners could possibly be a group set up in the country of Paraguay. Paraguay was once considered the safest location for Nazis after World War II. The dictator, who came to power less than ten years after WWII in about 1954, was Alfredo Stroessner, who was of German descent. His father was from Bavaria, and his mother was from a very wealthy Paraguayan family. Stroessner ruled as a dictator from 1954 to 1989 and was considered the most powerful dictator in the Americas next to Fidel Castro of Cuba. If I remember correctly, 95% of the Paraguayan people have European ancestral heritage of one form or another. There is also

'Asuncion A. G.' that could be named after Asuncion, the capital city of Paraguay. Spanish Jesuit monks originally established the city in the early 1500s. Many of the citizens of Asuncion have been known to be friendly to the Nazis. It has been speculated that Martin Bormann and other high-level Nazis lived out their lives in the city of Asuncion, Paraguay. Until more is known, however, I have no way, at this time, of verifying if these names are related to the organizations or groups just mentioned," said A.T.

"Are there others?" asked Robert.

"There are quite a few other names on the accounts; however, I couldn't even venture a decent guess for any of the rest of them," said A.T.

"It is my speculation the Senator felt there was some significant tie-in between the names on the accounts and the groups you have under investigation. Otherwise, it is very doubtful he would have the Professor provide this information to you,'" noted Robert.

"That would be a fair presumption, and it would be my guess there is a possibility the groups under investigation are receiving their funding or a part of it from the entities the Professor is listing with the money. As I mentioned before, 'follow the money.'"

"Better that task left to you than to me. Fortunately, I am just a 'leg man' for the Senator, and in the process, I am to provide the necessary security for you in order to be sure you get to see what you want and return safely. James is to provide the transportation and any information he can muster regarding the folks down in this area of the country. Other than that, there's not much either James or I can do to help you in assessing what seems to be a very sensitive political matter," said Robert.

"You mentioned your role was to provide the security for me in order to get the information I need and get me back out. Do you anticipate any problems or concerns? Should I be made aware of any particular problems?" asked A.T.

"Not really. As James mentioned to you earlier, A.T., I have been back in the forest location a number of times, and I have never encountered any difficulties. The new wrinkle involving the two people in the green Taurus is the only thing that would provide some new concern. However, they are going to be tied up with accident details for quite a while. We should be in and out before they can even get reorganized enough to get back at it. Of course, I am presuming the two people in the Taurus were following someone or something in this car."

"That was a puzzling matter, and hopefully, we will not see them again. My plan is to fly out tonight and head down to Houston, where the Senator has me in meetings scheduled with Bud Hawthorne for tomorrow. After the meetings in Houston, I am scheduled to go back to the Twin Cities for a few days, and then I'll be off to Washington in order to meet up with the Senator. I will provide him with my report and the materials I have been assembling. Are there any special words for the Senator from either of you? I will express my gratitude for the help I have received from both of you, and I will probably alert him of the people in the Taurus," noted A. T.

"Not from me," said James.

"Just tell him I will meet with him for our monthly meeting in Baltimore at the end of the month, and I will be ready to follow up on whatever the Senator wants me to do," exclaimed Robert.

"By the way, we may want to bury our cell phones along with your briefcase when James drops us off."

"Nothing doing! I will need to keep all of the materials I have received from James and the Professor with me, along with my laptop. Plus, I have already turned off my cell, and I will keep it just for emergency purposes, if you don't mind," said A.T.

"Suit yourself," said Robert. "Just keep in mind even if your phone is off, it can still be tracked with today's technology. As far as the documents from James and the Professor, along with your laptop, just be sure they are not too heavy or too bulky because we will be moving at quite a pace through some pretty rugged terrain," warned Robert.

James was able to get Robert and A. T. to the drop point in fairly decent time, given the fact that about two hours had been lost through the detours with the Professor and the two individuals in the green Ford Taurus. James reminded them that when he returned, his vehicle would be its natural red color. The plan was for James to then transport both Robert and A. T. to the Lexington airport where A.T. was to board a flight for Texas, and Robert was to take a return flight to Washington D.C. Everything seemed to go well as James dropped his two travel companions at the predetermined location and proceeded easterly on the DB Parkway to Hazard. Robert and A. T. slipped into the Daniel Boone National Forest on foot and headed south to the location where Robert intended to provide the information A. T. was seeking. The two of them hiked at a rapid and steady pace through very rugged terrain for over an hour. They would stop at regular intervals in order to rest and drink from the canteens Robert had provided. The countryside was beautifully laden with an artist's palate of color as the forest was alive with the vivid array of the fall tree foliage of oak, maple, hickory, walnut, and elder that was native to the region. Although many of the leaves had fallen, most trees continued to maintain a last grasp of the multiple colors that were indicative of the varying members of the species. The changing deciduous trees were set off by the varied greens of the pines and brush which had not changed color. The forest was quiet, except for the chirping of the birds and rustling of squirrels. Occasionally, a deer or a flock of wild turkeys darted in front of them.

Despite the labor of the hike through the hilly landscape, the trip was refreshing and invigorating for two men who appreciated the outdoors for all it had to offer. Soon the peaceful enterprise would end as the serious matters at hand would jolt them back to their mission. Robert broke the silence.

"You will soon see what you came out here to observe," said Robert while A.T. paused to take a swig of water from his canteen. "It isn't a simple matter of bean counting like your 'lunatic fringe' Professor friend was apparently content to do."

"I understand," said A.T. trying to observe Robert's eyes while Robert removed and wiped his dark aviator sunglasses on his shirt sleeve. "However, when it comes to the 'lunatic fringe,' you may need to count each bean in order to find out if there is any blend between the action they are taking and the financial support behind it."

"What you will see is anything but a proper blend. It may be more like a dangerous blend," said Robert, while the two of them continued their trek through the woods.

CHAPTER 5
A DANGEROUS BLEND

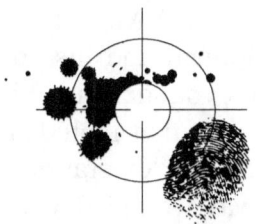

After another twenty minutes of hiking, Robert held up his hand signaling a stop. A.T. complied and watched as Robert pointed with one hand while using his sleeve on his other hand to wipe the perspiration from his balding head.

A.T. peered through the tall grass from their vantage point well above the valley below. It had been a long trip on foot through some of the most uncomfortable but beautiful terrain A.T. had ever experienced. The trip had taken over an hour, and he wasn't sure how far they had traveled. His traveling companion was far younger and had obviously been trained to handle any of the obstacles the land had to offer.

A.T. realized that the entire trip was risky, yet if he didn't follow this lead, the last fourteen months of research and investigation could be of little real value, especially if the Senator felt A.T. was not being fully cooperative. The entire endeavor was far more than he had bargained for, and it seemed that each new bit of information led to half a dozen new issues that made this particular task even more implausible.

From what the Senator told A.T., Robert saw action in both Iraq and Afghanistan. He served in the Special Activities Division

(SAD) or Special Operations Group (SOG) that was directed by the CIA. Although Robert was too young for active duty in Vietnam, he did engage in drop operations behind enemy lines and engaged in organized guerrilla warfare consistent with some of the original duties developed by the forerunner to the CIA, the OSS (Office of Strategic Services). In both Afghanistan and Iraq, Robert became skilled at developing information about enemy troop movements and resources at times before significant American troops were deployed.

Robert attended VMI and had graduated with a B.S. in mechanical engineering. He took courses under the "Modern Languages and Cultures Curriculum" while at VMI and had a talent for languages. He studied for a year at Marmara in Istanbul, Turkey, during a specially approved leave from VMI between his junior and senior years. He was well disciplined and his conditioning allowed him to appear at least ten years younger than his forty-four years. He'd been decorated with citations that included service with the secret "Operation Prime Chance" and "Operation Praying Mantis," during the Gulf War. Also, he was wounded while in Afghanistan. As a result of that injury, he had been nominated to receive the "Purple Heart."

Hiking through the Daniel Boone National Forest was like a frolic in the woods for Robert; however, for A.T. it was a bit more of a challenge. Although he enjoyed the hike, A.T. was getting far too old to be fighting his way through the thicket of brush in a vast wooded area with a former military skill artist. He felt that he should be at home with grandchildren, like the rest of his generation. The only problem was that he had children but no grandchildren. He did have a dog.

A.T. began to reminisce about his dog, a patient and deadly predator. When he was ready to strike, the dog would get totally silent and stalk with deliberate caution until he was within striking distance. A.T. had seen Remington bring down a fairly good-sized white-tailed deer with absolute skill. When hunting in a wooded area of a friend's farm, he had watched Remy move patiently and quietly from point to point while the deer came to the junction of two fence lines. The deer hesitated at the corner post and looked away, while less than thirty feet from him Remington moved quickly and decisively, using his front bulk to take the front legs of the deer out from under it as the deer was forced into the fence. Within an instant, the dog was at the throat of the deer, and it was quickly over. Some of A.T.'s friends thought that his dog's ancestry personified A.T.'s own personality. Remington was half Labrador and half Rottweiler.

His wandering mind was abruptly brought back to reality when he heard Robert ask, "Are you still with us? You looked like you were in a trance. You may want to focus on the task at hand. We came here for a reason, and we need to get back out soon."

"Sorry," said A. T. "My mind was in a better place."

"You can see, we've arrived at the location. If you move the grass and debris in front of you, be quiet and cautious. Also, be careful moving toward the edge, so you don't lose your balance," warned Robert.

A.T. stepped a bit closer to the edge. Beyond the parted clusters of weeds and brush, the entire valley below presented a panoramic view. Except for an old farmstead at the opposite end of the valley from the cliff, it was apparent that much of the valley had been recently cleared by large earth-moving equipment that sat menacingly near the farmstead where several buildings were under construction. A nearby parking area revealed every imaginable type of vehicle. Adjacent to the parking lot, A. T. counted at least half a dozen helicopters of various shapes and sizes.

At the far end of the valley and to their right, additional construction was underway. The construction crews presented a beehive of activity with trucks, cranes, and end-loaders moving about the building complex. At the opposite end of the valley, an airstrip was taking shape. Surveyors were laying out a grid work of streets and open lots in the center area. Also, in the middle of the valley near an old windmill and barn, a pasture hosted a significant number of personnel in military-style formations. A type of combat exercise over manmade obstacles was in progress.

"Is this what you wanted me to see, Robert?" asked A.T.

"Yes, this is what you're supposed to see."

"Who are those guys? What's going on? What are they doing in this remote -"

"They constitute a private security force. They have no official authority. I thought that you knew that. This is what the Senator said you wanted to see. Most of the men whom you see are part-timers. During their regular workweek, they have other jobs or do other things."

"So, are these types of operations part of Blackwater?"

"No! At least as far as we know they are not."

"What do you know about Blackwater?" A.T. asked.

"It was started by Erik Prince. He was also a former Navy Seal operative like me; however, he was active in Bosnia, Haiti, and the Middle East. He started Blackwater in the swamps of North Carolina near Moyock, where it occupies about 7000 acres. It also has a place in Illinois that is called Blackwater North. Blackwater was established as a 'Praetorian Guard' for the George W. Bush administration's war on terror, according to Jeremy Scahill, who wrote the book on Blackwater."

"So, are all of these men a part of that operation?" A.T. inquired.

"Not from what we know. Blackwater is different. It has about 2500 'soldiers' and keeps a database of about 21,000 former special forces troops. According to Scahill, Blackwater's leader and CEO, Prince, is a right-wing Christian mega-millionaire, who in the past helped bankroll the George W. Bush campaigns, as well as some Christian right-wing agendas. I believe that his father and sister were also big Bush supporters."

A.T. added, "I do know that Blackwater came under Congressional investigation by Congressman Henry Waxman's committee. Apparently, they were investigating the shooting deaths of about seventeen people at the Nisour Square incident in Iraq, along with some other Blackwater sniper activity done because of what became known as Order 17 that was signed by Paul Bremer while he was stationed in Iraq. Wasn't there an issue of immunity in regard to the snipers?"

"That's true. One point of interest for you is that a friend of mine, who was rather well up the Navy ladder, had a safety deposit box opened after his untimely death," said Robert. "Within the box were some reports that related to a military investigation by the Army's Third Battalion, 82nd Field Artillery Regiment of the Second Brigade. I have no idea how he gained possession of them. The Third Battalion reported on the incident at Nisour Square and made note of the fact that a number of civilians, including a doctor's family, were shot and killed. The military report states that it was unprovoked and was without justification. That is the same incident that finally brought Blackwater to the attention of the American public. It also created quite a bit of diplomatic backlash, not just from Iraq but from parts of the world as well."

"I remember that," responded A.T. "Is it true that similar people like the type of people who operate Blackwater were more than just friendly to the Bush administration and promoted the privatization of military operations?"

"I don't know," answered Robert. "I understood there were political operatives that included Dick Cheney, Donald Rumsfeld, Paul Wolfowitz, Douglas Feith, Zalmay Khalilzad, Stephen Cambone, Under Secretary of Defense Pete Aldridge, Army Secretary Thomas White, Navy Secretary Gordon England, and Air Force Secretary James Roche who had some sort of relationship with people affiliated with Blackwater. I also understood that Vice President Cheney and Secretary of Defense Rumsfeld were also a part of efforts involving 'Projects for a New American Century' started by neoconservative activist, William Kristol, in 1997."

"Getting back to the subject at hand and the people who we see down in that valley....you said there were other groups like them."

"No doubt about it," answered Robert. "Some are organized differently than others. Some are known as the 'Posse Comitatus;' some are operational under the Klan, and yet others have various other names."

"From my recollection, the 'Posse Comitatus Act' was initiated after Reconstruction and prevented the military from being used for or by law enforcement," recalled A.T. "It was passed back in the late 1870s and prohibited the use of any of the uniformed armed services, such as the Army, Navy, and Marines, as well as the National Guards of the States, from being involved in law enforcement exercises or efforts on non-federal property."

"That's true," responded Robert. "...unless there is a specific statute that would allow it, and I'm not familiar with any such statute. However, I do know that there are instances when the National Guard may act in order to enforce the laws of a given state. The intent of the act was to prevent the use of military force from becoming a national police force. But, as you know, the National Guard has been called in on various occasions to enforce the law of various states, as well as federal law on some occasions."

"I think that's right," guessed A.T. "I am aware that it has been used in matters of immigration, civil disobedience cases, and some drug cases. The original act has been modified several times and was even used for public control during the 'riots' in Los Angeles in the early 1990s. As I understand, it can also be used in cases of national disasters. I believe that was allowed under the Stafford Act."

"That's probably correct," said Robert. "But the 'Posse Comitatus' that I'm talking about is a group of people in the U.S. who identify themselves as a Christian body of activists, who are really survivalists, vigilantes, and anti-government groups. They are often anti-Semitic and anti-Catholic, and they hold beliefs very close to those of the 'white supremacists' and the KKK. The 'Posse Comitatus' is fairly well organized throughout the United States and has organizations in many of the fifty states. The information I have already disclosed to the Senator reveals that many of the members of these groups make up a good share of the people you see down there and in similar groups located throughout the U.S."

A.T. asked, "Where are they located? Are your contacts within their organization reliable? Would it be possible for me to get copies of the military reports that you spoke of?"

"Our friend, the Senator, already has them. You will need to ask him. I think that you should discretely take your pictures and make whatever notes you want; in other words, stay down and out of sight. We will need to leave soon. It's getting dark, and although I like to travel in the dark, it will take us much longer getting out than it took getting in."

"What was it that got you involved with the Senator, if I might ask?" A.T. inquired, as he continued to take notes and photographs.

"It was mostly religion."

"Religion? If you don't mind my saying so, that's an unusual reason. Are your reasons similar to those that James gave us in the car?"

"Not quite! As you know, I served two terms in Iraq and one in Afghanistan. I am a combat veteran and was wounded during action near Kabul. It was my third time around. I was lucky. Most of my men were either killed or seriously wounded. I had to be carried out most of the way. I learned then how some religious thinking twists some people as I became aware of torture and beheading of some of our troops who were captured."

"So, that's when you decided it was the radical Islamic religious beliefs that drove you to get involved with the Senator?"

"It was my first taste of religious fanaticism. But it took more to confirm my prejudice against religious thinking. That came about later while I was recovering in Germany. A very close and longtime friend of mine who was up for a promotion was granted leave from his D.C. post to visit me. He's the guy I mentioned earlier. He had his enemies within the Navy, including members of Naval Command at the time, who didn't want to see him get the promotion. They had him under observation for no reason other than to discredit him regarding his personal life. During my recovery process, the two of us spent a lot of time together while he was on leave.

"There were photographs. The photos were enough to generate an inquiry. My friend was quite irritated and learned in the process that the individuals who were pushing against his promotion were rather obsessed regarding their religious beliefs. Listen, he was a very dedicated naval officer and as loyal as anyone regarding this country. But, it was too much for him to just let it go. He made a public issue of it and held a press conference about the fact he was gay and proud of it. Because of policy at the time, he was discharged. The unfortunate thing is he took his own life because of the disgrace that followed him. I then got involved and did my own inquiry. Ultimately, I received his personal effects, along with a key to his safety deposit box. In the box I found evidence including some information demonstrating that he was under surveillance by an organized group of religious fanatics within the government; not just the military. Does that satisfy you?"

"In other words, you now have a prejudice against religion in general, and that's what is motivating you?"

"No. Not at all! I just have issues with narrow-minded individuals who use religion as an excuse to go out of their way to ruin someone's life," said Robert as he watched a dozen men crawl under a barricade on the obstacle course in the pasture below. "Now, let's get down to business and get the hell out of here."

"I presume, that, along with what happened to your friend, is what motivated you to volunteer your services to the Senator?" asked A.T.

"That's pretty much the reason... I had learned that the Senator was investigating certain behavior within the military which involved a particular religious movement operating in an unacceptable and improper way by attempting to force the religious conversion of new recruits and members within the military. Subsequently, I went to his office and volunteered my services. Since it was the same group that had caused me some personal problems, I wanted to help expose them. After the Senator had me checked out, I was called back into his office and offered my current position providing I was able to conduct my investigations and work in a professional manner. By then, I had been discharged for quite a while and was looking for something to do."

"Wasn't there quite a hassle regarding efforts to impose particular religious thinking in the military a few years ago?" asked A.T.

"There was," responded Robert. "In fact, there was and still is quite a movement in the military academies, as well as on most bases, to convert young soldiers and cadets to a fairly rigid line of religious thinking. The instance with the most notoriety occurred at the Air Force Academy a few years back when there was a lot of arm twisting to get the cadets to become a part of an evangelical group that was teaching on staff at the academy."

"I do remember that incident," said A.T. "It surprised me quite a bit since many years ago, I had been chosen to be one of the two representatives from the university where I was in school to attend the 'Culture Affairs and Foreign Relations' seminar the Academy holds each year. Back then the Academy seemed to be seriously oriented to military life in the Air Force, but there was no slant toward any religious affiliation. In fact, back then, the Academy praised itself on how evenhanded it was to all religions. When we toured the Air Force Academy Chapel, a point was made that there was a separate place for Jewish cadets and others to worship."

"That's ironic," said Robert. "If I remember correctly, when the religious issues began at the Academy a few years ago, it involved a Jewish cadet whose father had also attended the Academy. If my memory is correct, some of the instructors were trying to convert the Jewish cadet and it created some very serious issues leading to an investigation. The incident tended to cloud my issues in the Senator's mind, but at least he involved me, so I appreciated his confidence in me. Plus, being involved is helping me cope with the loss of a person who was very dear to me."

"I'm sorry; I didn't intend to get personal."

"Well, I don't know why... but for some unexplained reason, I didn't mind telling you. There aren't many people who know what I just told you. Of course, there are those in the Navy, but it doesn't matter. I left with an honorable discharge, and they left me alone. They were after him and got what they wanted. Later, I received a tremendous amount of literature and calls telling me how sinful my life was and that I needed to reform."

Robert continued, "The material that I received from the safety deposit box revealed that there were members of certain groups well planted in virtually every branch of the United States government. When I started to follow up on the material, I found that it was much more than a religious movement."

"So, your work for the Senator is demonstrating the movement involves more than religious differences and particular religious groups."

"Of course, and you should also know by now from the investigation that you've been doing. You asked what got me involved, and I told you religion. It's still the principle motivation as to why I am doing this. What is behind your involvement?"

A.T. began, "There were some specific issues involving me personally, and those were significant matters I choose not to discuss at this time. One of the Senator's committees was already investigating the same issues."

"Are you saying you just decided to work with the Senator simply because the two of you were pursuing a common cause?" asked Robert.

"No," answered A.T. "It is more involved than a common cause. Remind me to tell you when we are in a bit more relaxed environment."

"That's interesting, and it doesn't surprise me from what I've seen. Look, it's getting late. Are you about wrapped up here?"

"Let me get a few more pictures, and we can head out."

A. T. carefully moved around the scrub growth of bushes and trees; he took his photos, including some with a telescopic lens. He made hand notes on the pad he maintained in the top left pocket of his jacket. When he put his note pad back into his jacket and nodded to Robert that he was ready to move out, Robert cautioned, "Be sure that your camera and note pad are fully secure. In addition, from here on we don't speak, unless you've got an emergency situation. I will need to listen because it is getting dark, and our eyes will not be as reliable as in daylight. If you have questions, please ask them later and take these."

Robert handed A. T. heat-sensitive night vision glasses that were quite different than any he had seen before. They looked more like underwater goggles than night vision devices. Robert motioned for them to move forward slowly as he held his finger to his lips.

They hiked for about an hour, and A.T. noticed some of the markings Robert had made to trees on the way in. It was a good thing Robert was ahead of him; otherwise, he may have never found his way out. He had never been to southeastern Kentucky before and did not realize how much rugged terrain there was without evidence of habitation.

Suddenly Robert motioned for A.T. to drop down. A.T. complied and from his crouched position saw Robert dash back in the direction they had come. He then saw Robert reach for the gloves he had attached to the upper left portion of his jacket, and a loud ripping sound followed. At that moment, A.T. saw a vague figure, who was about ten feet away. Like a cat, Robert pounced on the shadowy image, wrapping his arm and hand around the head of the figure. The struggle was brief as Robert pulled the shadowy figure back and to the ground. There was hardly a sound, but A.T. did hear a moan. After a matter of seconds, Robert said, "Here, take this and hold down the first button by the green light. Don't let up on it, and don't touch the second button by the red light."

Robert then secured the subdued individual to a tree and wrapped a gag around his mouth. "He will come to in about fifteen minutes and should be able to remove himself from the tree shortly after that. That should give us enough time for a decent lead. Hopefully, there isn't a companion. We'll want to keep a look out, just in case. This guy's just a kid, and he's, most likely, a local who knows the woods and area well enough to provide some form of remote security. Do you have the device?"

"Yes," answered A.T. "What is it, and why am I holding down the button by the green light?"

"It's a form of GPS. As long as the green button is depressed, the guys in the valley know that the guy up here is okay and on the job. If the red button gets depressed, it is a sign that he's in distress and needs help. We'll keep it with us for about half an hour or so as we work our way out. We'll then put something on the button and leave it. That will give us a chance to reorient ourselves and get off this range. Just so you know, we have just over a half-hour more in the forest before we are out. Are you up to it?"

"I'm okay, and I'll be up to it. What was the rip sound that I heard just before you jumped that guy?" asked A.T. "Oh, and here…you can have the GPS back, if you don't mind."

"I was just pulling my gloves from my vest. They were attached with Velcro, but I had to crack a capsule inside the one glove in order to give our friend there a bit of a nap. It was best for everyone if I put him out for a while. Like I said, he will have a headache, but he'll survive," said Robert.

The forest was dark, and on occasion, rustling nearby prompted them to stop and listen. Usually, the noise was a deer or other wildlife; this time the noise was accompanied by the murmur of voices. Robert turned and placed his forefinger to his lips. He then directed them very slowly in a circular pattern around the voices. Sitting around a campfire in a clearing uniformed individuals seemed to be engaged in serious conversation. After waiting and watching for a few minutes, Robert motioned for A. T. to follow him as he moved farther away from what turned out to be a Boy Scout troop. The two of them continued through the forest for about another half hour when Robert signaled with his hand upward that they should stop.

A.T. thought they must be near the location of the roadway where James's vehicle would be. Robert told A.T. to remain while he checked out the area of the road marker and the Tollway. In addition, Robert said he would be back and A.T. should stay frozen in place until he returned. After what seemed like at least half an hour, A. T. heard a noise behind him. Startled, he turned and assumed a defensive position but then realized it was Robert.

"I located James. We should be able to get to the vehicle shortly. Let's wait for a few minutes and then move out. Sorry it took so long to get back, but I wanted to be sure there was no one curious about James's vehicle sitting along the road. We'll have James get us to the airport as soon as possible, so we are sure to make our flights."

After meeting up with James, A.T. and Robert learned that James had washed his vehicle and had enjoyed his visit with his friend, Ruth. He said she was able to provide some significant information about the death of his father. He learned of two possible witnesses who were having trouble with their consciences about the shooting. She provided their identities to James, and he had already spoken to one of them. According to James, the witness was going to be solid and was a well-respected member of a small suburb of Lexington.

In addition to the information relating to his father's murder, James learned the paramilitary group that Robert and A.T. observed earlier was a part of a larger organization. Recently, the group had visitors from Washington D.C. James was hoping to learn of some additional information regarding the visitors from D.C. within the next week or two. He also relayed troubling news that a "shadow government" of some sort was being formed. The information was sketchy at best. There was no explanation as to whether this 'shadow government' involved public officials in Kentucky or across the country."

James dropped Robert and A.T. at the airport in Lexington and headed back to Cincinnati with his new information. Things were looking up for James. He had been hoping for some good news, and he finally received some from his friend, Ruth. That was not the case for A.T., who wasn't so sure about his new information. He didn't know if things were looking up or just getting more complicated.

CHAPTER 6
SOMETHING BREWING

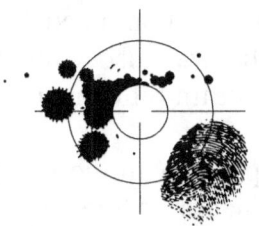

Hopping on a plane and sitting in a cramped seat for a number of hours after a major hike through the Daniel Boone National Forest was an experience that A.T. was not expecting to be enjoyable. He had plenty of new information to review considering the information from Robert, the packet from James, the package from Professor Brougham, and the new photos and notes that he had taken in the forest. However, the thought of working through any of the material while on the flight to Houston was too much to bear given the fatigue he was experiencing. Once on the plane, he found his seat next to a young mother and her six or seven-year-old daughter who immediately clamored for the window seat. After the usual pleasantries and introductions, A.T. sat back in his aisle seat. He noted the other people around as they were finding their seats. There was no way that he could begin to concentrate on the materials in his briefcase, so he decided to at least rest his eyes for a moment or two.

He knew once he checked into his hotel after reaching Houston, he would have a chance to get some sleep. The next morning, in order to be adequately prepared for his meeting with Bud, he would rise early enough to review some additional material he had placed on his laptop. They had scheduled a breakfast meeting at the hotel at 8:30, thinking it would allow them enough time to review the computer material, along with the information Bud was going to provide.

It was an understatement to say Bud Hawthorne was a real enigma. Although he considered himself an investigative reporter, he could be more accurately described as a political journalist. Some people viewed him as an investigative reporter "wanna-be" while others were a bit more severe in calling him a "political hack."

He did his own work as a "free-lance" type of reporter and was able to sell many of his stories to various news magazines and television groups. Apparently it depended upon the slant to his reporting as to which "news" entity was willing to pay for his work. Since he came from a well-to-do family, he could afford to work the way he did since he really didn't need to earn a living. Nevertheless, and as a matter of pride, he continued to fashion himself as an investigative reporter who was also willing to work with various elected officials who might find it convenient to work with him on a case-by-case basis.

Often Bud was compared with the late Robert Novak and that caused him great consternation. Although he was of a similar build in height, weight, and physical stature as Novak, Bud was a good bit younger and supported a full head of reddish blonde hair along with a well-trimmed mustache and small goatee.

Bud Hawthorne had been involved in politics for nearly his entire lifetime. His father was from London, England, and his mother from Providence, Rhode Island, so he had spent part of his youth on both continents and was a graduate of Cambridge University in England. It was through family connections that he enjoyed a rather privileged lifestyle. He had always been able to maneuver through life with jobs of opportunity. Bud had also held various appointed positions, including a short-term stint with the Cheney people in Washington. He left that position to become a "research assistant" to a member of Congress.

The job with the congressman lasted for a couple of years before Bud reconnected with the Senator, who was related to Bud's mother. Although the Senator did not represent Rhode Island, he would spend time with relatives there. As a result, Bud got to know the Senator quite well. After taking months to evaluate the material from Bud, the Senator decided to commence an investigation of his own. The investigation was initiated through a subcommittee to which Bud presented part of the information. The more politically sensitive and serious material was held by the Senator's office until he could decide what to make of it. The Senator wanted to be sure of himself before he revealed the volatile material Bud had produced. It was at that point that the Senator contacted A.T.

As far as the hike through the Daniel Boone National Forest was concerned, it was Bud, as well as the Senator, who wanted to be sure A.T. saw what Robert had to offer before taking him to a similar operation near Houston and an office complex in Houston where Bud determined that some of the organizational efforts were conducted by one of the groups under investigation. He did not realize Bud had a new batch of materials for him. Bud was already at the table in the restaurant sipping coffee when A.T. arrived. They exchanged greetings and ordered breakfast.

A.T. proceeded to engage Bud in some general small talk, having learned long ago that idle conversation was often important between people in order for them to reach a comfort level before directing their attention to the business at hand. Besides, A.T. was always interested in hearing more about Bud's background. Considering Bud's varied experiences with both major political parties, A.T. found Bud to be a curiosity, as well as the outgoing individual he remembered from their past encounters.

* *

Starting out of the hotel driveway, Bud got directly to the matters at hand. "We'll be going north of the city to view a field of training similar to what you saw yesterday with Robert. I'll first drive around part of the perimeter. It's my suggestion the photographs be taken from the car since we will later be going into the compound on foot and can't have cameras when we do that."

"What about identities?"

Bud explained, "That is not a problem on the first visit. They know a lot of people who join up are disgruntled about something, and the first visit doesn't always lead to a person joining up. Besides, they aren't going to disclose any secrets to a couple of guys who just come by and say they might want to join up."

"Do we need to worry about their checking us out?"

"Not at this point. If we came back for another tour and got serious, which not surprisingly a lot of people do, they would take the time to check us out. Plus, Billy is not going to show us anything considered top secret or secure."

"I can't believe we are going to do this -"

"While we drive to the facility, let me give you a background or outline of what I know," insisted Bud.

"Sure. Go ahead," A.T. agreed.

"About eighteen months ago, I was contacted by three different people at about the same time. After my interviews with all three, I felt that two of them were really trying to get the story out. Conversely, I felt the third was a plant, who was trying to find out what information I was getting from the other two. They all knew each other. It seemed unusual to me that there would be three people all at once trying to blow the whistle on the same enterprise. I was both careful and paranoid, so I let each of them do the talking, while I accepted what they gave me."

"Are you going to disclose their identities for my investigation?"

"You will meet each of them in due course. One of them has already met and spoken with you just yesterday. He wanted to personally meet you and hand-deliver some material directly to you. I trust you remember Professor Brougham?"

"I do, indeed. I am not quite sure how all of those financial records impact my investigation and how it all would tie into the assigned task from the Senator."

Bud reassured A.T., "I believe it will all make sense to you once you are able to review it, along with a new travel assignment I will discuss with you later today."

"More travel?"

"I'm afraid so. You'll need to travel to Geneva, Switzerland, and to Paris, France."

"Why to those locations?" inquired A.T.

"This matter has international ramifications, and you'll need to go to those locations. I will handle the travel arrangements for you and bring you up to speed on that element of the case. You'll need a travel companion for security purposes, and if you have someone in mind for that task, let me know, so I can arrange for his travel as well. If not, we'll get someone from Robert's team to work with you."

"Let me think about that. I need to think about both the travel and the travel companion. That's hitting me a bit broadside. I still practice law for a living and will need to consult the schedule. Plus, I'm not too keen on traveling to Europe right now. Besides, the Senator made it clear I could defer on parts of the investigation, if I so chose."

"True. However, I am rather certain you will want to take the trip. Let's discuss that later. At this point, before we get to the compound, I would like to set out some basics regarding where the investigation needs to go from here."

A.T. did not like the sound of what Bud was telling him. He didn't want to become part of someone else's plan or investigation. A.T. wanted to stick with what he believed were the serious infractions he found had taken place. Nevertheless, he would listen to what Bud had to say. He simply responded, "I'll agree to confer with you later about travel to Europe once we have the chance to put today's task behind us and after we have the opportunity to exchange information as discussed earlier. Still, I may need time to think about the travel part."

"Fair enough!" exclaimed Bud.

"The first segment involves both the structured and unstructured Constitutional 'Checks and Balances.' It's necessary to be aware of the fact that specific efforts have been ongoing for several decades to undermine those checks and balances. The second segment of the investigation involves various departments of our government and what's happening within those departments. The third segment of the investigation encompasses various domestic matters of influence upon the government and certain political interest groups that include what I call 'off-beat' religious groups, paramilitary groups, focused media groups, particular financial interests, dissidents, and other groups of interest. The fourth segment involves a group of foreign entities that have methodically targeted the first three segments in order to promote their own purposes.

"There is an interrelationship between each of the segments, and believe me when I say these efforts are well organized and were started several decades ago. In fact, the issue of gerrymandering is something that has come to fruition because of the desire of these groups, including and particularly the extreme right of the Republican Party, as they continue to position themselves with 'safe seats' in both Congress and the Senate. So far as I know, there is only one state that has a process that attempts to eliminate the gerrymandering nightmare, and that is the state of Iowa."

"The organization structure that you have defined is not quite the same as the one that I present in my preliminary report to the Senator," commented A.T. "However, most of the same elements you mention are there. Should I rewrite my report to fit your organizational scheme?"

"No," answered Bud. "The Senator's staff will be doing that, and for now, they are following my outline of the four segments. Ultimately, he and his staff will control the final report and disseminate it to at least two committees of which I'm aware. He will also be presenting to key members of both political parties some of the material that will not be in the reports. This dual presentation will occur before any official government investigations are commenced. The reason for that is simply because some of our government agencies have been seriously compromised at this point in time. Once the material is turned over to the Senator, the guidelines of the investigation will be well defined. There will be a system in place to catch certain individuals within the agencies because many of the answers will be known before directives are given."

"I trust that is an example you are making in reference to the Justice Department under George W. Bush, whereby he and his Attorney General, Alberto Gonzales, decided to remove perfectly good and honorable people from their positions as U. S. Attorneys and replace them with what Bush's brain, Karl Rove, called 'Bushies,'" inserted A.T. "From what I have learned, most, if not all, of the replacements were political operatives who were considered neither professional prosecutors nor individuals who had otherwise demonstrated a level of competency in the courtroom."

"That's a perfect example," responded Bud. "You are familiar with that situation since it directly affected you; however, let's suppose the same philosophy was used to alter every department of the executive branch in a similar way, whereby people of a certain political bent were hired into government positions purposely in order to move the process of government in a certain direction philosophically. Would it be shocking to you to learn such an effort had been underway for several decades and had been implemented while diversions were created elsewhere in terms of issues to keep everyone who might be concerned off track?"

"No, it wouldn't shock me at all," said A.T. "In fact, my investigation is showing that as early as 1971, hidden political efforts were underway and particularly orchestrated without executive order, mandate, oversight, or Congressional approval in order to politicize various departments, including the Department of Justice. I believe the midnight firings of Elliot Richardson and others by Richard Nixon may have been the beginning of a much more serious trend. Under President Ford, there was the suggestion by his then

Chief of Staff, Dick Cheney, to use the Justice Department in a number of ways that were considered legally questionable in order to go after a reporter for the New York Times. Then we experienced the nearly whole-scale efforts by Alberto Gonzales and Karl Rove to 'cleanse' the Justice Department of any U.S. Attorney who was not considered a 'Bushie.'"

"I'll have some information for you on that regarding Mr. Cheney a bit later. But let's continue with my overview, if that's okay," suggested Bud.

"Sure," agreed A.T.

"Up to this point, we have just been supposing such political activity to be exclusive to the executive branch alone," explained Bud. "Everyone knows with the power of the executive goes the constitutional power of appointment where the judiciary is concerned. Major political posturing takes place whenever a person retires from the Supreme Court or from the lesser courts, such as the circuit courts. The result is the positioning of political operatives within the judiciary, as well as the executive branch. No doubt it has always happened, but over the last couple decades, a serious number of incompetent appointees have been approved and now hold extraordinary positions of power over the public and the laws of this country."

"Although I agree completely with you," began A.T., "The Senate had to approve those appointments through its 'advise and consent.'"

"That's true," noted Bud. "However, the back door maneuvering became more prominent than ever before in the history of the country. At least in the past, the appointees had some level of pride and decorum, where they would try to demonstrate judicial competence and temperament. That was not the case when a large number of appointments were made during the last decade or so, but I don't want to get off track."

"Okay."

"It looks like we still have some time before we arrive at our location, so, if I may, I would like to briefly set forth what I believe is the second tier or segment that fits within the investigation. Your job is to follow my organization from here on, if you don't mind. While you do so, you will need to link each segment, since the activities under one undoubtedly tie to the other segments or tiers."

"That's not going to be a problem. In fact, I'm intrigued by what I am hearing so far."

"Good," said Bud. "Now, as to the second tier or segment that involves the various government departments such as the Department of State, the Defense Department, the Department of Justice, the Department of Energy, and Homeland Security, along with any others, such as commerce, interior, education, health and human services, agriculture, housing, labor, transportation, the treasury, and veterans' affairs, you may want to add these to your investigation, if you haven't already. As you know, all of these departments fall under the executive."

"Of course, I will," stated A.T. "Until now, I have merged my findings of the departments of government to the presidency and justice. I'll try to create a separate category for the cabinet tier or segment."

"While you're doing your investigation, don't forget the office of the Vice President. I have some significant information I can provide that will get you focused on what was done during the time that Dick Cheney served in the capacity of Vice President. As I said, I will address that later today."

"I thought Dick Cheney ran the vice presidency as if it could be operated outside the Constitution, and he was not bound by the same laws that governed the executive branch or the President. At least that was the popular conception and joke while he was Vice President."

"As you will see from what I know, it was no joke. He either really believed that nonsense, or he was simply thumbing his nose at all of us while he was Vice President of the United States. Even after he left office, he took the position that what he said and did while Vice President could not be challenged under the law by anyone or any government agency. When it was convenient, he would assert executive privilege. In those particular instances, he took the position that the Constitution did apply to the VP while in other cases he argued that it did not apply."

"I did know that."

"Good. We'll talk about that later, but for now, I want to visit a bit more about the second tier or segment involving the various departments within the executive branch. It has been disclosed to me that there were very large numbers of people hired in virtually every department, so long as they shared or would at least claim to share certain philosophies that fit a particular mindset. Although the plan to place such people in these positions became an orchestrated effort as far back as the early 1970s, it wasn't until the George W. Bush administration that it manifested itself in such a way that jobs would not be given or offered unless an individual would agree to espouse or accept a particular political philosophy."

"As I mentioned earlier, in my investigation so far, I have combined this tier or segment regarding the administrative offices and cabinet positions with the first tier or segment you have outlined as the balance of power segment. There are so many overlaps that until now, I didn't think of separating them," explained A.T.

"I trust you have found more than simply the politicizing of the departments since that has always been done to some degree."

"Absolutely, if there had been any oversight in place before the W. Bush administration took over, it was thrown to the wind. In many cases, the efforts to cover up what they were doing were very sloppy and without any administrative skill. I have also found the Republican Party did not expect to lose the election to President Obama, so there were numerous loose ends that stood out. Plus, the people who were supposed to handle oversight simply looked the other way or delayed processing the files for months and even years on end. At least that is what the investigation shows so far."

"Much of what you say has already been a matter of public knowledge; however, I trust that your investigation drills into some detail."

"It does," acknowledged A.T. "Would you like me to discuss some of that detail at this time? Let me get my briefcase so I can provide you with some specifics."

"No. Don't do that now. We are only minutes away from the compound, and I wouldn't want to get started on any details at this point. I trust the details you are mentioning are in the report that you will be providing for the Senator's review."

"That's correct."

"Then let's hold off on a discussion of the details at this time. Also, there are the next two segments. In addition to the first two I've just reviewed, there is the third segment involving certain domestic organizations about which it is more than just suspected that there has been significant undue influence directed to elected officials, particularly from certain political interest groups. Finally, the fourth segment involves a number of unique foreign entities that have become a matter of major consequence as far as the investigation is concerned going forward. I will discuss those two segments and what I have for you regarding Mr. Cheney after we have toured the upcoming facility and while we are on our way to the office complex these folks are using south of Houston."

For the next twenty minutes, while they navigated the roadways to the compound, Bud and A.T. discussed general matters relating to Bud's outline that he wanted A.T. to follow going forward. As promised, after arriving at the compound, Bud drove about three quarters around the part of the facility which was near various roads and streets. A. T. discreetly took a number of photographs in order to show the general scope of the facility. As they approached the entrance, A.T. placed his camera in his case and locked it to ensure its security.

Reaching the gate, they were able to see a cluster of buildings some distance from the gate. The entire facility looked like it had been a hospital or college campus of some sort at one time. It was old but in decent repair. Clearly, it was not as elaborate as the paramilitary base A.T. had seen in the Daniel Boone Forest the day before. Upon entering the compound, they were met at the gate by two individuals who were dressed very casually and seemed quite laid back. They noticed there were two other individuals in security-type uniforms in a guardhouse next to the entrance. The gate was already open, so they proceeded.

After entering, they stopped and were addressed by one of the casually dressed individuals who requested their names and purpose. Bud explained they had been invited by Billy Simonson to visit the facility and inquire about membership. They were told they should wait at the gate until Billy was paged and arrived. Then, they were directed to park their car in a parking lot adjacent to the entry. One of the casually dressed men opened the back door, and while he entered the car, he stated that he would direct them to their parking spot. There were only about a half dozen vehicles in the lot that looked large enough to accommodate at least fifty vehicles. With the car locked, they got out and were escorted back to the entry on foot. They noticed a man walking from the building complex about one hundred and fifty yards from the gate.

"Hello, Bud!" said the man coming from the compound. It was Billy Simonson, who was introduced simultaneously to A. T. by both Bud and the casually dressed man who had ridden in the car with them to the parking lot. Their escort then inquired of Billy about his relationship with Bud, and Billy explained he and Bud were old friends. Billy further explained Bud was from Rhode Island and was down visiting and wanted to see the facility since Bud was thinking about setting something up in Rhode Island. The explanation was enough for the escort who did not require any more. Bud told them A. T. had come from the upper Midwest and had been in the same business meeting Bud was attending in Houston. A.T. was surprised as to how open he was about the group and what they did.

A.T. turned and while he walked off with Bud and Billy, the escort also turned and began walking to a nearby clump of trees. The escort nodded to a wiry little man with a stand of very thin blondish-gray hair, protruding front teeth and familiar glasses that were wire-rimmed in nature. The little man nodded back at the escort, put his camera away, and pulled out his cell phone. In a moment he began speaking in an animated manner to someone on the other end of what became a rather protracted call.

Meanwhile, Billy directed Bud and A.T. to follow him to the building complex. As the three of them walked to the complex, Bud inquired of Billy, "I notice there aren't many people around, and there doesn't seem to be much security."

"Most of the guys are on a training exercise with a group up in Tulsa. I couldn't go because my mother-in-law is in the hospital. When you called, I thought it would be a good opportunity for me to show you the facility firsthand. Nobody comes in here unless they are invited," said Billy.

Bud then looked to A.T. and said, "Billy is one of the three people that I mentioned to you. So, now you have met two of the three people. By the way, Billy, for your personal information, A.T. can be fully trusted. He is working for the Senator on the investigation and was in the area, so I thought it would be a good idea to bring him by when I was here with you. I imagine that is not a problem."

"It's not a problem at all, especially since it is Saturday and almost everyone else including the command group is gone. By the way, A.T., it is nice meeting you. I want to warn you that you cannot take any pictures, and please don't ask any sensitive questions, if you know what I mean."

"That's understood," said A.T. "I'll just walk along and listen to what you and Bud discuss. If I have any questions, I will try to ask them in a general way that would reflect someone showing interest for membership purposes. That's so long as we don't have to provide any identification."

"You won't have to provide any ID here. It is everyone's belief that no one is going to come in here to investigate since any investigative type of questions would have significant 'tags.' Plus, these guys are proud of what this facility represents, and they are proud of what they are doing. They just believe they are displaying their patriotism. Most of them don't have any idea about any ulterior motives their leadership may have by training them in this facility. If this group were to become 'active' at any point in the future, be assured the leadership would have them convinced and in line with the thinking that whatever they do will be for the good of the country and a proper activity. They wouldn't know otherwise; nor would they challenge it," commented Billy.

There were about a dozen buildings and about half of them appeared to be in use. The first building they approached was a four-story building that looked like it had been either a dormitory or a hospital wing.

"This is our administrative building," said Billy. "We use it for on-campus lodging for our weekend activities. It also has a kitchen and a large cafeteria we use for meals when we are here for training. We also use it for general meetings and discussion groups. The main and second floors contain offices. Everything above the second floor is lodging."

The place was open, and no one was present except for a couple secretaries in an office adjacent to the large room that was used for meals and meetings. One other individual was sitting in a remote area of the large room and appeared to be working on his laptop, along with some papers that he had spread over the table. After walking through the facility, Billy took them out into a common 'green' area that was laid out with buildings on either side and a large one at the far end. There was a pattern of sidewalks that crossed the green area, along with a straight sidewalk that led directly to the one on the far end. The three of them walked directly to that building as Billy explained its purpose.

"This building hosts our gymnasium, locker facilities, private offices for special training staff members, and a gun vault. The offices are on the upper two floors, and as you will see, the lower area holds the gym, lockers, and vault."

"You have a gun vault?" inquired A.T.

"Big time," said Billy. "We will go around to the south entrance, and you'll see that it's right inside the door. I don't think we will be able to enter because it is probably locked. The guys on maneuvers in Tulsa no doubt took what they needed and locked up. It is considered a major violation of protocol and would lead to disciplinary action against anyone who entered the vault without proper authority and without being escorted in and out. There are strict sign in and out procedures for anyone and everyone who would enter the vault. The guns and the ammunition are both expensive. Our budget at this time is limited, therefore, the protocol."

"I would have guessed that the guys who belong to this type of organization would have their own firearms," suggested Bud.

"Believe me, they do and plenty of them. However, the training typically is done using the weapons locked up in here. They do require that the training be uniformly done as to all personnel. Each guy is permitted to qualify on two weapons of his own, but otherwise, he must use the weapons that are provided. You'd be surprised how particular they are about the training. The firing range is just east of the building; I can show that to you when we leave. I wanted to show you the gym and the locker rooms; they are really first-rate. The facility may not look like much on the outside, but inside it is state of the art with the latest in exercise equipment, mats for hand-to-hand training, and even video systems to record how each trainee is doing. That way a given individual can see what he is doing wrong and what he is doing right. Just off the gym there are interrogation rooms where some of us are trained in the various 'arts' of interrogation."

At that comment, the three of them entered the side door to the facility. They first walked by the locked firearms vault. There was a long case containing a number of trophies, awards, and plaques. A.T. was not able to take enough time to read the inscriptions, but he did notice that the display case presented a number of firearms familiar to him. It looked like the display of firearms was set up in some manner of historical significance. It contained some very old Colts, no doubt from the historical past of the state of Texas. A.T. also recognized a 38 caliber Smith and Wesson, similar to one he had used years earlier. He saw a 38 caliber Colt, an old Thompson machine gun, an Uzi, a Glock, and an assortment of rifles. In addition, a collection of shotguns and automatic weapons of every imaginable variety was also on display.

On the other side of the corridor opposite the vault and trophy case were some locked offices. The large gymnasium was at the end of the hall. They walked through the gym and turned to the east end of the building. At the east side of the gym were the locker rooms apparently designed at one time for either two separate teams or as separate facilities for men and women. One of the locker rooms was more comfortably appointed than the other, so A.T. presumed that it was the locker room for officers. The hall between the locker rooms took them to the east side of the building, and a very elaborate firing range with bleachers was set back next to the building, along with an observation tower. The bleachers and the tower were positioned so that any activity on the firing range could be clearly observed.

The remainder of the tour included a review of two large fields set out with obstacle courses and roadways. Billy explained that the fields were used for training for their own membership which included just over 550 people, as well as being used for maneuvers and training for guest groups that would come in from time to time. He mentioned that there was another group similar to theirs in the Houston area, and the two groups would train together about six times per year, alternating between facilities.

They came back to the main building where the cafeteria was located, and they treated themselves to some sodas and other items from the vending machines positioned on the opposite side of the kitchen. They then walked back to the parking lot near the entrance where they shook hands and parted company. Billy said he would expect an email from Bud once Bud returned to Washington. Bud explained that it might be a week or so but that he would send a proper note of thanks. Without any incident, Bud and A.T. were permitted to drive through the gate and be on their way. Billy spoke to one of the guards briefly and then walked back to the main facility.

* *

On their way out A.T. inquired, "From what you said, it is doubtful that Erik Prince has anything to do with these operations; however, I'm curious as to how he got all of his money to start Blackwater in the first place."

Bud explained, "Well, the story goes that Prince inherited about five hundred million dollars from his father, Edgar, who built up quite a business near Holland, Michigan, that supported the auto industry. They made accessories for cars, such as interior mirrors, map lamps, garage door opening devices, consoles, cup holders, and other items. After Edgar died, the family ultimately sold the business to Johnson Controls for about 1.35 billion in cash. The rumor was that Erik took the idea of a private military organization to his mentor, Navy Seal Al Clark. Blackwater was started. Prince bought thousands of acres near Moyock, North Carolina, at what was known as the Great Dismal Swamp. It's part of a 111,000-acre peat bog from southeastern Virginia to northeastern North Carolina. I think that is how they decided on the name, Blackwater."

"So, he really used an inheritance to set up Blackwater?"

"Yes, but as you know, he is really plugged into some of the most powerful politicians on the Republican side of the aisle. He won't do business with the Democrats, from what I've been told. He and his sister, who was and may still be very active in the Michigan Republican Party, have given large sums of money to Republican causes, as well as to George W. Bush. But you're right; initially it was started from money that he had inherited."

"Yesterday, Robert told me that there may be somewhere between 80 to 100 groups like the one we just saw. Are they all funded through local financial interests, or do they have the support of Blackwater?" A.T. questioned.

"As far as we can determine, Blackwater funds only its own operations; it has several in the U.S. and some organizations abroad, as well. We have no evidence that it is funding any of these other operations."

"Do you know where all of the 80 to 100 groups are located?"

"We do know of 83 such groups," said Bud.

"Where are the groups located?"

"It's difficult to remember them all off hand, but I can take a stab at some in your area. Let's see, you're from the Northwest. I know of operations near Spokane, Coeur d' Alene, Missoula, Boise, Butte, Great Falls, Billings, Sheridan, Casper, Cheyenne, Bismarck, Grand Fork …"

"No. Wrong area. I'm from the upper Midwest."

"Oh, that's right. Let's see…there is at least one in the upper peninsula of Michigan, one near Saginaw, Lansing, Toledo, South Bend, Terre Haute, Aurora, Rockford, Peoria, Dubuque, Milwaukee, Green Bay, Menominee, Duluth, White Bear, Brainerd, Mankato, Sioux City, Omaha-Council Bluffs, Mason City, Independence, Columbia, Springfield. I can't list from memory, but there's bunch. The guy who could tell you about all of them that have been fully identified is Robert. I don't think you need to get into that issue. The Senator just wanted you to see a couple of the actual facilities. He thought if you knew about them, it would make more sense to you in regard to your part of the investigation that is to be focused more on the political aspects that have been taking place within the government as they relate to the overall structure of the investigation I have been setting out for you."

"Okay. So far, you have given me two of the segments or tiers. You were going to lay out the remaining two tiers now, and those include the domestic organizations that might be involved in possible subversive activity and the final tier that relates to a group of foreign interests. Oh, and you were also going to give me some information on Dick Cheney."

"What you just saw and what you saw yesterday," said Bud, "fit within the third tier of domestic groups involved in possible subversive activity. As far as greater detail and the fourth group, I'll get to those a bit later today. I also promised some information regarding Dick Cheney, so we'll start with Cheney. However, first let's stop to get some lunch, if that's all right with you."

"Sure," agreed A.T.

Bud found a pancake house along the road just before they came upon the intersection of Highway 59 and I-610. The two of them were seated next to the window, and the waitress took their order. After several minutes, the waitress brought them their food. Bud noticed that his coffee cup and utensils contained some debris, perhaps from the last patron. He requested new utensils and pointed out the problem, especially the lipstick markings that remained on the cup and some food residue on the fork. The waitress took the cup and fork and with her apron attempted to remove the stains. Bud explained that it was not sufficient and he expected them to be clean through appropriate washing. The waitress tried to get by with the explanation that the cup and utensils were just "a bit tarnished."

CHAPTER 7
A BIT TARNISHED

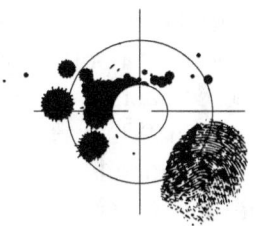

Bud finally received a clean cup and new utensils, and he and A.T. were able to eat their meals. After paying the bill and leaving a less than generous tip, the two of them got back into Bud's rental, picked up the I-610 beltway, and headed south. "Well," A.T. laughingly said, "Something that is just a bit tarnished shouldn't be too bad, should it? Perhaps some people shouldn't be so particular."

"I didn't realize you were going to side with the waitress. Let's suppose you're right. However, I know from the discussions about your investigation that you wouldn't like to be presented with something so 'tarnished' that you wouldn't have confidence in using it," noted Bud.

A.T. then asked, "Do you mean 'tarnished' like the office of the Vice President under Dick Cheney?" After they both laughed, A. T. inquired, "How did his career get started?"

"From an education standpoint, he got both a BA and an MA in political science from the University of Wyoming. It was after he flunked out of Yale."

"The press reported that he attended college for military deferments more than any other reason. Is that true?" A.T. asked.

"No doubt military deferments had a lot to do with it," Bud offered. "I believe he had a total of five deferments so he could avoid military service."

"I always got a kick out of former Minnesota governor, Jessie Ventura, when he referred to W. and Cheney as 'chicken hawks.'"

"That became a famous reference point. Cheney's deferments may be demonstrative of how convincing and manipulative he could be. He probably used the political connections he developed with the Republican Party in Wyoming to land a spot as an intern in the office of Congressman William Steiger. It was a widespread rumor that Cheney had been quite active in the Nixon campaign in the late 1960s and the early 1970s, so the contacts he may have developed then most likely helped get him the spot with Congressman Steiger. During that time, he also developed contact with Donald Rumsfeld, who had become the Director of the Office of Economic Opportunity. From there he expanded his resume through repeated contacts with the Nixon people. Some of the positions he held included a White House assistant job, Assistant Director of the Cost of Living Council, and the Deputy Assistant to the President when Gerald Ford took over as President. He received some notoriety at that time when he wrote an infamous memo to Rumsfeld that the Ford administration should use the United States Department of Justice to go after a reporter for the New York Times."

"If I remember correctly, weren't the suggestions by Cheney that the Justice Department be used as a political instrument considered to be of questionable ethical practices and possibly illegal?" A.T. asked.

"They were considered as such. Later, and perhaps due to some additional backroom politicking, Cheney became White House Chief of Staff under President Gerald Ford. That was when Rumsfeld became Secretary of Defense. Unbelievably, Cheney became the campaign manager for Gerald Ford's run for a full term as president in 1976. So, Cheney was building up plenty of political contacts, and who knows what kind, during the decade between the late 60s to the late 70s. The contacts were enough and of the kind that allowed Cheney to wage a successful campaign for Congress as a candidate himself and become Wyoming's congressman in 1978."

"You're kidding," said A.T. "I didn't know that."

"He was indeed elected to Congress. In fact, he was re-elected at least four more times and ended up being the House Minority Whip," Bud added.

"How did he become so popular in Wyoming?"

"As you know, he grew up in Wyoming and developed many political contacts within the Republican Party there. He used those contacts to get in with Nixon people, and when Ford became President, he slid into a void left by Rumsfeld. Plus, he and Rumsfeld developed a tight relationship. It also didn't hurt that he did his best to promote the oil and coal business in Wyoming. He even has a federal court building named after him in Casper."

"That's unbelievable."

"Well, a lot of people, especially the neoconservatives, believe Cheney has done some significant things, and no doubt he has. However, the problem is that he is known more for his negative influences and strong-willed positions on a variety of issues. Of particular note was Cheney's belief the United States should play an expansive role worldwide. The majority of Americans believe this was ill-founded and the cause of many of the economic woes the U.S. has today."

"I believe the single word for that is 'imperialism,' which we deplored when the British did it to us and later when Germany tried to do it to the world twice during the last century."

"That's where the trouble lies. Cheney seems to fit perfectly into the saying 'power corrupts and absolute power corrupts absolutely.'" Bud further explained, "As I mentioned earlier, he worked himself into a life of political appointments that led to political office, then back again into political appointments only at a higher level than before. In fact, as far as the U.S. government is concerned, he got himself into some of the highest positions possible, except for the presidency. He never needed that position since he was able to do more to promote his way of thinking as Vice President, where he felt he was beyond the control of Congress, the courts, or the public."

"Wasn't he the Secretary of Defense under Bush, Sr.?" asked A.T.

"Yes, he was, and he knew how to manipulate that position of power from the first day at the post. He went into office in 1989 and immediately found like-thinking people in Paul Wolfowitz, Donald Atwood, and Pete Williams to work with him. It was during his tenure as Secretary of Defense when the concept of 'privatizing' the military caught its stride. Later when he was Vice President, the 'privatization' of the military through groups like Blackwater became solidified and grew into the 'ex officio' operations they are today with very serious funds under contract. In fact, these 'privatized ex officio' military operations receive so much money from the U.S. government, and are now under such critical contracts, that our military often finds itself in a secondary position to the private contractors who have become responsible for everything from the protection of our diplomats to goods delivery to the military. Even the NSA has used private contractors. Remember the case of Edward Snowden in 2013."

"Wasn't Cheney able to promote the privatization under the guise of reducing the budgets of our own military?"

"That's correct," Bud said. "He reduced the U.S. military strength from 2.2 million troops to 1.6 million during the 1990s, and he also downsized the military budgets during the same period from $291 billion to $270 billion. The void has since been made up through the independent contractors. Then, on top of that, Cheney promoted an aggressive stance against Iraq, Iran, and North Korea, while he served both as Secretary of Defense in the 1990s and as the Vice President from 2000 to 2008. That seemed to fill the gap of alleged military need that was the result of Cheney's stance against those countries. Now the independent contractors receive hundreds of millions in funds from the United States. They took on more and more tasks under the 'privatization' scheme of Dick Cheney and others, who may well have had hidden agendas for those independent contractors."

A.T. remarked, "He couldn't have done this alone."

"He didn't. As I mentioned, he found allies within the government. He also found allies with the Saudis, especially through the aristocracy of Saudi Arabia. By the way, that alliance created some very serious issues with many of the Muslims who opposed having non-Muslim military personnel and bases in the Middle East. That amplified an already volatile problem. Ironically, in addition to the close ties with the Saudis, Cheney carved out a tight relationship with particular Jewish interests. He became a part of the board of the Jewish Institute for National Security Affairs (JINSA) before he became Vice President. In addition to that maneuver, along with Donald Rumsfeld, William Kristol, and others, he founded the Project for the New American Century. Its stated goal is to "promote American global leadership."

"That doesn't sound 'imperialistic,' does it?"

"That is its goal," continued Bud. "Mr. Cheney and his allies are willing to utilize every ounce of financial clout, independent contractor strength, and any other resource they can muster in order to get and maintain control of government positions in order to promote their idea of 'global leadership.' Their appetite is insatiable. They believe the average American citizen doesn't know enough to make important political decisions, and they believe that they do. Cheney has made the statement that he expects the U.S. to be involved in the Middle East at least throughout his lifetime or longer. He has repeatedly made that statement public."

"As to Cheney," explained Bud, "part of his understanding of the region was what he wanted to believe from limited information. He screened out what he didn't want to hear. As the old saying goes, 'my mind is made up; don't confuse me with the facts.' He was far more interested in hearing about the wealth of the region and what it might mean to have control of natural resources while operating through allies like the Saudis. It didn't hurt that he was so close to independent contractors like Halliburton."

"It would seem that both Cheney and the senior President Bush had an affinity for the oil industry," commented A.T.

"That's certainly true," responded Bud. "As you well know, in his younger years H.W. Bush worked for Dresser."

"I didn't realize that," said A.T. "Refresh my memory regarding Dresser."

"Dresser was a Texas oil industry company that Prescott Bush, H.W.'s father, helped establish," noted Bud. "George H.W. Bush was given a place at Dresser by a fellow Yale 'Skull and Bones' member. After his stint at Dresser, H.W. started his own company that was known as Zapata. It was a company that George H. W. Bush established with investments from two Oklahoma brothers. This was after George senior's namesake uncle, Herbert Walker, had financed Overby Oil Development Company. It had been established that Zapata or Zapata-Offshore owned and loaned a number of its ships to the country at the time of the Cuban Missile Crisis. I understand that was a part of 'Operation Mongoose' that was the CIA's name for an operation designed to remove Castro. Apparently in 1965 a hurricane destroyed some of the oil-drilling platforms. Zapata supposedly received in the neighborhood of eight million dollars for the loss."

"Very interesting" said A.T. "Getting back to Cheney, what exactly was the relationship with Halliburton?"

"When Cheney finished his last term in Congress, and while he was a director of the Council on Foreign Relations, he developed his own ideas of foreign policy. He was then at the Department of Defense, which he left when President Clinton took office. He stayed on at CFR until 1995 and then became the Chairman of the Board and CEO of Halliburton, where he remained until 2000. Halliburton merged with Dresser Industries, and Cheney was criticized for Halliburton's lack of what was termed 'proper accounting practices.' Cheney left Halliburton in July of 2000 and became the candidate for Vice President. His severance package from the company was to be about $20 million. As a result, his net worth has been estimated to be between 30 and 100 million dollars. It is reported he has an annual gross income of between 8 and 10 million dollars."

"It's no wonder he feels comfortable about spouting off."

"He regularly would spout off, and he didn't seem to care much about the facts. As you know, he made statement after statement during various television interviews that Iraq had weapons of mass destruction. He knew better from his trips to Langley to visit with mid-level agency personnel. It didn't matter to him since he wasn't on the front line. He was the main force behind the U.S. involvement in Iraq. W. didn't need much convincing because he thought his father hadn't gone far enough in the first Gulf War."

"W. seemed like such a cowboy compared to his father. What do you suppose was Cheney's real motivation for going into Iraq?"

"Coming from Halliburton, it would seem oil was an issue at the forefront," Bud began. "Also, remember Cheney was a member of the National Energy Policy Development Group. He was in comfortable company, considering the other members of the group included Enron execs. There was a big battle over documents during which the Bush administration was accused of improper political and business ties. The Supreme Court ruled the Department of Commerce had to disclose the documents, including those with references to companies that made agreements with Iraq for its petroleum. Cheney refused to release the documents under the argument of executive privilege. That's when the media began a series of stories referring to the office of the Vice President under Cheney as a fourth branch of government. Lawsuits were filed to disclose the Vice President's records."

"It didn't seem to bother Cheney when there were leaks about Valerie Plame at the CIA. So, records must not have been as important to Cheney."

"Cheney didn't care about her, and he felt it was one way of getting back at her husband, Joe Wilson, who had debunked Cheney's claim about nuclear arms materials and weapons of mass destruction being made available to Iraq. Richard Armitage, who was the former Deputy Secretary of State, later claimed that he was the source regarding the leak on Plame. Of course, by that time, the damage had been done. Scooter Libby, who was Cheney's chief of staff, had been found guilty of perjury and obstruction of justice because he had earlier stated that Cheney had authorized him to disclose classified information to the press regarding WMDs in Iraq. At least that is what *The National Journal* reported."

"Has any enforcement regarding the disclosures ever occurred?"

"No. Cheney has taken the position that the powers of the presidency allowed him to do what he personally thought was best. It is at this point where he used the powers of the executive branch for his own convenience. Otherwise, as we discussed earlier, he felt that the office of the Vice President was without regulation under the Constitution. Cheney is perhaps the strongest advocate of the expansion of presidential powers, including the expansion of the powers of the Vice President. Cheney considered many of the enactments regarding the executive branch such as the Foreign Intelligence Surveillance Act, the Presidential Records Act, the Freedom of Information Act, and the War Powers Resolution to be virtually a 'carte blanche' to the executive branch to do whatever the executive deems proper at the time."

"It's a good thing he's no longer in a position of power."

"He still asserts significant influence over some of the same elements that he did before and has written his memoir," said Bud.

"I haven't read it, but I've heard it is an interesting slant on history," noted A.T. "I understand that the 20 million emails that the Bush administration thought they destroyed may come back to haunt them."

"There will be a haunting," Bud said. "That has yet to come, and the public will be dismayed at the disrespect the Bush administration had for the Constitution, the laws, and justice in general. Cheney is in there with both feet. He and W., along with Karl Rove, think they can rewrite history; however, there are still some big-time skeletons that will be coming out of the closet. A lot of care will need to be exercised since it appears as though he purposely tied himself to many of the most confidential matters in government that were going on at the time. Because of those tie-ins, he has been able to avoid the scrutiny of Congress, the press, and the public. For example, when then CIA Director Leon Panetta reported to the Senate and House intelligence committees that Cheney withheld information from Congress about a secret counter-intelligence program, nothing was done. It is apparent that Cheney had probably woven himself into some of the actual intelligence reports in such a way that any revelation of what he was doing, including any purposeful misinformation, may be impossible to sort out. If the information were to be revealed, it might compromise the intelligence community and proper defense work."

"Is he a part of your investigation?" A.T. asked. "I ask because it is beyond any part of my efforts."

"You will see that his name will continue to crop up in your investigation. You will also see that he will pop up in virtually all four of the segments I have outlined. As far as my personal position is concerned, I doubt he knows I have been helpful to the Senator. I was not one of his 'star' pupils and not at the top of any list. Nevertheless, I have valuable information I have conveyed to the Senator. What I have been organizing and presenting goes well beyond Mr. Cheney. Keep in mind he served as a catalyst and as a moveable piece in the 'chess board' that others are manipulating behind the scenes. Don't get me wrong; he is a good and willing soldier for their cause. He's 'a real advocate.'"

"It often appeared that Cheney was more in control than W."

"In some respects he was," Bud confirmed. "Believe it or not, he tried hard to keep that image under wraps during his term in office. Cheney was working with a different group of people than W. was, and they wanted a lower profile. In contrast, W. loved the limelight, no matter how misdirected he appeared."

A.T. commented, "All I really know about Cheney is what has already been printed. So far, the investigative material that I have has very little to do with Mr. Cheney."

"Don't count on it. There are several members of Congress who are already engaged in their own investigations that deal with the former Vice President. Be sure to include any reference to him in your report. Even if it is redundant, the Senator will want to see it.

By the way, you do list your sources for the Senator, don't you? I'm sure he will want to see those sources, even if they are confidential."

"I do list all my sources for him. Even the confidential sources know the information will be conveyed to the Senator. In most cases, they are more willing to talk after they find out the information is for a United States Senator."

"The Senator is a former prosecutor and likes to see sources."

"I know. What surprises me is that he is a bit of a liberal."

"He's more of a moderate but people think he is liberal," noted Bud. "Now back to business."

"What comes next?" asked A.T.

"We've covered the first two segments. The third segment might include some religious groups or individuals, paramilitary groups, extreme media people or groups, particular financial groups, or other groups and individuals of interest whose purpose is one of agitation of the public."

"Do you mean like some of the conservative talk show hosts who exercise a disproportionate influence upon the public, such as Rush Limbaugh; Ann Coulter; Bill O'Reilly; Glenn Beck, who I understand is a friend of Senator Liebermann; Sean Hannity; Hugh Hewitt; Mark Levin, who I believe worked for former Attorney General Edwin Meese; Michael Medved, who is apparently a friend of your friend, Dick Cheney; Laura Ingraham, who was a former clerk for Justice Clarence Thomas; and Neal Boortz, who was apparently a speech writer for former Georgia governor, Lester Maddox."

Bud cautioned, "These commentators are entitled to their opinions and positions because the First Amendment allows them both the freedom of speech and the freedom of the press. The Senator is only interested in acts that may constitute violations of the law, and we are not aware of any of the people you mention to be in violation of any laws."

"What about those you have called 'off-beat' religious groups or individuals?"

"Many of the individuals and groups that fit into this third segment are aware of their Constitutional protections, and they use those protections to incite others. They are not completely stupid. In fact, they are cleverly using the Constitution and the laws in order to encourage others to act."

"I will remain objective. The same may be said about the paramilitary groups and individuals since they would also have certain rights including the freedom of speech, as well as the right of peaceful assembly and the right to keep and bear arms."

"That is true. As I said, the purpose of your investigation is not an easy task," reiterated Bud. The investigation needs to show that laws are being violated, and those laws are being violated for the purpose of certain groups attempting to overthrow our form of government."

"That might be; however, my focus is the DOJ and how it has gotten so far off track. This third segment that you mentioned seems to be far afield in regard to my investigation. How do the paramilitary or religious or financial people factor in?" A.T. inquired.

"You may be able to tie some intended subversive activity into each segment of the investigation. That is why the Senator thought it was imperative you have the materials Professor Brougham handed to you in regard to financial matters. You have already seen some of the paramilitary operations. It is the financial connections between these segments that will require you to travel to Europe. Professor Brougham may have given us some very key information. Once you tie it together, you will see the connection."

"What about the fourth segment that involves foreign entities?" asked A.T. "That has not been a part of my investigation.

"It is now," answered Bud. "It is this foreign element that is of the greatest concern to us since there is evidence they are determined to influence what happens in this country. They are interested in continuing to formulate the direction of this country, especially now that they have positioned themselves well in terms of influence over the other three segments I have outlined."

"How do you know they exist, and why would the Senator be interested in an investigation of this foreign element?"

"As I told you, there were three individuals who brought information forth about the same time. My first inclination was to do a story that would expose what was going on. However, when I found out what was really happening, I decided to contact the Senator," explained Bud. "After we spoke, we contemplated whether or not the information needed to be conveyed to law enforcement. We didn't have enough information to make an official complaint or report. The Senator met with an old friend who has been in the FBI for many years. He told the Senator of some concerns he had about the dissemination of information within the Bureau and the Department of Justice. He recommended that the Senator conduct his own investigation under the authority of his committee. Once more information has been obtained, a Senate investigation would serve a better purpose."

"What about a possible threat to national security? Wouldn't it be necessary to get appropriate law enforcement involved?"

"By contacting his friend at the Bureau, that step has been technically taken," responded Bud. "The information we have does not establish that there is an immediate threat. The potential threat is real, but it is long-term. The real threat is still being orchestrated. We needed everything we had already assembled in order to gather more information. We wanted to lock down what we could. The foreign element that is involved has been around for a very long time and moves very deliberately and with great patience. It is not a matter of trying to overthrow the government; they just want to take control through a very methodical process. They are far smarter and their plan, unlike any terrorist plan, has great potential for success."

"I don't think I understand what you are saying," remarked A.T.

"Let me use one example. You've already learned what was attempted at the Justice Department under the George W. Bush administration. By improperly terminating and replacing the United States Attorneys across the country, the Justice Department was politicized in such a way that it was being used to destroy people who were perceived as political enemies rather than remaining focused on crimes that had been committed. I believe your investigation up to this point has established how the manufacturing of evidence is used in order for people at the DOJ to charge individuals with fabricated acts where government agents actually orchestrate what appears as a potential crime. These people then use the Department of Justice to draw into the process various innocent individuals whom they wanted to 'get' for one reason or another. Usually, it involves a focus upon people whom they consider to be political enemies."

"I definitely know what you are talking about," observed A.T.

"Many of these cases were test cases to see how far they could go. Your case was one of those test cases," noted Bud.

"I did work especially hard to maintain a good reputation, and I believe most American citizens work hard to maintain a good reputation."

"As you know," Bud said, "that is not enough. If 'they' really want to set you up with a crime and 'get' you or anyone else, they are convinced they are powerful enough to do it."

"You're right about that," agreed A.T.

"As we know, you can now speak from experience," Bud added.

"I got your point. It was the misdirection of the Justice Department that got me involved in this entire matter in the first place. When I started to investigate it, I was appalled at how distorted the entire department was under the presidency of George W. Bush. In my opinion, it became a political arm of the 'lunatic fringe.' My investigation proved that to be true."

"Let me get us back on topic," insisted Bud. The foreign interests are the fourth segment you need to include in your investigation."

"I don't know. I don't have anything in my investigation so far that includes any foreign ties."

"Yes, you do. The material that Professor Brougham gave you provides the first bit of information that is needed in that regard. He should have given you both printed material, as well as several discs of balance sheets, account reconciliations, account material, some transfer documents, ledgers, and in some cases, copies of electronic deposits, transfers, and withdrawals. I'm sure there is more."

A.T. insisted, "I'm not the right person to handle this material. I don't have a finance or economics background. Shouldn't the Senator be using someone with an MBA to review and digest this material?"

"He has a couple of MBAs on it. They will digest the material for an analysis from an economics perspective. He wants you to conduct a follow-up investigation. That's why you will need to travel to Europe. There is a contact in Europe whose name I will provide. He is the third person who contacted me about an exposé. You met Professor Brougham, and you met Billy earlier today."

"Before you get me involved in a trip to Europe, please understand that I have other things to do here in the States, plus I technically still work for a living at my law practice."

"You are involved, and you can't back out now. The Senator is relying on you to complete the investigation he has outlined for you. You should probably plan to fly out as soon as possible. I'm sorry to hit you with new travel plans, but this work needs to be done before the next ten days are up. The Senator has some deadlines in regard to a meeting he has set up with some other members of Congress pertaining to the work you are doing for him. The trip to Europe will finish out the tasks at hand and will allow the Senator to bring some other trusted members of Congress up to speed. You are a key player at this point, and the trip to Europe is essential."

"Although I don't want to let the Senator down, I would have to adjust my schedule. I don't' know how much time I'm going to be able to spare. It will be only a day or two. Three days tops."

"You shouldn't need more than three days over and back. Your main purpose is to meet my contact because the two of you will be working together. From the meeting forward, he will be handling matters in Europe, the Far East, and the Middle East. You will be handling matters stateside. At this initial meeting, my contact in Europe will be providing documents that should match those that the professor provided. My contact is a banker in Europe. He will tell you what he believes you will need to do stateside regarding the various accounts, ledgers, etc. Once you return, you will have time to organize the materials as a part of your next report."

"Aren't you giving my report to the Senator?" A.T. inquired.

"I'll be meeting him in a couple of days, and I'll give him what you have provided. However, you will need to supplement what you have given me with a new report that includes the Brougham material, along with the material you bring back from Europe. If you have time, we would like to have it organized into a system that reflects the four segments we've been discussing."

"What exactly do you expect me to be getting from him, and why is it so important that I meet him?"

"If what he is telling me is accurate, you will see there are major connections between various worldwide organizations, mostly located in Europe, to groups here in the states that involve the fourth segment I mentioned. These groups have been active for decades, but their influence and involvement have become more intensified over the last forty years. It would be an understatement to say they have become entrenched in the political and governmental processes of this country."

"The problem is both you and the Senator are attempting to take me off the track of my investigation. It was my expectation that the focus of the investigation would be the Department of Justice and just how far afield it has gone, along with the FBI, in efforts to politicize instead of remaining focused on the enforcement of laws that have been violated," protested A.T.

"It's all tied together," responded Bud. "As you continue forward with the investigation, the undermining and politicization of the DOJ and the FBI are part of a much greater effort by some very powerful people who hold great wealth and political positions.

Once you follow the leads, you will find the connections to be real and truly dangerous."

"That may be true," noted A.T. "However, I don't want to find myself in a position when the investigation is over that I've been used and that nothing definitive gets done in regard to the misdirection of the DOJ and the FBI. There is far too much at stake for the core of my investigation to be overlooked or swept aside."

"Frankly, A.T., I'm surprised you would think either the Senator or I would attempt to use you. You will see that the material is relevant and ties very well into what you have been investigating. That is why I am introducing you to Jean Paul Valance. He is the banker whom you will meet in Paris before you travel to Zurich. The documents he presents will substantiate what Brougham provided. You'll learn that funds are being moved to and from the United States with purposeful intent to influence and infiltrate the U.S. government, as well as U. S. politics."

"I'm not sure I want to be involved."

"Believe me when I say you are the right man for the job. We couldn't find a useful skeleton in your closet, and we have done some real checking. Don't give up on us now since we are getting so close to exposing the orchestrated efforts presently underway to infiltrate both government and politics in such a way that the American public will suffer immeasurably if we stop now."

"I can't keep doing this. It's already more than I have bargained to do. If I accommodate you and meet with your European contact, what's his name, Jean Paul, will this then be the end of it for me?" A.T. asked. "I need to focus on a couple specific matters that my investigation shows involve me directly. I don't want to get too far off track with that endeavor."

"Trust me, you won't. Your personal interests and the specific matters to which you refer are tied directly to what you will be doing for us, with us meaning the Senator, his staff, a couple of Congressmen, and me. I get the first shot at a fully published exposé," informed Bud.

"Keep in mind I am quite uncomfortable with any other angle or approach to this investigation."

"Don't look at it that way," Bud said. "Keep your investigation objective as requested by the Senator. Be aware, however, that powers behind the scenes who want to remain behind the scenes are pulling the strings and calling the shots of what is going on here. It is far more organized than you realize and has been taking place for a very long time. It has been going on far longer than the late 60s and early 70s as you are postulating."

"So far, that is the time period during which efforts became well-organized without the public's awareness," noted A.T. "In that time period the investigation can establish organized efforts to plant people of specific philosophies within the various government departments, and it is when the Republican Party began to evolve into a closely held group of ultra conservative ideologues. The evidence on such matters is real and not something imagined."

"That's the track to follow," insisted Bud. "Substantiate what you find with documentation and hard evidence. As you step into this added arena we are presenting, you will find similar proof to bolster what has already been uncovered."

"Just so you know, whatever I find will be presented objectively and with evidence," responded A.T.

"That's understood and agreed. Believe me, if what Jean Paul was presenting didn't have a basis, he would not have been introduced to the Senator. I've done a pretty good job of screening the material so far. These powerful people remain behind the actual office holders and direct them. They have been described as invisible, subtle, watchful, and the interlocked real rulers of the country. Those are not my words, but the words of former presidents, Woodrow Wilson and Franklin Roosevelt, along with former Supreme Court Justice Felix Frankfurter. That's just naming a few of our better-known leaders who were aware of the presence of the invisible influence in this country."

"I'll agree to gather the evidence," A.T. noted, "but it will be up to you and the Senator to sort it out and present it. I want to return to my focus regarding the abuses that occurred within the Department of Justice. So, I will accommodate you on this European task, and when I return, I will need to meet with the Senator personally to deliver what I have to date. I will then respectfully request leave to finish my own designated purpose and investigation. Is that agreed?"

"Sure, as far as I'm concerned, it's agreed; you will need to discuss the details with the Senator when you return. I think that would be a fair way to proceed. Soon we'll need to exit the beltway, so I can take you to the office complex set up to administer some of the paramilitary operations that are underway at the various locations across the country, including the two that you have seen firsthand yesterday and today."

* *

It wasn't long after Bud's comment that he found the exit he wanted. He drove them to a fairly new office park not far from the beltway. There were about a dozen fairly modern buildings in the complex, which had a single two lane road that looped around it so that there was only one way in or out. Bud had been at the location before and drove to where the road started to loop back. The area was well-landscaped and wooded with large pine trees that had all of the lower branches removed and trimmed to about ten feet above the ground. There were curving sidewalks throughout with some water fountains and flower gardens strategically positioned. The center area around which the driveway traversed was also well-designed with four buildings of similar architecture placed apart from each other in an asymmetric fashion.

Bud pulled the car into a small parking lot near the point where three buildings were clustered at the apex of the curve. After parking the car, he and A.T. went into the first of the three buildings. It was four stories in height and had a glassed entry that opened into a two story foyer that contained chandeliers extending about halfway down from the ceiling overhead. There was an open balcony above the large foyer, and a coffee shop was situated in an expansive area at one end of the foyer. Other than a modest but tasteful sign that read, 'The French Roast,' the coffee shop was appointed with overstuffed chairs, along with some irregularly positioned tables with accompanying chairs. Besides a young attractive lady behind the counter and a few people sitting at a far table, A.T. and Bud were the only people present.

On the side opposite the coffee shop, there was a sitting area with a number of exotic trees that looked natural against the large glass windows surrounding the entire entry. Between the coffee shop and the area with the trees was a hallway for the elevator entry with two elevators on each side and a water fountain positioned at the far end of the hallway. The elevator bank and hallway were appointed in a light gray reflective marble that complimented the dark gray marble on the floor. There was an unoccupied guard desk positioned off to the side of the hallway leading to the elevators. With no guard present, Bud motioned for A.T. to follow him, and they proceeded to the elevators. Bud pushed the "up" button and took out his cell phone. The elevator door opened, and they got on and pushed the button for the top floor. While the door was closing, someone called out to get on the elevator; the door closed completely and up they went.

At the fourth floor, the doors opened, and the two of them exited. A.T. could tell that Bud had started to take pictures with his iPhone as he pretended to be talking to someone. The fourth floor had a glass barrier that allowed a clear view of the entire floor. There was an open area with secretarial desks, and since it was Saturday, there seemed to be no one present. However, around the perimeter of the secretarial area, several offices were fronted with glass and wooden doors. It was possible to see into the offices through the glass, and it was apparent that four or five people were busy working at their desks. Bud continued to take pictures while pretending to speak intermittently to an imaginary person on the phone and also to A.T. He was pointing out the interior of the floor and acting as though he was showing the building to A.T. The two of them got back on the elevator and traveled down to the third floor.

The third floor was configured the same as the fourth floor but displayed nearly a full workforce of secretaries and office individuals. This floor was quite a beehive of activity. Bud continued to take pictures while talking a bit louder than normal as he continued to display an animated conversation between the phone and A.T. After a couple minutes of this, one of the elevator doors opened. Exiting the elevator was a security guard and possibly one of the people who had been in the coffee shop below. They both simultaneously rushed to Bud and A.T. explaining the building was closed and Bud and A.T. should not be in the building because it was a private company. Bud held his phone to his side, and A.T. was sure he heard the iPhone catch a photo of the two men. Bud started to explain he was a realtor who was showing the building to A.T., who had flown to Houston to see about relocating his business in the Houston area.

After again being told the building was the office of a private business and not for sale, Bud told the imaginary person on the iPhone there was apparently some confusion since some people at the building had complained the building was not for sale. He then told the imaginary person he would call him back as soon as he found out why the building was no longer for sale. As the guard and his colleague escorted Bud and A.T. onto an elevator, Bud placed his phone into his shirt pocket. Then he produced a number of papers that indeed showed a real estate listing with photographs of the area and the outside of the building. While Bud presented the listing to the two individuals who began examining the papers, he pushed the button for the second floor. When the doors opened, Bud exited and amazingly his phone rang. He took it out, and A.T. was sure Bud was again taking pictures. Apparently, A.T. was the only one who noticed the photo action as the two men worked to herd the lingering Bud and A.T. back onto the elevator.

When they finally arrived at the main level, the two men handed the papers back to Bud and explained the building was not for sale and Bud's literature was outdated. Bud provided some excuses and threatened to fire his secretary when he got back to the office. It was apparently enough to placate the guard and the suit. A.T. was more than ready to leave; however, Bud insisted the two of them get a cup of coffee at the restaurant in the lobby called 'The French Roast.' Although it was unnerving to A.T., he agreed to join Bud for a cup of coffee and a piece of pie at the coffee shop.

The two of them ordered their coffee but learned there was no pie available. The shop had muffins, so they looked over the choices. Across the lobby from the coffee shop, a group of people were warming up musical instruments. Apparently, they were rehearsing for a later performance which was to take place in the lobby of the building. After warming up, the band began to play some "bluegrass." Although the style of music was not a favorite of A. T.'s, the band was pretty good. The band played through a couple of selections and would stop occasionally to make corrections. Once the band got going, A.T. fully expected someone to come out of the elevator flapping his arms and dancing on one leg. He was envisioning a scene out of *Deliverance,* but fortunately, there was no dancer hopping on a single leg, and he was happy to have been spared such a scene.

After receiving their coffee and muffins, Bud said, "Don't you think it's appropriate for us to take a break and savor the moment?"

"As the saying goes, 'you have more crust than a pie factory,'" said A.T.

"You should be thanking me for doing your job. By the way, I will email the pictures to you, so you can include them in your report."

"Thanks a lot. What kind of paperwork did you show those two guys?"

"It's an old listing of this building a realtor friend dug up for me. It was obviously part of an old listing book taken before this group bought it. It was an honest mistake," laughed Bud.

"Well, it was a well-planned effort," said A.T.

"I told you this morning I was going to be your realtor," commented Bud. "I'm always prepared. I trust you go prepared when you conduct your part of the investigation. Plus, if we hadn't been so lucky to find no guard in place, I was prepared to show him a fabricated listing, so we could try to talk our way in under other circumstances. Fortunately, we didn't have to show it. Now that could have been problematic."

"I suppose you have everything in place for my trip to Paris and Zurich?" inquired A.T.

"Not quite. You will need to line up another skilled party to travel with you. May I suggest your backup be someone whom you trust implicitly and who has skills, in case skills are needed? The sooner you can get information to me, the better."

"What do you mean, 'someone who has skills?'" asked A.T.

"It is always good to be prepared for anything. Keep in mind your investigation is very sensitive, and since you have material from Professor Brougham, there may be certain parties who would like to have you relinquish that information. Therefore, you may want to have an able-bodied associate, who is skilled in appropriate arts, to accompany you just in case..."

"If necessary, I can find such an associate to accompany me. So, are you and the Senator painting a target on my back and creating a dangerous situation out of what was to be a routine investigation?"

"No. You painted your own target the minute you started your own investigation. Truly, you are now in a safer mode since the Senator is involved. You have to keep this in mind as the investigation proceeds. It well might be sensitive to certain parties. You will need to start watching your back and have someone assist you. The Senator can provide such support, if you don't have someone in mind. Perhaps Robert could go with you."

"I appreciate the offer, but I think I can find someone who can help me out in regard to security. If he is unavailable, I might consider Robert. I want you to know with you and the Senator expanding the investigation, I have become paranoid. There are too many intricacies, and there is far more than I bargained to do."

"As is often said, 'just because you are paranoid, doesn't mean they are not out to get you.' From what you've experienced, you already know that. By the way, since you are going to France, don't you think it is a matter of synchronicity for us to be having a pleasant cup of coffee at an appropriately named coffee shop, 'The French Roast?'"

Bud's comment was not amusing to A.T., so he ignored it. He noticed, as they left for the airport, the emblem of the business displayed on the window of the building included a blue globe background. He was sure he had seen the emblem before.

Despite the unnerving experience at the building, the coffee did hit the spot. The cup of 'French Roast' he just finished wasn't too bad.

CHAPTER 8
FRENCH ROAST

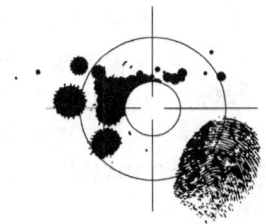

After departing the building complex where the 'French Roast Coffee Shop' was located, Bud drove the two of them to the George Bush International Airport. On the way to the airport, Bud and A.T. further discussed the four segments of the investigation Bud had suggested and outlined. Then A.T. bid Bud farewell and boarded his plane. He wasn't as tired as he had been when he flew to Houston, so a nap was not on the agenda. Instead, after sitting down, he tried to review the events in his mind, including those events that got him involved in the first place.

Up until this point, his investigation had been focused on particular matters relating to the Department of Justice. It also involved certain irregular political activity which bordered a fine line between legally permissible acts and outright violations of various laws dealing with improper and undue political influence occurring within the executive branch of government over the past couple of decades.

It was in 1988 when A.T. was again campaigning for Bush, Sr. that he met W. Unfortunately, he was not a bit impressed; in fact, he was disappointed by W. He thought W.'s efforts at flattery were superficial, while other people seemed to enjoy any such attention

W. would give them. At the time of senior Bush's candidacy, A.T. was thankful W. was not the candidate, and he mused how there could be so much difference between father and son. He met two of the three other Bush brothers and liked them far more than W.

At the same time, A.T. got a taste of the Pat Robertson campaign and its personnel. In A.T.'s opinion, those campaign activists were the worst political people he had met. Even at that time, some of the Robertson people were trying to insert their own manufactured religious beliefs into the political process. From what A.T. remembered, he developed the opinion that none of the supporters of candidate Robertson had either read or understood the Constitution of the United States, at least not in terms of the separation of church and state.

Subsequently, when W. became a candidate, A. T. made it clear he would not help in W.'s campaign or join any of the Bush administration's small business committees. A.T. was happy he had decided not to have any part of the George W. Bush administration and that especially held true when invitations came from then active Congressman Tom DeLay.

When A.T. started his investigation, the purpose had been clear and simple. Once the facts had been properly assembled, he would write a full report with specific recommendations relative to guidelines and oversight in terms of regulating and controlling the Justice Department and the grand jury procedures, along with a meaningful review of the ethical practices of each attorney within the Justice Department. The Office of Professional Responsibility or OPR, as it was known, had to be strengthened and greater impact of its investigations and findings had to come about. New recommendations would be made in reference to the qualifications and testing of individuals who made employment applications to the Justice Department for positions as staff attorneys.

It was known that two highly respected and well-regarded members of Congress had started investigations within their respective committees. House Judiciary Chairman, John Conyers, and Senate Judiciary Chairman, Patrick Leahy, had been conducting wide-range hearings relative to the criminal activity and unconstitutional acts by the Bush administration.

A.T. thought both committees needed to see and hear actual examples in which the politicizing of the Justice Department had resulted in the prosecution of innocent individuals. They also needed to be aware of the hardball tactics which had been employed by Bush era DOJ attorneys to attempt to force guilty pleas or convictions of innocents all due to prosecutorial misconduct including the concealment of exculpatory evidence, the fabrication of evidence, the falsified indictments, and the threats to witnesses to alter and fabricate testimony.

Members of the American Bar Association, the president of the Center for Constitutional Rights, and the president of the National Lawyers Guild, along with former Justice Department ethics attorneys, all gave speeches and wrote articles about the abuses within the Justice Department under the Bush administration. However, A. T. knew the committee members needed firsthand examples, so his investigation ensued. The "accidental" deletion of approximately twenty-two million emails during the Bush administration raised a new set of questions.

It was also obvious to A.T. the Bush administration would use claims of "executive privilege" as a means to cover up any illegal and unconstitutional acts, especially in terms of the Justice Department. He also realized as the Obama administration followed Bush into office, it had its hands full with a disastrous economy which was in large part created by the Bush administration. In addition, the Obama administration inherited two wars, one of which was incredibly ill-advised, and the other that was an international disgrace from a diplomatic standpoint. As Senator Sheldon Whitehouse of Rhode Island had reportedly said in 2009, "We could spend the entire next four years investigating the Bush years."

Republican leaders such as Senator Mitch McConnell of Kentucky and then House Speaker, John Bochner, publically stated they would do anything to assure that President Obama was a one term President. Apparently such statements must have meant that no sacrifice of the country's welfare was too great in order to make life difficult for President Obama. It was widely believed such thinking was part of the reason why the Obama administration left the George W. Bush administration free of any criminal prosecution.

Now, Bud had outlined a far-reaching investigation which went beyond any previously contemplated. A. T. had reluctantly agreed to expand his investigation into a new realm of activities along the lines outlined by Bud. Based upon what he had seen over the last couple days and what he had been given by Professor Brougham, A. T. realized more had to be done. His first task was to contact his old friend, Allen Aranda, who had served in both Interpol and with the U.S. Marshall's service. He was wondering if Allen would be interested in taking a trip to Paris and Zurich.

He and Allen were the same age and had followed many parallel avenues in their lives. They had been friends for many years and were very comfortable with the trust established between them. A.T. realized if he were going to travel to Europe, especially Paris, he needed to have someone who was familiar with the people and the area. While Allen had been with Interpol, he had been stationed for a number of years in France and operated out of the Paris office. He was quite familiar with Paris, the surrounding area, the people, and certain customs. Allen still had some active contacts in Paris, who had remained with Interpol. A.T. felt thiswould be important if he were to carry out the meetings that were to be set up for him by Bud.

When A.T. called Allen upon arriving back in the Twin Cities, he learned Allen was involved in planning a wedding for his daughter. Allen's daughter was a medical technician on staff at the Mayo Clinic, and she was marrying a physician, who was a staff internist at Mayo. Since Allen and his family were from St. Paul and had been active in the city for several generations, the wedding was planned for the Cathedral of St. Paul off Shelby Avenue. Allen said he was scheduled to be at the Cathedral that afternoon; therefore, the two of them could meet at the church. A.T. was hoping Allen, who was retired, would be able to travel sometime during the next week or two, so he kept his fingers crossed.

Allen was in a good frame of mind and appeared almost giddy. Apparently all the wedding plans were going well. Allen introduced A.T. to his daughter's fiancé and again to Allen's daughter, whom A.T. had met on several prior occasions. After various pleasantries and small talk, the Rector appeared, and Allen introduced him to A.T as well. Allen told his daughter and fiancé he would see them later for dinner. The Rector excused himself as he was called away for a telephone call, while A.T. and Allen walked toward the Avenue entrance where they could speak privately. A.T. asked Allen how he was enjoying his retirement, and Allen complained he had little to do. This seemed like a great opportunity for A.T. to ask Allen about the possibility of traveling expense-free to Europe. Although it was getting rather chilly outside, Allen and A.T. walked outdoors as they continued their conversation.

"A trip to Europe would be fun, especially after being more involved in my daughter's wedding than I had planned," exclaimed Allen as he displayed a broad smile. "I haven't been to Europe for years, and it would be great to reconnect with some of my old friends from many years ago while I was stationed in Paris. Could we put Paris on the list?"

"That's exactly where we need to go. Plus, we would need to go to Zurich, as well," said A.T.

"What exactly is going on, A.T.?" inquired Allen.

"As you know from my prior discussions with you, I have been involved in a self-directed investigation for just over a year now," explained A.T. "Nearly one year ago and after I had been working on the matter for a couple months, I was in contact with a United States Senator to see if I could get an audience before one of the subcommittees of the Senate Judiciary Committee. After I showed the Senator and some of his staff members what I had, they told me they were already conducting an investigation of their own. As it turned out, much of their investigation overlapped with what I was doing. Since I had done some work in the past for the Senator, he asked if I would be interested in having some official sanction and expanding my investigation. I said I would and that allowed me to broaden my scope for about a year now."

"So, I take it this has something to do with your situation?" asked Allen.

"It does, but because of the direction the Senator wants to take the investigation, it has expanded well beyond what I had originally targeted. As it turns out, Bud Hawthorne, who I believe you've met, is now doing some free-lance work for a couple of magazines. Bud had some sources bringing information to him, and he in turn took it to the Senator. I'm not sure just how much I am at liberty to tell you, except it involves some financial matters, along with some paramilitary activity. The financial matters require I meet with someone in Paris, and he in turn is to introduce me to a banker in Zurich, who is to provide some additional information which is to be directed to the Senator," said A.T.

"Are you sure of this? Do you know what you're getting involved in?"

"Yes and no! Just so you have some assurance, I can show you a copy of the letter from the Senator which sanctions the new direction of my investigation. I want you to see the letter so that you know I am not off on some wild goose chase," A.T. responded.

"That's not really necessary. I trust you, and you know that. However, just for the sake of protection for both of us, a copy of the letter from the Senator would be nice to have in case we have someone asking questions in Europe."

"A copy of the letter should be no problem, but let me be certain. I will inquire about it when I call the Senator and Bud to advise you have agreed to go with me."

"Wait a minute. I said a trip would be fun, and it's especially true if it is expense free, but I'm not completely sure. I do have some concerns. What is involved? What do we need to do? Is there any kind of danger? Is there any kind of security issue? Are we going to be just a couple of businessmen, or is there more involved? Neither of us is getting any younger, and we really don't need any unforeseen stress at this stage of our lives."

"To be very upfront about the matter, it could involve some danger. Bud told me to find someone 'skilled,' who could go along with me. I didn't want to mention your name until I first spoke with you. We are to be a couple of businessmen meeting with a banker. When Bud suggested I get someone who is 'skilled' to go along, I got the impression there could be some issues with security and there could be some danger. That is all I know for now, and I will understand if you choose not to go."

"Now you've got my interest. You have to know my 'skills' such as they are could not possibly be what they once were. I don't know if I would be an asset or a liability to you. By the way, your 'skills' can't be all that great anymore either. Aren't you taking on a bit more than you should at your age?"

"I hope not. As you know, I got into this whole thing for a very good reason. It's not your war, so I will understand completely if you decline the opportunity to see Paris at this time. I just felt I needed someone who I trusted implicitly; therefore, I thought I would ask you first. There is a former Navy Seal whom I met a couple of days ago, and I understand he is already working for the Senator. I've had a chance to see him in action and know he definitely has the requisite 'skills.' However, I don't know him well, and it would be my preference to have someone like you along. Besides, I honestly don't expect there would be any danger regarding what appears to me to be a routine trip to meet with a banker for the purpose of receiving specific information for a U.S. Senator. One would think such a task wouldn't involve anything too exciting."

"You never know… Let me shoot straight with you. I've been putting you on a bit. Bud did call me, and he was guessing you would be asking me to join you. He knows we are good friends, and he also stated he thought that someone with my level of 'maturity' would be a good assistant for you. My 'maturity,' indeed! At least he didn't call me 'over the hill.' Listen, I just liked the idea, and some excitement sounded good. I was hoping you would give me a call and ask if I would go along. When do you want me to make some calls to Paris? I can line up the right kind of support, if you know what I mean. A.T., this is the kind of thing that might just spice up my retirement. I have really been bored and helping plan a wedding has taken a lot out of me. I need some excitement in order to get rejuvenated," said Allen.

"That being the case, would you be available for travel in about two weeks? Although Bud said three days, I think we would need to plan for five to seven days over and back. Did you say you still had some contacts with the authorities in Paris, just in case we need to have someone there who could give us support at the right time, if we ever needed it?" asked A.T.

"Two weeks from today and back a week later will work for me," answered Allen. "The wedding will be long over and anything I had to do around here would be done. If you are making arrangements through Bud, I believe he still has my information; if not, he can give me a call. I still have friends in the right places. In fact, one of the guys I used to work with at Interpol is with the Paris police department and is still holding down a supervisory desk. If I remember correctly, he should be coming up for retirement in a couple years. He can provide whatever assistance we will need in Paris. As far as Zurich is concerned, I will need to check on that since I no longer have any active contacts there."

"If it is all right with you, I'll instruct Bud to make plans for the two of us in about two weeks," responded A.T. "Do you think that we will need anyone like my new acquaintance, Robert?"

"I don't believe so. Rene LePonte, my old Interpol buddy, should be able to get us some private assistance or better yet, some assistance from his department, if we need help. I trust that everything to be done will be totally above board."

"Of course, it is! Need you even ask?" smiled A.T.

A.T. and Allen ended their conversation with some general discussion about the wedding and Allen's recent efforts at attempting to remain physically active by playing some pick-up hockey games and jogging. Allen had been a first class distance runner in college. While in the military, he was a champion boxer with a multitude of ribbons and trophies to display for those efforts. He had been a remarkable athlete in his college days and since that time had maintained a significant physical exercise regimen. As A.T. departed, he felt confident he had made the best possible decision in selecting Allen for the task ahead. Naturally, he did not expect any problems or have the slightest expectation of difficulties; nevertheless, it was reassuring to know that Allen would be joining him in this endeavor. Robert would have been a better choice had A.T. expected any serious problems of any sort that really required someone "skilled" with tactical maneuvers. Allen, on the other hand, had connections and knew people in the right places, in case they ever got into a bind of any sort.

* *

During the next ten days the required arrangements for travel, lodging and meetings were set. A.T. made adjustments to his schedule and completed the necessary work relating directly to his case load of court appearances and client meetings. He wanted to be certain all matters involving his clients were current. He and his seven law partners, including Adam, maintained a medium-sized law firm of associates, who were assigned various tasks, along with attending hearings in A.T.'s absence. Everything he deemed necessary for the representation of his clients was in place. He was now free to travel.

It was never A.T.'s habit to travel with more than the bare necessities, and the forthcoming trip held no exception. The night before he was to fly out, he was packing his long distance leather bag and a smaller carry-on that was large enough to hold his laptop, files, toiletries, a change of shorts, socks, and a few other necessities. He had traveled this way for years and felt comfortable by taking less than virtually every other traveler he had ever met. Normally, he would send extra suits, shirts, and ties, etc. via DHL, UPS, or FedEx to his hotel.

Having already sent the suit/tie package earlier in the day, he was finishing his packing when he saw Jacci entering the driveway off Summit. The first thing that had naturally attracted A.T. to Jacci was her good looks. She had been the college homecoming queen and had won a couple of state beauty contests. However, she was far from typical in that regard. After he started dating her, he learned that she was an honors student. He had always been impressed with her intellect.

She held a Master of Arts with two degrees in psychology. Jacci was a psychologist who worked for a subsidiary of a large publishing house and had recently taken an early retirement when the opportunity arose. Most of her time was currently being spent with local projects and with her horses. She had been active with the local dressage club and had won numerous trophies. Their three children were grown and on their own. She was allowing herself to enjoy life, and A.T. was proud of that fact. She had always been generous to the community and to her work, so it was time for her to reward herself.

A.T. grabbed his bags and headed down the stairs to greet Jacci, who had been out riding.

"How were the horses?" he asked. "I see there are no broken bones, so it must have been a good day."

"The horses are good. Everything is pretty much set for the winter. So, since you're heading out for a couple weeks, I thought I would fly to Arizona to see my mother. I haven't been there for a while, and I think it would be good for me to see how she is doing. What do you think?"

"I think it would be great."

"I know she doesn't like the winters up here, but I'll assure her if she comes to Minneapolis we will take good care to see that she stays warm. Of course, I will entice her with a couple trips to Mall of America, so she can shop."

"The promise to buy some new shoes should do it," laughed A.T.

"Since this will be our last night together for a while, I think that it would be a good idea for you to take me to a very nice dinner," said Jacci.

"It's a date! A nice dinner and a fine wine would be well in order. Who knows, we may later find a way to entertain ourselves," urged A.T.

Later, the evening was all it was expected to be. Since the two of them always enjoyed each other's company in every respect, and because A.T. did not have to depart until the following afternoon, they slept late and enjoyed a quiet brunch together. That afternoon Jacci took A.T. to the airport where he would meet Allen for the trip to Paris.

* *

As A.T. kissed Jacci and reached for his two bags, he told her the same thing that he always told her when either of them traveled and that was how he had chosen wisely. She smiled, kissed him again, and repeated the phrase back. They both laughed, and A.T. left for the trip to Paris.

A.T. met Allen inside the terminal, as agreed. They checked in and proceeded through the security check including a pass through the new systems of body scans and scent detectors. They found their gate and waited to depart on the direct flight to Paris. They were fortunate to find Bud had booked them into first class. A.T. rarely traveled in first class because he felt it was an unnecessary expense. However, with a long flight to Paris, he appreciated the extra room the first class seat provided.

Allen explained he had made arrangements with his friend, Rene, who was planning to meet the two of them as they arrived at the Charles DeGaulle Airport north of Paris. As a longtime friend of Allen's, Rene LePonte had volunteered to take them to their hotel, so the car rental was cancelled. Allen explained that Rene was about eight months away from retirement as an inspector with the relatively unknown Paris Department of Special Investigations. The PSI, as it was termed, was a special department that had been established over twelve years ago. Its principal function was to investigate terrorism and radical activity. In Paris, the PSI always had its hands full. Currently Rene had been working on a number of cases dealing with the fluid travel between French Morocco and Paris. He was definitely looking forward to retirement.

Allen mentioned that Rene would assist them in any way possible. If necessary, he could spare at least one of his men to assist them for a couple days, however, not for the entire time. Unfortunately, Rene could not assist in regard to any travel to Zurich. A.T. did not foresee any type of difficulty. Yet, the help would not be rejected since A.T. was not at all familiar with Paris. He had only been there once before, while Allen had lived there for three years. Having some assistance in simply getting around was good news.

For the meetings in both Paris and Zurich, A.T. had been instructed to bring the Professor Brougham ledgers, spread sheets, and other materials since those items would need to be examined by Jean Paul.

Upon arrival in Paris, Allen and A.T. deplaned with their carry-on bags and went directly to the baggage claim area to collect their luggage. As A.T. was picking up one of the bags that Allen had brought with some gifts for his friend Rene, a gentleman of about six-two in height and decently fit asked if he needed any help. He tried to determine whether the man, who spoke perfect English, was from a particular geographic part of the world since, over the years, he had become fairly well-skilled at identifying accents. He felt certain that he was an American.

A.T. told the man that he appreciated the offer but that he didn't need any assistance. Then he recalled that the man had been on the same flight and had been seated a couple rows in front of Allen and A.T. on the plane. The man attempted to continue his conversation of small talk and commented on how difficult it was to travel abroad these days. He said it was important that Americans really stick together and then volunteered that he and his associate had a rental car with plenty of additional room, if A.T. needed a ride. A.T. declined the offer and joined Allen. After the man departed, he was joined by a much shorter man who seemed to visually assess A.T. and Allen while leaving.

"What was that all about?" asked Allen.

"I'm not sure, but I did notice he and his shorter friend were both on our plane. He asked me if we wanted to share a ride with them, and I declined. He also said we Americans should stick together," commented A.T.

"He was probably just trying to be friendly. A lot of tourists seem to feel a sense of comfort when they notice other Americans in foreign airports and elsewhere. I doubt it is anything to worry about; besides, we have our transportation already arranged. In fact, I believe that is Rene coming toward us now."

"*Tres bien! Bonjour, Allen!*" exclaimed Rene as he approached Allen and A.T.

"*Bonjour, Rene! Je vous presente Monsier A.T. Van Doren,*" said Allen.

"*Parlez-vous Francias?*" asked Rene as he shook A.T.'s hand.

"*Oui. Je parle un peu Francais, mais je...*" interjected A.T.

"*Je comprends,*" said Rene. "We will speak English. Welcome to France, A.T."

"Thank you. I'm sorry that my French is not better. I should have been better prepared; however, the trip came on short notice."

"Do not worry, my friend," said Rene. "We modern French understand completely. The English have given the world a rather universal language; you Americans have given the world a common denominator in terms of the dollar as a manner of exchange, which we like much better now that your Bush president is no longer in power. We French have given the world culture and beauty in the form of art, design, architecture, engineering, dress, style, and women, of course. Those of us who value the shrinking world understand cross-culture is good for the world as we all interact across the globe. The astute Frenchman has no problem using English."

"That's appreciated," said A.T.

"It's good to know that you are still 'full of shit,' Rene," commented Allen.

"And you are the same blunt, 'bull shit' American, Allen. Did I say that right?" asked Rene.

"You said it right. Thank you for coming to our assistance. I trust your wife, Michelle, and the five children are all well?" inquired Allen.

"Michelle is wonderful. She sends her regards and wants me to tell you when I retire in a few months, we will be coming to the U.S. to see the Epcot Center in Florida. She asks that you will be our guide there."

"Absolutely! It would be my honor."

"Great. I will tell her. She may want to plan a dinner while you are here, so let me see what she has in mind. The children are fine. My oldest has been in the Foreign Service and will be returning from Gabon in a couple weeks. My second son, believe it or not, is studying to be a priest of all things, so he is in Vatican City now. My older daughter got married several years ago and has given us two beautiful grandchildren. My youngest son is still at the university, and my baby daughter is still at home. They are all well and healthy. What about your family? If I remember correctly, you have a daughter and two sons."

"That's right. My youngest, the daughter, is a medical technician at Rochester and just got married. Both of my sons are in law enforcement, with one on the police force in Minneapolis and the other in the police department in Washington D.C."

"Just like their father. That is very good," said Rene as he turned to A.T. and asked, "What about you, A.T.? Do you have a family?"

"Yes," said A.T. "I have a lovely wife and three children who are all grown now and with their own careers.

"Wonderful," commented Rene, who then asked, "What exactly brings you to Paris? I understand from Allen you will also be traveling to Zurich."

"We are here to meet with a banker, and he is to introduce us to another banker in Zurich. Our assignment is from a United States Senator whose associate is a reporter who has set up an exchange of information that we are instructed to process and return to the Senator. It is of a classified nature. It involves U.S. interests both here in Europe and in the U.S. Hopefully, it is only a domestic matter for the U.S.; otherwise, we would be working through diplomatic channels. As I understand it, your government is not involved; therefore, we are handling the matter privately. Plus, at this stage, the investigation is preliminary. If it becomes more and does involve your government, the Senator will be in touch with the appropriate parties on this side and that would include any banking authorities," explained A.T.

"You understand," asserted Rene, "I cannot provide any proper assistance for you, unless I become officially involved. I can give you one of my men in an off-duty capacity, so long as he is properly compensated.

"That's understood," said A.T. "I have some limitations regarding what I may do in terms of compensation, but I do have some authority. Perhaps I could visit with him tonight or tomorrow."

"He is mostly not available this evening; however, I will make him available to you tomorrow morning. Here we do not start our day officially until about 10:00 a.m. Shall I arrange for him to meet you for breakfast in the morning? There is a decent café in your hotel. I understand from what Allen told me in an email you are staying at the *A La Villa Madame* Hotel while here in Paris," noted Rene.

"That should be fine. Will he be on duty, or will he be free to discuss a fee for his assistance with us during his off-hours?" asked A.T.

"He is off duty for the remainder of this week. He just finished a long weekend for us and returned from the U.K. I will have him meet you at 10:00 in the hotel café. His name is Jacques Bouline, and he is of average height. I'd say about six foot. He is forty-something and is quite fit. He has blonde hair and a mustache. He will want to know what this is about. He is a very honorable person, so you will need to be honest and direct with him. Just telling him that it is about banking will not be sufficient. He is a native of Paris and knows the streets and businesses well," said Rene.

A.T. said, "He sounds like the right man for us. I know Allen has lived here, but I have not; therefore, knowledge of the city will be helpful. I will tell him, as I told you, we are here to meet a banker about some accounts that may be subject to the agreement reached between the U.S. Treasury Department and various large European banks in regard to U.S. citizens maintaining accounts here in Europe without properly reporting the accounts and the earnings to the U.S. government. That's about all Allen knows, as well."

"Isn't it a matter that has already been under the scrutiny of the appropriate authorities?" asked Rene.

"It is. But there is some reason for the Senator to believe something more is at stake and complete reporting has not been taking place by certain groups. My task is to conduct a preliminary investigation. If what the banker knows is helpful, be assured the proper authorities will be made aware of what is taking place, and they will definitely be involved. In sum, I am on a fact-finding mission, and Allen has joined me in order to be a witness that the task is nothing more and becomes nothing more. What we learn will be turned over to the Senator."

"You don't intend to turn it over to me as well?" inquired Rene.

"I don't believe I am permitted to share the information with anyone. What I learn needs to go straight to the Senator," noted A.T.

"That makes my job difficult. Therefore, you may work with Jacques, if he is willing to help you. You must convince him you are within proper bounds. Should you or Allen get yourselves into difficulty, I hope you understand I may not be able to assist you. Consequently, I must warn you to be very careful. I will, of course, deny I have helped in any way. The only alternative is for you to get your Senator friend to make appropriate arrangements with his counterparts within government at this end. Permit me to warn you that you could be in dangerous waters. Let me suggest you contact your Senator immediately for the necessary arrangements," warned Rene.

"I understand," said A.T. "I have forewarned Allen that we may not have your sanction, and I believe Allen understands. Am I correct, Allen?"

"It is understood," agreed Allen. "We do not anticipate any type of trouble in any respect. As I understand it, we are to meet with the banker and exchange some banking information. It is a simple task and is no different than the type of routine business conducted every day. I would guess that the information we receive is the type of information that could be disclosed to your authorities without incident or question. Am I correct on this point, A.T.?"

"As far as I know, you are correct," said A.T.

"All right, gentlemen! It is your call. I will have Jacques meet you in the morning. You are free to make independent arrangements with him as an independent contractor while he is off duty. It will be up to him and his good judgment," warned Rene.

Rene delivered Allen and A.T. to the *A La Villa Madame Hotel* and advised them to proceed with the utmost caution. He told Allen he would check with his wife, Michelle, in regard to a dinner engagement for later in the week, after A.T. and Allen returned from the meeting with the banker in Zurich. Allen and A.T. checked into the hotel and retired to their rooms for a few hours before heading out to a local restaurant Allen remembered from years earlier. An early return to the hotel was in order, so the two of them could rest up for the next day.

* *

At 10:00 a.m. the next morning, Allen and A.T. met Jacques at the hotel café and reviewed what they believed would be a simple task of meeting a banker by the name of Jean Paul Valance. While they were eating breakfast, Jacques had his office check on Jean Paul Valance. He determined Jean Paul was indeed a banker and was, in fact, a vice president at Paribus. Jacques felt comfortable with the information he received on Jean Paul, who was regarded as a credible individual. Jacques agreed to assist Allen and A.T. in finding their way around Paris but cautioned he would be helping them as an independent contractor and not in any official capacity.

As a result of the investigation Jacques performed on Jean Paul Valance, he decided to share what he considered to be quite position important information that he had learned about Jean Paul. Jacques explained while Jean Paul was working at Paribus, he was granted a special leave of absence from the bank in order to work with French officials who were conducting an investigation relative to the Bank of Credit and Commerce International, otherwise known as BCCI, which at the time had earned the moniker "Bank of Crooks and Criminals." According to what Jacques explained, the BCCI was a bank funded by Saudi interests and had started as a Pakistani bank back in 1972 with much of its original funding provided by the

Bank of America and the CIA. The bank had been utilized by the CIA to move funds used by covert operations globally. Jean Paul had developed certain information in his private banker capacity important to French investigators, so he was hired as a special consultant.

Jean Paul was able to link a quiet and dignified Director of Saudi Intelligence, Sheikh Kamal Adham to former U.S. President George H.W. Bush when Bush was at the CIA. The BCCI was a private bank ultimately connected to various scandals and criminal activities that included terrorists, drug money laundering, Iraqgate, and the Iran-Contra affair, along with other violations. What was more astounding was the fact BCCI was involved in the funding of the Pakistani nuclear weapons program. Although it has been reported the FBI and other U.S. government agencies were aware of the illicit acts of BCCI, nothing was done. Ultimately when law enforcement in France and a state prosecutor in New York were ready to file criminal charges, the bank's operations in the United States were shut down. Because of the work Jean Paul had done for the French authorities, he was not only highly regarded but he received a decoration as well. What was not completely known was the motivation behind the cooperation by Jean Paul and Paribus; however, Jacques speculated it might have had something to do with the fact that Paribus was, itself, running into some difficulties with the banking regulators at the time. Jacques wanted A.T. and Allen to know the story behind Jean Paul, and Jacques believed Jean Paul was trustworthy.

The meeting with Jean Paul would take place after hours since it was a full work day for Jean Paul. Jacques stated he would not be able to assist until evening anyway because he needed to fulfill some personal tasks inasmuch as he had just returned from the U.K. on department business. A.T. provided the name of the restaurant at which Jean Paul had told him they would meet in the new business district known as *La Defense,* just west of main Paris. Jacques stated he knew the area well, and he would arrive at the restaurant on his own in a private way and position himself so he could observe A.T. and Allen in their meeting with Jean Paul.

* *

That evening Allen and A.T. hired a taxi and went to the upper level area of the *La Defense* business district near the 'Great Arc,' known as *La Grande Arche Tower*, where they were to meet Jean Paul. Allen told the restaurateur they were to join a *Monsieur Valance*. Jean Paul had already arrived, and they were immediately escorted to his table in a corner of the far end of the restaurant. Jean Paul, a gentleman in his fifties, was wearing a dark blue pin-striped suit and a pink tie with a wide paisley pattern. A.T. thought paisley must be back in style if a French banker was wearing it. He noted Jean Paul, who was fairly trim and tall, possibly over six feet two inches in height, was very dignified looking with a thin and neatly trimmed mustache. Jean Paul also wore a pink handkerchief in his suit pocket, and his hair was predominantly black with a salt and pepper look. He looked like a banker. Using impeccable English, he immediately greeted A. T. and Allen.

As he extended his hand in greeting, first to A.T. and then to Allen, he said, "Mr. Van Doren and Mr. Aranda, please sit down and join me. It is a pleasure to meet the two of you. Your friend, Bud, has told me much about each of you; permit me to say everything he said about you was quite flattering. I feel reassured to meet you both. Will you be interested in some wine? I have taken the liberty to order in advance of your coming. I believe you will enjoy this particular *Merlot*. It is one of my favorites."

"Yes, thank you," said A.T.

"Please. Yes!" urged Allen.

"Let me proceed to properly introduce myself," said Jean Paul as he poured the wine. "I am an officer with Paribus here in Paris. I have been with the bank for eighteen years, and in my current position, I am familiar with many of the more sophisticated transactions that occur beyond the day-to-day banking. The information I am going to show you does not involve our bank but other banks here in Europe and in the U.S. Kindly, first permit me to give you some background information.

"I met Bud when the two of us were students together at Cambridge. He and I have maintained a close relationship; in fact, our families have vacationed together both in Europe and in the United States. I have particularly enjoyed your Grand Canyon. It is the most amazing marvel of nature. I hope to see it again. I also believe you should know Bud and I, along with our wives, own a home on the French Riviera together with two other couples. It is a great retreat for us, and it works out well since we rotate use of it. Perhaps either of you or your families may someday want to enjoy it."

"That's quite an offer for having just met us," said A.T.

Jean Paul held up his hand and said, "Gentlemen, please realize I know much about each of you. In fact, I now have a rather detailed file on each of your impressive backgrounds. Had I not such a file, we wouldn't be having this meeting. The file was completed by our in-house security team, along with a friend of mine who is with the Paris police. I do have my own connections, and be assured that I would not conduct business with anyone with whom I am not comfortable. Forgive me for such an intrusion, but it was necessary given the highly sensitive information I am about to convey to you. Also, I recognize Inspector Jacques Bouline at a table behind the planter near the waiter's desk at the entrance. By chance, would you know him? Could he be tailing either of you? Does the Department know you are meeting with me? Forgive me, I ramble. Let us order our meals first, and then I will tell you what you need to know for your U.S. Senator."

Allen explained he was friends with Rene LePonte, and Jacques was offered on his off-hours to provide some assistance to Allen and A.T. in the event they needed a guide through the streets and the city. The meals were ordered, and the three of them enjoyed some fine French cuisine. During the meal, they discussed their families and Jean Paul's relationship with Bud. Jean Paul told them several stories that were both revealing and entertaining about Bud in his earlier days at Cambridge. Jean Paul laughed in a delightful manner until tears came to his eyes. As the meal and casual but polite conversation came to a close, Jean Paul reached below his chair and pulled out a briefcase. From his briefcase, he removed a large accordion-style file about two inches thick.

"Let me describe what I have for you and your Senator," said Jean Paul. "The documents I am presenting tonight need to be kept as confidential as possible. I am giving you a secure briefcase to assure the documents remain confidential. I was concerned about transferring the material electronically; therefore, you have some idea how important these materials are. If the briefcase is opened without the code I will give you to memorize, all of the contents of the briefcase will be destroyed by an acid activator. The gas is toxic; therefore, if that happens, do not allow yourselves to breath in the gas."

Jean Paul continued, "These documents, along with the remote drives and discs in this folder, are records of what are called high level financial transactions involving the purchase and the sale of certain types of bank instruments. The transactions fall within what is classified as PPPs or Private Placement Programs. The legitimate PPP documents are then filed with a proper regulatory agency, and in the U.S. that would be your Security and Exchange Commission. Typically, only an initial filing is required. Often, the instruments that generate the funds for these PPPs are known as MTNs or Medium Term Notes and BGs or Bank Guarantees. Transactions of this nature are performed in large denominations; typically, each transaction involves hundreds of millions of dollars. You, along with the Senator, will find these transactions have been occurring for a couple of decades between certain U. S. organizations and particular European organizations. The transactions are legitimate, so it is not a matter of the transactions being illegal in that sense."

"Then, what is the issue?" asked A.T.

"The issue is the transactions or I should say the proceeds from the transactions are being used to fund particular activities and organizations that manipulate the political process and the governmental organization of your country."

"Wait a minute," exclaimed A.T. "First explain, if you will, what the MTN or BG transactions are. That is something I'm not sure I understand."

Jean Paul explained, "Both the MTNs and the BGs are bank instruments created by certain major banks in order to raise funds for major financial endeavors. The MTNs are bank instruments created much like stock certificates. They are sold in private transactions by banks to specific corporations or individuals, who are selected because of the corporation's or the individual's ability to invest large sums.

"The instrument typically has coupons redeemed on an annual basis for interest on the instrument. The instruments themselves are bought and sold and usually have a maturity date ranging between seven and ten years. The BG or Bank Guarantee is an instrument typically issued for a major corporation but through a large bank. It is usually for a shorter term and normally does not have an annual interest. These bank instruments are, in a sense, a commodity transacted in an elite environment. Most of these instruments are registered with an appropriate banking authority or with a stock exchange under particular rules and regulations. You can find information about these instruments on the Internet, but I want to caution you not all of the Internet information is accurate. There is a significant amount of fraud taking place. That is one of the reasons why the transactions that involve such instruments are found in a very refined environment."

"If these are so legitimate, or at least the ones that you are addressing, why is there such a need for the material to be handled in such a confidential manner that Allen and I have unwittingly become couriers for Bud and the Senator?" asked A.T.

"You're conducting an investigation, right?" inquired Jean Paul.

"Right! But my investigation involves domestic issues in the United States. It involves matters within a couple of our agencies and perhaps some irregularities that involve individuals or groups influencing those agencies. I don't see how it would have anything to do with what you have just explained," noted A.T.

"Did you bring the materials a certain Professor Brougham gave you?" inquired Jean Paul.

"Yes," said A.T., who then opened his own briefcase to remove copies of the papers he had received from the Professor.

"I hope the briefcase you are using does not have any sentimental value to you since you will need to strip it of any identification materials and any other items you have in it. You will place all of those materials in the briefcase I am giving you tonight, along with the new materials I have been showing you. You will then want to dispense with the soft leather briefcase you brought. May I suggest you simply leave it beneath the table, but again I warn you to remove any and all traces of identification. Now, let me see the materials from the Professor," Jean Paul requested. He then took some very deliberate time to examine the documents A.T. had received from Professor Brougham.

Jean Paul laid out some of the documents from the Professor, and next to them, he placed some of his own documents. He pointed to the ledger and said, "Here, you will see from the Professor's ledger I have set before you that there are regular deposits of fairly large sums for a period of weeks and months. The amounts of the deposits are regularly made and are in the amount of seven and one half million each time. The intervals of the deposits are occurring on the same day each week for a period of twenty-four weeks or roughly six months. Now, notice this transaction sheet. This sheet represents a part of the trade transactions I mentioned earlier.

Please notice the deposits on the Professor's ledger correspond precisely to the wire transfers out of the account I have presented. Also, notice the wire transfers are made directly into the accounts provided by the Professor."

"Should we be discussing this here at the restaurant?" asked Allen.

"It's a perfect place," said Jean Paul. "We are reviewing bank matters and here, at least in this restaurant, such business is done on a daily basis. Patrons of the restaurant and the restaurant personnel know to stand back, unless they are motioned to come to the table. Open discussions establish there is nothing to hide and business is routine."

"That sounds okay. I haven't noticed anyone paying any attention to us. Should we continue?" urged A.T.

"Certainly," added Jean Paul. "As you see from the documents, the funds are then moved by wire transfer into the accounts that Professor Brougham has provided. Where the funds are going or what they are being used to fund, I have no way of knowing. That is information the Professor needs to provide to either you or the Senator."

"I noticed," A.T. commented, "I've checked on some of these and have noted that some are incorporated in the Channel Islands, some in the Bahamas, some in Turks and Caicos, and others in Switzerland. I am not familiar with any details because in none of the cases have I been able to determine the identities of the incorporators. I am still working on that matter. What I have found troubling is none of the corporations have been organized in the United States. Hopefully we will get some information about the people who set up the companies."

"Don't hold your breath," said Jean Paul. "I believe you will find most of the corporations with letter monikers will be using other corporations that serve on a routine basis as registered agents for others who do not wish to be identified. I am also sure those registered agents will not be willing to reveal the identities because they consider it a matter of a fiduciary relationship. So, the disclosure of the incorporators will be hard to come by."

"How is the information you provided going to be of benefit to the Senator?" asked Allen.

"The Senator will now have the identifiable source of the funds that were used for the transactions, as well as an idea of where the actual funds originate," said Jean Paul. "My files do contain the details in regard to the parties who are involved in the very trades and transactions that are occurring. Also, the volume and dates of the transactions are contained in my materials. Therefore, from my end, you are getting the necessary detail. That is why you must use the briefcase I provide. These materials should not get into the wrong hands, and they need to be delivered personally. As I mentioned, without the access codes I am giving you, A.T., the case cannot be opened. If it is opened without the codes, a vial will automatically detonate and the contents will be destroyed."

"Understood," remarked A.T. "The materials you are providing will give the Senator all he needs from you. Won't you be compromised by giving these materials to us?"

"Not at all," said Jean Paul. "My bank is not involved, and although the activity disclosed in the documents is not in violation of any of our laws or EU regulations, the disclosures may trigger more than just interest in the United States. That will be up to the Senator and his committee. I have spoken to the Senator through a conference call that was arranged by Bud. As a result of that call, it is my understanding the Senator may be aware of some potential violations of banking regulations in the U.S. The material was provided to me through a counterpart at one of the banks involved. He felt there might be issues, so he called for my advice. I then contacted Bud who, at the time, was contemplating an article for publication. He apparently decided to turn the matter over to the Senator. Be assured my bank does not have any possible exposure. I've already checked on that matter to be sure. The Senator will also be making the necessary contact with the proper parties at your Federal Reserve. I trust the two of you have some knowledge of how it operates in an independent manner from your government."

"I guess I knew it was separate, but I wasn't sure exactly how or why," said Allen.

"It is not a part of your government but a separate entity from your government," instructed Jean Paul. "Let me explain; as a European banker, I am quite familiar with your American banking system. In my position at Paribus, we work with your banks and your Federal Reserve every day. First, as a bit of American history, the Federal Reserve Bank was established by President Wilson and the Congress in 1913. It was set up under what was called The Federal Reserve Act. The idea was to preserve stability and banking integrity. It was in part designed so the average person would place funds into a savings account or other safe account with a bank. The bank could loan out that money to others in a manner that put the money to work in industry or other enterprise. It also, over time, has certain requirements on the banks in regard to the amount they may loan out and the amount they must keep in reserve, which I believe, is ten percent.

"As an institution, the Federal Reserve is broken down into twelve regional banks to placate the individuals who thought a single central bank would be too strong and would wield too much power. If I remember correctly, the twelve regional banks are New York, Boston, Philadelphia, Richmond, Atlanta, Cleveland, Chicago, St. Louis, Kansas City, Minneapolis, Dallas, and San Francisco. They each have a geographic area governed by the regional bank. From what I have read, there were two in the state of Missouri solely because a powerful member of Congress came from that state. Each of the regional banks manages a large sum of money; New York is the largest with over one trillion dollars under its management. A.T., your city, Minneapolis, is the smallest with about twenty-four billion under its management.

"The FED operates under a Board of Governors that includes a member from each of the twelve regions, along with board members appointed by your President. The President also appoints the Chairman. This board is supposed to advise the President, Congress, and Treasury Department. It is through the twelve regional banks that checks are processed, money is placed into circulation, and the banks throughout the country are regulated. On a more local level, the member banks elect six of the nine directors for their region of the Federal Reserve.

"The money supply is regulated in several ways, including the requirement that member banks hold in reserve so much of their deposits, lending to member banks through the FED discount window and through the purchase and sale of government securities. Today, there are also currency swaps with foreign banks, certain specific government-backed loans, and certain mortgages backed by the FED. There has been an expansion of banking operations of the FED, and much of that has occurred with the expansion of world markets, world banking, and world industrialization. The Federal Reserve has become an integral part of banking in virtually every corner of the globe. For an excellent book on the subject, you may want to read *Secrets of the Temple,* which is a superb description of the Federal Reserve by Mr. William Greider. The author is very credible and has wonderful credentials."

A.T. followed the instructions of Jean Paul and cleansed his soft leather case leaving it under the table. The copies of the material Professor Brougham had provided, along with the new material from Jean Paul, were placed into the new briefcase Jean Paul had provided. A.T. received the codes for the case, and after additional discussion, Jean Paul waved to the waiter who brought a mobile 'cellaret' with various wines, coffees, and several desserts to the table. Although the desserts did not interest A.T., he did find several of the coffee blends of interest. He ordered a particular blend that the waiter placed into a coffee grinder and then proceeded to brew the coffee from a brewing device on the 'cellaret.' The waiter then prepared desserts and coffees for Allen and Jean Paul.

The dessert and coffee atmosphere was relaxing while the three of them discussed a wide range of subjects. The only unusual incident after they had finished their meal was when a lady walked very close to the table and seemed to turn her ankle a few feet away. At first none of the men at the table reacted; however, as she remained in a slightly bent-over position while she appeared to be rubbing her ankle, A.T. rose from the table to see if he could help the woman whose back had remained turned. However, before he reached the woman and offered assistance, she appeared to regain her full posture and was able to flawlessly walk away. Since it seemed as though she was walking fine, A.T. returned to the table.

When he returned to the table, both Allen and Jean Paul were smiling. "What?" asked A.T.

"We noticed that you were quite ready to help the poor lady as she seemed to lose her balance," observed Allen.

"Why not?" inquired A.T. "Isn't that an appropriate thing to do, or is it customary here in Paris to allow a lady to fall down?"

"It is not customary to allow a lady to fall," answered Jean Paul. "However, you have to be careful since such an act could have been contrived. You have to remember that here in Paris some of the higher-class 'ladies of the night' engage in such maneuvers in order to start a conversation, especially with people whom they suspect are from out of town."

"So, is that what you think just happened?" asked A.T.

"No, I don't think that such was the case," smiled Jean Paul. "If it had been the case, the lady would have definitely allowed you to assist her, and she would have engaged in a sweet conversation with you."

"Well," said A.T. "There was no conversation; in fact, she never did turn around but seemed to stabilize herself and walked off before I could get close enough to help."

"What made you think she was of a high class, Jean Paul?" smiled Allen.

"Oh, it was her perfume," responded Jean Paul.

"You could tell from her perfume?" asked Allen with an incredulous look.

"Oui," answered Jean Paul. "I detected a very expensive perfume. We Frenchmen have very well-trained olfactory senses."

"Really," exclaimed Allen. "If that is the case, can you tell us the type of perfume the lady was wearing?"

"I have a pretty good idea," said Jean Paul. "On some special occasions I have purchased something similar for my wife. It seemed to include a scent of minty patchouli. If it's the same perfume, it's over three thousand dollars per ounce."

"Wow," exclaimed Allen. "Only you bankers seem to be able to afford that type of perfume."

"To say nothing of having such a good nose so as to detect ingredients of what did you say…patchouli," commented A.T.

"Yes, I have a good nose for perfumes, especially since my wife is a bit spoiled in that regard. We French really appreciate fine perfumes," responded Jean Paul. "Patchouli is an herb from the mint family that is generally raised in more tropical regions like Indonesia, Thailand, and Vietnam. Perhaps each of you gentlemen should purchase some of this fine perfume for your wives before you depart Paris."

"If we could afford it," said both A.T. and Allen almost simultaneously which brought a good laugh from all three of them at the table.

When coffee and dessert were finished, they left their table and proceeded to the entrance of the restaurant. There they met Jacques, who obviously knew Jean Paul. They exchanged pleasantries whereupon Jacques suggested that Allen and A.T. discharge the cab driver since Jacques would return them to the hotel. As Jacques was now under contract to assist them, it was determined the best course of action would be to allow the cab to proceed with another fare. A.T., Allen, and Jacques bid adieu to Jean Paul and left for Jacques's vehicle.

After the parking valet brought the vehicle, the three men headed for the hotel. It was a comfort knowing Jacques was at the wheel inasmuch as he had an extraordinary memory of the streets and the terrain. It was a good thing too, for within a matter of blocks from the restaurant, Jacques noticed a vehicle had been following them and turned down every back street to avoid being followed. Because the other vehicle remained behind them after Jacques had purposely driven a surreptitious pattern of repeated streets, Jacques alerted Allen and A.T. he was rather certain that they were being followed. Jacques explained that he would deploy a maneuver he termed the "coffee grinder," in which he would loop back over some of the same streets in his route in a progressively forward manner, simply as an exercise to confirm whether they were indeed being followed.

CHAPTER 9
THE COFFEE GRINDER

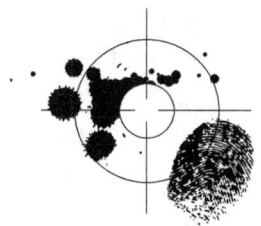

The methodology used by Jacques through the driving technique that he termed the "coffee grinder" lived up to its title. As Jacques left the *La Grande Arche Tower,* he proceeded down a number of streets and in rapid fashion turned from one to another. The following vehicle was still shadowing, so Jacques began more of a crisscross pattern and with it staying close by less than a block, Jacques ultimately went down *Avenue de Château–du–Loir,* then over *Rue Jean–Pierre Timbaud.* It appeared as though Jacques was losing the pursuing vehicle, so he finally maneuvered onto *Rue de l'Hotel de Ville* and then onto *Rue Ficatier.* With some additional maneuvering he hit *Avenue Charles de Gaulle.* This ploy took them to old Paris where Jacques commented that he noticed the vehicle behind was gone. They then proceeded to their hotel, *A La Villa Madame.*

Allen and A.T. felt like they had indeed been in a "coffee grinder" by the time Jacques approached the hotel. Unfortunately, due to traffic and some construction barriers, Jacques could not get close to the hotel, so he dropped A.T. and Allen a rather long city block away from the hotel. He said he would see them at 10 a.m. the next morning in the hotel coffee shop. The weather had turned cold, and neither A.T. nor Allen had worn topcoats, so they were a bit chilled walking toward the hotel. A.T. carried the new and rather heavy briefcase he had received from Jean Paul.

When they were nearly half the distance to the hotel, Allen noticed two people following them at a brisk pace. He warned A.T., and the two of them started to run towards the hotel as did the two people behind them. One of the people behind them was fast, while the other seemed to be outpaced. By the time A.T. and Allen neared a setback in the sidewalk, the first of the pursuers was only a few feet behind. Instinctively, A.T. and Allen went toward the setback that they now noticed was more of a service entrance than an alley. They turned into the setback and prepared to defend themselves. While they positioned themselves near what appeared to be several types of dumpsters for an anticipated upcoming assault, the first trailer turned the corner and slipped on something wet on the walkway. A.T. and Allen thought they would find a way out, but while they were seeking an escape or refuge, the second individual came around the corner. This second individual looked familiar. To A.T., it looked like the African-American who had been on the same flight from the U.S. to Paris.

Allen tackled the man, while A.T. used the briefcase to hit the man in the head. The blow stunned the man causing him to fall back against the building. Meanwhile, the first man was getting to his feet and grabbed for the briefcase. A.T. pulled the case away, resulting with the man reeling and losing his balance. The situation had placed Allen and the African-American on the ground while the second attacker lost his balance. A.T. ran over and extended his hand to Allen to help pull him from the ground. As Allen got back to his feet, someone hit A.T. from behind. The second attacker had given A.T. a body blow, and they both hit the ground. The briefcase tumbled from A.T.'s hand and slid across the setback.

One attacker reached for the briefcase, while the second got to his feet. He too went for the briefcase. Before either of them was able to get to the case, two more people entered the setback. The taller of the two new additions to the melee wrestled for the briefcase. However, before he could get to it, the first attacker turned, and the two of them immediately broke into a confrontation of hand-to-hand exchanges. Then the African-American grabbed the briefcase and turned to leave the setback. At that point, the shorter of the two new additions to the affray kicked him behind the knee, and he came crashing down dropping the briefcase in the process. The two of them began to go at each other in an aggressive battle involving a fairly skilled exchange of blows. It became readily apparent that the larger African-American was no match for the smaller individual, who kept driving hard until the African-American was forced to the rear of the setback.

While the four attackers were in combat with each other, Allen ran to the briefcase and tossed it to A.T., who was the closest to the entrance of the setback. Allen then dodged the two men fighting in front of him and took off running in the direction towards A.T., who had caught the briefcase as it started to scrape the ground. A.T. and Allen bolted for the sidewalk and ran, not bothering to look back until they reached the hotel entrance. When they turned to look back up the street, the two late additions to the mix were coming out of the setback. Neither of the two original attackers were anywhere to be seen. From that distance, it appeared the smaller of the two was either a woman or a small man with long hair. The lighting was not good enough to get an accurate view of the two who had emerged, and neither A.T. nor Allen wanted to take the time to offer any thanks. In fact, they were not sure that thanks were in order. Either Rene had placed someone on their tail for assistance, or there was more than one group of people interested in the contents of the briefcase.

Once A.T. was safely in his room, he received a call from Jacques. Jacques explained he had seen part of the confrontation, whereupon he apologized for not staying with them and for not getting them closer to the hotel. Jacques said he would come directly to A.T.'s room and would remain on alert for the remainder of the evening. A plan was already in place for A.T. and Allen to meet Rene for breakfast at 10 a.m. in the hotel restaurant. At that time, Jacques would leave and get a few hours rest before the second meeting with Jean Paul that would take place as scheduled at Versailles. Jean Paul had informed them that he wanted to visit in a more private place the next day in order to provide them with the identity of the individual whom they would meet in Zurich.

As promised, Jacques remained on watch near the entrance to A.T.'s room. From his position, he could also see the entrance to Allen's room which was a few doors down the hall. Jacques felt he could prevent any additional confrontations. During the waiting and watching process, he phoned a full report over to Rene. Rene said he would alert hotel staff members in case Jacques needed any additional help. Nothing official would be documented until the next day, if at all. Rene wanted to first visit personally with Allen and A.T. Although doubtful, the fracas of the previous night could have been a simple matter of street people trying to grab a briefcase thinking it had some monetary value.

* *

The night passed uneventfully except for a couple who seemed to be lost when they got off the elevator. Jacques noticed the tall man and the smaller woman with him acted a bit strange; however, neither of them seemed much of a threat to Jacques, who was in the prime of his life and totally confident in his training. Plus, he held police credentials he was not afraid to flash, if he felt the need. The couple tried one door, and when it didn't open, they left the floor and didn't return. At about 9:30 a.m., A.T. came out of his room with his newly acquired briefcase. After bidding good morning and thanking Jacques, he went to Allen's room and knocked on the door. Allen was ready, so the three of them went down to the café.

Rene was already seated at a table and sipping coffee when the three of them arrived. After greetings, Rene asked for a full report on the previous night's events. He was especially interested in receiving descriptions of the four individuals whom A.T. and Allen had encountered. Because it had been dark and the street had not been well-lit, it was difficult for either A.T. or Allen to provide adequate descriptions. Rene chastised both A.T. and Allen since they had previously been in law enforcement and should have been experienced in noting appearances. They then explained to Rene that not only had it been dark, but everything had happened so fast; therefore, any descriptions were going to be inadequate. Nevertheless, each provided descriptions that Rene meticulously noted on a pad. Allen was almost certain the smaller person in the second pair was a woman. Rene asked Jacques if he had a decent look at any of the four people. He unequivocally stated he did not; however, he did provide Rene with a description of the couple he had seen on the hotel floor after the incident.

There was not enough information to mandate an official report. Rene cautioned both A.T. and Allen that there may be something in the briefcase documents the two pairs of individuals wanted. He then asked A.T. if he could see the documents. A.T. said he had no objection; therefore, he set the codes and opened the briefcase. He showed Rene the ledgers, and assured him the information had something to do with the possibility of American citizens holding European accounts and funds that were not properly reported to the U.S. authorities. A.T. told Rene the materials would be turned over to a U.S. Senator as part of the investigation being conducted by a committee and the Senator was a member of the committee. Rene explained that he knew Jean Paul, so he believed the documentation would be worthy.

Rene made it clear he would assist both the Senator and A.T., if there were a need for his assistance. If assistance were needed from additional French authorities, Rene would make appropriate arrangements. He instructed A.T. to so advise the Senator and mention that a call of reassurance from the Senator's office would be in order. Rene felt such a call would be nice if it were to take place before he invited Allen and A.T. to dine with his wife and him within the next day or two. That would give Allen and A.T. time to proceed with their meeting with Jean Paul in the afternoon and take their trip to Zurich. As breakfast was winding down, Rene once again cautioned Allen and A.T. He offered his personal number, as well as his home phone. Before he left, he reminded A.T. to have the Senator call him.

After A.T. returned to his room, he made a call to the Senator's office in Washington D.C. and requested the Senator call Rene. During his conversation with the Senator's office, A.T. noticed that his room seemed different. Generally, everything was in place; however, items that he had left in the closet and on the bed had been moved. Fortunately, he had taken the briefcase and his personal identification materials with him. Although he had left nothing of consequence in the room, he decided to look through everything to be sure nothing had been taken.

Moving about the room, he sensed someone who wore a distinctly unique perfume had been in the room. Perhaps it was the cleaning maid, but it seemed the perfume was a bit more subtle and likely too expensive for a cleaning maid to use. Then he realized the perfume seemed to be the same scent he noticed the evening before while dining at the restaurant with Jean Paul. He wondered if he should tell either Rene or Jacques. However, after thinking about it, he decided not to since he didn't want Rene to think such an observation to be a bit overboard.

A.T. long ago realized one would never leave anything of value in a hotel room. Still, it was discomforting to suspect someone had been through his belongings. He changed and left to meet Allen. Noticing the door to Allen's room was open, A.T. entered. Allen was at the nightstand putting on his wristwatch and hanging up the phone.

"I've phoned the front desk to file an official complaint," said Allen. "Someone was in my room and moved my belongings. I don't think it was the maid because the bed is still unmade, and the tip I left on the dresser is still in place. Items I left on the bed were on the chair over by the window, and the bag left on the floor was on the bed and was opened."

"I too noticed someone has been in my room," commented A.T. "However, nothing seems to have been taken, so I didn't feel it necessary to call in a complaint. Was anything of yours taken?"

"Not that I can tell," said Allen, "but it is a bit disarming to come back to my room and find someone has been through my things." Allen noticed A.T. smelling the air and asked. "What are you doing?"

"Do you smell anything unusual?" asked A.T.

"Not particularly," answered Allen as he sniffed the air. "Well, it does smell good in here, and it doesn't smell like any aftershave that I would use. Why do you ask?"

"No reason. Never mind," said A.T. "Do you think we should change hotels?"

"Not yet," said Allen. "Let's see what the hotel security determines. I thought that they should be aware of the situation. Obviously, someone was looking for something, and I would guess is it's the contents of the new briefcase. When you couple last night's events with this incident, my concern is growing about our own safety as long as that briefcase is with us. Rene suggested we give the case to him for safekeeping, and he will have it for us when we have dinner at his home in a couple days. After dinner, he will be taking us to the airport for our flight back to the states, so it strikes me as a good idea."

"We can't," said A.T. "We will need to take the case with us to Zurich."

"Are you forgetting the case has a combination lock that would prevent anyone from accessing the materials inside?" asked Allen. "We could leave it with Rene at least for a while. Remember, if someone opened it without the combination, it would activate a vial and destroy the contents."

"That's true," said A.T. "But I don't want to run the risk of the contents being destroyed. Rene may believe his department could open the case without consequence and…"

"The briefcase might be a problem and may be placing us in some type of unknown danger," exclaimed Allen. "Rene is the best man I could imagine in regard to our having a 'straight shooter' when it comes to integrity and assistance."

"You're right, Allen," said A.T. "We need to trust somebody. Let's see if Rene would secure the briefcase for us, but I want to be sure he has spoken to the Senator first. If that checks out, then let's have him secure the case for us until we travel to Zurich tomorrow. I sense we may need Jacques's assistance in our travel to Zurich because, from what Jean Paul said last night, I will need to show the documents in the briefcase to the banker in Zurich. Go ahead and call Rene, and I will call the Senator to see if he has had an opportunity to speak with Rene."

* *

Jacques picked up Allen and A.T. at the agreed time and drove them to Versailles where they met up with Jean Paul for a late lunch and an informative stroll through some of the gardens. The walk served to be both relaxing and educational.

Quite candidly, Jean Paul explained that the materials he provided revealed matters of concern felt by many within the European banking community regarding changes in the financial world over the last decade. He reiterated what he had told them at dinner the night before about the purchase of the bank instruments by certain identified groups and their financial interactions. He explained that the transactions involved buyers and sellers of particular bank instruments and a relationship between the buyers to the sellers seemed to be most unlikely. He emphasized that when they went to Zurich to meet Claude Schmidt, they would learn the buyers and the sellers were parties which seemed to be natural enemies.

A.T. asked if Jean Paul would clarify what he meant and explain the transaction process so when A.T. and Allen met with Claude, they would have a better understanding of what was transpiring and why the documents were so important. Jean Paul explained that the U.S. dollar had become the world's common denominator in regard to major monetary exchanges and that particularly included the purchase and sale of bank instruments. The position of the U.S. dollar evolved over time since the end of the world wars. Most European countries, except for Switzerland, had been financially devastated, and the United States had grown powerful as both the industrial and financial leader of the world.

He explained that in terms of world-wide commerce, the United States was the only country with a global reach standing strong. Additionally, the European countries which had been on either side of the war were devastated in terms of population, economics, infrastructure, and relationships with each other. He continued to explain how each country had its own form of monetary exchange, and regardless of whether one held pounds, francs, marks, or other forms of currency, the rates of exchange would fluctuate drastically. It had become necessary for a commonly acceptable currency to be used, especially in banking transactions. Added to these considerations was the fact that many of the European countries had placed their gold supply across the ocean in what they believed was a safe haven, the United States.

Not all of the supplies of gold and other valuables, including ownership certificates of corporate interests, went to Switzerland. The United States was a beneficiary of many of the holdings, and the dollar at the time seemed to survive the world wars with the greatest degree of stability. Many countries and royal families moved their gold, jewels, certificates, and other valuables to the U.S. for safekeeping. The Swiss continued to perform the majority of the banking tasks of the world, but none of the European currencies were considered to be acceptable as the "common denominator" of exchange. The U.S. dollar filled this role. Confidence grew in the U.S. dollar in terms of its being the exchange medium for international transactions.

After the world wars, banks needed to expand their ability to finance a rebuilding world as did corporate and private interests. Bank instruments, such as medium-term notes and bank guarantees, became a desirable mechanism for making funds available to each country and allowed each country to maintain its currencies for stability. Using these bank instruments, each country could transact financial business through an acceptable method. Instead of different currencies being printed and thereby creating unknown inflationary issues and exchange issues, the bank instruments served a valuable function. There would be a set purchase price, a stated rate of return, and a maturity date. The instruments functioned well and have been in acceptable use by the larger financial institutions, certain entities, corporations, and the wealthy willing to invest through the instruments.

Jean Paul continued to explain it was obviously a marketplace for only those with means. The world wars, like all wars throughout history, made some people very wealthy and others very poor. Being in the right place at the right time was only part of it. He believed that dumb luck and connections, as well as planning in advance of a war's end, had a lot to do with financial success. The Swiss banks welcomed the wealth of both sides of the war, and this position allowed for the Swiss banking laws to be written with the idea of neutrality in mind. Accordingly, the protection of the identity of an account holder was one key to the success of the Swiss banking system.

In recent years efforts were made to modify the Swiss banking laws in order for disclosures of account holders to be mandated in certain circumstances. The efforts by the United States during the last several years fit within this category due to noted activity occurring in the previous couple of decades. Since the year 2000, many U.S. corporations and individuals took advantage of the Swiss banking system to park large sums of money to evade taxes in the United States. Jean Paul noted the catalyst of change in recent years was when UBS (United Bank of Switzerland) sent representatives to the U.S. to offer methods of moving funds to their bank. Jean Paul explained UBS ended up paying penalties of nearly one billion dollars and had to disclose what at first was believed to be over four thousand such account holders but may have ended up being over fifty thousand account holders, with an estimated average of over a quarter million dollars in each account.

According to Jean Paul, that investigation brought about the various investigations now taking place. Additionally, the investigation by the Senator was now a part of A.T.'s investigation as a result of the UBS event. Jean Paul explained once the investigations began, he was assigned by his bank to look into the matter. In the process, he contacted Claude Schmidt, a Swiss banker, who had been hired by the Swiss government to help sort out the growing problem. It was Claude who brought the matter at hand to Jean Paul's attention. They were old friends. Claude had explained to Jean Paul that he was finding an unlikely relationship involving several billions of dollars in transactions. The transactions involved a number of European entities, U.S. individuals and corporations with European subsidiary corporations, along with funds transacted through attorney trust accounts in Europe, particularly Germany and Switzerland. The matter also included some Latin American entities with relations in the Middle East.

Jean Paul said he had flown to Zurich to meet with Claude, who provided the documents Jean Paul turned over to A.T. However, before Jean Paul provided the documents to anyone, he wanted to be certain the documents went to the proper party in the U.S. Since Jean Paul and Bud Hawthorne were closely tied and Jean Paul trusted Bud, Jean Paul contacted Bud about the information from Claude Schmidt. Subsequently, the documents would be preserved and delivered to the designee of the Senator. A.T. was that designee. Jean Paul suggested A.T. do some research on his own in order to understand the process.

A.T. indicated he would research the matter regarding the bank instruments but did not understand why would Claude Schmidt with the Swiss government would flag the matter and contact Jean Paul if these were legitimate transactions? Jean Paul explained he would leave the details of such an explanation up to Claude but he could mention the fact the transactions involving certain purchase and sale of bank instruments involved particular interests in the United States and particular interests in the Middle East seemingly at odds with each other. Given the position of the United States in Iraq, Afghanistan, Pakistan, and Yemen, having the parties Claude identified involved in the same transactions seemed questionable at best.

The walk and conversation with Jean Paul was informative, but it created new issues regarding the transactions he described. Since Jean Paul insisted A.T. and Allen speak with Claude about the matter, the discussion on the topic ended, and the three of them focused on the beauty of the gardens. Jean Paul provided instructions indicating where and when to meet Claude the next day in Zurich. He also provided a written set of instructions which A.T. noticed were in French. He handed the instructions to Jacques, who acknowledged he knew the place having been in Zurich many times.

After arriving at the hotel, they learned hotel security had located a suite for them in a secure area of the hotel. Security moved their belongings, which A.T. and Allen assembled and left with the security office before proceeding to Versailles. The new suite had a couple bedrooms and a living area, which worked out well. Both A.T. and Allen felt somewhat reassured when they were informed the hotel would provide hall security for the night. Jacques was able to return to his home for a good night's sleep. There were no incidents that evening which allowed for a comfortable rest. The next morning Jacques gathered Allen and A.T. within the hotel lobby at an early hour since they needed to drive to Zurich for a midday meeting with Claude. Rene, who was also present, returned the briefcase to A.T. for the trip to Zurich.

* *

They started the drive before dawn as the trip was estimated to take about six hours if the roads and weather were decent. The meeting with Claude was set for three in the afternoon, and if it lasted a couple hours, they expected to be back at their hotel in Paris before midnight. Because Claude had an official role with the Swiss government, the meeting was scheduled at his office at the bank used by officials. Jacques had no trouble navigating to the office after a late lunch in Zurich. They timed their arrival at Claude's office, so the wait was only about ten minutes. Typical of a Swiss official, Claude was on time.

After preliminary introductions among all parties, the four men sat down at a table in a small conference room next to Claude's office. Since Jacques was a member of the Paris police department, he could be present at the meetings. Neither A.T. nor Allen felt there was any reason to exclude Jacques since he would be able to translate in the event there was a need to do so.

As it turned out, Claude spoke several languages, and the English he used on a daily basis was excellent. When the meeting started, A.T. opened the briefcase with the combination Jean Paul provided and placed the material on the table before him. Claude started the meeting by presenting his credentials.

"Gentlemen, as you know, I am the person who initially brought to Jean Paul's attention the materials A.T. has placed on the table. So you realize I am who I represent myself to be, I am showing you my credentials. You should also be informed that I have spoken to Jean Paul and Rene this morning. Please also be advised Jean Paul telephoned his contact, Mr. Bud Hawthorne, who was able to place your Senator friend on the phone during a call early this afternoon. The Senator told me you would have a letter of introduction from him. Is that true, A.T.?"

"It is," said A.T. while presenting the letter.

Upon examining the letter, Claude said, "I requested this even though I had you, Mr. Aranda, and Jacques provide identifying material to me in the outer office. I wanted to be certain. It is my understanding from what Rene LePonte told me this morning that you may have had some interested parties following you. I want to be sure the matters you have on the table before you are in the right hands and they do not slip into the hands of others, whom I am not able to verify. I gave them to Jean Paul, who I know extremely well, and he promised the documents would be delivered to the proper courier. I have been informed by the Senator you are the courier, Mr. Van Doren."

"Well, I guess I have unwittingly become a courier," said A.T. "That was not my initial intent and not what I bargained to do for the Senator. I don't understand why these materials were not either electronically sent or otherwise delivered through either common courier or a bonded courier."

"Because," interrupted Claude, "I believe the system in my office has been compromised. Jean Paul feels the same way about his IT system and office, in general. This is why he visited with Bud while they were on vacation. He personally presented the materials you have before you to Bud, but Bud did not want to handle them since he did not feel he had the experience to protect such matters. We believe the materials in front of you are volatile and could impact the national security of your country. They must be successfully delivered to the Senator.

"I have some serious concerns, especially after the night before last. First of all, why would neither you nor the Senator involve the U.S. authorities, such as the CIA or the FBI? It is their function both in the U.S. and abroad to handle all matters involving U.S. intelligence and security," commented A.T.

"Dear Sir, it is simply because your country's FBI and CIA are significantly compromised, especially in regard to matters involving the activities of the Middle East. This package involves matters of the Middle East," said Claude, as he poured coffee for the assembly.

"The fact the CIA and FBI are compromised to that degree, I find hard to believe," said A.T.

"Aren't you a former special agent, Mr. Van Doren?" asked Claude.

"I am, but the agents whom I knew and worked with were very honorable and would never betray their country," said A.T.

"From what the Senator explained on the phone today, I understand you yourself were betrayed by a couple of dishonest FBI agents. Did the Senator tell me wrong? I recall he also told me you had 'blown the tooter' on some other agents while you were once with the FBI," stated Claude.

"It's called 'blowing the whistle,'" said A.T., "and yes, I did bring a matter involving some fabricated security files to the attention of my supervisor when I was in the Bureau. That was long ago. It is also true I personally and fairly recently encountered some less than scrupulous agents who, in my opinion, should never have been allowed to be agents and, in fact, should be discharged and prosecuted themselves. However, that is a different matter. Even though I feel very confident some of the agents of today are not worthy to carry FBI credentials, I would think in terms of security issues that involve the Middle East, the FBI would be interested in detailing and protecting every possible security breach. I believe the Bureau would go out of its way to expose anyone who would attempt to undermine the U.S."

"Really!" exclaimed Claude. "In that case, let me tell you something you should know before we examine the documents. Here in Europe we are very mindful of what the U.S. does, and we watch very carefully. Your intelligence agencies have slipped considerably over the past decade or so. The two agencies that should be getting this information from me are the FBI and the CIA, but as I have said, they have been compromised. We believe both agencies have moles within their upper echelons and informants who are double agents misdirecting the U.S. intelligence agencies. The moles and the informants have their own agendas. Those agendas are not favorable to the United States. Let me give you an example. Are you familiar with a man called Ali Mohamed?"

"No, unless you are referring to the famous American boxer, Muhammad Ali, whom I believe is an honorable American," said A.T.

"Not the boxer!" admonished Claude. "I am speaking of a man named Ali Mohamed, who is an Egyptian whom I believe your government has now finally incarcerated. He was a double agent who betrayed the United States in many ways. He was known in Egypt as Major Ali Abdul Saoud Mohamed and operated with numerous aliases over time, including 'Bakhbola,' 'Bili Bili,' 'Haydara,' 'Abu Mohamed al Amriki' and 'Ali the American.' He was an Al Qaeda spy and became a U.S. citizen after he married a U.S. woman. Even though he had been on a travel watch list before he entered the U.S., he ended up becoming a U.S. citizen, joined the U.S. Army, even though much older than a normal recruit, went to Fort Bragg, and became a Green Beret. These are all well-documented facts. Both the CIA and the FBI knew who he was, and yet he was somehow protected while in the U.S. military. He essentially duped both the FBI and the CIA. As they say, 'he played the FBI like a small stringed instrument.' While in the U.S. military, he was allowed to travel to Afghanistan to meet with Al Qaeda officials and ended up training individuals who were close to Bin Laden. He himself became a close confidant to Bin Laden and revealed much about the U.S. training standards of Green Berets and other U.S. procedures. He allegedly transferred a significant amount of classified information he obtained at Fort Bragg to Bin Laden and Al Qaeda. Let me suggest you read a very well-written book on the subject by a five-time Emmy Award-winning investigative reporter and former ABC News correspondent by the name of Peter Lance. The book is entitled *Triple Cross.* It is an extremely well-documented book that includes copies of internal FBI documents with some excerpts from FBI 302s about how your security agencies had been compromised. I've been through my copy of the book several times."

"Is the information in the book the reason you do not want to provide your findings directly to U.S. intelligence agencies? What about your agencies here in Switzerland and in France?" asked A.T.

"In case you forgot," interrupted Claude, "I am a banker here in Switzerland, and my good friend, Jean Paul, is with banking in France. We work together and decided because of what we already knew and suspected, along with what we read in Mr. Lance's book, that we needed to get information directly to a higher authority in the United States. Your Senator is considered, at least by us, to be of higher authority. Besides, there are too many 'stove pipes' within the FBI, and we were afraid the information would not get to the proper authorities and would possibly dead-end within the FBI or the CIA. With what I have to tell you and with what we are providing, this information cannot be stalled because of individual domains within your security agencies."

"All of what you've said concerns me," said A.T. "In your view, are the U.S. intelligence agencies really balled up in 'stove piping' or 'walls,' such that information is not flowing to the parties of need within the agencies?"

"In a word, yes," noted Claude emphatically.

"If that is the case, then there must be something of critical importance and of imminent concern for you to try to open a live channel to a United States Senator, as you have through Bud and now through me. If I had known about this, I would not have allowed myself to become a part of such a transfer of information. I would have suggested someone much younger and with more recent training," insisted A.T.

"What I am going to tell you and what you will see in the documents is critically important and very sensitive. You are the right person to carry this information back. Your age is a benefit. We need a seasoned and well-educated individual, who is also levelheaded. We also need someone loyal to the Senator. On your return, there will be safeguards in place that will 'have your back.' Accordingly, we do not think you will have any additional problems in either Switzerland or France. You will be protected going into the United States. We cannot offer assistance there, but we have suggested Bud arrange something for you through the Senator. Bud said the Senator had a very good man in mind whom you've already met on a recent excursion; they may decide to use him. Here is another point; we need someone who has already been involved in an investigation. Many of the same people you are investigating are a part of what is concerning us. We need someone who can listen and learn about the documents in order to assure a proper explanation to the Senator. I will tell you how to read the documents and what the documents mean," explained Claude.

"So, what is so important about these documents that they need an explanation of such that a personal education is required?" asked A.T.

"The documents you received from an individual who had previously been employed by one of our targets are going to be helpful. I believe you received documents from a Professor Brougham, at least that is the name I have been given. His documents are ledgers, deposit records, and transfer records. Those documents, from what

Jean Paul has told me, relate directly to the documents provided. When you compare the documents side by side, you will be able to see they reflect a completed cycle between the professor's records and the records of earnings from bank instrument trades Jean Paul provided. Let me show you the specifics," explained Claude, as he proceeded to lay out the documents on the conference table before them. He then expounded upon how the earnings from the purchase and sale of bank instruments were transferred to the accounts on the ledgers and other records of the professor.

"I see the record of profits from the sales on Jean Paul's records, and I see the transfers to the accounts provided by the professor. I can also see the interrelationship between the entities shown on the documents. So far I understand; however, where is the issue of concern? Aren't these earnings records that represent legitimate transactions?" asked A.T.

"You are correct in that they represent legitimate transactions," agreed Claude. "However, the third set of documents represents financial interests out of Germany, Argentina, Brazil, Saudi Arabia, UAE, and the Far East. Do you see these?"

"Yes, I see them, but how are they relevant?" asked A.T.

"Let me show you the transaction codes," said Claude. At this point, Claude laid out the third set of documents and pointed out detail after detail on the documents. "As you see," noted Claude, "the transaction codes allow us to trace the originators of the funds used to purchase the bank instruments, and the parties who purchased the instruments originally are also identified. Now, here is a fourth set of documents, and these documents demonstrate that the same originators of funds are providing similar funding to separate groups, whom you will see are entities that have interests throughout the Middle East and not in the United States. In other words, the sources of the funds, and in many cases, the original owners of the bank instruments being supplied to what one would believe are U.S. interests, are also the same sources of funds and the same original owners of the bank instruments being supplied to various interests in the Middle East."

"It looks like the same parties are both providing the funds and the underlying instruments to two different groups, a composite of various parties that appear to be mostly of U.S. interests, and on the other hand, a composite of various parties that appear to be mostly of Middle Eastern interests," noted A.T.

"That's correct," affirmed Claude. "To put it simply, you have the same core entities providing both funding and bank instrument availability to two seriously opposing interests. More bluntly stated, you have some powerful financial interests from various European countries, along with interests from Argentina, Brazil, Saudi Arabia, UAE, and the Far East who have, for all practical purposes, joined together to fund two seriously opposing sides of current political interests in the world.

"You have within that mix religious extremists and political extremists in both the Christian world and the Muslim world being funded by the same entities. The United States seems to be the planned point of focus in the sense that the money is going to extremist groups operating in a clandestine way in the U.S. on the one hand and right wing extremist organizations on the other hand. You have two groups of organizations that are on the opposite ends of the political spectrum."

"Can this be?" asked A.T. "To what end? Since the media shows these parties are on the opposite sides, it would seem they would probably rather kill each other than share a common financial beneficiary. This could lead to some serious disputes or even a religious war of some sort…couldn't it? So, is someone or a group of parties trying to restart the Crusades?"

"That would be my concern. Actually, that should be anyone's concern. Plus, I am rather certain the extremist groups being funded don't realize their counterparts are also being funded by the same interests," stated Claude.

"That, I can't believe," said A.T.

"Or, you don't want to believe it," said Claude.

"I cannot imagine anybody even trying to foment that kind of discord in this day and age," said A.T. "I see no way our government would ever be a party to such an endeavor."

"From our assessment, it would not be your government. At least, your government would not officially allow it to happen," offered Claude.

"Are you sure of the identity of the groups being funded, and do you know how the funds are being used?" asked A.T.

"We are sure of the identity of the groups, but we don't yet know who the members are. Therefore, we do not yet have the identities of the specific individuals behind the groups or entities engaged in the financial transactions. We are trying to find the names of those behind the companies involved with the bank instruments and the movement of the funds. We know they are using proper corporations to register them and to serve as their registered agents. So far, we cannot pinpoint any violations of the law. We are working on that and so must you. Identifying specific individuals is one of the things you are to accomplish for the Senator," instructed Claude.

"I don't know how you would expect me to find the identities of the specific individuals behind the rather sophisticated shell game of corporations and other entities engaged in the trades. If you and your staff cannot drill down to the individual identities, I am at a total loss as to how I will be able to make such a determination," said A.T.

Claude responded, "We have run into a roadblock because what these investors are doing from a corporate structure appears to be legitimate both here and in the United States. However, devious individuals who do not wish to be identified can employ the use of certain corporations that properly serve as the registered agent for individuals who wish to protect their identities."

"Couldn't you trace the individuals through tax records and other public records?" asked A.T.

"Please understand," commented Claude, "everything those investors are doing appears perfectly legitimate and that includes proper corporate structures that pay their taxes and file all other required documents in a timely fashion. Many of these companies have been formed by other companies in foreign countries, and we are finding the same corporate structures are serving as the registered agent there as well. We are continuing to work on the identities, but it isn't easy, especially since some of these organizations have been around for decades, and the original parties may not even be living at this stage."

"I don't see how I would be able to help," stated A.T.

"When you were in the Bureau, you cultivated informants. That's what you should try to do, if you can," said Claude.

"I will do my best, but please keep in mind it will not be my priority to do so. If I come up with someone, it would most likely be by accident. Otherwise, my investigation will continue under the more conventional methods, and I will try to glean information from public records, newspaper articles, the underlying sources of the records and articles, and firsthand observations I am able to make from the leads developed. I will try to line up interviews with anyone I feel has information, and I will provide reports to the Senator. However, I have no intention of expanding my investigation beyond those elements that would be of proper investigative techniques. I have allowed myself to become more involved than I ever intended. At some point, the Senator will need to hand the baton over to someone else. I've taken this far beyond where I originally intended to go. I hope you can understand that," said A.T.

"I appreciate your position," commented Claude. "However, you will need to address that issue with your Senator. Unless you have any additional questions about the materials we have laid out here on the table, I will reassemble them for you to take with you in the briefcase. Always remember to use the codes when you open the case; everything inside will be destroyed if any attempts are made to open the case without the codes."

"I understand," said A.T. "Jean Paul explained that to me."

"I should tell you I am the one who gave the case to Jean Paul. So far, only the three of us know the codes. Be very careful, and from this point forward, do not let the briefcase out of your sight or possession," cautioned Claude.

* *

In the morning, A.T. and Allen would first go to Rene's office and from there they would go to Rene's home for dinner. It would be a relaxing homecoming of sorts for Allen, Rene, and Rene's wife. A.T. felt he would try to enjoy the evening and he would also try to keep his mind off the investigation and the contents of the briefcase that were in his constant presence.

The evening at the home of Rene and Michelle LePonte started early. Following cocktails and dinner, Rene would deliver A.T. and Allen to the airport for their flight back to the Twin Cities. As promised, Claude and Jean Paul had arranged for two individuals to provide protection for them during their return to the United States. A.T. and Allen had been introduced to the two security officers but were told to ignore them during the trip to the airport and to the States. All went well, and the return trip was without incident. The flight back would get them into the Twin Cities by late morning of the next day. Efforts to rest on the plane were problematic, so it gave Allen a chance to review with A.T. his life while in Paris many years ago. He explained how he met Rene and his wife.

The new daunting task of connecting the financial information provided by Jean Paul and Claude to what he already had was in the front of A.T.'s mind as the stewardess brought a refreshment cart along the aisle. A.T. was ready for something stimulating and refreshing, so he ordered one of the new iced coffee drinks. Unfortunately, the bottle he received had been shaken a bit. Therefore, when he opened it, a portion of the contents burst out and over the side of the bottle. A.T. used a napkin to absorb the spilled contents from the side of the bottle. That left a "foaming fringe" around the top and inside the mouth of the bottle.

To A.T., it felt as though the investigation he had started was growing exponentially well beyond anything he could have imagined. When he started, he recognized that the investigation would, as all investigations do, lead in unexpected directions. Now it seemed the entire matter was erupting into a "foaming fringe," and A.T. didn't want to be a part of an investigation with such ominous implications.

CHAPTER 10
FOAMING FRINGE

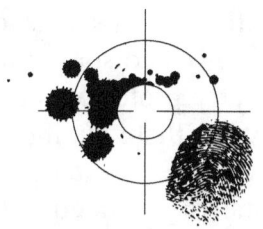

After arriving back in the Twin Cities, A.T. and Allen, along with all other returning passengers, were greeted by a large group of protesters upon their exit from the airport. The protest in progress had people who claimed to be a part of the "tea party" movement holding various signs. Apparently, a member of the current administration was visiting the Twin Cities, and it struck the organizers of the "tea party" group as important to stage a public protest along the exit from the airport. This particular type of protest was beginning to wear thin with the general public. To many Americans, they had become known as the "Lunatic Fringe."

The "tea party" protests had been going on for a number of years and had started as a protest by former dissident political operatives. The group's alleged purpose was far removed from the purported and stated purpose made to the general public. Its original cause, if there ever were one other than to disrupt the process of government, had been totally lost over the last eighteen months or so. The people behind the movement were some very wealthy individuals and some religious fanatics, along with former politicians and corporate interests bringing forth one staged protest after another.

The moneyed people and groups behind the movement were using both the disgruntled folks who had nothing to do other than complain and in many cases paid protestors to create the appearance that the protest was representative of the "small guy" and the individual. The real objective, however, was for the corporate interests and the well-organized politicians in the pocket of corporate interests to stir up discord.

Upon retrieving his car from long term parking, A.T. carefully tried to drive past the protestors. Slowing down to maneuver around the group of protestors, A.T. turned to Allen and said, "Once again, permit me to thank you for traveling with me and providing some great cover. Your contacts in Paris were really helpful. I will try to get a 'thank you' note out to them, especially Rene."

"You're welcome! It was my pleasure to go along," assured Allen. "It gave me a chance to do some traveling, and a little excitement never hurt anyone. The entire matter seems to get more intriguing as each new day unfolds. I really had some fun. I thought it was well worth it. Boy, these tea party protestors are going farther over the edge each time somebody lets them out into the streets. Look at that sign. I thought that was what they were promoting."

A.T. noticed that one sign stated, "Down with Fascism!" Yet, Fascism is precisely what the political operatives and the corporations funding the movement wanted. Instead of "one person - one vote," the corporations were more interested in "a million dollars – buys votes." Many of the private interests behind the movement had worked for decades to influence the government of the United States into a type of system that would fall under the control of large financial interests and corporations. The protestors were playing into the hands of those providing the financial support for them.

"It is doubtful that any of the sign bearers know what Fascism is, but they probably know what that swastika over on that sign represents. I wouldn't be surprised if the group we see here has a number of 'skinheads' within their ranks; those characters like to adorn their bodies with the swastika," noted A.T.

"That they do. Who knows, there are probably a number of their relatives included in the protest who are members of the K.K.K. You know, real 'God-fearing' cross burners with Christian-promoting hatred. Jesus would be so proud," quipped Allen.

Seeing yet another sign displaying a Nazi swastika left one to contemplate just how close the country was moving to a similar situation as the one Nazi Germany experienced directly before the

German state was taken over by the Nazis before World War II. The guy carrying the sign undoubtedly had no idea he was promoting the very fascist cause he was protesting.

"You know," said A.T., "the past several decades of orchestrated change within the U.S. government by some financial interests and certain corporations have stretched their tentacles into most aspects of the government in a very similar fashion to that of Nazi Germany. That all happened before the Obama administration took office."

"No doubt about it," agreed Allen. "Plus, look at that sign about spending. They must be trying to blame the current administration for what happened under the Bush administration. Of course, a lot of the protestors didn't like Bush either."

A prominent sign said, "Stop Big Spending." Once again A.T. mused to himself that the biggest spender in U.S. history as a President was George W. Bush. It was during his administration that the deficits grew to record numbers. Under W.'s administration, the national debt grew to a record of about $10.6 trillion, and the wheels were set in motion for that to continue no matter who succeeded W. as President. When W. took office, the National Debt stood at $5.7 trillion. By almost doubling the National Debt in a single President's tenure, George W. Bush nearly ran up the national debt faster than all of his predecessors combined and was just short of singlehandedly running up $5 trillion in debt. The Obama administration has had the unbelievable task of unwinding the huge cycle of spending set in motion during the Bush administration. A.T. also recalled it was under the George W. Bush administration the United States borrowed more money from foreign countries than all previous administrations combined.

A.T. observed in response to Allen's remark, "The fact that there was a budget surplus when George W. Bush took over from President Bill Clinton had been a matter the large financial interests and corporations tried to sweep under the table. The elimination of the surtax by the Bush administration benefited the large corporations and the large individual financial interests. Then W. proceeded to double the national debt. No doubt the beneficiaries of the Bush administration were the rich, the corporations, and the bankers whom he failed to regulate. Look at that sign."

This sign read, "Stop Bank Socialism." That sign in A.T.'s mind had to be of special interest to the banks because during the last several decades, at least going back to Ronald Reagan, bank oversight had been eliminated little by little. Under the presidency of George W. Bush, the remaining vestiges of bank oversight had been abandoned or unenforced. That led to the bank crises of 2008, and it was during W.'s administration that Congress presented a bailout to the banks of just under a trillion dollars all told. Instead of the banks using the money to open loans to the average person, the banks used the funds to consolidate their financial position, to acquire other banks, and to pay large bonuses to their executives.

What made matters worse in A.T.'s mind was a decision by the United States Supreme Court in January 2010 overturning key campaign limits on corporations. The ruling by a Court in the *Citizen's United* Case, allowed the political ideologues from an extreme portion of the Republican Party to open the floodgates of political contributions by large corporations. It would forever change the landscape of the electoral process in the United States, in which it would no longer be an electorate of "one person – one vote." In the process, the opinion by Justice Kennedy basically overturned a century-old practice of limiting corporate political involvement. The opinion struck down the McCain-Feingold legislation that had limited corporate financial influence over elections in the U.S. What seemed totally out of hand were the public comments by Justice Anthony Scalia who attempted to claim the unlimited allowance of large corporate funds into the political process was a form of "free speech."

A.T. reminded himself that the protestors had both the right of free speech and the right to peaceful assembly. However, it seemed the purpose of the financial and corporate interests behind the group was one of provocation. It was, perhaps, an unintended consequence of those freedoms as set forth in the Constitution. Nevertheless, thought A.T., they had those rights, and in our free society, those rights are protected.

Although there were many signs obviously designed to foment hatred and discord, the signs that encouraged bigotry and racial hatred were the worst. There were many such signs, and the obvious purpose was to stir up the hateful and bigoted fringe people who were already prone to violent and rebellious activity. What made the situation even more disturbing and volatile was the fact some of the protestors were openly carrying firearms. No doubt such open acts of displaying a means of violence were to bring the Second Amendment to the attention of the media.

A.T. thought about his "hero" Republicans and felt Abe Lincoln and Teddy Roosevelt would be rolling in their graves. Today, there was not a single elected Republican official on the national level who had the courage to stand up to the "Lunatic Fringe" which had taken over the Republican Party. Both the public threats and the private meetings of intimidation with what were once reasonable or middle-road Republicans had taken their toll.

* *

Despite A.T.'s personal objections, Allen convinced him to arrange for a conference call among the Senator, Bud, Allen, and A.T. for the purpose of exploring the possibility of setting up a safeguard system of getting the information to the public in the event the investigative work were to get stalled out indefinitely for one reason or another.

The greatest difficulty in arranging such a call was getting the Senator on the phone at a convenient time. Finally the Senator agreed to a time, and the call was set up. A.T. explained what Allen had suggested in a preliminary call to Bud, and that necessitated a decision from Bud before the Senator was included in the full conference call. It was all subject to the Senator's approval. If the Senator agreed, Bud would allow the material to be divided into four distinct areas that he would determine, and each separate piece would be disclosed to a member of the media, whom Bud would approve.

Under Bud's plan, only he and the Senator would have the full report, and the four trusted members of the media would have only one fourth of the report. By utilizing such a process, none of the four media members could make a complete disclosure without the collaboration of the other three. Bud, but none of the other reporters, would know the identities of the other three.

From Allen's perspective as the new member of the investigative team, he felt the public needed to be informed of what was going on behind the scenes. The Senator indicated he understood Allen's position; however, he felt the investigation needed to proceed unimpeded and any disclosure to members of the media, no matter how incomplete, might lead to separate efforts by investigative reporters or even worse, ill-advised publications. That had to be avoided.

Because of Allen's concerns, A.T. suggested an agreement be put in place through Bud restricting the amount of information that would be disseminated to any given reporter and with only a part of the information, the story of the matters under investigation could not be told with any credibility or accuracy, unless all four sources were to be combined. The Senator's office had already agreed to grant Bud an exclusive inasmuch as Bud had brought the matter to the Senator's attention in the first place.

It was also Bud who reminded the Senator of the close personal relationship between them, as a foundation of trust, and it was Bud who brought the basis for the investigation to the Senator. The Senator knew Bud would not allow the disclosure of information until appropriate or authorized "leaks" were received from a certain undisclosed public official's office. The Senator mused how he liked the check and balance system suggested by Bud, Allen and A.T. in regard to multiple investigative reporters having only part of the story. That way both the Senator, from an official capacity, and Bud, from a media perspective, could control the information that ultimately got disseminated. It would assure a complete story.

Bud concluded his pitch to the Senator by reminding the Senator Allen could be correct about the information never seeing the light of day if a committee were to bottle up the results. The Senator decided he would give the proposal some thought, and Bud should come up with a number of suggestions for the four journalists who would be the likely candidates to be given a fourth of the information. The Senator's office would have the final approval of four of the candidates that Bud would offer, and the Senator explained that he might have certain guidelines that would need to be followed in order for there to be assurances that no early disclosures occurred and that the information was complete once a decision was made for disclosure.

There was one other matter A.T. brought to the attention of the other three members of the conference call. A.T. noted that as things were progressing and as things stood, he was now in the middle of an investigation that had taken on a life of its own. It had gone far beyond anything A.T. ever intended to investigate. Besides, he was a practicing lawyer with a full contingent of clients, partners, associates, and support staff that depended upon his remaining active in the practice of law. An additional concern was the fact he was now the only party who had all the material gathered by virtue of the investigation.

He didn't like the responsibility of having all of the documents, including the material from Professor Brougham, the bank records from Jean Paul Valance and Claude Schmidt, along with the photos and other documents. Finally, he noted if copies of the material were to be divided with one-fourth to four different investigative reporters, he would still have all of the information that the Senator's office had. He, therefore, suggested the Senator's office take over the investigation and secure the original materials, so he could serve as a consultant only.

The Senator denied A.T.'s request and insisted only A.T., Bud, and the Senator's office have complete files. The Senator explained that he chose A.T. because of their past work together and professional relationship. He assured A.T. the investigation would most likely conclude within the next eighteen months or so, and A.T. had plenty of competent staff that could operate the law practice without him.

Allen wanted to offer one additional person to the mix for the Senator to consider. Allen's candidate was his longtime lady friend, who worked for one of the major wire service companies. Both the Senator and Bud knew her and felt she would be as good a confidante as the six mentioned by Bud. The Senator said he would try to have an answer back to all parties within the hour and he would personally be on the phone to discuss his decision with them. A.T. and Allen waited in A.T.'s office while Bud, who was in D.C., indicated he would travel back to his home near Baltimore, where he would take the call.

Just over an hour passed when the Senator's office was on the phone to administer the conference call among the Senator, Bud, A.T., and Allen. The Senator came on the phone to advise he had made his decision regarding four of the people suggested as media confidants who would each receive one-fourth of the information with the understanding that Bud would coordinate the division of the materials with A.T.

The Senator's office had run down a CV, or curriculum vitae, on each of the seven potential media confidants, that included Allen's suggestion, and the Senator personally made phone calls to the individuals on the suggested list. The Senator provided the names of the four final and selected confidants. As it turned out, Allen's lady friend was one of the individuals chosen. Allen expressed his gratitude, and the call ended.

Allen and A.T. had taken the calls from the Senator in A.T.'s office and considering it was time for dinner, Allen suggested the two of them meet Allen's lady friend at a nearby restaurant. Since Jacci was in Arizona visiting her mother, A.T. agreed. Allen's lady friend, Cynthia Brownell, was a professional reporter who, upon graduation from college, had been hired by a national newspaper. After several years with the newspaper, she went to work for a major news service where she continued to work. Her grown daughter was in college. Since she and Allen had both been divorced, and they seemed to have many interests in common, some mutual friends had arranged for a blind date. That was eight years ago, and the two of them were still together.

A private room at the restaurant was arranged for the meeting. A.T. double checked to be sure the briefcase provided by Jean Paul was securely locked in the law office safe before he and Allen left for the meeting. When they arrived, Cynthia, who was punctual to a fault, was already in the room enjoying her first glass of wine. She got up from the table, so she and Allen could embrace each other. She gave Allen a welcoming kiss and turned to A.T., who hugged Cynthia before the three of them sat down. After a few minutes of small talk and ordering their meal, Cynthia, who could be rather direct, asked, "Well, A.T., what's this all about? It sounds like you've managed to get both yourself and Allen into something intriguingly sensitive from what the Senator told me."

"Would it do any good if I told you I was working on something simple that grew beyond my wildest imagination? Also, Allen was looking for some real excitement, and that's when the investigation took on a life of its own," said A.T., as he tried to minimize his role.

"That's not good enough, A.T.! Knowing about your dogged determination and your penchant for trying to rectify some record somewhere, I can't imagine you were working on anything simple. Plus, I can definitely believe Allen was looking for a way to get involved in some sort of intrigue. When Allen told me he was traveling to Europe with you on a routine matter, I suspected it was anything but routine," said Cynthia.

"Well, it was routine when it started," replied A.T.

"Let's cut to the chase. What's really going on?" Not only was Cynthia direct in her questions and demeanor, but her perky personality was reflected in her petite and alert presence as well. So, it was no surprise to A.T. when she shifted herself toward the front of her chair, drew her long blonde hair back from her forehead, crossed her arms in front of her, intensely looked directly at A.T., and said,

"I'm listening. This better be good. You and Allen had better have a good story because a serious explanation needs to materialize."

"First, Cynthia, I want to be sure that anything I tell you will be kept in the strictest of confidence, and any materials Bud Hawthorne provides will be kept in a secure location. Is that agreed?" asked A.T.

"That's agreed. I already had to promise fidelity on the matter to the Senator and to Bud. Both of them called me before I had a chance to even call Allen. If what the two of them have told me is true, it would seem we are discussing some major issues that will ultimately need to be brought to the public's attention, as well as to the attention of Congress, and ultimately, to the attention of the U.S. Attorney General. Bud assures me I will be included in the major part of the story's release but I must wait until he receives the okay from the Senator to proceed. He said he would write the lead story that will precede the main story by two to three days. I told him that would be too long and the main story would need to follow by a day at most. We are still negotiating that matter. I also wanted to know who the other reporters would be, but he has refused to tell me. In fact, he said I would not be informed of their identities until the day he breaks the lead story. At that time the four of us who have been given portions of the remaining information would be brought together in order for us to be able to collaborate for the follow-up story or stories. If I am going to agree to all of that, the story better be really good."

"It's good," said A.T.

"Are you at liberty to give me some kind of idea what is involved?" asked Cynthia.

"As long as I have your word it remains confidential, I am at liberty to give you an overview without the details, documents, or other evidence. What I tell you will be of little value without the hard evidence. Keep in mind information is continuing to be developed, and additional evidence is being acquired," explained A.T.

"So," asked Cynthia with her arms still crossed in front of her. "What's the story?"

A.T. proceeded to inform Cynthia about his being falsely accused, exonerated, and subsequently deciding to investigate the whole situation.

"Isn't this something that should be handled by the current administration and the Department of Justice?" asked Cynthia.

"No. It would look too political. Besides, they have their hands full trying to undo the unbelievable mess the Bush Justice

Department left them. Also, the Senator decided it was best to leave the President out of it because of the political nature of the entire matter," warned A.T.

"Okay. So, what did you find out in your investigation?"

"Plenty and none of it very good," A.T. said, continuing, "I found there were efforts by my own party, the Republican Party, to undermine and politicize the Justice Department; those efforts went as far back as the Nixon administration. I'm sure that is no surprise to you or anyone else. If you're old enough, you'll remember when Nixon was President, he ordered his Attorney General, Elliot Richardson, to engage in an illegal act and to fire the special prosecutor, Archibald Cox. When Richardson refused, Nixon put more pressure on, and Richardson, along with his Deputy Attorney General, William Ruckelshaus, resigned. Those types of efforts have been intensified by a group of operatives within the Republican Party to this day…"

"That was a long time ago. So, how does that tie into today?"

"To supposedly fill the void left when so many of Nixon's people were indicted, several self-proclaimed party experts, including Dick Cheney, Don Rumsfeld, Karl Rove, and others stepped forward. They were all deeply involved in trying to mold the Republican Party and the Presidency back then but avoided the limelight. In the process, they were able to promote their own careers quite well within certain Republican groups. The three of them were not a part of any prosecutions regarding the Watergate scandal; therefore, they were able to stay active within the Republican ranks and over time continued to position themselves within the party and within the government."

"I didn't realize that all three of them went back that far," commented Cynthia.

"They do," said A.T. "At any rate, they were all deeply involved in the transformation of the Department of Justice during W.'s administration."

"What about the Hatch Act. Doesn't that prevent such politicking by administrative personnel?"

"That seemed to have been ignored, as was the earlier act called the Pendleton Civil Service Act that provided a standard of merit for professionals instead of their political affiliations. In fact, when Ms. Goodling testified before Congress, she stated she was told by those up the ladder that when it came to the appointments of administrative law judges in regard to immigration, she did not have to follow the Hatch Act."

"What about the firings of U.S. Attorneys during the George W. Bush administration?" asked Cynthia. "I heard it was far more egregious than the Elliot Richardson issue during the Nixon administration."

A.T. replied, "It was, and yet nothing was done about it. There were eleven top U.S. Attorneys fired by the Bush administration allegedly because they were not the proper kind of Republicans. They were not 'Bushies,' so they were 'persona non grata.'"

"That's interesting," responded Cynthia. "I didn't realize so many had been hammered."

"It has often been suggested many more USAs were forced into retirement since W., along with Gonzales, Cheney, and Rove, wanted to remove them and insert more 'Bushies.' The new individuals who interviewed for their jobs were often screened by Monica Goodling or Kyle Sampson, who would bluntly and improperly ask questions about their political loyalty to W. They would also ask questions about religion, as I understand it. They wanted to be sure the people appointed were of the 'right' religious beliefs. The Bush administration people, including Goodling, who have been called before Congress, have taken the Fifth Amendment, which they have a right to do. Of course, it does add to the speculation."

"So if I understand you correctly, the investigation is primarily focused upon the transgressions of the Bush administration. From what the Senator said, it seemed that there was much more involved. Is that right?" Cynthia inquired.

A.T. continued, "My initial investigation was focused upon the misconduct and ethical violations of the Bush Justice Department. That was where my investigation started; however, the further I got into the matter, the more apparent it became that actions well beyond the Bush Justice Department were cropping up as red flags. As a result of that, I contacted the Senator, and the entire matter grew into a full-fledged investigation that went well beyond my initial focus."

"How was that so?"

"The investigation revealed voting issues and irregularities in many races for public office including Congressional seats and Senate seats. Unfortunately, some Republican office holders were trying to use the power of their office to force criminal charges against their Democratic opponents and to discredit Republicans who didn't agree with their position or philosophy."

"I believe I read about that in one of the McClatchy newspapers," said Cynthia. "Didn't I read that in the *Albuquerque Journal*?"

"I'm sure you did. You know, even Gonzales refused initially to fire Iglesias; however, apparently after Senator Domenici met with W., Iglesias was fired. But that's one of the particulars in terms of how efforts were made to influence elections while undermining the Justice Department at the same time. So, at the top levels of government, there were issues with House seats, Senate seats, and within the Executive Branch of government. In addition to the Justice Department makeover, efforts to undermine the top echelon of other departments were also occurring. The investigation is finding whole-scale changes in other departments. There were the improper appointments of administrative law judges coming into issue; and appointments and hirings within the State Department, the Defense Department, plus much more. It would be difficult to find any department of the Executive Branch not politicized during the eight years of the Bush administration."

"That's not a surprise. Politicians are the same regardless of party."

"Not from what I am finding. Laws were being broken and not only the law; protocol, as well, was being thrown to the wind. Once you receive your share of the materials, it will become clear to you that the Executive Branch of government was being revamped not only into a Republican hierarchy but also into a 'Fringe-thinking' hierarchy. That, in turn, as you will see, had a direct bearing on government contracting including the 'privatization' of many of the tasks once done by the U.S. military, the State Department, the Defense Department, etc. And don't forget the Commerce Department, Banking, Treasury, and others were restructured in such a manner that essentially removed the necessary oversight which most likely would have eliminated, or at least forestalled, the economic catastrophe of recent years. Remember during most of the Bush years, there was a Republican-controlled Congress that went along with the Bush era changes."

"With all due respect to your investigation," Cynthia interjected, "shouldn't these matters be handled by a proper law enforcement group such as the FBI or by Congress directly if you don't think Justice is the proper avenue?"

"The investigation is also showing the Bureau itself has been compromised and at a fairly high level. The fear is if the material were turned over to the FBI, it would get either stalled or die at the hands of a plant within the Bureau. It is in the hands of Congress; that's why the Senator is involved."

"A single Senator doesn't count for much, if this matter is as involved as you say."

"Just so you know, it isn't a single Senator. You already know he's involved, but he's not alone. There are at least three other Senators, and one of them is a Republican. Additionally, there are nearly a dozen Congressmen and Congresswomen, who not only know about it but who are involved with the direction of the investigation. There are about as many Republicans as Democrats from the House side involved. There is very serious concern about what is happening to the Republican Party."

"From what I know about the current makeup of Congress, there are some interesting people who have become very powerful in that body of government. I have been working on a piece involving a network of politicians who are related to the 'C Street' group. That involves some interesting developments, but I don't want to go into what I am working on at this time. I am preparing a story on them that is less than flattering," commented Cynthia.

"I'm not surprised," exclaimed A.T.

"In addition to Congress, shouldn't the courts be involved in your investigation? Shouldn't they be informed, as well?" inquired Cynthia.

"No. This will probably end up as a legislative matter. This is not yet a matter for the courts. It may come to that, but I doubt it. There are problems with the courts being involved at this stage. Plus, it is becoming more and more apparent that there have been problems with the courts, as the past several decades have seen political ideologues rather than scholarly jurists going onto the courts."

"I suppose that is why we have the Supreme Court we now have?"

"It is not only the Supreme Court, but all of the Circuit Courts, and many of the Federal District Courts were affected as well," A.T. elaborated."

"Bush was better at relating to the type of people he appointed rather than to someone who had good academic credentials, wasn't he?" offered Cynthia.

"True. So anyway, you had all three branches of the government very deeply affected during the Bush administration. However, there is more. As you know, your profession, the media, has often been called the 'fourth estate' or more bluntly, the fourth branch of government. That was not overlooked by any means over the course of the last couple decades."

"That's definitely true," said Cynthia, "call it 'assault media.' When I started as a reporter, there was a lot of credibility given to the media because of its objectivity. Members of the media felt they had an obligation to provide an objective and honest view where the facts did matter. Now, it's getting more and more difficult to sort out the real from the fictional. As the saying goes, 'It smells but sells,'" said Cynthia.

"That's obviously true," observed A.T. "Nevertheless, keep in mind the government can't really police that very much, except perhaps to restrict how much of a media market can be owned by one person or group. That was somewhat thrown to the wind a few years ago, so the problem has gotten worse. Now, what we are finding in the investigation is this phenomenon is not accidental. We are seeing a concerted effort to buy up control of as many media outlets as possible in order to influence what the public sees and hears. Foreign interests are definitely in the mix like never before. That's partly due to a recent decision by the U.S. Supreme Court."

"It sounds like you're investigating something that has been going on for decades in the three branches of government and with the media. I take it there is something more involved than the usual political posturing and power plays. Is my guess correct?" Cynthia inquired.

A.T. exclaimed, "You're correct! The investigation is beginning to reveal outside interests working behind the scenes in such a way they are attempting to claim control of each branch of government, along with the media. Unfortunately, we have been gathering evidence that substantiates it is beyond planning and is actually taking place.

"These groups have orchestrated a particular movement allowing them to infiltrate each of the branches of government and the media. The evidence also demonstrates these efforts have been in place, as you mentioned, for several decades. Furthermore, they are very close to moving the country to a particular point from which there may be no return. These efforts involve some particular methods of conducting government activities that compromise the democratic process. The evidence is also showing certain financial interests causing this influence are benefiting in terms of control over the government and the manner in which government is administered. A lot of money is changing hands, and it is going into the hands of the very few. At this point in the United States, over 90% of the wealth is in the hands of about 5% of certain people and their corporations.

"There is a reason why there has been such a push for that to happen," continued A.T. "The evidence the Senator and I are gathering is what will be provided to the subcommittee and what will be ultimately revealed to the public. Hopefully, we can get it done before too much more time elapses. Time is really of the essence. The Senator has concerns about several items that I have provided. The fact the Department of Justice and the Federal Bureau of Investigation have been compromised is only a part of it. The paramilitary groups are a major concern since there is some evidence some of them are actually planning a coup d'état. Personally, I don't see that happening, but it's a part of the investigation. There is also some grave concern the 'tea party' segment of people within Congress might be able to block legislation to the point of obstructing the operation of government. The Senator and I believe there is a segment of the Republican Party that intends to make it look like there is an impasse in government due to differences between the two political parties by creating false issues relative to matters like health care, abortion, 9-11, gun possession, revenue, tax increases, and other such subjects."

"That's a very serious contention. Can you give me a hint as to what this evidence will show?"

"No. I am not at liberty to provide any details at this time," A.T. replied. "I have been assigned to gather the information and the evidence. Believe me, it has gone way beyond my original investigation of what happened in the Justice Department over the past decade. The Senator and his committee will make the decision about disclosure. The only reason the media, through Bud, is involved is to be sure there is a check of some sort in place. As I understand it, Bud will be at liberty to make a disclosure, if the matter gets totally bottled up in the subcommittee. I do not know what the triggering mechanism happens to be. That's between Bud, the Senator, and the other members of Congress who are aware of it."

"Checks and balances are the purpose of the three branches," remarked Cynthia.

"The system and use of the 'checks and balances' won't work until the subcommittee has the information and until there is some assurance the evidence can be presented to the public. That's where the media comes in. The media will be the vehicle to get the public involved. The public will need to know what is going on and what is at stake."

"Surely, you could get the Justice Department and the appropriate investigative agencies involved if this is as intricate as you imply."

"At this point, we are confident some of the people who were hired at Justice over the past decade were a part of the groups who are attempting to take over the operations of our government. The evidence already gathered reveals virtually every department of government has been 'salted' with operatives of the groups moving to reform the government to their own liking from within."

"I'm not sure I understand."

"There are outside interests that include people and groups both within the United States and from outside the country. If they had not tried to make so many changes so quickly, those efforts would have been harder to detect."

"For what end?" asked Cynthia. "It sounds like a conspiracy theorist's idea or some sort of fictional account."

"It's not fiction," affirmed A.T. "It is definitely real. It is happening and has been evolving for decades. The purpose is one of power, and with power over the various governmental agencies comes control. Wealth can be and has been channeled into the hands of fewer and fewer people and the companies those people control. The investigation and the evidence demonstrate it has taken place. To reverse what has already occurred will take not just years but decades. Naturally, the powers behind the movement are hoping to regain control of the presidency since that is where they were the most successful during the eight years of W."

"It sounds like they could get back in and continue what they have started. They could undo whatever corrections have been made, couldn't they?"

"Not if the public is made aware of it. The hope is if the Senator's subcommittee can do something about it, with proper controls in place, the process of reversing what has already been done could happen sooner. If it doesn't, the same people and companies that have molded or altered the government to what it is now will continue to do so. You and everyone else in this country will experience fewer and fewer overall freedoms. Instead, there will be manipulated elections and less and less economic flexibility."

"So, do you have any particulars as to who or what groups are behind making this change occur?"

"The identities of individuals and groups include mostly domestic names. However, there are foreign interests too; at this point, we are trying to determine their identifies. Allen and I have recently received some new information and documentation that will help identify both the people and the groups from abroad. Of course, in order to dig deeper into the process and in order to reveal some of the actual identities, we will need more than what we now have. We will need a break of some kind."

Cynthia asked, "What about the domestic people and groups?"

"The investigation identifies individuals who have some influence in the media, certain religious factions, particular corporations, individuals with money behind those corporations, paramilitary groups, and others who have been working for years to bring the transformation of our government about," explained A.T. "What's worse is they are preparing to enforce those changes, if necessary. In addition to learning the identities of the foreign individuals, we are also digging deeper into some of the individuals here in the U.S. who have attempted to keep their identities hidden."

"What kind of break are you talking about?"

"We will need to have more than the documents we have recently been given. We will need to come up with an informant who has direct knowledge and who can identify the particular individuals. That may be very hard to come by. At this point, I don't know how I will approach this dilemma. When I was in the Bureau, sometimes we would get lucky, sometimes we would get a lead from someone, and yet other times, we would be following one lead and get information that would open a door. So, I just have to hope something breaks. Who knows, maybe someone with the media will have something for me, like Bud did. How about it, Cynthia, any ideas?" asked A.T.

"I'm sorry, A.T. I don't have anything for you at this point. The stuff I have been working on is really pretty mundane, except for the 'C Street' file, and I don't have anything that would seem to have a tie to what you are pursuing. Plus, I have quite a bit more to do on my own story. Let me assure you, it does not involve the intrigue you are pursuing. I am not seeing anything that has a foreign side at all."

"If you come up with anything, please keep me in mind."

"If I come up with anything, I'll let you know, but I hope it is not something that will set you and Allen off on another excursion around the globe. You'd like that; wouldn't you, Allen?" asked Cynthia.

"Just let me know if it involves travel or something that will get my adrenaline stirred," commented Allen.

"Perhaps after dinner, I might come up with something to stir your adrenaline," smiled Cynthia.

They all laughed at her comment and finished their meals. A. T. picked up the tab. Allen and Cynthia left together while A.T. walked back to his office which was only a short distance away. He sorted through a stack of phone messages, checked his emails, and looked through the letters and pleadings his secretary had placed on the relevant files on a conference table in his office. He knew he would have the weekend to catch up, but it looked as though everything was in order and there was nothing that stood out needing immediate attention. He placed his laptop in a soft leather shoulder bag and then went to the safe to retrieve the steel briefcase Jean Paul had given him.

* *

A.T. said good-bye to a couple of young attorneys who were still working at their desks. He then left through the back door in order to proceed up the alley giving him quicker access to the parking lot where he left his car. Walking up the alley, he noticed what looked like a shadow slip under the light that illuminated the middle part of the alley near the rear exit to a theater backed up to the alley. It was getting dark, so shadows at that time of day were common, especially in late autumn. He was familiar with the potholes and knew how to traverse the alley in a bit of a zigzag pattern. With the one soft case over his shoulder and the steel case firmly in his right hand, he continued toward the middle of the alley where the light provided some less than adequate guidance.

Since he was getting tired from the earlier travel and a bit worn out from the discussion with Allen and Cynthia, he thought about hitting the shower when he got home and having a relaxing glass of wine. In the morning, he would be meeting an old friend, whom he had called earlier.

An early snowfall was expected overnight, and it was already getting cold. Usually A.T. would have his first cup of coffee while he took his dog out for an early walk; however, since both A.T. and Jacci had been out of town, Remington was situated at a nearby kennel. Thus, in the morning, he would wait and have his first cup of coffee at the bakery. A.T. remembered the bakery had good coffee, and he thought positively about having a relaxing meeting with his old friend. He was looking forward to the first cup.

Once again, he thought he noticed a shadow near the alley dumpsters. That seemed odd. Perhaps it was an employee who was dumping some waste from the movie theater. Other than office staff, the only people who knew he was leaving the office at all were the two individuals who he had just spoken with on the telephone. The call had been from people from the past who had recommended A.T. provide the information from his investigation to a reporter who was with *Fox News.* There was no way he would be providing anything to *Fox.*

When he reached the recessed portion of the alley where the fire escapes were located, he instinctively ducked as a man lunged out from behind a dumpster. The man had something that looked like a knife, and it seemed to be pointing at A.T. A.T. drew back, catching the man's wrist with the briefcase he had received in Paris. The item the man was holding fell to the ground and careened across the alley. At that moment, A.T. grabbed for the man's wrist while twisting and bending it back on itself. The man fell to the ground. Despite the wrist hold, the assailant was skilled enough to maneuver himself free. In a fluid motion the man was able to flip back around. Then it appeared as though the assailant either sprained or broke his wrist. Either that or the assailant dislocated his shoulder in the process. In a countermove, he was able to push A.T. against the brick exterior of the back of the theater. A.T.'s face scraped against the brick building.

Feeling a surge of adrenaline, A.T. shoved the larger man up against one of the dumpsters. The extension arm or truck receptacle of the dumpster caught the assailant directly in the back. A.T. thought to himself: *That had to hurt. Now the playing field might just be a bit more even.* It didn't seem to matter as the man came at A.T. again. That was enough for A.T. to realize this was no mugger. It was apparent this guy had been trained.

The attacker kicked A.T. in the groin, and A.T. bent over in reaction to the blow. The assailant again hit A.T., but this time it was a hard hit to the left side of A.T.'s face. A.T. started to go down hitting the back of his head against the dumpster. Pain jolted his ankle when he tried to break the fall. This time A.T. came down on his wrist and winced in pain.

While A.T. was on the ground, the assailant turned momentarily to look for the item that had been dislodged from his hand earlier. When he looked away, A.T. didn't miss the chance. He was able to kick the side of the assailant's knee, which caused him to lose his balance. At that point, the assailant stumbled on one of the potholes in the roadway and fell to the ground. A.T. crawled on top of him, locked his two hands together, and came across the assailant's head with a blow to the side of the man's face. With the man's head turned to his right, A.T. came back again with his hands clasped together and caught the man under the chin with as much force as he could muster. The man reached for his throat, and A.T. hit him again as hard as he could in the nose. It appeared as though the man was losing consciousness.

A.T. stood up and watched the man gasping for air. Quickly A.T. padded the man down for an ID, but he couldn't find any. Instead he found two cell phones in the man's jacket. He noticed the item the man had been carrying was a can of mace. A.T. picked up both the briefcase and the can of mace and sprayed the man in the face for good measure. Using one of the man's cell phones, A.T. dialed 911 to report a disturbance in the alley. After he hung up, he left for his car. It seemed the less time spent in the alley the better, especially if the assailant was not alone. A.T. felt the responders to the 911 call could provide aid to the man and attempt to get his identity. No doubt the police would be called, and under the circumstances, A.T. didn't want to be identified.

CHAPTER 11
THE FIRST CUP

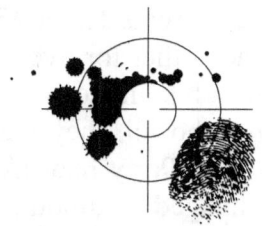

The next morning the simple task of walking along the cold parking lot to the old bakery was difficult enough against the bitter wind, but having to carry a box of bottles and documents over the rough and rigid surface of snow and ice made every step tricky, especially with a sprained ankle. A. T. felt sure he must have looked like the fondly-remembered television character of many years ago called "Chester," who was the deputy to Marshall Matt Dillon on the old hit TV series *Gunsmoke*. Remembering that old "western" and his own childhood brought a smile to his face. That was the favorite show of just about every kid back then. *Ah*, thought A. T., *the good old days!* He didn't have a care in the world then and just knew life was good.

Regardless of the pain A.T. felt, he moved cautiously with his newly-acquired limp until he finally reached the side door to the old bakery. The bakery had been around for over a hundred years and had been in the same family until recently when it was sold to become a part of a larger bakery chain. A.T. didn't like chains. However, habits were hard to break, and this bakery had served the purpose of a convenient meeting place since he came to the Twin Cities. Opening the door, he smelled the combined, rich aromas of the newly brewed coffee and the freshly baked breads. This blended aroma always hit a nostalgic spot. It reminded him of a long time ago while growing up on the family farm.

As he entered the door to the south side of the bakery, he looked at the first row of booths and the adjacent tables where he usually sat with friends virtually every day. Although he thought he sensed being watched, that was not apparent as he looked around the bakery. No one bothered to look up when he entered, so he felt somewhat reassured. Generally, he would recognize some of the customers, but today no one looked familiar. Will would be there soon, and they hadn't seen each other for about a year. It was critical he and Will catch up, but more importantly, he had something to give Will he could trust with Will only.

He had always felt certain he could trust Will Blake implicitly. The two of them had known each other for over thirty years, and during that time, Will had served as his mentor in a number of ways. Both of them were Republicans who felt they had been disenfranchised when an extreme wing of the Party had taken control. They were not alone! So much had changed, and both Will and A. T. had seen it all unfold from a "ringside" seat. Both of them had been involved to a greater degree with the Party than either wanted to admit. In addition, both men had been quite skilled at waiting out the political changes of the time. They had become trusted friends. They were the kind of friends who could sense the attitude of the other.

It was Will who offered A.T. a position with his law firm after A.T. had finished about seven years of public service, including a couple years with the Bureau and about five years as a prosecuting attorney. The two had met each other on the opposite sides of the table in a criminal case that found Will defending the son of a prominent local family. A.T. was the prosecuting attorney on the case. Like A. T., Will had also been in the Bureau and had retired early after enjoying a rather remarkable reputation as a result of some work he had done during the Korean Conflict while serving as a cryptographer in helping break North Korean codes. Although he wasn't hired for that purpose, Will had displayed some exceptional talent in deciphering codes and was moved within the Bureau to that unit. He was now in his eighties but still displayed the aggressive mind of a thirty-five year old. With Will, the wheels were always turning, and his wit was always well placed.

After entering the bakery, A. T. found several vacant tables next to the row of booths near the south wall. It made sense to select a table near but not directly next to the door because the first table always caught the blast of outside air during the cold winter days. The table he selected was close enough to the door that the box he was carrying could be easily placed on the floor while remaining in plain view between the counter and the booths and yet out of the way of patron traffic. A. T. removed his topcoat and limped to the east counter to order. The east counter was the main counter and extended across the entire side of the interior in front of the work area reserved for the bakers and the service help. About two-thirds along that side of the building, the counter broke to the northwest at a sharp angle.

Once at the main counter on the east side, A.T. ordered two ceramic cups for coffee and two glasses of water. He felt confident that Will would be arriving fairly soon. Will was often late in an acceptably social way. It was not intentional; he just always ran late, even in his younger years. The clerk handed A.T. the empty ceramic cups and two glasses of water on a tray. Patrons would generally select their own interest in coffee or tea from the central service area, so the cups were provided without content.

Because the center counter was close, he poured a half-cup of the strongest coffee and hobbled back to the table. By just taking it one-half cup at a time, the coffee stayed hot, and he limited his consumption. Not only did his leg hurt; his face still felt hot from the scraped injury to his cheek, and his wrist throbbed where a slight contusion was obvious. As he looked around the central area, he felt somewhat reassured that no one was looking in his direction. The information he had been compiling was the kind that would make just about anyone paranoid.

When A. T. took the first sip of his coffee, an announcement over the bakery PA system sounded, "Mr. Van Doren, your order is ready!" A. T. stopped! What order, he wondered? He had his cups and water. He didn't place any other order. He looked up and panned the bakery. He didn't notice anyone acting unusual or looking in his direction. After taking a few moments, A. T. cautiously got up from his chair and went toward the section of the main counter where the orders were placed.

"Hello, Mitzi! You called my name for an order?"

"Oh, yes, I did, Mr. Van Doren. Here are the two 'bear-claws,' the blueberry muffin, and the ceramic cup, but I thought it was the other Mr. Van Doren, perhaps your father, who placed the order. He gave me the name of Van Doren when I asked for a name."

"The other Mr. Van Doren?" asked A.T.

"Yes. I believe he and Mrs. Van Doren, I assume, are sitting over there." Mitzi pointed to the most remote table in the bakery at the very northwest corner of the building where an elderly couple sat patiently.

"Well, I'll be…," said A. T. "Will you do a favor for me? Here's a tip in advance if you will carry the tray over to them. I need to go to my table and gather my coat and some other items."

"I sure will, and thank you for the tip!"

A. T. went directly to his table that had constantly been within view. He placed his half-cup of coffee on the tray with the other items. Once he had his topcoat back on, he checked the pockets to be sure the two items were still there. They were. He picked up the box and the tray with its contents on top and proceeded to the northwest corner of the bakery.

Mitzi had already delivered the tray of sweets by the time A. T. arrived at the couple's table. Everyone started to smile! A. T. set the box and tray down. Will got up from the table, and immediately the two friends embraced. A. T. then moved to the other side of the table to the presence of the lady, whom he kissed on the cheek and addressed by saying, "Marjorie, I didn't realize you were coming too. This is a double treat! How are the two of you?"

"I'm well, A.T., but Will needs to get out more. He is driving me crazy with all his arguing with the evening news and his pacing about the house."

"Well, Will, are you really trying the patience of this saintly lady?"

"I'm doing that to be sure, so when she is canonized, they will have good reason to name a few churches after her."

"The two of you look great. As I said, this is a double treat."

"Sit down and tell us how you have been," said Will. "I noticed you were limping a bit and …what did you do to your face?"

Will sat back down, and A. T. took a chair opposite Will and Marjorie. Given their age, neither of them had changed too much since the day A.T. first met them. In his prime, Will had been about six-four in height. However, due to his age, he was now a bit shorter yet still stood in a dignified manner. His swept-back gray hair and his erect stature almost gave him the appearance of arrogance, but he was a gentleman whose personality didn't include any of the behavioral qualities of an arrogant man. Marjorie was slender and tall for a woman of her vintage. She was about five-eight, and her grey hair matched Will's, although hers may have been touched up a bit. Regardless of age, they were young-thinking and open-minded. For that reason, A. T. thought their true age would never show.

Will had taken up a saying of former California Congressman Thomas Lantos, who was often quoted as saying, "A mind is like an umbrella; it doesn't work unless it is open." Marjorie had been a lifelong resident of the city and came from one of the city's founding families. She and Will had been childhood sweethearts and even attended the same college. Both had started law school at the same time although Marjorie had never finished. She and Will had gotten married while the two of them were in law school. Marjorie was way ahead of her time since she was the only female law student in their class. While today there are probably more women than men attending law school, back in Marjorie's college days, not many women even thought about being attorneys. Although she hadn't finished, it was an accomplishment and a credit to the good student she was. They started a family after Will's graduation, about the same time he received his appointment to the Bureau by J. Edgar Hoover. The two of them had four children, who were all in the same age range as A. T. and Jacci. Marjorie, the extrovert, picked up the conversation.

"What have you been up to during the last year or so? We haven't seen you for far too long, and we hadn't heard about you. Usually, we hear something, but this time it was so long we thought you had disappeared from the face of the earth."

"Actually, I have been quite busy with the practice of law, and as you might have guessed, some 'especially designated' work."

"You're still doing that?" questioned Marjorie, who insisted she be called by her proper name. She detested anyone who tried to use an informal salutation and attempted to call her 'Marge.'

"Easy, Marjorie!" said Will. "You know we don't speak of those things."

A. T. responded, "It's okay, Will. Actually, the 'especially designated' work was originally of my own doing, and an assignment I gave to myself; however, that changed when your friend, the Senator, got in touch with me."

"A self-assigned task?" asked Will.

"It was something I felt I was forced to do from what I had accidentally come upon. But first, where are my manners? I brought something for you. Actually, it is for the two of you. Even though I didn't know you would be here, Marjorie, I have something for each of you." A. T. reached down to the box and removed the coffee tray, placing it on the table. He then opened the box and began to remove a couple of bottles one at a time and said, "First of all, for you, Marjorie, I have some Disaronno Amaretto, and for you, Will, I have some Laphroaig Scotch. Both are pretty good in their respective genres. You know, for occasions of celebration."

"You're so sweet!" said Marjorie.

"Well done, good sir!" said Will. "We can use these to help keep us warm on these bitter cold nights."

"It's my pleasure! Bitter cold nights, for sure! I believe we have been setting some records for low temperatures, and we're about to get heavy snowfall from what I understand," said A.T. "In fact, I have a few other items I think the two of you will enjoy as a result of my recent trip to Paris and Zurich. You will find an assortment of collectible items from each of my stops along the way and some chocolate." A. T. then pulled out a few items from the box. When he started to demonstrate the items, his mood changed to a serious one. He then spoke softly and deliberately, saying, "Will, there are also some documents you may want to review, and those docs are mixed in with the old newspapers I've used as filler for the collectibles and the bottles. Please don't show any concern, in case anyone is watching. Also, please keep in mind that you don't need to keep any of them. If you don't want to keep them, I'll stop by to pick them up and share a hot toddy with you. I did want your opinion about what I have found, and these documents will give you a pretty good idea. If you do keep them for me, and until I identify where they go, I suggest the securest of locations."

"Well," said Will, "First of all, thank you for the kind gifts! You're catching me a bit off guard regarding the apparent 'special contents' of the box. It would seem you have a lot going on here. First of all, though, what happened to your face, and why the limp? Next, any hint about the documents? You don't need to explain the purpose of the newspaper disguise; I understand that. In general, what kind of documents are they?

"In reverse order, I'm sure they are what the Senator discussed with you. At this point, they are not sanctioned. When I began my own investigation and was encouraged by the Senator to expand it, I started to see something of grave concern. When I followed the money, it kept getting more and more serious. After I had gotten so far with the investigation, our friend, the Senator, called me in and set both me and the investigation in a new and more involved direction."

"I think I will go to the ladies room," said Marjorie.

"Marjorie, you know I trust you implicitly; feel free to stay," said A. T.

"I'll rejoin the two of you in a minute, but I do need a break," said Marjorie as she left the table.

"As you wish, Marjorie," said Will. "Now A.T., first tell me about the limp and the face. Do these maladies have anything to do with the documents?"

"Yes," replied A.T.

"Well, how did it happen…what happened?"

"At first, it seemed to be out of the blue. But after I thought about it, I came to believe that it may be related to my investigation. It may have started yesterday morning. Early in the day, after Allen Aranda and I had returned from Europe…you remember Allen, he used to be the U.S. Marshall here back in…"

"Sure," said Will. "I remember Allen. He's a good man. If he went to Europe with you; he was a good choice."

"Thanks. He was a good choice," continued A.T. "In any event, after Allen and I returned, I called some of the people I worked with on sensitive issues before, whom I thought I could trust. Unfortunately, the investigation developed some unexpected troubles since Allen and I apparently attracted some attention in a setback by our hotel in Paris, and then last night I had a bit of an altercation in the alley behind the office as I was heading over to my car. As a result of the altercation, I was able to come up with a bit of evidence that might prove to serve as clues regarding the assailant."

At this point, A. T. pulled two cell phones from a pocket in his topcoat. One was a fairly new iPhone, and the other was a pre-paid cell. A. T. continued, "I used the pre-paid phone to call 911 to report a disturbance in the alley. I took the phones and what I thought was a knife but instead found a can of mace. I then grabbed the metal briefcase I had used initially to hit him and walked as calmly as I could to the ramp and got into my car. This morning I had one of my son's IT guys download the entire contents of both phones. The data seem to have some connection to the research I have been doing. Obviously, this guy is reporting to a number of people. A couple of the names are similar to the names on the materials that have been given to me as evidence and that I will turn over to the Senator. However, most of the names are unknown to me, so I'm going to be running them down."

"You know, A.T., you're lucky."

"With all due respect, Will, when you are fighting for your life, the old instincts come back. The guy was definitely trained. What do you make of it?"

"First of all, you're obviously onto something. Second, you've hit a serious nerve. And third, you're in over your head. Don't' misunderstand me. I don't mean you can't figure it out, nor do I mean you can't finish this to your satisfaction...but...you need to bring in some help. The question is whom do you trust, and who would be discreet enough to use?"

"That is the question and one reason why we needed to talk today."

"Well," said Will, "As you know, my son-in-law is a Congressman, and I am totally confident he can be trusted in every respect. Plus, he may be able to provide some help in the right places. He knows our friend, the Senator, quite well. In fact, they socialize on occasion, as I understand."

"I was hoping you would say that," said A. T.

Will continued, saying, "That's not a problem. You know that he would be more than willing to help you. In addition to him, there is Blaine Jeffers on the west coast, who has always been both helpful and discreet."

"First of all, Will, thanks for offering the assistance of your son-in-law. I had hoped you would contact him for me after you review the documents. Let me clear it with the Senator first, just so we are all on the same page. Second, I believe Blaine Jeffers would be excellent."

"Don't worry about my son-in-law; he will do it and probably get right on it. Of course, you check with the Senator first."

"You will see in some surprising documents some witnesses were trying to tie the loss of two former United States Senators, Mel Carnahan and Paul Wellstone, to the political 'Fringe.' Both died in plane crashes about two years apart, and those incidents were uniquely similar. I believe former Senate majority leader, Tom

Daschle, even alluded to the eerie similarities between the two plane accidents in his book, *Like No Other Time*. Getting back to your son-in-law, don't get me wrong, I'm fairly comfortable that the fringe may leave your son-in-law alone given his committee status, etc. But again, I need to verify with the Senator before you contact your son-in-law."

"In regard to my son-in-law, let's use him to aid us but under no circumstances, at least at this juncture, should we use his name or the name of any staff members who might come forward to help. I believe your current approach in keeping this tight and controlled makes sense."

"That will work, but I don't like the idea of using staff members since we have no way of knowing if any of them are plants in his office. If we could work directly and discreetly with him personally, it would be a great help. He would need to see the documents I am giving to you today, and the docs will need to be kept at a secure location. I only have three more copies."

"He and our daughter visit a couple times each year, so the documents you give me could be used for both his review and mine. My role will need to be limited because of my age; however, I can use my contacts to help."

"That will be more than sufficient. Please remember I don't want you, your son-in-law, or any family members exposed."

"A. T., I've been doing this longer than you, so I am comfortable about protecting my family and myself. However, I don't think I ever had an incident as you've just described. What about your family?"

"At this point, there would be no reason for them to be in any danger since they have no knowledge of what I have found. This was mostly a solo operation by me until the Senator brought me together with others he already had working on the matter. I am the one with the documents someone seems to want. Plus, I have purposely kept everything from my family except my son who, as you know, has his own contacts with both the CIA and the NSA. He has done some work for Langley through his business. His company does some work with them on a case-by-case basis. Even though he is also an attorney, he spends most of his time developing new electronic devices. His background as a patent attorney comes in handy in that regard. My one daughter is a research assistant for a professor at Portland State, and he is a well-known moderate Republican.

In regard to my other daughter, she has taken her husband's name, and he is with the State Bureau of Investigation. You may remember that she was a Special Agent with the State Bureau herself. They can handle themselves. So you know, there is always protective surveillance when necessary for each of my children and their families. Plus, there's Remington."

"Well, I didn't know about your interest in a securities firm, but I can guess which one. I've seen your dog, and I certainly wouldn't want to meet him alone without your being there. I don't know about your electronics system, but I trust that it is sufficient. It would be a good idea to double your efforts. What about Jacci?"

"At present, she is at an 'undisclosed location," said A.T.

"Very funny, A.T.," said Will. "So, she's like Dick Cheney used to be?"

"Actually, she is with her mother in Arizona, but they will be flying back together tonight. I will be picking them up at the airport, and I will be sure that the security guys redouble their efforts at the home here in the city."

"Good! Now, what about some help? What about Blaine? Why don't you call him, A. T.? That way the two of you can discuss what you have, and you can make the decision on the spot whether you want to get him involved?"

"That's a good idea, Will; however, don't forget I am already working with Allen. After I give these copies to you, I will have three copies left. If Blaine gets involved, he will need a copy for any work he might do; plus, the Senator will have to approve. I will want to retain a copy myself that I will need for my report to the Senate subcommittee. The final copy I've reserved for the media. I've promised the Senator it would be divided into four parts with each part given to one of four media members whom the Senator has approved."

"Be careful dealing with the media. Many of the media people today are directly or indirectly tied to the 'Lunatic Fringe.' You already know how tied together many of those sources have become, especially with Rupert Murdock having his fingers in so many outlets and stations. With the *Wall Street Journal* that has been added, he must have nearly fifty percent of the total market by now. In any event, permit me to agree with the Senator's idea that you divide the fourth package into pieces with some going to reporters of several media concerns. That way you will force collaboration and a checks and balances between them so when the story does break, it will be a collective effort where all sources have a built-in system of checks.

The final product will be more complete that way, and with several sources presenting at the same time, the story gets better coverage."

"Actually, it was Bud Hawthorne's idea. You remember Bud, don't you?"

"I do. I always thought he was a pretty decent guy; however, he's probably not the most objective reporter by today's standard –"

"True, but Bud is in step with the Senator. In fact, he originally brought the matter to the Senator's attention. Then I got a call out of the blue from the two I had not realized were aware of my investigation. Those were Wilson and Johnson."

"Were they both on the line?"

At that point, Marjorie returned to hear the names. Marjorie sat down and looked A. T. in the eye and inquired, "Did you say Wilson and Johnson? Are you referring to 'Squeaky' Brent Wilson and 'Big John' Harry Johnson?"

"Well, yes," said A.T. "I've worked with them before on a couple of special assignments, and I've known them since the early seventies."

"Those two ne'er-do-wells nearly got Will killed on a trip they all took many years ago to Saigon when the U. S. was trying to get the troops out under some guise of negotiations. They took care of their own hides and were going to leave Will there to try to survive on his own. It was fortunate Will caught up with some reporter friends and got back to the airport in time. Those two idiots nearly cost Will his life. They should probably be sitting in jail for all of the questionable past acts they have done."

"Now, Marjorie," said Will, "you don't know. They may have just gotten wires crossed like they said. Besides, I never considered them too dangerous other than through the mistakes they would often make. I often viewed them as a 'Penn and Teller' or better yet, a 'Dumb and Dumber' type of act, except they were supposed to be doing something serious. Besides 'Penn and Teller are too smart and clever to be compared to 'Squeaky' and 'Big John.' How is it that you know them, A.T.?"

A.T. explained, "Actually, I met them in about 'seventy-two.' I had gotten an invitation to attend a series of meetings taking place in Washington D.C. for the 'Committee to Re-Elect the President.' I had just left the Bureau and had taken a job as an assistant prosecuting attorney."

"There were groups developing within the CREEP Committee that had other purposes, and the meetings just gave these groups the opportunity to meet some of their own kind and band together. They have had their own agendas since then and have become more and more focused in their designs. That is why the Republican Party is the way it is today. They now have the inside track, and little by little, they have simply taken a big share, if not, most of the control," said Will.

"What I am finding and what the documents clearly show is there is a fully functioning and powerful quasi-government group placed within the Executive Branch of the United States. It has some pretty fanatical promoters in positions that could do some real damage. Actually, there are several groups linked with many of those people who probably don't even know they are linked. There's a very intricate system in place from what the documents are showing. It includes members of Congress, several members of the Justice Department, people in the Defense Department, people at State, and politicians at every level of government. However, the real serious operatives are not even elected or appointed officials, yet they affect the daily operations of the government.

"Many government-initiated programs that have been brought to fruition during the past several decades have placed 'Lunatic Fringe' operatives in very key positions. For example, the creation of the office of Homeland Security has many of these folks in position, and they have seemingly done some harm to the various branches of law enforcement, such as the Bureau and the Agency. Some of them brazenly refer to the United States as 'the Homeland.' Who knows, maybe they will be calling it the 'Fatherland' next. Even the more legitimate and thoughtful conservatives don't agree with the 'Lunatic Fringe.'

"Some of the more extreme religious thinkers were really used by the 'Fringe.' Even John Dilulio, who was known as a fairly serious religious person, got an eye-opener when he realized the 'Fringe' was just giving lip service to 'faith-based initiatives.' He was perhaps naïve, even though he was allegedly a scholar. In fact, it was reported that Dilulio felt Karl Rove was a part of a political arm running the White House, at least while Dilulio was on staff. Additionally, I believe it was Dilulio who said that it was the 'reign of the Mayberry Machiavellis.'"

"That's a good way to say it, and I believe it was the consensus at the time," said Will.

"From the references in the investigation that relate to W., it appears as though he believed he was in complete control. However, that was probably not the case. As you know, he has an incredible ego. However, it is likely he was subject to the will of the 'Fringe' since they were able to get him in discussions where he would believe the ideas were completely his. That, of course, was not the case. He was politically smarter than most people think, but many people believe he was still very skillfully manipulated. I doubt W. knew he was being manipulated most of the way through his presidency. Cheney was the most powerful, but some commentators believe Rove was the man directly responsible for keeping W. on track for the benefit of a quiet group operating behind the scenes."

"You say W. was smarter than most would think? Will asked. "Boy, I find that hard to believe."

"Actually, the guy could be quite affable and convincing. One-on-one, he was very relaxed and could make his point better than anyone else with a rather limited vocabulary," offered A.T.

"Have you met him? How well do you know him?" inquired Will.

"Yes, I have met him more than once. It was when I worked for his father's campaign the first time in 1988 against Reagan in the primaries. If I remember correctly, it was back before W. was governor of Texas, and he seemed only interested in things that made him feel good. He didn't seem very serious about much of anything, so I was quite surprised he actually ran for President. He was a perfect fit for some of the 'Fringe' interests since the family name was good for political purposes and political contacts. It was rumored about Washington he was one of the axe men for his father's administration. Most people don't know that. If you were on staff and got a note from W. back then, you had to know it was trouble. The 'Fringe' loved the qualities W. offered, and they felt they could manipulate him. Plus, they loved the Bush name. But before we discuss that, let me get a new cup of coffee because I have gotten to the bottom of the cup, and I've just tasted some rather bitter grounds."

CHAPTER 12
BITTER GROUNDS

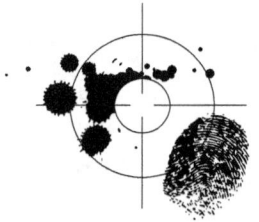

A. T. left the table and went to the center service counter to pour himself another half cup of coffee. He had offered to get more coffee for both Will and Marjorie, but they declined. In order to get rid of the grounds while at the service counter, A. T. rinsed the cup with some hot water from the dispenser usually used for the patrons who were drinking hot tea. After rinsing the cup, he poured another half cup of the strong coffee that he had chosen earlier. When he looked up, it was natural for him to look at the bank of windows near the front of the bakery. As he did, he stopped. It was beginning to snow, and the wind had picked up. The snow was blowing from the northwest at the windows; however, it wasn't the snow that caused him to stop. Looking out the window, he thought he was seeing the ghost of the man that he had encountered the night before.

A. T. squinted and looked again. Facing the southwest, the man now had his back turned against the wind. He was talking to a woman, but A.T. was unable to make out any details or features of either the man or the woman. The man seemed to be about the same height as the one A. T. had encountered the night before. He was wearing a full-length dark, possibly black or navy blue, topcoat. The female was wearing a woman's beige dress-coat and had a "Russian-style" hat covering her long blonde hair. Cautiously, A. T. started to limp to the door, but soon the two people outside the bakery walked in the other direction to a car. Reaching the main door, A.T. visually followed the couple's path to a dark blue 'Navigator;' the man opened the car door and reached in for a package he handed to the woman. A.T. presumed they were leaving, so he decided to go back to the table. Out of the corner of his eye, he noticed the two people walked a short distance to a small red car.

No doubt A.T. was still jumpy from the night before. There would be no reason for the guy from the night before to know where A.T. was. In addition, A.T. presumed the man would still be under treatment at the hospital, assuming the 911 call had been successful. Besides, this guy was with a woman, and the two of them seemed more interested in getting to their cars and transferring the package. A.T. surmised he was really getting paranoid about the whole thing. Why, in the first place, would he try to tie the event of the night before to the research and investigation he was about to provide to Will?

Having satisfied himself that the man he saw was not the same man as the night before, the limping A.T. arrived at the table where Will and Marjorie were waiting. After sitting down, A.T. asked, "Well, where were we?"

Marjorie piped up, "As you noted before you left to refill your cup, that last sip of coffee must really have been bitter. Perhaps you ate some of the bitter grounds at the bottom of your cup? Your face has a sour expression."

"Oh, I was just imagining things or seeing things," said A.T.

"Perhaps you've been at this too long, and you need a break. Let me suggest we pick up the conversation at another time," offered Will.

"No. As long as the two of you have time, I would like to tell you a bit more so you are up to speed on the general subject matter before you dig into the paperwork."

"In that case," said Marjorie, "You were about to tell us what you felt the 'Lunatic Fringe' was up to that was so pressing."

"There are many reasons why I believe it is pressing, but the reason of greatest concern is that evidence shows they have been at it since at least 1972 and possibly before. The documents and evidence I have found are quite disturbing. The 'Fringe' doesn't believe the general populous can govern. To the 'Fringe,' the matter of voting is a placebo for the masses. It is their opinion that they know what is best for the people and if they control all significant segments of government, they can placate the public and operate with impunity as they see fit. They believe if the people are fed the right information through the media, education, and government publications, the public in general will be happy to enjoy what the 'Fringe' decides is right for them. They want to dominate everything from mindless television, to influenced media, to what is important in education, and what religious practices are best. The control of wealth, the media, education, and religion are the items of thrust for those behind the 'Fringe.'"

"You're overly concerned about the politics of the 'Fringe,'" said Will.

"I have been concerned about that and wanted to be sure I wasn't placing too great an emphasis on political differences. Yet, every time I tried to step back from what the witnesses were saying, there would be a new outright violation of the law. Even after the FISA, you know the Foreign Intelligence Surveillance Act, was changed, there were still more violations. There were targeted members of Congress. There were dossiers on members of the news media. There were dossiers on anyone who publicly opposed the 'Fringe.' There were dossiers on candidates. There was the manufacturing of materials and documents that would make opponents of the 'Fringe' look bad. There were threats to people who intended to expose the activities of the 'Fringe.' The 'Fringe' would even collect evidence on the family members of their opponents for the purpose of forcing their opponents to back off or to discredit the opponents."

"Perhaps you have gotten too polarized yourself due to your own beliefs and from being at your investigation too long, A.T.?" asked Marjorie.

"No, at least I don't think so. The evidence is so convincing and there is so much of it. Some of the witnesses, who didn't want to be identified, said the only way they would agree to identity disclosure would be if they were called before Congress. Otherwise, they are not talking. The 'Fringe' is entrenched into so many facets of government and witnesses are scared."

"Entrenched in government in what way? Can you provide some general examples?" asked Will.

"There is Homeland Security. The development of that agency happened fast and furious under W's administration. It was an effort to bring all segments of national security under a single point of control. According to the witnesses and the documents, Homeland Security was planted to the hilt with people who were 'Fringe' thinkers. They are political. I believe that for the most part the Bureau and the Agency are truly interested in doing the right thing under the Constitution and the laws of the land. However, there are those who will do anything to promote their own self-interest while working for those agencies. That is the same apparent agenda of many of the individuals who were brought into Homeland Security under the W. Bush administration."

A.T. continued, "Much is deceptive. For example, when Katrina hit, it gave people within W.'s administration an excuse to divert funds into 'special ops' of their own, instead of getting the funds and help to the Gulf Coast. That's just another or, should I say, a series of misappropriations. There were scapegoats, but that was on the surface. The same was true of the 'border security' issues. According to documents from a retired professor, significant funds were diverted. The 'Lunatic Fringe' is deeply involved, and they have an agenda. However, there isn't time to discuss it here or now.

What do you mean?" asked Marjorie.

"I have taken the time to 'log' or record and index the statements of key members of the Bush administration against what has actually occurred. Let me give you some examples. W. said that he didn't believe in large government, yet once he took office we ended up with the largest Executive Branch in the history of the country. Over three hundred thousand people worked for the Executive Branch during his tenure. Then W. said he would balance the budget. Yet in his administration, the budget was the most 'unbalanced' in the history of the country. W. also said there would be great economic times; yet when he left office, the deficit was around $11 trillion, which is the largest in the history of the country. During W.'s administration this country borrowed more from foreign powers than all previous administrations combined," noted A.T.

"You haven't even mentioned Bin Laden," noted Marjorie.

"That's right," agreed A.T. "He said he would get Bin Laden. He didn't, yet we had opportunities to do so in both Afghanistan and Pakistan, and we didn't get him until Obama became President. The Bush administration started a war in Iraq under false pretenses. Many of the military authorities are outraged at how George W.

Bush and Dick Cheney had weakened the military. Many lives have been lost for a private and ill-advised war that has only satisfied the apparent benefit of segments within private enterprises," noted A.T.

"There were a lot of people who made a lot of money on the wars in Afghanistan and Iraq," inserted Will.

"Sadly, I would guess that would be true. Through the creation of Homeland Security, the control over law enforcement and intelligence gathering is at the focal point of the control the 'Fringe' has been seeking for some time. Please remember they were trying to do the same thing to the Attorney General's Office and to some degree succeeded. It became a political enterprise. There is a direct link between the political arena and the control the 'Fringe' has sought for years. Unfortunately, their overzealous activity has caused them to cross the line."

"I do remember the mess Attorney General Gonzales created, and even when Congress had evidence, he seemed to simply slip away with a resignation. I was wrong about his successor, Mukasey." said Will.

"Remember," said A. T., "there was concern about the issues of torture and surveillance. Mukasey simply passed it off before Congress and basically evaded both issues. There was more going on at the time that was hidden. I cannot believe the emails and letters I've seen that provide insight regarding the efforts to change the makeup of the United States Attorney offices across the country. There was an awful lot which seemed to disappear under Mukasey's tenure. I cannot tell whether he had direct knowledge or if there was a wholesale effort to keep much of the activity from him."

"I can see why you need some help, A.T., but this is pretty overwhelming. I will do what I can. After you speak with the Senator about my son-in-law, let me know. He should be a real ally for the Senator and for you in this endeavor. Congress should be in adjournment soon, and he is expected to be back here in the Midwest," said Will.

"Wait, there's much more," said A. T. "During the Reagan administration, the 'trickle down' philosophy of economics was reintroduced, and it became a hallmark of every administration that followed since. One thing President George Herbert Walker Bush called correctly before he became the Vice President under Reagan was that such an economic policy was nothing more than 'Voo Doo Economics.'"

"Voo Doo Economics?" questioned Marjorie.

"That is the famous 'trickle down' economic principle by which the money is made available to the rich, the corporations, the insiders, and the big contributors because they will supposedly spend the money promoting business enterprise and put people to work," explained A.T. "It is a philosophy that conflicts directly with the Keynesian basic economic philosophy. These two philosophies have been at the polarized sides of the economic spectrum for over sixty years. The Keynesians, a name taken after Lord John Maynard Keynes, the author of *The Economic Consequences of the Peace,* postulated among other things that wealth needed to be made available to the masses since they were the ones who bought most of the products such as cars, washers, dryers, etc."

A.T. continued, "Keynes was one of the major attendees at the 'Bretton Woods' Economic Summit in New Hampshire after World War II. One of the objectives was to find a way to reestablish a world economy that had been devastated by the war. After World War II, the only major countries with their economies still somewhat intact were the United States, Canada, Switzerland, and Australia, as I understand it. The gold was then concentrated in the U. S., Canada, and Switzerland. Those countries became the bankers of the time. Credit was established upon trade among nations. Gold-backed currency became the U. S. dollar with gold then at about $35 per ounce. The non-communist countries would be able to trade with this new system in place, and the countries in both Europe and the Far East could rebuild their economies. The war had been economically devastating. The famous Marshall Plan and the World Bank were two of the offspring of this postwar development. Keynes was the principal architect of this plan that I briefly mention. The plan was far more intricate than I have described. In any event, the World Bank became the lender to the world, and the U.S. dollar ultimately became the common denominator. We have gone through some tough strains on the dollar; however, we are at a crossroads for it."

"What do you mean tough strains on the dollar? It's not like the depression that my folks spoke of, and I barely remember," said Marjorie.

"The tough strains most people don't realize happened during two administrations," responded A.T. "The first was during the Kennedy administration. The world needed more dollars, and the gold supply didn't support additional dollars. A 'forfeit' system of finance was put into place. It was a methodology that allowed import and export transactions to underlie guarantees. It was a form of guarantee developed under Napoleonic Law. It was akin to the issuance of U. S. Treasuries. I don't think that it involved any new U. S. Treasuries but bank instruments from major world banks instead. Letters of credit and bank guarantees were used," said A. T.

"Weren't there other changes, as well?" asked Will.

"Yes," A.T. responded. "Later during the Nixon administration, a new crisis was looming with the limitation of the gold supply. This would have been around 1971. Nixon met with his Treasury Secretary; I believe a Mr. Connelly. He also met with Paul Volcker, who was then an Undersecretary of the Treasury. Now there were a couple of real egos, but they were also bright men. To appease the concerns of countries like the UK, Germany, and Japan, gold was to be valued at its then market price of about $350 per ounce, rather than the $35 per ounce that had been established at the Bretton Woods conference in 1947. Of course, today the price of gold per ounce has nearly quadrupled and comes in just under $1,300 per ounce if I am not mistaken. In my opinion, both the Kennedy administration and the Nixon administration actually saved the U.S. dollar, the U.S. economy, and the world economy because of their actions. However, now there is a new crisis facing the United States because of the economic situation created by the past several administrations and especially the W. Bush administration. Several documents indicate that safeguards were purposely set aside."

"Yeah, the Bush people sure have made out better than bandits," said Marjorie. "You and my husband should each become a Democrat like me."

A.T. interjected, "Democrats have profited as well. You know former President Bill Clinton received over thirty million dollars to help close a major uranium deal in Kazakhstan for a Canadian industrialist. I believe Clinton is to get another one hundred million dollars from that deal. It isn't clear, but I believe those funds are to go to a 'Clinton charity,' such as his library. But, rather than dwell on this, let me mention a few other subjects."

Will asked, "Do you mean there's more?"

"Unfortunately, yes," said A.T. "There are now issues with the Federal Reserve because of the actions and inactions of the Bush administration. The OCC had been stacked where possible with 'Bushies' of another type, and they are from the 'Lunatic Fringe' as well."

The OCC?" asked Marjorie.

"It is the Office of the Comptroller of Currency. It regulates the national banks through examinations and certain rules. It also handles the FDIC."

"I thought that was the FED. You know, the Federal Reserve," said Will.

"They are two separate agencies. The OCC is a part of the U.S. Treasury and was established way back in 1863 to help finance the Civil War, while the modern Federal Reserve, as we know it, was started in 1913 under President Woodrow Wilson. It is an independent organization that is not a part of the government but is regulated by Congress and the Office of the President through appointments. Lots of folks don't like it, but it does add stability away from politics to a certain degree that OCC cannot," said A.T.

"The FED has long been the target of many Americans, mostly because it is run by the banking industry," said Will.

"And here I thought the economy was controlled by the oil companies," said Marjorie.

"Okay," said A.T. "They control a portion of the economy, no doubt, and more and more of it. The oil industry has been entertaining the 'Lunatic Fringe' for some time. By controlling the price of oil, the 'Fringe' can control the price of food and all other commodities and needs. They are not alone. The media industry is partially in the grips of the 'Fringe,' and the impact the media has is what is often called the 'Fourth Estate.' By controlling the media, the 'Fringe' can influence the thinking of the country, including whether the country goes to war and stays at war, even if it can't afford more wars. With people like Rupert Murdock and his influence over politicians on both sides of the aisle, the 'Lunatic Fringe' has a significant foothold in both political parties."

"There seems to be so much interconnection between many of the major political issues of our time and the big financial interests. Now, you are telling us that these problems are interconnected and tied to the 'Lunatic Fringe?'" asked Marjorie.

"From what the evidence shows, there is no doubt. It is intentional. It is deceptive, and it is focused on control of all critical aspects of our society. There are even deceptions that involve travel, personal restrictions, social functioning, personal identification systems, communications, and monitoring. I am not going to go into each of these topics now. It will be evident to you as you review the material. I have gone on longer than I should have, and I need to stop bending your ears. Plus, you will need to be on your way home before the snow gets too deep," said A. T.

"Don't worry about the snow. Charles has driven us as he does almost everywhere now. It is very rare for either of us to drive. He has been with our family for about twenty years," explained Marjorie.

"Well, I'll be…," said A.T.

"You look surprised and shocked. I was sure that you knew that," observed Marjorie.

"That's not the reason of my apparent shock. It is something else…the man from last night is standing over by the main counter, and he is with a blonde lady. I was right! I thought I saw the two of them outside the bakery earlier when I got a new cup of coffee. They were getting something out of a dark blue Navigator, and I thought they had left. At the time, I wasn't sure it was the same guy. It was snowing, and I didn't get a good look. I'm surprised he is here. The question is - why is he here?" A.T. wondered out loud.

"It is a public place, A.T. Just ignore him," said Will.

"Now… that is going to be hard to do. He is coming straight for us," remarked A.T. "This will be interesting!"

The features of the man were much more distinct in the light of the bakery. He was well over six feet tall, maybe six-four. He was reasonably fit and muscular, yet he seemed to be carrying a few extra pounds. The man demonstrated a self-assured gait and moved decisively toward the table where A.T. sat with Will and Marjorie. His hair was cut very short, and it looked like he was losing most of it at the front of his head. Perhaps that is why it was cut so short. He had dark soulless-looking eyes. The nose seemed as though it had been broken more than once, probably years ago and had never been set properly by a doctor. He demonstrated a cynical looking smile that seemed accentuated by his scrapped face.

The man grabbed a chair with his right hand from the next table and slid it over to the table where the three of them were sitting. He looked straight at Will, then Marjorie. He took a few moments to assess them and said, "How are you nice people this beautiful day?"

Before anyone could say anything, he slowly turned his attention to A. T. to speak again. A.T. started to stand up, and the man calmly held out his hand and warned in an almost singing tone, "Please relax and sit down! Nothing is going to happen but pleasant conversation.

My, but you seem a bit jumpy today, and it is such a nice day. At least it's a nice day if you like the beginning of a snowstorm."

Before A. T. or anyone else could say anything, the man continued the one-sided conversation, "You're a very lucky man, 'Prometheus.' I believe that you have a couple of things that belong to me. It would be neither considerate nor advisable for a person of your reputation to take something that didn't belong to you, now, would it?"

A.T. stared straight at the man and said, "What did you call me?"

"You are Prometheus, aren't you?" said the man.

"You've got the wrong guy. It was the wrong guy last night," said A.T.

"Now, now, Prometheus!" scolded the man as he waved his finger at A.T. "I thought you would prefer to be called by your 'file name,' rather than the derogatory name some of my friends call you." The man placed the point of his index finger on the table and drew an imaginary circle, then withdrew the finger and punctuated the imaginary circle with a point in the middle. "As you will learn, there are those in my industry that call you 'ATV,' and that doesn't mean 'All-Terrain Vehicle.' Although those are your initials, Albert Thomas Van Doren, the industry folks refer to you as 'ATV' or 'A Traitorous Villain.' It does have a modern ring to it. And, you have earned it. You have built quite a reputation over the last couple years…mostly a reputation of what we consider to be that of a traitor."

A.T. looked the man straight in the eyes and said, "You and your kind are the traitors. It is no wonder the civilized world refers to you as the 'Lunatic Fringe.' Do each of you slither from you own dedicated holes, or is it just a cave of despair?"

"Please don't be rude," said the man. "You are not in a position to criticize us. We are in control of more than you realize, and we don't need unassuming and naïve 'do-gooders' like you running around screwing things up. We are making it better for everyone. The general public cannot handle responsibility, and they are much better off to let those of us who are professionals run the government and allow us to do our jobs. Operating a government is too much for the average person to worry about. The average person is better off just going to his job, enjoying what he is given, and enjoying his life within approved activities like watching television and going to church picnics on Sunday. Professionals need to be able to function without people like you trying to impede the progress."

"That's not democracy as defined by anyone," interrupted A.T. "Your 'Fringe' friends are running around espousing democracy on the one hand, while doing everything they can to prevent its functioning on the other hand. Virtually everything you nuts are doing is undermining democracy."

"This country, my dear sir, is obviously the best example, and therefore, the best place for us to implement our form of democracy," said the man.

"Your form of democracy? Really…isn't the proper term for your taste in government called oligarchy? What do you mean, file name?" asked A.T.

"Just like the Greek character, 'Prometheus,' you are trying to deliver fire to man and cheat the gods in your personal attempt to render to the masses what rightfully belongs to the gods, or in today's parlance, those in power. You realize in ancient times, the term "god" meant the leader of a community. Back to point, due to your interference, Prometheus, you are going to bring about the creation of Pandora, and that will lead to the exposure of many evils and hard work for man when the contents of Pandora's box are released. You are literally messing with powerful leadership beyond your imagination. Like Prometheus, you will be lucky if all that happens to you is being chained to a mountaintop where the eagles will eat at your liver over and over each new day."

"That is a distorted version of Prometheus," said A.T. "At least you should read a book to get a real idea of the actual Greek legend. But, of course, you people in the 'Lunatic Fringe' either don't read or can't read. So, in order to spare me of having my liver eaten anew each day, you decided to give me a break by attempting to murder me."

"You're a fool, and stop referring to the "Fringe' in regard to me," interjected the man. "Neither my people nor I am a part of your so-called 'fringe.' And when it comes to Greek mythology, please be assured I know such mythology very well. It was a minor of mine when I attended Yale. In fact, I am the one who gave your file name to you. I was speaking figuratively. By the way, there was no effort to murder you last night. That I could have done easily and before you would have known what was happening. I was expected to scare some sense into you. It was my intent to have you turn over your files and investigation. By scaring you first, then demanding the files, we felt you would ultimately agree to be reasonable. At that point, I was going to make the demand thinking you would be too unnerved to continue your 'misadventurous' investigation. Obviously, my associates were wrong. Now it is getting more than serious. It is getting personal. I believe you have three items that belong to me."

"What are you talking about?" asked A.T.

"Don't be coy with me, and don't take me for a fool," said the man, his voice rising to the point where patrons at a nearby table began to look.

"Gentlemen!" said Marjorie. "You're beginning to disrupt the patrons."

"I'm so sorry!" said the man to Marjorie as he smiled and looked toward the people at the next table. He looked directly at the other patrons and continued as he addressed them, "I get a bit too excited when I tell my old war stories. Please forgive my excitement." He then looked back at Marjorie and said, "Look Margie, don't get involved in something that doesn't pertain to you, okay?"

Everyone could see Marjorie's eyes narrow, and at that moment, it looked as though she would stare a hole straight through the man. Instead, she simply smiled and said, "Oh, forgive me. I just thought it was getting a bit boisterous for a bakery. Perhaps you should leave."

Will started to laugh out loud, and the patrons at the other tables must have thought someone had told a joke as they all smiled and nodded. Then Will leaned toward the man, got very serious, and said, "Look sir, I don't know what this is all about, but you have been on the borderline of seeking eviction from this place, and you are being very unkind and rude to my wife and my friend. If you don't leave, I will be certain an appropriate complaint is filled and the police escort you to a facility designed for people like you. I am serious; do you understand?"

The man looked at Will and relaxed back in his chair. He eyed Will, then Marjorie for a moment. He paused and sighed, "Well, I am going to leave the three of you, but before I do, let me mention a couple of very important things. First of all, I certainly hope both you and your wife have enough good sense to avoid having anything to do with what it is that 'Prometheus' here is up to. He is in over his head, and he has irritated the wrong people. Second, I expect any discussion that 'Prometheus' has had with you will be forgotten. Third, I trust this box contains only what it appears to be - bottles of liquor and some 'knick knacks.' If there is more in here, I will want to see it." He then began to shuffle through the newspapers that were used as protective filler.

A.T. grasped the man's hand to stop his shuffling of the papers and said, "These are gifts I have presented to my friends. There is nothing in there that should be of concern to you. Have the common decency to refrain from molesting these gifts."

The man looked at one of the old newspapers that was part of the filler and decided to accept A.T.'s plea. He stopped shuffling through the box. Had he continued to rifle through the newspapers, he would have ultimately gotten to the documents. He removed his hand from A.T.'s grip, then placed his hand on his knee and looked directly into A.T.'s eyes and issued a warning. "If you don't give me the items that you took last night, this matter becomes personal. I mean very personal. Now, do you have them with you, and will you give them to me?"

"Let me just say," said A.T., "the Identification Bureau of the police department is in possession of what you may be seeking." It was partly the truth but not the whole truth because A.T. still had the two cell phones and had only given the mace to the PD. "I have asked for prints to be analyzed for the purpose of identification. Since we had not been properly introduced, I thought it would be a good idea for me to find out exactly who you are."

"That was really a dumb thing to do. Unfortunately, you are making this very personal. I will need to see if the police department will release the phones since I will tell them they were dropped out of my car on the street accidentally when I got out last night. Naturally, I will make no claim for the mace. By the way, they will not find any prints. You're not as observant as I thought. I was wearing surgical gloves. Someone with your background should have noticed that detail. One final item, it only seems fair you know who I am, so I will tell you. My name is Gerald Peterson, and I am currently working for a private entity that has a good reputation. If I named it, you would not recognize it. I can assure you. Additionally, that same entity owns some very well-respected hedge funds. Here is my card. You will not find anything negative about me. I am covered and covered well."

A.T. studied the card and replied, "So, your cover is hidden within some hedge fund, and according to the card, there are four addresses: New York, Washington D. C., San Francisco, and Rome.

You have an interesting combination of locations. Is that where the money is today?"

"There are lots of funds at our disposal, and it comes from various sources, if it is of any concern to you," said Gerald. "Now back to business. Are you willing to give me the paperwork you have wrongfully taken possession of?"

"Why would any boring material of mine be of interest to you? What gives you the idea you would be interested in anything I have? Please explain exactly what types of documents are of interest to you. Maybe I can help direct you to the proper party," offered A. T.

"I can see this is a waste of time, so I will be saying good-bye for now. However, I'm sure our paths will cross again. In fact, you can count on it. Ultimately, I will obtain the documents. We know what you have for the most part, and we have already started to discredit some of the more questionable documents, the witnesses, and you. Please be assured your little adventure is going to come to an end very soon," explained Gerald.

"Are you threatening me in a public place, in front of God and witnesses?" asked A.T.

"Please! Don't take the Lord's name in vain. Now, you've been warned. I tried twice to approach you. Once was their way, and now I've tried my nicer way. The third time will be more direct and will yield results. You have my word," Gerald promised as he got up from the table and put his chair back at the nearby empty table. He stared at the floor, looked up at A. T. for a moment, and turned to leave. He stopped and turned around and provided a final word, "It's too bad it has to come to this. You are creating a worse situation than you realize." Before A.T. could respond, Gerald walked to the front door of the bakery where the blonde lady was waiting. They spoke for a moment, and the two of them left.

"Imagine, the audacity of that guy!" exclaimed Marjorie.

"There's a lot more going on here than I thought initially," said Will. "You are obviously onto something, A.T. As soon as I get back to the house, I will call my son-in-law to see exactly when he can get out here. Don't worry, I won't let on as to what we have nor will I say anything over the phone. I will simply mention to him that Marjorie and I ran into you and had a very pleasant conversation with you until that character from the alley interrupted us. That will be enough. He will put two and two together fast enough."

"Thanks, Will," said A.T. "I really appreciate it."

At that point, Charles, the driver for Will and Marjorie, came over to the table to inform Will and Marjorie he had the car running and it was starting to snow more than before. Charles recognized A. T., and the two of them exchanged pleasantries. He suggested to Will and Marjorie they should start for home. He then shook hands with A.T., bid him farewell, and picked up the box. He turned and headed toward the side door where the car was waiting.

"I certainly didn't mean to get the two of you involved in this matter to the extent that I have, but I truly do appreciate your help," said A.T.

"Look," remarked Will, "we're here for you. We have always been good friends, and we've all done this before. Please be careful, and don't be afraid to get the authorities involved, if necessary. We need to go, but before we do, let's have a final toast to your good health and good luck." At that, Will raised his cup. Marjorie followed with her cup, and so did A.T.

A.T. said, "Bottoms up," and all three clicked their cups in a toast. They gathered their coats and hats while chitchatting about the weather as they walked to the side door of the bakery. A. T. said good-bye and hobbled to his Chevy Tahoe parked east of the bakery.

He waited until Will and Marjorie's car had passed; then he backed out to leave. Their car turned to the left in the direction of their estate. When A.T. turned to the right to proceed down the adjacent street, he kept a watchful eye to the mirrors in case the Navigator followed him. Sure enough, the dark blue Navigator turned and began to follow A.T.

A.T. decided to take a convoluted route. He was definitely being followed because the Navigator also took every side street he had taken. Finally, A.T. turned onto a controlled access roadway he needed in order to drive home. Once again, the Navigator turned to follow him.

Along the sides of the road were intermittent small banks of snow that had been plowed to the side by the road crews. The Navigator had been over a block behind him when he entered the main road; however, now it was closer. A narrower shoulder than normal ran along the outside lanes of the four-lane highway on each side as a result of the snow plowing by the maintenance trucks. The four lane roadway was a divided highway with a raised median between the two eastbound lanes and the two westbound lanes. Some snow had accumulated, causing the central surface to be about a foot above the curb.

At this point there was no other traffic but the two of them heading east. A.T. moved into the outside lane and sped up. After proceeding for about two miles, A. T. noticed the Navigator had moved into the outside lane behind him, and it wasn't slowing down.

CHAPTER 13
BOTTOMS UP

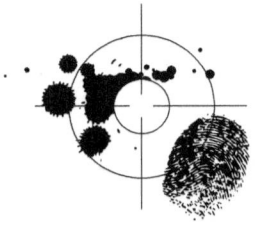

The Navigator was still speeding up, and A.T. felt certain he was going to get rammed from behind. Waiting until the last possible moment, A.T. hit the gas and turned into the lane near the median. The Navigator missed and was now adjacent to A.T.'s vehicle. He could see Gerald look over with a smile. At that point, A.T. thought Gerald was simply trying to put a scare into him and he would drive off. However, that didn't happen. Gerald slowed his Navigator and pulled in behind A.T. The next thing A.T. experienced was a heavy jolt that caused his Tahoe to swerve on a patch of packed snow. A.T. sped up, and then Gerald again hit him from behind. The vehicle lurched forward. A.T. hit the gas again and moved away from Gerald. Quickly, Gerald was coming at him again, and it appeared to A. T. that Gerald was attempting to get an angle on his car's left rear corner.

A.T. hit the brakes hard, and the ABS system took over. The Tahoe locked down on all four tires, and the Navigator hit directly in the middle of the truck bumper rather than the left side. Both vehicles began to slide from the impact. A.T. then turned in the direction of the slide and hit the gas. All four wheels moved the vehicle away from the Navigator, and he was able to straighten the truck out along the outside lane. He sideswiped a small bank of snow piled up along the side of the roadway before he was able to regain complete control of the vehicle. He looked into the rearview mirror and saw the Navigator was coming at him while straddling the two lanes.

This time it looked like Gerald was going to make contact on the left corner for sure. A.T. pulled the Tahoe to the right as hard as he could along the shoulder and hit the brakes. The Navigator just missed the left rear corner. It then hit a patch of packed ice and snow. That was it. Gerald could not control the Navigator. As it spun by A.T., it hit the snow bank on the shoulder, went over the bank and down into the ravine. The Navigator rolled over twice and skidded on its roof sliding sideways until it was stopped by a large oak tree at the bottom of the ravine.

A.T. knew he was lucky. Had Gerald caught him in the left corner of the bumper, he would have been forced over the bank and into the ravine instead. Never did A.T. think he would be thankful for snow and ice in the middle of the road.

Slowly, A.T. pulled to a complete stop and got out of his truck. He then began hobbling down the embankment. It was never a good time to have a bad ankle but heading down a fairly steep, snow-covered highway grade was painful and difficult. The snow on the embankment was already over a half-foot deep, and getting down to the Navigator was not a fast process. It took a while to get to the steaming and hissing overturned car. There did not appear to be any fire, nor was there any odor of gas or burning material.

The vehicle was completely "bottoms up." As A.T. approached the vehicle, he noticed it had spun around with the driver's side to the roadway and the passenger's side against the oak tree. A.T. could see that Gerald was upside down bunched up in a heap against the window of the door on the driver's side. His body was pressing down upon the window against his head and his already bandaged left arm. A.T. bent over and tried to open the door in order to check on Gerald's condition. The door was stuck, and there did not appear to be any movement from within the vehicle. It was going to be necessary to break the glass; however, A. T. didn't have anything with him that would be of assistance in that regard. He tried the door again, and as he did, he heard a woman's voice say, "Back away!" Looking up, he saw the blonde woman from the bakery coming down the embankment toward him with what looked like a tire iron raised high in her left hand.

Immediately, A.T. moved away from the vehicle and must have instinctively raised his hand. The woman said, "I said back up! I'm not going to strike you, so relax."

"You'll need to excuse me, but I don't often have someone come at me with a raised tire iron," said A.T.

"It's for the window, you idiot. I have no intention of hitting you. I was following the two of you and saw the accident. You guys are crazy to be driving like that. What were you doing? It looked like the two of you were trying to kill each other," the woman said angrily.

"He was the one trying to force me off the roadway. I was driving defensively. Aren't you the blonde lady who was in the bakery?" asked A.T.

A.T. observed something very unusual about the lady. She was blonde, and he was sure she was the same female who had been with Gerald in the bakery. Now, however, he noticed for the first time while she was close to him that her uniquely colored eyes seemed to have the appearance of someone with Asian ancestry. He noted the blonde hair didn't seem to match her other features. There was a grave look of concern on her face as she ordered A.T., "Here, take this car jack and see if you can break the window. I am a nurse by training, and I need to check his condition. Also, be careful not to make matters any worse."

A.T. took off his topcoat and placed it against the glass nearest Gerald's face. He then took the tire iron (not a car jack as the woman had said) and swung at the window at its farthest point near the front of the vehicle in order to minimize any effect that the glass would have in regard to the position of Gerald's face. A.T. struck at the glass again and again. Finally, the glass broke through, and he was able to chip away at the window without causing any additional injury to Gerald. A.T. wrapped his topcoat around the inside of the remainder of the window as he and the female changed positions outside the vehicle. With the topcoat as a protective cushion, A.T. was able to force the remaining portion of the window outward onto the snow.

Gerald fell forward with part of his head and arm coming out of the vehicle. The woman held his face and his shoulder allowing Gerald to slide forward and partially out of the open window. Gerald groaned and opened his eyes. He started to speak, but the woman stopped him, saying, "Just try to breathe as normally as possible. Let me know if you can feel your extremities and if you have any pain."

"I can breathe, but it is difficult in this position," complained Gerald. "Can you help me get out of here? I do have some pain, but I think that I can move if you will help me out."

"We'll need to try to release the seat belt and move you out with caution, and you will need to check to be sure you can help us get you out," said the woman. She then stuck her head into the vehicle to unlatch the seat belt. After what seemed like minutes, she pulled her head from the vehicle and ordered A.T. to help, "Please help me very carefully move Gerald out of the window. Gerald, tell us immediately if you feel any pain, and we'll stop. Do you understand?"

"Yes, I do have some pain in my legs, but otherwise I just have some aches." Gerald started to move himself out of the window with the help of A.T. and the woman. Gerald yelled, "Hold it! I am having trouble with my legs. They seem turned around, and I can't move any farther forward."

"Can you feel your legs? Can you move them?" asked the lady.

"Yes, I can feel sensation, and I can move them, but I can't seem to get them turned around the right way in order to get out," said Gerald.

At that point, two additional people who had come down the embankment joined A.T. and the woman. They were paramedics who explained that they had been traveling with their ambulance in the opposite direction when they noticed two cars appear to slide into each other. They had turned around as fast as they could under the conditions and came to the scene. While the paramedics were explaining their timely arrival, A.T. thought to himself: *Two cars sliding into each other was no accident.* A third paramedic had brought a stretcher from the ambulance, and the three of them were strapping Gerald to the device when a police officer started down the embankment. Apparently, the paramedics had called him to the scene.

While A.T. put his topcoat back on, he and the female watched the paramedics remove Gerald from the ravine while the police officer returned to his vehicle to use the radio and get a mini-clipboard. He motioned to A.T. and the woman to come up the embankment to him. The climb was difficult for A. T., but he followed the female upwards. At first he noticed she didn't seem to have any problem climbing the embankment despite the rather high-heeled boots she was wearing. She demonstrated some athleticism while she moved skillfully and rapidly through the snow and up toward the roadway. However, before she reached the top of the road, she slipped down toward A.T., who instinctively reached out to prevent her slide. When she started to fall backwards down the embankment, her coat blew upward and A.T. caught her posterior with his good arm. She was wearing wool slacks that were form-fitting. He could tell she was very fit and shapely, at least in that part of her anatomy. He pushed her upward as he said, "Bottoms up!" Then he started to slip back down the embankment himself.

The woman turned and scowled at him with a penetrating glare. He shrugged his shoulders and shook his head. She seemed to smile as she turned toward the road. Regaining her balance, she reached the top of the roadway and straightened herself while looking back at A.T. She started to say something but apparently changed her mind and walked directly to the police officer. A.T. took a bit more time getting his balance; then he proceeded to the top of the roadway. Walking to the police vehicle, he noticed the woman was already providing a statement to the police officer. By the time A.T. arrived, it appeared she had already given her identity and other contact information.

She told the officer the icy road surface had caused the two vehicles to slide into each other, and it was an accident that couldn't have been helped under the circumstances. In her opinion, neither party was at fault; it was just one of those unfortunate things that happen on bad roads. Since she had already provided her contact information to the officer, A.T. did not determine her identity. However, he thought he would be able to get that information from the police officer at a later time.

The officer then turned to A.T. for identification and a statement of what had happened. A.T. was careful to not be accusatory of Gerald regarding what he himself had perceived to have happened. A.T. reported he thought Gerald had been driving too fast for the road conditions. When asked if he knew Gerald, A.T. replied he had just met him for the first time this very morning, and although that was an accurate statement, it was not the whole story. A.T. did not mention the incident of the night before and purposely avoided saying anything more about his suspicions or the conversation at the bakery. Following A.T.'s statement and after handing him some accident forms to complete, the officer asked to view the damage to A.T.'s vehicle. When the two of them walked to the vehicle, the female came along, apparently to be in a position to hear any additional conversation.

After viewing the vehicle, the officer noticed another police vehicle was pulling to a stop on the shoulder of the roadway. The officer made sure he had handed A.T. the accident report forms and verified the contact information. As it began to snow again, the officer turned to A.T. and said, "Your vehicle looks fully operable, so you should be able to drive it away. I trust you are not injured. If you are, you need to tell me now. If not, I will need to examine the other vehicle with the other officers. Then I will head down to the hospital in order to interview the other gentleman, who is being taken away by the ambulance. The two of you may go, but please be assured I will be in touch with each of you if there is anything else I need from you. Good luck with your car, and please be sure to include your insurance information on the forms I have given you. They need to be filled out completely with the original copy mailed to the address shown on the envelope. You will need to have that mailed within ten days or less." He then looked at the woman and said, "And you, miss, are free to go as well, but in case you think of anything else you may have forgotten to tell me about the incident, here is a card with the police department number. I have written my name on the bottom of the card. Thank you for your help. Good day to the two of you, and you, sir, be sure to send in the accident report I provided. Thanks to the both of you, and try to be careful on the roads."

Once the officer had left, A.T. began looking through the forms he had been handed. The woman turned and said to him, "I believe it might be a good idea for the two of us to meet somewhere to discuss the events that have just happened."

Surprised, A.T. looked up from the documents. For the first time, he noticed the woman was fairly tall, and he tried to guess her height. While the two of them stood on a reasonably level spot on the pavement, he was a couple inches taller than she was. He remembered that she had boots with heels. Since he was not quite 6' 1," he was guessing her to be about 5' 9". He said nothing but studied her face. Her unusual green eyes, with a touch of amber, seemed to sparkle when she spoke. With her now standing fairly close, he noticed she had a small irregularly shaped birthmark under her left eye. He tried to observe whether she was wearing a wig or if she had dyed her hair to the blonde color. She was watching him intently with her eyes moving directly as his eyes moved over her face. She then turned to look in the direction of the police officer and noticed the officer had gone down the embankment with the other officers and the ambulance had already left.

Looking around and making certain there were no other people in the area, she abruptly turned toward A.T., reached to the top of her forehead, and pulled off a blonde wig along with her Russian styled hat. She removed a hairpin from the back of her head, shook her shoulder-length raven-colored hair, smiled, and said, "Look, I'll be honest with you, and I would like you to be honest with me. We need to talk, and it is getting too cold out here for the pleasant conversation the two of us will want to have. Since I am not from this city, permit me to suggest we meet at the restaurant in the lobby of my hotel, or you can suggest an easy place for me to find where we can get something hot to drink."

"Really! Now, that comment has me even more intrigued than I've been for the last twenty-four hours. To say the least, the last day has been intriguing enough. All right…what would you prefer… there's the old bakery back up the road where we were, or there is a coffee shop in a shopping mall just a couple of blocks away," exclaimed A.T.

"At this point, I would like something hot, but I don't want to go back to the bakery," replied the female.

With that, A.T. suggested the two of them go up the street to the mall where a coffee shop stood directly inside the mall entrance that faced the roadway. A.T. thought this would be a good time to find out about this mysterious woman and her friend, Gerald. More importantly, she said the meeting was for his sake and they needed to talk. He wondered what else they had planned for him. Was he in real danger, or were they just trying to put in a scare? Plus, from an investigational standpoint, he didn't know anything about this woman, not even her name.

They got into their own vehicles and proceeded the short distance to the mall. The woman stayed directly behind him on the roadway. After he parked near the mall entrance, she parked her vehicle next to his. He got out and waited for her to join him on the sidewalk. She had wrapped herself tightly in her dress coat and fur-trimmed Russian styled hat, which she placed back on her head since it had come off with the blonde wig.

Once inside the mall, the two of them selected a table near the back of the coffee shop and although private, it opened to the general public. A.T. pulled back the chair for her and offered to assist with removing her coat. A.T. couldn't help but notice this very attractive woman was extremely well designed. It must have been a natural instinct for him to smile as he observed her form. He noticed her features were quite stunning, and she seemed to recognize his observations. She turned and expressed a most enchanting laugh. Then she shook her head and sat down.

Once seated, she noticed the food court was self-serve. She looked over at the large menu above the somewhat distant counter and said to A.T., "Like I said, I would like something hot. Would you mind bringing me a very large hot chocolate?"

"Of course," said A.T. "Would you care for anything else?"

"Not now, thank you, but depending upon the size of the cup and the length of our conversation, I may want a refill a bit later."

After removing his topcoat and placing it on the chair next to the woman, A.T. started for the counter but remembered the two cell phones in the pocket of the topcoat. He returned to the table, retrieved his topcoat, and turned toward the counter.

His coffee shop companion exclaimed, "There must be something in the topcoat that is important to you, or have you felt a sudden draft?"

"Neither," said A.T. as he put his topcoat back on. "I just haven't warmed up from the cold or the trip down the embankment earlier."

"Well, I think it is quite comfortable in the mall, and I notice a heating unit right near the table," she said.

A.T. was generally pretty quick on his feet, so he said, "You just reminded me of a clever story. There is this monastery near here where the monks take a full vow of silence and each –"

She interrupted, "Perhaps we could hear the story after we have the chance to sip a warm beverage?"

"Certainly," he replied setting off in the direction of the counter while putting his topcoat back on.

At the counter, A.T. ordered a large hot chocolate and a medium coffee. To make conversation, he asked about a couple of menu items while the clerk began preparing the drinks. He turned to notice his companion appeared to be checking her makeup in a small compact. She was also talking either to herself or to someone else through the compact that could have been a Bluetooth or phone. It didn't look like she was talking to herself because she seemed a bit animated in conversation. She looked in A.T.'s direction, smiled, and stopped talking to the compact. Everything was causing him a new form of concern. Why couldn't he take anything at face value anymore? Everything around him seemed to heighten his senses these days.

When the drinks were ready, A.T. paid for them and for refills at the same time, just in case refills became necessary. When he walked back to the table, he felt the vibrating motion from one of the cell phones. That prompted him to amplify his limp and walk slower back to the table. Finally, the cell phone stopped. That seemed more than just coincidental. It was too delayed for it to be a call from the woman, but it could have been a call from whomever she had called. Perhaps, that person was now trying to call one of Gerald's two phones in A. T's coat pocket. He would be sure to put the coat over a chair away from the woman, so if the phone rang again, the phone's vibrator could not be noticed.

"Here we go...'Hot and Sweet!'" said A.T., as he approached the table.

"How's that? Oh, you're referring to the drinks!" she said with a smile.

"Yes, the drinks. Here is your large hot chocolate," commented A.T., as he placed the drink before her on the table. He set his coffee down and removed his topcoat, placing it on a vacant chair at the far end of the table. He sat down and looked at this unfamiliar female, who was pressing the newly-acquired drink to her lips while looking directly at him.

"Well!" She said with a grin on her face, "Was it as good for you as it was for me?"

"What are you talking about?" inquired A.T.

"I'm speaking of the liberty you took with me when we were climbing up the ditch to the highway," she said, with a mischievous smile.

"Look," noted A.T. "You were starting to fall, so I simply reached out instinctively to keep you from tumbling back down to the bottom of the ravine. I did not take any liberty with you, and I nearly fell back down into the snowy ditch myself. I do not take liberties, and I don't appreciate the accusation. Besides, I am a happily married man."

"My...how sensitive," she said. "I was trying to make some effort at humor in order to lighten the conversation. I don't think a tense conversation is in order under the circumstances, and I don't think much can be accomplished if our discussion begins with any stress. In fact, didn't you mention a story about a monk before you went to get the refreshments? That's one way to break the ice. As long as the story is not offensive, I wouldn't mind hearing it."

"The story is not offensive, and besides, I don't like offensive stories, so I don't tell such stories. I was simply reminded of this particular story because it demonstrates the merit in listening and assessing what others have to say. I am quite interested in what you have to say."

"I'm also very interested in what you have to say, and I am a good listener. So, what's the story?" she asked.

"You mean the story about the monks?" A.T. questioned.

"Yes, let's start with that since it might break down the apparent hostilities between us," she insisted.

"It so happens there was this monastery of monks not far from here. Every monk who ever joined the order was sworn to a vow of silence as a part of the individual dedication to the order. However, each year a single monk, and only a single monk, was permitted to speak during Christmas dinner. No one else was permitted to speak; however, each subsequent year, one other monk was permitted to speak. Since the abbey was based upon seniority, the order of speaking allowed for the oldest monk to speak during the first Christmas dinner. Then at each successive Christmas dinner, the next senior monk was permitted to speak and on down the line. So as the story goes, the first year at the Christmas dinner, the first and eldest monk stood by his chair after everyone had eaten, he cleared his throat, scanned the room full of the other monks, and simply said, 'The soup in this place is too hot!' With that, he sat down with nothing more to say. An entire year elapsed before it was the turn of the next eldest monk. As expected, he rose, cleared his throat, looked about the dining hall, then at the oldest monk who had spoken the year before and said, 'I disagree; the soup in this place is too cold.' Having said that, the next eldest monk sat down, and the silence continued for another full year. Finally, at the Christmas dinner of the third year, the third eldest monk stood at the conclusion of the dinner, cleared his throat, looked at the monks remaining in the hall, then looked at the two older monks and calmly said, 'That's it! Unfortunately, I've decided to leave the monastery and the order after all these years. There is far too much bickering, and I do not wish to tolerate such discord any longer.'"

The woman's reaction was a simple smile and a negative shake of her head as she rolled her eyes. She cautiously stated, "I don't mean to be presumptive, but since it appears as though you are the elder of the two of us, would you care to go first and provide an explanation of just why it is that you are causing so much attention and so much aggravation to my friends? I am willing to be a patient listener."

"It is undoubtedly true about my holding the senior position; however, if you don't mind, I would like to defer to you. Perhaps we should hear from you first. I believe that would be in order inasmuch as you and your friend seem to be following me. It also seems apparent you know something about me, but I know nothing about either you or your friend, other than what he mentioned earlier at the bakery down the road. Permit me to say what he said was more cryptic than sensible."

"All right, I will start. Sometimes mistakes are made, people get carried away, and they get reckless. When that occurs, actions often get out of hand, and those actions get categorized in the wrong way. Diplomacy and deliberate discussions are usually preferred by sensible parties, so matters that may have been misconstrued and misunderstood don't get completely out of control. When such circumstances occur, everyone involved needs to take a step back and take a deep breath," said the female.

"Presumably you are speaking of the actions of your friend, Gerald. You need to forgive me if I seem a bit on edge. I would imagine his activities would cause even the calmest individual to be a bit intense, so you need to appreciate my position. But before we discuss him, let's speak of the former blonde who now sits before me. So far, there has been no name, a disguise, a clever number of diversions, and a tendency to direct the conversation and possibly even the events of the day. So, if you don't mind, I would first like to know whom I am addressing and something about the mystery lady across from me at the table," said A. T.

The woman reached for her purse, pulled out several items, and placed in her lap. She took the first item and presented it to A.T., saying, "Since I already know about you, and I am familiar with your background, your request is fair. Here is my U.S. passport. As you can see, my name is Samantha Nguyen-Plantagenet-Henderson. I was born in Vietnam, but I am a citizen of the United States. Does that satisfy your inquiry?"

A. T. examined the passport he was handed and inquired, "How do I know this is really you? I can see the picture matches the present appearance before me. However, how do I know this isn't a duplicitous passport? I am also curious as to why you happen to be carrying your passport with you."

"I thought you would be skeptical, so here is my California driver's license and my AAA highway assistance membership card. The passport is authentic and can be verified. I have it in my possession because I do a lot of traveling on a moment's notice. You will see the other two forms of ID are consistent. Are these sufficient forms of identification for you? I don't plan to ask you to cash a check for me," stated the woman, with an expression of satisfaction on her face as she seemed pleased with her own sarcasm.

"Well, I notice the three documents match and some of the apparent vitals such as height and features seem to match," said A.T. "However, I have no way of verifying what you have provided. Some of the vitals don't seem to make sense, such as the date of birth. I am also a bit puzzled by the name. Here, let me give these back to you."

"What you said makes it a nice way of addressing age and my name in a diplomatic sense. A diplomatic discussion is what I had hoped for. Obviously, I am a bit older than I may appear. With all due respect, I'm probably fifteen to twenty years your junior. Let's just say I come from a good gene pool," she said. "I was born to a French-Vietnamese mother, who was native to the Kontum region or area in the Central Highlands of Vietnam. She in turn was the child of a French Foreign Officer, my grandfather, ergo the French name, Plantagenet, and a well-regarded lady from a long-standing and highly noted family of the region, my grandmother, whose maiden name was Nguyen. That name is a bit like being called 'Smith' in the U.S. My father was an American, who was assigned to South Vietnam in the 60s. His cover was that of the United States State Department, but in reality, he was "on loan" from a Special Forces group of five men who worked through the CIA at the time. He and my mother were married in Kontum. I was born there on March 29, 1964. I have a younger brother, who was also born four years later, and I have a younger sister who was born here in the States. Obviously, we are citizens of the United States."

She continued, "Due to the circumstances occurring during the Easter Offensive with attacks by the North Vietnamese in 1972, the

Kontum area was seriously threatened. That happened right around the time of my eighth birthday. My father arranged for my mother, my brother, and me to fly to the States, where my grandparents met us in California. At the time, they lived in the San Bernardino area, and that's where we lived for about sixteen months, until my father came home to join us. He moved the family to San Diego, and that is where my younger sister was born. Subsequently, my father went back to Vietnam several times and later he was assigned to various locations throughout the world. He would return to our home in San Diego when his leave permitted. Our family stayed in San Diego for the most part. My father remained in the service until he retired."

Then she added, "You don't need to know where my family now lives, and if you ask, I will choose to not tell you. You could see from my documents, my name is Samantha, and as far as I know, the name has no special significance other than a name my parents chose. Henderson is obviously my father's family name, and you will find he is the third generation of his family to earn distinguished military honors from the United States. I am a graduate of both Yale University and Stanford University. I also became a certified RN while serving in the military. My specialty is languages, and I am fluent in five languages including English, Vietnamese, French, Japanese, and Russian. Does that satisfy your curiosity?" asked Samantha.

"Actually, it serves to increase my curiosity," said A. T. "Travel on a moment's notice...did you say?"

Samantha looked annoyed and said, "At present, I am an independent contractor. Considering my background and political interests, I found I could live comfortably and see some interesting parts of the world with all expenses paid simply by handling some special assignments from time to time. My father's connections were helpful. You and I are a lot alike in that respect because we both get paid to conduct investigations for people who either cannot take the time or who do not have the expertise."

"Well, we are not alike in the sense that the people who hire me as an independent contractor for investigations are authorized to take action on behalf of the United States Government either through a Senate or House subcommittee or through the office of an elected official. My work, you see, has a legitimate basis to it," said A.T.

"So, you don't think the work I have been asked to do by various government officers or others is authorized?" asked Samantha.

236

"I couldn't say if your assignments and work have been authorized because I have no idea what you have been asked to do or for whom you are working. I will say it is my guess if the work you have been doing is like that of your friend, Gerald, it is outside the realm of proper authority on the one hand and of a purely political nature probably prohibited or against the law on the other hand," commented A.T.

"How arrogant!" exclaimed Samantha. "What gives you any authority or basis to presume the work I perform is anything but an assignment with proper authorization, as well as for the good of the country?"

"For starters, what I am finding in my investigation is a series of acts which appear to be violations of the law and cannot be shielded under the pretext of immunity or legitimate government authority. What I am finding are matters of questionable politics, pure and simple. Judging from the way the acts were performed, it would seem they are prohibited under various statutes, as well as the Constitution," said A.T.

"Oh, really!" exclaimed Samantha leaning forward in her chair to look A. T. directly in the eye. "Would you care to tell me exactly what it is you think you have found? By the way, as I understand it, you are doing this on your own, so you have no authority to be proceeding down this misguided path. You don't even have a mandate from anyone in Congress. You are doing this wholly on your own and without any authority to do so. Isn't that right? Oh, and besides, the acts you have been investigating are long gone; they are history, and no one is interested in what was done months and even years ago by an administration that is no longer relevant."

"Not so fast!" said A.T. "I was directed to investigate certain matters involving the United States Congress and particular acts considered to be violations of the Constitution, as well as other statutes I have already mentioned. That investigation led to other related matters, so my investigation continued after my initial report was filed with a United States Senator."

"But the W. Bush administration is done, and if I am not mistaken, your investigation relates to the Bush-era politics. What possible motive could you possibly have to continue? Truly, it is a waste of time," noted Samantha as she placed her face nearly nose-to-nose with A.T. who was leaning forward.

Immediately A.T. observed what he first perceived as a birthmark under her left eye to actually be a tattoo. The tattoo looked like a

Maltese cross. If it were a birthmark, it would have been an unusual twist of nature. A.T. couldn't hold back. He inquired, "Please forgive me, but that is an interesting mark under your left eye. It doesn't appear to be a part of the original art work."

"Do you always have a problem staying on subject? It isn't a natural mark," she commented as she sat back and rubbed her left hand over the mark. "It is a tattoo I personally prefer, and it has a special significance to me. Plus, it is my business, isn't it!" she exclaimed.

A.T. immediately responded, "Yes, it is your business; however, for someone to display such a mark so openly, it would occur to me you would be proud enough about it that if someone asked, you would willingly explain it."

Patronizingly Samantha explained, "The tattoo, if you must know, represents a special reminder to me and to the world that I belong to a very unique and renowned group of people who are dedicated to a better world as a better place. It tends to keep me focused each day when I look into the mirror. My father was a member, just as I am. Does that satisfy your rude request?"

"Not completely," said A.T. "If it is a Maltese cross, does it mean you belong to some secret society which is a part of German history?"

"No, no. It's not a part of any German history," exclaimed Samantha. "Let me give you a bit of a history lesson. The Maltese cross is the adopted emblem of the Order of St. John. Its origin was from ancient Assyrian interests, and it was adopted by a group of Christian crusaders in the middle of the twelfth century. It actually symbolizes the 'Cross of Promise.' The Knights of Malta adopted the symbol when they were first known as the Knights Hospitaller. As knights, they were both skilled in the medical arts, including knowledge they obtained during the Crusades from the people in Jerusalem at the time, and they were also very skilled warriors. When they were driven out of the Holy Land, they settled in Cyprus. They later moved to Rhodes. Some say they were rivals to the Knights Templar in vying for the interests of the church. As it turned out, much of the property of the Knights Templar in France, Germany, Spain, and England was given to the Knights Hospitaller.

"Also, it has been alleged some of the Templar fortune came into the hands of the order sometime after the Inquisition. Later, when the Muslim leader, Suleiman, defeated the order, they moved to Malta, where they solidified the order until 1834. The order was renamed the Knights of Malta and after 1834, the order moved to Rome. It is there where many of today's leadership reside, and they maintain a very good standing with the Catholic Church. Today it is known as the Order of St. John, and we members believe we have been especially endowed to lead the world in many respects. The order only accepts people of noble heritage through generations or individuals who have demonstrated particular talents, loyalty to the church, and dedication to purpose. The order does involve itself in a helpful way with governments and the power behind those governments. You may already know from the documents you have that the order is significantly involved in the world of banking. I am a member of a group within the Order of St. John, as was my father. We are proud to be dedicated to such a noble service. I wear the tattoo as a reminder of that service, and it is the Maltese cross. Does that satisfy you?"

A.T. sat back in his chair and studied Samantha intently and asked, "So, that's it. Your organization is trying to see what I know about your activities, and whether or not I found out how they might be trying to subvert the government of the United States. Which are you, a member of nobility or one of the dedicated servants, or both?"

"Don't be a fool," exclaimed Samantha. "The order of St. John is not subverting the government of the United States. Your petty investigation won't have much, if any, effect on the Order of St. John. You can have your investigation. We are only interested in some of the documents you might have in your possession that could belong to us. The documents don't belong to you. They were stolen from us, and we simply want them back. I am certain you don't want to keep what does not belong to you or to your friend, the Senator. And for what it's worth, I am both from a family of nobility, and I am a dedicated person with special talent, including my language and martial arts skills the order recognizes as valuable."

"I don't doubt you have convinced yourself of some noble cause; however, I am trying to do what is right by my country. My investigation will continue until all of the facts are known and are in the hands of the proper parties, including the Senator," stated A.T.

"It's my country too, so don't be a jackass," exclaimed Samantha.

"Excuse me! You should want my investigation to continue until certain parties who were overtly undermining the government process are brought to justice. I would think such an effort on my part would be applauded by you. Besides, I've never had a lady call me a 'jackass,' especially since most people know I am a Republican,'" said A.T.

"Very funny, but if you would act like a gentleman, I wouldn't call you names you don't think you deserve. You can continue your investigation, only without involving us. Those documents you received in Kentucky belong to us. Therefore, I'm asking you nicely to give them back to us," ordered Samantha.

"Did you say Kentucky? How do you know about Kentucky? Unless you and your friend Gerald were –"

"We were there, and we were in Paris, and we were in Zurich. Actually, it is lucky for you we were in Paris," said Samantha.

A.T. sat back in his chair, obviously stunned. He looked hard at Samantha and said, "Do you mind explaining just what you were doing and why you were following me?"

"Actually," explained Samantha, "we weren't following you, initially. Gerald and I were assigned to follow Charles Brougham who had done some accounting work and some financial planning for a group to which I have some close ties."

"I trust that is the Order of St. John or the Knights of Malta," commented A.T., as he took another sip of coffee.

Samantha explained, "Yes and no; however, the group requesting my assistance is related to those two groups, and don't ask me how or why because I am not at liberty to tell you. In any event, Mr. Brougham had taken some documents that belonged to this group, and they wanted them back. We were assigned to visit with Mr. Brougham and insist he give us the documents. That's when you and your two friends showed up. We had a very difficult time identifying the three of you. In fact, it wasn't until your trip to Europe that we were actually able to identify you and your other friend who traveled with you to Paris. The other two in Kentucky we haven't yet identified, but we will. The meeting you had with Mr. Brougham threw us for a bit of a loop, and we noticed he had transferred the paperwork to you. We decided to follow you and contacted some other friends of ours to tail the professor. He may be a skilled accountant, but he is terrible at trying to conceal his whereabouts."

"So you had someone continue to follow the professor? What happened to him, if I may ask?" inquired A.T.

"He was followed, and that's all I am at liberty to tell you," said Samantha.

"Don't tell me," interrupted A.T. "Your group had him killed and probably on site."

"We don't kill people, and we don't have others kill people," she retorted. "Our people are quite civilized and don't engage in violence."

"Shouldn't you tell that to your friend, Gerald?" inquired A.T.

"You've got Gerald all wrong. He is a very skilled individual and usually performs his assignments with a clear conscience."

"That's not what I experienced on the roadway just now, nor is it what I experienced last night in the alley when he attacked me."

"I don't know about last night, but I believe today's incident was simply what it appeared to be. It was an accident. Most likely the two of you were just demonstrating some uncontrolled testosterone in trying to see who could better handle a car in the snow."

"That certainly was not the case. Although, I will say Gerald's driving skills seem to leave the door open for serious speculation. I saw what his alleged driving skills were today when he went into the ditch. I also saw a demonstration of his driving skills along the Middle Fork of the Rockcastle in southeastern Kentucky, presuming he was the driver instead of you. Oh, and I also saw a sample of his driving skills in Paris, again assuming he was the driver in the car behind us."

"You've just been lucky. Perhaps you lead an enchanted life. He was the driver all three times, and all three environments were strange to him. However, don't be too harsh on Gerald because he and I saved your behinds near your hotel in Paris."

"Let's face it, the guy is a really awful driver... Wait! What do you mean you and Gerald saved our behinds in Paris?"

"After your arrival in Paris at the airport, he and I noticed you had a tail on you. Obviously, someone other than us was interested in either your travels or what you were carrying. We had flown into Paris the day before and waited for you and your friend, who we finally did identify. We observed you had two people following you, and they, in fact, were on the same flight. I'm sure you didn't notice."

"We noticed. I mentioned to my associate that I was asked by another gentleman at the end of our flight into Paris if I needed help with my carryon while we were at the baggage carousel. I never thought I ever appeared as feeble. I thought it was odd at the time, but I made a note of him, and I suspected he was one of the men a day later near the hotel."

"Really? Describe him for me," requested Samantha.

"The man on the plane was an African-American, who was about six-two and relatively fit looking although a bit flabby in the midsection. He was probably about two hundred and thirty pounds or so, and I'm sure he was one of the men near the hotel in Paris," said A.T.

"So, you did observe him. Perhaps you're not as oblivious to the world around you as I imagined."

"Yes, I did observe him, and as I said, I mentioned him to my associate. By the way, I'm not oblivious to the world around me. Anyway, thanks for the assistance near the hotel. If the two people who came along were really you and Gerald, you have my thanks. I actually thought you, and apparently Gerald, did a masterful job of handling those two. Until now I had mistaken you as a small man, no offense, and —"

"Don't you think we women can be trained in martial arts? What a chauvinist!"

"I never said or implied that," interrupted an agitated A.T.

"I know you didn't," laughed Samantha. "By the way, there is no need to be upset, A.T., if I may presume to call you that."

"Please, I would prefer it over Mr. Van Doren," interjected A.T.

"That's good and a start at our settling down a bit," said Samantha. "Permit me to suggest you might want to switch to either decaf or hot chocolate. However, I appreciate your thanks for the help we gave you in Paris since I presume the thank you was sincere."

"It was, and it is sincere," answered A.T. "I should probably have you thank Gerald as well, but I'm not sure that he will accept my thanks."

"Gerald is okay," responded Samantha. "He can get a bit excited at times. Just so you know, he and I each have skills. Initially, we thought the two men in Paris would be more of a challenge; however, they were quite easy, and I thought the one I handled, the African-American, was quite soft considering his position and all."

"What do you mean his position and all? Do you know who he is?"

"Yes, I do know who he is. I've been able to identify him; however, I don't know his friend just yet, but that will be easy," answered Samantha.

"Well, who is he?" inquired A.T.

"Not so fast!" cautioned Samantha. "As I said, you have something that belongs to us. Actually, you have paperwork, and you also have a couple items that belong to Gerald. You give me those items, and I'll give you the identity of the guy tailing you," said Samantha smiling and drawing herself back in her chair as proud as a Cheshire cat.

A.T. thought about the proposition. Under no circumstances was he about to give up the material from Professor Brougham. Nor was he about to give up the material given to him by Jean Paul or Claude. The two cell phones of Gerald's, however, were a different matter. He had already had the SIM chips copied, so he felt he had all he needed from the phones. Although, for her to be asking for them now and for Gerald to go to the extremes he had to get them, obviously the phones were items of some importance. A.T. imagined if Gerald lost the phones, it was likely his superiors, whoever they were, would be more than just unhappy. He realized he had more than one bargaining chip, and Samantha had perhaps some questionable information about one of the men in Paris. A.T. held the upper hand, and he was not about to lose it. "Here's what I would be willing to do," said A.T. "Imagine there might, for discussion purposes, be a couple of cell phones in the hands of certain people and those same cell phones might be a source of professional and permanent embarrassment if they turned up missing. Wouldn't it seem fair if there were an exchange of two phones for what is probably a matter of questionable identity regarding the man who attacked me in Paris?"

"The identity is not questionable. If an exchange is made, you will see what I am talking about. So, it's not a deal unless I get the phones and the documents," insisted Samantha.

"I am so sorry," said A.T. "Such a transaction would be -" At that moment, one of the cell phones began to vibrate in A.T.'s topcoat. It seemed louder than normal, causing both A.T. and Samantha to turn toward the coat. When the vibration continued, he thought to himself: *Gerald must be nearly deaf. Why would he have the vibrator turned up so loud?'* After the phone continued to vibrate, Samantha looked at the topcoat and then to A.T.

She asked, "Aren't you going to answer it?"

At that moment, A.T. decided to call her bluff and said, "Why yes, hold on a second…" as he got up from his chair and moved toward the coat sitting upon the chair at the end of the table.

Samantha got up as well and exclaimed, "No. Don't answer it. We'll make the trade. The two phones for the identity. Besides, I don't feel comfortable carrying around that kind of identification."

"What kind of identification?" asked A.T. as the phone stopped vibrating.

"First, show me the phones and the documents, and I'll show you the identification," said Samantha.

"Nice try," commented A.T. "The documents are not a part of the trade. There is no deal involving the documents."

"The folks up the ladder will not be pleased. At some point, you will need to give us the documents, so it is better now rather than later."

"No documents," insisted A.T. "The documents go to the Senator. So, are you saying if I don't give you the documents, you're going to have someone try to force them out of me at gunpoint or under the threat of death or worse?"

"We don't threaten at gunpoint. We don't kill people; however, torture is another matter," noted Samantha with a big smile.

"Well, then, that settles it. The documents will go to the Senator."

"There are other means at our disposal that will convince you to turn the documents over to us," suggested Samantha.

"Sorry, the answer is still 'no,'" said A.T. "I suppose I'll now have to face either water boarding or some form of sleep deprivation."

"There are means other than water boarding and sleep deprivation. Suit yourself, but don't say I didn't warn you. You know, certain people can make life pretty miserable for you," she cautioned. "For now, you can just get the phones out in order for me to properly identify them, and I'll show you what I have."

After being satisfied they had an agreement regarding the trade, A.T. went to his coat and pulled out the two cell phones. He said, "Here they are; now, what's the name of the guy whom you trashed in Paris, and what kind of ID do you have on him?"

At that point, Samantha reached for her shoulder bag and extracted a thin black item about three inches wide by five inches in length. A.T. couldn't believe what he thought he was seeing. He was quite familiar with the item because he had carried one himself many years ago. She offered it to him with one hand, while extending her other hand for the two cell phones. The exchange was made as he placed the phones on the table in front of her and received the small packet from her. He was amazed at what he now held in his hand.

While she examined the two phones he had taken from Gerald the night before, A.T. deliberately opened the item she had given him. The credential case and the credentials for an FBI Special Agent made the agent's identity quite clear. He exclaimed, "How did you get this and when?"

"I took it off the agent while I had him pinned down on the street next to your hotel in Paris. The guy was a real 'wuss.' The FBI either needs to do a better job of training, or it needs to hire better people. As big as he was, he was a pushover when it came to a real fight. Frankly, I've faced a lot tougher just in training sessions. When I had him pinned down against the wall, he twisted to get out of my hold, and that's when I took the credentials out of his coat pocket. I started to move away from him, and lifted my knee directly into the bottom of his jaw as he was trying to stand up. That blow to the head about did it for him. I think I may have put him out," she said with an absolute air of confidence.

"Really? As I remember him in Paris both on the plane and later by the hotel, he looked a bit overweight but seemed pretty fit," recalled A.T. "I do think you may very well be in some kind of trouble by lifting these credentials from him."

"No, you're the one in trouble," smiled Samantha. "Now you've got the credentials you will need to explain, and if I don't miss my guess, as long as you refuse to give up the documents Professor Brougham gave you, you are in more serious trouble with my benefactors."

"Is that a threat of some sort?"

"No, not at all! I am very serious when I warn you about your future," insisted Samantha. "You cannot imagine how miserable they will make your life. One thing after another will come at you. There will be legal problems. There will be new charges. There will be difficulties in the world of finance. You will face a constant barrage of difficulties every time you turn around. I have seen what they have done to others, so I just thought I would warn you. If my recollection is correct, you have already stepped on some toes, and that is why you encountered the problems you have in the past."

"So, I take it that your threat, or excuse me, warning, is your way of telling me the Knights of Malta or the Order of St. John will use whatever connections they have to make my life miserable?" A.T. inquired. "Just so you know, I'm now used to it as some unimaginable things have already been done to me. Isn't just trying to mug me in an alley enough, or isn't bodily harm sufficient these days?"

"Please get this straight. It isn't the Knights of Malta or the Order of St. John you need to worry about. They aren't going to waste their time with you. However, there is an affiliated organization some of us belong to that you should be concerned about."

"So, neither the Knights of Malta nor the Order of St. John will dirty their hands, but your affiliate organization will. Is that right?"

"Right," said Samantha.

"Does this affiliate have a name, and is it sanctioned by the Knights or the Order?" A.T. asked.

"They are called the triple G Knights or GGG Knights," said Samantha. "Gerald and I are not officially sanctioned by either the Knights of Malta or the Order of St. John. In fact, he is with a different group which also has membership in the GGG. As I told you earlier, they are good and worthy organizations. We have some members in our GGG who like to help out."

"Well, from what you just told me, I'm so sure that would be true," said A.T. with as much sarcasm as possible. "Now, let's see, the GGG. I suppose that stands for something like God's Great Guards or some such noble name. I take it the GGG is some sort of enforcement arm of –"

"Actually, it's nothing quite so flamboyant," smiled Samantha. "It is an international organization and simply stands for Good Government Group. We help promote good government, and in the process, we encourage others to let themselves be known in areas of religion, government, laws, politics, advertising, media coverage, public protests, and so on –"

"I get it," interrupted A.T. "The GGG stands behind the scenes and encourages others, who agree with your basic philosophies, to take the front lines. From what I've seen, there are plenty of people out there dumb enough to comply. That way you can help mold their thinking as long as it's compatible with your group's idea of good government, providing they can even think. While such benevolence is taking place, you remain quietly out of sight. You simply nudge them in the 'right' direction, and I suppose you help their funding along the way."

"We do nudge them in the 'right' direction, but their philosophies, if they have any, are quite different from ours. The front line groups, as you call them, are people with short-term agendas and petty grievances. On the other hand, we do have long-term objectives and follow certain philosophies. The GGG simply helps encourage them with funding and staged empathy," said Samantha. "It is not the GGG you are really after. Believe me."

"In other words, the GGG you work for stirs up factions of the public so long as those elements suit your purposes," A.T. insisted.

"It's sort of like that," said Samantha. "Many times some people just need to be encouraged."

"Like the 'Lunatic Fringe;' and I trust the less educated, the better," asserted A.T.

"You have much to learn from your investigation," insisted Samantha. The GGG is not a part of the 'Lunatic Fringe.' You will soon see the GGG is quite different from the 'Fringe.'"

"I see," said A.T. "The GGG wants to be altruistic as it tries to create 'a new world order' that fits within your group's philosophy whether it is religion or government or whatever and so long as your plan is followed. Does that about sum it up?"

"Not at all," answered Samantha. "However, since it is apparent you wish to be antagonistic and hold to your own belief about the GGG without completing a proper investigation and in order to satisfy your short-sightedness, let's leave it at what you just said."

"I suppose all of us should be so grateful that we have you folks around to show us the way," said A.T. leaning back in his chair with a smile and a shake of his head.

"You can be as cynical as you wish. Perhaps it would be better for us to discuss the documents you will want to give me. First, though, would you mind getting me something more to drink? Perhaps, just some hot water this time," ordered Samantha, offering up the empty porcelain mug.

Plain hot water?" asked A.T. while placing the credential case into the inside pocket of his suit coat while getting up from the table.

"Please. Plain hot water," she said.

CHAPTER 14
HOT WATER!

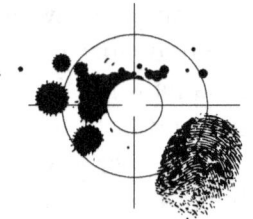

After reaching the counter of the coffee emporium, A.T. ordered a coffee refill for himself and some hot water for Samantha. The clerk provided a new cup for Samantha and while the clerk was getting the coffee refill, A.T. had the opportunity to observe Samantha at the table. She was carefully examining the two cell phones she had been given. In fact, it appeared she was scrolling through an application on the iPhone as if she were looking for a particular number or message. While watching her, A.T. believed he knew exactly what he would do with the FBI credentials she had given him. It was always a critically serious matter for an agent to lose his credentials. Moreover, if the credentials were lost in the wrong place and at the wrong time, it could be devastating to an agent.

Once he had the opportunity, A.T. planned to dictate an affidavit that would accompany the credentials when he gave them to the Senator. He would detail the entire matter that related to the credentials, and he would include the full information that he had received regarding Samantha's identity. It was his plan to personally deliver the credentials, the documents from Professor Brougham, the materials from Jean Paul, the documents from Claude, and the latest findings of his investigation to the Senator.

Upon receiving the coffee refill and the hot water, A.T. returned to the table where Samantha was still searching the contents of the phone. He interrupted her apparent intensity and said, "Those are the two phones I took from Gerald. I didn't use them to make any calls, except a call to 911 when Gerald was recovering in the alley."

"It doesn't matter to me if you used them or not," she said. "However, I imagine you either reviewed or downloaded the data you wanted. Tell me, does that include the emails?"

A.T. tried to act surprised and asked, "You mean you can download the emails off those phones? Wow, I didn't know that."

"Don't take me for a fool," she said. "Why can't you just try to be straight with me? I have been very up-front with you. I gave you my identity, not that it will do you any good. I have told you about my interests and the group with which I work. Don't you understand I am really trying to remove you from a situation I'm sure you don't want to be in?"

"I am truly grateful for your concern, but you must understand I have agreed to perform a task for a United States Senator, and I have no intention of failing him.

"Under Bush's tenure, the Justice Department, for example, actually was complicit in the creation of various scenarios in which the orchestration of potential criminal activity was masterminded by members of the Justice Department and by certain agents within the FBI. Real criminals went free, and any oversight of serious criminals, like Bernie Madoff, was virtually nonexistent. It was that period of time when the FBI even looked the other way when it had key terrorists within reach. They either got away or were successful in 'conning' their way out of the FBI's reach."

"Like I asked," said Samantha, "Why should that concern you?"

"Because it was some unscrupulous individuals within the Department of Justice who attempted to involve me in one of their efforts to orchestrate a crime out of nothing. Between certain members of the Justice Department and a couple of misguided and egocentric agents within the FBI, there was a concerted attempt to involve me in something with which I had no involvement and with individuals whom I had never met. In sum, I was forced to get involved, and now I will not be happy until there are sweeping reforms to the Department of Justice and the grand jury process. It just so happens my quest coincides well with what the Senator is doing. Needless to say, I am more than happy to help."

"Why would they try to involve you supposedly in something in which you weren't involved?"

"When I was in the Bureau, I was one of the young agents who blew the whistle on one particular agent who had been fabricating the contents of some security files. That might be the reason. Or, perhaps it was because I refused to work with certain people within the George W. Bush administration who asked me to be a part of something of which I wanted no part. Of course, it may have been because I crossed swords with some of the Pat Robertson people during a presidential campaign in 1988."

"Sounds like you made some political enemies. Do you think someone was carrying a grudge?"

"Any one of those three situations could be at the heart of it. I will ultimately find out, and once I do, I intend to pursue the proper judicial avenues to be sure it doesn't happen again to anyone. One thing is for certain, I was never a part of any criminal activity or conspiracy. It is a shame I now have to spend so much of my life attempting to seek total vindication. However, if I can help bring about proper reform to a corrupted system and eliminate the prosecution of others who are innocent, I will have accomplished a great objective."

"Perhaps it was just accidental someone included you in a process to get others who were involved in improper activity."

"That I will never believe, unless the people in the Department of Justice and the FBI at the time were totally incompetent. In actuality, I believe the Bush Justice Department was trying to prove they could bring charges against anyone at any time and for any reason to suit them."

"Sometimes accidents happen. Can't you just leave it alone and leave our people out of it? All I want are the documents Professor Brougham gave you. Those documents, discs, memory sticks, and other materials are copies of items that belong to our group. If you gave them back, you could still continue your personal quest," said Samantha.

"It's too late for that. I have made a firm commitment to the Senator, and I will keep it," answered A.T.

"It sounds like your battle lies with the ghosts of the Bush administration and not with our group at all. Just leave us alone, and we will quietly leave you alone. The materials you have from Professor Brougham are all we are interested in receiving from you. Leave us out of it," urged Samantha.

"For your information, the materials from Professor Brougham, along with other information I recently received, show your group and others at the heart of the controversy. If one examines the materials along with the other items developed through the investigation, it is apparent those materials implicate your group as one that may have been playing a role behind the scenes," A.T. responded.

"That's a stretch. You could never prove such a connection. I think both you and the Senator are out on a limb," Samantha reasoned. "Our group is only interested in good government and the political process. The material of Professor Brougham doesn't belong in your scheme of investigation."

"That's where you are wrong, Samantha!" insisted A.T. "Any time there is outside influence in the political realm to the point of stepping outside the law to force a particular philosophy, it has a direct effect on other factors such as the fair administration of justice."

"And you're helping in that 'worthy' cause?"

"Yes. At least I believe I am," answered A.T., as he sat back.

"Well, well. How noble of you!" exclaimed Samantha.

"I believe it is a noble cause. Plus, I believe, or certainly hope, it will help everyone regain some balance within the political arena."

She looked at A.T. with an irritating smile and said, "Here I thought you were one of those people who wanted to go after the people in the Bush-Cheney administration for all of their alleged acts of misconduct and high crimes and misdemeanors."

"No. That's a task for people like former Congressman Kucinich of Ohio. I just want to help unwind the changes they made to the DOJ, the FBI, and the grand jury process," explained A.T.

"Isn't the stuff from the Bush Administration water over the dam? Besides, they are no longer in power. What's the point in going after them?" asked Samantha.

"Now that you say that, it causes me to rethink what I just said. It is true most of the acts were committed by certain political individuals in the W. Bush administration who no longer hold the power. However, many of the former office holders have converted to regular civil service employees, so they are protected from termination unless and until any connection can be made to a specific criminal offense," responded A.T.

Samantha interrupted, "But, as I said, that is all water over the dam or under the bridge. Now, you're just shadowboxing. People have forgotten about the transgressions of the W. Bush administration, to say nothing of the same type of politicizing that was done during the Clinton administration. Everyone wants to move on. You are beating a dead horse."

"Not so!" declared A.T. "What I have found is not the remnants of some simple mistake or inadvertence. The investigation unfolds a story of a very grave nature, and the findings undermine the very fabric of this country. The damage has been far-reaching and has compromised the standing of the United States in nearly every aspect of our democracy. The acts that have my attention were not accidental but by design and were administered in a very cunning way through a puppet who was probably an unassuming pawn to power brokers of the worst kind. They have used everyone they could, and the public will be shocked to learn the truth."

"Boy, are you angry! It's too bad what they did to you, and I guess I would be more than upset if it had happened to me or a member of my family," said Samantha. "However, our people didn't have anything to do with it, so please give me the material the professor gave you, and I will be on my way. Plus, I will put in a good word for you."

"You'll put in a good word for me? How nice of you!" exclaimed A.T. "Your people have been actively funding many people in the United States. It would be interesting to know exactly what these folks do. From what I understand, it might be possible many of the election laws and many of the regulations designed to control the lobbyists of this country have been violated, and it appears as though your group may be involved."

"Look, it's getting late, and I have a plane to catch. Plus, I need to get to the hospital to check on Gerald," noted Samantha as she checked her wristwatch against the large mall clock that was a part of the obelisk campanile near the center of the mall. "You are obviously very passionate about the investigation that you are doing, but I implore you to leave us out of it. Is there anything I can say to persuade you to change your mind and give me the materials that you received from Professor Brougham?"

"Sorry, but the answer is no," replied A.T. "As I said, it appears your group is far more involved than you may realize. I don't think they have told you everything they are doing, nor do I believe they have been totally honest with you."

"I'll keep that in mind, but just so you know, I've been with the group for over ten years, and I believe in them and in what they represent. Now, I need to get going as I need to check out of my hotel and also see Gerald before I leave town. In the event you do change your mind, let me give you my card," said Samantha presenting a nondescript business card with phone, fax, and email address.

A.T. came around the table and helped her with her coat. While he was wondering how such a gentile-appearing lady could come off so hard-nosed, she smiled and thanked him for the assistance. She then left the mall, and A.T. returned the cups to the coffee vendor in the food court. He realized time was running short for him as well; he needed to travel to the airport to pick up Jacci and his mother-in-law who would soon be returning from the Southwest. A.T. noticed the mall clock again, and he calculated that he had enough time to dictate the events of the day into a document for his report to the Senator. He was quite eager to find out more about the agent who had unwillingly relinquished his credentials to Samantha during the scuffle in Paris. He was also quite curious as to why an agent from a most likely assigned location in the United States would be following him to Paris.

* *

Once back in his office, A.T. began to dictate the new materials into a report. He had previously submitted reports to the Senator and utilized a format similar to one he had used as a prosecutor.

The time flew by during the dictation and organization of the materials. He had already downed quite enough coffee to remain alert for hours; therefore, he moved through the task at hand without break or interruption. Because it was the weekend, a limited number of attorneys were working in the office. Those who were at the office were sufficiently busy with their own tasks of 'catch up.' The hour was approaching for him to pack up what he had on his desk and place it in the office vault for security. He was not about to leave such sensitive material on his desk or in his office. After he locked the vault, he walked through the office and bid a 'good weekend' to the attorneys who were busy working at their desks.

The drive to the airport was uneventful; the snow had subsided, and it appeared the airport traffic was winding down for the week. After parking his car, A.T. went into the terminal and waited at the baggage carousel designated by the monitor for the incoming flight from Sky Harbor. Although the carousel began to turn, it was about ten minutes before any luggage started to move through the conveyor. About fifteen minutes later, he could hear a familiar laugh in the background. Jacci had such a delightful laugh, and whenever he heard it, it would invariably put him in a good mood. Looking toward the sound, he saw Jacci and his mother-in-law riding down the escalator, so he walked over to greet them. When she reached the end of the escalator, Jacci surveyed the area and immediately noticed A.T. They embraced, and although neither of them approved of what was termed PDA (Public Display of Affection), an exception for them was whenever either had returned from travels. They embraced with a long hug followed by an affectionate kiss. A.T. then hugged his mother-in-law.

Jacci noticed the limp in A.T.'s walk and inquired about it, but A.T. replied he would explain the limp later.

While the three of them walked over to the designated carousel, a woman's voice summoning A.T. came from directly behind them. The voice was vaguely familiar to A.T., but he wasn't sure of the identity that matched the voice until he turned and saw her. Samantha was walking at a fairly rapid pace up to A.T., Jacci and Jacci's mother. When Samantha got next to them, she gave a big hug to A.T., and then raised herself up as if to kiss A.T., at which point he attempted to remove himself from her tight hug. As Samantha was being pushed away, she looked at Jacci and exclaimed to A.T. while she was still attempting to hug him, "Aren't you going to introduce me?"

While he removed himself from her attempted embrace, A.T. calmly said to Jacci, "This is Samantha Nguyen-Henderson. She works for a group that she identifies as GGG. Personally, I'm not sure what the group really does, nor am I sure what Samantha really does since I just met her earlier today. Samantha, this is my wife, Jacci."

Jacci, obviously amused, extended her hand to shake Samantha's outstretched hand. Samantha then turned to A.T.'s mother-in-law and inquired, "And you, ma'am, you are –"

"She happens to be my mother-in-law, who is known as 'Sunny,'" A.T. interrupted.

"Hello, Sunny and Jacci. A.T. is being coy. We have known each other for some time." She then looked at A.T. and said, "Wasn't it during your trip about two weeks ago to Kentucky when we first met? And then, of course, we had quite a time in Paris. Didn't we, my dear?"

"Very funny," said A.T. keeping his narrowed eyes on Samantha while he addressed Jacci and Sunny. He explained, "Samantha and another member of her GGG group were tailing us both in Kentucky and in Paris, according to what Samantha told me earlier today." Continuing his glare at Samantha, he said, "Let's not try to make something more out of what really happened than the facts. Just stick to the truth, if you can, Samantha."

"Well, however you want to slant it, A.T.," said Samantha, turning to walk away as if she had been jilted. She turned and said to A.T., "I warned you. But, suit yourself." She turned to Jacci and Sunny and said, "You ladies are free to believe whatever you wish, but I must go now since it is apparent A.T. is going to treat me this way. That is very troubling to me, especially since he has something which belongs to me. I do hope you come to your senses, A.T., and at least return my things to me." After sensing she had made a sufficient scene, Samantha abruptly turned and walked away.

While A.T. was standing somewhat stunned, Sunny laughed and said, "Sounds like you're in some hot water, A.T." She nudged Jacci to see if she could get a reaction from her.

"Maybe more than hot water," said Jacci as she started with her enchanting laugh."

"Listen to me," said A.T. noticing his wife's luggage rolling around the carousel and went to retrieve it. "Today was the first time I met that lady."

Sunny shook her head. "I think that you at least owe Jacci and me a nice 'welcome home' dinner during which you can explain your real relationship with that very attractive lady."

"It's a date, ladies," said A.T.

* *

After dropping the ladies at the house, A.T. proceeded to pick up Remington from the kennel. In addition to an elaborate security system for the home, A.T. and Jacci allowed their one hundred and forty pound Rottweiler-Labrador dog to have free reign over the entire home as an additional measure of security. The dog, along with the security system, was all they felt they needed to adequately protect the home. They also felt comfortable in the fact they never kept anything of real material value at the home. A.T. had developed a practice of never taking casework of any nature to his home, thereby eliminating any chance of a lost or compromised file.

By the time he had returned home with Remington, the ladies had rested. They were in the process of dressing for dinner. A.T. noticed that Jacci was dressed informally; thus, he was able to judge how he would prepare for the evening. While he and Jacci were getting ready, she mentioned she had made reservations at one of their favorite pizza restaurants. It had become one of the more favorite local restaurant chains in the Twin City area. A.T. was ready for a relaxing evening.

The evening was one of the most relaxing times A.T. had experienced since before he had left for Europe several weeks earlier. He was able to get his mind off the investigation and was actually able to laugh with Jacci and Sunny while they watched their humorous waiters. There was no question that the young man deserved a generous tip, and A.T. made sure that such was the case. After all, anyone with such a magnetic personality, along with the prompt service, deserved to be treated well.

Upon returning home, Sunny chose to retire while A.T. and Jacci decided to have a relaxing glass of wine while they listened to one of their favorite operas by Puccini, *Turandot.* Since Puccini died before he completed the opera, there were three versions of the finished work. Of the three, they preferred the version completed by Franco Alfano known as *Alfano I,* which they had once heard performed in St. Paul when they were a young dating couple. Perhaps it was that memory which allowed them to behave toward each other as if time had not changed a thing. When they were alone together, they often felt young and vibrant. They had a tendency to bring the best out in each other. The entire evening was a treat as they relished each other's presence and company.

The next morning was Sunday, and for an additional treat, they decided to attend Mass at the cathedral. After Mass, they ran into A.T.'s friend, Bob Billings. Bob had been the court reporter who traveled with A.T. across the country when they were taking the numerous witness statements for the initial investigation. Bob already knew Jacci, so he said hello. He was then introduced to Sunny. For years A.T. and Bob had worked together. A.T. especially liked Bob because of his extraordinary competence. Plus, he was one of the few court reporters who could still take shorthand statements if his machine was not available or the statement location did not allow for the time or space for a transcriber machine. Bob was getting up in years and had retired, but he would always find time to help A.T. He was fully grey-haired and a bit stooped over now, but in his day, he had been both a swimmer and a soccer player of some acclaim.

The four of them walked to their cars and it started to snow. Christmas was less than two weeks away, and most of the church decorations and the outside holiday decorations of the city were displayed in great splendor. Bob mentioned he needed to speak to A.T., so he was invited to join the three of them for brunch at a nearby restaurant. It was obvious Bob had something on his mind, and from the way he behaved, it seemed urgent. A.T. sensed Bob was reluctant to say anything in front of Jacci and Sunny; therefore, A.T. suggested the ladies engage in the breakfast buffet while he and Bob took a moment or two at the table to visit.

Bob was eager to tell A.T. what he had recently learned from one of the witnesses who had been previously interviewed. Bob explained since the witnesses were instructed they could read the transcripts of the statements before they signed them, they each had received Bob's card, so they could contact him. A witness who had been with the Department of Justice during the Bush administration and who now practiced law privately had called to advise he had been contacted by a couple people with whom he had worked while at Justice. One of the two people had been asked to leave the Department of Justice because of some irregularities traced to his office by the Attorney General. The other had taken over some of the cases of the first and was still working for the DOJ.

Apparently, both of the individuals who had contacted the witness were concerned about some of the emails, memos, and interoffice communiqués they believed the witness still had. As it turned out, the witness still had the documents and was told to destroy them if he valued his future and any career. It was obvious the former Justice attorney, Osborne Leeds, who was now in a D.C. law firm was calling the shots. The witness explained the material he possessed implicated both of the other attorneys in political intrigue whereby the office of the Attorney General was used to target political enemies who had no real criminal involvement. Because of the power of the office of the A.G., those targeted individuals were charged with fictitious crimes in order to eliminate them as they were considered a danger to the "Bushies" and their overall objectives.

A.T. asked if the documents were available or if they had been turned over to the two lawyers who had made the call. Bob advised that the witness stated he turned over the documents but had first made copies for A.T. The witness was especially concerned since some of the documents involved A.T., as well as other innocent individuals who had been targeted. The witness did not want to be a part of any case that targeted innocent individuals, and he did not want to be a part of a cover-up. According to Bob, the witness stated he would meet A.T. and Bob at a prearranged location and would deliver the copies. He also stated he wanted whoever was directing the investigation to know he did not have a willing part in the matter of attempting to set anyone up with a crime. Apparently he wanted to clear his conscience.

Then A.T. inquired if Bob knew where the witness wished to meet. Bob indicated it would be in the Washington D.C. area as the man had taken a job with a law firm there. A.T. advised Bob he would be in D.C. during the coming week. However, he wouldn't have time to stay too long because he planned on returning to the Twin Cities for Christmas. A.T. indicated he would arrange for the lodging and travel but instead of just the two of them, he would ask Allen if he were available to travel along. One of Allen's sons was a detective for the Washington D.C. police department, and A.T. thought it would be helpful if Allen and his son were informed of the visit and subsequent interview. Bob agreed to make contact and promised to call A.T. later that afternoon to confirm the trip and accommodations in D.C.

With the matter of the witness settled, A.T. and Bob decided to head to the buffet line. The brunch was plentiful and generous. After eating perhaps more than appropriate, the four of them left. A.T., Jacci, and Sunny headed for home, where A.T. would begin his arrangements for the forthcoming meetings with the Senator and others in Washington D.C. He first called Allen to see if he would be able to travel along. Next, he contacted one of the Senator's aides whom he knew well enough for a Sunday call. The aide would call A.T. back by the end of the day with meeting times and places. In the interim, Bob had contacted the attorney witness and had determined they would meet him at Dulles International Airport.

When A.T. made the travel arrangements, he thought it was odd the witness wanted to meet at the airport. Bob explained the witness altered his travel plans to New York in order to stay in Washington long enough to meet with A.T. and Bob, thereby accommodating A.T.'s schedule. A.T. then booked the flights. The schedule allowed him a couple days at home to help Jacci prepare the house for the Christmas family gathering. A.T. also booked a hotel for Allen, Bob, and himself in the downtown D.C. area and rented a car for travel. Both he and Allen were quite familiar with Washington D.C. since each had lived in the area many years earlier as they were both government employees in earlier days.

During the time before the travel to Washington D.C., A.T. busied himself with the final touches to his report for the Senator, as well as some file review of various pending cases. He allowed a comfortable amount of time to confer with other members of his office and staff who were actively working on the cases A.T. had assigned to them. Work on the cases seemed to be going well, and he was pleased his attorneys and staff members were efficiently preparing the cases that still involved A.T. Each year he would reserve three or four of the more interesting cases for himself. The time zipped by, and before he realized, it was time to head out to D.C.

The night before his departure, he once again took Jacci and Sunny to one of their favorite restaurants in the Twin City area. The Twin Cities boasted some of the best restaurants in the Midwest and a couple of the finest in the country. For this particular occasion, they decided to treat themselves to one of the best in the area. The atmosphere was relaxing although it took a few minutes to get seated. The restaurant was decorated to the hilt, and it seemed everyone was in a festive mood. Jacci had arranged for them to dine with several other couples in a private area near the back of the restaurant. All of the couples had been friends for many years, and all were set to enjoy the outing that had become an annual event. Jacci would typically plan the evening with a couple of her friends from her former employment and her bridge group. There was always a modest exchange of gifts, and everyone had a great time. It was during this time of year when this particular group would gather to enjoy their long-lasting friendship.

The evening was capped off with everyone enjoying a dessert of individual taste and a toast to 'good health and good fortune.' The night was memorable for many reasons, but when A.T.'s serving of 'banana flambé was spilled by the waiter causing the table to catch fire, the room erupted in uncontrollable laughter at the expense of the poor waiter who apologized profusely. No sooner had the waiter put out the fire on the tablecloth, than the coffee pot he had started on the nearby 'carrier' stove, where the temperature had been set too high, began to boil over. While it was boiling over, someone lifted his glass and proposed a toast to a Merry Christmas and an exciting new year of great adventures and "boiling over" good times. Everyone joined the toast as they concluded a great evening.

The following morning A.T. met with Allen and Bob for their flight to Washington D.C. The trip was to be a precisely choreographed series of events starting with a meeting with the attorney witness after their arrival at Dulles International. Once they had completed that meeting, the three of them would travel to downtown D.C. and get situated at their hotel. Since it was a Saturday, the three of them planned to have dinner with Allen's son and his family at a restaurant in Arlington that was about halfway from downtown to the residence of Allen's son.

Because there was so much sensitive material in the briefcase Jean Paul had given to him, and the case required a code entry for access, A.T. intended to keep the briefcase under his watchful eye the entire time. Upon finding his seat on the plane, A.T. placed the briefcase under the seat directly in front of him.

CHAPTER 15
BOILING OVER

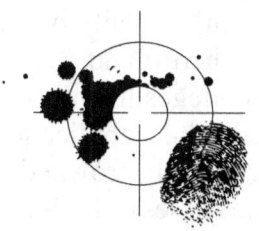

Upon their arrival at Dulles International, A.T., Allen, and Bob exited the designated arrival gate of their flight and shortly after walked into the corridor. Allen's son, Eric, had used his security clearance as a Washington D.C. detective to gain access to the terminal in order to meet them as they arrived. After a warm greeting, the four of them continued down the corridor.

On the way to the main terminal, they were approached by the attorney witness, whom A.T. and Bob immediately recognized. Bob introduced the witness to Allen and his son. The witness, George Orville Felthaus, who went by both George and Orville, was a young, mid-statured attorney with a fair complexion, who had been a part of the George W. Bush political organization in his home state of Florida. He was in his early thirties, just short of six feet tall, and displayed a perpetually positive appearance. As a reward for his political help during the 2004 presidential campaign and due to his relationship with a group of lawyers from South Florida who were known as the 'South Florida Contingent,' Felthaus had been given a job as a staff attorney at the Department of Justice, where he had worked until 2009 when he left for a job with a Washington D.C. law firm.

Felthaus had graduated from Liberty University and Regent Law School. He became known as a witness through the Senator, whose staff had determined Felthaus had received and authored several emails that had come to the attention of Bud Hawthorne. Bud, in turn, had received various items of interest through one of his informants, who wanted to remain anonymous. Once confronted with the emails, Felthaus decided to come forth with a fairly complete story about efforts made to populate the Department of Justice with individuals who shared a unique religious and political philosophy.

The emails, along with the statement by Felthaus, confirmed there had been a concerted effort to place within the Bush Justice Department as many individuals as possible who shared a particular religious advocacy, along with a uniquely conservative view. The practice was active and nearly a daily occurrence at Justice during the tenures of both John Ashcroft and Alberto Gonzales. Applicants who had graduated from colleges like the ones attended by Felthaus were more than preferred while applicants from some of the Ivy League schools were particularly frowned upon. The names of the individuals hired and some names of individuals denied employment because of their lack of certain beliefs were also provided by Felthaus, along with the emails and his testimony.

While Allen and his son excused themselves to visit about family, A.T. and Bob escorted the young attorney to a fairly quiet seating area for a statement. Bob took the statement by shorthand. A.T. couldn't help but reveal his curiosity, so he began by asking, "Tell me, Mr. Felthaus, why did you request we meet you here? We could have utilized a number of more appropriately comfortable places a lot less public."

"That's true, but I particularly chose the airport for two reasons. First, it is very public. I don't think anyone would attempt to do anything to me while everyone is milling around, plus it would be difficult for them to get weapons inside the terminal. I say this because I want you to know I have been threatened. I was told if I spoke to you, my life might be in danger. Some individuals, who want to be sure the information I have is never revealed, know I have already given information to you in an earlier statement. Since I have a good idea who is behind the threats, I take them very seriously. In fact, I have notified the Senator's office, as well as some trusted members of law enforcement. As a result of their concern, I have taken a leave of absence from my job, and I may never return there because some members of the firm have asked me to stop providing information. Between the Senator's office and law enforcement, I will be provided a safe location with protection for up to a year, at which time the Senate hearings should take place. Once I publically testify, it would be far more difficult for them to do anything to me."

"Who are the individuals that have threatened you?"

"I won't tell you. I already told the Senator, along with members of his staff who sat in during my discussions with the Senator."

"You said there were two reasons for our meeting here, and I take it from what you just said the second reason involves your flight plans."

"That's correct. I purposely rescheduled my flight so directly after we visit, I will be able to fly to my initial destination. I will be met by an escort who will locate me in a safe place with a useable identity and a job."

"If you have spoken to the Senator, why are you meeting with us?"

"The Senator wanted my sworn statement taken independently, and he wants the materials I have with me to be made a part of your official investigation and the reported record. When he asked me to contact you, I decided it would be best to contact Bob due to the fact I believe, at least from what I know, all of your phones have been tapped."

After Orville was sworn in as a witness by Bob, who was a certified court reporter in several states as well as Washington D.C., Orville asked if he might provide an initial statement on the record. It was agreed he could make whatever statement he wanted.

Orville began, "Let me first provide you, Mr. Van Doren, with a bit of a warning. Some of the people with whom I have been affiliated have held high level positions in the Department of Justice in the past, and some are still buried within the department, simply waiting for the national political landscape to change back to Republican control. You are a major target, and they regret they were unable to 'get you' the first time. They are still reeling from that and from the complaints you made against some of their brethren. I don't think they are planning any physical injury to you, but they are definitely going to try to bring you down. Most likely that will come out of the Department of Justice once they find a way back to the top positions. Hence, if you have felt a bit paranoid, you have good reason. You are a target."

"That doesn't come as a surprise to me, but for the sake of this investigation, I will need the names and the positions of the people who would want to do this to me or to any others who step in their way. Can you provide that kind of information?" inquired A.T.

"Yes, I can," commented Orville handing a package to A.T.

"This package contains some emails and some letters identifying the specific individuals who are after you and others. There are a couple of 'thumb drives' that contain some recordings of conversations I made after this entire matter took on a life of its own. It has grown way beyond anything I could have imagined. You will see in each of the conversations, I am a participant, and I believe each recording was made properly under the law. These guys are all attorneys, and they are sometimes considered the brain trust of a political operation that is taking place and has been in place for years behind the scenes within the Republican Party. They have separated themselves a bit from other political operatives within the Republican Party because they are convinced they are much smarter than what they are calling 'political hacks.'"

"So, I take it they don't just dislike my political thinking or political contacts. Apparently, they also do not like the thinking of some of their own kind within the current Republican Party," said A.T.

"It goes way beyond what you are doing and well beyond you personally. You just got in the way when you didn't fold at the time they first had you charged with a federal offense. They didn't expect it to turn out the way that it did, and they didn't expect you to survive the charges. However, they were never seriously interested in you until you started speaking out against the Republican Party and began irritating them with some of your revelations. After you were able to overcome the charges, and once you started to investigate them, they included you in their current plans to destroy the reputation of anyone who got in their way. Your investigation has been the last straw. Let's say you've hit a nerve or two."

"Perhaps some of the nerves I have hit involve investigative matters the Senator and his friend, Bud, have dropped into my lap."

"I don't know about that," said Orville, "but you are now considered one of the individuals whom this group of attorneys intends to discredit and otherwise target."

"What about you?" A.T. inquired. "It would seem you would be in greater danger than I am. As I understand it, you have some critical emails that delineate potential criminal offenses. May I presume some of that information would be contained in the package you just provided?"

"We will get to the package, which definitely does contain information exposing criminal activity. You have to understand these people are also attorneys who have worked with the Justice Department. Their personal goals reach well beyond any agenda of the Bush administration and well beyond anything Alberto Gonzales or President Bush and others in the Bush administration envisioned. These clever guys wanted to completely control the Department of Justice for themselves and build a dynasty of power. As I've said, they have their own agenda. At first, I was a full believer in what they wanted to accomplish from both a political and religious perspective because it seemed logical that the 'right' kind of thinking be in place at Justice. However, the more I listened to them, the more I realized these guys were not at all religious. Deceptively, they were merely using those of us who were. The main principals involved are only interested in political power they believe they can have through their ultimate control of the Justice Department. They have very close ties to elected officials in Congress and the U.S. Senate. The group of 'friends' they have extends to governors, other elected officials, non-elected officials and some extremely wealthy individuals. I believe they also are working with some groups out of Europe."

"What about your safety?" A.T. again considered. "You have mentioned me, but what about you?"

"I am comfortable knowing the Senator has made arrangements for my safety. Besides, I believe I must do the right thing as Jesus would have wanted it. The Lord would have wanted me to come forward with the truth. I want my conscience to be clear, since I believe more harm than good will come from the attorneys who were taking control of the Justice Department under W."

"Well, let's look at the material you have given me, so I will be able to ask you some questions about this group of attorneys and –"

"No!" interrupted Orville. "If you don't mind, you can examine the package later when you have time to do so. I will need to give my statement without direct reference to the material I just provided. My statement will need to be extemporaneous as much as possible. I do have a flight to catch, so please let me supply the information you need from me that I think the Senator wants included in the record."

"But for the record, I will need you to identify each of the emails and discuss at least to some degree the contents of each of them," requested A.T.

"Well, in that case, we better get with it because there are 344 emails contained in the package," commented Orville. After hearing that comment, A.T. immediately removed the stack of emails and began to have Mr. Felthaus identify some of the more significant ones, along with a brief explanation of each. It was a tedious effort and time consuming as Felthaus had warned, but they finally accomplished the goal due to the 'spot on' questions. It was more than apparent to A.T. what he had received from Mr. Felthaus was a treasure trove of information that could definitely be used for the Senator's investigation, as well as the ultimate prosecution of a significant number of lawyers who were indeed trying to take control of the Department of Justice for their own political objectives.

Nearly two hours elapsed. During that time, people would come and go, with some of them inquiring as to what they were doing. Inevitably, once they saw Bob taking notes, the patrons of the airport terminal who noticed them began to assume A.T. and Bob were newspaper reporters. Finally, Orville insisted he summarize the remainder of his statement, considering he would soon need to prepare to leave for his flight to New York.

"Okay, sorry to take so much of your time, but we needed to properly identify and review some of the more important emails. Please feel free to provide whatever statement you wish. At this point, I believe that we have most of what we need," said A.T.

"As I said, in addition to this group of attorneys having the intent to put pressure on various individuals at the Justice Department once they can regain control of it, they are interested in ultimately controlling the DOJ completely. They have a plan in place to accomplish this end, and they believe by controlling Justice, they can control the judicial system of the United States. They are working with others, including some powerful Republican Senators and a few Congressional members who believe they can also mold and control the judiciary through the Justice Department and through court appointments to the bench over time by virtue of their control of the DOJ. The plan they hatched over twenty years ago was coming into fruition during the George W. Bush administration. They were very patient and, as I mentioned earlier, the timing was perfect under the tenures of John Ashcroft and Alberto Gonzales. There are so many of their philosophical brethren in place already due to the multitude of appointments and hires made during the Bush presidency that they believe they will have the ability to accomplish their objective of control over Justice if they can get another sitting president similar to George W. Bush. They loved the fact he hated lawyers. Therefore, W. was more than willing to see the DOJ change, especially under his friend, Alberto."

"You knew this because of your position?"

"The group to which I belonged believed once Democrats took control of either the presidency or of Congress, the 'salting' of the Justice Department would be far more difficult," responded Mr. Felthaus. "Therefore, as much as possible was done to position 'right thinking' attorneys during W.'s tenure. People like Karl Rove did what they could to try and force the Democrats into nominating Hillary Clinton because they were sure they could prevent her from getting elected. They were surprised Obama got the nomination. Once he did, people like Rove exclaimed, 'We can't lose!' Rove and others never thought there was a chance Obama would ever get elected. And, Rove along with others, never thought President Obama would defeat Mitt Romney, who they believed was another W. That way my friends at the DOJ could continue what they had started. Several key attorneys from our group were placed in charge of elections. Personally, I believe fate had its hand in bringing about Obama's election and re-election. Let me assure you if the Republican ticket of McCain-Palin had gotten elected or if the ticket of Romney-Ryan had gotten elected, my friends from South Florida and elsewhere would have moved even more aggressively to lock down the Justice Department. No one can imagine how deep-seated their plans already are."

Then A. T. asked, "So, has the Obama administration made any effort to purge the system?"

"Not at this point, and I don't think they can. Our people are so well entrenched and cannot be removed without cause. As I said, there are so many individuals within the Department of Justice already who cannot be legally removed; it is fair to say the plan by these attorneys to take control of the Justice Department is well under way. Over time, and if the right Republican Attorney General is back in place any time soon, the plan will continue to unfold. Some day the Justice Department of the United States will be so powerful it will be able to ruin the lives and the careers of anyone who steps in the way. Also, as you know, a very high percentage of the candidates for judicial positions come from the Justice Department. Therefore, the list of candidates for judicial positions will most likely be from the lists of individuals who are of the 'right' philosophy and who have been placed into positions within the Department of Justice in one way or another. Besides, who will ever contest them; after all, they are attorneys that hold positions in the DOJ. To them, the Obama Justice Department is a temporary setback. If you think about it, it is quite a plan."

"I have to agree from what I've discovered through the investigation," said A.T. "I've tried to tell the Senator I thought such was the case, but he had me following other leads that involved banking, political campaign contributions, paramilitary groups, and other political activities including the Republican Party itself."

"The Senator is not wrong," insisted George Orville Felthaus. "The efforts by these groups to take control of the Justice Department are only a part of it. Originally, a plan was set in motion by some seasoned politicians to take control little by little of every major department of the government with a particular emphasis on State, Defense, Treasury, Commerce, Interior, and the Intelligence Community that includes all agencies, particularly the FBI and CIA, the EPA, and Justice. They even had plans for the Department of Agriculture. The plan to take over the various offices was masterminded over thirty years ago under people who were in nonelected positions under Nixon. From what I know, he wasn't even aware of its happening. That's what I have come to understand because some of the people in my group go back that far. In the process, the plan was to take control of the Republican Party as well. For all intents and purposes that has already happened. Personally, I don't think it can be undone because too many of the same people and those of the same philosophy already have control of the Republican Party. I have been offered a position there in order to buy me off, but my conscience has gotten the better of me."

"You said the Senator is right in having the investigation reach beyond the Department of Justice, and you claim other departments are involved as well?"

"Absolutely! The Department of Defense had been seriously compromised both during the George W. Bush administration and before. So much of what the Defense Department had done was privatized with private groups actually having about as much money through the contracting process that Defense had itself. Several private paramilitary groups have profited greatly and are now extremely powerful both financially and politically. In some cases, their equipment and their personnel are as good as or better than the government's. The paramilitary groups are so deeply entrenched, and the government is so dependent upon them; it would be nearly impossible to unwind that entire process. What's worse is the government cannot function without these groups. It is very worrisome since efforts are now underway to try to tie these paramilitary groups that are contractors of the U.S. government to the many loosely organized regional paramilitary groups across the United States. Ironically, the leaders of the paramilitary contractors have similar philosophies to the guys I have been dealing with at Justice, and they all have similar philosophies to the people running the Republican Party."

"That doesn't surprise me," A.T. remarked. "It is not the Republican Party I've been a part of in the past. Instead of it being the party of Abe Lincoln and Teddy Roosevelt, it has become the party of who knows what."

"What may surprise you is there are now meetings taking place that would tie the paramilitary groups together for an even stronger power base. They hope and expect it will have the ability to manage a major part of the political thinking of this country, along with the administration of justice in this country, with the means to enforce a particular agenda through force, if necessary. Ultimately, there is a plan for these groups to function as an enforcement arm for the DOJ. Just think about what the results might be if a major political party, along with organized paramilitary operations, were coupled with control of the justice department," Orville cautioned.

"It would be quite devastating and difficult to bring into check. The United States would probably end up being nothing better than a banana republic. What evidence do you have the attorneys that have infiltrated the Department of Justice have paired up with the paramilitary groups and the Republican Party? I don't think the Senator realizes the extent of the infiltration of the Department of Justice."

"You will see confirmation of that from the documents and other material in the large envelope I have given you," stated Orville. "Please guard that material with your life. The people behind the efforts to establish their own shadow government within our government are serious, and they now feel they have the ability to coordinate the factions mentioned."

"What about funding all of these endeavors?" A.T. asked.

"For much of it, they are using the U.S. government's own treasury in one way or another. As I mentioned, they probably have just short of two hundred people they know they can count on within various positions at Justice. They are already friendly and in step philosophically with some very powerful paramilitary groups that receive obscene sums of money working as contractors for the U.S. government. Plus, there are the political contributions the Republican Party receives from corporations, along with contributions received by certain Republican candidates. Most of the big money comes from corporate interests; however, there is a major outside interest that I have heard about, but I have no clue who or what it is. If I understand it correctly, it involves old-time foreign money. I overheard some conversations about foreign money from a major source that had both a religious and a political agenda for the United States. Don't forget the religious interests here in the States. Sadly, I must admit those funds are substantial, and they are coming from parties I had agreed with until I saw what they were planning to do to our country. I want my hands to be clean of what is going on and what is about to happen."

"Can you provide me with more detail? So far you have touched on a number of subjects that have many people worried and concerned," interjected A.T.

"Documentation pertaining to my information is in the envelope. You will need to sort it all out in conjunction with the investigation you are doing for the Senator." After having said that, Orville looked at his watch and glanced at the large clock near them in the terminal. "Time has run out. You have my statement and the materials. I do need to make a restroom stop before I head out to my flight. If you need more information or an additional statement from me, you can contact me on a secure phone the Senator gave me himself. Please do not call me on any of your phones, A.T., because I have very good reason to believe all of your phones have been compromised. Now, permit me to run off to the washroom and head over to board my plane."

At that point, George Orville Felthaus shook hands with both A.T. and Bob. A.T. and Bob said goodbye and advised Orville he could review his statement for accuracy once it had been reduced to typing. Then Mr. Felthaus grabbed his carry-on and headed down the corridor to the nearest facility.

As Orville walked to the restroom three individuals dressed in maintenance clothing followed his moves. While one of the individuals pushing a rolling dumpster followed Orville into the men's room, another placed cleaning cones at the entry and proceeded into the rest room. The third individual stood at the entry and waved to other patrons stating the floors were going to be cleaned and waxed as routine maintenance. Orville yelled to the maintenance man that he would be a minute, whereupon he was told he could take his time. Since Orville was already in the stall, he did not see one of the other maintenance men checking under the stall doors to see if anyone else was occupying a stall. Finding no one in a stall and after the last patron left, one of the maintenance men went to the door to be certain no one else entered. The remaining maintenance man then disabled the restroom camera in the lavatory area.

When Orville exited the stall, he went to the lavatory to wash his hands, first setting his case down nearby. While checking his hair, the one large maintenance man calmly approached Orville, smiling at him as he turned on the water at the next lavatory. Abruptly, and with the rapid movement of a cat, the large maintenance man brought his right hand up to Orville's face and immediately placed a rag over Orville's mouth and nose. After a struggle and a few breaths, Orville fell to the floor. He was picked up by the maintenance man, dragged to the nearest stall, and placed in a sitting position against the inside wall. The maintenance man again placed the rag over Orville's nose and held it there until Orville passed out. He then slipped out of his maintenance outfit, thereby revealing a full dress suit of clothing underneath. He tossed his maintenance overall in the dumpster, as well as a black toupee that covered his bald head and removed a fake mustache. He grabbed Orville's bag and started to the door.

A significant "burn" type of scar ran from over the left eyebrow upward onto the center of the bald head. He also displayed a scar under his left eye. He nodded his head and winked a beady eye to the other two maintenance men who left the cones in place as they both stepped back into the restroom where each went to a different stall to change. Once the overalls were removed, the two revealed casual attire. One stepped into the stall where Orville lay motionless and checked Orville's limp body. He nodded to his partner and shut the door.

* *

After discussing Orville's statement for about fifteen minutes, A.T. and Bob decided they should join Allen and Eric. They motioned for Allen and Eric to join them as they walked toward the center of the terminal. With the presumption that Orville had said his goodbyes and headed out to catch his own flight, the four of them proceeded to pick up the rental car and their additional baggage on their way out of the terminal. Allen decided to ride with his son, Eric. They would then meet A.T. and Bob at the predetermined dinner location in a couple of hours.

A.T. and Bob enjoyed the drive over what they fondly remembered as the Washington Parkway to downtown Washington D.C. and proceeded to their hotel.

While at the hotel in the afternoon, A.T. was able to integrate the Felthaus material into the report. When he finished his report, A.T. called Bob, grabbed the briefcase, and went to the hotel lobby to meet Bob for the ride to the dinner engagement.

During the drive, they discussed some of their earlier days in Washington when they had taken statements of witnesses that had been assigned to them in regard to a corruption case and a class action lawsuit which ultimately led to a major campaign contribution case involving a large private U.S. corporation and various politicians on both sides of the aisle. There were a number of humorous incidents during those cases causing both A.T. and Bob to laugh as they neared the location for the evening dinner. Upon parking the car themselves, A.T. took the briefcase and the two entered the restaurant. The maitre d' escorted them to the table where Allen, Eric, and Eric's wife, Sharon, were already seated.

After A.T. and Bob were introduced to Sharon by Allen's son, Eric, A.T. inquired, "Where are the grandchildren? I expected to meet them as well."

"We thought it best under the circumstances they remain at home," said Allen.

"If I may ask what circumstances...are they in one of their school activities?" inquired A.T. placing the briefcase on the floor near his chair.

"Oh, I'm sure you wouldn't know, but we have some distressing news," said Eric.

"What news?"

"It seems your witness, Mr. Felthaus, was discovered in the restroom," Eric added.

"What do you mean discovered in the restroom?" Bob asked.

"As usual, I had the scanner on in my car," Eric explained. "Just as we were coming up the driveway to my house, we heard a report that a man described as a fair-haired individual in his mid-thirties was found in one of the men's restrooms at the airport. It seemed odd, and although the description of the man was abbreviated, it sounded strangely familiar to me, so I called in to my office to see if I could get some details. It was then I learned the man found at the airport was identified as an Orville Felthaus. I tried to get as much information as I could. I also informed the department that we had met him at the airport earlier when he was in the process of providing a sworn statement. As you might have expected, the department wants to get a statement from you. No doubt they will want to know what kind of statement you were taking and why. We'll need a copy of that statement."

"My God!" exclaimed A.T. "I can't believe it. Although Felthaus said he had been threatened, I never expected anyone would do anything to him. For Christ's sake, we were in a very public airport."

"Apparently, several people located him in the restroom and drove out the other individuals. There is some video recorded before one of the assailants disabled the system. It appears as though there were three of them. There was no evidence of a weapon, but some clothing and a rag with chloroform were found in a dumpster. Virtually every police department in the area, along with TSA, is trying to get some identity on the three individuals who were partially seen on the video. I've been asked to work on the case in cooperation with all metro units and with TSA. At some point, I will need to take an official statement from both you and Bob. It is a bit fortuitous I hold the position that I do. Although I must strictly follow proper procedures, we can work out the timing."

"Naturally we will cooperate in every way possible," said A.T. "However, the statement taken from Mr. Felthaus for the Senator will need to be transcribed and will be provided to the Senator. I'm not sure I can just give that statement to you. I will need the Senator's okay."

"With all due respect, the Senator is not going to be able to prevent us from having a copy of the statement by Mr. Felthaus. My department will need a copy of the statement in order to assess it for motive. Because of the circumstances, I have been assigned to the case; therefore, I will need a copy of the statement and both you and Bob will need to provide a statement to me as well. Right now, let's order some food before we speak of details," said Eric as he motioned for the waiter to come to the table.

After all orders had been placed, A.T. attempted to reach the Senator but was unsuccessful. He also left messages for two of the Senator's aides who were also unavailable.

"As you know," explained A.T., "Bob will need to have some time to transcribe the statement of Mr. Felthaus because it was taken down in Bob's own system of shorthand."

"Well, Bob, how long will it take you to reduce the statement to a transcript?" asked Eric.

Being quite astute and cautious by nature, Bob realized he needed to answer as carefully as possible. He knew he had already transcribed most of the statement earlier at the hotel. Not wanting to leave a copy on the hard drive of his computer he left at the hotel, he had placed it on the memory stick he carried with him. Keeping this information in mind, Bob decided to hedge. He said, "It will probably take a couple of days after I get back to the Twin Cities before I can get a complete copy out."

"That's not good enough. We'll set you up at the department headquarters tonight, so we can have a copy before the end of the day. Also, after we have eaten, I will need to have the two of you provide a statement of your own. I'm really sorry about this, but at minimum we have an assault and possibly even a homicide, depending on the condition of Felthaus, and that's my line of work. Both of your statements and the reported statement of Mr. Felthaus will need to be in my hands before midnight at the latest," urged Eric.

"Couldn't it wait until sometime tomorrow?" urged A.T. "I have an early morning meeting with the Senator, and I thought after I spoke with him, we would have a better idea about timing the Felthaus statement."

"Sorry, but I can't wait that long. I will need to get your statement, Bob's statement, and a copy of the Felthaus printed statement by midnight. Did you say you were meeting with the Senator tomorrow? Isn't that a bit unusual? Tomorrow is Sunday."

"Actually, it is not unusual. It is generally early on Sundays when the Senator meets privately with me, and it's usually at a major landmark here in Washington," commented A.T.

"That's interesting," said Eric. "Nevertheless, I will need to get statements from you and Bob tonight, and I would like to have a copy of the Felthaus statement yet tonight as well. I will ride with you and Bob to the detective bureau where we will take the statements. Feel free to contact the Senator's office as you need to, but we will need to act tonight on this matter because of the nature of the situation."

After Eric's comment, the first course of the evening meal, mostly salads, was served. While the waiter was moving about the table, A.T. received a call from a member of the Senator's staff. He excused himself from the table after making certain Bob kept the briefcase for him.

A.T. went to the outside of the restaurant to complete his conversation with the staff member. While he was explaining the bizarre set of events that had occurred upon his arrival in Washington, he noticed a large bald-headed man dressed in a dark suit just outside the restaurant. The man seemed to be about six feet four or taller. As the man lit a cigarette, A.T. noticed he had what appeared to be a scar just below his left eye. He also had what appeared to be either a birthmark or a fairly large burn type of scar, possibly a former burn, above his left eyebrow. It extended partly over the front of his bald or shaven head. The man pretended to be observing the young valet who was parking cars; however, it seemed apparent to A.T. the man was trying to listen to A.T.'s conversation. A.T. finished his discussion with his back turned to the man and then hung up the phone and walked back to the entrance.

The bald man stepped in front of A.T.'s path and inquired, "Would you like a cigarette?"

"No thanks," said A.T. as he maneuvered around toward the door.

"Well, I just wanted to talk to a friendly face and you look friendly. You see I'm from out of town and came in to visit with some lawyers about a case I have. You don't happen to be a lawyer, by chance?" asked the man.

"Yes, I am a lawyer. Now, please excuse me, I need to get back to my table," said A.T.

"Well, I'm a lawyer too, and I'm referring a case to a large Washington D.C. firm that specializes in stolen property and slanderous statements made by people who don't do the proper research. What type of law do you practice? Of course, I am assuming you are a practicing lawyer and not one of those lawyers who gets himself involved in politics," probed the man.

"Sorry," pleaded A.T., "but I need to get back to my guests. They are waiting for me, and it appears you are blocking the door."

"Oh, forgive me, but I thought you might be interested in talking about stolen property or slander. That's my specialty," continued the man.

"Sorry, but I really don't have the time to discuss such subjects. Besides, those are not subjects of interest to me. Now, I really must get back to my table."

"I thought those might be subjects of interest to you. Here, let me get the door for you."

Just then two fortunate events occurred. The door opened, and Allen came out looking for A.T. In addition, A.T.'s phone rang. Allen stepped around the man and stood next to A.T. while A.T. answered the phone.

Stepping farther away from the door, he continued, "Yes, Senator. What I told Lisa is true. It all happened since we got to the airport. We are at dinner now, but we will be heading downtown to the detective bureau as soon as we are finished. We have been asked to provide a statement. No. We don't know if he is conscious or even dead... Yes, we did get it, along with the materials... The detective bureau wants everything we have... Well, do what you can with a call, but I am pretty sure they will want everything Felthaus provided. I presume he's in the hospital or morgue. Isn't that normal procedure? Yes, we will still meet as planned, but I thought you should be aware of the recent chain of events... Okay, I'll see you then."

Upon finishing his call, A.T. with Allen at his side, turned and noticed the bald man had worked his way fairly close to them. He observed that A.T. and Allen were looking rather intently at him when he said, "I can see you gentlemen are busy, so I apologize if I seemed a bit forward in trying to strike up a conversation earlier." The bald man then began walking down the sidewalk. Both A.T. and Allen observed two other men who seemed to be waiting for the bald man at the end of the sidewalk. Since they thought it was an unusual encounter, they told everyone at the table in the restaurant what they had experienced.

After hearing what happened, Eric telephoned the detective bureau and went outside the restaurant to see if he could observe the individuals whom A.T. and Allen had described. He walked up and down the sidewalk but did not observe anyone in the area, except for the parking valet who was pacing about the front entrance while waiting for the next customer. Eric inquired of the valet whether he had seen where the men had gone and was not surprised the valet was unable to help.

Eric returned to the table and explained the conversation A.T. had with the man seemed very unusual under the circumstances; therefore, Eric asked for an undercover car by the Arlington police department and an unmarked car by the Washington D.C. detective bureau to be dispatched to the area in order to scour the vicinity for three men. The camera recording from the airport did provide some decent footage of two of the men, but neither of them was bald. Eric felt there might be a possible connection between the man A.T. had encountered and the two men he had seen down the sidewalk; consequently, he ordered the area to be combed for a possible lead.

After dinner was finished, Allen and Sharon left for Eric and Sharon's home while A.T., Bob, and Eric headed to the detective bureau in downtown Washington D.C. Eric explained that all of the departments, including the Capital police, worked on such matters as a homicide with a very smooth method of cooperation, sharing information quite readily with each other. He also explained TSA would have a representative at the detective bureau, along with a number of other related law enforcement agencies. When they arrived, they were escorted to a conference room and inquiry was made of A.T.'s briefcase. He explained it was a secure case with highly classified information for the Senator. That seemed to satisfy everyone present, so he kept the briefcase.

Before the interview began, a representative from the Senator's office was permitted to join. A.T. recognized the Senator's aide, Lee, and introduced him to Bob, Eric, the plainclothes individual from TSA, and another detective who had joined them in the conference room. During a general conversation among the room participants, the door opened and everyone sat stunned. Entering the room was a TSA investigator, who was leading none other than a very alive Orville Felthaus into the room. Everyone rose to a standing position simultaneously. A.T. was closest to the door and exclaimed, "Orville, from what we were told, we all thought that you were dead. It's good to see you are still with us!"

"I feel like I'm dead or near dead," said Orville. "I've been at the hospital for the last several hours where they gave me some medication which I've chosen not to use. I feel rather sick from what they forced me to breathe at the airport, and I'm fighting a major headache."

"Should you even be up and around?"

"Everyone felt it was necessary I be moved from the hospital, and the doctors saw no reason not to release me. The police are moving me to a safe location as soon as possible, but first they wanted me to stop by here for an official statement. I wanted to see you guys to let you know I'm still around. Since we all seem to be on the same side, no one had any issues with my talking to you first before they find a safe place for me. Everything I had with me was taken by the guys who assaulted me and that included my plane ticket, along with details of the identity materials and location items the Senator had lined up for me."

"Does the Senator's office know?" inquired A.T.

"I didn't," exclaimed Lee, the Senator's aide.

"The Senator probably didn't have time to tell you, Lee, since I just now telephoned him. He knew you would be here and asked that you call him directly. Obviously, something needs to be done about the other arrangements you made for me," said Orville Felthaus.

Before Lee could respond, Eric interrupted and said, "Don't do anything just yet about those arrangements since we want to see if someone tries to make any contact with the company where Orville was set up for employment, and we want to stake out the condominium where Orville was going to stay. We believe we might be able to catch one or two of these guys, so let me speak with the Senator about the arrangements he made for Orville before you do anything."

"Let me call the Senator, if that's okay," said Lee.

"Let's go to my office," said Eric. We will speak with him together on a speaker phone. Since he knows Orville is alive, we will all need to work together to keep the lid on this matter. Actually, I didn't expect to tell A.T. or Bob, but the Senator said it would be okay to do so since they were working on a confidential basis for the Senator on matters specifically related to Mr. Felthaus."

"What about the statement Mr. Felthaus gave at the airport? Do you still need it?" inquired A.T.

"That issue remains undecided, but I have spoken to the Senator. At this point, we've agreed you do not need to provide Mr. Felthaus's statement since we can now speak with him ourselves. However, we will still need statements from both you and Bob before the night is out," commented Eric as he and Orville left for his office.

After Eric left, both A.T. and Bob provided statements about what they had observed at the airport and at the restaurant. The details of the Felthaus statement were not discussed as it was anticipated that at a future date the Senator would agree to give up the statement. However, for the time being, the Felthaus statement was to remain confidential for the Senator's office and the committee.

A.T. and Bob took Eric to his home after the statements; they then proceeded back to their hotel for the night. The plan was to meet Allen back at the hotel restaurant the next morning for brunch at about 11:00, after A.T. had finished his meeting with the Senator.

Once back at the hotel, A.T. and Bob decided to have a nightcap in the hotel lounge. They were warned to not discuss the fact Orville Felthaus was alive and well. In fact, both A.T. and Bob were warned that because of the information they had received from Mr. Felthaus, they too might be in danger. They were cautioned to be extremely careful. A.T. was happy the briefcase had continued to remain with him.

At the hotel bar, A.T. decided he needed something hot and sweet, so he ordered an "Irish Coffee." Bob thought it sounded good, and he ordered the same. When they were having a second round, they observed an altercation in the nearby lobby. With their beverages and the briefcase in hand, they went to the entrance of the bar as it opened to the lobby and observed two men in suits taking a man down to the floor. The two men were police officers who cuffed the man on the floor. After he was cuffed, one of the undercover men ran out the door as if pursuing another individual. A.T. asked a nearby patron, an attractive woman who appeared to be in her mid-thirties, what had happened. In an animated and gushing manner the woman explained there had been three men in the lobby earlier, and as they headed toward the bar area, the two undercover detectives grabbed the one man while the other two ran out.

"She seemed to be pretty excited about what happened," commented Bob, while he watched Allen and Eric walk over from the desk of the concierge.

"We thought it might be a good idea to keep an eye on the two of you, and it paid off," said Eric. "The video from the airport matched two of the men who were just here and will now be in custody in regard to the Felthaus matter. One was cuffed here in the lobby, and the other will be caught because we had a couple of men directly outside."

"For that good bit of detective work, we are both grateful, aren't we, Bob?" prodded A.T., who noticed that Bob had wandered back over to the attractive lady. When Bob started an additional conversation with her, A.T. called out, "Bob, we need you over here."

A.T. said to Bob, "It would be a good idea to minimize your conversations with other patrons since you have no idea who they are or whether we can trust anyone under the circumstances."

"I know," said Bob. "But she was so excited about what happened. I was trying to comfort her. Besides, she was so 'hot and sweet.'"

"When it comes to 'hot and sweet,' let's stick to our drinks," instructed A.T., while turning to Allen and Eric to see if they were interested in a nightcap. Because Eric was now off duty and had heard over his radio that both fugitives were now in custody, he and Allen agreed to join A.T. and Bob for a nightcap.

They decided that they had enough excitement for one day. Allen and Eric headed out for Eric's home, while A.T. and Bob headed to the hotel guest office and computers in order to wrap up some details by using the thumb drives they brought along.

Once finished, they met at the hotel office center and sent the electronic version to the secure cloud vault system. They destroyed the hard copy of the transcript in the shredder that had been available. Bob noted even if someone would attempt the impossible task of piecing together the hard copy of the transcript, it would be nearly impossible to decode since over the years Bob had developed his own system of phonetic transcription.

While Bob was finishing the destruction of the hard copy of the transcript, A.T. made certain he made an extra copy of a portion of the new materials that would be provided both to Bud Hawthorne, pursuant to the earlier agreement with Bud and the Senator as well as a copy of a portion of the new materials A.T. planned to provide to Blaine Jeffers. As a part of the methodology for maintaining the security of these sensitive items, A.T. took great pains to see that all of the items were transferred to the secure multi-server cloud vault system. Once finished, they left for their respective rooms for the evening. Although it was difficult to sleep, A.T. did his best, knowing that he would need to meet the Senator at 6:45 the next morning.

CHAPTER 16
HOT AND SWEET

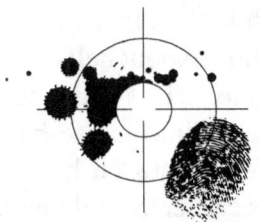

The next morning arrived more quickly than anyone wanted, especially for A.T., who awakened at 5 a.m. after a fitful night consumed by concern over the contents of the briefcase that seemed to grow more and more sensitive with each passing day. Everything, including the newly acquired material from former Justice Department Attorney Orville Felthaus which he had placed into the briefcase for the Senator, was still in place.

In preparing to go out for the day, A.T. felt reassured in just over an hour, the briefcase and all of the original documents would be in the hands of his friend, the Senator. His copies of the complete materials were on the independent hard drive in a bank safety deposit box and on the multi-server cloud vault system at a co-location bunker.

He was happy the day of the meeting with the Senator was finally here and no additional instances relating to the documents had occurred. He and Bob had decided the night before that they would meet at the hotel restaurant for an abbreviated breakfast as they would later be meeting with Allen and Eric for an 11:00 brunch. Bob had agreed to drive A.T. to the Lincoln Memorial for his meeting with the Senator. Then Bob would give himself a tour of the sights in Washington D.C. because he had not been at The Mall area for several years.

At the designated time of 6:45 a.m., Bob dropped A.T. at the foot of the Lincoln Memorial. In the distance, a lone siren wailed; it was probably an ambulance on its way to a hospital. Overhead, a plane rumbled as it was no doubt either flying in or out of Reagan National. Birds chirped away, and a squirrel chatted in the area of The Mall. Enjoying the fresh crisp air, he took a deep breath and turned to head up the long stairway.

A.T.'s only real concern was the briefcase and how it might appear to any of the security personnel in the area of the Memorial. Looking to the top of the stairs, he noticed there were only two people, whom he was certain were security guards. One of them started walking down the stairs toward A.T., while the other moved to the top of the stairs directly above A.T.'s position. About halfway up the first tier, someone called from street level up to A.T. It was Lee, the Senator's aide, who had just exited from a black limo at the base of the Memorial. The limo must have just arrived because it had not been there when Bob dropped A.T. off moments earlier. Simultaneously, the Senator got out of the other side of the limo and was waving to the man coming down the stairs toward A.T. The man stopped, nodded to the Senator, and started back to his former position.

"The Senator would like to have you join us in the limo for a short ride first. Then the two of you will be able to have your private meeting back here at the Memorial," said Lee.

"I'll come right back down," acknowledged A.T. thinking to himself: *Great, I get to ride in one of those cramped limos.* A.T. detested limos since every one he had been in was very uncomfortable. The seating was always bad, the space was poorly designed, and the ride was usually bumpy. When Lee opened the door for A.T. to enter, he was instructed to sit in the back seat next to the Senator. Immediately, he noticed how comfortable and spacious the car was; then he recalled that the only limos that he had ridden in before were either airport or hotel shuttles. Lee positioned himself across from A.T. and sat down next to Lisa, the Senator's staff member, whom A.T. had telephoned the night before from outside the restaurant in Alexandria regarding the Felthaus matter.

"How have you been, my good friend?" inquired the Senator, extending his hand to A.T. who placed the briefcase on the floor. The two of them vigorously shook hands.

"I've probably been less stressed and more myself on the other occasions when we've been together," said A.T.

"I have no doubt about that! How are Jacci and the family?"

"Fine, Senator, and how's your family?"

"Just fine," exclaimed the Senator in his somewhat raspy voice. "As you know, my children are all older now with children in college and beyond. It is just a task keeping up with all of their activities and travels, to say nothing of their budding careers. But it's keeping me young, and the family gives me my best touch with reality since nothing here in Washington seems very real anymore."

"I can believe that from all I read and hear," commented A.T. as he noticed the Senator motion for the driver to begin a predetermined route.

Apparently, the Senator intended to have a rolling conversation not only with A.T. but with Senate aides, Lee Mattson, Lisa Browning and the driver, Samuel Bernstein, taking part as well. A.T. recognized the driver, Samuel Bernstein, who had been used in the past for a number of special assignments and deliveries for the Senator. It was obvious the driver was a very trusted friend, as well as an employee.

"A.T., let me apologize for getting you more involved than was originally planned," said the Senator. "Please realize this happened because of our past work together and because of the trust I have in you. No one else, other than Bud, had gotten so far into this matter. Since Bud does not have the training or background for this type of work, I needed you to expand the investigation into a couple of matters that were being tied to the work you were already doing. Plus, I knew you were motivated due to what happened to you under the Bush administration."

"Thanks for those kind words. It is true I am motivated due to what was done to me. Of course, at the time you asked me to expand the investigation and look into certain paramilitary and financial operations, I was baffled. However, I am now getting a bit of an appreciation as to how and why they are connected," A.T. responded.

"Unfortunately, as you now know, for the past several decades there has been a concerted effort by hidden interests living in the shadows to drive the government and the country into a specific direction intended to promote and follow a unique philosophy. Since the *Citizens United* case was decided by the United States Supreme Court, large financial interests have taken the funding of the political process in this country to a new and very dangerous level. That decision essentially emasculated the 'McCain-Feingold Campaign Reform Act' and now large corporations, certain alleged non-profits, and in many cases, unknown and foreign interests are pumping untold amounts of capital into political campaigns thereby undermining the "one person-one vote" principles upon which our elections are supposed to be based. That in turn has allowed for the elections of individuals who would essentially "stack" agencies such as the DOJ and the FBI with political operatives whenever certain individuals with particular political agendas get into office. What Professor Brougham and the European bankers have given you directly relates to what you are investigating. There are always special interests trying to have their way with the government and with the political process. However, this time it is different. Of a major concern is the ability of these outside interests to control the administration of justice, so it isn't just a matter of philosophy," observed the Senator.

"What do you mean?" inquired A.T.

"Due to what we now know, there was a group of individuals that formed a coalition of sorts in the late 1960s. They first devised a plan whereby they would work their way into key appointed offices within the government starting with the Executive Branch. In order to accomplish that task and to get themselves into certain positions of power, they needed to be a part of the political process. They chose the Republican Party as the best vehicle to get them where they wanted to be. There was always a very conservative wing within the Republican Party, and that's where they first went to work since they felt very conservative Republicans would be the closest to their philosophies and a comfortable place where they would be accepted. By talking a good game of 'conservatism,' they would ingratiate themselves with the far right within the Republican Party. The trouble is the far right of the Party doesn't even realize how they are being used, and I'm sure the party people have no real idea what these folks are really hoping to achieve. The conservative wing of the Republican Party is being used by a very devious and well-organized confederation. They have been setting up a 'shadow government' for nearly fifty years."

"From my relationship with the Republican Party and from my own past experience in my early days with the Party, I can vouch for the fact that there was always a very conservative faction within the party," noted A.T.

"As I said, this group started to form in the late 1960s," reiterated the Senator. "They were able to work themselves into key positions. Some were electable and others were not, but in all cases, they were successful in gaining position after position by appointment, if they could not get elected. They stayed somewhat together and helped each other move upward at each opportunity. Today they have money behind them. Lots of money!

"They've remained active within the Republican rank and file and maneuvered themselves deeper and deeper into positions within the government, as well as the Party. What has come into existence is a coalition of extreme social conservatives, advocates of a private military, a group of lawyers from a very extreme faction of the justice department and some very wealthy contributors. Collectively they continued to observe the type of young people who were joining the Republican Party, so they actively recruited others like themselves. As their numbers grew and as they methodically helped individuals of their own kind gain positions within the Party and positions within the government, their carefully orchestrated power base within both the Party and the Executive Branch of government became ever more solidified."

A.T. asked, "How are their philosophies much different than so many of the conservative Republicans that make up a significant portion of the Republican Party?"

"One thing that definitely makes this country so great is because our system of government allows for all different philosophies and points of view," the Senator responded. "However, I'm sure your investigation is showing, the neo-cons that now control the extreme right of the Republican Party are not the same as your father's Republicans. The extreme right wing of the Republican Party is non-compromising in their philosophy. It's either their way or the road. They are using the system against itself in order to control both a major political party and the government process as well. Some of what they have done has been accomplished legally, but some of it, the part that concerns me, has been done illegally. Plus, you now know, there are both domestic and foreign interests helping to bankroll these groups. Those are a couple reasons why the investigation is being conducted and why you're involved. There are two issues that trouble me greatly, and I realize those go a bit beyond your current investigation."

"What are those? I would really like to know since I want to limit my investigation to the misconduct of the DOJ, the FBI and the abuse of the grand jury process. I don't feel comfortable with the expanded investigation," explained A.T.

"In that case let's talk about some items that do relate to your investigation. First, there are the voting machines and the manner in which votes were counted as a result of the widespread use of those machines. When violations occur in that environment, it directly involves the DOJ and the FBI," began the Senator. "Second, there is the matter of the missing emails from the White House during the George W. Bush administration. That too should involve the DOJ and the FBI."

"As you well know," responded A.T., "both of those matters go well beyond the scope of my investigation, and I don't see how the two matters are related."

"Let me tell you how I think they are related," said the Senator. "Have you ever heard of a man named Michael Connell?"

"No, I can't say I have," answered A.T.

"For your information," exclaimed the Senator, "he was a person who was involved in the 'black box' drama of a few years ago. He was a voting technocrat from Akron, Ohio, who worked hard for the Republican Party. At one point, Mr. Connell was under a subpoena and court order to come forth and testify about any role he may have had in regard to the election machinery in place in Ohio in 2004. He became a crucial witness in regard to the tabulation of votes and how such tabulations related to the voting machines in Ohio. Mr. Connell was also the founder of a company called 'New Media Communications,' and it was alleged his server or servers were used to bundle some of the White House emails during W.'s presidency. There was a lawsuit that made such allegations public."

"What happened?" asked A.T.

"No one will ever know," answered the Senator. "Mr. Connell died in an airplane crash while his plane was approaching the Akron-Canton Airport. It was simply regarded as an unfortunate incident, and that, as far as I know, was the end of it. Now that would be something for one of your investigations."

"No thanks," said A.T. "With all due respect, Senator, my investigation has been redirected far beyond what I ever intended. Please don't even ask me to do more."

"Wouldn't you be interested to see if there were any connections between the airplane crash of Mr. Connell and those airplane crashes that took the lives of former Senator Ted Stevens of Alaska in August 2010 or of Senator Paul Wellstone of Minnesota, your own state, in the fall of 2002? Or what about the airplane crash of former Missouri Senator Mel Carnahan in October 2000 or the airplane crash of former Louisiana Congressman Hale Boggs in 1972? They were all key people who oddly enough died in airplane crashes that seemed a bit mysterious. There are some interesting theories about all five of these airplane crashes. Wouldn't you also be interested in learning exactly who was on board American Airline Flight 587 back in 2001 or the mysterious TWA flight 800 that crashed after takeoff near East Moriches, New York, in 1996?"

"No, no, no. I would not be interested. I'm sorry, Senator, but don't ask me to do more. My hands are full enough with this investigation. I don't need or want anything more on my plate. I am interested in judicial reform, along with some changes at both the DOJ and the FBI. I want to see some realistic and serious changes to the grand jury process and some real accountability in regard to both of those departments," answered A.T.

"Be prepared to run into some resistance. You're taking on a couple of institutions where the people in power won't like having someone looking over their shoulders, and the last thing they want is any form of meaningful oversight. For us to look into something being done illegally is all the reason needed; however, in this case, there is something that is unnerving and problematic," cautioned the Senator.

"What's that?"

"The people behind this enterprise have faces. I know many of them since I've been around Washington so long. They are up to no good."

"What are you saying?"

"The individuals behind this evolving enterprise are expecting to control all major aspects of our government without allowing it to be a part of the democratic process. Some of these people are not electable. In fact, some have unsuccessfully run for office, and now they are trying to control others who can get elected by funding those campaigns."

"It would seem at some point in the near future the country might just be heading to a one party system if the Republicans continue to isolate themselves from mainstream America," observed A.T.

"I certainly hope not," was the Senator's response. "I value the give and take of the two party system, but I sincerely fear if the

Republicans continue down this path of the current uncompromising conservatism, the Republican Party will soon become a shell of itself. In my opinion, this is especially true if the Republican Party continues to embrace the views of Grover Norquist or the views of the John Birch Society. Needless to say, those views are far afield from the thinking of mainstream America. At least that's my view. I like and look forward to the dialogue Congress has had in the past on issues of real concern to the public. An awful lot has changed from the days when I first came to Washington. Unfortunately, the current Republican leadership has catered to the fringe interests, and there is no longer a give and take dialogue in Congress. It is bad for the country and is hindering the country's ability to solve the many problems, be they financial, domestic, foreign, or otherwise. The failure of Congress to fairly evaluate and compromise on issues today is seriously crippling the U.S. and the world as well. Please recall what the fringe portion of the Republican Party's elected officials did in regard to Susan Rice before she withdrew her name as Secretary of State and what they did to former Senator Chuck Hagel on his appointment as Secretary of Defense. I've become familiar with Ms. Rice from her testimony before my committee, and I personally know Chuck Hagel - two fine people. I'm simply saying the picture is much bigger than your limited concern about the grand jury process and the DOJ."

"Although I have agreed to incorporate your suggestions into the expanded investigation, for the most part, I plan to direct my principle focus on the grand jury process, the DOJ, and the FBI. If the investigation demonstrates that the political process is involved, it seems it will just be something we will have to endure," observed A.T.

"Just be careful. Behind the scenes, there are those who are bending the rules. Part of the investigation my office is doing in conjunction with a Republican Senator is to determine who these folks are and how far they are willing to go, including compromising the law," said the Senator.

"Am I missing something?" asked A.T.

"Let me give you a few examples. First, by controlling the voting process, they can control the outcome of elections. Who can say electronic voting systems cannot be particularly programmed? We know it has been done, for example, in both the Ohio election results of a number of years ago and in a Delaware primary during the 2008 primaries. We have some proof, but we need more and we are currently having trouble connecting the dots in regard to this matter. In this regard there is also a very serious effort by Republican controlled legislatures to gerrymander certain Congressional districts throughout the country. Second, by controlling a major political party, those behind the scenes believe they can control about half of the political process. Third, by controlling the media, or at least a significant percentage of it, they can manipulate public opinion. I believe it is a fair statement to say that over fifty percent of the media is under the direct control or the influence of this same group or similar thinking groups. Fourth, and here is where the most serious danger lies, by controlling the executive branch of government, especially the presidency, they can control the day-to-day functions of the government and many of the major decisions that would affect the country, both here and abroad."

"That's quite a list," interrupted A.T.

"Wait, there's much more," insisted the Senator. "Fifth, by controlling the Department of Justice, they can control the judicial process by determining which laws are enforced and how the laws are enforced. You've already experienced that firsthand. Plus, by controlling the Justice Department, including various operations within Justice, such as investigative agencies, they can control the administration of the judicial system. By "salting" the Justice Department with their own people, they can also influence the makeup of the appointments to the judiciary. A very high percentage of the judicial appointments come from the Justice Department. Six, by privatizing much of what the military does, they can dictate how the Department of Defense functions and how the domestic enforcement of certain laws will be achieved. Seven, by having the people intimidated by certain religious philosophies and thinking, they have a particular type of control over portions of the public by emphasizing certain acts. It becomes a matter of "public" conscience. In this regard, and you might remember, the State of North Carolina even had proposed a single religion as a state religion. That is unequivocally unconstitutional. Eight, by controlling the economic considerations as to who does business and what happens in the marketplace, they can at least 'favor' their own kind in terms of wealth, contracting, banking, business license, and markets. That was never more evident than during the George W. Bush and Dick Cheney administration. But I honestly believe

W. was unaware of the extent to which this shadow government had entrenched itself."

"Obviously, you are aware of more than I have found, but I can vouch for much of what you say being true in regard to the Department of Justice, and that is simply based upon my investigation so far," said A.T.

"Let's talk about what you have found so far. Can you provide a summary for me?" asked the Senator.

"Yes, I can," answered A.T. as he reached for the briefcase. "At the top of the documents in the briefcase, you will see my report. Here is the briefcase Jean Paul Valance gave me. Jean Paul said he had spoken with you about the documents he provided, but he wanted the documents to be protected and the originals delivered personally to you. So, he gave me this special briefcase that, if opened incorrectly, would discharge an acid that would in turn destroy the documents inside."

At that point, A.T. demonstrated to the Senator how the briefcase needed to be opened with specific codes and turns of the latches near the handle. Once he demonstrated the workings of the briefcase and told the Senator the case would soon be in the possession of the Senator and his staff, he removed the materials and placed them on his lap.

"Here is my report to you," said A.T. "The report starts with a synopsis of the investigation and is followed by the report itself in an outline format. There is a table of contents, then the report details, and finally an exhibit list that relates to the other matters contained within the remaining files also included with a set of exhibits within their respective files. Do you want me to go through the report?"

"That won't be necessary. Just summarize for me what is in the report; then give me a general overview of each of the files, the contents of each of those files, and how each relates to the main report."

"The report that was amended last night because of the Felthaus matter begins with an assessment of the Justice Department and what was going on in that department during the Bush administration. In regard to that department, various violations of law were committed pertaining to the hiring process of attorneys. It also details the questionable practices relative to the termination of United States Attorneys, who wouldn't march to the specific political instructions being routinely sent down by both the Attorney General at the time and the Bush White House. There is a file folder with the exhibits that substantiate this, and you might find a pleasant surprise or two involving admissions by several former employees of the Justice Department. Some admissions were made before one of the committees here in Washington or were made public through the media or otherwise.

"The Felthaus portion of the file includes a significant number of emails he has provided. Those emails demonstrate there was a concerted effort by individuals both outside public office and in public office to influence the matters I just mentioned. Some of the evidence is pretty overwhelming. At minimum, it is a fair statement to say the Justice Department was seriously compromised, and laws were routinely broken during the Bush administration. The next four folders contain exhibits relating to the portion of the report that deals with the Justice Department. From a couple of the emails I have particularly marked, you will see that these people believe they can control voting, selected prosecution, political enemies, the judiciary and access to the courts," said A.T. as he handed the four file folders to the Senator.

"What's next?" asked the Senator.

"The next matter set forth in the report relates to the paramilitary groups springing up throughout the country. There are far more of them than I ever imagined. From what I have been able to document, there are 174 such groups that have been identified. So far, they are not all connected, but some of them are. The next three files relate to these groups. Some of them are well-funded and others are receiving funds from outside the United States, which itself constitutes illegal activity," explained A.T.

He continued, "It most certainly could be construed as subversive activity since in nearly every one of those instances, there are enumerated plans to 'overthrow' the U.S. government. Most of these groups are connected to individuals who are known to have 'fringe' or seriously reactionary ideas. From what has been determined, none of these groups are tied to radical Muslim groups; however, some have ties to the Middle East. There are definite ties to organizations in Europe, and some that are tied to South America and South Africa. Some of them have sympathies to the Timothy McVey matter, while others can be tied to the Waco matter and still others, believe it or not, are tied to the same people showing up in some of the emails Mr. Felthaus gave us in regard to the DOJ."

"I'm not surprised. That's why I wanted you to see what was going on in Kentucky and in Houston," commented the Senator.

"The second file relates to two of these groups. You will find pictures of an operation in Kentucky you asked me to view, and there are two sets of pictures that deal with operations near Houston," responded A.T.

"Have you found any ties between those groups and any of the mercenary corporations that have contracted with or that are now contracting with the United States Department of Defense or State or the government in general?"

"Yes," answered A.T. "There are connections between individuals who were and are members of corporations that have contracted with the government, and those are detailed in the third folder of exhibits that relate to this part of the report. So far, there is nothing showing a direct tie to the corporations but only ties to individuals who either are or were a part of those corporations."

"Is there proof?" asked the Senator.

"Yes. "As the report explains, there seem to be some religious overtones involved. You will see what I mean when you look at the third file that relates to the paramilitary," commented A.T. while providing three more file folders.

"These paramilitary groups have always been a bit of a concern, and, in many if not most cases, they are advocates of the overthrow of our government. Some believe the government is illegally constituted, and that belief gives them cause to seek the violence they have been known to employ," noted the Senator. "What else do you have for me?"

"The next batch of materials involves the world of finance and the channeling of funds between foreign banks and banks here in the United States. Simply stated, it appears there is some serious money laundering going on that both Jean Paul Valance, the French banker, and Claude Schmidt, the Swiss banker, have detected in terms of transactions and the movement of funds," said A.T.

"I'm sorry you had to have that thrown at you the way it was and at the last minute, but it was somewhat spontaneous the way it all came about," observed the Senator. "Some of the details developed after you left Washington the last time we met in my office. Bud called and said he had heard from a new informant who had information about some foreign groups that were developing a funding chain to some of the paramilitary groups here in the U.S. Bud's informant, in this regard, turned out to be Professor Brougham, and he was really elusive. The word is the professor had gotten away with some documents that would apparently verify that there were funds being shifted about and that the funds involved some foreign bank accounts and foreign money interests. When the professor contacted Bud, you were already on your way to Kentucky, and the professor was driving across the country attempting to elude the people who wanted the documents back. Ironically, the professor was driving up to Tennessee, as I understand it, so it was arranged for you to meet him while he was en route."

"That's interesting," said A.T. "The professor said that he was traveling west rather than north when I met him in Mt. Vernon, Kentucky. Apparently, he was providing whatever story appeared convenient to him at the time. He said he had been in Florida but wanted to get the documents specifically to me since Bud told him where I was heading. It was interesting we were able to connect. The documents he provided proved useful and worthy from what both Jean Paul and Claude told me. First, let me give you the documents the professor provided." At this point, A.T. handed to the Senator the files, the thumb drives, the CDs, and the zip drives the professor had given to him weeks earlier. "There are records of corporate and individual contributions to certain groups tied closely to the Republican Party; however, there are no direct contributions to the Party itself. Some of the names of the people involved will stand out immediately since quite a number of them are well-known individuals who have been active in the Republican Party."

"I trust none of these 'contributions' or transfers of funds went to any Republican official or candidate or Party organizations?" queried the Senator. "I can't imagine anyone would be that stupid."

"That's correct," answered A.T. "In every case I have documented, the funds have gone to private accounts, certain non-profit corporations, or interest groups. On a few occasions, funds have gone to individuals, presumably as a sort of consulting fee. I don't know if those individuals or groups have in turn contributed to the Republican Party or to candidates or to any officials. However, I presume if one were to follow the money, he could find out. Please don't ask me to do that." Having said that, A.T. provided a fourth set of files to the Senator.

"No," said the Senator, "I'm not going to ask you to do that. I have an individual in mind to check on that item. In all likelihood, you already know him. For now I will withhold his identity, but I am pretty sure you may know him from your past activity within the Republican Party. He would be in a better position to 'follow the money.' Is there anything else?"

"Thanks for sparing me the task of tracking down the contributions. As you can see, I have provided four groups of files, and those files break down into fifteen separate files with details and exhibits. You have four files on the Department of Justice; four files on the paramilitary groups; four files on the financial matters, including Professor Brougham's file with electronic data; and three files that relate to the politics of the investigation," explained A.T.

"That's great, A.T. I knew you would come through for me. I will never be able to thank you enough for your work on this matter. Hopefully, I can make it up to you in the future on a properly-commissioned endeavor. Even though I have given you official sanction to conduct the investigation you have, the funds were limited except for your expenses. I believe we addressed that the last time you were here in Washington. We are almost back to the Lincoln Memorial, so let's wrap up the business regarding the files. Then you and I can have a bit of a private chat as we walk up to see our good friend, Mr. Lincoln," commented the Senator.

"Sure. You're welcome for my part in this case, and I will submit my expense report sometime within the next couple of weeks. Now, in addition to handing over the briefcase, I do have one more item of curiosity and of significant interest," said A.T. while he reached into the pocket of his suit coat.

"Why don't you discuss anything else with me as we take our walk up to see Lincoln, okay?"

"Okay," said A.T. handing the briefcase to the Senator while he again demonstrated the latching mechanism. The limo stopped at the base of the Lincoln Memorial, whereupon A.T. and the Senator exited the car and started their climb up the stairs. It was now over an hour since they had left the Memorial earlier that morning. Small groups of people were gathering at different spots along the stairway. The two of them ascended the stairway and engaged in casual conversation with the Senator commenting on the fact that it appeared as though it would be a clear crisp day for the country's capital. A.T. took the hint and continued the small talk about the weather and how Washington D.C. had changed since he lived there many years earlier. Reaching the top, they discussed the impact of

President Lincoln upon the country as the Senator guided A.T. to a rather secluded spot near one of the pillars.

"Thank you again," said the Senator. "Your work, as usual, was very well done, and I presume discreetly so."

"I'm not so sure that it was done discreetly," said A.T. while handing the Senator the FBI credentials that had been given to him by Samantha Nguyen-Henderson.

"What's this?" asked the Senator.

"FBI credentials," answered A.T.

"Well, my good friend," laughed the Senator, "I can see that. The question is how did you get them?"

"That is one bizarre story that unbeknown to me started at the time I first met Professor Brougham in Kentucky. Apparently, he had a tail on him at that time. However, that tail, actually two individuals whom I have since met under very unusual circumstances, started following me instead of the professor once they suspected I had received documents and other materials from him."

"That would have been some weeks ago, right?"

"Correct! At the time I was with your special assignment guy, Robert, and his friend, James."

"I know James quite well and was a good friend of his father, Dr. Robbins."

"That's what he told me. Later while we were in Paris, we were on our way to our hotel when we were attacked by two men. While we were engaged in that confrontation, two other individuals appeared out of nowhere and came to our aid. It turned out that those two individuals were the same two who had started tailing us in Kentucky and were the same two people who had been tailing the professor. After that incident, I became even more paranoid about this investigation."

"I'm glad that you are telling me this. Is it a part of your report?"

"No. I thought it best that I tell you this privately."

"That's a good idea. Not that I don't trust my staff implicitly, but you never know how leaks occur. But, tell me about these credentials."

"I'm coming to that. After the scuffle in the alley near our hotel in Paris, Allen and I realized that the contents of the briefcase were too valuable. While the four other individuals were engaged, we took off for the hotel and immediately contacted Rene, who had one of his police inspectors come to the hotel to maintain a watch over us for the evening and to start a discrete investigation. Then a day after our return, I was leaving my office after some late work and was confronted as I was heading to my car. We had a scuffle, and I got lucky. I got his identity and a couple of cell phones that he was carrying."

"So, when you got his identity, is that when you got the credentials?"

"No. The credentials were handed to me the next day. While in a coffee shop, I was approached by the same guy who wanted his phones and the documents the professor had given me. He said that he is an independent contractor and may be working for a group called the GGG or the 'Good Government Group.' Have you heard of them?"

"No. I've never heard of them. What do you know about them?"

"I was told by the partner of this Gerald Peterson, that the two of them are with this GGG entity, and it either has or had some ties to the Knights of Malta or the Knights Hospitaller. Do you know who they are?"

"No, I don't, other than the fact that they were an ancient order of some sort. I thought they had something to do with the Crusades. I thought that they had disappeared long ago."

"Apparently, they are still around. The person who provided this information to me is the partner to this Gerald Peterson character, who, I might add, is a terrible driver."

"Getting back to the credentials –"

"It was Peterson's partner, one Samantha Nguyen-Henderson, who provided the credentials, along with the information I just gave you about the Knights of Malta and the GGG. I have no idea why they wanted the materials I received in Europe. However, and as you will see, those documents are linked to the financial documents Professor Brougham gave me. In fact, this Samantha Nguyen-Henderson did tell me they wanted the professor's documents because those documents belonged to 'them.' By 'them,' I assume it is this GGG organization for which she works. I exchanged the two cell phones I took from her associate, Peterson, for the credentials. Now why would someone with FBI credentials be following me?"

"That is a good question, A.T. Let me do some digging since any agent who loses his credentials is most likely in trouble well over his head in the first place. Meanwhile, you had better find out about Gerald Peterson and Samantha Nguyen-Henderson."

"I do have some information on her because she willingly allowed me to see her passport, license, and a credit card."

"How did you manage that?" asked the Senator.

"She volunteered it when she was trying to prove to me she was earnestly trying to 'help' me in her attempt to regain the cell phones of her accomplice and the documents of the professor."

"So, you gave her the phones but kept the documents?"

"Yes. That seemed to placate her," explained A.T., "but she did warn me the GGG was a powerful group that would ultimately try to force me to give up the information I held. Now that information is yours, except for the copies that are a part of the deal you made with Bud Hawthorne regarding an ultimate exclusive for him and his designated press buddies once your investigation is ready to be released. Just so you know, I did get the SIM chips copied earlier in the day, so the phones were really of little value to us from that point forward, plus we got our hands on those credentials. I trust when you check on the credentials, it will be through strictly confidential sources within the Bureau?"

"Please be assured it will be strictly confidential through some trusted friends I have with the FBI," the Senator responded. "Without going into detail, I have good reason to believe that there is a group within the Bureau that has its own hidden agenda. Perhaps that is what you have already encountered with your own case. Be well assured that I will check it out and let you know. In the meantime, I would like you to follow up on this GGG entity and find out what you can. Perhaps starting with this Samantha."

"With all due respect, Senator, I really don't want to have to deal with her ever again. I would respectfully like to beg off on that one."

"I understand your concern. Perhaps once you get to know her, you might really like her," laughed the Senator.

"Come on, you know me better than that! I really think she is dangerous. Plus, my part of the investigation is over," insisted A.T.

"You're too deeply involved," noted the Senator. "I need you. You already must know I will need your testimony when the hearings begin, so you really need to stay involved in the investigation. Just get me some information on this GGG; right now it would seem this lady is the best source or lead you have. You said you got her identity, so track her down and find out what the GGG has to do with the professor's documents or with any other matter that relates to our investigation. I will let you off the hook on the other matters involving the political side of things, and I will get Robert to follow up on the paramilitary issues. As far as the financial matters, I will get Bud more involved since he and Jean Paul are such good friends."

While they finished their conversation, an argument was developing across the stairway and down a flight from where they were standing near the pillar. The argument across the stairs was heating up, and it was apparent the lady, who had her back turned and who was facing northeasterly toward the Federal Reserve Building, was raising her voice at the man who was looking up toward A.T. and the Senator.

The man abruptly turned away, and the Senator said, "Look, A.T., that is a Republican congressman whom I know fairly well. I do need to talk to him, if you don't mind."

"No, not at all," said A.T. "Go ahead, although it would seem his lady friend is a bit distressed with him. Do you think this is a good time?"

"The timing couldn't be better. I know him well, and that lady is not his wife. His wife is blonde, much shorter, and would never be involved in an argument in a public place. Let me simply walk over and say hello. I think it would be beneficial for me to do so. Plus, it might have the effect of calming the lady down."

"Good luck, Senator! Please remember to keep me posted on the credentials."

"I will. Don't forget to check on the GGG for me," said the Senator while heading down the stairs in the direction of the congressman.

A.T. watched the Senator move briskly down the stairs and noticed the congressman had broken off his conversation with the lady, who seemed to turn away from the congressman. She appeared to be trembling and shaking. It was apparent the congressman had seen the Senator and was attempting to elude him; however, the Senator was both cagey and spry. He was no fool. He had been in Washington for a long time and knew how to manipulate a situation with the best of them. A.T. watched the Senator catch up before the congressman could get to the base of the Memorial. A.T. thought to himself how much he would like to hear the upcoming conversation between the Senator and the congressman. Instead, he found himself walking toward the lady. Perhaps it was a natural instinct that he had to try to comfort people in distress.

When A.T. approached the lady, she must have sensed his presence for she turned and looked directly at him with tear-laden eyes and a slight trace of smeared mascara. He nearly lost his balance on the stairs for he couldn't believe what he was seeing. The weeping lady was none other than Samantha Nguyen-Henderson. He wanted to call to the Senator to let him know that the very person whom they had been discussing was right here at this very moment, but then his mind started analyzing the situation. The congressman and Samantha were presumably a couple of some sort. His mind started racing. This couldn't be intentional; at least not with her crying so profusely. Her mood seemed genuine with emotions well beyond any acting that he had ever seen. He reached out for her as she seemed to sway on the stairs. When she seemed to fall forward, he caught and steadied her.

"What the hell are you doing here!" she exclaimed. "Have you been following me? Here you are again, attempting to take advantage of me. You can let me go."

A.T. was speechless. He thought that there was no delayed response from this lady in any given situation she seemed to encounter. He was marveling at how fast she seemed to change her attitude from moments earlier when she seemed to be in considerable distress. He thought to himself: *this lady really seems cold and calculating.* But then as if she sensed his thoughts, she once again broke down and started crying.

"That bastard used me. He promised he would leave his wife and file for a divorce before the holiday season, and now he completely backtracked on me. I really thought he and I had something very special," she lamented.

Before A.T. could comment, she continued, "For over three years we've been together. I know I have spent more time with him than his wife has. He says it's for the sake of his children he had to change his mind about us. But that's a bunch of bull! He thinks he is going to run for president someday, but that will never happen. At least that isn't going to happen as long as I am around. No one is going to double-cross me like that. I never thought he was so selfish! What a liar! I should have known better than to get involved with a politician."

A.T. didn't know what to say. He simply said, "I'm sorry."

"Why should you be sorry? Oh, don't tell me that. You guys all stick together, so whatever he does is okay. You men are all the same."

"I just said I was sorry. What did you expect me to say?"

"Nothing. Just be quiet. I need to think, and I just want to be left alone. Just go away!"

"All right," said A.T. starting down the stairs. He really was glad she told him to go since he didn't trust her as it was.

"No. Wait!" she commanded. "Walk me to my car. I'm sorry I yelled at you. You didn't deserve my wrath. I'm a little bit emotional right now. Please walk with me. I need to have someone with me for a few minutes, if you don't mind…By the way, what are you doing here? You aren't following me, are you? Tell me the truth. You at least owe me the truth."

Not that A.T. owed her anything, but he would tell her the truth. He didn't want to tell her too much, but he didn't think it would matter if he told her he had been meeting with a friend of his who just happened to be a United States Senator. If she wanted to imply anything from that, it was her prerogative. So he said, "I was just meeting an old friend of mine. We go back many years; when I'm in Washington, we meet."

"At the Lincoln Memorial early on a Sunday morning when there is no one else around?" she asked. "It sounds a bit fishy to me. You were delivering the documents we talked about a few days ago, weren't you?"

"All business now, right," commented A.T.

"No, I don't even want to talk about business," she said as the two of them started walking down the stairs. "However, let me just warn you one more time about the people with whom I work. They are pretty relentless, and you seem like an awfully nice guy to have to go through what they might have planned for you. You've been pretty nice to me, even if I have been more than just ornery to you."

"Thanks for the warning, but I got into a particular investigation for reasons of my own, and I am not about to turn and run with my tail between my legs at this point." stated A.T. thinking to himself about the rare opportunity that might be at his feet. The Senator wanted him to find out more about the GGG organization Samantha was a part of, so A.T. decided to play out the situation that had now presented itself. However, he would handle it very deliberately so she would never suspect that he was going to get what additional information he could from her. "Where are we headed?"

"I left my car over by the Department of State building. It isn't far. My friend, the congressman, stood me up last night, so I called his home this morning. His wife answered, and I'm sure she has known about us for some time. Either that or she is a complete idiot. So, I tried to tell her when she answered that her husband stood me up last night, but he got on the phone and she immediately hung up. I'll bet there was an interesting conversation between them after he and I talked. Anyway, he said he would meet me at the Lincoln Memorial, so I knew it was going to be bad news. Otherwise, he would have come to our place that we both have occupied together for three years now at the Watergate."

"The Watergate, over at Foggy Bottom?" asked A.T.

"Yes. There isn't any other Watergate I'm aware of, and besides, no one refers to the area as Foggy Bottom anymore. We have an apartment there. Actually, it is in my name, but he and one of the companies he once owned pay for the place. I think his ownership in those companies is in some kind of blind trust. That will be interesting when it comes to who pays what and for how long it stays in my name. I can afford it myself, but I'm going to make him pay, not just for that but for some other items I have in mind. I'm not like some disposable mistress. I'm independently well-off, and I can put him through the paces if I decide to do that."

"Why did you park near the Department of State, considering the Watergate isn't that much farther?"

"I thought I would be able to get closer to the Memorial than I was permitted. The changes in security have altered everything in this city, but I still love it. Although my permanent residence is on the West Coast, I've always loved my stays here in D.C. The excitement of the city and feeling the pulse of the country has gotten into my blood. I don't know what exactly I will do now in terms of spending time here. My company's office is in New York, so perhaps I will move my second home and office there. Although, I hate to give up the apartment here, I –"

"Your office is in New York. Where is it, exactly?"

"Hey, we decided we were not going to talk about business."

"Fair enough," he said as they continued to walk to her car, discussing the features and advantages of living in the nation's capital. A.T. explained he had lived in Washington many years ago while he was an agent with the FBI and for a brief period when he was doing some special work for a subcommittee for the United States Congress. Once they arrived at Samantha's car, she realized he had to walk back to the Memorial. A.T. explained he needed to call a friend of his in order for him to be picked up for a brunch meeting at 11:30. Since it was only 8:35, she invited him to join her for a cup of coffee at a coffee shop near the Watergate.

Once at the coffee shop, Samantha and A.T. were directed to a table at the far end of the restaurant. After being seated, Samantha excused herself for a trip to the ladies room while A.T. used his phone. By the time Samantha returned to the table, she had composed herself and seemed to have regained her charismatic self.

A waiter came to the table to take their orders. Samantha ordered breakfast, while A.T. requested juice and coffee. He began by asking her how she was feeling. He could tell the question was unpleasant for her, so he immediately changed the subject and commented about the high level of activity in the restaurant.

She interrupted his small talk and redirected the conversation. She stared with an expression of gratitude, "Thanks, A.T., for being there to comfort me at the Memorial. I really appreciated the fact there was someone there to talk with after my bout with the congressman. Your presence was timely. You're sure you weren't following me?"

"Actually," A.T. responded, "it was purely coincidental that you and I were in the same location today. Frankly, when I saw you today, my first reaction was to leave you alone. After all, I am still more than irritated with the stunt you pulled at the Minneapolis airport when I was picking up my wife and mother-in-law."

"Well, I can't say I am sorry for that. I was irritated with you for not giving me the documents from Professor Brougham. Plus, I was a bit irritable. I was at the top of my game, and I was actually hoping to make more of a scene than I did. It didn't seem to bother your wife much. Apparently the two of you have a strong relationship. Quite like the one I thought I had with the congressman," said Samantha. "I still find it hard to believe you weren't following me today."

I was not following you, period!" exclaimed A.T.

"Sorry. Actually, I am glad to see you, and again thanks for providing some comfort," said Samantha as she sat back in her chair sipping her coffee. "Come to think of it, our running into each other is a bit fortuitous. I know I said I didn't want to discuss business, but I feel an obligation to at least tell you some of my superiors have asked that I reconnect with you to see if I could reason with you about the documents the professor gave you. They also wanted me to find out what else you are up to. I submitted my report and my superiors know about our encounters in Kentucky and Paris. They also know about the incident in St. Paul and your altercation with Gerald. I thought under the circumstances, I should put the cards on the table and let you know that. I really meant what I said about the fact they usually get what they want and if they get too upset with you, they will make your life a living hell. I hope you don't mind my being so direct, but you seem like a decent guy, and I don't want you to have to go through what they are capable of doing to you."

"Samantha, I appreciate your warning, but I am doing what I believe is right and necessary. It may sound trivial, but I honestly feel I am doing the right thing. Just so you know, I will continue my investigation as long as I feel it is necessary. That is just the way it is."

"Please call me 'Sam.' That is what everyone who knows me well calls me, and at this point, it seems we have gotten to know each other well enough to be on a more informal basis."

"Okay, Sam. So far my experience with you is that you have been bluntly direct. To speak on more informal terms might help us get to know each other better and just what ticks in each other's mind. I have always believed in putting 'the cards on the table,' particularly to show where I stand. You will see I am devoted to what I do, and once I make a commitment to something, I stick with it. Frankly, from your end, I would like to know more about your GGG group, as well as the modern day Knights of Malta. Perhaps we could start there, so I know how seriously to take the threats about their activities against me and –"

"Wait, wait, wait…I am not threatening you at all," said Sam, as she deliberately placed her cup on the saucer and leaned forward to look him straight in the eye. "I am doing you a favor by warning you. I am doing it simply on my own because I know what they can do, and I just don't want you to get in over your head with something far bigger and more complex than you could imagine. There is, as there has always been, a 'chess match' going on, if you will. It has been going on for centuries, and it has recently been turned up a notch in order to fit within today's world of politics, economics, technology, and business interests. From my guess, I would say perhaps you are too naive to imagine what is really at stake."

"Please don't call me naïve or underestimate me or what I know or don't know," cautioned A.T. "I am more aware of what is going on and what is taking place than you obviously realize. The investigation became expanded because of what some elected officials wanted to learn in regard to not only the Justice Department but other areas of government as well. I'm just curious as to how 'your people' fit into the equation."

"You said 'some elected officials' wanted to learn… What did they want to learn? What government officials? Is one of those government officials the person with whom you were meeting at the Lincoln Memorial? Forgive me, but I actually didn't notice either you or your friend or friends at the Lincoln Memorial since I was a bit preoccupied at the time."

"The person I met with is one of several elected officials interested in learning more about what appears to be a concerted effort to establish a 'shadow' government within various departments, agencies, and political organizations that deal with the government on a daily basis. So there! Now that I've told you about my involvement, would you mind reciprocating and let me know a bit about the GGG entity you claim to have as your employer?"

"The GGG is not my employer," Samantha corrected. "I am an independent contractor. I thought I told you that back in St. Paul over a week ago. I just happen to have performed many contract assignments for them. In fact, during the last several years, they have been my principal."

"What about the Knights of Malta?"

"That's a different story altogether. I have a direct relationship with the Knights of Malta because of my family and heritage, the French ancestry, but they do not establish contract enterprises, at least as far as I know. However, there is a relationship between the two organizations. It was because of my relationship with the Knights of Malta that I was given an introduction to the GGG and probably how I got my initial contract with them. I have completed several contracts for the GGG. This one shifted from Professor Brougham to you, so I don't mind telling you that you are now the focus of the contract."

"So, if I give you the documents from Professor Brougham, you can complete your contract, and the GGG goes away as far as my life is concerned. That's presuming it is not a contract to terminate me. Tell me, honestly, if you can manage to do so, are you under contract to eliminate me?"

"Don't you listen to anything I say? I told you the GGG does not kill people. I don't kill people. I have certain skills that include martial arts, but I am not a contract killer and wouldn't do such a thing if asked. Besides… that is not something they would ask me to do."

"So, is the next option to attempt to beat the hell out of me?" asked A.T., as he sat back in his chair and laughed.

Samantha picked up her cup, glared at him and said, "Giving back the documents is no longer an option. Not now anyway. It isn't quite that simple at this point. You have probably made copies of what Professor Brougham gave you, so I will need all copies, as well as the originals. Plus, as our investigation has progressed, it appears as though you have additional information you may have received in Europe, Texas, and Kentucky. Therefore, I will need to see what you have acquired from those locations –"

"I see… so you were following me for reasons that went beyond the materials of Professor Brougham and –"

"Wait. There's more. You have mentioned the Justice Department and other government offices and related entities. I would want to see what your investigation reveals in that regard."

"With all due respect, Sam, you can go to hell. Under no circumstances will you ever see the results of my investigation, especially as it relates to the Department of Justice. What I have found is serious, monumentally critical to the security of this country and will undoubtedly lead, or at least should lead, to the prosecution of people who have compromised the Department of Justice. You will never see that material. Plus, you will not see the material I obtained in Europe or the material from Kentucky or Texas. Besides, all of the material I assembled during my investigation has been delivered to a proper party within the United States Senate. I couldn't give it to you if I wanted to, and I don't want to."

"That's most unfortunate. I will have to report that to my friends at the GGG. I can't protect you anymore. I will see if there is another option, but since you have taken the position you mention, I have run out of choices. I have tried to warn you. There will be nothing I can do without special instructions. So, unless I receive something additional in terms of instructions regarding you, this will probably be the last time we will see each other. It is probably better that way since you at least tried to be nice to me today."

"Your work and the GGG sound pretty ominous. At least our mutual friend, Professor Brougham, no longer has you tailing him. By now, he is undoubtedly on to his new life without the GGG breathing down his neck."

"Oh, Professor Brougham is on to a new life all right, but I don't know exactly what it is."

"What do you mean?"

"The GGG found him."

"So, what did the GGG do to him?"

"I have no idea. I was redirected to follow you and to intercept the documents and other materials you have…or had. All I know is the GGG caught up with the professor. Remember what I told you. He was crazy to think he could get away. He was a trusted contractor of sorts, so what he did was not acceptable."

"Is it fair to make the presumption that the professor is 'pushing daisies?'"

"No. That is not a fair presumption. I already told you the GGG does not murder people. All I know is what Gerald told me a few days ago. He was told that Professor Brougham was no longer a problem. That was the end of the story."

"How is Gerald? I imagine he is out of the hospital now?"

"He's been out. You may have made an enemy there."

"Why? I returned his cell phones to you."

"I don't want to talk about him. Are you going to continue with your investigation, or is there some way I could reason with you?"

"I will continue it for now. I was trying to beg off with the people with whom I had been working and not continue. Now, from what I am reading between the lines regarding the GGG, I think I will recommit to the investigation, and do what I can to see there is a full disclosure and the people involved get prosecuted."

While Bob approached the table, Sam held out her cup for a fresh cup of coffee. A.T. complied and was pouring the hot beverage as Bob said, "Hello A.T. and Miss –"

Looking up at Bob while pouring a fresh cup for Samantha, A.T. responded, "Hey, Bob, thanks for stopping by. This is Samantha. Samantha, this is Bob. Now, you and I need to get to our brunch meeting."

Before Bob could sit down, A.T. rose. Samantha also rose, shook Bob's hand, and before A.T. could react, she turned A.T.'s face toward her with her hand, rose onto her toes, and kissed A.T. on the lips. When A.T. pushed her away, she smiled and said, "As the saying goes, 'parting is such sweet sorrow.' Thanks for being so nice to me. I am sorry we won't be seeing each other again. Have a good life." Then she turned to Bob, smiled, and left the table in the direction of the restaurant entrance.

CHAPTER 17
A FRESH CUP

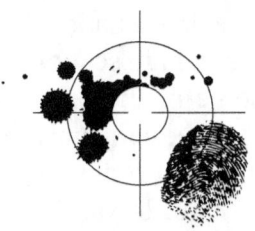

"She seemed sweet," said Bob, watching with a smile as Samantha appeared to be accentuating her graceful departure from the table.

"She's not sweet," noted A.T. "She is treacherous, conniving, and a focal point of real danger. She's what you might call a real lightning rod."

"Really," protested Bob as he continued to watch Samantha walk away. "You at least have to admit she is hot!"

"Be very careful, Bob. She's the kind of 'hot' that causes permanent burns. It would be best to disregard her, considering she works with the enemy. There is far more to her than you might imagine; plus, she and her Republican congressman lover just broke off their relationship this morning."

"Is that so? How did you find that out? More importantly, if you don't mind my asking, how do you even know her?" asked Bob.

"I ran into her at the Lincoln Memorial when I was meeting the Senator," said A.T. who then explained the details of the encounter with Samantha on the steps of the memorial. He also told Bob about his past meeting with Samantha in the Twin Cities and how Samantha fit into the investigation.

"Knowing you as I do, I'm sure you will want to see just what role she plays in the over-all picture," noted Bob grabbing a cup from the table in order to have some coffee.

"That may not be the case this time. There is far more here than I ever imagined. Excuse me, but we'd better head over to our meeting with Allen. You can get a fresh cup once we get there," commented A.T. as he took the cup from Bob, using the cup as a pointer to the wall clock, and placing it back on the table.

The two of them left for the predetermined meeting with Allen, his son Eric, and Eric's family. The brunch was held at a family-friendly restaurant set up for various forms of family entertainment to supplement the good food. Allen's family was especially proud of the oldest boy who was about to enter his senior year at a private high school in the area. He had become a national wrestling champion in his sophomore and junior years in high school. He was starting to receive scholarship offers from some of the best wrestling programs in the country, including three Midwestern universities that had wrestling programs of high acclaim: Iowa State University, the University of Minnesota, and the University of Iowa.

* *

After spending over two hours at the restaurant, Allen joined Eric and his family in returning to their residence. A.T. and Bob took the rental back to the downtown hotel where they were staying. The plan was to pick up Allen the next morning and return the rental car to Dulles International, where the three of them would board their plane for a trip back to the Twin Cities. As they entered the hotel, A.T. and Bob decided to retire to their rooms until about 6:00 that evening, when they would join each other at the hotel restaurant for their evening meal.

Upon opening the door to his room, A.T. noticed the blinking light on the desk phone, indicating he had a voice message. He accessed the message and learned he had received a call from someone who identified himself as an old friend, a Father Bert. A.T. searched his mind and recalled his past close friendship with a Catholic priest named Albert Wendling, who went by Bert. He probably hadn't seen Bert for over thirty years. He considered how odd it was that Father Bert knew he was in Washington. What even seemed problematic was how Bert would know where to find him. Something was obviously not right about the call. Nevertheless, curiosity overtook him, so he listened to the entire message.

The caller, who identified himself simply as A.T.'s old friend, Father Bert, was hoping to meet A.T. in the hotel lobby yet before the day was over. A four o'clock meeting at the lobby was suggested by the caller, who said he would be waiting there. A.T. was too curious to pass up the matter and was hopeful it really was his old friend. However, he had misgivings, so he called Bob. Bob was unavailable, and A.T. left a message telling Bob that he intended to meet an old friend in the hotel lobby after four and Bob should plan to join them, if he could. A.T. also called Allen to tell him of the call. He told Allen he was suspicious of the caller since it was very puzzling as to how and why he would have a call at the hotel when only family and close friends knew where he was staying. He expressed concern that someone might be tailing him or impersonating his old friend. Allen told A.T. that he and Eric would come to the hotel as soon as they dropped the family at Eric's home in Virginia. They would not be able to get there for about an hour, so A.T. decided to wait until well after four before showing up. That would give Allen and Eric time to get to the hotel just in case they were needed and in the event the call was somehow related to the Felthaus matter.

At approximately twenty minutes after four, A.T. went down to the lobby of the hotel. He was both cautious and anxious. While he hoped he would be meeting his old friend, Father Bert, that possibility after all these years and at this location simply did not seem likely. A.T. was vigilant and felt reassured he had called Allen and left a message for Bob. As he approached the lobby, he noted plenty of activity, so his anxiety subsided to some degree. He looked around but did not see anyone who looked remotely familiar. He certainly didn't see Father Bert.

After twice walking slowly through the lobby, he went to the front desk to inquire about whether there had been a priest in the area of the lobby. To his amazement, he was told a man who was wearing black and who might be a priest was sitting alone at the far end of the lobby reading some documents. The clerk pointed to an area where a black topcoat had been draped over one of two stuffed chairs near a glass-topped coffee table. A.T. decided to walk over to look around the area designated. When he arrived at the area, no one was nearby, so he decided to turn back toward the elevators. When he did, he heard a quiet voice behind him say, "It is so good to see you again, my son."

Turning, A.T. saw a large man dressed in black and sporting a priest's collar. The man was far too tall to be Father Bert. It definitely wasn't Father Bert; however, A.T. did recognize the man. It was Gerald. Almost instantaneously A.T. said, "What the hell are you –"

"Now, now, my son, you should know better than to use such language, especially in the presence of a priest," laughed Gerald.

"You're no more a priest than I am a monkey's uncle."

"Well, let me say you are definitely wrong about me; however, I must say I was unaware of your being such an uncle," quipped Gerald.

"If you were really a priest, then it is clear the Church is reaching to the bottom of the barrel. Oh wait, don't tell me…you're a defrocked priest, and I imagine the reason for dismissal is probably –"

"How uncharitable you are! Really, Prometheus! First, you swear with a rather loud voice in the presence of a priest while everyone is watching. Then, you refuse to believe a priest who tells you who he really is. Also, of course, remember you even assaulted this very same priest in an alley near your office…but don't worry…I will do my best to grant you absolution, providing you are willing to state your confession. Perhaps, we should sit down. Let me offer you a comfortable seat here in the lobby next to my chair. Permit me to suggest you begin with an Act of Contrition. How about it?" asked Gerald while pointing to one of the large stuffed chairs near the one holding his black topcoat.

A.T. was so angry and stunned he nearly followed his immediate reaction, which was to leave. In fact, he turned to leave, but instead, due to his curiosity decided to stay. He sat down in one of the two stuffed chairs once he was certain Gerald presented no immediate danger and had already seated himself in the opposite chair over which Gerald had draped his topcoat. A.T. then stared at Gerald, cleared his throat, and asked, "It seems as though you've regained your health since the traffic incident when you took your car into the ditch."

"Those roads were terribly slippery," said Gerald sarcastically. "I'm quite well. The doctors only held me for a day and gave me a clean bill of health. There are a few bruises but that's about it. How are you doing? The limp seems to have disappeared for the most part."

"I'm doing fine," answered A.T. "Now, what is this all about? How did you know about Father Bert, and what kind of charade are you now engaged in as you apparently find yourself enjoying some fictitious role as a priest?"

"Well, 'my son,' for your information, I am actually a priest. I was ordained in 1989. I remained at the Vatican for a number of years before I was assigned to the archbishop of San Francisco here in the United States. Unfortunately, I was reassigned due to a misunderstanding, and I ended up back in Vatican City for a while before once again being reassigned to Monsignor Levada, who had been the archbishop in San Francisco. When I was reassigned, he had just been appointed to a new position known as the 'Prefect' or head of what is now recognized as the 'Congregation.' But that was a while back and now, I am operating under a special assignment which involves some coordinated efforts with the Knights of Malta."

"Forgive me," said A.T., "but I find all of that hard to believe –"

"You'll have to do better than that for absolution," quipped Gerald.

"I don't expect absolution from you and wouldn't ask it of someone like you. How do you know Bert?"

"I don't personally know him," said Gerald. "However, I have done a great deal of checking on your background and learned you're quite a creative investigator. You do have a knack for thinking well outside the box. From our investigation of you and from the file we have on you, I learned of your friendship with Father Bert. So, I checked him out as well. I'm afraid he marches to a bit of a different drummer than most priests."

"He marches to a good drummer. Fortunately, he's not marching to the same drummer you are apparently hearing. What are you? Wait, don't tell me…you are part of some newly-devised military branch of the Vatican," said A.T. smiling at his own effort at humor.

"You're not far off base, my friend. I am a priest, and I happen to be affiliated with what is known as the 'Sacred Congregation of the Holy Office.'"

"What 'congregation' might that be? I'm sure it isn't the same one that Father Bert belongs to -"

"For those of you who are uneducated and claim to be Catholics, let me give you a bit of a history lesson. No doubt you've heard of the 'Inquisition,' where the good Church had to rid itself of the many heretics who were found in certain parts of Europe, particularly

France and Spain, where the Cathars had to be placed in check. For your information and edification, the fruits of the Inquisition manifested themselves particularly around 1244 at the Castle of Montsegur. Since then, for the very salvation of their own souls, the Church has found it necessary from time to time to police certain members who drift from the proper and meaningful agenda."

"Oh, I see. You are telling me the slaughter of the two or three thousand Cathars and the elimination of their opposition to many of the peculiar teachings of the Catholic Church were for their own salvation?"

"So, you do know some of your Church history. How impressive!" complemented Gerald. "What you probably don't know is that the office of the Grand Inquisitor has remained throughout history as a part of the Church in order to assure the 'proper frame of mind,' or the true faith, as we see it. The Office of the Inquisition became the 'Sacred Congregation of the Holy Office' in 1908; later, in 1965, it was renamed as the 'Congregation for the Doctrine of Faith.' In May of 2005, Monsignor Levada became the 'Prefect,' upon succeeding Cardinal Joseph Ratzinger, who, as you know, unfortunately recently resigned his position as Pope. With a new Pope from Argentina, we will see if anything changes. I believe my role will be the same."

"Are you telling me former Pope Benedict the XVI, Joseph Ratzinger, was the head of the successor office to the Grand Inquisitor? I can't believe such an office would still exist. Nor do I believe that the Church would condone such an office. You're clearly full of it, and I don't believe a word of what you are telling me. Frankly, I believe you would say or do anything to accomplish any end that suited you. Besides, it has nothing to do with what I am doing, and I certainly hope such a fantasy has nothing to do with what you are up to with your strange and mindboggling behavior."

"Believe what you want, but I am telling you the truth. I am truly a priest. Although I may have at one point encountered a bit of a glitch in my career, I have earned my way back into good graces. It helps that I have some very powerful allies within the hierarchy of the Church. I now enjoy the privilege of working special assignments, and I also serve as an envoy to the Knights of Malta and to the group Samantha had to blab about, the GGG. She needs to be a bit more careful in what she tells people."

"So, may I presume your position grants you certain privileges that allow you to harvest information from sources across the globe and that, in turn, gives you access to private information? If that is then the case, you obviously don't need to keep bothering me. Apparently, you can get the same information I have from your other sources. So, why don't you simply leave me alone?"

"I obviously don't have access to all of the information you may think; however, I do have access to a great deal of information. The material you received from Professor Brougham needs to be returned to a party whose interests may not completely vary all that much from your own. The other information you apparently have, we need to see. We merely are curious as to where your simple investigation is going and what exactly you are piecing together. Believe me when I tell you that you are in way over your head. Please don't underestimate my ability or resources. I know all about you, your associates, and your friends."

"First of all," began A.T., "I very seriously doubt my interests would be the same as your group's, whatever that might be in reality. I think you are bluffing, and I'm guessing the information which you claim to have is probably what the average person could find over the Internet."

"You are dead wrong, my friend. You have no idea of the information and the databases maintained by the Catholic Church," cautioned Gerald.

"So, now it's 'my friend,' instead of 'my son.'"

"Don't try to be clever. I'll give you an example. Let me tell you about your friend, Father Bert. He left for South America many years ago when he sought a move from the Catholic Church you attended and where you first met him. Apparently, he thought he could make some sort of difference in the world if he got actively involved in events taking place in South America. In my opinion, he was a bit misguided and far too idealistic."

"Well, I always had the highest admiration for Father Bert. I realize the Holy Spirit would move him in a different direction than most priests; however, one has to admit he is a very serious and well-intended priest. I believe that -"

"I wouldn't blame it on the Holy Spirit," Gerald chided. "However, I don't want to talk about Father Bert. I want to talk about you and your salvation. Let's start with your returning the documents you received from Professor Brougham and assuring me that copies will be destroyed."

"And if I can't or won't? What then? Are you planning to ambush me again in some dark alley? Are you a current 'hit man' for the Church? Your friend and partner, Samantha, told me the folks at the Knights of Malta and the GGG don't kill people. Assuming that to be true, does my new concern become one with my own Church? In regard to killing people, may I presume the same is true for the Church as well and they don't kill people? Oh, I forgot the Church had no qualms about slaughtering hundreds of innocent people during the Inquisition. But from what Samantha told me…today you just make people's lives miserable," said a dismayed A.T.

"Tut-tut! Poor Samantha! She is not exactly what you would call a close friend. Nonetheless, she is a friend. Our friendship is one of accommodation. We trust each other and are at least friends due to the activities the two of us perform for our superiors. Outside of our work, neither of us has many friends. She is a co-contractor who approaches our investigation, as you might call it, from a different direction than I do. She was assigned to follow the professor and needed my help. Once you received the documents from him, we were reassigned to follow you. Oh, by the way, I do remember you from an earlier time on the same day as the incident with Professor Brougham."

"Oh, do you really? I don't ever remember knowing about you at any point before the incident in the alley; however, Samantha told me it was you and she who were in the car along the Middle Fork of the Rockcastle River. Then days later, it was the two of you who were following us in Paris."

"That's true. Incidentally, do you know who else is following you?"

"Not exactly, but I have some idea…besides, a friend of mine is checking the matter out for me."

"Okay…since I imagine you feel your friend, the Senator, will find out for you, I will leave that subject. Although, I will tell you I do know who else has been following you, and I could certainly provide that information for an exchange of documents from you," said Gerald.

"Sorry, but I'll find out from my own sources. No deals," insisted A.T.

"All right, have it your way," retorted Gerald. "On the same day as the Rockcastle incident, I had an early meeting with some people from Houston and Chicago at the Minneapolis airport regarding some funding assistance for a rally that was to take place later in Minneapolis. They were staging an event and obviously needed some financial assistance. I believe their rally was scheduled about ten days later when the President and certain key members of the Democratic Party were in the Twin Cities for a major speech regarding the economy."

"You don't mean the 'tea party' rally?"

"We simply took an advisory position although we were asked to help with some of their major financial issues by providing some additional funds. We took a 'pass.'"

"At the time some friends were dropping me at the airport, so I could meet up with Samantha at the Lexington airport. She said she had been following the professor and he was at a hotel in Mt. Vernon, Kentucky. She wanted some assistance in bringing him in. Since that is one of my specialties, I was being sent down to Kentucky to help her. I was okay with her request, considering most of my work in the Twin Cities was complete. You know what is ironic?"

"What?"

"We were probably on the same plane to Lexington."

"What a small world! That almost makes us related."

"You really can be a smartass!"

"Of course, but only when I am forced to deal with people like you. Besides isn't that unusual language for a priest?" asked A.T.

"I am trying to be civil and work something out with you," exclaimed Gerald. "I was told I should reason with you and offer a solution to you. Once we reached an agreement and presuming that we could, I was instructed to simply let you disappear back into your mundane life."

"Both you and Samantha have been so helpful, you are actually helping me make up my mind," A.T. stated. "I now believe I will continue to do more work for the Senator. I thought my work had been completed, but now I'm changing my mind, and I believe I should agree with his renewed offer to me relative to additional assistance."

"You insist on involving yourself in matters that should be of no concern to you. As I've often said, 'Samantha talks too much.' Samantha is undoubtedly skilled, but in my opinion, she is an amateur. She is so naive. She is basically a good person and comes from a very respectful lineage; at least one side of her family does. That's why they like her so much."

"So, do 'they' like her because of her Catholic background, or is it her French background, or her Vietnamese background, or is it because she provides blind loyalty to the distorted cause of the GGG, or is it because she is a part of today's Inquisition, whatever that might be?"

"They like a lot of things about her, and it's none of your business. As far as your comment about the Inquisition, it was necessary to rid the world of a vast number of heretics. Today, the Church does not engage in warfare nor does it kill people. If you were a good Catholic, you would know that. You're not a Muslim sect sympathizer, are you?"

"No. I am not a sympathizer to any of the radical fringes of any religion be it Muslim, Christian, Jewish, Hindu, or otherwise. Nuts belonging to any religious fringe are a danger to peace, regardless of how you slice it."

"You just don't know enough about the struggle taking place between good and evil -"

"From which or whose perspective…is it yours?"

"Not mine. The struggle has been going on for centuries, and until recently, many people were willing to allow it to be buried outside the public eye. Today is much like the past, except we are a bit more sophisticated in attempting to bring about the necessary change. It is different today than in the day of the Cathars."

"What if someday it were determined the Cathars were right all along? That would really make the Church look bad, especially in regard to what all of Christianity has been taught. For now, that's enough about the unfortunate history of the Inquisition. You said 'they' liked Samantha. Just who are 'they' who like her so much?" A.T. inquired.

"The people with the Knights of Malta and the GGG like her. Because of her family ties, they have taken her under their wing. I believe that her grandfather was French and properly connected. She has quite a family lineage on the French side. Her mother also came from a good Catholic family located in Southeast Asia. Of course, it helps that she is very bright, uniquely skilled, and fluent in several languages."

What about you?" asked A.T. "Are you from supposed 'acceptable' lineage, along with being otherwise skilled and fluent in several languages?"

"As a matter of fact, I am. Now, let's get back to the subject. Although I personally may not be willing to forgive you for your transgressions, my contractors are. Plus, as a priest, I understand the importance of forgiveness. They are willing to forgive you for what you have done, and although I still have issues with what you did in the alley and on the roadway the next day, I can bring myself to a state of forgiveness. You see, I can be magnanimous," said Gerald as he spread his hands in a sweeping gesture.

"Oh, I have no doubt of your magnanimity. I'm sure -"

Gerald interrupted by trying to impose on A.T.'s conscience, "For example, I am willing to overlook the fact you don't have the good sense to thank Samantha and me for saving you in Paris, and I'm even willing to forgive you for complicity with Professor Brougham and his theft of property that does not belong to him. However, you will need to cleanse your conscience and be forthright with me. You can start by returning the documents the professor stole. Surely, you don't want to be associated with his thievery?"

"In regard to the documents the Professor willingly gave to me, you should know those documents are now in the hands of a United States Senator who is conducting an investigation that somehow involves those documents. Therefore, you will need to contact the Senator's office. When and if you do, perhaps his subcommittee will have some questions for you."

"Why would you do such a thing as to give those documents to a United States Senator? Are you an idiot?" asked a provoked Gerald.

"Obviously, I don't have the same interests as you do. Frankly, I can't think of a better place for those documents than in the hands of a Senate subcommittee."

"Why are you involving yourself in these matters?"

"Because I was personally drawn into this mess by being falsely accused and subsequently indicted for something with which I had no involvement. It's really none of your business," exclaimed A.T. "What about your involvement? I think it's fair for me to know what the other side of the table is thinking and why."

"Believe me, I am not the other side of the table! I've already told you I am a priest and a dedicated servant of the Church. As I said, I have a special assignment as an envoy to the Knights of Malta and the GGG. In actuality, it is the GGG Committee that is directing the activities at this point. It is a large committee with some of the world's most influential interests occupying a position at the table. I have been permitted to be present before the Committee on several occasions. Let me assure you its membership is quite impressive. They are powerful."

"So, you were drawn to the power. I should have guessed it; you are impressed with power-based organizations like the Church and the GGG."

Gerald held up his hand to stop A.T. from continuing and said, "It wasn't only my being a priest with certain special obligations that led to my being selected for my current task. It was also because of my educational background and knowledge of certain matters."

"That doesn't tell me much at all," remarked A.T.

"In addition to being an ordained priest, I have multiple degrees. I thought I mentioned that to you at the bakery in Minneapolis. In addition to undergraduate degrees in philosophy and languages, with an emphasis on Ancient Greek, I also have an MBA and a PhD in economic engineering."

"No offense, but as a result of our first encounter, I never would have guessed you would have the educational background that you do."

"Virtually every priest is well-educated," stated Gerald confidently. "Certainly, I have been privileged to have been granted the right to further my education several times at the expense of the Church. I am deeply grateful and loyal partially because of that fact and because of my beliefs."

"So, was it the economic engineering background or the martial arts training that brought about the tail on Professor Brougham?"

"Not the martial arts," noted Gerald. "That is something I have simply continued as a private means of keeping fit. I do train daily. To answer your question, permit me to say a significant part of my work with the Church has been in the realm of finance. I am engaged in what has been recently categorized as 'shadow banking.' It is a well-known banking practice within the industry which I can explain to you some other time. The professor was assigned to perform some of those banking tasks on a rather daily basis for the GGG. That's how I got to know Professor Brougham initially. We had often worked together in the past."

"You mentioned 'shadow banking,'" noted A.T. "Isn't that what got the Vatican into some serious trouble back in the 1970s and 1980s with a well-publicized banker by the name of Roberto Calvi?"

"That wasn't the Vatican's fault," answered Gerald. "That was a situation where the Vatican had invested funds and was defrauded."

"Well, that's a good story; however, the media seemed to have reported it differently," commented A.T. "From what I recall, Banco Ambrosiano had hired Calvi, and then proceeded to launder money into all kinds of off-shore accounts; got the bank involved with the Samoza dictatorship in Nicaragua and the Sandinista rebels, along with some funding to a solidarity group in Poland. If I remember correctly there was a television special in the United States on the subject, and it reported that Calvi had been hanged from a bridge in London and somehow a Masonic lodge was involved, along with several other suspicious deaths and the mafia. At some point, over three billion dollars were found to have been missing, and I thought the Vatican had agreed to pay part of that money back against some claims."

"Some of your facts are correct," responded Gerald. "However, the Church was an innocent victim. Like you, it got wrongfully implicated and was a victim."

"Not the same," exclaimed A.T. "I wasn't involved. In actuality our company had actually been victimized."

"So had the Church," retorted Gerald. "Now, what about the documents Professor Brougham stole?"

"As I have told you," said A.T. "Those documents have been given to a United States Senator for his further investigation. If I may ask, what did you or, more particularly, the GGG do with him once he was located?"

"That is a matter I shall not disclose; however, I can tell you he is safe and secure on a nice island where the GGG maintains some offshore operations. He has been given the opportunity to again assist the GGG from his island location. The choice will be his."

"What if he just decides to leave the island?" asked A.T.

"He can't. It is too remote, and he is supervised. There are only certain times departure from the island is permitted, and it is doubtful he will be leaving the island anytime soon. He is a valuable asset and perhaps today even more valuable since he decided to leave the United States when he started on his adventure and headed to Mazatlan."

"So, he is essentially a prisoner?"

"I assure you he has all of the comforts he could ever want. He is properly situated with others like himself who have a past history with the Church, the Knights of Malta, or the GGG. They really have it made. They can either help or not. It is up to them. They all usually agree to help after proper re-indoctrination."

"That's most reassuring. God only knows what that must be like."

"There you go again taking the Lord's name in vain," Gerald scolded A.T. "You do need to clean up your behavior."

"That's really choice coming from you. I feel sorry for the professor."

"He is none of your concern."

"I'll need to think about that. So, is he supposed to be back working on your 'shadow banking' enterprise?"

"It is not my enterprise. 'Shadow banking' is a system that has been around for some time but became very popular between 2000 and 2008. It was sort of an off-ledger or non-banking 'banking' system."

"You said it became popular during the years between 2000 and 2008. How interesting it just seemed to correspond with the very years George W. Bush was President of the United States."

"Perhaps that had something to do with it, but in actuality, 'shadow banking' intensified during that time in both the United States and Europe. Groups like the Vatican, certain pension funds, insurance companies, investment banks, hedge funds, money funds, and other non-bank institutions got seriously into the 'shadow banking' business during those years. Of course, we at the Vatican have been in the banking business for centuries. 'Shadow banking' was just a new wrinkle. It has developed into quite a system of acceptable finance. Some of your well-known companies such as Bear Sterns and Lehman Brothers are what you would call regular players. Today, 'shadow banking' is a critical part of the global financial system. It allows companies to privately borrow funds from sources as I have just mentioned. We believe it is a very good system and vital to world financial stability."

"So, essentially you're saying it is an unregulated system of world finance that allows some privileged companies to borrow from private sources where funds get channeled from the investors or private entities to certain corporations. Is it fair to presume there is some profit incentive, as well?"

"There is, most certainly! There are often fees, as well as the difference in the interest rates between what the entity pays the investor and what it receives from the borrower. Banking officials in the United States and in Europe have publically praised the 'shadow banking system' as an important and growing segment of the world's economy. The best part, at least up until now, is that it has been virtually unregulated as it operates outside the banking system and the mandated regulations of the system. If you've heard of 'sweep' accounts, then you've heard of a part of the system. Unfortunately, a lot of the 'do-gooders' in Washington are trying to change the system and bring it under some regulations."

"Would it be fair to presume some of the information contained within the documents Professor Brougham gave me were details of the 'shadow banking' that involves the people directing you?" asked A.T.

"That's correct. You're not nearly as dumb as you look."

"If that is your effort to try to be nice, unfortunately, it's not working. This conversation is over," said A.T. rising from his chair to leave.

"Please sit back down and permit me to lay out a plan of information exchange that may appeal to you," urged Gerald. A.T remained standing long enough to observe among the mix of hotel patrons that Allen and his son, Eric, had positioned themselves at two opposite ends of the lobby with Eric near the main entrance and Allen at the elevator bank. Then, he also noticed Allen had collared Bob while he was exiting the elevators. As A.T. nodded to Allen and Bob, Gerald noticed and casually turned to look in the direction of the elevators. When he turned back to A.T., he said, "Wasn't that one gentleman with you in Paris?"

"He was, and allow me to observe you are not as dumb as you appear," said A.T. while he looked down at Gerald, who was still sitting as calmly as before. Both men laughed as A.T. sat back down. "Now, tell me about your proposed exchange."

"I have told you, and I'm sure Samantha told you, we are interested in retrieving the documents that you received from Professor Brougham. You have those documents, or as it stands now, you have conveyed those documents to your Senator friend. We are no fools, so we feel certain you have copied the Brougham documents. It was a mistake to give the documents to the Senator, but I will relay that information to see how that now delicate matter needs to be processed and handled. However, you have other documents or at least copies of other documents of material you received from your European contacts. It will be too messy for us to attempt to get those documents from the boys in Europe; therefore, you may want to part with your copies so we can assess what you now have. Then we can handle damage control, for I believe once you see the full picture, you will want our explanation. Who knows…you may even be convinced we are on the right track and you could be helpful. In return, I might be able to provide some valuable information regarding certain individuals within the Department of Justice, whom you undoubtedly would consider to be 'plants' for a certain ideology that you apparently feel is detrimental to that Department."

"Why would I imagine you would want to do that, unless it was to eliminate certain individuals whom you would consider weak links? Plus, how would I ever know if you were providing accurate information or even the full extent of the identities of the individuals who have been 'salted' into that Department?"

Gerald continued, "I can't assure you I will be able to identify everyone who interests you, but you will be able to cross-check some of the names from the emails you recently acquired at Dulles when you arrived here in D.C. I won't guarantee you will have the identities of all the people within that Department. It is true some of the people who will be identified are individuals we no longer believe are trustworthy, and frankly, that is because they are real amateurs. They need to be identified."

"It sounds like you are offering up some scapegoats, and just how is it you know about an acquisition at Dulles?"

"In regard to Dulles, I happened to be following you. While at Dulles, I ran into a number of other priests whom I knew and who were attending a conclave here in Washington. Perhaps we were a bit too obvious since there were five of us. Isn't it interesting that if there is a group of priests congregating together, no one ever looks carefully to see if they recognize any of them? You looked right at us and didn't recognize me at all. Although that was accidental, I need to remember that ploy for future stakeouts. It must be the guilty conscience of the public in that they don't want to be too observant of a group of priests."

"I certainly didn't expect to see you, especially dressed as a priest," commented A.T. "What about the incident at the airport? Is it fair to presume you or your other friends had something to do with it?"

"On the contrary!" rebuked Gerald. "A couple of the priests happened to be entering the men's room after three or four people were leaving. The one priest couldn't wait, so he bypassed the service cones just as some other individuals left the facility. That's when the guy was discovered in the toilet stall. Unfortunately, I got there well after the fact and was only able to learn that the guy who was found in the men's restroom had provided some documents to an investigator directly before he was assaulted. The undercover detectives came, so I wasn't able to get any further details. Since I had seen you there, I put two and two together and presumed you were the investigator to whom he was referring. It was purely accidental. I like to think of it as an act of God."

"I wouldn't go that far. Now it is you who should be careful about taking God's name in vain," suggested A.T. "So, after the alley incident, did you think you needed three or four priests to subdue me at the airport?"

"Don't be absurd! I told you," Gerald reiterated, "the other priests were in Washington at a conclave of specifically invited clergymen for a rather confidential matter that happened to have been organized by my superior. I was scheduled to attend after I had set up this meeting with you. I also mentioned, I had been instructed to follow you until this meeting could be arranged."

"So, now I know several things of importance. First, you were following me, and I assume such a 'tail' included this morning. Second, you were specifically trying to set up a meeting with me. Third, you were scheduled to attend a conclave of clergymen here in Washington. Fourth, you had something to do with poor Mr. Felthaus -"

"Hold on! I had nothing to do with Mr. Felthaus," chided Gerald. "Until yesterday, I had no idea who he was or that he had worked for the Justice Department. I told you I know who else has been following you, and I believe I can also tell you why. However, that information will come at a price to you, and it will involve the documents you received from Professor Brougham and from your friends in Europe. Regarding the other reasons you mention, you are correct, except I lost track of you earlier this morning until I saw you with Samantha at a coffee shop. Ironically, our conclave is at the Watergate, and I was entering the coffee shop when I noticed you and Samantha were already there. It was my presumption she had located you and was already approaching you about the exchange of information I have just mentioned. I trust she was unsuccessful since I have not heard from her yet today."

"Your friend, Samantha, and I were not able to agree to anything. In fact, from what she told me, I have pretty much decided to continue to work with the Senator."

"Sometimes, Samantha can be a bit of an amateur. Did she tell you we are willing to work with you so long as an exchange of information is made and providing we are assured that there are no remaining copies of the information that relates to the GGG? We really don't care about your investigation relating to the Department of Justice. In fact, we are willing to give you some critical information about what has been going on at Justice over the past decade or so."

"Just why would you be willing to do that?" inquired A.T.

"Let's just say what had been going on at Justice before President Obama got elected is not the sort of thing we would condone. Permit me to also say the plans of those folks may just lead to a result that would complicate what we have been meticulously and methodically attempting to accomplish for a long time."

"So, it would appear there are some efforts that involve a bit of cross purpose maneuvering between your group and this other group, even though your two groups have been working together to some unknown and questionable end. Did I guess that correctly?"

"I will not provide details to you at this point since you do not have an agreement with us. Let's just say some of what we are intending to accomplish allows for us to ally ourselves with certain other interests, but it is not what you have termed 'the other group,'" Gerald explained. "However, it also needs to be said that although our interests and the interests of certain other groups may be similar in some aspects, be advised that those interests differ markedly in other respects."

"That conundrum is something I will need to think about," commented A.T. "However, at the outset and to me, it's apparent there is really little difference between your intentions and the intentions of the others that -"

"Don't judge us too hastily or too soon. When you decide you are ready to listen, we should sit down and speak seriously. I am confident you will see we are well-intended. We are really interested in good government operations that transcend the simple daily lives of the average person," explained Gerald.

"Well-intended as to your perspective, I'm sure," asserted A.T.

"I have been instructed to provide you with the option of sitting down in order to discuss matters," repeated Gerald. "In the meantime, permit me to suggest you hold off on any further distribution of the banking materials or the Brougham materials you possess. If I were you, I wouldn't wait too long to make a decision. Please think my offer over seriously and plan to give me a call soon," said Gerald while presenting A.T. with his nondescript card that contained a Vatican logo, along with Gerald's name and two phone numbers. A.T. was not convinced, considering the many efforts at forged documents he had seen through the years.

While A.T. examined the card, Gerald must have sensed A.T.'s thinking so he added, "One of those phone numbers is for the one cell phone you returned to me through Samantha. The other number is a new number you can use in order to leave a message in the event I do not answer. I will take your call as soon as I can, and I do hope you do call me very soon. I would suggest sometime before the week is out. That gives you five days, including Christmas Day, and I'm sure you would not want to ruin the Christmas holiday for either of us. I seriously suggest you call in order for us to meet. So you know my schedule, I will be here in Washington until Christmas Eve; then I will be flying back to San Francisco, where I will remain until New Year's Day."

When A.T. placed the card into his shirt pocket, he commented, "You're threatening me again! I will continue my investigation and -"

"That might be precisely the right thing for you to do, presuming we become allies. Our people can really help you. By our joining forces, who knows what might be accomplished," urged Gerald.

"Once again, threats do not work with me."

"The threats, as you wish to call them, are simply warnings, and if Samantha had been doing her job properly, she would have spelled that consequence out to you in plain English," commented Gerald.

"What could you possibly mean by that?" asked A.T. "Why would I want to even listen to what you and your group have to offer?"

"Quite simply stated, the GGG finds many of the instrumentalities of government that were convenient for certain specific purposes in the past in order to discreetly bring parties of interest into check were overworked during the George W. Bush administration. Two of those vehicles were the United States Attorney General's Office and the grand jury system. Through that overuse for very obvious political purposes, there now stands a good chance reform to both is dangerously close to a reality. The fact that the Attorney General's Office and the grand jury system, along with some other government policing vehicles, were commonly used for political purposes by people of a certain political philosophy, has compromised our ability to use those systems methodically and strategically as we have for many years prior to recent times."

"Compromised by people like you and groups like the GGG, apparently."

"No. You really are naive about what is really going on in your own political party. At least our investigation shows that you are still a registered Republican and were a former party leader in your state. May I presume that is still true?"

"For what it's worth, I'm still a registered Republican," said A.T. "I don't like what has happened to the Party."

"Then you should know there are currently three well-known and significant factions within the Republican Party that are actively working behind the scenes to gain master control of the Party. Don't think for a minute moderate Republicans like you are even within the competition," asserted Gerald. "Moderate Republicans essentially have no voice in the Republican Party today, and you should stop deluding yourself into thinking you have such a voice."

"I never thought I had been completely disenfranchised."

"Well, you have, and that is of concern to the GGG."

"You're concerned for me as a moderate Republican?" asked A.T.

"We're not the least bit concerned about you. Harness in your ego! However, we are quite concerned about the Party." Gerald explained, "Today, the Republican Party lacks the balance it once had and may very well be headed for extinction as a viable political party. For your information, the three current factions vying for control of the Republican Party include the alleged 'tea party' group funded partly by the Koch brothers finding support with former political operatives like Newt Gingrich, Dick Army, and their allies; the second group involves the Libertarians who find leadership through the likes of Ron Paul, Rand Paul, and their supporters; and the third group is a loose confederation of former Bushies and their operatives, such as Karl Rove. However, we now believe there is a fourth political faction within the Republican Party you may have just stumbled upon within the last couple weeks. Their efforts are designed to give them elements of control within virtually every department of government."

"Sounds to me like your group, the GGG."

"That's hardly true! But I have told you more than I should have. There is much more I can tell you, but it will only happen if you are able to come to your senses and sit down with us in a meaningful way.

It would be wise for you to make that decision soon. In that regard, I would expect a call from you sometime before the beginning of the New Year. You have my card," said Gerald rising from his chair and extending his hand to A.T., who took the gesture to mean the meeting was over. Since A.T. had nothing more to discuss, he rose and shook Gerald's hand.

Gerald put on his topcoat. He then walked with A.T. to the elevator bank where Allen and Bob were standing. A.T. introduced Gerald to both Allen and Bob, after which Gerald walked out of the hotel.

Bob looked at A.T. and said, "It looks like you could use a drink."

A.T. answered, "Either a double scotch, a double espresso, or both."

CHAPTER 18
A DOUBLE ESPRESSO

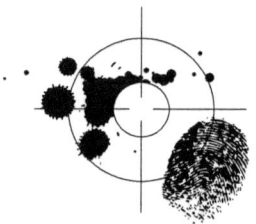

It was late enough in the day, so when they reached the hotel bar, A.T. opted for a double scotch rather than a double espresso. He figured he would need the double espresso the next morning. It was going to be difficult enough to sleep after the meeting with Gerald; therefore, any additional caffeine was the last thing he needed. With Allen, Allen's son, Eric, and Bob, A.T. proceeded to discuss the recent encounter and Gerald's proposal that A.T. meet with him after the first of the year for the purpose of collaboration. The general agreement was to continue with the investigation that the Senator had requested, especially since Gerald's offer was intriguing.

The next morning Allen met A.T. and Bob at the hotel restaurant before the three of them departed for their return trip to Minneapolis. Although the trip was uneventful in regard to the flight, upon arrival at the Minneapolis airport, A.T. noticed a person he believed was the same African-American gentleman whom he had met while disembarking the flight in Paris weeks earlier. At the airport, the man simply looked away after he noticed A.T.'s glance in his direction. The fact that this man was at the Minneapolis airport coupled with the proposal of the day before from Gerald suddenly presented two reasons to call the Senator.

After returning home, A.T. spent the day with Jacci, with the two of them discussing recent events, along with the upcoming plans in a couple of days for a family Christmas dinner with the children and their spouses. A meeting at the firm was set for a late morning eat-in brunch in one of the office conference rooms in the main downtown office. All seven partners were in town and available due to the fact each of them was preparing for his or her family get-togethers for the upcoming holidays.

Although the associates, including Adam, were not a part of the meeting, they would be informed of the decision by the partners regarding A.T.'s continued involvement in the Senator's investigation. The decision was an easy one for the firm. A.T. proposed he would go 'of counsel,' for as long as his investigation for the Senator was required to proceed. It was anticipated the investigation would continue for up to two years. Other than the firm formalizing the modification to A.T.'s relationship through an agreement, case transitions would be taking place over the next couple of months. He was now ready to call the Senator with his commitment.

To make the call, he decided to walk the half-block up the street from his office to a nearby coffee shop that offered several nooks where an element of privacy was present. The walk allowed him to think about his approach to the Senator and also about the conditions he would place before the Senator for continuing the investigation. He was confident the Senator would listen to his conditions since it was becoming quite apparent A.T. was now an integral part of the Senator's objectives.

When he entered the coffee shop that was laid out in a rectangular store front, he noticed one of his favorite nooks was available. He also noted the shop was relatively empty during its typical lull before the lunch hour. It was about 11:20 in the morning, and the coffee shop crew was busy preparing food for the usual rush of noontime patrons. The shop served soup, salads, and sandwiches in addition to its well-known coffees, which made it a popular stop for many of the busy downtown professional and clerical personnel. The day's weather was favorable, so A.T. expected that within 45 minutes or so the coffee shop would be a bustling hive of activity. His timing was good.

When he stepped to the counter to order, a hearty voice from behind him said, "Why don't you order a double espresso. I hear that it is very good, and it will keep you alert."

When A.T. turned, he realized that the voice belonged to the same African-American who had been on the flight to Paris weeks earlier and who spoke to him at the baggage carousel at the Charles De Gaulle Airport. He was also sure it was the same person whom he had seen at the Minneapolis airport two days earlier as he, Allen, and Bob returned from Washington. He was confident this was the same man whom he and Allen had encountered near their hotel in Paris and the same man whose FBI credentials had been "lifted' by Samantha. Trying not to appear too stunned, A.T. turned and said, "Thanks for the suggestion; however, I generally like a simple but strong cup of coffee."

The man extended his right hand. A.T. shook it and stated, "You do look familiar to me. Didn't we meet at the Charles De Gaulle Airport a couple of weeks ago?"

"As a matter of fact, we did," said the man. "My name is Wilbert Edison, and I am an investment banker from the greater LA area. My firm has offices throughout the United States, including the Twin Cities."

A.T. recalled from the identity on the credentials that the man's real name was Norvell Emerson.

Despite his immediate dislike and distrust, A.T. tried to be pleasant. "That sounds like an interesting profession. I really don't have much to do with the banking industry."

"I'm surprised. Here I thought you were one of those attorneys who was involved in the banking business," said the man.

"Why would you think that?" asked A.T.

"I had been making inquiries here in the Minneapolis area for a good finance attorney, and I was given your name. I was just on my way to your office when I saw you pop into this coffee shop," commented Wilbert.

"It really must be a small world in order for that to be the case," observed A.T., "especially since we were on the same flight to Paris a couple weeks ago."

"That really is a coincidence, don't you think?" said Wilbert.

"More improbable than anything one could imagine. Now, who was it that referred you to me?" asked A.T.

"I'd rather not say. It was another attorney here in Minneapolis, and I don't think he wanted me to reveal his name."

"In that case, there is no way I would even consider taking your case."

"Why not? I thought you lawyers were always looking for work."

"No, thank you. Now, if you'll excuse me, I am going to find a nice quiet nook to enjoy my coffee."

"Don't you at least want to hear about my case and what my company can do for you? There might even be a large retainer in it for you."

"Again…no, thank you!" said A.T.

"Please don't be so hasty. At least allow me to give you my card," said Wilbert while handing A.T. a bogus-looking card that identified the bearer as an investment banker with a company by the name of 'New Vista Mesa.' A.T. took the card, looked at it, and handed it back.

"Why don't I call on you sometime in the near future?" offered Wilbert insisting A.T. keep the card.

"No, thanks," said A.T. heading to the secluded table. He noticed Wilbert or in actuality, Norvell, left the coffee shop and turned down the street. A.T. was able to observe Wilbert/Norvell get into a waiting black sedan about halfway down the block. Although he couldn't see the driver clearly, he was rather certain the driver was the man who had been with Wilbert/Norvell in Paris. Once seated and after taking a couple sips from his cup, he assured himself there was no one nearby and dialed the Senator's private number. Since the Senator was unavailable, A.T. left a message. After a period of ten minutes or so, the Senator called back.

"Hello, A.T.?"

"Yes."

"Are you alone and in a position to speak privately?"

"Yes, I am."

"All right, we can talk. I trust the call is quite important since you called on this line."

"It is. I have decided to take you up on your desire that I continue with the investigation. Accordingly, I have some requests I feel will be acceptable."

"What are your requests?"

"Simply that I be compensated at the usual rate and through the subcommittee budget. Additionally, I would want my work to be properly sanctioned by an appropriate letter from your office with the letter specifically delineating that the investigation I will be performing is an authorized endeavor with proper authority, directives, and protections set forth with clarity in a succinct manner above your signature."

"That's agreed and not a problem. Consider it done. Now what is the urgency of the call?"

"It is two-fold," began A.T. "First of all, the identity of the man who was following me along with the lady, Samantha, whom I have previously mentioned to you, has been made known to me. He set up what he called a 'chance meeting' with me in Washington at my hotel before I left. He said his name was Gerald Peterson. He mentioned that, along with the Samantha lady, he was with the GGG organization. Additionally, he said he would help us identify certain individuals who have compromised the Justice Department and elsewhere within governmental agencies. Apparently, his group, the GGG, has been involved with and has been working with certain individuals within our government for some time. He alluded to the fact that now there is a new player or players who seem to be encroaching upon the past efforts of the GGG. He said the GGG has some interest in exposing those individuals. He tells me he can give us names and relationships."

"That is good news. By all means, plan to pursue that avenue."

"There's a catch."

"What's that?" asked the Senator.

"He wants the material Professor Brougham gave us, along with the papers I received in Paris from Jean Paul and the documents we obtained in Geneva from Claude. Apparently the GGG is somehow intricately involved, and it sounds as though they want to minimize their exposure."

"What's his connection, if you know?"

"He was blunt about that. He claims he is a properly ordained priest and is working for both the Vatican and the GGG. He also claims to be some sort of emissary to the GGG group from the Vatican. He stated that for not just decades but for a much longer period of time, the Vatican has been involved behind the scenes while trying to influence key individuals within our government. He made no effort to conceal that fact and seemed somewhat proud of it."

"That is nothing new. The powers behind the scenes in Washington have known about the Vatican's distant but well-placed interest in our government for a very long time," commented the Senator.

A.T. inquired, "Did you know about any financial dealings the Vatican has had with the Federal Reserve?"

"No...but that sounds quite intriguing, along with the fact someone with the Vatican knows about your investigation and wants some of the documents. That's something that would be of interest. Now, what about this GGG? I've never encountered them before. Have you?"

"I haven't, no. The only thing I know at this point is the GGG group is apparently the group that also employs Samantha. She is identified in my last report to you. Ironically, she is the same lady who was with your friend, the congressman, at the Lincoln Memorial," explained A.T.

"Did he give you contact information?"

"Yes, he did; however, he expects me to be able to deliver the documents from Professor Brougham and the documents from Europe to him if I call him back."

"That's interesting," stated the Senator. "Does he know you gave the documents to me?"

"He knows I gave them to a member of the U.S. Senate, but he doesn't know who."

"Let me think about how I want to handle this matter. I can tell you that I do want you to make contact and follow through. I am especially interested in finding out what he can tell us about certain people within the Justice Department and other government agencies. I am particularly interested in any campaign contributions. Let me think out the document matter, and I will get back to you on that. Does he know about the plan you and Bud devised regarding the release of the material in segments to members of the media if a full Senate investigation does not take place?" questioned the Senator.

"No."

"Good. Now, what else do you have for me?"

"The second reason I called pertains to the FBI Agent whose credentials I received from the Samantha lady who's a friend of your congressman buddy. I saw him at the Minneapolis airport when Allen, Bob, and I returned from Washington D.C. In addition, he confronted me about ten minutes ago here at a local coffee shop that I frequent. He gave me a bogus name and card. Apparently, he doesn't know we have his credentials or that we know his real name."

"That's also very interesting. I've been doing some checking on him with some of my close friends at the Bureau."

"That's great news," said A.T. "What have you found out?"

"You won't like it. My sources tell me he is being watched by certain other agents within the Bureau. They believe he is dirty and is a part of a covert segment within the Bureau that seems to have an agenda of its own. You already know his real name is Norvell Emerson. And, most importantly, he is a part of an FBI task force that attempted to implicate you in the matter that was ultimately dismissed.

"The former head of that FBI task force was forced to resign as he was originally charged with several felony counts and has since pled guilty and has been sentenced. Several of the prosecutors were written up by OPR, you know, the Office of Professional Responsibility. At least one of the assistant attorneys from the DOJ in Washington was forced to resign from the Department of Justice. My sources tell me although the task force was purportedly set up under the guise of legitimate purposes in an attempt to ferret out white collar crime, it is being used for other purposes. Its hidden purpose seems to have been to serve as an experimental enterprise on behalf of a certain group within Justice to go after individuals who are perceived as political enemies of the covert segment I mentioned and is now under scrutiny as it operates within the Department of Justice, including the FBI. One of the apparent and undisclosed purposes of that task force was to try to connect political enemies to suspected criminals and then the task force would create a criminal enterprise of some sort. In their eyes, they were accomplishing two purposes, namely, entrapping some known criminals by creating and operating a criminal enterprise and then connecting those suspected criminals to their perceived political enemies. They would get an indictment against all of them and, as you personally know, the rest is history," explained the Senator.

"Why would they want to target me in such an enterprise?"

"One of my sources told me your name had come up as an individual who was getting too close to some of the financial systems put in place for funding certain political processes. Does anything come to mind?"

"No," A.T. continued. "The only thing that would have come close was a few years ago when I was assisting a client in the client's attempts to locate venture funding. Any contact I made was done in order to conduct due diligence on various venture sources, and I might add all of them were turned down or ruled out by my client as a result of the due diligence I had done. As a matter of fact, because of the company's spending a considerable sum on various venture sources, an official complaint was filed with the FBI. As it turns out, the FBI task force from another FBI Field Office never even bothered to check its own indices. In a related case involving a venture source that defrauded my client out of $450,000, I filed a lawsuit and obtained a judgment when that group thumbed its nose at the lawsuit and the service of process the local sheriff served upon them. That individual later filed for bankruptcy and was discharged from his debts," said A.T.

"What happened then?" asked the Senator.

"The FBI agents conducting the task force never bothered to check my earlier complaint with the FBI or the fact that the same people were involved or that the guy whom we had a judgment against claimed that he had performed alleged trades that were sanctioned by the Federal Reserve. That is always one of the first things an agent is supposed to do. It was never done. They never bothered to interview me. Had they done so, I could have tied many of the 'bad players' together for them. I even remember that particular con artist calling to tell me that an FBI agent had interviewed him about me. Therefore, it is my guess the work I was doing for the client stirred some interest in the fraudulent funding sources, and as a result, they tried to implicate me by diverting attention from themselves," continued A.T.

"It might even be more than that. Perhaps in your due diligence, you were getting too close to some sort of banking interest or enterprise the bogus venture groups were using, and those people or groups were being covered by certain people in the Bureau," commented the Senator.

"That scenario is a definite possibility. The one venture source that had defrauded the company client out of $450,000 was tied to the other group about which our complaint had been made to the FBI. It was a venture group operating out of Las Vegas, and it turned out the other venture funding group was introduced by a member of the first venture group, a fact that was unknown at the time. That second venture source, the one who had been sued in civil court, had divulged in at least two depositions that he had acquired over ten million dollars and the funds were being kept for him in an attorney's trust account that I believe was in Europe somewhere. Later, when that particular defendant testified before the bankruptcy court, he stated he had been wrong in his earlier testimony. Obviously, he was lying one time or another. He even lied to the bankruptcy court when he told the court he had never been served, yet there was a certified affidavit by the deputy sheriff who had served him. In addition, one of his former partners was present when that defendant was served by the deputy sheriff," added A.T.

"Perhaps there is a connection. We'll need to check it out. I can tell you that you were targeted and that the task force was being used as an instrument to implicate individuals whom the task force knew were innocent. Other rules and regulations, including those of the FBI Handbook and the Undercover Ops Manual, were violated as well. I learned from my contacts at the Bureau about an internal investigation that was and is underway. Some FBI Agents and a couple of prosecutors will soon be charged with criminal violations themselves or will be asked to resign. They are attempting to identify with greater particularity those involved, along with some of the attorneys at the Justice Department. My contacts have asked me to see if you would cooperate with them in learning more about this particular operation within the Justice Department. In that respect, your independent investigation would prove helpful," the Senator insisted.

"I can see why. They have some serious problems within the Justice Department, and obviously, not all of them involve this particular task force," said A.T.

"That's correct, and I believe that is why nothing further was done to any of the prosecutors in the Siegelman case or FBI agents that handled the Stevens case."

"Did you discuss the lost credentials of FBI Agent Emerson with your friends at the Bureau?"

"I did, and in fact, I gave the lost credentials to the Assistant Director. He said he would be using the credentials as additional evidence in his case against Agent Emerson and his associates," explained the Senator.

"By 'associates,' may I presume such would include some of the attorneys at Justice that Mr. Felthaus has mentioned?" asked A.T.

"Indeed! And for that reason alone, it might be worthwhile for you to re-contact this Gerald individual of the GGG to see if he really has information that would be beneficial to us. Did you say he wanted an answer before the first?"

"He does, but don't forget he wants the documents we received from Professor Brougham and the documents from Paris and Geneva."

"I want to think about how I want to have you handle that matter." The Senator continued, "In regard to the Felthaus material, if Gerald asks about it, tell him the material from Felthaus would be our means of determining whether his information is accurate and helpful. Tell him we are taking a big risk in working with him, and any exchange of information would have to remain confidential between us and his superiors. Tell Gerald before we exchange any information, we will need some verification, other than a business card, in regard to his having a capacity of some sort with the Vatican and the GGG group of people. See how much information you can get about the GGG membership."

"I'll give him a call, and see what I can work out and whether or not there's more I can find out about him and his alleged connection to the Vatican and the GGG. I'll also see if I can learn more about this GGG itself. What about the FBI agent, SA Norvell Emerson? What do you want me to do in regard to him?"

"From what I understand, he is already under investigation by one of the Assistant Directors, along with several others at the Bureau and at the Justice Department. I don't think we want to stir that matter, but we do need to find out what he is up to in regard to our investigation and why he was in Paris."

"Yes, but how exactly do we follow that matter without stepping on some toes at the Bureau?" inquired A.T.

"That's a good question. Let me have a private lunch with one of the Assistant Directors who has routinely been working with me on the entire matter my subcommittee is addressing through your investigation. He and I will exchange the necessary information as this situation unfolds."

"So, is this FBI Agent a part of what is going on?"

"We believe so," said the Senator. "It is our impression he is working with a group within the FBI and the Department of Justice being molded into a segment expected to position themselves into key spots within the Bureau, Justice, and the Judiciary."

"That's far more serious than I suspected based on my investigation."

"I presumed as much, and that is why I diverted your investigation to certain financial matters, paramilitary groups, and political portions within the Republican Party. You were a natural for me because of your background. I knew you would be able to piece the investigation together, and as I'm sure you are aware, this matter is far more serious and dangerous than any of us expected. Needless to say, that is why I have so many Republican members of Congress willing to work with us on this matter. For the sake of their own party, they are perhaps more fearful than we Democrats are of what is happening. I am doing everything I can to make sure this investigation stays clear of any politically motivated agendas and that key people from both parties are informed," explained the Senator.

"At this point, I'm not surprised at anything," said A.T. "The client I represented had even gone to the trouble of hiring a law firm with expertise in compliance. The client had a Regulation D Memorandum prepared in advance of attempting to secure any venture funding. Both the client and I wanted to be sure everything was done in full compliance, regardless of the fact there had been so many efforts by Congress to deregulate the financial industry."

"That was really very careful thinking on your part and on the part of your client," the Senator responded. "However, so much has been done to deregulate the finance industry, it is no wonder the investment bankers, venture capitalists, and other supposed financial experts are getting away with what they are and in the process are attempting to implicate the innocent. By implicating innocent individuals through orchestrated entrapment efforts, the folks we are after think they have thrown us off track by prosecuting people who can't defend themselves. To my way of thinking, the Congressional efforts to deregulate the finance industry have allowed for the DOJ, the Bureau, and other agencies to try to get creative in orchestrating environments for crime instead of relying upon laws designed to regulate and bring enforcement to the financial industry."

"From my perspective, that has certainly been the case," observed A.T. "Now, as a point of interest, what exactly do we know about Agent Norvell Emerson?"

"The most important thing we know is he is overly ambitious and will do just about anything to enhance his position within the Bureau. From what we know, he is being used primarily due to his unbridled ambition. He is trying to make up for his shortcomings in terms of education by exerting himself within the Bureau. He has been quite ready to volunteer for many available assignments and tasks. His expertise, if he has one, is to 'set up' people. He has even 'set up' some of his fellow agents in order to advance his own career. In the past, he has 'set up' people at a major airport, some people involved with corporate stock matters, and certain individuals in several drug cases. He came in from the greater L.A. area as an undercover police officer and was able to get an invitation to the FBI's 'National Academy' as a law enforcement officer. He then pulled all of the strings he could in order to get an appointment to the FBI Academy and later in order to become an agent. His specialty with the greater L.A. drug task force when he was a police officer, as well as his current specialty with the Bureau, is to 'frame' people. He is known as an 'entrapment expert.' That is how he has moved up the ladder at the Bureau. He was given a Supervisor's Desk at one point but got busted back down to the street. It is doubtful he is fully aware of what the internal group within the Bureau is really up to, but he has been more than willing to be a part of it so long as his volunteering pays the dividend of advancement for him within the Bureau."

"He sure sounds ambitious," A.T. noted.

"There's no doubt about it," said the Senator. "It is my suggestion you keep Agent Emerson at arm's length and avoid any additional contact until I am able to get a better indication from the Assistant Director as to how we should handle this matter. Meanwhile, I would like you to make contact with Gerald in order to determine if he can prove his identity. If he can prove himself to your satisfaction, I urge you to work with him on the basis of what we have discussed."

"I'll do what I can to get in touch with him and see what develops. What about the letter from you of confirmation of the assignment?" asked A.T.

"It will be sent out yet today. If you need to reach me, use this phone number; I will be leaving Washington for the holidays this afternoon. Give my regards to Jacci and the family, and don't be hesitant to call me."

"No problem and thanks. Please give my regards to your wife, children, and grandchildren, as well."

"Thanks. By the way, have you given further thought to providing a copy of the materials to Blaine Jeffers?"

"I called him last week. He wants me to fly out to San Diego after the first of the year. I didn't mention anything over the phone to him since I decided the subject matter was too sensitive, and I didn't want him guessing about it. I'll take a copy with me when I head out after the New Year."

"Okay. Take care, and have a great Christmas and New Year's."

"Please do the same. Talk soon. Bye."

In A.T.'s mind, all was settled. He would be able to finish the 'of counsel' documentation for the law firm and be ready to dig back into the investigation. He finished his coffee and thought about how he would approach Gerald sometime between Christmas and the New Year.

Although A.T. was a firm believer in matters of synchronicity, he didn't expect matters to unfold so quickly. When he stepped out of the coffee shop, he encountered a panhandler who was sitting on the street with a sign requesting assistance since he was "out of work." He had a coffee cup in his hand that he pushed in front of A.T. It was a scene out of a cheap novel, yet it had an impact. As A.T. approached the man in order to give him some cash, the man extended the cup that contained a white piece of paper. The panhandler motioned with the cup to A.T. to take the paper. When he took the item, he noted it contained a simple message that read, "Contact Gerald immediately." While somewhat stunned, A.T. subconsciously placed a couple small bills into the cup and took the note. The panhandler said "thanks" and disappeared down the street.

Since A.T. retained the private phone numbers Gerald had given him at the hotel in Washington, he decided to make the call to Gerald on his car phone while on his way home. Although he tried to reach Gerald several times, contact wasn't made until A.T. was about halfway home. Gerald identified himself, and after some pleasantries, he got to the point.

"You might be in some danger of being compromised by some of the people whom you are investigating," said Gerald.

"So, you and your GGG and/or the Vatican are trying to compromise me? Thanks for the warning," A.T. responded.

"Don't be a fool," asserted Gerald. "I'm trying to help you and to demonstrate some good faith efforts with you. My superiors want to work with you, and in that process, they believe you may need our assistance more than you realize."

"So that's why you are having a disguised panhandler tailing me?"

"He's not tailing you. Everyone knows you spend too much time at certain coffee shops. It doesn't take any great investigative efforts to determine that. The man who delivered the message to you is a private investigator whom we often use in the Twin Cities. The disguise was my idea in order to get your undivided attention. It looks like it worked."

"It was a bit unnerving to say the least. Obviously, I will need to start changing my habits."

"That's a good idea; you should give that fact serious consideration, especially if you are going to continue any investigation."

"What makes you think I am going to continue my investigation?"

"That's what you told me back in Washington D.C.," Gerald said.

"So I did," responded A.T. "You said I might be in some danger from the people whom I am investigating. Would that be from the GGG?"

"As I've told you, you will not be in danger from my superiors; however, I've also told you, they can make your life much harder to live. It is not my superiors whom you need to fear. Perhaps you don't yet realize it, but you have hit a nerve and are irritating that nerve with your continued investigation. It is apparent those political forces are the very ones positioning themselves to take control of the Justice Department and other government agencies. I've been telling you we have some common interest."

"So, is a part of that common interest one of protecting me from this unnamed force?"

"It is simply because you have documents we want and for the further reason your investigation might be very helpful to us," said Gerald.

"Then, first tell me exactly what kind of danger it is that you believe I am facing. Can you also identify parties who are attempting to place me in danger?"

"The danger you face is that you already have learned too much about what this political group is attempting to accomplish within the Department of Justice and elsewhere within the U.S. government. This political group that is behind the scenes and better organized than you might imagine already believes they can place you in a position where they can bring criminal charges against you, thereby taking you out of the investigation you have been doing. They weren't able to do that the first time, but they are intending to double their efforts and literally 'get you.'"

"You mentioned a 'political group.' What group is that, and what do you know about them?"

"Not so fast. We need to work out some kind of arrangement first regarding the documents."

"Before I discuss that any further, you will need to tell me at least something about the 'political group' you mentioned and that you imply is trying to set me up,' inquired A.T.

"I can tell you this 'political group' is operating mostly within the Republican Party although there are some Democrats who are also involved. At this point, it is somewhat loosely organized, but it is organized. It also involves some individuals who were unelected officials who worked in several administrations, including the Nixon, Ford, Reagan, H.W. Bush, and W. Bush administrations. And most significant of all is what your investigation has stumbled across, and that is the money sources pulling the strings behind the scenes. The group operates under the name of LESTER. That is all I will tell you at this point."

"Tell me exactly why this is so important to you and your 'people.' It certainly is not due to an altruistic urge to help cleanse American politics."

"It's not," Gerald agreed. "Sorry to repeat myself, but our members have been doing this for a long time. We believe the process we follow is a proper and legitimate one. Plus, we don't want to see the overthrow of the U.S. government. We like it the way it is. It serves our purposes well, and it currently serves the world better than control by some radical group."

"That's interesting. But let's say, just hypothetically speaking, that I would be willing to work with you and find a way to deliver the Brougham documents and the Paris documents to you. What's in it for me other than to presume the GGG and the Vatican will leave me alone?"

"That should be enough; however, I told you in Washington, we can deliver the names and connections of many of the people at Justice and in other departments of government. We can identify with some detail the people and their connections to the fringe interest groups that actually do plan to take over the U.S. government utilizing their plants within the government that have been set in place for some decades now."

"You'll have to do better than that," said A.T.

"What if I could deliver some letters and emails that specifically set out organizational efforts, directives, agreements, and plans for a series of major meetings that will commence within the year?"

"That's intriguing, but you'll need to tell me more."

"I will tell you more, but that won't happen until we reach some type of agreement," Gerald said.

"Okay. Let's say I could deliver the documents. What is the procedure?"

"Let me set out the terms first," said Gerald. "You deliver the original Brougham documents and destroy any and all copies. I'll need assurances of that. Next, you provide all of the original documents you received in Paris and assure me any and all copies have been destroyed. Finally, I want copies of whatever it was Mr. Felthaus gave you at Dulles International. You can keep copies of that material for your records."

"That will not work. Let me tell you what we are willing to do -"

"You said we. Who is 'we'?" Gerald questioned.

"You already know I am working with a United States Senator and one of his committees. That is the 'we'!"

"Okay. Now, how about the terms I just outlined?"

A.T. explained, "Here is what we are willing to do. First, we can give you the original Brougham documents; we keep copies; and we want Professor Brougham to be made available to us and removed from his island prison. Second -"

"Wait, wait. Nothing doing," Gerald protested. "He works for the GGG, and he will be happy to continue to work on the island. He is not a prisoner. Plus, we do not want any copies of his documents in anyone's hands."

"What I just presented to you are the only terms to which we will agree in regard to Professor Brougham."

"That's not what I expected. I will speak to those above me to see what they say. If Brougham is made available, we will need to know the purpose and what your intentions are with him. About that, I am sure. As far as the copies, I will have to see what I am told in that regard. There will have to be some measure of confidentiality and non-distribution. What about the documents from Paris?"

"In regard to the Paris documents, we might agree to provide copies of those documents; however, we will keep the originals. In any copies we provide to you, the names of our sources and perhaps the names of other parties identified in the documents will be redacted."

"That doesn't sound doable. The names are important to us, and we definitely do not want copies of those documents floating around. However, I will check with those above me who make the decisions. What about the material Mr. Felthaus provided?"

"In regard to the Felthaus material," A.T. replied, "I've been instructed to tell you under no circumstances are you entitled to that material. That came to us as a part of our investigation, and it is our way of cross-checking any information you might provide to us relative to the DOJ."

"You said that you were instructed to tell me. Who instructed you?"

"The Senator instructed me in that regard himself. So, these are the terms to which we would agree. Plus, you could tell me more about the GGG connection with the Vatican and how this entire matter is important to your people at both the GGG and Vatican. It's that simple."

"It's not that simple."

"What then?" A.T. questioned.

"If we reach an agreement, we can discuss it but not before. Are you sure the terms you set forth are complete and final?"

"From what I have been told, the answer is 'yes.'"

"Look," said Gerald, "It's late in the day. Why don't I meet you somewhere, and the two of us can have a comfortable drink together. I understand you appreciate a good 'Irish Coffee.'"

"No thanks. Besides, I thought you were in San Francisco until after the first?"

"That's where I will be in about twenty-four hours; however, I'm in the Twin Cities, where I typically stop on my way from Washington to San Francisco. Why not take a moment to relax and join me for an 'Irish Coffee' or some other beverage of your choice?"

"Not at this time," responded A.T. "If we are able to come to terms and develop an agreement, perhaps I will take you up on that invitation in San Francisco. Presuming you really are a priest, I trust an 'Irish Coffee' is a good disguise. Have a Merry Christmas!"

CHAPTER 19
AN IRISH COFFEE

Pulling into his driveway, A.T. received another call from Gerald, who went directly to the point. "I almost forgot to give you a final warning. Since it appears we may be working together, I felt duty-bound to call you back to once again warn you about the individual who is following you."

"Are you referring to the man I encountered in the coffee shop a bit earlier?" asked A.T.

"That's the one. I will caution you to stay away from him. We are still checking him out, but we can tell you some interesting things we do know."

"What's that?"

Gerald explained, "We know he is an FBI Agent, and we suspect he is tied to the people within the Justice Department who are carving out their own organization within the Bureau and the Department of Justice."

Not wanting to tip Gerald off to the fact Samantha had already informed him over a week earlier about the tail in Paris and that the individual was an FBI Agent, A.T. remained silent. He didn't want Gerald to know Samantha had already given him the agent's "lost" credentials.

A.T.'s silence must have lasted too long since Gerald interrupted the silence and said, "Are you still there? I am very serious about this warning. The guy who approached you at the coffee shop has been tailing you for weeks, and he is one of the people whom Samantha and I stopped near your hotel in Paris. Does that give you enough to make you concerned?"

"No doubt about it," said A.T. "I have been concerned about the guy for some time. I don't know exactly what he is up to or why he is targeting me. Can you give me some insight?"

"All I am at liberty to tell you at this time is that our sources tell us he is a part of the group we have been watching, which I mentioned to you earlier. We believe he is trying to place you in a compromising position. We don't know why for sure, but we think it has something to do with the documents you have and the investigation you've been conducting."

"I have gathered that. I've been checking him out as well. At this point, I need to know more, so if you have more information, it would be appreciated."

"As I learn more," Gerald said, "I will let you know. For now, stay away from him. That is the best advice that I can give you at this point. I will try to call you sometime before New Year's Eve. See if you can get some latitude regarding terms from the Senator, and I will see what I can do with my superiors."

The two men bid each other farewell again. Approaching his driveway, A.T. noticed Adam's car parked at the front of the house. He knew that in two days his son and two daughters, along with their spouses, would be joining Jacci and him for Christmas dinner at the family residence. Therefore, he presumed Adam had stopped by with some items for the holiday. After parking his car, A.T. went into the house and found Adam and Jacci seated in the study having a casual conversation.

Adam rose and hugged A.T. Jacci immediately stated she had just begun brewing some fresh coffee and suggested she prepare an Irish Coffee for the three of them. Adam declined the Irish version of the coffee and requested just black coffee because he rarely consumed any beverage that contained alcohol. While A.T. and Adam discussed some matters related to the law practice and Adam's company, Jacci prepared the drinks and returned to join the conversation. At the first moment of opportunity, she said, "Adam has something for you."

"What might that be?" asked A.T. when he noticed a broad grin spreading across Jacci's face. At that point, Adam reached into his pocket and pulled out a small box and presented it to A.T.

A.T. said, "Christmas isn't for a couple of days, so you're a bit early." Opening the box, his expression turned to a stern look, while Jacci giggled. A.T. looked back and forth between Jacci and Adam and said, "I've told all of you for years now I don't need a hearing aid. Not that I don't appreciate the gift and the idea of the gift. For the gift, I am grateful. However, my hearing isn't that bad, and I'm just not ready to start wearing a hearing aid."

"Easy, Dad," said Adam. "Let me explain what it is that you have in your hand. It is something I put together with my IT department."

Adam, in addition to being an attorney, was an inventor who had developed several "high tech" items for the communications industry including a number of 'state of the art" video systems. He, along with A.T. and several other individuals, had started their own company that designed various systems utilizing video communication formats. The company had its own Information Technology division, and it was that division that had developed the device according to Adam's explanation.

"What you have in your hand looks like a hearing aid, but it isn't. Well, actually, it does have hearing aid capabilities, but it is also something else. A couple days ago, Mom told me you were going to continue your investigation for the Senator. I thought if that were the case, I could prepare some nice technical items for you. This is the first one. Although it looks and operates as a hearing aid, it actually includes a transmitter with a small 'subscriber identity module' or SIM chip embedded within the device. It has a small and efficient battery that holds a charge for several hours. It is also designed to utilize some of the natural body current in order to maintain a charge for a longer period of time, if it is properly installed in the ear. The battery portion and SIM chip are designed to fit within the crease behind the ear, allowing stability from the side of the head. We've used some of the new 3-M adhesive to allow it to remain in position." At that point, Adam removed another box, a bit larger than the first, and presented it to A.T.

"This is a nice cell phone, and I appreciate the gift, but I like the iPhone I use on a daily basis," said A.T.

"This is not your typical cell phone," said Adam opening the back of the phone. "This is the receiver for the ear piece you are holding. Although this is a fully functioning cell phone, it is far more. It will pick up and record what you are hearing and transmitting with the 'hearing aid' device you are holding. It is possible for you to leave this cell phone at a remote location, such as a car, so long as the distance is not more than a mile or two at most. This device will pick up any discussion you are having and record it. Additionally, the phone can be used in a conference mode that will patch the discussion it receives directly to another party anywhere in the world. So, for example, if you leave this cell phone portion in your car and are transmitting from the hearing aid device, the cell phone can also be used to add another party in a conferencing mode so long as you set the call to the third party in advance of your using these two items in combination with each other."

"Really," said A.T. "Here I thought you and your mother were trying to get me to wear a hearing aid."

"Not that you don't sometimes need one," commented Jacci.

"What makes you think that's not intentional selective hearing," offered A.T. while smiling at Jacci. He examined the ear portion of the device, and in looking back at Adam, noted, "This could come in handy. I've always been in favor of using new technology, and it would seem this could be very useful. As I think back over time, I could have used this in many different cases."

"Our concern," said Adam, "is really one of safety. From the sound of things, your investigation for the Senator is getting more and more complicated each day. Based on what Mom is telling me, you have encountered some rather tense situations lately. This device could be one way of assuring your safety during the investigation. We have beta-tested it, and so far we believe it is ready for 'prime time.' Our hope is to market it to various police departments because it is far superior to the conventional and even the newer electronic 'bugs' law enforcement is currently using. I suggest we take some time either today or tomorrow to try it."

For the next three hours, A.T. and Adam ran tests on the hearing aid transponder and the receiver system throughout the Twin Cities. It seemed to work better than expected. They found the device would actually work at a distance of just under three miles and without disturbance in even the busiest parts of the downtown area. The test included patched calls to Jacci, who received and recorded the calls on the home answering machine. To be sure the device would work with a long distance call from its phone portion, A.T. called both

Rene and Jacques in Paris to wish them a happy holiday. Various lengths of time for the calls confirmed the system would work.

With the confidence of the system in hand, A.T. returned home from the "on road" tests of the new device. He spent the remainder of the day assisting Jacci with the Christmas dinner plans. Adam would return with his wife, while Rachael and Renee, along with their husbands, would also be present for a celebratory day of fun. The afternoon before Christmas, with all of the preparations well in hand, Adam, Rachael, and Renee, along with their spouses and several neighbors, stopped by to join A.T. in a "pick up" game of ice hockey in the backyard, which they had flooded. The game was the right prescription for relaxation and fun. The audience included Jacci, their two daughters, and Jacci's mother, who was included in all the festivities. She always added an additional upbeat dimension to the family. The event put everyone in a joyous mood for the next day.

Christmas Day was an eventful and joyful experience with A.T. and Jacci entertaining as usual. After church, the family convened at about 12:30 at the residence on Summit. Everyone had a great time with plenty of food to eat and some lighthearted moments during a gift exchange. Much fun was made over Adam's earlier gift to A.T. Jacci especially enjoyed recounting the event and the expression on A.T.'s face when he thought that the hearing aid was intended solely for any deficiency A.T.'s hearing had been displaying in her recent conversations with him during which there was no response.

As in past years, the entire family spent the late afternoon assisting at a dinner and food distribution center for individuals who were having a tough time with the economy. Each year A.T. and Jacci would help fund the organization and would assist in the clothing and toy drive. The entire family had become regular fixtures at the event and this year was no exception.

When the family was departing the distribution center during the early evening hours, they were approached by two men. A.T. immediately noticed one of the men was Norvell Emerson, the FBI Agent who used the name Wilbert Edison. After pausing to assess the encounter, A.T. introduced the first man as Wilbert Edison to his family and waited for Emerson to introduce his companion. Emerson caught the hint and introduced his companion as George Tarkanian. Emerson stated the man introduced as Tarkanian was his mentor and superior with the investment banking firm for which they both worked. He stated they were interested in contributing to the distribution center but had gotten there too late since the doors were closing. To A.T. it sounded like a Paul Ryan tactic. When Ryan ran for Vice President, he pretended to be helping at a relief center by washing dishes that had already been washed. A.T. told Emerson/ Edison and Tarkanian they could contribute the following week during regular hours, and A.T. gave them a phone number for the center.

A.T. bid the men farewell and turned with his family to leave. While walking to the nearby parking lot for their vehicles, Emerson said, "Oh, A.T., as long as we have made this chance encounter, perhaps we could take a moment to discuss something with Mr. Tarkanian because he will only be in town a couple days longer."

A.T. turned and said, "For heaven's sake, man, this is Christmas Day, and I plan to spend the remainder of the time with my family. Permit me to suggest the two of you do the same. There is nothing so urgent that a discussion needs to take place at this moment in time. Have a Merry Christmas." A.T. and his family proceeded to their cars.

"Sorry," said Emerson while he and the newly-introduced Mr. Tarkanian followed the Van Doren party to the cars. "Mr. Tarkanian would like to take just a moment of your time to discuss your banking interests in Paris, and then we will let you go. I'm sure once you've heard what we have to say, you will want to visit with us as soon as possible."

"No thanks," said A.T. as he and his family continued to walk toward the vehicles that were a short distance away. He then paused a moment and turned to say, "...and by the way, I don't have any banking interests in Paris or anywhere else that would be of concern to you."

"Please, just a moment more," pleaded Emerson directly before A.T. opened the car door. "Mr. Tarkanian and I are following a rather pressing schedule and need to do something with Mr. Tarkanian's funds before the end of the year. You see, he would like to work with you and your friends in Paris, along with the ones here in the U.S. In order to do that, he would like you and your law firm to set up a couple corporations for him that would be able to work with an offshore company that has a significant amount of funding behind it."

"Believe me when I tell you that you are asking the wrong person," said A.T. "I have never worked with any offshore companies in my life nor would I. Personally, I am very suspicious of any offshore endeavors. Perhaps you should get someone to introduce you to Mitt Romney."

"Look," pleaded Emerson, "We obviously have gotten off on the wrong foot. We want to work with you. Frankly, we know you spoke to some rather high-ranking bankers while in Paris, and we simply would appreciate an introduction to them. We would like to meet with them, but we need an introduction from you."

"Under no circumstances would I introduce you to the people with whom I met in Paris. They are not venture capitalists nor are they investment bankers. My purpose in meeting with them is a confidential one and cannot be disclosed to you. There are client confidentialities and besides, what business is it of yours to have been following me in Paris or anywhere else for that matter? The fact you were in Paris and attempted to encounter me there is already a matter of concern to me. Under such circumstances, I cannot help but be suspicious of your intentions," noted A.T. as he continued to open the door.

"Sorry about that, but we were hoping to get an introduction to you while in Paris. That is why I tried to introduce myself to you at the Charles de Gaulle Airport. We heard you and your firm were involved in the venture funding business and -"

"You heard wrong! I have never in my life been involved in the venture funding business nor was my client. And once again, let me assure you the people with whom I met in Paris are not in the venture funding business. Now, good evening," said A.T. as he finished opening the door and slid under the steering wheel.

Emerson asked with a final plea, "What about the investment of Medium Term Notes and 'Shadow Banking'"?

"I had never heard of 'Shadow Banking' until days ago," said A.T. "You are barking up the wrong tree, believe me."

"If you can help us, we can make you very rich. We can share profits with you. We can even make you a partner in the business. We can make it worth your while if you would at least introduce us to the people in Paris and others here in the United States that -"

"Not a chance," said A.T. closing the door and starting his car.

"Perhaps I could call you tomorrow," yelled Emerson. A.T. began to back the car out of the parking space. After finally leaving the area, the Van Doren family regrouped at the family residence on Summit for an evening snack of sandwiches and desserts. Both A.T. and Adam were anxious to see if the hearing aid device had worked, considering they had opened a phone line from the device back to its companion phone portion that had been left in A.T.'s car. Before they had departed earlier in the evening, they had also opened a line from the phone portion of the device that was left in the car to the home phone answering system. They were pleased to learn the entire evening, including the conversation with Emerson and Tarkanian, had been captured by the system. A copy of the conversation was made for the Senator.

Their best efforts were made toward enjoying the remainder of the evening with the usual eggnog toasts and desserts. By the time the evening had ended, everyone had put the incident involving Agent Emerson and his associate out of their minds. A.T. had decided he would wait until the following Monday to contact the Senator about his discussions with both Gerald and his encounter with Agent Emerson. He thought the taped conversation with Agent Emerson would be interesting to the Senator, as well as to the Assistant Director with whom the Senator had been working. It was apparent the agent was up to something, and it somehow related to Paris and certain financial matters. Without additional information, this issue had to remain a mystery until A.T. could develop more from his investigation.

* *

The next day was spent resting, with A.T. assisting Jacci in some household chores that typically arise after a holiday celebration. By noon, the two of them had finished the "clean up" portion of the house and decided to spend some time together touring the city to view some of the decorations that were well-known attractions in various neighborhoods throughout the area. After their self-guided tour, they decided to have their evening meal at one of their favorite restaurants. Since Sunny had chosen to rest rather than tour the city, they returned to their residence to collect her for the upcoming dinner. Once at the restaurant and in order to wait for their table, they were escorted to the bar area, where they positioned themselves in a corner with two oversized and comfortable chairs. They all ordered some holiday cheer in the form of "Irish Coffee," considering they all enjoyed it from time to time.

From their position at the bar, they were able to see one of the large flat panel television screens showing the local news. At a moment during the broadcast, A.T. held up his hand to Jacci and Sunny when asking them to turn around to see if they could also hear what was being said by the news anchor. The picture showed several men dressed with coats identified with the FBI emblem and lettering. The men identified by the news as FBI Agents were escorting two individuals with familiar faces, namely Norvell Emerson and his friend, Mr. Tarkanian. The news report noted unauthorized access and disclosure of confidential documents and violations of the Intelligence Identities Protection Act of 1982.

Jacci inquired if those weren't the same two men who had met up with them at the food distribution center the previous Christmas evening. After A.T. nodded in the affirmative, he pointed to the subtitle feed at the bottom of the screen indicated that the two men, who were identified as FBI Agents, had been arrested by the FBI Office in Minneapolis for apparently using their position with the Bureau and a special 'task force' for accessing unauthorized records and transferring confidential information to outside sources.

A.T. commented to Jacci that what they were seeing was significant in several ways including his recollection of what the Senator said about the agent known as Emerson, who identified himself as Wilbert Edison, being under investigation by the FBI. He commented to Jacci that he knew the FBI regularly investigated the illegal and improper acts of its own agents. He mentioned he would now need to contact the Senator about what he had just seen and read. Jacci insisted he wait until the next morning and to forget about the matter at least for the evening.

For whatever reason, perhaps a perverse sense of satisfaction due to the arrest of Norvell Emerson and an agent identified to A.T. as Tarkanian, A.T. was able to enjoy the evening with Jacci and Sunny. He found himself to be in a particularly jovial mood. The evening meal and subsequent activities were especially relaxing and enjoyable. He thought it was poetic justice that two of the men who had been going out of their way to improperly implicate him in their ill-orchestrated enterprise had been nailed. Although he didn't have a full picture or complete details of what they were up to, he was more confident than ever that his counter-investigation was on the right track and that sooner or later he would have both answers and satisfaction.

The next morning A.T. placed a call to the Senator's private cell phone. After explaining the events of the night before and after apologizing for the call, A.T. was put at ease by the Senator who had heard the same news broadcast that had hit the national circuit. The Senator told A.T. he had received advance notice from his friend at the Bureau that the arrests were going to be made. The Senator stated some unauthorized access and disclosure of classified information had been made with certain records compromised by the agents. There was also the improper disclosure of covert agents that brought the Intelligence Identities Protection Act into effect. He stated he didn't want to bother A.T. on Christmas Day with the information. After hearing what the Senator had to say, A. T. was happy he had apprised the Senator of his encounter with Agent Norvell Emerson and the other agent, whom he learned from the Senator was another FBI Agent whose real name was George Teller. The Senator informed A.T. that after the latest conversation with the Assistant Director, the two of them wondered if A.T. would enjoy the opportunity to question both Emerson and Teller, along with a couple of FBI Agents who were a part of the internal investigation.

A.T. was overjoyed to hear the request and answered in the affirmative. He cautioned the Senator that time was becoming an important factor because their new acquaintance, Father Gerald, wanted an answer relative to the proposed exchange of information sometime after the first of the year. Also on the agenda was a possible meeting with Blaine Jeffers, whom the Senator also knew. A.T. did not mention the fact that he had his own agenda in contacting Blaine. He did not inform the Senator of what he had discovered several weeks ago when he retrieved his old computer and found an interesting email from Julian Tilson-Gould, a former member of the White House staff under W. He believed that it was unlikely that the Senator would know her. Besides, he was on a personal quest in an attempt to find out if there were a connection between staff members under W. and the indictment wrongfully rendered against him.

The Senator told A.T. to make arrangements to meet both Gerald and Blaine. Since one was in La Jolla and the other in San Francisco, the Senator suggested after the first of the year, A.T. plan to travel to the West Coast for meetings with each of them. The Senator promised he would call A.T. back immediately after the first of the year with his decision as to how the exchange of information with Gerald should be handled. He thought he had a plan but wanted to run it by his friend, the Assistant Director at the Bureau. He asked A.T. if he still had a copy of the portion of the documents that were to be entrusted to Blaine. When A.T. said he did, the Senator told him to have the documents ready and that it was a "friendly" Republican Senator who had suggested Blaine Jeffers as a possible custodian of one set of the documents. The fourth copy would still need to be placed with a trustworthy party who would be able to work with the others holding portions of the confidential documents. A.T. agreed, and the conversation with the Senator ended.

The remainder of the week between Christmas and New Year's was spent relaxing and organizing things at the law office that A.T. had left a bit unattended. The break from the investigation proved to be the right change of pace for A.T.

On the second of January, and as agreed, the Senator called A.T. with the proposed terms for the information exchange with Gerald. The terms were short and direct. The Senator would allow for the original documents of Professor Brougham to be returned to the GGG entity, with full copies being retained by the Senator's office and investigators. In exchange, the GGG would have to agree to produce Professor Brougham for deposition and allow him to be made available to testify before Congress, if it were deemed necessary by the Senator. Copies of documents received from George Felthaus would not be provided and would have to remain confidential.

The Senator particularly noted if the Felthaus documents were to be provided, it would only be after the information regarding the individuals in the Justice Department known to the GGG was disclosed to A.T. He also informed A.T. he would be granted the opportunity to review and compare the Felthaus documents against the new information from the GGG. It would be exclusively up to A.T. as to whether the Felthaus documents could be released in the event there was satisfaction showing some of the same parties were identified in both the Felthaus documents and the GGG documents. After getting the terms straight from the Senator, A.T. telephoned Gerald for the purpose of arranging a meeting in San Francisco. If the terms were met after the meeting in San Francisco, A.T. planned to meet with Blaine in the San Diego area.

A.T. presented the proposal to Gerald directly after he concluded his call with the Senator. After presenting the Senator's proposal, Gerald said he would call back within the day.

Gerald called back within several hours to advise A.T. he had the authority to reach an agreement. He said, however, the logistics of bringing Professor Brougham forward as a witness were a matter that would need to be delineated with certain conditions, including the waiver of any potential prosecutorial efforts. If the GGG understood it would not be challenged or charged with any criminal activity relative to Professor Brougham, arrangements could be made for his being presented as a witness. Gerald also wanted assurances the GGG would not be the subject of any investigation by the Senator. A.T. stated he could not agree to such a proposal and he did not have the authority to do so. Gerald insisted that the meeting proceed despite this unresolved "loose end."

Arrangements were made to meet Gerald in San Francisco within a couple of days. It was now up to A.T. to attempt to arrange for a meeting in San Diego with Blaine and hopefully with Julian. In the call to Blaine, it was as if time had stood still. Both A.T. and Blaine were able to pick up with their relationship, and in the process were able to discuss 'old times,' along with reminiscing about old political events and meetings of years ago when A. T. had still been active in politics.

A.T. dialed the private number for Blaine and left a message for him to call back. Within less than a minute A.T.'s cell rang. It was Blaine.

"A.T., this is Blaine. How've you been, and how were your holidays?"

"I couldn't be better. The three kids were here with their spouses, so we had a great time. The problem was eating too much."

Blaine replied, "We had one great time after another. Two of our boys brought their sweethearts back for the holidays. Our third boy hasn't gotten himself involved with anyone yet and still has been focusing on sports. He has a couple college scholarship offers to play football, and he is considering that as a possibility. Our youngest will just be going into high school, so he's been running all over the place and spending far too much time with the latest computer online 'gaming.' He just wants to grow up so fast. Having three older brothers doesn't help. How's Jacci?"

"She's wonderful! How about Angel? Is she still as involved in the political world as before?"

"She is. At present she has been working as the chairperson for one of our Republican Congressional candidates. They were roommates in college, so they're old friends and have been involved in some of the same groups for years. In fact, I think they are still in a bridge club together. So, she remains quite active with her social circles and politics taking most of her time. However, we still get to spend time together and that usually includes an evening cocktail of Irish Coffee we both enjoy after the evening meal."

"That sounds like a nice way to end the day. By the way have you heard from Julian?"

"I have but I haven't set anything up for you yet. She and her family have moved to Palm Springs, where she's been writing her memoirs. Since she and I are still active in Republican politics, I will see her from time to time. You're sure you want to meet with Julian?"

"Absolutely!" exclaimed A.T. "It's always good to catch up with old political friends. In our earlier call you said something about a meeting in early January. Is that still a possibility?"

"I believe it is," answered Blaine. "Let me call you back on that. I'll try to be back in touch within a half-hour or so. Talk then."

The call ended with A.T. looking at a silent phone. It was the same old Blaine. After hanging up, A.T. reminisced about Blaine. He recalled that Blaine Jeffers seemed to be one of those individuals who had been born to be in politics. It was Blaine who had introduced A.T. to the benefits of a late afternoon 'Irish Coffee.' Blaine had instructed A.T. that 'Irish Coffee' was the drink of the politician who didn't want it to appear as though any alcoholic beverages were being consumed. Blaine was extremely outgoing and always managed to be the center of attention, wherever he went. In college, he had been active in virtually every type of political activity that was available on campus. He had been a fairly good student since studying came easily for him. Upon graduating, Blaine was accepted into graduate school and began work toward a master's degree. However, he tired of the rigors of studying, and much to his parents' chagrin, he enlisted in the Navy. He served his full term, and returned to Southern California with the sole purpose of entering the political arena. Another well-known fact about Blaine was his fondness for the ladies. Wherever he went, the ladies followed.

Blaine wasn't opposed to making the best out of his good looks and his compatibility with the opposite sex. He made special use of his "attributes," particularly through the political process and from his own direct involvement in the Republican Party. It was through his political contacts that he met his wife. As it happened, the father of Blaine's wife was a staunch Republican leader in California and a close personal friend of Ronald Reagan. Blaine met his father-in-law during a major political rally held in Newport Beach. After the first meeting, the two of them became allies and close friends, despite the difference in age. As it turned out, his father-in-law had an extremely attractive daughter. Blaine was immediately drawn to the daughter, named Angel, and she was attracted to Blaine. Consequently, his attraction to the lady who became his wife was twofold. To add to the mix was the fact Blaine and Angel found they had a number of mutual interests, with politics being only one.

In addition to Angel, arguably a misnomer, being the daughter of a very prominent Republican, she was, in actuality, the perfect complement to Blaine. While in college, she was much like Blaine in the sense she was quite fond of the opposite sex. Plus, the fact that she was extremely attractive allowed her a seemingly endless line of suitors and partners. It was inevitable she and Blaine would meet each other at a Republican rally where the after-hours activities were enough to challenge those of any Shrine or realtor convention.

Blaine and Angel immediately connected and developed more than just a mutually strong attraction for each other. Rumors always travel far and wide, and in the case of Blaine and Angel, who ultimately became husband and wife, certain stories found their way out, including a particularly juicy one. At a time directly before their engagement, the two of them were sitting behind a piano on the piano bench in the plush study at Angel's family residence in Palm Springs. They were not playing the piano but were otherwise engaged when Angel's father came into the study in order to pour himself a brandy from the hidden bar along the bookshelf area. After Angel's father entered the study, he stopped abruptly when he noticed his daughter and Blaine were in a compromising situation. Pretending to not see them, he went to the hidden bar behind the bookshelves, where he fumbled around with glasses and bottles, while making a considerable amount of noise with the hope that the two at the piano would make themselves less conspicuous.

The ploy worked and necessitated Angel replacing certain clothing items and slipping off of Blaine's lap where she had been facing him on the bench. Once she had dressed and situated herself next to Blaine on the bench, Angel began to play holiday songs on the piano, while the two of them attempted to sing. Angel's father took the cue and came out from the concealed bar behind the bookshelf to say 'hello.' After somewhat of an embarrassing conversation, Angel's father asked to see Blaine privately later in the day. As a father, he had become aware of his daughter's less than stellar reputation.

Subsequent to the conversation between Blaine and Angel's father, later in the day Blaine proposed marriage to Angel. A wedding date was set. The two of them have remained happily married since that time, with four children to show for their relationship. Both of them have remained active in Republican politics in California with each of them wielding their own unique power base within the party. The fact that Angel's father was a forty year veteran of the Party with long-term contacts was more than helpful to both Blaine and Angel.

A.T. knew Blaine would most likely remain in politics in one fashion or another, so it made sense to contact Blaine if it became necessary to take a current pulse of Republican activity. Ironically, Blaine had never run for office himself but had preferred to remain in the background as a Party officer. It was a good bet that Blaine and Julian had maintained contact over the years, due to their mutual interest in Party politics, as well as each other. At least A.T. would be able to reopen the door with Julian through Blaine. Regardless of the outcome, a meeting with Julian was expected to be fruitful in getting up to speed as to what was happening within the Party.

After completing the call with Blaine, A.T. decided to call Gerald in order to make specific arrangements for the two of them to meet in San Francisco. The plan would be to meet Gerald first and then fly down to meet with Blaine and Julian. At the time of the call, it seemed Gerald was somewhat preoccupied. Thus, the conversation was brief with Gerald's suggesting the two of them meet in the Old Mission area. When Gerald learned A.T. had never been to the area, he proposed that they meet at the old "Mission Dolores," otherwise known as Mission San Francisco 'de Asís.' Since A.T. was always interested in historical sites, the idea struck a chord. The meeting was set for Wednesday, and although Gerald felt they start by attending Mass at 7:30 that morning, A.T. declined since he claimed he would be traveling. Accordingly, he was not sure where he would be staying or how long it would take to reach the Old Mission area from the hotel. He didn't want to make a commitment he could not keep. Besides, it didn't sound like a good time to A.T. Additionally, A.T. was suspicious that

Gerald would want to start a meeting by attending Mass. He still found it difficult to trust Gerald. He wasn't convinced Gerald was actually a priest, as he had claimed.

Once he firmed up the time and date with Gerald, A.T. made calls to each of his law partners in order to set up a meeting for a final review of the new 'of counsel' agreement with the firm. Once the document was approved and signed, A.T. would be free to spend most of his time on the continued investigation for the Senator. While he was sending the emails to his partners, he received a call from Blaine, regarding the meeting with Julian.

"Hello A.T. This is Blaine. I set up the meeting with Julian and by the way, Angel says hello."

"That's great! Tell Angel hello!"

"I will, but we're hoping you will be able to tell her hello yourself when you come out. Would it be possible for you to join us next Friday evening? We are having a party at the La Jolla Country Club, and we were hoping you could attend. In fact, we would like to have Jacci come along as well. What do you think?"

"That's an intriguing invitation, but I don't think Jacci will be able to come because her mother is visiting from Arizona. I believe my mother-in-law will be here for at least the next two weeks, so Jacci will be unable to get away."

"Tell her to bring her mother along," encouraged Blaine.

"Thanks, but it sounds as though they have already made some plans to meet with friends of Jacci's mother."

"Okay, however, if she changes her mind, let us know."

"I will and thanks."

"What about you? Are you available next Friday?"

"Friday might work. I have to be in San Francisco on Wednesday and possibly Thursday morning. I could fly down from San Francisco on Thursday and be available to meet with you on Friday, so long as it wouldn't be an imposition. I don't want to be a party crasher."

"You won't be a party crasher, and besides, I believe there will be a number of people there whom you should know."

"Is that so?"

"You wanted to catch up with Julian, didn't you?"

"Oh, yes, I did. I take it she will be there."

"She'll be there with bells on! She said the two of you needed to talk. She was afraid you were mad at her."

"Why would that be?" asked A.T. innocently.

"She didn't say. She just said she was surprised you would even want to speak with her. She did say she definitely wanted to talk with you at some point and thought the two of you could visit privately while you were out here. She said she might owe you an explanation…if that makes sense."

"Well, that's interesting," said A.T. feeling encouraged he might finally get to hear some of the explanation of facts that had long eluded him. He thought to himself: *Julian at least owes me that.*

"We'll let the two of you discuss whatever it is that seems so important to you, but I don't think you will want to do it at the country club on the night of the party. There will be too much going on. Why don't you just plan to engage in some general conversation that night, and I will set up a dinner meeting for us on Saturday? We can discuss it then. That's providing you don't mind if I tag along. How does that sound?"

"That sounds fine. So far as I'm concerned, it wouldn't bother me to have you listen to my discussion with Julian. See what she says. Okay?"

"Sure! Once you know where you will be staying, let me know, and we will have someone pick you up on Friday at about 6:30. It will probably be one of the boys. That way you don't need to get a map for the club. By the way, some of those attending might be dressed a bit formally because it is our annual 'Holiday of Politics' party. We've been holding the party for about ten years, and it has become one of the more upscale parties of the winter season. A lot of Party officials, including some elected officials, will be there."

"I hadn't planned on bringing a tux, so perhaps I should pass on the party and plan to hook up with you on Saturday instead."

"Nonsense! You and I are about the same size. Why don't I have one of my sons bring a tux for you when he picks you up Friday night? I insist. In fact, I received a call from a friend of mine who said you and one of his colleagues in the Senate were visiting and you might have some interesting information for me. He mentioned some paperwork. Does that make sense?"

"It does; however, I don't think we would want to discuss the paperwork in a party atmosphere. The subject matter is a bit delicate; therefore, why don't we plan to meet at a coffee shop when I'm out there."

"Okay, that sounds good. If it is so serious, then we should discuss such matters, perhaps over a cappuccino on Saturday, and plan to have fun at the party the night before. We'll see you next Friday. Take care," said Blaine and he hung up.

A.T. looked at the silent phone, and thought to himself, 'That's the same old Blaine. To anyone who didn't know Blaine, they would most likely think he was either upset about the conversation or rude. However, that was the way Blaine always finished his phone discussions. Once A.T. was able to make hotel reservations, he would send confirmation to Blaine in order for arrangements to be made for one of Blaine's sons to accommodate him with a tuxedo.

Since A.T. was unable to get Allen to join him due to Allen's vacation plans that included a late January Caribbean cruise with Cynthia Brownell, he decided he would instead pack his new hearing aid toy simply as a safety measure relative to any conversation that might prove unique during his trip to California. The purpose of the device would be to assure anything A.T. said would not be later misconstrued or misquoted. After all, he was simply trying to preserve his own part of the conversation. Next, A.T. sent the documents designated for Blaine to the hotel in San Diego via registered courier and directed to his own attention.. With everything seemingly in place, A.T. planned to enjoy the next several days and the weekend with his family before he needed to prepare for the trip.

CHAPTER 20
A TIERED CAPPUCINO

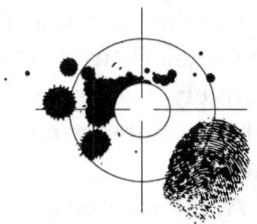

The Tuesday flight to San Francisco was a late arrival that allowed
A.T. to check into his hotel in the downtown area just before
6:00 p.m. At the front desk A.T. picked up the registered package
containing the documents and located his room. He telephoned
Gerald to confirm their meeting at Mission San Francisco de Asis
at 9:00 in the morning. Gerald asked if he could send transportation
for A.T. That was a red flag in A.T.'s mind. He didn't want Gerald to
know where he was staying, so he advised that he had a rental and
would meet at the agreed time the next day. A.T. spent the evening
reviewing the documents he had assembled for Gerald. He wanted
to be sure that all of the names that he was unwilling to reveal had
been redacted from the materials from Europe.

The next morning A.T. traveled to the Mission District and took
time to drive around in order to become familiar with the streets
and landmarks. At about ten minutes before 9:00 a.m., he found a
parking spot and walked over to the Mission. There on the steps
of the Mission Chapel was a waiting Father Gerald who, after the
greeting pleasantries, insisted on giving A.T. a private tour of the
interior of the chapel and the nearby basilica. Gerald was actually
dressed as a priest, and during the tour, it was apparent he was

personally familiar with everyone, including the groundskeeper, the Parochial Vicar, and the Deacon, to whom A.T. was introduced.

After Gerald provided a thumbnail history of the Mission chapel, along with some history about Father Junipero Serra and Father Francisco Palou, he suggested that he and A.T. take a stroll down the street. He stated he thought a relaxing walk would allow the two men to discuss the documents, along with what Gerald termed "important other matters." Gerald directed the walk eastward for several blocks since he planned a lunch at the 'Monk's Kettle,' which turned out to be a very busy and noisy place.

During the walk, the two men discussed in general terms the documents Professor Brougham had given A.T. weeks ago in Kentucky. The outside hope was to obtain some form of cooperative efforts regarding a number of the other entities that also appeared on the documents. This was particularly true of the "targeted" individuals and corporate entities actively shown as both the recipients and the originators of funds being transferred to questionable political sources in the United States.

Both the Senator and A.T. harbored an outside hope they would be able to convince Gerald's superiors to make the professor or others available as witnesses. They were also keenly interested in the whereabouts of the professor. As absurd as it sounded, they wanted to pursue the status of the professor. If neither Gerald nor the GGG provided any answers, a new segment of the investigation would be in order as it would seem more apparent than ever the GGG had something serious to hide.

Before arriving at the "Monk's Kettle," a general agreement had been reached. According to Gerald, the GGG was willing to allow the documents provided by Professor Brougham to be copied and retained by the Senator and his investigation with the understanding the documents were provided voluntarily by a cooperating witness who would not be the subject of the investigation. It was not as though the GGG had any choice in the matter; therefore, its decision was simply a perfunctory act. From the Senator's perspective and as A.T. had advised, that part of the agreement was not necessary but reached in order to placate Gerald and the GGG.

After entering "Monk's Kettle," A.T. and Gerald were escorted to a table against the wall set for four. It bothered A.T. that the setting was specifically noted by the waiter for four and that the place was so loud. Being true to his nature, A.T. bluntly stated, "Have you noticed we have a setting for four? Isn't this place a bit loud for casual conversation?"

"We will soon be joined by two others for lunch," said Gerald. "This restaurant is always a place of high energy. That is part of what makes it so unique. Don't worry; I didn't bring you here to have you shot and left at a table near the wall. I told you we don't kill people. Besides, you haven't given me the papers we agreed upon. Where are those promised documents?"

Annoyed at Gerald's bizarre sense of humor, A.T. pulled out a chair next to the wall. He waited for Gerald to sit down as a matter of courtesy for what he believed was a role-playing priest, and then said, "I wasn't expecting you to murder me. That wouldn't seem appropriate conduct for a priest, assuming you are indeed a man of the cloth. The place also seems a little too public for that type of activity. It just seems awfully loud for conversation. In regard to the documents, please be assured they are in a safe place, where I will take you when it is time for the exchange. You said we will be joined by two others. I didn't expect that."

"They are fine people. Well, they are now. One of them you have already met. The other is such a pleasant and capable person. They should soon be here. I trust you don't mind picking up the tab for four instead of two. You know they never pay priests very well," noted Gerald.

"I'm prepared to pick up the tab. By the way, you promised some documents for me in the exchange," responded A.T. "If I recall correctly, those documents were to detail the recent activity within the DOJ, along with names, emails, and other matters. What about those items?"

"The documents will be with our two additional guests. We're a bit early, so why don't we plan to order a preliminary beverage," suggested Gerald as the waiter approached the table. The two of them ordered with A.T. requesting a coffee and Gerald a Tiered Cappuccino.

"With all we are doing for you and the Senator, it troubles me that you are not willing to remove us from the investigation," noted Gerald.

"It is simply because we do not have all the facts at this time. I can tell you there is ample evidence from what we do have to demonstrate a trace of funds going into the hands of several politically active groups here in the United States. Some of those groups are advocating either separatist movements or succession efforts that include violence against the government. At this point, we cannot exonerate your friends at the GGG from such activity. Therefore, the investigation continues," explained A.T.

"We are not interested in the violent overthrow of the government," said Gerald. "At this stage, we are willing to assist you due to the fact some of the same parties you are targeting present concerns to us as well. As I told you in Washington, our people have been trying to assist the United States government in positive ways ever since the country was founded. We are not the 'bulls in the china shop' that certain other groups present. They are clearly unskilled in the nuances of promoting good government causes. We agree they are dangerous and they present serious problems. That is why we are offering to help you. Let me assure you under no circumstances should we be bundled with them."

"We haven't yet come to the conclusion one group of outside finance of the American political process is better than another, at least not at this stage. Frankly, there are quite a number of outside groups presently 'on the board' for investigative review. That's about all I can tell you at this point in time," remarked A.T.

"Let me be bold enough to tell you that there is more than just one group you are investigating advocating the overthrow of the government as you and I know it. Therefore, if that is the criteria, you would be spending a lot of time for nothing if you were to include us. To include us would be a monumental waste of resources. Let me assure you we can be very helpful to you and we are not the enemy. For example, much of the information I believe we have for you that relates to the Department of Justice doesn't involve the violent overthrow of government; however, it does involve a very detailed and methodical plan to use the Justice Department as a major tool in shaping the politics of the twenty-first century and also who ultimately will hold power," detailed Gerald.

"Can you be more specific?" asked A.T.

"By controlling the Department of Justice, almost every aspect of government can be made to fit within the grasp of those who are clever enough to hold and administer power from that department. Ultimately, the courts can be controlled, including justices serving at virtually any level. Everyone knows if an individual has worked as a United States Attorney or as an Assistant United States Attorney, that person has a better chance of being named to a judicial position.

Having been at the Department of Justice is a very powerful item to have on a resume, especially if the person is interested in becoming a judge," noted Gerald.

"So, you're telling me you can demonstrate that the people whom Mr. Felthaus was willing to identify are attempting to position themselves in the Department of Justice in order to 'salt' the judiciary?" asked A.T.

"Not just the judiciary," warned Gerald. "Every aspect of societal control crosses through the Department of Justice. Just think about it. The major arms of national law enforcement, including your friendly FBI agency, are operated through the Department. The investigations of anything or anyone fall within the authority of the DOJ. An investigation can be commenced about anything. The DOJ enforces the law of the land. Voting regulations come through the Department of Justice. The appointment review for administrative law judges, United States Marshalls, District Court Judges, Appellate Judges, and the Supreme Court justices comes through the DOJ. The magistrates through the judges all find their approval or rejection through investigation done by some department within the DOJ, such as the FBI that, as you know, derives and maintains its existence through the DOJ. The enforcement or non-enforcement of any specific law whether it involves commerce, the environment, transportation, agriculture, food and product safety, pharmaceuticals, medicine, immigration, social legislation, civil litigation, licensing, defense contracts, foreign exchange, intellectual property, and virtually every other aspect of government passes through the Department of Justice in one way or another."

"Don't forget the grand jury," urged A.T.

"Certainly, it includes the grand jury and just about everything else that relates to any law of this country. I wasn't trying to place a limit on it by citing the examples I did," said Gerald. "I just wanted to make the point that the people who you need to be concerned about have specifically targeted the Department of Justice as their principal objective. They have already taken up positions throughout the department, and in the process, they have kept specific relationships with particular major law firms vibrant and active. The people we have been tracking are some of the same people about whom you are now just learning. You will find, if you haven't already, these people are very clever and have a very well-orchestrated system of taking control of the Department of Justice. We can offer some significant assistance. We are in a position to make you look very good at your job."

"Any effort to make me look good in my work will be appreciated," smiled A.T. "Some of the information we have and the information we expect to obtain from you in regard to the Department of Justice would involve other possible violations of various statutes and would relate to the politicizing of the Department."

"That's what I expected, and that is where we can help you," noted Father Gerald. "Although we suspect your concern is the politicizing of the Department of Justice during the George W. Bush presidency, the politicizing was set in motion long before he was President. It may have manifested itself to a great degree under Gonzales, but you will see it was going on long before that and involves a group of attorneys who have a bit of their own agenda. A large contingent of these attorneys comes from a specific group that organized themselves before they came to Washington D.C. Today, the group includes attorneys from Washington D.C., major law firms throughout the country, specific law schools, and a contingent of attorneys who had worked their way into the DOJ years ago. There is already significant evidence a large percentage of recent DOJ lawyers were drawn from a handful of law schools carefully selected during the term of Mr. Gonzales. They have a set agenda with one of their main objectives being control of the Department of Justice, along with molding the DOJ toward their political ends. They understand power."

"We realize that. We are trying to get to the bottom of it and see just how bad it has gotten. Hidden agendas are always the sorts of things that raise red flags. That might be true of the agenda of the GGG as well. For that reason, I cannot tell you that you are going to get any kind of 'free pass,'" cautioned A.T.

"That's understood," said Father Gerald. "We don't want or need a 'free pass.' I believe when the smoke clears, you will find what we do is perfectly proper and we have been doing it for many, many years. In fact, you will find our groups have been helping the governing process of many countries for centuries. If it had not been for our guidance and help, many countries would have foundered. In my view, you will find we have been beneficial to Western Civilization in many respects and have helped stabilize many governments over time."

"That's a sales pitch if I've ever heard one," commented A.T. "Please understand the investigation is being done because of various irregularities discovered in the process of three separate investigations. The Senator's office was aware of each of the separate investigations and believed there was evidence that the three were being tied together by a particular group with a wealth of funds behind them. The Senator believes the people with the money are attempting to unify the three segments under investigation. The Senator also believes these 'behind-the-scenes' financial interests felt it would be expedient for the three segments to be joined into a common enterprise."

"If I may ask," inquired Gerald, "what three investigations?"

"First, there was my independent investigation regarding certain abuses occurring at the Department of Justice. Next, there was an investigation by an investigative reporter regarding some hidden financing of certain political activity. Third, there was an independent investigation of certain paramilitary groups that have been organizing and training with impunity within the United States. It appears as though the paramilitary groups have made no qualms about the use of violence against the government. Evidence developed that the three investigations were coming up with some common names of individuals who were attempting to tie the three groups together in order to position themselves to drastically change the government here in the U.S. It was the Senator's office that identified the tie-in, and it was the Senator who changed the course of the investigation of each of the three of us who were pursuing our own efforts. He felt it was beneficial to bring the three investigations together. That's how we have reached this point."

"Don't forget all of our friends in the media," added Gerald. "They are deeply involved with what is happening in the world of politics today."

"There's no doubt about it. However, due to the protections accorded to the media under the Constitution, it would be too complicated to include them. To include the media would immediately result in a diversion from the strength of the three investigations under way. Bluntly stated, we are already having enough complication in terms of the investigation when it comes to the financial part of the work that is unfolding. The decision by the U.S. Supreme Court relative to corporate funding has made that part of the investigation more difficult, however, not impossible."

"So, the media is out, but the financial interests are in," chastised Gerald.

"That's correct. A decision was made for us to focus on the three areas I mentioned to you."

At that point, the waiter brought the beverage order. Gerald used the opportunity to summarize what he was hearing. Taking a spoon to taste the cappuccino in front of him, he said, "So, the three investigations become one; it is much like my cappuccino. It is but one drink comprised of three layers or stratified items with the espresso on the bottom, next the agitated hot milk, and topped with a steamed froth. I like some chocolate, sugar, cinnamon and other delicacies on the top. I know that isn't a proper cappuccino, but it is the way I like it, and they always accommodate me here."

"I see, and I suppose your analogy would be a colorful and tasty way of describing the three-pronged investigation that -"

Gerald interrupted, "Did you know legend has it that it was a group of monks who discovered some Turkish coffee left abandoned when Christian armies held off the Turks as they were nearing Vienna to overtake the city in about 1683? The coffee alone was too bitter, so the monks developed the cappuccino drink by adding sweetened milk, sugar, chocolate, and sometimes cinnamon."

"I didn't know that, but it wouldn't surprise me. From the pictures I've seen of monks, it would appear as though they drank plenty of cappuccino with, no doubt, large portions of chocolate and sugar. Perhaps you could analogize the investigation to your drink, although I don't think there are any delicacies when it comes to this investigation," said A.T., as he looked up and, to his surprise, saw Professor Brougham wandering about the restaurant.

It must have been the surprised look on A.T.'s face that caused Gerald to turn and exclaim, while waving to the professor and a tall blonde lady who seemed about six inches taller than the professor, "Here they are now! I told you we would be meeting someone you knew."

The professor saw Gerald wave and immediately started toward the table with his lady companion. Once the two of them reached the table, Gerald pulled out a chair for the lady and began introductions. "Gretchen, this is A.T. Professor, you have already met A.T. Say hello to your old acquaintance. A.T., please meet Gretchen Locksley. Gretchen is a close friend of the professor. The two of them met a bit over a month ago, and since then, they have been inseparable."

"Really," said A.T. while greeting Gretchen with a hand shake, "Nice to meet you, Gretchen -"

"You may call me Ms. Locksley," said Gretchen as she shook A.T.'s hand with a firm grip that seemed to last an uncomfortably long time.

"Okay! Good to meet you, Ms. Locksley." A. T. turned to the professor and said, "Nice to see you, professor, although I am a bit surprised."

"Why would you be surprised?" interrupted Gerald. "You said you wanted to speak to the professor again. So, here he is."

"That's true," noted A.T. while waiting for Gretchen and Professor Brougham to sit down. "I'm just surprised from what I was led to believe -"

"You can't believe everything that you hear," laughed Gerald. "As Gilbert and Sullivan reminded us, 'things are seldom what they seem; skim milk masquerades as cream.'"

"'Very true, so they do,'" answered A.T. with an effort to let Gerald know he was familiar with the line. "However, I was led to believe the professor was at some remote island, and it wasn't quite described as a vacation spot. I had visions of our good professor being chained to a desk and being forced to process numbers and some bank instruments as investments for the GGG." A.T. paused, then continued, "I'm happy to see such is not the case. How free is the professor to discuss matters?" asked A.T. while turning to size up the professor's new friend, Gretchen. He then added, "Tell me, Gretchen, I mean Ms. Locksley, are you the professor's handler? Although I see he is not joined to you with any form of restraint, is there a control system involved or is the professor a free man?"

"Whatever would cause you to say such a thing? Frankly, I'm shocked you would imagine such to be the case," responded Gretchen. "I met the professor on a vacation island, and the two of us just hit it off. We have become very close friends. Actually, he approached me, and we simply started to enjoy being together."

"Sorry, if my comments seemed insensitive," urged A.T. "You will have to forgive me, but I was led to believe the professor might have been under some sort of restrictions."

"You will simply have to stop listening to Samantha. She has a real imagination," noted Gerald.

"And here I thought you and Samantha were working partners," exclaimed A.T.

"We have been assigned to some of the same tasks. I guess you might say that is done as a sort of check and balance. She has her superiors, and I have mine. Although we answer to different people, often the interests of our superiors are common. We have often been assigned to work together on matters of common interest." After the somewhat abrupt comments about Samantha, Gerald waved down the waiter in order to divert attention to the task of ordering lunch. Once everyone had placed an order, A.T. felt it was time to take some initiative.

"Professor, how is it you have come here today?" asked A.T.

After first glancing at Gerald and then Gretchen, Professor Brougham cleared his throat and said, "I was informed you wished to visit with me about the items I provided several weeks ago in Kentucky."

"That's true," said A.T. "I do want to visit with you about that, but first tell me, if you will, what caused you to change your plans. I thought you had planned to retire to an undisclosed location somewhere in Mexico or South America."

Again, the professor looked at Gerald and Gretchen before he hesitated with a response. A.T. was sure he had seen Gerald nod affirmatively before the professor said, "I guess you might say I changed my mind. I have been convinced I shouldn't have been so rash as to remove the documents and provide them to you. I had contacted a friend of mine who works for the Senator and was told the Senator wanted you to have the documents as a part of an investigation you were conducting."

"True enough," said A.T.

The professor continued, "I have come to the realization I was wrong, and the people who were paying me deserved more from me than what might have been construed as a betrayal of sorts. I now know the accounting and banking work, including the formulations of various world markets and trades I was performing, were for a good cause. I just wasn't able to view the entire picture in a proper perspective. Did you know the people who actually hired me have been working for centuries in their efforts to make the world a better place for all of us?"

"Really," said A.T. as he looked at Gerald and continued, "I've recently been so informed. Why I was just told this very day by our good priest friend, Gerald here, that certain entities such as the GGG, the Knights of Malta, and I presume the Catholic Church have been doing their level best to helpfully guide many individuals and even countries for centuries to be sure governments across the globe followed certain proper and 'altruistic objectives' in order for the people of the world to benefit from such leadership. Isn't that right, Father Gerald?"

"There is no need to be so sharply cynical," warned Gerald while scowling at A.T. and then looking at the professor and Gretchen. "You have to understand our friend, A.T., is inherently a suspicious man. He is a lawyer, after all. He is also the sort of guy who wants to think the worst thing of others before he has completed his investigation. However, I am certain once A.T. opens his mind and his heart to the point where he can objectively view the evidence he has, along with the evidence we will provide, he will see things a bit differently. A.T. just needs to realize there are degrees of awareness and levels of culpability. Nothing is simply black and/or white."

"Forgive me, Father, but I thought in the eyes of the Church, it was only black or white," said A.T.

"Now, now, A.T," warned Gerald. "Shouldn't you be a bit less critical and a bit more gracious, especially since we are about to help you. In fact, we are about to make you look very good in terms of your investigation. You will see we are not your enemy but a very close ally. Wouldn't you agree, professor?"

"Most assuredly," volunteered the professor after again clearing his throat. He continued, "I was suspicious too; in fact, I was getting downright paranoid. Now, after I have listened to the whole story, and after hearing what others are up to, I am fully convinced Father Gerald is correct. Actually, I am disappointed in myself for causing so much trouble and for giving you the documents in the first place. I clearly overstepped my bounds. At this point, I would like to do what I can to make things right."

"From what I have already determined through my investigation, it is impossible to turn back the clock. The material you gave me in Kentucky has already been processed, and it is now an integral part of our investigation. In fact, one of the reasons I have agreed to talk to Gerald is with the hope he will make certain documents, as well as you, available to the Senator as the investigation continues. From what we have seen in the documents, it would be a good idea for you to step forward with testimony. It is our belief your testimony could serve to clarify many points," insisted A.T.

"We certainly agree," said Gerald. "That is the very reason why I asked the professor to join us today. You see, once you understand the banking statements, the transfers, and the investments our group has made, it will become quite clear at least three of the parties appearing on the documents will be fully exonerated. You will see the Vatican, the Knights of Malta, and the GGG have acted appropriately and properly. In fact, you will see any transaction that involves our people is well within the ruling by the Supreme Court. We have been right all along. We have been making contributions right in line with what the Court has said. Isn't that right, professor?"

"That's absolutely correct," said the professor.

"Just as a point of clarification," inquired A.T., "aren't there four Catholics on the Supreme Court right now?"

"Actually, there are five with Catholic backgrounds. But why should that be of any concern?" asked Gerald.

"No reason," answered A.T. "I was just thinking out loud." At that point, A.T. turned his attention to Gretchen and said, "Tell me, Ms. Locksley, isn't all this discussion a bit boring to you? Perhaps we should change the subject to a more commonly acceptable topic. In that regard, I was wondering if a discussion about martial arts or firearms might be of greater appeal to you."

"I see what Father Gerald meant when he warned me about you. You can be very abrupt and misdirected," asserted Gretchen. "Why on earth would you think such a subject would appeal to me?"

"Sorry," said A.T. "but I couldn't help but notice a fairly large bulge from inside your handbag and a bit of a 'clunk' sound when the purse was dropped to the floor earlier. From the size of the bulk, it looked like it might be in the form of an Austrian 'Glock.'"

Gerald smiled and leaned back as if he were enjoying the turn the conversation had taken. Then he looked at Gretchen and said, "Why don't you tell A.T. what it is that you do, Gretchen?"

At that point, Gretchen leaned forward over the table in A.T.'s direction and said, "I am a licensed private investigator in several states, including California. One of my assignments was to protect the professor, as well as some other individuals whom we believed had been threatened or otherwise compromised. We didn't want anything to happen to them. While I was assigned to the professor, the two of us became a bit enchanted with each other's company, so it made my job easier in terms of protecting him. I still have to watch over others who may be in danger from time to time. Charlie understands. We each have our jobs to perform. He is cool with that, aren't you, Charlie?"

The professor sat back, smiled, and said, "Absolutely. Besides, it was Gretchen who helped me see I had made a mistake in making the materials available to you in Kentucky."

"I see," said A.T. as he turned back to Gerald. "How does all of this sit with you, Father Gerald?"

"Why, fine, just fine," smiled Gerald. "These two people seem to be well-suited for each other in my opinion, so I think it's just fine."

"What about the professor being made available as a witness for me? Are you okay with that, as well?" asked A.T.

"I'm fine with that, as well," assured Gerald. "In fact, I am confident when the Senator hears what the professor has to say, he will be satisfied none of our folks have anything to hide and there will be no reason to include any of our people in any continued investigation. I believe I can go even a step further when I assure you the Senator will be most pleased when he learns we have some of the same concerns as he does about some of the funding being used to help pave the way for a number of the paramilitary groups. What's more interesting is that once you see what we have for you, there will be great pleasure in your reading. You will find we are able to pinpoint some of the violations occurring within the Department of Justice by the very individuals whom you are trying to identify. So, you will also become a believer in our ability to help you. I've said before; we will end up making you look good."

"If what you say is true, you will make my day. Perhaps we could see some of that material at this time. I understood you to say earlier it was going to be delivered. Is it then fair to presume the professor has the material with him?" asked AT.

"He has a briefcase with him," answered Gerald, who then turned to the professor. "Did you bring everything I requested?"

"I did," said the professor. "Most of the material was given to me by Gretchen yesterday with the specific instructions I bring it to you today. So, it was decided the two of us would bring it. We thought once we delivered it to you, we would tour some of the historical landmarks in the area before heading back. Isn't that right, Gretchen?"

Gretchen looked at Gerald for what seemed to be some sort of approval and said, "That's all right, isn't it?"

"Certainly," assured Gerald as he took the briefcase from the professor.

At that point, the waiter delivered the meal. The discussion turned to some of the historical landmarks in the area. Gerald seemed quite familiar with the landmarks of the entire metropolitan area. It was as if he had lived in the greater San Francisco Bay area his entire life. As a result of the discussion, the earlier tension that seemed to be present at the table disappeared for the most part. Everyone, including Gerald, seemed to enjoy Gerald's descriptions of the landmarks he punctuated in his narrative with considerable wit and detail as nearly every unique feature of the area came into discussion. After hearing the entertaining stories Gerald provided during the meal and after considerable time was spent in general discussion, the meal was finished and the waiter began clearing the table. A.T. thought it would be a good moment to refocus on the document exchange and the availability of the professor for testimony.

"Since I do have a departure scheduled for later today, I trust it isn't too presumptive of me to once again raise the issue of the document exchange," suggested A.T.

"Sure," said Gerald. "I will bring the briefcase provided by the professor with me if you take me to the location of the documents you have promised. We can make the exchange at that point. How does that sound?"

"That works for me," offered A.T. "We will need to walk back to my car. We can make the exchange there. Now, what about making the professor available for testimony? I will need to have some contact information for the professor and -"

"That will be handled through me," interrupted Gerald. "You know how to reach me, and it will be through me that you will be able to arrange for the testimony of the professor."

Taking Gerald's comments to be a clue, the professor and Gretchen slid their chairs back from the table and they got up to leave. Gretchen looked at the professor, then to Gerald, and said, "We will be going now. Charlie and I will want to see the sites before the afternoon is over. I trust that you, Father Gerald, will let us know whenever it is necessary for us to be at a particular location for any testimony."

Gerald and A.T. also both rose from the table, and Gerald answered, "That's correct. I will be in touch with you when it is appropriate. I hope the two of you have a nice day. Thank you for joining us. Have some fun touring the sites."

After the professor and Gretchen shook hands with Gerald, they waved to A.T., said their goodbyes, and left. A.T. and Gerald sat back down. The waiter presented the bill that A.T. paid, as promised.

Then A.T. said, "Well, Father Gerald, shouldn't the two of us head out as well in order to make the appropriate document exchange?"

"Agreed," said Gerald. "Remember, we are serious about making the professor available to the Senator. Once again, I want to assure you that after you see the documents we are providing and once you hear the testimony of the professor, you will be confident none of our people have anything to hide. You will find us to be in full compliance with the law."

"I guess time will tell, and we shall see," said an unbelieving A.T.

The two men left the "Monk's Kettle" and headed back to the Mission. A.T. directed Gerald to his car, where the two of them exchanged the documents. Gerald urged A.T. to maintain contact with him and to be sure to call if there were any questions about the documents provided. Each of them got into A.T.'s vehicle and took a few moments to review what had been provided from the other. Once each seemed satisfied they had received what had been promised, they agreed to be in touch. A.T. then took Gerald back to the Mission and dropped him at the front walk. Once he observed Gerald heading up to the Mission, A.T. drove off and returned to his hotel room to pack for his trip to San Diego.

As it turned out, A.T. had enough time left to get to the airport at a comfortable pace. The flight to San Diego was uneventful and smooth. Upon his arrival, he picked up his additional luggage and his rental car. When he checked into his hotel, it was getting late, so he decided to have dinner at the hotel restaurant. The hotel clerk gave him a package delivered for him by special courier. It was the package he had sent to himself. It contained copies of the documents assembled with portions of the material that had been provided in Kentucky by the professor, along with portions of the material from Paris and later from Mr. Felthaus. The documents were to be given to his old political friend, Blaine Jeffers, pursuant to the plan, there would be four sets of documents in the hands of four different and trusted individuals.

* *

The following day proved to be relaxing and allowed A.T. to compare the documents and names contained on the documents received from Gerald with the material previously assembled from the professor, the trip to Paris, and Mr. Felthaus. A.T. was surprised to see how detailed the documents from Gerald were. As he reviewed the documents, it became apparent that Gerald's superiors were attempting to disclose and target a significant number of individuals, many of them civil service employees, who had been hired between 2003 and 2008 in the Department of Justice, the Bureau, and the Executive Branch of government. For a bonus, there were names of individuals in the private practice of law, as well as individuals who were currently with the State Department and the Department of Defense. Included in the material were private memos from within the GGG between individuals whose names had been redacted. Those memos made it clear the GGG was concerned with the vast number of hires of people associated with organizations the GGG considered to be problematic.

Throughout the day, A.T. continued to read over the materials. Although he found the information related to the Executive Branch, the State Department, and the Defense Department during the George W. Bush administration interesting, he reminded himself his focus, the focus of the Senator's investigation, had to remain on the particular groups within the DOJ, including the Bureau, the financial world, and the paramilitary groups. He could see what Gerald was saying about there being a connection relative to some newly-identified corporations as certain transfers of funds were being made through corporate entities into particular paramilitary organizations. None of those transfers seemed to involve the GGG, the Knights of Malta, or the Vatican, so in that respect, Gerald was right. If that were the only issue, those entities would be ultimately excluded from further investigation. It would be the Senator's call once all of the information was assembled.

A.T. could also see a pattern of hires within the DOJ and the Bureau that showed a disproportionate number of individuals who had been tied to extreme political and religious groups. The unbalanced number of attorneys who had been hired from a limited number of large law firms and universities with unique religious ties was also a matter of concern. It became evident a predominate number of new attorneys and new agents for the Bureau had been hired based upon their answers to particular questions focused upon unique political preferences that bluntly resulted in answers that favored rather extreme political positions. Some on the list included well known neo-cons. The memos also confirmed a large number of lawyers left the DOJ to join a number of large law firms located in specific geographic areas. The number of new lawyers from Florida and from Washington D.C. and religious schools seemed to stand out on the pages.

In regard to political contributions, he noticed Gerald and his superiors made no attempt to hide their corporate contributions. Contributions from the GGG, a corporation owned by the Knights of Malta, and from a number of companies related to the Catholic Church showed significant dollars being contributed to candidates in both the Republican and the Democratic Parties. Those contributions and money transfers did seem to be in proper order, and there were plenty of them from little known companies that typically had a benevolent name of one sort or another in the title. Those entities would need to be researched. Apparently, Gerald and his superiors were attempting to prove to the Senator such contributions from their groups were within the guidelines of the Supreme Court decision and contributions were distributed equally to both sides of the aisle.

A.T. was interested in finding some connection between Gerald's GGG, the Knights of Malta, and the Vatican directly to anyone within government offices other than elected officials. However, he could find none, even after several hours of searching the records. In a similar search relative to the paramilitary groups, he could find no connections to the GGG, the Knights of Malta, or the Church. However, during his examination of the records, he did notice a number of repeated contributions by companies with unknown names showing a stream of contributions to certain paramilitary groups within the U.S. Given the fact that Gerald was providing this information in such an open format, A.T. was led to believe these unknown corporations were without ties to the GGG, the Knights of Malta, or the Vatican. It was also apparent whoever was behind the production of the documents wanted A.T. and the Senator to bring to ground the identities of those newly-named entities.

A number of "good government" funds could be identified regarding contributions to organizations, including some colleges and universities with religious connections. Those same "good government" funds were showing contributions to a number of the paramilitary groups and to a number of political organizations that were shown to have had ties to some of the law firms and attorneys who had been hired by the DOJ and by the Bureau. Those contributions would need to be researched in order to determine whether or not there was a concerted effort to fund paramilitary entities and other groups that had demonstrated a hostile attitude toward the functioning of the United States government.

The day passed quickly and A.T. became fully engrossed in the new materials from Gerald and the professor. Since it was already mid-afternoon, and he had the remainder of the day and the evening free, he thought that he would go out for dinner at a restaurant where he frequently dined when he was in town. The Republican function Blaine had invited him to attend was the next evening, so A.T. decided to spend the greater part of Friday doing some research on the Internet relative to the new names mentioned in the newly-produced material from Gerald. He knew he could access the offices of various Secretaries of State in order to learn what he could about the many new corporate names. It would be a bit tougher to track down the offshore companies and the foreign corporations and entity names disclosed in the materials.

Just as A.T. was preparing to leave for dinner, he received a call from a "blocked" phone number. Normally, he had a policy of never taking such calls but instead waited to see any message left on the voicemail. In this case, he took the call and answered abruptly, "Yes?"

After some pause, a recognized voice said, "A.T.?"

"Yes."

"This is Julian. How are you?"

"Fine, I'm fine! How are you?" inquired A.T.

"I've been well. I hope and trust you have also been well. Also, I was pleased to hear from Blaine that you were interested in speaking with me."

"Based upon some of our discussions of a few years back, I thought it would be good for us to talk. I came across an email and -"

"Please, A.T., not now. But please, I want you to know I didn't want you to be upset with me, and I felt you might think there was a reason to blame me for what happened to you. First of all, let me assure you I did not know the extent of what was happening a few years back, and I felt I owed you an explanation," interrupted Julian.

"In that sense, we are on the same page. I would like to discuss the matter, and that is why I asked Blaine to line up a conversation between us," said A.T.

"Yes, that's what I presumed," assured Julian. "I hope you don't mind my calling; however, I thought it would be best if the two of us spoke privately before tomorrow night. I know Blaine wanted us to wait until tomorrow, and we can certainly visit then, but I thought there might be a need for a more private conversation between us before then."

"That's a very good idea; however, I don't think a phone conversation would be appropriate," answered A.T.

"I agree, and I don't think it is necessary for Blaine to know that we talked before tomorrow evening. Would you be willing to accommodate me in this request?" she asked.

"Certainly, I too don't think that it's really necessary for Blaine to hear what we have to discuss between us. I know you and Blaine are good friends, so when he suggested that he be a part of the conversation, I felt it would be okay with you," noted A.T.

"We are very close friends, but in this instance, I don't believe he needs to hear everything we have to say to each other. Some of what we have to discuss should be strictly between us. When we see each other tomorrow night, we could discuss old political times and some of our better days in the world of politics and government. Would you agree?" she urged.

"I do agree. So, when we see each other tomorrow night at the Republican event, we can simply discuss the politics of years ago," agreed A.T. "Now, what do you have in mind in regard to a meeting? I just finished some work, so I could meet yet this evening."

"This evening won't work for me because my husband and I are planning to attend a dinner with some other couples. What kind of schedule do you have tomorrow, particularly during the morning hours?"

"At present, my plans are flexible as I will be doing some research. I could be available at about any time. What are you thinking?"

"Would you be able to meet me at 10:00 for coffee?" asked Julian.

A.T. agreed to the time. Julian described a restaurant at Coronado near the naval station. She indicated the restaurant at that hour was quiet, and they would be able to have a private conversation. She claimed she wanted to clear the slate and square things with A.T., who felt reassured since his memory of Julian was of a person who had a tough time being insensitive or vicious in anything she did politically or otherwise. After A.T. hung up the phone, he felt somewhat reassured the meeting with Julian the next morning would at least clear his mind about many things, including exactly how it came to be that he had become a part of the nightmare he had experienced over the past four years.

CHAPTER 21
GINGERBREAD LATTE

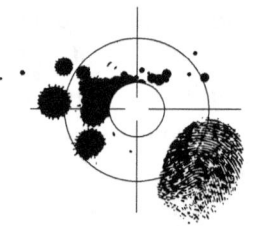

A.T. arrived right on schedule for his meeting with Julian. As usual, she was ten minutes late. Although they had known each other for what seemed to be a political eternity and had run across each other during numerous political meetings and events in the past, A. T. had no recollection of Julian ever being on time. He was certain she prided herself in being fashionably late. He was also confident she took advantage of everyone due to her good looks and charming personality. She was a natural politician, except for her tardiness. A.T. was sure her attractive physical presence and her gracious personality had everything to do with her political popularity. She was presumably smart enough, with documentation supporting a degree from Yale; however, she never recognized her own presumed intellect as a point of strength. Everyone who knew her expected she would rely more upon her mental abilities than upon her physical presence, but that was not the case.

While he was thinking about how Julian must have perceived herself and the need to promote her own presence rather than her natural abilities, she entered the restaurant without stopping at the maitre d' desk but looking around the room for A.T. When she noticed him, she came directly to the table in her methodically deliberate walk. It was a naturally slow and elegant gait. To A.T. it seemed she had an issue with her five-foot-six inch frame since she always appeared to be stretching her posture upward, including the use of high-heeled shoes in order to look taller. Since she was a well-formed woman and a bit thin, she naturally seemed taller than she would have if she had been heavier. While careful about her appearance, her neatly trimmed shoulder-length wavy, almost curly, blonde hair with some barely noticeable grey highlights was a bit wind-blown when she arrived. Typical of Julian, she wore a well-tailored dark blue pinstriped business suit with a very striking multicolored scarf at the neck. She always seemed to find an article of clothing to accent her normally conservative attire.

A.T. rose from the table as Julian hugged him and gave him her typical air-kiss. To any observer, it would have seemed they were close and dear friends. Despite the outward appearance, each of them had learned over time to be cautious of the other. That was due to the fact they had both been involved in the Republican Party for many years. While Julian followed a more conservative philosophy within the Republican Party, A.T. had been involved with the now nearly-dead moderate wing of candidates and party activities. The two of them had been allies on numerous occasions when the interests of the candidates they supported within the Party found it necessary to unify for a common goal.

One event of common interest had occurred many years earlier while both of them were young activists in the Party. That event included some efforts by several factions of the Party in an attempt to curtail the Pat Robertson rogue group that entered the Party in 1988. That year Julian and A.T. both found themselves part of a coalition formed for the purpose of stalling the efforts of a significant block of Pat Robertson supporters and nonparty members who were trying to take over party politics through some of the local party organizations. The coalition included supporters from within the various campaign camps of George H.W. Bush, Bob Dole, John Connelly, Pete DuPont, and Pat Buchanan. The coalition was successful in its attempts to curtail the Robertson supporters. It was probably that act among others that helped set in motion the determination of the Robertson people to work behind the scenes to try to take control of the Republican Party, wherever it could. Those efforts had since manifested themselves in the current Party structure and philosophy. Decades of party maneuvering had paid off for the Robertson faction now well in step with the "tea party" movement.

Both A.T. and Julian had been supportive of Bush 41; however, they parted company when it came to Bush 43. Julian was intensely loyal to W. but A.T. was not. Julian had been so loyal to W. that she worked feverishly hard during his campaigns. That was no doubt why she ended up working at the White House for most of the eight years while W. was in office. During that period of time, the relationship between the two became significantly strained. A.T. didn't want to have anything to do with W.'s administration and had been asked on numerous occasions if he would participate in campaigns and leadership committees. In every instance, he refused. Although he respected President Bush, Sr., A.T. did not care for W. As a consequence, he had refused every overture to get involved with either the campaign efforts or other positions offered. Plus, A.T was satisfied at the time to engage in the quiet practice of law. He felt Julian had taken his refusals to get involved personally. Like other Bushies, she considered A.T. 'persona non grata.'

Perhaps she had hoped the intense hug and air-kiss would be enough for the strained past to be forgotten. When A.T. moved a chair for her at the table, she raised her hand and said, "Why don't we go out onto the patio to have our meeting. It is such a pleasant day." Since A.T. had no issue with the suggestion, he picked up the briefcase he had with him and nodded to the maitre d' in the direction of the patio. Immediately the maitre d' caught the glance and the hint. He walked over to the patio doors and opened them while he waited for Julian and A.T. He immediately escorted them to a table that had a nice view of the ocean. Once at the table, Julian again picked up the conversation. "How have you been during these past several years?"

"I've been as well as could be expected, especially since I had to overcome some misplaced efforts that nearly ruined my life." A.T. then paused since he caught himself sounding as though he was mired in self-pity. He changed his mood to sound more upbeat and said, "Actually, I've been fine. It's really good to see you. How have you been?"

"I have been quite well; thanks for asking. After President Bush left office, I decided to take some time to relax and enjoy life. My husband and I were able to take several vacations, enabling us to see parts of the world we had always dreamed about. Our two children were able to travel with us on a couple of the trips."

"That sounds like a good way to recharge after all the hard work you were undoubtedly a part of while working at the White House. So, in addition to your travels, have you essentially retired?"

"Yes, in a way. I have been working on a book about my time at the White House. It has taken far more out of me than I expected. I have found writing to be a bit laborious at times. Plus, I have had the opportunity to engage in some lecturing. It's not been to the point of an adjunct professor or anything like that, but there have been far more invitations and engagements to serve as a guest speaker at the college level and with the media than I ever expected. So, I've stayed pretty busy. What about you? I trust you are still busy with the practice of law, or have you retired?"

"No, I've made no effort to retire. Until recently, I continued to practice law; however, a great deal of time had to be spent assisting attorneys who had to be hired to defend me on a matter of serious concern. It was a clear case of misplaced efforts by certain parties who decided to exercise the power of their positions in order to see how far they could go. Frankly, this is one of the reasons I wanted to visit with you, but I imagine you knew that. Am I guessing correctly?"

"You are, and I am sorry you had to go through what you did. First of all, I want to thank you for breaking the ice and offering to set up this meeting. When Blaine told me you had inquired about me and a possible meeting, I was so happy. Seriously, I was sure you were still mad at me and you would never speak to me again. As you know, I can't bear it when people won't talk to me. I try very hard to be friends with everyone, even if they have differing political views from me."

"Why would you think I would be angry with you, Julian?"

"You know very well, A.T. It was because of what happened several years ago in regard to the 'Business Forum.' After our emails and after it seemed as though our conversations were getting more and more strained, I felt our friendship was over and you would end up hating me forever. I simply don't want to be at this stage in my life with people hating me. I'm mostly out of active politics and want to sleep at night knowing I have not been the cause of anyone's grief."

"It's true there was a bit of a strain during our conversations and emails of the past; however, I sense there was more to it. Would you agree?"

"I suppose I would have to agree. I trust you are referring to what happened to you?" she asked.

"That's a good guess. Why don't we start by your telling me exactly what 'they' were hoping to do and why they did it?"

"I don't know what to say. First, you need to know I only know about part of what happened. I'm willing to tell you the whole story, as I know it, but I'd rather you not repeat what I tell you. I am going to be talking a bit 'out of school,' and other people don't need to know. I don't even want you to tell Blaine. Is that agreeable?"

"I won't tell Blaine; I have no reason to tell him. However, if what you tell me has something to do with the official investigation, I may be required to include what you tell me in my reports. Therefore, I can't -"

"What 'official' investigation?"

"I have been asked to work on an investigation that deals with national security in the sense certain groups employed within the government during the George W. Bush administration worked in concert with some political action committees and corporations we believe had been breaking the law as they attempted to populate the Executive Branch of government with appointments. I believe the evidence will show they went well beyond the permissible guidelines allowed for appointments. It is evident these people based their efforts exclusively upon political philosophies and political loyalty instead of merit."

"But that's always what happens in a political world. You know that," said Julian, as a waiter approached the table to take orders.

A.T. began to hand Julian one of the menus provided by the maitre d'; however, she waved him off and looked at the waiter to place her order. She said, "I'll have a large cup of your 'Gingerbread Latte,' with some extra honey and some extra sprinkles of ginger over the whipped topping."

After the waiter took her order, she looked at A.T. who ordered a bagel with cream cheese, along with an orange juice and a coffee. After ordering, A.T. looked at Julian and commented, "It would appear as though you have some familiarity with the menu. You ordered a 'Gingerbread Latte?' I've never heard of it before, but I haven't been personally too fond of embellishments beyond regular coffee. Would you care for anything else?" asked A.T. thinking to himself: *How appropriate for Julian to want something with the gingerbread.*

"No thanks," said a smiling Julian. "You were talking about political appointments. I fail to see the problem."

"Julian, there are some very serious issues relative to various appointments during W.'s term in office. From my perspective, many of those were through the DOJ while run by Alberto Gonzales. In fact, there have already been a number of Congressional hearings on such matters. The investigation also disclosed there might be a particular group of individuals who have been attempting to influence the administration of justice and our government in an improper and illegal way," stated A.T.

"Boy, A.T., I don't want to be involved in anything like that. So, as far as your investigation is concerned, I don't see how I could possibly help. Besides, I'm not sure I would want to -"

"From our past conversations of a couple years ago together with a few other items I have uncovered, I suspected you knew more than you had been willing to say until now. I don't mean to be difficult, but I do think it would be in your best interests to disclose what you know in order to be in the position of a witness rather than a part of any investigation. I am rather certain you were involved in some discussions about the DOJ, and a few of those discussions involved me."

"How can you say such a thing?" asked Julian defensively.

"In addition to my investigation, along with information the Senator has provided, I now have copies of particular information I received under the Freedom of Information Act. I know more than you realize," said A.T. while stretching the facts a bit beyond his complete knowledge.

"I don't really like this, A.T. I didn't do anything wrong!"

"Julian, please understand I am not trying to implicate you in something you didn't initiate or promote. There is no interest in targeting you."

"That's good to hear. Besides, as I said, I didn't do anything wrong."

"I didn't say or imply you did," stressed A.T. "However, I am certain you were involved in some conversations that could prove uncomfortable. Regardless, I only want to visit with you in order to find out the extent of what you know. At this point, I don't think your involvement would be anything other than that of a witness."

"I don't want to be telling you anything that is going to require me to step forward and testify," Julian said. "Just so you know, I was never involved in any of the appointments or other activity regarding the DOJ. I did sit in on some of the interviews for offices that were available or created for specific individuals. I am also aware of the fact there were individuals in the administration who wanted to use the power of the DOJ to curtail certain activities by others outside the administration who were considered 'obstructive' by some people in the DOJ. I believe that is the word used on a couple of occasions. Please keep in mind I don't want to say anything that will hurt President Bush or the Bush family. You know I am very loyal to them for my political career and -"

"I realize that. Let me assure you my investigation has a focus that deals with particular individuals who were breaking the law. It would serve no useful purpose to target W. or his family if he wasn't aware of the full impact of what was going on. It's always been a question as to what W. actually knew about the day-to-day operations of the DOJ; however, it is believed others within the White House and the administration did know what was transpiring. That includes using the DOJ as a tool to punish certain individuals, especially other Republicans who were considered 'obstructive,' as you so well stated. Apparently, there was some thinking that if the administration targeted their own uncooperative Party members, the Democrats wouldn't do anything about it and would let it go."

"So, as I understand it," said Julian, "you are really interested in people other than President Bush. If that is the case, I might be willing to discuss with you some of what happened. As you might expect, there were certain people in the administration whom I did not like very well, including the Vice President and Karl Rove. Now, having said that, I don't want to be considered a vindictive person, and I am not going to be a whistleblower."

"I expected you might say that," assured A.T. "We already have a couple of former employees of the DOJ who have come forward. They have agreed to testify, and they will be witnesses. Perhaps you already know, the sworn testimony of Monica Goodling before Congress was significant in that it helped confirm the direction of this investigation."

"Tell me about this investigation?"

"The investigation I am doing has a focus upon individuals and groups that have been working deliberately to place themselves in key positions within the government in order to unduly and improperly influence the administration of justice."

"How will that involve the former President or the Vice President and their staffs?"

"As I told you, from what I have seen, I don't believe that the former President was aware of everything going on, nor do I think he was properly advised from a legal standpoint. In other words, he got some very bad legal advice. It seems he was willing to rely upon the advice he was given," assured A.T.

"So, who are you after, if I may ask?" questioned Julian.

"I've already told you, there is evidence certain individuals and particular groups pursuing a set political agenda for several decades are using the political arena to take positions of influence within government through appointments. They are using those positions to literally 'get' individuals whom they consider to be political enemies, and that uniquely and particularly involves people within their own party, the Republican Party. It would seem they have found ways to do this through the Justice Department without being held accountable."

"Hearing this from you is important to me considering I was contacted by a friend, whom I will not identify, who works for a Republican Senator," said Julian. "He told me you were doing an investigation, and he thought you would be contacting me. He said it would be okay for me to talk with you since the Republican Senator was also involved in the investigation. However, he wanted me to assure you I was not personally involved other than to sit in as a witness. He also told me you were doing your investigation for a Democratic Senator. If that's true, I am very disappointed. I can't believe you would work for a Democrat."

"Why not? I'm interested in finding out what is going on within the Department of Justice. From my perspective, the DOJ under Alberto Gonzales got seriously off track and abused the office. Clearly, Gonzales and those with him were using the DOJ for political purposes. In my view, it was not for the proper administration of justice for which the office was intended."

"Even if that is the case, it doesn't do our Party any good to have our own people investigating whatever your Democratic friend thinks is important."

"It's not the case of party politics, Julian. It's a matter of doing the right thing for the country," instructed A.T.

"There are always political appointments. There always have been. Nothing has changed. You and I both know that having been involved in politics for as long as we have," said Julian.

"Not so! As it turns out, there was a whole lot more going on. From the information I have been given and from the investigation I have done, I can now see why the Senator wanted the investigation expanded. We have been tracking some of the funding sources that are a part of the enterprise to 'salt' the Executive Branch, particularly the DOJ, with specific people from groups that do not favor the continuation of our government as it now operates."

"You mean different than the Democrats want it to be."

"No, Julian. Certain laws, such as the Hatch Act, are written for a specific reason, namely, to keep those who are employed by the government working in an objective manner that is fair to all citizens. That includes not playing politics through an appointment or hiring into a position or office of responsibility within government. There is evidence of the Hatch Act being violated on a daily basis during W.'s administration, and that was especially true of the Department of Justice during the period of time Alberto Gonzales was the Attorney General."

"Was that it?"

"That's enough, but there were other issues as well."

"For example?" inquired Julian.

"There were voting machine issues; there were the improper appointments of people into judicial positions, particularly Administrative Law Judges; there were the improper appointments of people into positions of USA and AUSAs that were purely political and not based upon merit; there were efforts to indict political enemies, especially people within our own Republican Party; and much more."

"In other words, you are saying Alberto Gonzales was a rogue A.G., and that's where the problem lies, right?"

"No. It isn't that simple," explained A.T. "Gonzales didn't engage in these activities on his own. There is evidence he had support from the White House and that included staff members of both the President and the Vice President."

"You know, A.T., I am having some real problems with this."

"Why?"

"Because it is a violation of the 11th commandment to which President Reagan referred. Essentially, it is forbidden to speak ill or otherwise act against one's fellow Republican," commented Julian.

"If you don't mind my saying so, that is so absurd it isn't funny. I always thought such a statement was ludicrous and counterproductive. Is it okay for those who control an office to go after their political enemies while others are only left to chastise such activity? The idea of making up a commandment to suit one's own purpose with the implication that because the word 'commandment' was used, the idea should somehow have some significant effect, is totally without basis or reason. It only works for those holding the power, thereby allowing them to 'get away' with anything they believe suits their purposes or objectives. Perhaps it is one of the reasons why the Republican Party has become so isolated from both the truth and the mainstream of public thinking."

"It keeps the Party operations and philosophy in line."

"That's certainly true, especially if the Party operations and philosophy benefit 'fringe' thinking. When you follow such a rule, you're allowing yourself to be manipulated into a corner, Julian. Be cautious of who is doing the manipulating."

"I'm not being manipulated by the Robertson people or 'tea party' people or others like them," said Julian.

"Really?" asked A.T. "How do you think so many people who are either devotees of Robertson or others like him have gotten such a strong following within the Party and in politically appointed offices?"

"I can answer that," responded Julian. "Karl Rove thought it would be a good idea to align with those people as a part of the 'base.'"

"That's a well-known fact, and look where it has led."

"Where?" demanded Julian.

"People with a philosophy like Robertson now have a disproportionate amount of representation within the Party. They have even boasted as to how many graduates of his university now hold positions within the government, and that particularly includes the DOJ. Besides, didn't the very conservative religious people have a falling out with Karl Rove because he used the religious groups for voting purposes and then later made fun of them for their beliefs?"

"That's true. They did. In my opinion, they were right. Rove used them just like he has a tendency to use everyone. I heard some of the complaints against Rove on that issue while I was working at the White House. In that instance, I had to side with the religious people," Julian admitted.

"I understand. But aren't we getting a bit off track? I'm interested in the abuses that occurred, and I'm looking for proof of such abuses.

I'm not interested in anyone's religious beliefs. However, I am interested in their political beliefs, if those beliefs are so distorted and slanted that the beliefs end up causing them to bend the law in order to promote their own political ends," stated A.T.

"Is that what you think happened?" questioned Julian.

"In part, I do think that is what happened, but more importantly, I believe it was their interest in the power and the control of the government that gave rise to the violations of the law to such a degree they felt they could get away with using their positions to further their cause and their beliefs. In addition, perhaps as a bit of a surprise to you, I believe there were a number of people within the administration under W. who felt they were so clever, they could manipulate the DOJ and, in some cases, the Executive Branch of government in such a way that they would place their own people into positions of power and then use those positions to campaign and attack anyone whom they perceived to be an enemy."

"Aren't you overreacting to what you believe the investigation is showing? In fact, aren't you too close to it to really be objective?"

"I have often worried about that, and on many occasions, I just wanted to stop being a part of the investigation. Every time I would feel I should stop, there always seemed to be some new evidence that proved I was on the right track. Each time, I became more convinced that if I didn't continue with the investigation, the matter would continue to go unchecked. If it remained unchecked, those who masterminded the efforts to take over the DOJ would continue to mold the department deeper and deeper into a vehicle they could use to control the judicial process of this country. That thought alone kept me going. It didn't and doesn't have anything to do with party politics or my Senator friend. If anything, his direction of the investigation has tempered my zeal."

"If I decide to help, A.T., it will be for two reasons. First, I didn't like what they did to you. There was no reason for it. Second, my friend in the office of a 'Republican Senator' told me I should feel comfortable in dealing with you since you were well-regarded and trusted by both senators. Well, I guess there is a third reason. I just don't want to have your past situation on my conscience. So, what do you want from me?"

"I'd like to be able to conduct a full interview in a question/answer format. Additionally, I would like to conduct the interview before a certified court reporter, so the statement could be used for any and all purposes."

"Boy, I don't know. Can I think about it?" asked Julian cautiously.

"Sure. I would need to line up a court reporter, and I haven't done that at this point because I didn't want to be too presumptive. However, I would like to visit with you now, if we could, just to get an idea about what happened and what you might say. Would that be all right?"

"That would be fine. If I do provide a statement later in front of a court reporter, where would it take place?"

"We could do it out here or in D.C. What would you prefer?"

"Actually, I would prefer to do it in Washington D.C., and if you don't mind, I would like my friend, the Republican Senator, or a member of his staff whom I know, to be present.

"That would work out just fine. In fact, I think that is a very good idea. Why don't we plan to do the official statement in D.C.? So, today we'll speak informally about the matter. Then I will have an idea of what we might expect in terms of a later and more formal statement."

"That sounds like a good idea to me," said Julian. "You're not recording this, are you?"

"No," answered A.T. who realized he had not even given a thought to the possibility of using the 'hearing-aid' device Adam's IT department had designed for him. "Would you be willing to just tell me of what and how you remember the situation to be?"

"Sure," began Julian. "You'll remember, a former and at the time very prominent congressman tried to get you to join the 'Business Forum.'"

"I remember. If we are thinking of the same congressman, I recall he was convicted. However, his case was reversed on appeal."

"That's the one. Both he and W. were getting frustrated with a number of you who wouldn't cooperate, so it was decided to put some pressure on those of you who wouldn't join. The former congressman had expressed his frustration to a couple of attorneys from the DOJ who happened to be at the White House for a different meeting that related to another topic."

"What was that topic?" asked A.T.

"There were a number of attorneys within DOJ who wanted to target certain Democrats and also some Republicans who had become problematic to the administration. When instructions were sent down the pipe to the USAs in various federal districts, it turned out a number of the USAs felt the White House and some of the upper levels of the DOJ were attempting to target individuals without a proper basis. It was causing some of the USA offices across the country to divert their already limited resources away from ongoing investigations and prosecutions," reported Julian.

"Presumably, that was the lead-in to what ultimately led to the dismissal of quite a number of United States Attorneys, as well as the subsequent Senate and House hearings regarding the dismissal of several excellent USAs, as I recall," offered A.T.

"That's right. The matter became a major issue with some of the personnel at the White House. Both Cheney and Rove got excited about it, and they in turn got W. all worked up, along with Gonzalez. It was then decided to try to assemble some evidence of misconduct as to the various USAs who were not cooperating. Wiretapping at that time was pretty widespread, and the people from the upper levels at DOJ felt they had 'carte blanche' to tap whomever they decided. The guys coming over from DOJ at the time were really aggressive and certainly put on a good show for the President and anyone else who would listen."

"So, how did that ever involve me?"

"There were some people from the DOJ who were speaking with the President and Mr. Gonzales. The meeting prior to their meeting involved the 'Business Forum,' which the former congressman had been discussing with the President. The DOJ people heard the end of that meeting, and your name was one of the names mentioned in regard to business leaders who had stated they would not agree to help."

"So?"

"One of the DOJ attorneys specifically heard your name mentioned. Apparently, he was a Robertson supporter years earlier when you were one of the attorneys who was interpreting the rules at a state level when Robertson was trying to get on the primary ballots and when there were some issues about Party membership and voter registration. This attorney said he recalled that a number of Robertson people were required to switch parties or had to register as Republicans in order to vote as Republicans."

"I don't recall that. Perhaps there was some requirement in some of the states where a person needed to be a member of a specific political party in order to participate in that party's nomination process. I don't remember being that involved in any such issue, so I'm at a bit of a loss as to -"

"It doesn't really matter, and I'm not sure I understand all of what was being discussed. However, he said he recalled your name, and he expressed curiosity about why the former congressman had mentioned you. So, the former congressman told him."

"Apparently, I'm missing something," said A.T.

"You can put two and two together. The DOJ guy was about to go into a meeting regarding certain United States Attorneys and Assistant USAs. They were also talking about wiretaps, and I did hear them discuss how open-ended the wiretap matter had become. There was some feeling expressed that they could wiretap anyone they wanted under the guise of national security."

"Go on…"

"The former congressman was intrigued, and he pulled out a list with quite a number of names of reluctant businessmen. Your name was on that list. So, I think it was fair to assume whoever was on that list was going to have his or her phones tapped."

"That wouldn't make any difference to me because I had nothing to hide. If they wanted, I would have granted permission. I have no recollection of ever having a phone conversation I was not willing to have disclosed," stated A.T.

"Oh, really? They must have thought so because a couple weeks later, there were some taped conversations that included your saying some unflattering things about the President."

"That could well have been the case. I make no bones about the fact I probably said some unflattering things about W. So what? That's not a crime, and I'm certain I'm not the only person who has said unflattering things about W."

"Just know this…it was enough to get his attention. He was ticked off. He didn't think that you would say such things," said Julian.

"I fail to see how that would matter," said A.T.

"It had enough of an effect to allow for some of the people at DOJ, who had a problem with you, to obtain a full reign as to if and how they would include you in some of their various enterprises to involve political enemies in predetermined activities designed to create various traps," Julian explained.

"Involve me in what enterprises?"

"They had set up several task forces to try to couple their political targets with some fairly unsavory characters they had been watching in terms of possible criminal activity. Several of the task forces were designed to take heat off the DOJ for its failure to police the financial industry where a large array of investment bankers, like Bernie Madoff, were robbing people blind," said Julian.

"That was a well-known matter as far as the public was concerned. Most of us believed it was due to the lack of any oversight of the financial markets during W.'s time in office," commented A.T.

"There you go again, blaming President Bush."

"Isn't that a line out of Ronald Reagan's debates in 1980?"

"What?" asked Julian.

"Never mind. I thought it was a line used by Reagan during his debates with Jimmy Carter. Anyway, back to your discussion about the task forces. You were discussing their genesis."

"At the time, it was clear the administration and especially the DOJ and FBI had dropped the ball regarding Madoff and others. The President was upset that it was making his administration look bad, so several task force operations were set up."

"Wasn't it a bit late? Madoff and others had been running wild and unrestrained for years. It was a time of virtually no oversight from the way I saw it," noted A.T.

"The guys from DOJ thought they could divert the public's attention if the task force concept was implemented in order to make it look like the administration was going after white collar crime. The guys at DOJ suggested the task forces could be used for potential white collar crime, potential election and campaign violations, and a number of other areas where investigations could be conducted. With the new rules relative to wiretaps since 9/11, someone at the meeting suggested the task forces could be used to go after various individuals who had been 'unsupportive' and essentially political enemies."

"Could you elaborate?"

Julian explained, "It was believed through the implementation of various task forces, a system could be set up to trap people into fabricated investment plans or suggested election law violations or what appeared to be corruption, where the government supplied the necessary environment. It was designed after the drug task forces in which past efforts had been successfully made to get people involved in drug trafficking, even if they didn't want to be."

A.T. questioned, "Even if they hadn't been in the past?"

"Correct. The task force could essentially target whomever it wanted. It had worked in the past and essentially had the sanction of the courts that repeatedly upheld law enforcement efforts to trap individuals in the drug world that it couldn't otherwise get. It was a fairly intricate plan whereby the task forces would set up an operation, supply the money, supply the drugs along with everything else, and then try to implicate people in it. They wanted to do the same sort of thing with the financial markets and in so doing, they could just about implicate anyone they wanted."

"What kind of operation?" asked A.T.

"They would use the task force to set up an enterprise that could lead to a potential criminal act. They would try to draw into the task force enterprise those who had prior 'run ins' with the law. They would also try to draw into the task force enterprise other people whom they did not like and who they targeted for reprisals due to any statements or actions made from a political sense. In that way, the task force would try to couple some political enemies with individuals who were known to have worked at the edge of the law."

"That might have worked in the drug world where people might have had a predisposition to involve themselves with drugs. However, as to white collar or election matters, it sounds pretty bizarre. It would take some doing to try to get innocent individuals drawn into something like that, especially white collar crime or campaign matters"

"Not true! The guys from DOJ suggested they simply set up a bogus company that had a stated objective to deal with business in one way or another. They would then invite the businessmen they wanted to include, along with the potential criminals, to meetings. The DOJ guys would tell the businessmen anything they thought would potentially draw them into a meeting."

"That's interesting. As I look back at the efforts to entice me to come to a meeting, I had received no less than seven invitations to attend meetings set up by a company that stated its purpose was to help small businesses. The funding group said my client's project was so appealing to them, they would pay for all the expenses of travel, lodging, etc. The client's Board authorized me to take the trip."

"Did you ever find out how they had gotten your name or your client's name?" asked Julian.

"I did. A year before the invitation, I had filed an official complaint with the FBI through one of its Field Offices. The complaint was about a venture group that had taken the client's money and failed to perform. The one FBI Field Office where I had filed the complaint determined I had been a victim, along with the client. Then, and contrary to Bureau guidelines and policies, another Field Office, the one with the task force, didn't even bother to check the FBI 'indices.' If it had done so, it would have seen I had filed an official complaint against the very people who introduced my client and me to one party the task force was targeting. I've never seen a worse excuse for an investigation than that one. Bureau procedures were thrown to the wind, and proper investigative techniques were never followed. That resulted in quite a number of loose ends from which, I'm sure, a number of real criminals walked free."

Julian inquired, "Did you have proof of your filing the complaint and that you had been victimized?"

"Absolutely!" exclaimed A.T. "There must be at least a dozen letters back and forth between me, the FBI, the Marshall's Service, and the Assistant United States Attorneys in the district where we filed the complaint. Plus, we retained copies of the check and direct deposits to the client's account of the funds recovered by the FBI for us. Clearly, we were victims who had filed a proper and timely complaint."

"Then, why are you going through all of this?"

"It is because they wrongfully charged me through one of those ill-conceived task force operations. It took some monumental efforts to ultimately get the matter dismissed, and that was only because cooler heads took over at the DOJ. You don't know what it's like, Julian, to be falsely accused and then to spend a good share of your life trying to clear your name."

"You're saying you had acted properly the entire time?"

"I absolutely did!"

"Then, how did they include you in the indictment?"

"Apparently, one of those task forces from a different FBI Field Office decided to pursue me, even after I had told them I wouldn't trust over 90% of the people involved in the venture funding business. It was the task force that introduced me to people whom I had never seen or met before. There was a stack of materials about three to four inches thick that I provided. When they continued to refuse to discuss the client's business plans, I left for home."

"Then what happened?"

"They kept calling me and requesting I assist them in regard to the due diligence on the venture group. I had repeatedly told them to get credentials of the venture group. It was the venture group against whom we had filed a complaint that gave us the name of an alleged federal official. Presumably, the task force was after the alleged federal official. I told them to get the credentials. They ignored my repeated warnings, apparently knowing all the while there were no credentials. The task force even missed an opportunity to find out who it was at the Federal Reserve who might have been assisting the alleged 'bad guys.' They were invited to a meeting within the Federal Reserve office, but the task force chose instead to meet at some hotel," A.T. explained.

"You're seriously saying they missed an opportunity to investigate?"

"Without a doubt!" replied A.T. "It was a very poorly-conducted investigation. As you know, I am a former agent, and I have often wondered why the undercover agents didn't take up the alleged 'bad guys' offer to meet within the Federal Reserve office. If they had, they would have determined who at the FED was working with the 'targets,' how they were going to get access to the office of the FED, who was letting them into the office, who they were going to meet within the office, where in the office they were going to meet, what kind of paperwork was going to be presented, and how any investment was going to be processed through the FED, along with who knows what other information could have been obtained."

"So, you're saying they may never find out?" asked Julian.

"That's absolutely correct. In fact, it occurred to me that they really didn't want to find out. My guess is things were getting uncomfortable for whoever it was within the FED that they wanted to protect. Therefore, they diverted the meeting to a hotel and that eliminated a link to the operations within the Federal Reserve that they wanted to conceal. If it had turned out there was something going on that involved people within the FED, it would have been another black eye for the administration. After the Madoff scandal, they couldn't afford for it to become public."

"Do you think there was more to it?"

"I think there was far more to it and the investigation was either botched intentionally or due to total incompetence by the FBI agents that made up the task force. Frankly, I can't imagine the FBI agents could have been so incompetent. However, after doing my own investigation into the background of the case agent, I could see why things got so screwed up. The case agent was so intent on promoting his own career within the Bureau, he was doing anything he thought would benefit him, regardless of the consequences to the Bureau or anyone else. His agenda was solely to make himself look good. The bottom line is either his superiors were totally incompetent, or they were trying to cover up something at the Federal Reserve during W.'s administration."

"Will you stop blaming George W.! It wasn't him. If you want me to help you, then you will stop trying to blame him all the time."

"If you want me to do that, then you need to give me the kind of information I can use in my investigation. I was really in the dark considering I did not know the people whom they introduced to me at the meeting. Then I didn't hear from anyone until a couple of agents arrived at my door to inform me they had a warrant for my arrest. I presumed that you knew all of this."

"I only knew some of the DOJ attorneys wanted to include you in their task force efforts. Some of the people working at the White House thought it would be a good idea to teach you a lesson, so they went along with the DOJ lawyers who were trying to implicate you. It had something to do with your path crossing their path a long time ago. I think it was politically motivated from what I heard."

"What did you hear, and what lesson were they trying to teach me?"

"In part, I guess the lesson was that you don't turn down powerful people when you are asked to do something," Julian explained. "Although, it seemed like much more and apparently involved an ideological dispute of years earlier."

"Now you're speaking of the 'Small Business Forum?'"

"That would be a good guess. However, it is only part of the story. When I called you, I had been told by one of the DOJ attorneys to see if you were willing to work with the 'Forum.' Actually, it seemed as though he was hoping you wouldn't. He was really interested in implicating you in something the task force was creating. In fact, I believe if the President had said to stop, the DOJ attorney who was pushing it would have still continued to go forward on his own, regardless."

"Apparently, I wasn't the only innocent person they went after. I've managed to research that particular task force. As it turned out, there were a number of problems with that task force. There were issues of withheld documents and evidence; there was the improper access of documents; there was the threatening of witnesses; there were problems with the full disclosure of tapes and purposeful alterations of those tapes; there were improper wiretaps; there were improper dealings as far as certain plea bargains in some of the task force cases; also, there were a number of other issues that are just coming to light. The FBI has some serious problems with the activities of several task forces, especially that one," elaborated A.T.

"So, are you going after the FBI too?"

"No. That is not my style or my interest. However, I am interested in going after the specific individuals who were at DOJ and the FBI back then. They were the ones who were intentionally violating the public trust and who were abusing their positions. They need to be identified and brought to justice themselves. I fully intend to pursue that, no matter what."

"Is that what your friend, the Democratic Senator, wants?"

"He and your friend, the Republican Senator, are interested in bringing a number of people to justice, and that includes individuals at the DOJ and the FBI. The reason this investigation has gone well beyond what I originally intended is due to what 'my' Democratic friend and 'your' Republican friend in the United States Senate want. They obviously see a different and more global picture than the one I saw in my initial investigation. Therefore, if you can help in terms of providing names and any other evidence, that is what I will need in order to satisfy the directives I have been given."

"Here's what I am willing to do for you," said Julian. "I have already discussed this with my friend at the Republican Senator's office, and he suggested I talk with you first. He wanted to be sure you were not attempting to target me, and I wanted to be sure in my own mind you were not going to target W. If those are the ground rules you are willing to follow, then I can help. I can provide you with the names of the people at DOJ and those from within the White House who were a part of the group that specifically wanted to target political enemies. I can also provide the specific names of the people at the White House who set in place the guidelines and rules for any new appointments and the removal of those who didn't cooperate with internal directives and desires. Additionally, I can provide some emails that will substantiate whatever information I supply. I can do all of that so long as I know I am not going to be a target of any investigation and you are not making some effort to make W. look bad."

"Julian, I cannot promise any kind of immunity. However, from what I know, there has been no effort to include you in any investigation. If you feel you need some sort of immunity, you need to speak with your friend within the Republican Senator's office. If someone decides to set an investigation of W. in motion, it will be at a much higher pay grade than where I am sitting."

"Because of the content of some of the emails and since I was involved in some meetings where political matters were discussed," explained Julian, "I really may need some assurances that I personally will not be a target."

"I didn't realize you were that deeply involved," said A.T. with some surprise.

"I might have been, so let me talk to my friends in the Republican Senator's office. If they can provide me the necessary assurances I feel I need, I will make up the list you need of the people who were directly involved, and I will make copies of the emails and other items that might be relevant. None of that information will be made available to you until I receive some assurance in writing that I am able to freely disclose without personal ramifications. I also want to be sure I am not violating any laws by making any of the expected disclosures to you. I hope that is acceptable to you since I am not a 'Wikileaks' type of person."

"It is agreeable; as long as I will be able to take your statement before a certified court reporter, with your telling me the identities on the record. In addition, if there are emails or other documents that support what you state on the record, we will want copies of those as well. Would that be agreeable, and if it is, how long before we can meet in D.C. in order to record your statement?" asked A.T.

"I will make some calls, and I will request an answer in writing from my friends in Washington D.C. I will ask that they transmit the letter that includes my protection by email and on proper letterhead. I also want them to tell me just what I may disclose, and how far I can go in that disclosure. I understand from Blaine you will be at the dinner. Is that correct?"

"It is. I plan to be there. I trust we can have a private meeting at some point because I don't think it would be a good idea for us to be exchanging documents in front of so many people," urged A.T.

"That's probably a good idea; however, you realize the people at the dinner are all going to be Republicans. It is a Republican fundraiser, you know."

"I realize that, but still, I don't think the exchange of any letter in the presence of others would be a good idea."

"I agree. We will work something out. When are you scheduled to leave?"

"I have a flight scheduled after twelve on Sunday."

"That sounds good. It will give us time to meet tomorrow. If it's okay, let's plan to meet sometime. I will let you know when and where tonight at the function."

"That will work," said A.T. as he picked up the tab and assisted Julian with her chair. They said goodbye and planned to see each other at the fundraiser that evening.

CHAPTER 22
THE CUP RUNNETH OVER

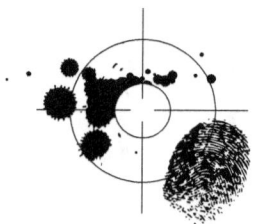

Upon returning to his hotel, A.T. first checked to be sure the documents he had delivered to himself were still in the room safe where he had left them. A.T. continued to feel apprehensive about giving the material to Blaine; however, the Senator had approved the release after apparently clearing the matter with his Republican colleague who was working with him on the subcommittee investigation. Certainly, A.T. and Blaine had been old friends with a long-term relationship; yet, the two of them had not seen each other for a few years. It was fair to say the level of trust that once existed was not quite the same as it had been in the past.

Since it was still early Friday afternoon and before five o'clock on the East Coast, A.T. decided to call the Senator with a status report. The first effort resulted in the need to leave a voicemail, which he did. Finally, as he was about to exit his room for a mid-afternoon coffee break, the phone rang. He checked the caller ID and noted it was the Senator. He thought to himself that the Senator was responding at a fairly late hour for a Friday. He thought it would be best to make the call as brief as possible.

A.T. answered, "Hello, Senator. I'm sorry to be bothering you so late on a Friday. If you would rather talk at a different time, just say."

"Actually, this is a very good time, A.T.," said the Senator. "My wife and I are about to leave for a dinner engagement. I'm sitting here waiting for her to get ready, and based upon past experience, it might be a while. How has your trip been so far?"

"It's been better than I expected. First of all, I met with Gerald in San Francisco. He agreed to our terms; however, he wanted to be assured of some type of immunity for his friends at the GGG, so long as they were cooperating with us on the investigation."

"What did you tell him?"

"I told him I was not in a position to make any arrangements, and I didn't have any authority to discuss such matters. I also told him it was probably in their best interests to cooperate with us."

"What was his reaction?"

"Despite his request, he said he was prepared to proceed regardless and that he had the authority to work with us. He also commented that the fairly recent decision by the Supreme Court supported all of their corporate activities in regard to political contributions."

"I guess we'll know once all of the investigative reports come back. I do wish you could find out more about this GGG entity. I had a couple of staff members checking on them, and they were not able to find much at all. Perhaps in your next discussion with Gerald, you might try to pursue that angle," requested the Senator.

"I'll try. I already have an excuse to speak with Gerald again considering he opened an unexpected door for us."

"He did? In what regard?" questioned the Senator.

"Do you remember Professor Brougham and the documents that he provided several months back?" A.T. replied.

"I do, indeed."

"To my great surprise, Professor Brougham met us for lunch and appeared to speak freely about his relationship with the GGG."

"That is a surprise," noted the Senator. "I got the impression from your earlier report that he may have either disappeared or he was being held against his will by the GGG."

"That's what I was led to believe by Samantha Nguyen-Henderson. If you will recall, she has been identified as an independent contractor for the GGG and the Knights of Malta. I'm guessing you will remember her as the lady friend of the congressman whom you saw on the steps of the Lincoln Memorial when we met there."

"I remember. Plus, I saw that in the report. I can give you some new information on her. If you'll remember when we met at the Lincoln Memorial on that Sunday, we broke off our conversation when I saw the Republican Congressman whom you mentioned and whom I thought might be helpful to us. After I encountered him at the base of the Memorial, he and I had a chance to visit about a number of things. He was a bit distraught, and he kept looking up toward the lady that he had been meeting on the stairs. When we looked up, we saw you with her. It looked as though you were attempting to comfort her by giving her a handkerchief. I then realized the lady was your new acquaintance, Samantha Nguyen-Henderson. As it turns out, she and the Congressman were involved with each other. He was very serious about keeping his relationship with her strictly confidential. It was obvious he didn't want his wife to know about it."

"I found out the same thing although from what Ms. Henderson said, it sounded like the wife of the Congressman knows about her. In fact, I took Ms. Henderson for coffee with the hope of getting her to settle down a bit. She was quite upset and apparently believed the Congressman was going to leave his wife for her. However, when she learned that was not the case, she became quite agitated. Evidently, the two of them had been together for some time," informed A.T.

"For about three years from what the Congressman said," noted the Senator.

"She thought that it had been longer," interrupted A.T.

"I suspected such to be the case. In any event, the Congressman is going to help us, so we need to handle the matter with your friend, Samantha, quite delicately," noted the Senator. "It turns out the chance meeting of the Congressman on the steps of the Memorial has been quite beneficial. It is more than obvious the Congressman doesn't want his relationship with your new friend, Samantha, to become a matter of public knowledge. That information will be quite helpful in my getting the Congressman to work with us on some new legislation relative to the 'Citizens United' case. It now appears I will be able to count on one more vote when the new bill that I will be proposing gets into the House for consideration. Plus, this particular Congressman will be able to bring a number of more moderate Republicans over for the vote when it comes up."

"That's pretty sly of you, Senator," commented A.T. "Sounds like you are working the political system a bit due to the Congressman's indiscretion with Samantha. The dirty world of politics seems to have reared its head. However, I don't see why that would affect my investigation."

"A.T., it has everything to do with your investigation," the Senator responded. "Try to understand there is far more at stake than your personal grudge with the DOJ and the FBI. You've got to try to get over what happened and understand there are bigger concerns, and that is part of the reason why the two of us are working together again."

"My focus is to get some oversight in place where the grand jury process is concerned," insisted A.T. "Although I think the 'Citizens United' case was a disaster, my goal with the investigation is to see changes to the grand jury process come about. I thought the two of us were working toward that same objective. It sounds like you now have a different goal in mind, Senator."

"Relax, A.T.," warned the Senator. "Both your efforts and my objectives with the investigation strike a common cord when it comes to doing something to 'right the ship,' as they say."

"I wish you had mentioned this sooner," said A.T. "I thought we had an understanding that the investigation's main objective was to set in place some grand jury oversight and get the process originally intended back to what it was. I want to see the elimination of the political aspects that have become a part of criminal indictments."

"It still is part of our objective," answered the Senator. "However, there is a greater good that can be accomplished if the investigation serves two purposes, namely, new legislation that changes 'Citizens United' and a look at the possibility of changing the grand jury process. That's why I think you need to stay in contact with this Samantha lady. It strikes me that she can be quite helpful in our obtaining our objectives."

"Well," said A.T., "it's starting to sound more and more like our objectives are quite different than what I originally thought when I agreed to expand the investigation. In regard to Samantha, frankly, I don't ever expect to see her again, and any contact information I had for her, I submitted with my report. In conjunction with our past practices, I didn't keep a copy," commented A.T.

"Okay," said the Senator, "I was hoping you might get in touch with her in regard to the GGG, if you are not able to learn anything new about them from Gerald."

"I guess that would be possible if we can't get what we need from Gerald. However, you will need to get someone to dig out her contact information from the file, since I had not planned on seeing her again. I really don't see how she could possibly be of any help in regard to the goal of getting us to bring about grand jury reform.

"As I've already said, there is more than one objective that can be accomplished here. The 'Citizens United' case affects us all, and by your continuing the investigation as I've laid it out for you, we will be able to use some of the same information in regard to that matter, as well as gain information that could be used for grand jury reform," instructed the Senator. "Go ahead and try to see what you can learn from Gerald first. Tell me about the meeting with him and Professor Brougham. That caught me really off guard. Did the professor seem to be there voluntarily?"

"Yes and no," answered A.T. "He came separately with the additional documents that Gerald promised. The professor said that he had been wrong in giving us the original documents in the first place. He sounded as though he was repentant in front of Gerald. He said he had changed his mind about the GGG and now claims they are a benevolent organization. But I need to mention his presence at the luncheon was unique in the sense he was accompanied by a woman named Gretchen Locksley. I personally felt she might be his 'handler,' but when I bluntly asked about that being the case, everyone present, including the professor, denied it. Both he and Gerald stated the professor would become a willing witness for us. I got the impression the GGG believes it can convince us through the professor that it is an honorable organization."

"Well," said the Senator, "it doesn't hurt for us to let them tell their story. Perhaps by doing that we will learn what we need to about the GGG. Do you know how to get in touch with the professor?"

"No, not exactly. Gerald insisted any contact made with the professor would be through him at one of the numbers he gave me."

"Did you give them the documents we agreed to provide?" asked the Senator.

"I did and I am impressed with what they gave us. There are letters, emails, and even an excel spreadsheet that identifies individuals within the DOJ, the FBI, State, Defense, and others within the Executive Branch, who are allegedly plants within the DOJ for the purpose of helping whoever is working behind the scenes to alter the direction of law enforcement by making the DOJ a political instrument. It would seem the GGG is as interested as we are in exposing these people.' The question is 'why?'"

"I'm sure you remember the, now former, FBI agents, Norvell Emerson and George Kowalski, whom I believe you knew as George Tarkanian."

"I certainly do," said A.T. with some expected disdain.

"You're going to be able to conduct an interview of both of them when you get back to Washington."

"That sounds like a dream come true. How did that come about?"

"As it turns out the Assistant Director of the Bureau, said he preferred that an interview be conducted by my committee in order to take him off the hook. The Bureau has already done its interviews and didn't want to initiate any additional requests for interviews of the two dishonored agents. Therefore, he asked if I had plans to conduct interviews of the two. I told him I felt it was quite important that my committee conduct its own independent interviews. He agreed. I told him I would ask you to conduct the interviews, and he thought that was a great idea, especially due to your background. He will probably sit in on the interviews with you, but that would be simply to make certain his office was aware of anything new that came up. Will that work for you?"

"Sure. Will I have access to any of the interviews the Bureau has done with the two former agents?"

"No. However, you will have free reign to ask any questions you want. Should I be scheduling the interviews for any time soon?"

"Perhaps sometime late next week might work. I need to get back to the Twin Cities. I leave here on Sunday and will be back there in the evening. I will be going to a Republican fundraiser with Blaine tonight, and as it now stands, I will meet with Blaine and Julian Tilson-Gould privately tomorrow."

"Did this Julian know about your situation?" asked the Senator.

"Yes, she did. She was at the White House when the whole situation developed around me. A couple months ago, I ran across an email she had sent, and I felt there might have been a tie-in to what had happened. She said your colleague, the Republican Senator, or someone in his office, had tipped her off that I might be contacting her. She was quite cooperative. I just thought you would have known about the fact she had spoken to your counterpart."

"I didn't know that, but that should be good news. It demonstrates to us that my colleague, the Republican Senator, is as serious as I am about getting to the bottom of these new groups that have arisen over the past few years. They have started to pour significant and questionable sums of money into certain campaigns. Perhaps you didn't know this, but some of the 'tea party' people have targeted the Republican Senator. They will be trying to defeat him in a primary coming up in the next election cycle. He believes the people who are now under investigation are somehow tied to some of the people behind the 'tea party' movement. I would imagine she might have some very valuable information for us; however, I would doubt if it involved the 'tea party' folks since they typically have a disdain for George W. Bush."

"It sounds like she does have some knowledge, but at this point I doubt it would involve the 'tea party.' It does look like she might give us some real insight into what was actually going on within George W. Bush administration, at least as far as some of the unusual and troubling appointments that were made and why."

"Well, as long as the information we receive from her is not classified," commented the Senator. "We don't want to allow her to get into trouble accidentally. I'm sure I need not remind you we are interested in statutory violations and political campaign contributions that will lead to the prosecution of those who have ill designs for our system of government and the need for change as to who and how political contributions are made."

"With all due respect, Senator, I am well aware of my assignment. So far, and in my view, the investigation had a sole focus of acquiring the necessary evidence that will prove the violations of which you speak, but I thought the focus was grand jury reform; now, it sounds like there is a second objective that I was unaware existed. In any event, I believe Julian will be significantly helpful in that regard. Also, for your information, she expressed some genuine dislike for a number of key people in W.'s administration. However, she is really fond of W. and doesn't want anything to cause him or his family any grief. She has a dying loyalty to W."

"That's understood. I am very happy to hear she will cooperate. I am thinking my colleague, the Republican Senator, is hoping to surprise me with Julian being a key witness for us. Don't let on that you informed me of her coming on as a witness. I will act pleasantly surprised when her Republican Senator informs me that she will be coming forward."

"So long as she gets the letter she wants, it will be some good news for all of us. I plan to visit with her tonight about a possible deposition in Washington D.C. perhaps as early as next week. As you might expect, she will be at the Republican fundraising event this evening, along with Blaine and some others whom I suspect I might remember from years ago. So, with the addition of Julian, along with the additional information from Gerald, plus the possibility of more information from Professor Brougham and the depositions of Norvell Emerson and George Kowalski, I would say we are on a roll."

"Wait, there is more," added the Senator. "I have more good news."

"What's that?" asked A.T.

"The two guys who were caught at Dulles International in regard to the attempt on the life of Orville Felthaus decided to provide what information they had regarding the attempt on Felthaus. The Transportation Security Administration was also able to get some of the videos from the airport with good shots of each of these fellows. The problem was with the third guy, who was clever enough to avoid the cameras. Of course, we now think he may be identified as well, due to the statements from the two accomplices."

"That is good news," said A.T. "but how exactly will that help us in regard to the investigation?"

"First of all, it gives us a direct link to the group of attorneys within the DOJ who have been trying to mold the DOJ into their own idea of enforcement and control at several levels directly below the top levels of appointments at the DOJ. These two guys have been formally charged and have told us they have worked for the third man before. We are learning more and more information about him. We are rather certain of his identity and are very close to bringing him in. If it's the guy we think it is, he is already within our reach and under surveillance. We think he will be able to confirm some identities that will give us the information we need," explained the Senator.

"That is good news. With all of the breaks we have had the last couple of weeks, it makes me feel like we are really on track."

"I would say so," said the Senator. "In fact, A.T., one might say our 'cup runneth over.'"

"Hopefully, our good luck will continue. Let me try to see how tonight and tomorrow go with Julian and Blaine. If I can obtain some commitments from each of them, I will be able to lock down some times for next week and plan a trip into Washington D.C. for the depositions of the agents, Julian, and whoever else we decide to get in front of the court reporter."

"That would be great," urged the Senator. "Why don't you give me a call on Monday after you've returned to St. Paul. If you can remember, try to see if that court reporter friend of yours, Bob, is available. I've always liked his work. You may want to also get in touch with Allen to see if he would like to come along. He may be helpful in several ways, including the fact he was with you during your meetings in Paris."

"I'll give you a call on Monday, Senator. Any special time?"

"Why don't you call either late afternoon or early evening. I will be on the hill for some meetings and a vote that involves some security issues. So, until then, have a good evening and a great tomorrow," said the Senator, while sounding like a news anchor in hanging up the phone.

A.T. looked at his watch and felt he still had time to grab a cup of coffee, so he started out the door. Just as he was closing the door to his hotel suite, he received a call from a 'blocked' number. At first, he was a bit hesitant to answer, but then he thought it might be the Senator with some last minute instructions. He took the call.

"Hello, Mr. Van Doren?"

"Yes."

"This is Lon Jeffers. My father said I should deliver some tuxedos to you. The hotel desk won't give me your room number, so I was wondering what I should do? Dad gave me this number and told me to call you to let you know. I'm in the hotel lobby with my brother and -"

"I'm on my way down," said A.T. "I was heading down to the coffee shop for a coffee break. I'll meet you and your brother in the lobby in just a few minutes." A.T. was already near the elevator by the time the call was over. After getting to the main floor, A.T. went straight to the lobby where he observed two young men holding several tuxedos. He approached them and said, "I haven't seen you boys since you were quite young. From the looks of the two of you, I would say that you're the two older boys. Is that right?"

"Just about," said the older of the two. "I'm Lon, but you probably remember me as Lonnie. I'm the second son. This is my younger brother, 'Gee,' whose real name is Grayson. We call him 'Gee' because he's not very fond of his real name. Our older brother, Blake, is going to be one of the ushers tonight, so he's getting ready for the fundraiser, and our youngest brother is playing ball tonight," explained Lon as he handed three tuxedos to A.T. "Here are three tuxedos. Dad didn't know which of them would fit, so he sent all three."

A.T. thanked the boys for the tuxedos and arranged for them to pick him up later for transportation to the dinner. Since A.T. had three tuxedos in his hand, he decided a stop at the coffee shop would be out of the question. Instead, he decided to get a large cup of black coffee to go, so he went to the coffee shop and ordered the coffee. As A.T. was about to get his large coffee from the clerk, he heard a familiar voice from behind him say, "Well, I'll be, if it isn't my old friend, A.T. It's been a long time, good buddy!"

Just then A.T. turned to see a very large man standing right behind him. It was an image out of the purposely forgotten past. Next to him stood "Big John" Harry Johnson, whom he had worked with many years ago. A.T. immediately knew if "Big John" were there, then surely "Squeaky" Brent Wilson wasn't far behind. The two of them always traveled together, and the last time A.T. even thought about them was when he met Will and Marjorie Blake at the old bakery in St. Paul before the holidays. He recalled neither Will nor Marjorie had anything good to say about the two companions. A.T. tried to hide his surprise when he turned and extended his hand in order to greet "Big John." A.T. said, "Hello, 'Big John.' Where is your buddy, 'Squeaky'?"

"I'm right here," said a voice as 'Squeaky' stepped out from behind 'Big John.'

A.T. shook "Squeaky's" sweaty hand and said, "I just knew you couldn't be far behind. What brings the two of you to San Diego?"

"We're vacationing here in the Southwest, and we just happened to be at the same hotel as you," said 'Big John,' who did virtually all of the talking for the dynamic duo. "What brings you out here?"

"Just some political events," said A.T. "I've been catching up with some old friends I knew back when I was active in the political arena. In fact, I was just about to get ready for one of the events I hoped to attend this evening. That's why I'm holding a couple tuxedos. I would love to stay and visit, but I am a bit pressed and will need to change fairly soon."

"I heard you had given up on politics," said 'Big John.' "Are you going to get involved as a candidate, or are you just getting into the back office again?"

"Actually, neither," responded A.T. "I've been invited to meet with some old political friends, and in the process, I was invited to attend a meeting set for this evening."

"Looks a bit formal," observed 'Big John,' while 'Squeaky' grasped the cuff of one of the tuxedos to assess the fabric.

"Just a small gathering," noted A.T. pulling the tuxedos away from 'Squeaky's' hand. "What have the two of you been up to?"

"We've been working for a couple of brothers who are rather prominent industrialists."

"Really? Who? Have I heard of them?" inquired A.T.

"Oh, we're sure you have, but we really aren't at liberty to disclose. You know; we perform some special assignments and that sort of thing," said 'Big John.'

"What type of assignments?" asked A.T. "It's not something that would get you into any trouble, would it?"

"Of course not! With our past history of conducting discreet investigations and that sort of thing, we have been employed by these very reputable brothers to check on things for them from time to time. Our superiors would prefer we not discuss our tasks with other parties," warned 'Big John.'

"Why, I thought we had such a good past relationship that the two of you could discuss anything with me. However, if you want to be that way, I guess I will just have to be left out. Besides, I do have to change for this evening. I don't wish to be rude, but I must get ready in order to be available for my ride that should be here before too long," commented A.T. turning to leave.

"What room are you in?" asked 'Squeaky' when A.T. walked away.

Since it was unusual for 'Squeaky' to do much talking, A.T. grew suspicious. He had already grown a bit paranoid about the investigation and felt there was a good likelihood 'Big John' and 'Squeaky' were up to something. Being cautious, A.T. turned back and responded, "Why don't I give you a call when I return. What is your phone number?"

"Rather than go through all that, why don't the three of us plan to meet at the hotel restaurant tomorrow morning. Since we are all at the same hotel, we could visit during breakfast and catch up," offered 'Big John.

"What a great idea," said A.T. "Why don't we plan to meet for breakfast at 8:30 here in the coffee shop?"

"That sounds good," said 'Big John.'

A.T. left for the elevators, realizing he was probably the subject of some investigation or 'tailing' that 'Big John' and 'Squeaky' were doing. He suspected the two 'old friends' probably already knew which room he was in. His only hope was that they had not already broken into the room. If they hadn't, he was sure they would. It would now certainly be necessary to do something with the documents A.T. had brought along for Blaine. He would also have to decide what he would do with the new documents he had received from Professor Brougham in San Francisco while under the watchful eye of Gerald. Although both sets of documents were in the room safe, A.T. was certain the room safe wouldn't be enough to stop 'Big John' and 'Squeaky.'

When A.T. returned to his room, he set down the coffee, hung up the tuxedos, and immediately checked the safe. He had placed a small piece of tape on the lower edge of the safe door and out of sight before he left the room so the tape might serve as an indicator should someone open the safe while he was out. If someone had, there would be nothing he could do; however, he would at least know someone had tampered with it.

He checked the tape on the underside of the door and noted it was still in place and unbroken. He opened the safe and saw for himself the documents were in place and undisturbed. That was a good sign, but he would have to do something because he felt confident 'Big John' and 'Squeaky' would find a way into the room and the safe. He thought of the perfect solution. The material he had brought along for Blaine, he would divide, place in envelopes, and then in the suit pockets of the two tuxedo jackets that he would not be using. He would return the two unused tuxedos to Blaine's sons.

The documents he had received from Professor Brougham and Gerald in San Francisco were more of a problem. A.T. decided he would take those documents to the hotel office center just off the lobby. The hotel was well-equipped with the technology he needed. He would scan the documents through his travel computer and drop them directly onto a thumb drive he had brought along. That way he could bypass the computer's memory. He would email the scanned documents directly from the thumb drive to his own office computer in St. Paul. He could also send a courtesy copy to Lee Mattson, the Senator's aide, whose email he had memorized from past transmissions. After A.T. had done that, he would shred the documents through the shredder in the hotel office center.

After finding that one of the tuxedos fit fairly well, he dressed and loaded the other two sets of clothing with the documents to be delivered to Blaine. A.T. checked his travel computer to be certain there was nothing of value on it. He generally would use the travel computer for two purposes, namely, to video-conference back to St. Paul or elsewhere and to prepare the documents he needed by directly accessing a thumb drive while working "off-line." His only concern was the transmittal of documents by email through the laptop. Although he could delete the emails, even an amateur could recover such an email. Once he finished using the laptop for the day, he would disable it before he left for the fundraiser. That would prevent an 'on site' recovery.

While back in his room he decided to telephone Jacci. It was a regular habit for him to call each evening while out of town in order for the two of them to catch up on each other's day. Normally, the conversations were routine and rarely was there any special news; however, on this particular occasion, Jacci said she had received a curious visitor at the house.

"Do you remember your old political 'friend,' Leslie?" asked Jacci.

"Yes," answered A.T. "What about him?"

"He stopped by under the excuse of delivering a certificate for you; however, it seemed he had more on his mind," said Jacci.

"Tell me more," urged A.T. "It's really odd that, after many years of not hearing from him, he has been in contact a number of times over the last several weeks. Did he say what was on his mind?"

"It seems as though he had several things he wanted to mention," explained Jacci. "First, he wanted to know where you were. Next, he said that even though the two of you were never close, he always admired you and because of that he wanted to again warn you that he felt the investigation you were conducting was not a good idea. He said there were people, whom he wouldn't mention, that had expressed concern about your continuing with the investigation."

"Oh, is that all," exclaimed A.T. "It sounds like Leslie was just using the certificate for an excuse to find out where I was."

"What about the warning regarding the investigation?" asked Jacci. I never thought your getting involved in this investigation was a good idea. That's why I asked Adam to have his IT people come up with some safety items for you. But what concerns me most of all is the fact that after all of these years the Senator has come out of the woodwork to try to get you to merge your investigation with whatever it is he is trying to assemble. Even though we have always been friends with the Senator and his family, don't ever forget, A.T., he is a political animal who is pretty clever at getting people to do things for him. I always felt it was unusual we never heard from him after the indictment. We only heard from him after the case had been dismissed, and you were in the clear. Although I don't trust Leslie either, in this instance, I agree with him in that this investigation could be more of a danger than you realize, and I agree the Senator is probably using you.

"Up until earlier today," said A.T. "I thought the Senator and I were on the same page as far as the investigation is concerned; however, after my conversation with him, I'm not so sure."

"What did he say that changed your mind?" asked Jacci.

"From what the Senator said," noted A.T. "it seems as though he is more interested in gathering information that would give him evidence to have the 'Citizens United' case nullified with some new legislation, possibly even a Constitutional amendment."

"Refresh my memory," insisted Jacci. "What's 'Citizens United'?"

"That was the Supreme Court decision that essentially allowed private corporations and very wealthy individuals to shelter large campaign contributions into nonprofit companies for political purposes," noted A.T.

"Oh, I remember now," said Jacci. "Whatever the case, A.T., please be extra careful since, after talking to this Leslie character, I have a feeling some people are most likely watching you and that can't be a good thing. Plus, I'd be extra careful in doing too much for the Senator, especially if it begins to appear as though he is using you for his own political purposes."

"I promise to be extra careful," assured A.T. "Plus, I couldn't end my day without at least saying good night to you."

"That's what I want to hear," said Jacci. "Be extra careful."

"I will," answered A.T. "Bye."

"Bye."

Upon finishing the call, A.T. made certain the computer and documents were safe. He finished placing the paperwork for Blaine into the other two tuxedos for Blaine's sons. A.T. went down to the hotel office center while formally dressed and carrying the other two tuxedos. He looked around the area to be sure "Big John" and "Squeaky" were not in sight. He entered the hotel office center, scanned the documents onto his thumb drive, emailed the documents to himself and to Lee, shredded the documents that remained, and waited for Blaine's two sons to arrive. Upon their arrival, he handed them the two tuxedos that he was carrying and asked the two boys to wait, while he took his laptop back to his room. He returned to his room and disabled the laptop. With the thumb drive placed on a lanyard that he hung around his neck and the hard drive safely in his pocket, he proceeded to the lobby to rejoin Blaine's two sons.

**

The drive to the country club went by quickly. When they arrived, several cars ahead of them were being transferred to the hands of the valet crew. While they waited, A.T. explained that contained within the inside suit pockets of the tuxedos was some very confidential and important paperwork for their father that was sealed into several envelopes. The boys were given specific instructions to be certain the tuxedos and particularly the documents were safely delivered to their father's study or room at the family home. A.T. was deposited at the front entrance to the club, and the boys drove off.

After entering the country club and noting the location of the "Republican Spring Blockbuster" event from the posted events calendar, A.T. received directions from a young girl, who was dressed in an outfit with the country club label on the lapel. Upon arriving at the ballroom designated for the event, he noticed a fairly large crowd had already gathered. Inside, a desk had been set up for registration. When he identified himself to the two young ladies at the desk, he reached for his checkbook and was immediately told by the one closest to him that his contribution had already been made. She then handed his name tag to him.

A.T. accepted the name tag and casually commented that the contribution must have been made by his rich uncle. The young lady smiled and said the rich uncle must be her future father-in-law as A.T.'s pass was presented to him by a young lady who stated she was engaged to the eldest son of Blaine Jeffers. The other young lady quickly commented it had to be a rich uncle since the dinner was a twenty-five-thousand-dollar-per-plate affair. A.T. thought either Blaine must really want to see me, or he's so rich a sum like twenty-five thousand dollars for an old political friend comes from a rather remarkable reserve from which he wouldn't miss such a large amount. He clipped on his name tag and thanked the young ladies.

He scanned the room for familiar faces and felt a bit uncomfortable, considering there wasn't a familiar one he could see. The room was set up with a long elevated table at one end. It looked as though it was set for about a dozen people, some of whom had already taken their seats. The remainder of the room was configured with large round tables set for eight people each. An orchestra was playing the Italian composed overture of Giacomo Puccini's *"Gianni Schicchi."*

The ballroom had a rather elaborate bar set up to the right side of the main entrance. Although the bar area was a bit crowded, he noticed some space, so he decided to order a drink of some sort. With such a large and unfamiliar crowd, he thought he might need to place a fairly strong order, so he ordered double vodka on the rocks, no vermouth. After he received what appeared to be a rather generous portion with what might have been quadruple vodka, he heard a familiar voice behind him.

"It must have been a rather strenuous day to order such a healthy beverage, or one would sense a serious drinking problem." A.T. turned in the direction of the voice, where he saw Blaine Jeffers and his wife, Angel.

A.T. smiled and extended his hand to greet Blaine, who instead gave A.T. a big bear hug that almost cost A.T. his drink. After the hug, A.T. turned and stepped back. He gave a gentle hug and kiss on the cheek to Angel, who looked as stunning as ever. She appeared to be wearing a rather expensive and fashionable gown, probably a BCBG. Angel looked the same as she had the last time A.T. saw her, probably fifteen years earlier. She was one of those fortunate people who simply didn't age. With a large grin, A.T. said, "Boy, is it a treat to see the two of you. You both really look great. It's as if time has stood still. It's hard to imagine you could possibly have grown sons, and let me add, very fine young men at that."

Angel smiled and said, "It sounds like you're getting political already and you just got here."

"Not political at all, Angel. I really mean it. You haven't changed at all. You really look as beautiful as ever," said A.T. He turned to Blaine and added, "You are a very lucky man, along with superb taste and good fortune, to marry such a beautiful creature as this Angel standing next to us. Plus, you're looking pretty good yourself."

"Thank you, A.T.," said Blaine. "You're looking the same, as well. That tux fits very nicely. I thought it would. Unfortunately, I've picked up a few pounds, so that particular uniform just doesn't work for me anymore."

"Thank you for providing this fine garment," A.T. responded. "Also, thank you as well for the invitation and a place at the table. It is awfully generous of you. I haven't been to a political event like this for many years. I hope I can remember how to behave."

"Just don't start dancing on the table like last time," kidded Blaine since he knew from past experience that A.T. had always remained quietly in the background at such events. The three of them had a good laugh. While they were still laughing, a young man appeared. With his arm outstretched, Blaine motioned for the young man to come closer and said, "A.T. please meet our oldest. This is our son, Blake. Blake, say hello to a dear old family friend, A.T. Van Doren."

"Hello, Mr. Van Doren. I've heard some wonderful stories about how you and my dad kept the Republican Party on the proper path many years ago. It is my pleasure to see you again, sir."

"The pleasure is mine, Blake," said A.T. "The last time I saw you, I was on the sidelines with your folks and Mrs. Van Doren. We were watching you play soccer, as I recall."

"That had to be a while back," said Blake. "I must have been in grade school because I haven't played much soccer since then."

"Blake is serving as one of the ushers for tonight, A.T.," said Blaine. "Perhaps he could show you where you will be sitting. We have place cards for everyone. You have to remember since we are Republicans, everything needs to be organized properly. I've arranged for you to be at a table with several people whom I believe you will enjoy. In fact, I think you will have a surprisingly good time. I will probably need to get close to my own table since they will be starting fairly soon. After the meal, we will have a good speaker. If it's all right, Blake will show you to your table."

"That would be great," responded A.T. "There is one thing I should mention. You might want to be sure to fully examine the two tuxedos your other two boys are taking back to your house. It would be a good idea to check the inside pockets. Thanks again for this tux. It fits quite well."

"You're welcome. I will check the tuxedos out fully. I trust that will be in accord with what I've been informed by a mutual friend from the United States Senate," noted Blaine.

"It is," said A.T. following Blake to the table set near the middle of the room. On the way to the table, A.T. and Blake encountered Julian and her husband, Bernie Gould. A.T. had met Bernie, who was considerably older than Julian, at several prior political events. Upon seeing them, A.T. smiled and extended his hand to Bernie, who was a step ahead of Julian, leading her by his other hand. A.T. and Bernie shook hands; A.T. turned and gave Julian, who appeared to be wearing a fashionable "Cynthia Rowley" evening gown, a kiss on the cheek and a slight hug. A.T. said, "Hello! It is nice to see you both. How has life been for the two of you?"

"It has been great," said Bernie. "We haven't seen much of you for the last few years, A.T. Hopefully, all has been well, and no doubt the law practice has kept you too busy to pay much attention to the political world."

"I've been quite busy, thanks. It's true I've tried to stay clear of the world of politics, Bernie, and that is no doubt the reason why you haven't seen me at any political activities for several years now."

"Well, it's good to see you back in the mainstream. We've actually missed some of your more levelheaded comments. The Party has nearly gone over the edge, and it's a good thing to see moderates like you back at functions like this. Hopefully, we will see much more of you from now on. Let's try to catch up later after dinner. We would love to visit with you, wouldn't we, Julian?" said Bernie as he turned to Julian.

"That would be very nice. We'll try to catch up with you after dinner," agreed Julian. "Until later, A.T., but now we should be getting to our seats, right, Bernie?"

Without further comment but with an affectionate nod, Bernie again took Julian's hand in order to lead her to their table. Blake escorted A.T. to his assigned table, where A.T. noticed his place card was set forth in a bold and stylish calligraphy at a table already nearly full.

A.T. observantly counted six people already seated at the table and began introducing himself to those present. To his immediate left was an elderly woman who reminded A.T. of a lady from a famous T.V. commercial for a burger company. In the commercial, the lady kept asking, "Where's the beef?" The woman's name was

Ethel, and she was there with her husband, George, who was seated to her left. He reminded A.T. of the character, 'Mr. Granger,' of the British sitcom, *Are you Being Served?* They were a delightful couple, and A.T. learned they had both previously worked for the Scripps Medical Research Institute. The couple next to them was quite a bit younger.

The man who sat next to George was a young attorney, and his pretty, young wife was a physical therapist. To her left were a man of about fifty and his older sister. They had been active in the Republican Party in Orange County and had come from a large, well-connected family that had apparently owned several of the orange and lemon tree groves that had been displaced by urban development in the areas of Irvine and Newport Beach. It sounded as though their family also had some involvement in the development of the rail system that ran from LA to San Diego. There was a vacant seat between the sister and A.T. When he glanced at the calligraphy on the card, it appeared to say, "Sir Henderson." A.T. wondered if some Brit with a title was the missing guest. Everyone at the table was pleasant and quite outgoing. Conversation was fluid and animated. All of the people at the table seemed to be enjoying their beverages.

Old George managed to control the conversation. If he felt someone was not adding enough to the discussion, he would ask them a question in order to get their political perspective. Apparently, George thought it was time to get A.T. more involved in the conversation, so he asked, "Tell me, A.T., what do you think of all of these stupid 'tea party' people trying to take over our Party. Don't you think the Republican Party has had quite enough of their bullshit?"

"Now, George, watch your language. You're out in public and among polite company," said Ethel.

"What did I say?" asked George, who was obviously expecting an immediate response from A.T. Apparently the answer wasn't forthcoming fast enough, so George pushed on, "Well, speak up, man. What do you think of all the nonsense they have been putting the Party through?"

"Personally, I'm not a bit fond of the 'tea party' people, and I consider it quite an affront to our founding fathers that today's 'tea party' would use the name they have chosen. I believe they have maligned the name 'tea party,' and they have degraded the principles behind the original movement and revolution of over two hundred and thirty five years ago. I would imagine our founding fathers are rolling over in their graves," answered A.T.

"I'll bet you're right about that. If nothing else, our founding fathers, who were extraordinarily intelligent men in my opinion, are seriously affronted by today's 'tea party' losers, if for no other reason than because today's 'tea party' doesn't have a good brain in the entire group. I've never seen such a mass of stupidity. They are ill-advised, ill-tempered, ill-informed, poorly educated, poorly read, and just plain stupid, if you ask me."

No one asked you, dear," said Ethel, who immediately laughed at what she perceived as her own humor.

"It doesn't matter, Ethel," said George as he waved off her comment. "What do the rest of you think? What about you, young man? You're a lawyer, aren't you? What do you say?"

"I'm in agreement with what has been said so far. Aren't we here tonight to start a resurgence of real Republican thinking? Aren't we trying to resurrect the real Republican base which was once one hell of a lot broader than the 'tea party' activists?" asked the young lawyer. "In fact, I thought tonight's speaker was going to address the inactivity of the non-tea party Republicans and how we take the Party back."

"That's why I'm here," interjected the middle-aged brother. "Like most of the people here, my sister and I come from a family of respectful means. However, we are different in that our family includes some Hispanic heritage that dates back a very long time. We feel the current movement of the Republican Party has excluded us for the most part due to the fact we have Hispanic heritage. As an aside, I don't mind mentioning our family presence in Southern California goes back for at least ten generations. It is my belief the Republican Party is changing its base to include many closet bigots. We are people of reason, and perhaps that is what caused an early family bond with the Republican Party as far back as the 1860s."

"I don't think the 'tea party' group is made up of closet bigots, Manuel. They are outright bigots," spoke up the sister. "Keep in mind this is the reason your wife refuses to come to these functions. Plus, I would add I personally believe today's 'tea party' is really a front for some very wealthy people, far wealthier than we are, who are trying to move the public in a specific direction. Meanwhile, those obscenely wealthy individuals follow a plan designed to protect their petroleum and chemical-based interests."

She continued, "These guys have a lot of money, and if they see anything that cuts into their bottom line, they throw more money at the 'tea party' people, so the 'tea party' can mobilize and try to sway public opinion. The problem is the 'tea party' base is just as you have said, George, they are ill-advised and poorly educated. They don't realize that they are being used. Everything they have done so far has been to undermine what most Americans really want in terms of fair and honest politicians. In my opinion, the people using and funding the 'tea party' don't really care two bits about the 'tea party' base. That base and the religious fringe are being used for the sole purpose of promoting some very wealthy and politically ambitious people. I would have to agree the 'tea party' folks are either too naive or stupid to see how they are being used."

"By golly, there is hope for the youth, after all," said George. "I want to compliment you young people for giving your opinions. Ethel and I thought that we, as moderate Republicans, were a dying breed and we were no longer welcome in the Party. I was thrilled to death when I learned of tonight's gathering. I ran into people tonight whom I haven't seen for well over a decade. Like me, most of them slipped into the woodwork when W. became president and started to cater to all of the 'fringe' people."

"It's not just your generation, George," interrupted the young lawyer. "If the youth of America are ever going to be considered a part of the Republican Party, the existing Party leadership and particularly the 'tea party' people are going to have to come to the realization they cannot run the party and expand its base, unless they stop operating the Party through oppression and bribery. They are running the Party like a dictatorship, and that will need to end."

"Personally, I can't stand the women in the 'tea party,'" said the sister. "They make women look one dimensional. Sarah Palin, Michelle Bachman, Sharon Angle, Christine O'Donnell, along with that lady governor in Arizona, all make women look stupid. Believe me, there are a lot of women who resent being categorized as some beauty pageant contestant who can't at least read a newspaper of some kind. We need more women in the Party like Elizabeth Dole to come forward. She may have been a bit conservative for my blood, but at least she was a smart woman who didn't compromise the role of women in this world."

"Sis may be the only woman's lib Republican," said the brother.

"I disagree," said the physical therapist, sitting next to her husband, the lawyer. "There are a lot more women in the Republican Party who want good spokespersons for women. Those of us who have used our minds to accomplish something are usually too busy to get involved in the public eye. Plus, I personally believe there is a serious character deficiency of some sort common to the women whom you have mentioned."

"You are probably right," said the brother. "Both my sister and my wife are like most women who are both offended and fed up with the fluffy, air-headed Republican women who get all the attention. You'll have to admit most of the women who attempt to stand at the front line of Republican politics are, as you say, suffering from some character deficiency. Other women like my wife, my sister here, and you," said the brother as he looked directly at the physical therapist, "are too busy attempting to fulfill several roles that include careers and family obligations. I've been trying to get my sister here more actively involved."

As the brother was finishing his statement and paused to look up, A.T. noticed everyone else at the table, as well as those at the surrounding tables, had stopped talking and began to look in the direction directly behind where A.T. was sitting. A.T. decided it might be a good idea for him to look around to see what had caught everyone's attention.

When A.T. turned and saw for himself, he nearly dropped the drink he was holding. There deliberately being escorted toward the table by young Blake Jeffers was the picturesque Samantha Nguyen-Henderson. She was dressed in a mauve-colored avant-garde 'Marchese' evening gown. It was a single shoulder strap dress that was floor length with a long slit that ran from the floor nearly to the hip on the left side. In her pinned-up hair, she wore a sparkling ringlet device that seemed to contain some diamonds. Around her neck she supported a thin triple band necklace that displayed a center row of emeralds with what appeared to be a row of diamonds above and below the emeralds. From what he remembered about Samantha, A.T. thought showing off was a typical behavior of hers, but more importantly, what was she doing here and why?

A.T. stood up when she approached the chair next to him. Immediately, he sensed a unique fragrance of perfume he had remembered from his meeting with Jean Paul in Paris and again at the coffee shop in the mall after Gerald went into the ditch.

Samantha waited for A.T. to pull back her chair, obviously enjoying the stunned look on his face. A.T.'s jaw must have dropped a bit as Samantha smiled and said, "Aren't you going to help me with the chair, A.T.? Oh, and you can close your mouth now."

A.T. moved the chair back for her, and took another look at the fancy calligraphy on the place card. He then realized the name on the card was "Sam Henderson" and not "Sir Henderson." It was the calligraphy that had thrown him off. There was no way on God's green earth he expected to see Samantha at a high priced Republican fundraiser or ever again for that matter. He looked across the room at the table where Blaine was standing with his glass raised high in an effort to salute A.T.'s table. A.T. smiled and shook his head. It was obvious there was a lot going on behind the scenes, and the invitation to A.T. for his attendance at the function was apparently no mere accident. There was undoubtedly going to be some intriguing new information he would want to hear before this night was over.

After Sam was seated, A.T. commented to Samantha, "That's a very pleasant fragrance I sense you're wearing."

"Thank you; do you like it?" asked Samantha.

"It is very nice," answered A.T. "I'm rather sure I sensed it once before and some time ago."

"You probably did," commented Samantha without missing a moment. "I was wearing it the night Gerald and I defended you near your hotel."

"Actually, I don't recall it from that time because there was so much going on, and you were some distance away from me since you were involved with one of the attackers."

"As you'll remember," whispered Samantha, "Gerald and I were defending you from that FBI agent whose credentials I handed to you in exchange for Gerald's phones."

"I remember full well," noted A.T. "However, I remember the scent from earlier that same evening."

"I'm sure you do," responded Samantha. "I was near your table when you were sharing some documents with the man who we are still attempting to identify. My plan at the time was to stop and introduce myself; however, after I reached your table, I wasn't quite sure how to approach you. I wanted to retrieve the documents the professor had given you, but it would have been too obvious. By the time I reached your table, I decided it would be better to follow you and try for an accidental meeting where I could bump into you and cause you to drop the case. Since that opportunity never occurred, Gerald and I decided to follow you to your hotel. As it turned out for you, that course of action was a good thing."

"Tell me," inquired A.T. "do you always dress formally when you engage in a street fight?"

"Are you trying to compliment me or insult me?" asked Samantha. Before A.T. could respond, she said, "For your information, I was dressed in business attire and didn't expect to have a street encounter. I would think you would be forever grateful to me and that you would be pleased to see me this evening."

"It is good to see you," responded A.T. "The thing of it is, I never actually expected to see you again, and I certainly never expected to see you at an event such as this. However, allow me to observe that you somehow seem to fit in perfectly."

While Samantha laughed, A.T. couldn't help but notice three things were happening simultaneously. The waiter was circulating around the table with a coffee pot and was pouring coffee into any cup that had not been overturned on its saucer, which included the cup at Sam's place setting. As the waiter began to pour coffee into her cup, someone bumped the table while A.T. happened to be focused on the necklace Sam was wearing. Sam only noticed A.T.'s eyes and said, "My eyes are up here, A.T."

"I was looking at your necklace and at the coffee cup," pleaded A.T.

"Sure you were."

"Really, I was and by the way, the waiter just spilled some coffee by your cup. The cup is running over," said A.T. who then sarcastically continued by saying, "perhaps he was looking at the necklace, as well."

At that moment, the waiter caught himself looking below Samantha's neckline. He immediately stopped pouring. He apologized and began to sop up the spilled coffee with the tea towel he had draped over his arm. Sam immediately reacted and slid her chair back and took the linen napkin at her place setting and began to absorb some of the coffee as well. She was trying to handle the matter as if nothing at all had happened. A.T. offered to assist, whereupon she turned to him and curtly said, "Just what would you propose? I thought the young man handled it well, and since I've used the napkin, I may need another."

"Consider it done," said A.T. so he offered and exchanged napkins with her. "It would seem something out of the ordinary occurs every time I run into you. These meetings will need to come to an end."

Sam thanked A.T. for the napkin exchange and said sarcastically, "Tonight, you didn't run into me. This meeting was planned, and I believe it will be of immeasurable benefit to you. A lot of people are already on the same page, and that is where you will need to be."

"Really?" inquired A.T. "Then perhaps you should explain to me what apparently everyone else already knows."

When Sam noticed everyone at the table had grown silent from their other conversations and were focused instead upon A.T. and Samantha, she said, "We'll talk later, but for now, let's enjoy the dinner, the other guests, and the speaker, who I understand will be worth hearing. Now, you said that you were looking at my necklace before the coffee spill. Is that right?"

At this point, everyone at the table seemed to snicker apparently wondering if A.T. and the waiter for that matter were really looking at the necklace. No doubt they were also wondering exactly what Samantha meant when she said the meeting between she and A.T. had been planned. To avoid further diversion to whatever was imagined by the other guests, A.T. said, "Indeed. If you don't mind my saying, the necklace is a very stunning piece of jewelry. It is very pretty."

"Thank you," said Samantha as she placed her hand over the necklace. "It is a family heirloom my French grandfather gave to my Vietnamese grandmother on their wedding day. Before it was mine, the necklace had been in my grandfather's family for many generations and that included ancestors of a French nobleman and his lady who were my great-great-great grandparents."

"Well, it is a beautiful accessory, and if I may say so, you wear it with both dignity and class," said A.T. while he tried to dig himself out of an uncontrollable set of circumstances that had placed him in an unenviable and uncomfortable position.

At that point, old George came to the rescue and said, "Young lady, you look like a princess of great renown. You have brightened this table and the entire room with your elegant presence."

"Thank you, kind sir," smiled Samantha. "However, there are so many beautiful ladies at this table, and I am honored, as well as humbled, to simply sit in their presence."

A.T. thought it was getting a little deep, so just as the second waiter was bringing the initial course of food, he asked, "Does anyone know what the subject matter of tonight's speech will be?"

The young lawyer answered and said, "It will address just how it will be possible for us to take back the Republican Party from all of the crazy people who have hijacked it."

That comment generated considerable discussion. While they were engaged in their discussions on the subject, A.T. leaned over toward Samantha and quietly asked, "Not that I can't wait, but could you give me some clue as to what is going on?"

"It's going to be a speech about politics within the Republican Party," answered Samantha.

"That's not what I mean, and you know it," whispered A.T.

Samantha leaned back toward A.T. and quietly said, "My benefactor wishes to meet with you regarding your investigation."

"Is your benefactor here?"

"No, I am to set up the meeting tonight, but let's talk later."

"Okay," whispered A.T. "I will be interested to hear how this all came about and how it is I'm feeling a bit on the outside of things at this point. I'm not sure what is going on but -"

"Let me see that napkin that was used to blot up the spilled coffee," said Samantha. She then asked for a pen, and A.T. complied. She drew a large circle around a large stain or 'spill spot.' She explained in a whisper while drawing a large circle, "Here is your investigation. As you will see, there are many other spots. Let me circle those as well. These are some of the many things that are happening. You, sir, need to connect the 'spill spots,' and along with the assistance of my benefactor, I am going to help you accomplish that objective. There is much you do not know about what is happening behind the scenes. For one thing, A.T., you are being used by your Senator friend. Secondly, you have aroused the attention of some very powerful people who want to put an end to this investigation of yours. Later, after the speaker has finished, we will meet along with Blaine, Angel, Julian, and Bernie. I will explain and arrange a meeting with my benefactor."

"I don't have your number any longer," said A.T. "I submitted it with my report."

"How could you!" said Samantha attempting to look shocked. "And here I thought that you would carry it with you forever."

"Very funny," said A.T.

As he said it, Samantha once again took the napkin and wrote her phone number on it. She made an indelible imprint from the lipstick from her lips upon the napkin and whispered, "There, my number and my signature in mauve. Now, don't forget. I'm sure that you will always treasure it."

At that point, while A.T. was placing the napkin in his inside coat pocket, George said, "I don't mean to interrupt, but they are trying to serve you two birds with the next course of food. The poor waiter has been patiently waiting at your chairs to do his job. Let him put the plates in front of you, at least. You should be able to discuss your personal problems after the dinner."

For A.T., the entire evening had gotten out of control, and he felt he was being manipulated by Samantha and his friends. He expected to get to the bottom of things as soon as the dinner was over and the speaker had finished. On the other hand, he was happy Samantha was going to introduce him to her benefactor. Although A.T.'s focus had been the Department of Justice, the Senator wanted A.T. to find out more about the GGG and others, in the complex array of information being acquired through the investigation. A.T. thought: *It is just like the Senator said, "The cup hath runneth over."*

CHAPTER 23
SPILL SPOTS

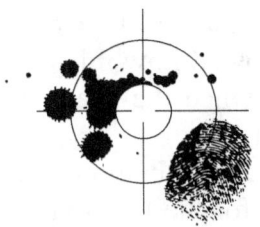

The meal proceeded with continued discussions among the guests at the table. A.T. and Sam participated with the others and dropped their private exchange about Sam's benefactor. Although the series of surprises that had confronted A.T. throughout the day, particularly the surprise of Samantha's presence at the Republican fundraiser, were churning over and over in his mind, he tried to be as cordial as possible to everyone at the table, including Sam, who had really irritated him. He wondered why it was that this woman kept popping up and why she seemed intent on causing him so much grief. However, if a meeting with her benefactor would prove beneficial, the investigation could take on an entirely new and fulfilling direction. He felt he should be happy about the situation instead of angry; however, he didn't appreciate the fact that others had been so instrumental in planning his life as of late.

The meal was extraordinary although probably not worth the twenty-five thousand dollars per plate. However, the company at the table was enjoyable enough to take A.T.'s mind off his own world of limitation that the investigation had created. In addition, the keynote speaker was very refreshing and thoroughly humorous in his presentation. It appeared as though he had been collecting excerpts of many of the political speeches given by some of the more public 'tea party'-friendly people, including Newt Gingrich, Mike Huckabee, Dick Army, Rick Perry, Herman Cain, Sarah Palin, Michelle Bachman, Wisconsin Governor Scott Walker, Florida Senator Mark Rubio, Texas Senator Ted Cruz, and others. It even surprised A.T. when the speaker called Mitt Romney, George W. "light." In that regard, the speaker had plenty of quoted gaffs and incomprehensible statements made by Mr. Romney, including the "binders full of women" statement that made the attendees laugh out loud.

The speaker especially seemed to enjoy comparing the misguided and misleading statements about history and the Constitution made by the 'tea party' segment to the actual historical events and portions of the Constitution, as well as case pronouncements that showed how misleading and absurd the 'tea party' statements were. Once the speaker finished, those present provided a standing ovation.

At the end of the speaker's humorous dissertation, he provided what he termed a recipe for the Republican Party and some of the 'tea party' politicians who had moved aggressively into the Party limelight. Because the speaker was so proud of the recipe he had authored for the occasion, he made it available in printed form for each of the guests at every table. To say the least, it was an interesting piece of work, and read:

THE CURE-ALL REPUBLICAN 13 STEP RECIPE

Before beginning, be sure to use a steel pot, as in former Republican Chairman, Michael Steel. Also be sure to have a decanter, being mindful of Eric Cantor, for distribution to all followers who will agree to drink the brew. Then be sure to build a large fire and follow these instructions:

First – Find an admitted and self-proclaimed witch, such as Christine O'Donnell, former Tea Party candidate for U.S. Senate in Delaware, to administer the "spin."

Second – Place the cooking pot at a unique Angle, similar to a unique angle as presented by former Nevada Republican candidate, Sharon Angle.

Third – Mix in a well-known "Palindrome" that does the same thing backward as it does forward, like former Alaska Governor Sarah Palin; then, blend in the following manner – "stir, madam, stir."

Fourth – Throw in a uniquely-fruited huckleberry from the Huckabee plant.

Fifth – Add one Romney sheep, otherwise known as a Romney Marsh Sheep, typically raised by the British farmers near Kent, England.

Sixth – Throw in some stiff and uncompromising element, such as a "walking stick," otherwise known as a "walker," like Wisconsin governor, Scott Walker or a "cane," such as the once befuddled candidate, Herman Cain, in order to give the mix some stiff and brittle texture.

Seventh – Add the antler from a Buck similar to former Colorado Republican Senate candidate, Ken Buck.

Eighth – Be sure to add an "idea" of Newt (as in former Republican Speaker of the House, Newt Gingrich) to the mix as it comes to a full boil, and it continues to boil over. The "idea" of Newt will undoubtedly create the disaster desired.

Ninth – For added deviation, throw in a ten Pence, (like Republican Congressman Mike Pence) a piece of British currency that is worth the meager sum of about 19 cents in American currency. It's like ether and highly flammable.

Tenth – Pour in a generous portion of Koch (like Koch Brothers, pronounced Coke) to assure the right amount of "flow," as in "cash flow," to the mix.

Eleventh – Throw in a paw, as in Tim Pawlenty, the former governor of Minnesota, in order to assure the appropriate clawing ingredient.

Twelfth – Use a Bush, preferably a "W" branch, to stir the entire brew.

Thirteenth - Use an actual Miller, such as former Alaska Republican Senate Candidate, Joe Miller, and have him present in order to supervise the mixing process so that it will never be complete.

Upon Boiling – Sit back and enjoy some Bach music to remind you of Tea Party/Republican Congresswoman, Michelle Bachman, and before you, you will have a brew fit for a harsh, bigoted and unreasonable King or Duke, as you are reminded of the outrageous statements of Iowa Congressman, Steve King or former Louisiana Congressman, David Duke. If the brew is good enough, it should be fit for a "Ryan" otherwise known as a "little king," very much like a Paul Ryan. As such, it could be a real "taxing" event. The brew is guaranteed to provide endless nightmares as your mind goes cruzing, like that of Ted Cruz. Be certain to keep a mint handy, like former Senator Jim DeMint. It will be useful when you set out and try to feed this brew to the public.

And Remember – In its efforts at government "Shutdowns," the Tea Party Republican contingent was able to accomplish what some anti-American elements were unable to do through their activities.

To his surprise, A.T. did not notice any boos or grumbling. He expected at least some of the audience would be uncomfortable about some of the references in the recipe, especially in regard to a couple of the Republicans named, particularly W. He expected to hear some muttering; however, there was none, not even from Julian.

After the speaker had finished, the attendees began to break up for the evening. A.T. made it a point to shake hands with everyone at the table. Samantha walked around the table with him and did the same.

Once they had exchanged comments and well-wishing, Samantha pulled A.T. aside and told him it was time to find Blaine and the others. When they headed toward the table where Blaine and Angel had been sitting, they saw Blaine motion for them to come to an area near the back of the room. Already gathered with Blaine were Angel, Julian, and Bernie. They were engaged in active conversations and smiling, so A.T. felt nothing too drastic should be on the agenda.

Upon joining the huddled group, each of them warmly greeted Samantha and commented upon her appearance and the fact they had not seen her for some time. It was obvious each of them knew Samantha well. A.T. did his best to hide his surprise; however, he did say to Blaine, "I didn't realize Samantha was connected to Republicans."

While Samantha turned in the direction of A.T. and smiled, she allowed Blaine to explain, "Samantha has been involved in Republican politics for many years. In fact, her brother was one of our candidates for Congress a number of years ago. I guess we expected you knew, considering her brother was the Henderson whom you met in the past."

"Sorry I never made that connection," A.T. responded. "Is he still active?"

"Yes and no," said Blaine. "Every so often he shows up and gets active. Then he gets disgusted with the way the Party has been going, and he drops out of sight for long periods of time. If he would simply stay active, I think he would have a good shot at public office. He is very well-liked and people listen to him. Unfortunately, he disappears every time he thinks the Party is self-destructing. We haven't seen him for well over a year. Recently, I believe he has been involved with a 'think tank' of sorts. He will appear on television now and then and comment on national and international issues. Quite a few people in the media like him because of his former military and Defense Department background. I don't think he is here tonight. Let's ask Sam."

"No, he's not here," interjected Sam. "He said he didn't want to get back into the political arena until the Party comes to its senses. I think he has been enjoying his life as a commentator and supposed expert." She turned to A.T. and said, "For your information, A.T., I have been involved with the California Republican Party since I was a teenager. I've been to many Republican activities over the years. My father was a very active member of the California Republican

Party. Years ago, he was one of Arnold's early supporters for governor."

"I guess surprises never cease," smiled A.T. "I take it your family is not too excited about the 'tea party' contingent of the Party."

"That's correct," answered Sam. "Truthfully, there really aren't many 'tea party' supporters here in California. In a general sense, the Republican Party in California is still fairly moderate. Of course, you're not here to discuss politics, are you, A.T.?"

"Bluntly stated, no," answered A.T. "I made a vow to myself to stay clear of politics, and after tonight, I see no reason to go back on that promise. I'm here to see my old friends, Blaine, Angel, Julian, and Bernie."

"Behind your visit is a purpose. Isn't that correct?" asked Sam.

"That's definitely true," said A.T.

"Then, let's set up the meeting, Blaine," commented Sam as she looked directly at Blaine.

"All right," agreed Blaine while waving to the other three people in the group. Once he had the attention of Angel, Julian, and Bernie, Sam and A.T., he said, "Let's all plan to meet privately at a restaurant tomorrow afternoon. It's too late to meet tonight, and what we have to discuss is the sort of thing that would be better done in a quiet place. Permit me to suggest we meet late tomorrow afternoon at one of my favorite restaurants up at Cardiff-by-the-Sea. It used to be called 'Charlie's on the Ocean.' In fact, it still may be closed, but the restaurant next door is also quite good, and it is still open. Let me think...I believe it is called 'The Beach House.'"

"Are you familiar with that location, A.T.?" asked Samantha. "I could pick you up at your hotel tomorrow before we decide to meet and -"

"Thanks, but I know the restaurant area fairly well. I've been there at least a half-dozen times when it was 'Charlie's.' I am also aware of 'The Beach House' and have eaten there as well. I'll just plan to meet everyone there tomorrow," A.T. responded since he didn't want Samantha to know where he was staying. Plus, he really didn't trust her.

"Good," said Blaine. "Why don't we all try to meet at 'The Beach House' for a late lunch or an early dinner, say about three?"

"That won't work for us. Bernie and I have some activities planned for one-thirty, and I don't think we'll be done by three," interjected Julian.

"Then, how about an early dinner, say about five-thirty, at 'The Beach House' location?" responded Blaine.

"I really don't need to be there," said Bernie. "Why don't the rest of you plan to have dinner without me?"

"It's up to you," responded Blaine. "If it's okay with everyone else, let's plan for a five-thirty dinner at 'The Beach House.'"

"If it's all right with everyone, I don't think I would get too much out of another political meeting. I wouldn't mind spending the time with my new daughter-in-law-to-be. We have some planning to do," insisted Angel.

"Well, how about everyone else?" asked Blaine. "Will a five-thirty dinner meeting work for the rest of you?"

Everyone else agreed to the five-thirty engagement. Once the time and place had been set, and while still congregated in the back of the room, the six of them continued to discuss family, friends, and some politics. Julian took A.T. aside and told him she had been given instructions as to how she could proceed and that she would be able to provide a reported statement to him in Washington. She said they would discuss it further at 'The Beach House' the next day. Now A.T. was trying to figure out how he would be able to have two separate conversations with Julian and Sam during the same dinner engagement the next day. He chatted a bit more and purposely tried to avoid any more political discussion.

When he looked out across the room, A.T. noticed the remaining guests continued to discuss politics within their groupings. He also noticed Blaine and Angel's two younger sons had appeared at the door to the ballroom. He took that as his clue to excuse himself and head back to his hotel. Following his good-byes to the group, the two young men were able to get A.T. back to his hotel in record time. This allowed him to dictate a series of notes relative to what he had been told by Julian and also by Samantha.

* *

After dictating the notes, he decided to relax. He was looking forward to the late afternoon dinner set for the next day. It would be a real accomplishment to have Julian's deposition. Even having to go to Washington to get it done would be fine; plus, he could regroup with the Senator. The added promise of getting to meet Samantha's benefactor might also prove useful to the Senator; however, it was doubtful such a meeting would benefit the efforts to expose the people in the Department of Justice who had taken the Department so far off track. Yes, he thought, tomorrow's meetings held great promise.

Once his notes were submitted electronically to a secure server in the Twin Cities, A.T. decided to again call Jacci. During the call with Jacci, he learned the Senator had left a message on the answering machine in St. Paul when the Senator had been unable to reach A.T. earlier, probably due to the fact A.T. had turned off his cell phone during the Republican Fundraiser. Jacci explained the Senator's message noted he had been unable to reach A.T. and stated the Senator was hoping A.T. and Jacci could both come to Washington in a week or so when A.T. was scheduled to be in town. The Senator had suggested that both A.T. and Jacci join the Senator and his wife during a "fund drive." The message also mentioned there would be certain individuals at the "fund drive" the Senator felt A.T. should meet in regard to the value A.T. was adding to efforts toward legislation designed to counter the "Citizens United" case.

"I thought your investigation was focused on reform to the grand jury system, the DOJ and the FBI?" inquired Jacci.

"It is," answered A.T.

"Well," exclaimed Jacci. "It sure sounds as though the Senator has a different idea about the investigation. It's starting to sound more and more like he is trying to get you involved in the political world and possibly using your background, including your background as a former Republican official, in order to help him in some fundraiser or in some other way."

"If he is," responded A.T., "he certainly has disguised those intentions from me. I do know he is working to change the decision of the 'Citizens United' case, but I got the impression some of my work was simply a side benefit to him in those efforts."

"Promises are quickly made and readily forgotten when it comes to politicians of every stripe," said Jacci. "Call it woman's intuition or whatever you wish, but after the voice mail message from the Senator, I think it is quite obvious the Senator is focused on his own agenda and objectives when it comes to your investigation."

"I promise I will listen to the message when I get back, and I will try to seriously evaluate the relationship I have with the Senator," commented A.T. "All of us have been friends for a long time. Now, as to more important matters, how is everyone there; I trust all is well."

"All is well and everyone is fine" answered Jacci. "Today Rachel and I went for a trail ride and set up a riding lesson for later in the week. I did notice a strange vehicle driving around as I was coming and going. But, I think I was just getting paranoid after all that has happened."

"Are all of the security systems in place?" asked A.T. "That kind of activity bothers me. Did you get a license plate or a description of the car?"

"I did," said Jacci. "I turned it over to Mike Mission, our old private investigator friend. I ran into him and his wife, Ann, at the grocery store. He said that he would check it out."

"Great," exclaimed A.T. "How are Mike and Ann?"

"They are both well and seem to be enjoying an early retirement," offered Jacci. "They said they would like to get together when your schedule lets up a bit. It's late here, I'll let you go. Take care. Love you."

"Love you too. Take good care. Bye."

"Bye."

The conversation with Jacci left A.T. worrying about her and what might be going on. He knew if his friend, Mike Mission, said he would check out the car, he would. Without a doubt, Mike was possibly the best and most thorough investigator A.T. had ever met inside or outside of law enforcement. Plus, Mike was a very trusted friend.

While thinking about the upcoming day, he was not excited about the breakfast meeting he had scheduled with "Big John" and "Squeaky." That thought prompted him to check the room safe to see if there had been any effort to enter it while he had been out. Sure enough, the tape on the bottom of the door had been broken. It was apparent someone had been in the safe. He was satisfied he had done the right thing in sending off the material electronically earlier in the evening and deciding to shred the paperwork. He had left nothing of importance in the safe.

* *

A.T. met at the hotel coffee shop the next morning with 'Big John' and 'Squeaky.' By the time A.T. arrived, the two of them had already selected a table in the corner of the main room. They continued a conversation between themselves and didn't notice his arrival. As he walked near their table, he couldn't help but overhear

'Squeaky' tell 'Big John' to ask about the investigation and about the happenings at the airport in Washington D.C. Hearing just that brief comment spoke volumes to A.T. and gave him some advance notice of the subject matter of the meeting.

When 'Squeaky' finally saw A.T. by the table, he immediately stopped talking and sat up straight. 'Big John' rose from the table for a greeting. A.T. knew the Senator would not have given information to these two; therefore, they had to have gotten their knowledge from someone who was on the other end of the investigation. Also of significant interest was the fact they had obviously been tailing A.T. and were willing to do about anything to get information. That was presuming they were the two who had picked the safe in the hotel room. A.T. greeted them feeling sure this was going to be an interesting meeting.

'Big John' offered, "How are you? I hope that you slept well."

"I did, thanks," A.T. responded. "How have the two of you been? It's been quite a while since I last saw either of you. If my memory serves me correctly, you guys were working for BP regarding that big oil spill in the Gulf a couple of years back."

"You have a good memory," responded 'Big John.' "We have moved on to bigger and better things."

"Really?" asked A.T. while pulling out a chair to sit down. "What happens to bring you to this hotel on this particular occasion?"

"We just happened to be in the neighborhood," said 'Big John.'

"Come on," smiled A.T. who decided the best method with these two was to immediately place the cards on the table. "That's a bunch of nonsense, and we all know it. The chances of the two of you being in the same hotel at the same time of my trip here is less likely than the earth coming to an end within the next ten seconds. Besides, as I stepped to the table just now, I couldn't help but overhear your normally silent sidekick provide some last minute instructions to you about inquiring of my investigation and about happenings at Dulles International weeks ago."

"You haven't changed," inserted 'Squeaky' crossing his arms and sitting back in his chair. "You always show the chip on your shoulder. You could at least try to be nice. We've never been anything but nice to you."

"That's debatable," answered A.T. "Sorry if I am too blunt for you, but there doesn't seem to be any reason for us to be anything but up front."

"We are engaged in a political investigation ourselves. It's a lot like your investigation. In fact, why don't you tell us about your investigation?" insisted 'Big John.'

"There's not too much to tell," answered A.T. "But first, aren't the two of you a bit old to be conducting an investigation?"

"We're still fully capable," responded 'Big John.' "You're no spring chicken yourself. Shouldn't you be back practicing law in the Twin Cities?"

"I still practice but on a limited basis," answered A.T.

"So, what are you investigating?" asked 'Big John.'

"It is a confidential matter being conducted for a Senate subcommittee," said A.T. "What about your investigation?"

"We are conducting an investigation for a large family concern based here in the U.S. It is operated by a couple of family members, and they have instructed us to search out and identify any individuals who might be attempting to disrupt their operations here in the States. They have reason to believe organized labor and other liberal groups are trying to undermine their operations and organizations," said 'Big John.'

"If that is why you are tailing me, you're barking up the wrong tree. I have never done any work for unions," A.T. stated bluntly.

"We weren't tailing you until you stepped into the picture several weeks ago in Washington D.C. Because of where and when you appeared on the scene, it was necessary to follow you, and it needed to be determined exactly for whom you were working and who you were contacting. It is the expectation that certain individuals are trying to interfere with a political process operating in the open for many years. Recently, you seem to be popping up wherever and whenever certain individuals show up. You were showing up on numerous occasions; therefore, we were instructed to see exactly what you were up to. How's that for putting the cards on the table? That's what you like, isn't it? The cards on the table," said 'Big John' as he sat back in his chair with a gratifying smile. At that point, the waiter noticed A.T. had joined "Big John" and "Squeaky." Since the two table companions had obviously already eaten, A.T. ordered coffee and juice.

After placing his order, A.T. said, "That's right. I like to see the cards on the table, and since I'm not a gambler, I like to know where the risks are. Right now, it would seem our investigations might well be at odds. Exactly what do you or your superiors expect to find out?"

"They just want to know who is causing so much grief and why," answered 'Big John.' "They believe they are simply following the same political process that has been in place in this country from the beginning. It's a process others have been using, so it seems only right that several can play at the same 'game.' They believe some of the interests that have been running this country for so long are sensitive and worried about the fact our superiors have now moved into a position of power and the 'old guard' that had been in control for so long is worried they will lose their influence and control."

"Worried about what influence and control?" asked A.T.

"The 'old guard' politicians and power brokers of the past are worried they have lost control of the political process and they are losing control of the government they have operated for far too long. The old Republicans, the Democrats, the labor unions, the educators, the eggheads, the Eastern Establishment, and the 'do-gooders' are all worried people like our employers are a threat and that the control of the political process and the government is changing. Frankly, 'Squeaky' and I agree with our employers, so we have been very willing to help. Plus, we get paid well for what we are doing. It's nice to be working for people whom we like and for a cause we believe in," said 'Big John.'

"If that is the case, why would you be so interested in conducting an investigation of the people whom you and your employers view as a threat? If your employers have obtained the type of control that they have, why would they be so worried that they would need to hire the two of you to perform an investigation, and why would you be tailing me?" asked A.T.

"Our employers want to stay informed about those whom they perceive as enemies," answered 'Squeaky.' "The enemies of our employers are our enemies as well. They mean us harm. As to you and your role, let's just say there are people who are tied to our employers who do not like you personally. They have not liked you for some time. It goes way back, and their only regret is they were unable to get you the first time."

"So, it's personal then?" asked A.T.

"To some of the people who are associated with our contractors, it is," said 'Squeaky.' "As to it being personal to our employers, the answer is no. They don't give two hoots about you; however, people close to them do. Certain people of interest want to bury you, and the fact you are involved in an investigation for a Democratic Senator gives them all the additional reason they need. They consider you to be a traitor to the Republican Party, and they remember back quite a number of years when you tried to block their candidate in your state. They remember that, along with some unkind things you have said about their group."

"I'm sorry to hear about their grudge. Although I'm getting an idea about who they might be, I couldn't be sure unless I hear more. Would you mind telling me who they are?" A.T. inquired.

"As to their identities, we are not at liberty to say. Let's just say they are powerful, and they believe you stood in the way of their attaining certain goals in the past," stated 'Squeaky.'

"They sound pretty vindictive to me," commented A.T. in order to try to provoke a revelation as to the identity of the individuals 'Squeaky' was trying to protect.

"On the contrary. They are good Christian people," inserted 'Big John. "In fact, they hold many similar religious beliefs and philosophies to that of our contractor. Some of them have worked together in the past and have even gone to some of the same colleges. They are a part of a very large network partially funded by a major religious leader and by major industrialists. This country has lost its religious way, and it needs to be brought back to the Christian way in terms of government and politics. After all, our founding fathers intended it to be a Christian government."

"Is that what you really think? Is that what your employers really think?" inquired A.T. "What about the separation of church and state?"

"The methods in place in this country are designed to undermine the wealthy people who have worked hard to achieve what they have in life. There is too much socialism and too little religion. That's what is ruining our country," said 'Squeaky.'

"Which is it? What is it that is ruining our country?" asked A.T. "Is it too much socialism or too much religion?"

"Don't try to be funny. It's too much socialism," answered 'Big John.'

"Wow. You guys have gone over the edge," commented A.T. while taking a sip of his coffee. "Perhaps you could tell me how this involves me, and after that I will take my leave of you and this conversation. But wait! What was that little tidbit of information I overheard about Dulles International as I was arriving at the table. Perhaps, you would be interested in giving some -"

"There is no point in discussing that matter, unless you are willing to share some of your investigation with us," interrupted 'Big John.'

"Now, you both know better than to ask me to share an investigation being performed for a United States Senator," cautioned A.T.

"It works both ways, A.T. We would like to reason with you and have you share your investigation with us. If you do, possibly we could discuss important things. However, you need to go first," said 'Big John.'

"Why on earth would I do that?" responded A.T. "First of all, it sounds like there are members of your group who would do just about anything to try to 'get me,' as you put it. Additionally, it is apparent to me that you guys are somehow involved with a particular faction of the radical efforts to control the Party. Plus, it sounds like your backers are religious nuts, along with some people of means who believe their money will be enough to change our way of government into their 'own image.' For those reasons, I fail to see any reason why I would share anything with you."

"Suit yourself," interjected 'Squeaky.' "Sooner or later we will have our way, and you will end up just another 'do-gooder' on the garbage heap. Our people can and probably will squash you like the cockroach you have turned out to be."

At that comment, A.T. couldn't contain himself and began to laugh, seemingly without control. The other patrons in the coffee shop looked toward their table and began to smile. A.T., still laughing, noticed the attention from the other patrons and said in the general direction of the other patrons, "That was one of the best stories I have ever heard."

'Big John' and 'Squeaky' tried to smile at the other patrons, 'Squeaky' said, "Laugh now, A.T., but we will have the last laugh."

"Gentlemen, if I may use that term, it has been interesting, but I see no point in remaining any longer," said A.T. "I trust each of you will have a nice day. There will be no need for you to continue to follow me. If you would like an itinerary, just say so, and I will write one up for you."

When A.T. got up to leave, 'Big John' said, "Don't worry, we will always know where to find you. Have a nice day, if you can."

"I can, and I will," said A.T. while offering to shake hands with each of them knowing they would be forced to comply considering most of the people in the coffee shop were still watching their table. After shaking hands with them, A.T. left to pay his bill. He immediately went to the main desk and checked out with a request that the hotel send someone to his room to assist with luggage. Although there was very little in the form of luggage, he wanted a member of the hotel staff to take his belongings to the entrance of the hotel, so they could be placed in his rental car that he requested be brought to the entrance. Going to the elevator, he looked into the coffee shop to see if his two "friends" were still there. They were. He then went to his room.

A.T. quickly packed. While he waited for the bellhop, he decided to dictate some notes about his meeting with 'Big John' Harry Johnson and 'Squeaky' Brent Wilson, two aged investigators who were never considered to be slouches by any means. Their threats could be real or just plain smoke; however, due to their longevity in the arena of quasi-government investigations, A.T. decided to take their threats seriously. After dictating his notes relative to the meeting, he decided to use his laptop to email those notes through the hotel Wi-Fi to the Senator's office and others, including Adam. Once his luggage had been picked up, A.T. took the elevator to the main floor.

Passing by the coffee shop while walking from the elevators to the hotel entrance for his departure, he noticed 'Big John' and 'Squeaky' were still engaged in discussion at their table. At the entrance of the hotel, the rental was ready, and the bellhop was at hand with the luggage. A.T. slipped the luggage into the trunk, tipped the bellhop, and drove off. Because it was a Saturday, he called his secretary at her home in St. Paul in order to have her line up hotel reservations in the Irvine/Newport Beach area for the upcoming night. He then got on the phone to the airlines and had his departure flight changed to the next morning out of the John Wayne Airport. Shortly thereafter, his secretary called back to advise him she had made hotel reservations for him at a hotel in the Fashion Island area of Newport Beach. With everything set, he decided to find a restaurant where he could spend some time before he prepared for the dinner at 'The Beach House' later in the day.

The time was well-spent allowing A.T. to organize his new notes and outline the material he would need for the next trip to Washington D.C. The Senator had sent him an email that provided two optional dates for a major meeting for the review of the investigation and the witnesses. In the email the Senator also mentioned he had left a voice mail and had hoped A.T. would include Jacci on his next trip to Washington and that he had some folks he wanted them to meet at a fundraiser set up on the Senator's behalf.

While he was in Washington, Julian's deposition would need to be included within the timeline, along with the depositions of the two former FBI agents who were already scheduled for meetings between their attorneys and FBI officials in the capital. The two dates the Senator suggested were at either end of the already scheduled interviews set by the Bureau for the two agents. A.T. would need to coordinate with Julian and with Gerald in order to see if Professor Brougham would also be available in Washington. He would see Julian shortly, so he would know of her schedule before the day was out.

A.T. thought it would be a good idea to text the Senator. He communicated:

Hv bn to Rep. dinr lst nt. J.T-G wil hlp & depo n DC. Bg Srpise! Enctrd Sam. Wil set mtg w/benefctr GGG. Mtg tnght. for Docs to B.J. Wil cnfrm dates. AT

A.T. sent the text and felt the Senator would be pleased. Now, he just needed some dates from the Senator for Julian's deposition in Washington D.C. Any new information Felthaus might have regarding the DOJ would no doubt prove helpful.

* *

The afternoon disappeared, and before he knew it, the time had come for him to head over to 'The Beach House' location in order to meet Julian, Blaine, and Samantha. The drive to 'The Beach House' was comfortable, and upon his arrival, A.T. noticed Blaine was directly in front of him, already handing his keys to the parking valet. At that moment, A.T. heard his iPhone beep. It was a text from the Senator. While he waited for the valet to come to his car, he read the text:

Gd jb & thks! Anxus to h'r wht Sam hs re GGG. T'l B&J hlo! Set depo fr wk aftr nxt, ethr M or F. Mdwk sv f Bu agts. Alrdy set. Gt Prof to DC f depo too, if psbl. Tlk sn. S.

He slipped the phone into his shirt pocket and looked up. When the valet approached A.T.'s car, Blaine was about to enter the restaurant and noticed A.T. was behind him in the parking area. He waited while A.T. got out of his rental, grabbed his briefcase, and handed the keys to the young parking assistant. As A.T. handed the tuxedo that he had barrowed back to Blaine, two men greeted each other and entered the restaurant. A.T. noted the absence of Angel. Upon entering the restaurant, the maitre d' immediately addressed them.

Blaine told him that the two of them were expecting two ladies and a gentleman, so there would be a need for a table for five. As Blaine began to describe Julian and Samantha, the maitre d' said he had already seated two ladies matching that description at a window table, so they could observe the waves hitting the "breakers," but there was no gentleman with them. While the maitre d' escorted Blaine and A.T. to the area, Julian and Samantha appeared to be engaged in a pleasant conversation. They both were laughing and sipping what looked like Chablis of some sort. A.T. noted that Bernie was not with them.

As A.T. and Blaine reached the table, the ladies stopped their discussion but continued to smile and laugh. They each extended their hands upward for a greeting from the two men. Blaine sat next to Julian, so A.T. found his seat next to Samantha. Blaine said, "Very nice to see you, ladies, on this fine and sunny afternoon. I trust you have been enjoying the view. I see some surfers out there. I would think it would be too cold, but young people can handle about anything these days. It would be good to be that young again." He placed the napkin on his lap and looked at Julian sitting next to him and said, "So, Bernie must have decided to hit the links instead of listening to our political discussions."

"You guessed that right. He and some of his cronies are out golfing. I see Angel has apparently also bowed out for the dinner," said Julian.

"Yes," answered Blaine. "She and our future daughter-in-law wanted to do some shopping and decided on a dinner of their own. This will give all of us a chance to have a frank discussion about the investigation A.T. is doing and see just how we can help."

"But first of all, hello, ladies! It's good to see both of you," said A.T. "Permit me to say you both look relaxed and pleasant enough to pass for part of the younger generation that seems to be prevalent in the restaurant this afternoon. Judging from the table settings and the partially filled glasses in front of each of you, I'm guessing Blaine and I will need to find the waiter just to catch up." While the ladies giggled about their early imbibing, A.T. motioned for the waiter to attend to the table. He and Blaine offered another round for the ladies and then each placed his own order.

"That was a nice comment, A.T.," said Samantha. "I didn't know you were so capable of being complimentary or graciously diplomatic. It was appreciated, wasn't it, Julian?"

"Let me tell you, Samantha," interjected Julian, "in days long past, A.T. could hang with the best of them. Don't forget; he used to be a politician himself; in fact, he held a number of offices within the Republican Party years ago."

"That's not completely fair, Julian," said A.T. while looking at Blaine for some help. "I really meant what I said. Plus, I thought it might be nice to relax a little bit before we got down to the business at hand."

Blaine smiled and said, "Keep going. I'm enjoying this. In fact, A.T., I haven't seen you in a relaxed mood for many years, so this is good." He looked at the ladies and said, "My apologies, ladies, for being a bit abrupt when we sat down. I probably should have -"

"I'm enjoying it too," interrupted Samantha. "In the few months I have known A.T., he has always been so serious. I thought he was without a sense of humor and was sure the investigation was getting to him. I often wondered if the man could even smile."

"He has a good sense of humor, or at least, he did have," said Julian. "Years ago, A.T. was a lot of fun to be around. I did not like the change that took place within you. Once again, I want to apologize for any role I may have had in bringing about the circumstances that led to the entire matter."

"We don't want to get you back into a bad mood," inserted a concerned Blaine. "Let's keep you in a good mood. I see our beverages are coming. I'm sure that will help."

After placing the drinks on the table, the waiter took their order for dinner. Before and during the meal, the mood was once again elevated to a pleasant and enjoyable level. By the time the meal was finished, everyone was having a fun time recalling some of the good humor of the keynote speaker from the last evening. A.T. thought it was a good time to speak to Julian about the deposition in Washington D.C. He wasn't sure how much to say, so he approached the subject a bit delicately.

"Julian, as you know, I will be flying out tomorrow, and I was wondering if at some point, I might have a word with you."

"A.T., if it is about the deposition in Washington, I have no problem with discussing it in front of Samantha and Blaine," responded Julian. "These two have been dear friends of mine for many years, and there really are no secrets among us. Why don't we discuss it now?"

"If that's all right with you," said A.T. "let me begin with the possibility of a deposition date. Have you decided to provide a statement, and if so, would the week after next in Washington D.C. work?"

"That would be ideal," answered Julian. "Both Blaine and I will be in the capital for some other business then, so that would work perfectly."

"Great! Would either Monday or Friday of that week work?" asked A.T.

"Let's book it," responded Julian. "I've checked with my contacts, and they have given me a green light to proceed as long as the conditions that were outlined before still apply."

"As I've said," answered A.T., "I can't provide any terms of immunity; however, I can tell you the investigation involves neither you nor W. I have no authority relative to any immunity. So, that's all I can -"

"Don't worry about the immunity issue, I worked that out myself with some of my contacts who are already involved in the investigation on the Republican side," interrupted Julian as she turned to Blaine and continued, "Did you know A.T.'s investigation is under the direction of a Democratic Senator? Isn't that a violation of the eleventh commandment?"

"I suppose it is," laughed Blaine. "But, from what I understand happened to A.T., I can see why he might work with a Democrat."

"What happened?" asked Samantha. "I've heard bits and pieces but not the whole story."

A.T. looked at Samantha, then turned to Julian and said, "Perhaps Julian can provide the best explanation. That's why she's giving a deposition."

Julian perked up and explained A.T.'s past situation to Samantha. "It happened while I was working at the White House under W. A.T. had been asked to be a part of the Business Forum. In fact, he had been asked several times with requests coming from both the White House and from a key congressman's office -"

"It was not something that interested me," interrupted A.T.

"In any event," continued Julian, "Some of the high ranking people at the White House and at DOJ thought if the DOJ went after some Republicans who didn't 'play ball' with the administration at the time, then an example could be set as a warning to other Republicans who wouldn't cooperate. It was discussed and felt that the Democrats wouldn't intervene since the targets would be Republicans. It would be much like the Senator Stevens matter. You know, certain people in the White House at the time felt if examples could be made of certain Republicans who didn't 'play ball,' others who weren't being supportive would fall in line."

"They openly discussed that?" inquired Samantha.

"They did," answered Julian. "They had their discussions in front of me while I was sitting there. Apparently, they thought I was some kind of office bimbo. At the time, they didn't know who I was," explained Julian. "This guy from DOJ wasn't a high ranking official, but he was high enough. He stated he remembered A.T. from years earlier when the DOJ guy had been working on the campaign for Pat Robertson, who was running for president at the time. Apparently, A.T. had worked against Robertson and made an enemy, at least with this DOJ guy.

"There were all kinds of people coming into the government back then. As you probably remember, there were Cheney, Rove, Gonzales, as well as John Ashcroft before him, and the President often talked about some of the United States Attorneys who had been appointed. When certain congressmen wanted the USAs to target specific investigations and found the USAs wouldn't do it, there was a very significant effort to change personnel at DOJ. Even before that, there was a group of attorneys from Florida, some others from Kentucky, Ohio, and other states, and also from Regent University law school who had made it known they were eager to become a part of the Justice Department. That's where a lot of the DOJ personnel came from when both John Ashcroft and later Alberto Gonzales were Attorneys General. They wanted people who were loyal from a political standpoint, first and foremost. Eastern Establishment attorneys, except for a few, were in serious disfavor with W., John Ashcroft, and Alberto Gonzales. Plus, there was a significant undercurrent to get people who held certain beliefs, religious and otherwise. There was also a serious effort by some of the people from Florida, Ohio, and Kentucky to 'load up' the department with people of their own thinking. They were trying to build their own dynasty within the DOJ."

Wanting to know more, Samantha requested, "So, then what happened?"

"I had heard A.T. was going to be included in the indictment," said Julian, "so I called and sent emails to A.T. trying to get him to agree to serve on the 'Business Forum.' Unfortunately, I never heard back from him. The next thing I heard was that A.T. had been indicted, along with some people whose names I did not recognize. I have really felt bad about this whole thing, and that is why I'm trying to help now."

"What happened to the indictment?" Samantha questioned.

"It was ultimately dismissed," answered A.T. "Through my legal counsel, an excellent attorney by the way, we filed our motion to dismiss, which remained pending for over a year. Finally, when Eric Holder took over as AG, the new head of the division decided to review the file, and then filed an application to dismiss on behalf of the DOJ. Once that was done, the judge dismissed the case."

"That's one heck of a story," commented Samantha.

"Look," interrupted Blaine, "Julian and I need to get to another meeting, so if the two of you don't mind, we need to get moving. Since you have a commitment from Julian for a deposition, you should be set, A.T."

"That's right," said A.T. "However, I did want to visit a moment with Samantha in regard to her telling me about a meeting with her benefactor. Could all of you stay a while longer so I may set up that meeting?"

"Samantha can stay," responded Blaine. "She is not a part of the meeting Julian and I have to attend. Julian and I have to plan for another upcoming political event, so the two of you can stay here and visit as long as you wish. By the way, I'll be picking up the tab on my way out. If the two of you decide to order dessert, it will need to be on a new tab."

Both Samantha and A.T. thanked Blaine for his generosity, and A.T. expressed a special thanks to Blaine for the tux and the ticket for the fundraiser the night before. After Blaine and Julian left, A.T. moved to the other side of the table, where Blaine and Julian had been seated, with the breakers and beach now to his right while facing Samantha. As he watched Julian and Blaine leave through the front entrance, A.T. observed, "I'm surprised those two would be attending a meeting on a Saturday evening, especially one that involves planning another Republican event."

Samantha smiled and asked, "How naïve are you, A.T.? The only event those two are planning is one that involves the two of them."

"What!" exclaimed A.T. "I can't quite believe that. It seems that Angel and Bernie would be suspicious of something like that; plus, I thought such a relationship was something of the long forgotten past."

"Nope! You're wrong again. I've known the two of them for a long time, and for at least twenty years now, they have had something going. I'm positive Bernie knows about it. In fact, he is the one who brought Julian and me here tonight, knowing full well Julian was going to end up with Blaine. When he dropped us off, I heard him tell Julian to not make it too late and to have Blaine get her back at a respectable hour. They appear to have what we in California call an 'open marriage.'"

"I would have never guessed it was continuing between them. What about Angel? Isn't she suspicious?"

"I'm sure she is, but she tolerates Blaine's interest in Julian, I suppose, since it's just one other woman and not a string of them. She knows Blaine for what he is. He can't help himself, and besides, both Blaine and Angel are in love with the same person, namely Blaine."

"You can really be a bit nasty," said A.T.

"Come on! It's the way we Republicans function on the sly," said Sam.

"If it's okay with you, I would like to change the subject. I thought we were going to visit a bit about your benefactor," commented A.T., purposely reopening the issue of Samantha's benefactor. "Oh, by the way, how will you be getting home if Bernie is the one who dropped you and Julian off here?"

"You're my ride, so you will have to make the most of it," said Samantha. "Now, since you want to get down to business, let's talk business. You seemed a bit surprised when I told you last night that my benefactor wanted to meet with you and discuss your investigation, so -"

"Wait! What do you mean I am your ride? Ride to where? In regard to last night, frankly, I was surprised to see you at all. To have you tell me your benefactor wanted to speak to me was even a greater surprise. I would like to start by having you tell me his or her name and -"

452

"You are my ride home, and I trust you will be a gentleman and accommodate me in that regard. Why should you have been surprised to see me? I told you when we first met I had lived in Southern California and my family was well connected. My benefactor isn't a man or a woman; it is a committee of benefactors, so you will have to agree to meet the committee."

"I'm always a gentleman. At least I think so. Don't you think it would be better for me to call a cab for you? And, of course, I was surprised to see you at the Republican function. I didn't know just because you were from Southern California and allegedly 'well connected,' you would be at a Republican event. Plus, I felt a bit put out since it seemed that everyone knew you would be sitting next to me. That must have taken some planning on somebody's part."

"You are not going to call a cab. You are going to be that perfect gentleman and escort me home once we have our little chat. I'll admit my sitting next to you last night at the Republican event was a bit of a setup. I was with Blaine and Julian when you called a couple months ago and tried to set up that meeting with Julian. So, we did some planning. Ironically, my benefactors had wanted me to start tailing you; talk about coincidence. It was a plan made beyond all of us. Now, let's talk a bit about your meeting with my superiors."

"I know, and you need to know, I will behave myself if I am to escort you to your home; the question is whether you will behave yourself. I find it hard to believe coincidence had anything to do with the planning that went on. Now, let's talk about 'the where' and 'the when' as to the meeting with your superiors?"

"I am shocked you would question whether I would behave myself," smiled Samantha. "Now, as to my superiors, do you still have the napkin from last night when I gave you my phone number?"

"You have to realize I still don't completely trust you," said A.T. as he reached in his pocket to produce the napkin. "Here is the napkin with the 'spill spots' and your phone number."

"Well, at least you used the word 'completely.' So, you must at least trust me somewhat by now, especially since I saved your behind more than once. Ah, we're making progress. In fact, A.T., I can provide some detailed information for you that will perhaps open your eyes a bit in terms of just who you can trust. For starters, I can tell you as a verity that you may have placed far too much trust in that Senator friend of yours who is making promises to you."

"How do you know about any promise the Senator might have made to me?" asked A.T.

"As I said," replied Samantha, "I have a number of contacts on 'the Hill,' and they are not all Republicans. Let's just say there might be certain people within the Senator's office who use information to their advantage."

"That might be true, and perhaps that's how you picked up what you believe is reliable information," noted A.T. "However, the Senator is a former prosecutor himself, and he knows how much reform is needed to the grand jury system."

"Oh," responded Samantha, "he is a former prosecutor all right, but he may be one of those who was in the office long enough to realize that it is influence over the acts of a grand jury that make prosecutors as powerful as they are. Frankly, A.T., your friend, the Senator, may not want to see that changed. You could be feeding the information of your investigation to the wrong person.

"I can't believe that," said A.T.

"Believe what you want," commented Samantha. "I am trying to prove to you that you can trust me; that is all. You will find out in time I am being truthful with you. Just think about it. Now, back to the business at hand, I see you have the napkin with the 'spill spots,' the phone number, and most importantly, my lipstick signature. I noticed you had it in your shirt pocket right over your heart. How touching."

"Here's the napkin. I don't have a shirt pocket over my heart. Now, why is it so important, other than the fact it contains your number?"

"Look at the 'spill spots.' Last night I circled this one," said Samantha while pointing to the spot that she had circled.

"I can see that. Like you said last night, it supposedly is to signify my investigation, and the other spots are -"

"Let me have your pen again," requested Samantha. She then redrew circles around other spots on the napkin. She explained, "This big spot I marked last night is your investigation. These other spots represent other matters related to your investigation. My superiors want to discuss those other items or 'spots' as they relate to your investigation."

"Apparently, I'm missing something. Why would your superiors be so interested?" asked A.T. "You will need to be more specific."

"These other spots represent other activities either directly or indirectly related to your investigation. For example, let's say this spot represents some of the funding and the banking that is working the political process." Then she pointed to another spot and referenced it as paramilitary organizations; then another spot represented the shell corporations; yet another spot was representative of the media; another spot was representative of government offices, including the DOJ; a different spot was representative of government contractors; another spot was representative of voter organizations; the other spots she explained represented education, religion, unions, regulations, commerce, etc.

After listening to her explanations and watching her continuing to draw circles around the 'spill spots,' A.T. asked, "What does all of this have to do with me or with my investigation?"

"I have been trying to spell it out for you," she said somewhat perplexed.

"Apparently so," responded A.T.

"You, my new and dear friend, are in a very good position to connect the 'spill spots' or, as is most generally said, 'it's up to you to connect the dots,' and do it in a meaningful way that benefits your Senator friend and my benefactors at the same time," explained Samantha.

"Me? Now, I'm a dear friend?" responded A.T. "Aren't you starting to sound like the Senator? My investigation started in regard to some irregularities at the DOJ and the FBI. It included the improper and illegal activity of former and some current members of the DOJ and the FBI. It started as an investigation into exactly how and why they had gotten off track as the department became politicized under W. and his two appointees, John Ashcroft and Alberto Gonzales. My interest was to explore just how far the DOJ got sidetracked into investigating political enemies instead of doing its real job in prosecuting actual criminals."

"That may be; however, now you are in the unique position to connect the dots or as you can see from this napkin, you are in the fortunate position of connecting the 'spill spots', and I am going to help you. Of course, you will also need some help from my benefactors, whom you shall meet very soon."

CHAPTER 24
CONNECTING THE SPOTS

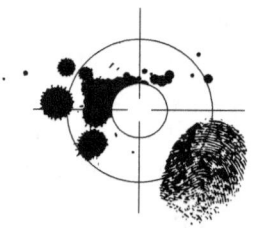

As the lyrics to "Let's Dance" were playing in the background, A.T. asked Samantha, "Just when do I get to meet these alleged superiors of yours? You keep talking about your benefactors, and it is my presumption the illusive benefactors are from the GGG or the Knights of Malta, whose tattoo or brand I see you still proudly wear on your cheek under your eye."

Listening to A.T., Samantha seemed pleased he had noticed the detail. She smiled and asked, "Do you want to dance?"

"Sorry," said A.T. "I'm not a dancer. Besides, I've never seen anyone dance here. I don't think they would appreciate dancing."

"Oh, I was referring to the song in the background," smiled Samantha. "I wasn't talking about physically dancing but dancing to the tune of what has been happening in terms of your investigation and how I can help you. So, let's start by dancing seriously. I'm talking about a close dance, a very close dance. In other words, let's stop dancing around the issues. I want to start by first discussing your investigation. I need to know more about your investigation, so I can really help you. For example, what was so important about the documents in Paris, and how exactly do those documents relate to the material Professor Brougham gave you in Kentucky?"

"What about Professor Brougham?" inquired A.T., who was trying to see if Samantha and Gerald were in communication with each other.

"Please stop playing games with me, A.T.," responded Samantha in a very direct fashion, holding the napkin up to A.T. as a school teacher might hold a spit-ball to a student. "You are going to have to start being more direct with me. I know about your meeting with Gerald, Professor Brougham, and Gretchen. Do you take me for a fool?"

"Frankly, I don't know how to take you, Samantha, and at this point, I really don't know what to think of you. You keep presenting new and different facets of your personality. I'm trying to determine whether or not I can trust you. You have to admit that for a person in my shoes who keeps seeing you pop up in the most unlikely places, it is not easy to lower one's guard and expect a fully open and forthright discussion that -"

"If anyone should have her guard up," interrupted Samantha, "it should be me. Don't forget you entered my life while I was conducting a surveillance of an individual, your professor friend, who had stolen some very valuable documents from the people who paid me to attempt to bring that professor to justice for stealing."

"Come on," responded A.T. "Neither you nor your 'benefactor' was ever going to bring Professor Brougham to justice, at least not in the normally accepted sense. The fact of the matter is you were trying to catch him and bring him back into the hands of your superiors, so they could detain him probably forever and a day. There is no way either you or your superiors would take the matter involving Brougham to the authorities. The material he had, and provided willingly to me, was so sensitive to your superiors that they would have done about anything to bury the professor and hide the material. Let's face it, your superiors are involved in the transfer of large sums of money to various political interest groups here in the United States. From what I see, there is no doubt your superiors are doing their best to influence the political and governmental process. Who knows, they are probably involved in money laundering as well."

"Please hold your voice down, A.T. There is no doubt the various organizations operated by my superiors are and have been influencing the governmental process and the political process of this country for far longer than you can imagine. Perhaps they have been at it since before this country even came into existence. But understand my superiors are not involved in any money laundering and never have been. What they do and what they have done has been in place for a long time and let me assure you it is within the letter of the law. Perhaps you and your Senator friend are confusing what we do and have done with the activities of some other groups that are also revealed as a part of the documents you received from the professor. Believe me when I tell you there is a very big difference between what my superiors are doing and have been doing and what the 'fringe groups' are doing. The difference is so dissimilar and so problematic that GGG is trying to acquire the necessary evidence itself in order to stop the questionable efforts of the 'fringe.' That is why we are trying to help you.

"Just think about it," Samantha continued. "How many times have I helped you, and how many times have you received help from Gerald? There was the time in Paris. There was the meeting in St. Paul when I gave you the FBI agent's credentials. There was the meeting that Gerald set up in San Francisco with Professor Brougham. There are the additional documents he presented to you just the other day. Now, there is a very rare opportunity I am offering with an introduction to my benefactors."

"Perhaps there is a matter of defining the word 'help,'" said A.T. "I didn't request your assistance in Paris; as far as the other times -"

Samantha interrupted A.T., saying, "Perhaps not, but it was a good thing for you that Gerald and I were following you, or you might have met a rather unfortunate fate at the hands of the two rogue FBI agents who were following you. Let's not argue about it. There are instances in which we have tried to help you."

"Allen and I could have handled them ourselves in Paris, and as far as the other instances, my guess is you were trying to influence my investigation toward your way of thinking," said A.T.

"From what I was observing in Paris, you needed help," said Samantha. "Those two agents were bad news. I don't know if you realize it, but they have been fired and charged with a series of criminal violations that even involve national security. The issues are serious enough that they are now both in Washington D.C. on a very tight leash."

"Tell me something I don't know about them. I've known about their arrest and about the charges against them for a number of days. There is no question they are bad news and should never have been hired by the Bureau in the first place," A.T. stated.

"That is undoubtedly true. But did you know there are more agents within the FBI than just those two who are a part of the 'fringe group' that believes they will ultimately be the principal enforcement arm of justice in this country under a new and far-reaching agenda within less than a decade? It's not just the Department of Justice or the FBI that have been infiltrated, yet so far that has been the thrust of your investigation. There is a concerted effort taking place designed to forever change the landscape of government in this country. In fact, those fringe interests feel confident they have the skeletal framework of a shadow government already in place." instructed Samantha.

"Samantha, you sound like one of those conspiracy theorists," insisted A.T. "There would be way too much involved in order for such a wide-reaching effort to take hold in this country."

"I am not a conspiracy theorist. If anything, I have learned from all of the 'conspiracy theorists' accusations about GGG and the Knights of Malta that it is very dangerous for anyone to follow any conspiracy theory," responded Samantha. "My superiors have been accused for years. However, what is happening at the hands of 'fringe' interest groups is real, and it is very well-orchestrated. Do you want to hear about it?"

"Go ahead. I'm listening."

"Long before I came to this country, there were efforts in place by some very wealthy Americans who wanted to change the entire process of government in the United States," explained Samantha. "You have heard of the saying, 'follow the money.' That's what we've been doing."

"By 'we,'" interjected A.T., "I presume that you are referring to the GGG and the Knights of Malta?"

"There are more groups and entities than just those two that are involved with our committee," explained Samantha. "When you meet my benefactors, you will also be introduced to quite a number of other powerful individuals who represent other interest groups that have helped mold the government of the United States since before it was a country."

"So, when you tell me to follow the money," said A.T., "you mean as to other groups but not the GGG or the Knights of Malta or the Vatican or other members of this special committee. But shouldn't I be following the money that applies to your benefactors, the GGG, the Knights of Malta, Gerald's Vatican, and the others to whom you have made reference?

"No doubt our people have money and lots of it," responded Samantha, "but they are the good guys, and their interests for the United States have been for the public good. My benefactors are not like the 'fringe' interest groups."

"But, of course. Your people are the good guys. Forgive me for forgetting that important point," A.T. said sarcastically.

"Stop and listen," insisted Samantha. "Our people make their presence known through proper channels, and any funding from my benefactors is clean money and goes to certain organizations within the letter of the law. We have been very particular about that. You will also find we do not try to change the government process. We don't mess with religion. We don't try to take over political parties. We don't provide funds to paramilitary groups. We don't force social issues upon the public. We have never made any attempt to infiltrate government agencies such as the DOJ, the Bureau, the Executive Branch of government, or other government offices. We do not use force unless we find it necessary to defend those who become vulnerable, like you and your friend in Paris. We use reason, and we try to meet with individuals whom we believe can make a difference in keeping with the principles of fair governance, individual freedoms, one person - one vote, and a system of fair play."

"Forgive me if I regard your statement with some reservation and some doubt," interjected A.T. "As an example, Gerald's presence as an operative for the GGG comes from the direction of the Vatican, doesn't it? Haven't funds been transferred to certain political think tanks? Isn't your committee providing funds to a number of college and university groups? Isn't there a considerable amount being spent on lobbying? Don't your groups funnel money to certain 'straw men' corporations that support particular political candidates? Aren't there strategic meetings with members of the media on a routine basis? Plus, my encounter with Gerald near my office wasn't an accident. At least these are some of the things my investigation has shown as we have followed the money from a couple of your groups listed on the ledger sheets we have."

"Those are all true statements," acknowledged Samantha. "Additionally, you will find in each instance such funding is being done through the proper and legal guidelines of permissible activity. We have quite a number of lawyers who work on a regular basis for us. Some are on retainer, and others work for us on a case-by-case basis. Whatever we do, we follow the law. The people who we are investigating and who you are being directed to investigate do not follow the letter of the law. In fact, they seem to do about everything they can to avoid the proper channels. Once they gain a position of power, they see how far they can go and flaunt their authority. The laws and the rules are simply minor obstacles to them. By now you have seen what the 'fringe' interests have done whenever they have become governors, congressmen, senators, members of the judiciary, and even members of the DOJ, which I believe you have seen firsthand. Now, let me tell you why."

"All right, why?"

Samantha continued, "It's because they don't expect to be challenged. They want to take control. They want the kind of power that allows them to force people to do things their way. We don't do that. We definitely try to influence and try to persuade people to feel our suggestions and ways are the correct ones. We don't always succeed; however, we have learned over time it is best to 'roll with the punches' and work with people, even if they don't agree with us. Part of our underlying philosophy is to allow people to govern. We definitely do not support dictatorships, and we do our best to prevent dictatorial activity across the globe. Our people have been doing that and helping for a very long time. Overall, I believe you will find the GGG and the Knights of Malta are working for the betterment of man and have been doing so for centuries."

"Or, shall we say they have at least convinced themselves they are and have been. Whether or not it's true might well be another matter," insisted A.T.

"Think what you will," answered Samantha, "but I am offering you an opportunity to expand your investigation in a helpful way that will assist you in actually uncovering the type of illegal activity you and your Senator friend are trying to piece together. You may not like what we do or what we have done over time, but let me assure you, at least on this point, your interests and our interests are the same. We are really in step with you in that we want to curtail the currently unbridled activity the 'fringe' is using to take over the government. If you allow us to help, you will find the 'fringe' is better organized than you realize."

"It would seem you are trying to wear me out," said A.T. "Now, let's say for the sake of argument the Senator and I agree to work with you. What do you, or your benefactors, expect to get out of any alliance between our investigation and the information you and your benefactors allegedly have?"

"Before I answer that, let me make one thing crystal clear," Samantha began. "Gerald's interest and the interest of his superiors are not completely in step with the rest of the GGG committee. You should know Gerald and his superiors come from a religious perspective, and that perspective has a lot to do with their thinking."

"That seems obvious to me," agreed A.T.

"What you probably don't know is they actually believe the 'Fringe Movement' we keep talking about is influenced by the dark side of the spiritual world."

"Oh, brother!" A.T. remarked, rolling his eyes. "Here we go."

"They really do believe that," continued Samantha. "They believe the 'fringe' is under the total influence of the devil and there is proof the actions of the 'fringe' are so contradictory to logic and so intertwined with the subjugation and denigration of man and his freedom that the Prince of Darkness is behind the actions and workings of the 'fringe.' At least that is what Gerald and his superiors have told the GGG."

"You guys can't really believe that kind of nonsense," exclaimed A.T. "If the GGG believes in that stuff, they have got to be crazier than I could have ever imagined."

"The GGG committee doesn't believe that stuff," Samantha reassured.

Samantha, then continued, "Still, Gerald and his superiors from the Church do. Considering they have been on the committee longer than anyone else, members listen to them. However, I am not aware of any other members with that belief or position. The GGG allows its members to hold to their own beliefs and takes such statements by Gerald's superiors to be the sort of thing that might be said by anyone who comes into the committee with such strong religious backgrounds."

"Thanks for sharing that bit of information, and let me make one thing very clear regarding such attitudes," said A.T. "If the Senator felt for one moment any help from the GGG or the Knights of Malta or any other such entity was based upon such thinking, there would be no effort to discuss any level of cooperation. I'm still waiting to hear one good reason for there to be any form of cooperation, and such a reason cannot be based upon some religious or emotional issue."

"That's understood and completely agreed with," Samantha said. "I was just trying to tell you the GGG does have its own differences, and Gerald and his superiors on the GGG have their own beliefs and ideas about things. The point is although the GGG members may share some common objectives and concerns about the 'fringe,' there are differences within the group. That's what I'm saying."

"I'm becoming more convinced than ever the GGG is a group of strange bedfellows, and unless there is some very compelling reason I haven't heard so far, I see no reason for the Senator to stick his neck out and try to work with the GGG," said A.T.

"I will be able to give you some compelling reasons. However, before I do, I wanted to explain something about the committee and Gerald. I wanted to be sure you knew not all of us are coming from the same perspective as Gerald and his superiors. Now, let me explain exactly how the GGG and the Senator's committee might work together in a common point of interest. Once my benefactors meet you, and if they feel comfortable to the point where they believe you are trustworthy of the information they have, certain members of the committee will be able to unofficially convey the information you need in order to connect the funding of the 'fringe' operations being orchestrated by certain individuals who once worked at the White House under several Republican presidents. These names of individuals, particularly one, are names you will immediately recognize. Once you become privy to that information, you will be able to connect the various aspects of your investigation to specific individuals."

"Can you tell me in a brief synopsis what exactly I will learn that is different from what I have already determined?" asked A.T.

"We at the GGG have compiled a chart showing the flow of funds from particular financial interests, including named individuals who have been channeling funds through shell corporations, both for profit and non-profit, using patriotic names intended to give the look and feel of benevolent enterprise. Those shell corporations in turn have channeled funds to the media, protestors, candidates, paramilitary operations, religious spokespersons, private trusts, family businesses, relatives of public officials, blind trusts set up for public officials, and retirement programs for former public officials.

Most of the investments made in regard to these enterprises are contrary to the money laundering laws of the United States, and many of the funds are set up rewards paid to public officials after they retire.

Samantha went on, "It is apparently the belief of these 'fringe'-friendly donors that they are successfully circumventing the law by providing the 'reward' to the public official after the official leaves office and subsequent to his performing in a certain way during his tenure in office. Our lawyers have told the GGG most of these financial vehicles have been set up to avoid the laws relative to bribery and money laundering statutes. The lawyers for the GGG, and believe me they are good, are of the firm opinion the many trusts, accounts, corporations, non-profits, lobbying concerns, and other entities set up to evade the law actually fall directly under violations of various statutes due to the deceptive way that such entities are created."

"So, if I understand what you are saying correctly, the lawyers for the GGG believe it is through the various trusts, business funding, shell corporations, etc., that it can be shown there are violations of the laws relating to money laundering and the paying or bribing of public officials due to the way such entities are created and administered?" A.T. reiterated.

"I thought you would appreciate the subtle nature of what I was trying to explain. The GGG lawyers are certain that since the funding entities are in actuality created to reward a public official for tasks performed while in office but not paid until the official leaves office, it is no different than paying the official while in office. According to these lawyers, the violations are the same regardless as to when the money is paid," Samantha explained.

"Are you telling me you have evidence proving such to be the case?" asked A.T.

"That is exactly what I am being told by the GGG," answered Samantha. "Did you ever wonder how so many politicians become rich in a matter of months or just a few years after leaving office or even while still in office? Did you ever wonder how some of the former government employees, including certain former members of the DOJ and FBI, become so well-off after they have left government service and joined a particular firm that engages in lobbying or security or 'good government?'"

"Your people have proof?"

"They have proof," Samantha reassured A.T.

"During the entire time I was an FBI agent and a prosecutor, I never ran into anyone I thought would be a part of such a program," insisted A.T.

"That might be," commented Samantha. "But they are out there, and we will be able to show proof it happens even at that level, especially when you have people you're trying to investigate, such as your 'friend' whose credentials I lifted in Paris."

"My take on him is that he was interested in promoting himself within the Bureau for upward positioning," insisted A.T.

"That might be true today, but that type of person is the one who will agree to make promises while working for the government and then accept the agreed-to reward after he leaves public service," said Samantha.

"What about the GGG or the Knights of Malta, or other such entities that are a part of the GGG committee?" asked A.T.

"Not one member of the GGG, as far as I know, has a single program where former government employees are hired and rewarded with a 'post task' job of some sort," claimed Samantha taking a sip of her coffee. "In fact, when your investigation was discussed in my presence at the last meeting of the GGG I was allowed to attend, this issue was specifically discussed because all members wanted to be sure every member of the GGG was totally free of any such activity. All of those present confirmed they did not have any such programs in place."

"If what you say is true, it would be my guess the Senator, as well as all other members of the subcommittee regardless of party affiliation, would be quite interested in hearing what your benefactors at the GGG have to say," asserted A.T. "However, I will tell you the same thing I told Gerald. From what the Senator has told me, there will be no promises of immunity, and if any were to be made, they would have to come directly from the subcommittee under very strict guidelines. I have no authority. Plus, we will need proof and witnesses."

"That was also discussed, and it is understood," assured Samantha. "I've told you on repeated occasions, the GGG has nothing to hide. It has been operating for years, perhaps under different names, but it believes it can show it has operated fully under the letter of the law."

"All right, set up the meeting with your benefactors. Now, tell me again exactly why the GGG wants to help," A.T. requested.

"The GGG feels if the investigation becomes a 'shotgun' effort to try to taint all political corporate contributors in the same light, there could be either a witch hunt of sorts or new legislation that would undermine all efforts to promote good government enterprise," explained Samantha.

"In my humble opinion," said A.T., "such legislation would be an excellent idea. I don't believe any form of corporate funding should be allowed when it comes to politics in this country. With the corporations allowed to fund any political idea no matter its content or directive, the 'one person – one vote' becomes totally undermined, and interest groups end up dictating the policies and direction of the country. I'll guess that is not what your GGG committee would want to hear; however, that is what the Senator seems to want and why he believes there should be integration between my investigation and his committee. The Senator and I may have slightly different objectives; however, our separate investigations appear to complement each other. At this stage, Samantha, I trust the Senator whom I've known for years. We have worked together before and there is a mutual trust between us. Unfortunately, I cannot say I have heard anything here that would lead me to trust you as I have the Senator."

"Well then," insisted Samantha, "I will need to tell you a thing or two about your 'trusted' friend, the Senator. Your friend, the Senator, is only interested in enhancing his position within his committee in his efforts to get a compromise between both parties relative to changes impacting campaign contributions. He wants to overturn the 'Citizens United' case, and he is working toward a compromise with Republicans. It actually sounds like he may have the attention of a number of Republican Senators in that regard. However, in regard to your dream of grand jury reform, you are deluding yourself if you think the Senator will be helping you."

"I don't believe you," responded A.T. "The Senator has made assurances and a hearing before his committee will take place regarding the issue of oversight when it comes to the activities of the federal grand jury process. He also promises to seek certain oversight reforms relative to the DOJ and FBI."

"A.T.," Samantha warned as she leaned forward and very close to A.T., "you are naïve. The Senator is a politician."

"I know he is a politician," exclaimed A.T. "But the Senator is also a former prosecutor, and he knows how out of control the grand jury system has gotten."

"No doubt he does; however, it is because he was a former prosecutor that he will drag his feet when it comes to real reform," boasted Samantha.

"Then prove it," urged A.T.

"What if I could replay for you a voice mail from my former Congressman partner," offered Samantha. "What if the message detailed the fact the Senator approached my former significant other with a proposition, and when he asked who you were, the Senator provided your name to the Congressman? He divulged that you were working on an investigation you believed had something to do with grand jury reform when in reality the Senator boasted that the investigation would also be used as evidence for reform to the funding of political campaigns. In fact, the message makes it clear your friend, the Senator, was pressuring my former significant other to essentially vote for the Senator's bill when it came to the House since it would not be a good idea for my Congressman's affair with me to be made public. Apparently, my former partner thought it expedient to let me know about it in a voice mail, and I have kept the message."

"I can't believe it," said A.T. "I would have to hear the message myself, and if it were true and if I could verify it was the Senator on the call, I would immediately confront the Senator with it. So I guess I would need a copy of the voice mail."

"All right," countered Samantha. "I could make a copy of the voice mail for you and you can present it to the Senator. But wait... there are some things I would need to delete from the voice mail since there are some personal matters my Congressman friend said that neither you nor anyone else needs to hear. The reason it was a voice mail in the first place was because I wasn't taking any calls from him. I can make a copy of the voice mail, but it will need to be cleansed of certain personal matters. Will that suffice?"

"How will I ever know if the voice mail is real and if the recorded voice on the machine is really your Congressman friend?" asked A.T.

"You can go ahead and ask him," answered Samantha. "I really don't care if you do; however, there are certain things I will want to delete. Plus, I am putting something on the line here. I am offering proof to you. You said you weren't sure if you could trust me and that you did trust the Senator. Now I am offering proof in order to demonstrate to you just who you can trust."

"How will I know your former Congressman friend is referring to the Senator?" inquired A.T.

"He mentions him by name, and he is very specific in his discussion about it," noted Samantha.

"I don't know," said A.T. "It's a recording of a private conversation, and I don't want to be a part of -"

"You said you wanted proof, and that is what I am willing to offer," concluded Samantha.

"Let me think about it," responded A.T. "What if the Senator -"

"If you want to debate the matter further, we can do that at my place. Right now, though, I would like to have you take me home. In a few days I will set up the arrangements for you to meet my benefactors who are a part of the GGG."

* *

The suggestion to leave was in order considering they had been at the restaurant for several hours. Reluctantly, A.T. had agreed to take Samantha to her West Coast residence that turned out to be in the same general area as 'The Beach House.' While pulling up to the gated community to which she had directed him, she handed him a card that activated the wrought iron entry gate. They entered the complex, and she guided him to the condominium where she lived. After he pulled up to the unit, he got out of the car, opened the door for her, and began to escort her to the door of her condo. She suddenly walked to the back of the vehicle, bent over the wheel well, and then seemed to trace an imaginary line back to the rear bumper, where she leaned under the car. A.T. watched her seemingly abrupt actions; he couldn't help but notice how nimble and athletic she seemed. At that point, she looked up and noticed him watching her.

She said, "While you're there apparently enjoying the view, I found this for you."

When she held up her hand which was holding a small box with a couple of wires, A.T. exclaimed, "What the hell is that?"

"It sure looks like a transmitter to me," answered Samantha. "Obviously, you have someone who is very interested in knowing your whereabouts. Any idea as to who may have done this?"

"No! Wait! It could have been a couple of old investigators, a real odd couple, whom I've known for some time. A lot of people who have been in the private investigative business know them. They pop up now and then in unusual places. I ran into them yesterday and agreed to meet them for brunch this morning at my hotel. Shortly after, I checked out and gave them the slip. They were still visiting in the coffee shop when I left the hotel."

"What do they look like?" asked Samantha.

"They are strange looking. One is tall and quite big. The other is small and tries to remain silent, while the big guy does the talking," explained A.T.

"'Squeaky' and 'Big John,' no doubt," said Samantha.

"You know them?"

"Everybody knows them. They're a couple of characters you would typically find in some dime novel. Their paths and mine have crossed on a number of prior occasions. At one point, they wanted me to work with them," Samantha said.

"They wanted you to work with them? In what regard if I may ask?"

"Those two are deeply involved with a group of people who have a specific idea about how our government is to be run. They have significant ties to a faction that has been active in the Republican Party as far back as the Nixon administration. They obviously have friends in high places, and the people they know are still active in both the Republican Party and offices within the government. They knew of my involvement with the GGG and wanted me to open the door to the GGG for their organization. LESTER wanted a position at the table. I tried to set up a meeting, but to no avail. GGG knows all about LESTER and want nothing to do with them. In fact some of the information the GGG will most likely share with you involves the very people behind these two characters. I told you that you needed to connect the spots. What you will learn from my benefactors is that once the spots are connected, your own investigation will make more sense, and you will see how the people behind 'Squeaky' and 'Big John' fit into the picture."

"That's interesting! So, I take it you were unable to work with them?"

"That's correct. I never really had any intention of working with them, but I agreed to take their proposal to the GGG. Needless to say, their proposal was soundly rejected. As a result, our two friends hate me. Apparently, they think I somehow blackballed them and their friends. In reality, I had very little say in it. Nevertheless, those two have been carrying a grudge against me ever since."

"I wouldn't think you would have much to worry about with those two. They are about as incompetent as it gets," noted A.T.

"Don't underestimate them," insisted Samantha. "They're deceptive. They are simply the 'red herring' front of something far more sinister taking place."

"What do you mean?" asked A.T.

"Those two aren't working alone," said Samantha. "They never do. They are the decoy. They are the front of a more serious enterprise of some sort. Chances are good that they were trying to throw you off track during your breakfast meeting while someone else was doing the dirty work, such as installing this interesting device on your car. I will further guess this same someone is tailing you. Any ideas about who this might be?"

"None," answered A.T., "except they indicated they were working for people who helped fund the 'tea party' movement. At least, that is what they said. I did know they had done some free-lance work after the BP oil spill, so I inquired this morning, and they said they were done with that deal and were now working with some folks who shared the same philosophy as theirs. I jokingly guessed the money people behind the 'tea party,' and they didn't deny it."

"Do you want this as a souvenir?" asked Samantha while presenting the device to A.T.

"Sure, I'll take it. It might come in handy as a piece of evidence depending on how this investigation goes," said A.T. taking the device and walking Samantha up the set of stairs to her door. She handed him the key after she inputted a code onto the door panel. He then unlocked the door, and she entered. A.T. looked at Samantha and shook his head. He then said, "Have a good evening. I will wait for your call regarding the meeting with your boss."

When he started down the stairs, Samantha said, "A.T., wait!"

He turned and asked, "What?"

"Be careful," warned Samantha. "There is probably going to be someone following you. You need to be on guard. If you get into a bind, give me a call; I can either send help or come myself."

"Thanks for your concern," he said as he smiled. "I believe I will be all right. You be careful yourself. The offer of assistance goes both ways. If you are the one who is being tailed, and you need my help, let me know. You have my number."

"I do, thanks," she said reaching into the pocket of her jeans. "I almost forgot. Here's the napkin with my drawings and my number. I really meant it when I offered to assist if you ever need help."

"Thanks," said A.T. accepting the napkin diagram from her. "Do you want me to come in to see if everything is okay?"

Samantha smiled and said, "Is that the real reason you are offering, or is there another reason?"

"That's the real reason," insisted A.T. "As I've said, I truly am a happily married man. I just wanted to be sure that you will be okay?"

"I'll be okay, now take care," giggled Samantha closing the door.

* *

A.T. double-checked below his vehicle in order to see if there were any other devices that might have been planted. Being somewhat satisfied there were no more, he got into the car and headed back to the wrought iron entry gate into the condo complex, which opened directly before he approached it. He left the complex and decided to take I-5 north to the Irvine/Newport Beach area. Nearing the main street in order to reach I-5, he noticed a dark blue BMW had pulled out over a block behind him. The driver was not visible. He thought it was just a coincidence and his paranoia was getting the better of him. However, as he followed several streets in order to reach I-5, the BMW remained behind him and had even appeared to race through a light changing to red.

He entered the approach onto I-5 and proceeded northbound. Over the course of the next several miles, he varied his speed to see if the BMW was still behind him. Although it was dark, he was rather certain he had pinpointed the BMW when it navigated various lane changes while weaving between other traffic in what appeared to be an attempt to remain a close distance behind him. Its headlights were of the newer xenon HID halogen LEDs and quite distinguishable from most of the other vehicles on the road, so it was fairly easy to track. From Oceanside to San Clemente, the 'cat and mouse' game between the cars continued at varying speeds. A.T. decided once he got near San Juan Capistrano, he would drop off I-5 and onto the Pacific Coast Highway in order to see if the BMW followed him. When he made his move, the BMW did also.

At Laguna Beach, he decided to engage in a maneuver or two and head back to I-5, which took him north over local 133, then southeasterly down 73 to I-5. When he reached I-5, he took the ramp south back toward San Diego. Once at the next interchange near San Juan Capistrano, he dropped off I-5 and found a fast food restaurant near the intersection, where he pulled off into the lot. He noticed the BMW bypassed the fast food place, either intentionally or otherwise. It continued up 74, and A.T. immediately headed back toward the intersection. He entered I-5 heading south again, and once he reached the Pacific Coast Highway, he doubled back north moving fast without risking too much attention for speeding. The natural pace of the traffic was fairly rapid, so he was pleased. He followed the Pacific Coast Highway into Newport Beach in the area of Fashion Island and decided to weave through various streets until he reached the general area of his hotel. Since there were several hotels in the area, he opted to park his car in the monitored lot at a hotel near the one where he was staying. He knew the area fairly well, so he felt he could follow some of the side streets and remain obscure from the greater movement of traffic, all the while keeping a lookout for the BMW.

Once at his hotel, he double checked his room in order to be sure it was secure and had a ready exit. In the morning, before his flight, he would call the rental car company to tell them the car wouldn't start. He would provide them with the location and would take the hotel shuttle to the John Wayne Airport in order to return to the Twin Cities. With that plan in mind, A.T. settled down for what he hoped would be a restful sleep. After a call to Jacci, he made sure his luggage was packed and ready for departure as soon as it was daylight. Following a long day, he felt exhausted and sleep enveloped him quite quickly.

The next morning, A.T. called the rental car company, and left for the airport on the shuttle much earlier than necessary. He felt there would be less chance of anyone being up and ready to tail him at that early hour. There was no sign of the BMW, and he was relieved. Once at the airport, he organized his notes since he would only be in the Twin Cities for a few days before he headed to Washington to meet with the Senator and members of his staff. The Senator had texted A.T. to inform him that he had set up a meeting at the W Hotel in downtown D.C. with various witnesses who had been involved with the investigation. Ironically, the text sounded like the Senator was following the same "game plan" Samantha had suggested. It appeared as though the Senator was also trying to connect the dots or as Samantha graphically demonstrated on the napkin, the "spots." The question now in A.T.'s mind was whether he and the Senator were connecting the same dots or spots. It seemed more and more significant that a meeting with Samantha's benefactors would be beneficial to both the Senator and to A.T. in terms of tying things together.

* *

Following an uneventful flight, A.T. arrived back in the Twin Cities on schedule. It was early enough for him to take Jacci to dinner at one of their favorite restaurants in St. Paul. After she met him at the airport, they drove to their home in order to relax and change for the upcoming night out. It was precisely what A.T. needed after the stressful trip to the West Coast. The evening presented itself as the sort of deviation from conducting interviews and writing reports that was well needed and deserved. When they were together, it was as if time had stood still for A.T. and Jacci. In fact, the next few days allowed the two of them to spend more time together than they had for months. For three days, the two of them spent time exclusively with each other. They were able to take a couple of nearby road trips to see sights they had not experienced for a long time.

After the three days of relaxation, reality returned to A.T.'s world when he received an early morning call from Lee Mattson, the Senator's lead aide. Since there had been no effort to work on the investigation during the past three days, the call was the sort of jolt that always seems to take place. It finally appeared the investigation was getting closer to a conclusion, and it was A.T.'s hope the major part of his work was about over. He knew the call from the Senator's office would come sooner or later. Plus, he had to confess to himself that he was interested in seeing if a meeting with Samantha's benefactors was going to occur. He hadn't heard from her and recalled she had promised she would call him with a time for the meeting with the GGG. Since he hadn't received her call, his first expectation when the phone rang was that it would be Samantha, but it was Lee instead. He would now need to schedule the expected trip back to the nation's capital.

The Senator had called a meeting through his aide, Lee, who had been with the Senator for nearly twenty years. Lee had always been direct, and this time was no exception. He told A.T. a major meeting had been scheduled by the Senator. He said most of the people whom A.T. had contacted regarding the investigation would be brought together for a seminar-style review of testimony and evidence before the Senator took the next step in moving the matter into committee hearings. On behalf of the Senator, Lee had booked some rooms at the downtown W Hotel since the accommodations held the necessary meeting rooms and lodging at a neutral site in what he believed would be a useful and reasonably secure environment.

A.T. made appropriate arrangements for the flights and other travel-related issues that included Allen, whom A.T. wanted along in the event he needed assistance. Since the meetings were to last the better part of a week, A.T. contemplated the possibility of Jacci accompanying him on the trip; however, she would be training with her horse for its first dressage show of the year the week following the Washington D.C. trip. Therefore, she declined the opportunity to once again visit Washington and some old friends, including the Senator and his wife. Plus, Jacci insisted she didn't feel comfortable attending a political fundraiser.

After making the necessary call to Allen and getting the travel and accommodations arranged at the W Hotel, it appeared all was set for the final stages of the case. Upon finishing some calls and after stopping by the law office to catch up with other cases and the progress of work being done, A.T. headed for home with the realization he would soon be back in the exciting mix of the final stages of the investigation. While driving to his house, he received two calls. The first was from Adam, who said he had something new to present to A.T. Naturally that piqued A.T.'s interest, so he was ready to see what was in store for him. While he was hanging up the phone, he received a call from Samantha. He was somewhat happy to hear from her since he had become concerned about the BMW that had been following him on his last night on the West Coast. It had crossed his mind that the same people following him might have also been following her. Fortunately, she was fine and had not encountered any difficulties. He was relieved, even though he was more than confident she was fully capable of handling herself.

It turned out, she was also going to be in Washington in the next few days. She didn't explain why, so he presumed she might be trying to make up with her Congressman boyfriend. It was none of his business, so he didn't ask. Samantha did have some news about her benefactors. She said the GGG Committee was planning to meet at their New York office in just over a week. Either it was a stroke of luck, or strings were being pulled behind the scenes in order to accommodate the already booked schedule that was on A.T.'s calendar. A.T. agreed to make himself available for a trip to New York during the week directly after the trip to D.C.

"By the way, Samantha," asked A.T. "are you still planning to provide a copy of the voice mail message you mentioned regarding the Senator's discussion with your significant other?"

"Former significant other," corrected Samantha. "Yes, I can do that, if you insist; however, by now I had hoped you would have developed enough trust in me that such would not be necessary. When we meet in Washington, I will have an edited version for you. I would ask and trust you would only use the recording if it became absolutely critical; and if it is not needed you would return it to me without attempting to copy it or allow anyone else to hear it,"

"That's agreed," answered A.T. "So you know, I really do want to trust you, and if the voice mail turns out to be accurate, I will have to admit I may have been wrong about you all along. I would also like to see and hear exactly what your benefactors at the GGG have to say before I would say I completely trust you."

"I am confident when you hear the truth about what is really going on behind the scenes, you will definitely trust me. I am certain of it, A.T. I thought I had proven myself to you time after time. Sooner or later you will see I am not your enemy but a very good and worthy friend, if not more," said Samantha in a soft and reassuring voice.

Although her last comments troubled him, A.T. let the matter stand and said good bye to Samantha.

* *

A.T. was looking forward to seeing Adam and discussing anything new taking place in the world of technology. Adam had been splitting his time between his new technology company and the law office where he had been working on several patent applications and a number of copyrights for his company and for some clients. A. T. was pleased Adam was finding time to meet with him before he left for Washington again. An enjoyable and relaxing evening was expected as Jacci was planning a dinner of favorite dishes. Adam and his wife were planning to join A.T. and Jacci. Rachael and Renee and their spouses were also invited; however, all of them had other plans and were unable to attend.

When A.T. left the office, he reminded Adam of the dinner. Adam indicated he had a bit of a surprise for A.T. Later that evening, Adam proudly displayed a new suit he had brought for A.T. The suit looked just like one of A.T.'s favorite blues, but it was a new suit with some technical innovations.

Embedded into the button loop of the left lapel was an extremely fine wire disguised as a thread woven into the fabric. A service club lapel pin was a miniature camera that became activated when it was inserted into the lapel buttonhole. Two thread-thin wires were woven into the coat fabric upwards to the seam along the shoulder where the fine fiber followed the seam to the back of the collar at which point the two main sections of the coat met. There the thread-thin wires entered the inside of the coat to a point where the "hang loop" of the coat was typically positioned, along with a normal brand label. The loop for hanging the coat connected with a thin wire threading that served as an antenna which extended along the shoulder seam. A special label inserted into the brand label turned out to be a mini-transmitter and a battery of unique design that would provide the necessary charge for the camera. Once inserted, the device would activate the system and would open a wireless link to a cell phone. This specially designed system would require that A.T. carry an additional cell phone and also remove the transmitter and battery package at any time when traversing through a security system.

While Adam's wife helped Jacci with the evening meal, A.T. and Adam experimented with the new suit coat and the video that would transmit to the special cell phone, where it could be either recorded or transferred via an open phone line to a remote location. Surprisingly, the new video devise worked quite well. Adam explained the system was designed as a safety device for A.T., especially after consideration was given to the tense and dangerous nature of the investigation A.T. had been conducting. For nearly an hour the two of them experimented with the new system before being told the table had been set for dinner.

CHAPTER 25
CAREFULLY MEASURED

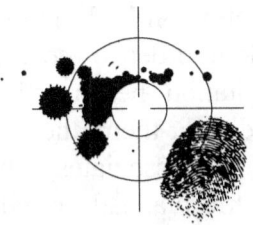

The driver of the "imperial blue" BMW 750Lix was in no mood to slow down for anyone or anything while finally leaving California after spending nearly a week following the movements of the two people he had been assigned to watch. He was especially angry that one of the subjects had given him the slip and had left for the Twin Cities three days ago. The other person had just boarded a plane for the nation's capital, and she had turned out to be nearly as elusive as the first. He knew he would soon be back on the trail of both of them. However, he still had to complete his final task in securing documentation from a "special source" that would create the impression of bona fide credentials in the medical arena. Once that task was completed, he needed to get to Washington D.C. as quickly as possible.

Impatient by nature, he gradually found the tedious driving along I-15 toward Las Vegas from LA to be getting on his nerves. He was becoming more and more irritated with the various DOT obstacles along the roadway, including the pylons that demarcated the separation of on-coming traffic, as the four lane highway had become a two lane "snails-paced" affair. Finally, he had enough, so he took the nimble BMW through the pylons and moved into the lane designated for oncoming traffic. Ahead of him in his lane there had been a number of semi-trailers, campers, and cars driven by all kinds of personalities, and he couldn't bear having to be a part of their monotonous lives any longer. He was able to get around no fewer than a dozen vehicles when at the last moment he swerved back through the pylons in order to avoid a head-on collision with an oncoming RV that he subsequently noticed from his rear view mirror had ultimately slipped off the roadway and into the bed of gravel being prepared for a new hard surface. He wasn't sure if the vehicle had overturned, but he felt he couldn't worry about it since he had perfectly measured his return to his lane in time to save himself and his car.

Wiping the perspiration off the top of his bald head, he suddenly remembered he was required to make a call he had been trying to delay. Despite the construction on I-15, he found it necessary to drive at whatever speed possible in order to meet the deadlines he faced in Washington. If he got a citation, he knew it would be "handled" by LESTER. For all that he did for them, they owed him more than one favor. Plus, the two very odd associates, who had been assigned to work with him while in California, had caused part of the delays due to their overly deliberate practices. After their part was done, the two of them had flown out a day earlier so they had probably provided some form of report to the committee in advance of the call he was about to make on the blue tooth integrated into the vehicle's sound system. The call was initiated and went directly to the private cell phone.

"Hello Victor! Where are you?"

"I'm on I-15 and heading east as fast as I can."

"Good," said Osborne. "I don't know why you don't take a plane like everyone else. You need to be in position the day after tomorrow."

"I know where I have to be and when," answered Victor. "I've never failed you yet, and you very well know why I don't fly. I prefer to use my own vehicle and equipment. You know the equipment I use is not the stuff that is going to be processed through any airport regardless of our connections. And under no circumstances am I going to allow for any of my 'special items' to be shipped by anyone. It was bad enough I lost a couple devices including a very expensive transmitter a few days ago."

"Why would you worry about losing something like that? We always take care of expenses and pay extremely well besides," noted Osborne.

"True, but I have rarely lost any of my surveillance equipment, and when I have, it usually means the subject is aware of being tracked," said Victor. "I pride myself on -"

"Fine, fine," interrupted Osborne. "So what if Mr. Van Doren and Miss Nguyen Plantagenet-Henderson know someone has been following them? Big deal! Did you get the credentials I told you to procure?"

"I did," answered Victor. "By the way, 'Big John' and 'Squeaky' do as little as possible and expect me to do everything. Are those two the best we could find to help me?"

"They are very loyal," insisted Osborne. "They will not let us down. They have proven themselves before. Besides, they are the two best 'cover up' artists I have run into. Plus, they have a lot of contacts, including a number of well-placed people within key government offices that include the office of one particular United States Senator who is determined to cause us some grief. And as a point of interest particularly to you, a certain Mr. Felthaus may have resurfaced if our plant in the Senator's office is correct on the information he has."

"Felthaus?" inquired Victor. "Isn't that the guy we put to sleep at Dulles?"

"That's what we thought had happened," responded Osborne. "However, it seems as though this Felthaus guy is still floating around and has become a witness of sorts for the Senator."

"In that case," said Victor, "permit me to suggest you speak to your 'cover up' experts, 'Squeaky' and 'Big John,' since they were supposed to pick Felthaus up from the restroom under the guise of a couple of paramedics. Apparently, they didn't get their part of the job done. I did my job and put Felthaus to sleep as I was supposed to. Your two incompetent friends were to pick Felthaus up for questioning. Obviously they failed, and now we have another problem your 'clean up' artists need to handle."

"Don't worry about it," responded Osborne. "If the story from the Senator's office is correct, 'Squeaky' and 'Big John' will handle it."

"Next time let's plan to do it my way," insisted Victor. "My way is permanent, and there are no loose ends."

"I sense there may soon be a time for that," said Osborne. "Once you're back here in Washington, we may need to discuss such a matter."

"Perhaps if you think you can do my job better, you should come out in the field with me. I'm sure you could do such a good job," noted Victor with considerable cynicism.

"Don't get cute with me," asserted Osborne. "Keep in mind while you are working on specific assignments, I have to be responsible for the big picture, and I personally have assured the financial people on Wall Street and the political action committee, along with our folks at the DOJ and the FBI that we at LESTER will perform. You, more than anyone else, should know my sole purpose in this prestigious law firm is to coordinate special functions for the power brokers and that includes keeping a keen eye on the happenings of Congress. Therefore, I have to pick people who I can trust and that includes 'Squeaky' and 'Big John,' who have provided me with the right kind of contacts within Congress. When do you expect to be back?"

"Since I have two full days and one night ahead of me, I should be there on time. If I can average seventy-five, which I am pretty sure I can, and allow myself twelve hours for stops, fueling, and rest, I should be on location at the W Hotel in Washington D.C. before the Senator's meeting takes place. 'Squeaky' said he would call me with details relative to the locations of both Van Doren and the Henderson bitch. Once I have that information from him, they will be in my sight until we need to put our ground plan into place. Is there anything else?"

"No, well…yes…" answered Osborne. "Give me a call every eight hours or so in order for us to coordinate any changes in plans. I want everything to be properly choreographed. If, for any reason, you are not available or are behind schedule, I need to know in order for us to modify our expectations. It is critical we get our hands on 'all' of the paperwork Van Doren and the Henderson woman have. By the way, no need to call her names. Keep in mind this is business. There can be no loose ends. None! No exceptions! I trust you understand and I will hear from you routinely. Is that understood?"

"It's understood. I just hate to have any woman think she can out-maneuver me," said Victor, abruptly ending the call thereby beating Osborne to the punch. Then, as a matter of purely vicious aggression, Victor activated the car's cigarette lighter, and patiently burned to death a small bug crawling across the dashboard.

* *

While Victor and Osborne had been discussing their next move relative to A.T. and Samantha, A.T. was enjoying some quiet time with his family in St. Paul. It was now the day before A.T. needed to travel to Washington D.C. for the third time in a matter of months. While intently watching Jacci carefully measure the coffee grounds she placed into the coffee maker for their morning coffee, he thought to himself the same patience was true of his report on the investigation. He knew his final report for the Senator had to be carefully measured. He didn't want to lose sight of his main objective in bringing about grand jury reform. The report that was nearly complete would be finished when he arrived in Washington. The testimony of each witness also needed to be carefully measured.

The following morning, A.T. could feel his mood change markedly. While the atmosphere of the night before had been lighthearted and seemed to match the gracious sounds of the Mozart selections playing in the background on the home sound system, the new day began to the bombastic sounds of the Wagnerian overture that had been the choice of the public broadcasting channel playing as the alarm activated the radio. The selection of Wagner continued while A.T. dressed and prepared his travel bag for the trip east. Jacci was already in the kitchen when A.T. arrived in time to help her prepare breakfast.

Since it would be nearly two weeks before A.T. would be back in the Twin Cities, he was happy he had been able to spend some time alone with Jacci. The two of them finished a leisurely breakfast before she took him to the airport for his flight to the East Coast. It was A.T.'s hope this would be the last trip for a while, and he felt comfortable with the general nature of the investigation.

In Washington he would be meeting with the Senator before organizing the witnesses at the W Hotel. There would be an additional meeting and the interview with Professor Brougham, who would undoubtedly be accompanied by Gerald. Also, there were the possible depositions of the two former FBI agents the Bureau had under close watch while they were still in the nation's capital. Once these loose ends had been satisfied, A.T. expected to be introduced to Samantha's benefactors in order to see if there would be any benefit from their meeting.

Arriving at the airport, Jacci dropped A.T. in front of the terminal. He kissed her good-bye and entered the airport to be processed through the entry point where he noticed Allen was already waiting.

The two of them caught up on the events of the past several weeks with each recounting how refreshing it was to have a break for some time with family and friends.

Upon their arrival in Washington, they were met by Eric, who brought them up-to-date concerning the two airport personnel who had been arrested for the suspected murder attempt on Orville Felthaus. There were several unfinished leads regarding the third member of the team that had assaulted Mr. Felthaus at the airport about two months earlier. Nothing concrete was discovered, so the third member of the group continued to remain at large.

Eric was able to provide a detailed description of the suspect and also provided a composite rendering to both A.T. and Allen. Although the composite drawing seemed to have some resemblance to the man whom A.T. had a glimpse of in the BMW behind him on I-5 a week earlier in California, he didn't think it was a strong enough resemblance to mention it to Eric. Therefore, he kept the matter to himself. Additionally, he didn't have a license plate number or any other identifying items of significance to offer.

After checking into the hotel, then calling the Senator's office, A.T. was informed a meeting had been set up that evening at the FBI Headquarters, where the Senator would be joining A.T. and Allen at the office of a Deputy Director, a good friend of the Senator. The two terminated agents and their attorneys, along with two DOJ attorneys, would be in attendance, with a quiet interview of the two former agents taking place.

Through their attorneys arrangements for a plea deal had been made between the DOJ attorneys and the former agents. The two former agents would now be providing additional information to the Senator and A.T. At A.T.'s request, Allen was also permitted to be in attendance for the statements the former agents were to provide.

A.T. was told the order of business for the next day would be to meet with the entire body of witnesses at a suite adjacent to a large conference room set up at the hotel for the preliminary review of witness testimony. Allen planned to assist A.T. in organizing and moving the witnesses through the preliminaries at the hotel. He would then spend some time with his son, Eric, in discussions relative to the missing Felthaus case suspect. By the end of the week, A.T. hoped to reach Samantha and set up a meeting with her benefactors.

* *

That evening, A.T. and Allen had the benefit of Eric dropping them at the designated entrance to the FBI Headquarters. There, they were welcomed by an agent and offered a specific sign-in register, much like the old "number one register" A.T. remembered from his days as an agent. They were escorted to the office of one of the Deputy Directors, who was already in conference with the two former agents, their attorneys, two attorneys from the DOJ, and the Senator.

Introductions were made of everyone present. It was specifically noted that A.T. had been authorized to conduct certain investigative tasks on behalf of the Senator's office and Allen, a former United States Marshall, had been assisting in that regard. After the introductions, the Deputy Director got out of his chair and personally provided a document of confidentiality to both A.T. and Allen. They were each asked to read and sign the confidentiality agreement allowing disclosure only through the Senator's investigation, including a disclosure of pre-drafted "Minutes of Testimony."

The Deputy Director provided a summary of his understanding of the situation, including the "plea deals" pertaining to the two agents. That summary was followed by an outline of the arrangement between the DOJ and each of the defendants, the former agents. The Deputy Director asked the attorneys for the former agents and the former agents themselves if the DOJ rendition was accurate, and all agreed the rendition was correct. It was duly noted that by special permission from the Senator, the Deputy Director, the DOJ, and the attorneys for the former agents, A.T. would be permitted to ask specific questions of each of the agents in regard to the investigation he had been conducting.

Before A.T. began taking the depositions of the two discredited agents, the Deputy Director had a private conversation with him. During the conversation, the Deputy Director revealed to A.T. that the Bureau had also determined there was an active group of agents within the agency who were operating with their own plan of action. That plan of action was directly tied to a group of politicians and members of the DOJ who had been infiltrating the FBI for the purpose of molding the Bureau into an instrument of enforcement that would undoubtedly have a political agenda. The Deputy Director described the agenda to be one where the intent was to shape the

Bureau into a powerful political entity able to direct investigations against perceived political enemies and/or individuals who came into the cross hairs of those individuals who were contemplating the slow and methodical control of the FBI.

The Deputy Director told A.T. he had been identified for several reasons, including the fact he had some political enemies at the DOJ. A.T. was also told he was in a position where he had become a target as an experiment in order for certain people within the Bureau and at the DOJ to see just how far they could go with the power they had already acquired. The information conveyed to A.T. was done confidentially for the purpose of assuring A.T. that the Bureau wanted to work with him.

Continuing, the Deputy Director acknowledged the Bureau had run into a significant number of internal problems that had not been properly monitored, especially beginning from 2000 forward. He wanted to assure A.T. and the Senator that efforts were being made to ferret out the problems within the agency, including the private agendas by agents and groups of agents. It was, therefore, made clear by the Deputy Director that the information given to A.T. stayed confidential. With an agreement from A.T. regarding such guidelines, he was permitted to take the depositions.

For the next three hours, A.T. deposed the two former agents. It was evident through the process that former Agent Norvell Emerson was quite hostile and seemed to blame A.T. for his arrest and for the charges against him. Former agent Emerson had been a police officer in the greater LA area before being accepted under special circumstances by the FBI. He had developed a knack for drawing people into drug activity and was regarded by the legal community as an "entrapment specialist." While at Quantico, Virginia, he made the most of his training period to develop contacts within the Bureau, and he wasn't afraid to use them.

His rise within the ranks of the Bureau was fairly rapid since he volunteered for every unique and available task that came along. He had cultivated favor with a number of supervisors, a SAC, and a couple of individuals at the Bureau in Washington. His testimony revealed he had spent considerable time "working" his superiors for special assignments and often volunteered to use his skills as an "entrapment specialist."

Former agent Emerson had worked himself up to a position as a Relief Supervisor and ultimately Supervisor before he was "busted" for various activities that took him beyond the FBI Manual and the FBI Rules and Regulations. From his disclosure, it was apparent former Agent Emerson would do anything he could to advance his own career within the FBI. His ambition was what led him to former Agent George Kowalski. Emerson had discovered that Kowalski had come to the FBI as a fairly well-recommended individual. He was the son of a state judge and was connected to several older FBI agents who provided recommendations for him.

The depositions revealed Kowalski had an uncle who was an FBI agent and both Kowalski and his uncle were a part of a very conservative religious group. Kowalski and some DOJ associates had convinced their supervisors at both the FBI and the DOJ to set up a special "task force" specifically designed to seek out individuals who allegedly would be likely to be involved in the financial world. The special "task force" was permitted to create a dummy corporation designed to look like it was an investment banking concern of some sort with the stated ability to provide financing to small businesses. This "task force" had the ulterior objective of indirectly aiding certain "friends" at Wall Street and the White House under President George W. Bush, who planned to have the Bureau focus upon political enemies while diverting attention away from any regulation of Wall Street itself.

To Kowalski, the skills of Emerson seemed ideal, especially since Emerson had a track record of being an "entrapment specialist." At first Kowalski did not reveal the hidden agenda of the task force specifically set to trap individuals whom his associates within the government believed were detrimental to the furtherance of set political agendas. Through Kowalski's deposition, A.T. learned an orchestrated effort was in place by a conservative/separatist political group to position as many people as possible with similar philosophies in both the DOJ and the FBI. Their idea was to ultimately control the enforcement of the laws in the United States, especially those relating to Wall Street, through a selective process. Over the past four decades, and particularly the last twelve years, a very defined and closed group of attorneys, along with some politically active individuals, formulated a plan to mold the DOJ and the FBI into entities that could control political enemies. A significant number of these individuals came to the DOJ and the FBI as a collective group with a set agenda during the George W. Bush presidency. He called the group the "Good Collective" or the "Southeastern Mafia."

When asked if the 'collective' had anything to do with the Italian Mafia, he answered it did not. He stated the "Southeastern Mafia" was considered to be a clever name and once others within the DOJ and FBI heard of them, they would leave them alone. According to Kowalski, by controlling the DOJ and the FBI, the 'collective' or "Southeastern Mafia" could dictate which laws to enforce and how to enforce them. He stated foolish laws, such as environmental laws and oversight laws, were ridiculous and should not be enforced. He further stated the 'collective' believed certain laws relating to education and laws protecting labor unions should not be enforced. Kowalski said the "collective" felt the same way about the civil rights laws and certain voting laws.

Individuals who were creating problems in the view of the "collective" or "Southeastern Mafia," could be eliminated through the DOJ and the FBI in various ways by certain task forces. It was the feeling by certain individuals at the DOJ that A.T. had stepped on some political toes, and because of his background, A. T. was a perfect test case. The general feeling was if the 'collective' could indict a former FBI agent and prosecutor simply by drawing him into a meeting and introducing him to some other individuals who had questionable backgrounds, they could target just about anyone.

When asked about Emerson, the explanation was that Emerson was so blindly ambitious and determined to "set up" people, he was an ideal choice for the "collective." Kowalski explained the 'collective' members in both the DOJ and the FBI were willing to use the talents and ambition of individuals like Emerson in order to further their objectives. In fact, the 'collective' loved people like Emerson, whom they felt would do about anything to get ahead, even if it meant selling out their own mothers.

Kowalski was asked if he would provide a list of individuals in the DOJ or the FBI whom he knew were a part of the "collective." He stated he had already spoken to the Deputy Director and the Senator privately about that matter, and that was what he had agreed to do in regard to the "plea deal" he had made with the DOJ. Otherwise, he would not reveal the identities, especially with former Agent Emerson present.

Former Agent Emerson refused to provide any additional information and felt he had been "set up" by former Agent Kowalski and others within the FBI. He thought he had made some enemies at the Bureau because he had turned a couple of agents in for certain violations of FBI rules and regulations. If it had not been for the investigation A.T. had started, the entire matter would have never been noticed or acted upon. In his final comments, he told A.T. he had made a permanent enemy and he would do what he could to get even. At that point, Emerson's lawyer and one of the DOJ attorneys cautioned Emerson such threats were totally out of line and constituted a wrongful threat and likely the obstruction of justice.

Following the depositions which were reported by the DOJ's own court reporter, Allen called Eric, who took A.T. and Allen back to their hotel. Once back at the hotel, A.T. and Allen decided to have a nightcap in order to unwind before turning in for the night. The depositions of the two former FBI agents had been both revealing and unnerving, especially for A.T. Nevertheless, it was at least a form of closure on the issue of how and why A.T. was wrongfully charged in the first place. Plus, the depositions gave more credibility to what Julian had told A.T. While the two of them met over a cocktail, A.T. confided in Allen that he felt he had a very strong case to present to the Senator's subcommittee relative to reform to the grand jury system, the DOJ, and the FBI. In that sense, it was a bit of a celebration for both A.T. and Allen who had worked hard to get the pieces of the investigation to the point of presentation to the committee.

* *

The next morning, A.T., attended a private, early breakfast meeting with the Senator for the purpose of reviewing the "Minutes of Testimony" and the upcoming meeting discussions with the expected witnesses. A.T. was feeling very good about the investigation and was looking forward to the meeting with the Senator.

The 'minutes' of the expected testimony of each witness were handed to A.T., who immediately read over the document while the Senator went through the breakfast buffet line and chatted with a number of people he recognized at the restaurant. By the time the Senator had returned, A.T. handed the copy back to the Senator with some notes in the margin for the Senator to review. While the Senator reviewed A.T.'s notes, A.T. went through the buffet for his breakfast. When he returned, A.T. noted an extra chair and asked, "Were we expecting another person?"

"Initially, we were," answered the Senator. "Actually, I expected Lee Mattson would have been able to join us; however, he just called and informed me he needed to meet with his attorney, Osborne Leeds."

"Did you say Osborne Leeds?" inquired A.T.

"Why, yes. Do you know him?" asked the Senator.

"I certainly know who he is," said A.T. "Apparently you haven't had a chance to review all of the materials. At some point during the course of the investigation, the name, Osborne Leeds, came up as being a member of a group called LESTER, which is an acronym that stands for Legislative Enterprise of Study to End Restrictions. It is a highly funded political interest group to which Professor Brougham seemed to give special attention in terms of utilizing its funding strength from both domestic and foreign interests in order to eliminate all forms of oversight and to alter certain functions of government. LESTER sounds like the very type of enterprise you are trying to eliminate in terms of political influence and contributions capitalizing on the 'Citizens United' case."

"If this LESTER is such a group, I will need to pay special attention to any reference to them in the materials; however, I want to apologize that I haven't had a chance to completely review the materials you have given me. I'm sure my staff has," noted the Senator.

"No doubt your staff, including Lee, has reviewed the material and perhaps that is why Lee is meeting with Osborne Leeds, who, as I understand it from the professor's materials, is one of the principals behind LESTER. Plus, if I am not mistaken, it was a man by the same name, Osborne Leeds, who used to work for the DOJ and was involved in the indictment that was dismissed. If that is who Lee is meeting, I think you might have reason to be concerned, Senator, especially if Lee has seen the material on LESTER."

"I think you are overreacting," said the Senator. "I'm sure it is just coincidental. Lee has been with me for many years, and if there is anyone whose loyalty I would not question, it is Lee. Why don't we review the proposed 'Minutes of Testimony.' Since the investigation is nearly complete, what is your impression?"

"I am quite excited about moving forward with the presentation on the matter of oversight in regard to the DOJ, the FBI and the grand jury," answered A.T. "After last night's depositions of former agent Emerson and former agent Kowalski, I am especially encouraged. They have now confirmed they acted in deviation of Bureau guidelines and regulations and that there has been a group within the Bureau and at the DOJ with agendas not compliant with the law. Of special concern is the fact the 'Southeastern Mafia,' as they call themselves, are purposely not enforcing certain laws, including laws that would apply to Wall Street. That same group, while well-planted within the DOJ and FBI, is also attempting to set up innocent individuals in order to divert attention from regulations that apply to Wall Street and investment bankers. The testimony of these two former agents confirms what Julian told me and what Mr. Felthaus has told us about the Department of Justice being used as a political tool against individuals who are perceived as political enemies.

"Also," continued A.T. "I noted from the 'Minutes of Testimony' I just reviewed, there is a Willis Flowers from the DOJ, who has a wealth of information regarding the efforts by the alleged 'Southeastern Mafia' group of attorneys within the DOJ. He indicates he became aware of the fact these people have their own agenda to convert the DOJ into a political arm and they use the grand jury system to taint political enemies. He says they are using indictments by the grand jury system as a political tool. That clearly undercuts the purpose of the grand jury. Additionally, you have my testimony substantiating the improper use of the grand jury system by the FBI and DOJ in order to punish certain individuals. I am quite excited about getting these witnesses and their testimony in front of your subcommittee for the purpose of getting some significant grand jury reform in place."

"Hold on, A.T.," exclaimed the Senator. "I believe you might be missing the point a bit here."

"What do you mean?" asked A.T.

"The testimony you describe is all true and definitely useful, but it also demonstrates there is a significant amount of outside influence, with much of that influence being directed by certain financial sources."

"That's true," interjected A.T. "It is demonstrative of how those special interest groups have extended their voice into the halls of government to the point of compromising the grand jury process, along with the operations of the DOJ and the FBI."

"Yes, but you are missing the bigger picture," said the Senator. "The 'Minutes of Testimony' also include a number of other witnesses that focus upon the direct influence of big money interests over the working of our government. Take, for example, Bud Hawthorne.

His initial work coupled with your investigation is what drew my attention to how special financial groups were exerting undue influence in the political process, and the internal workings of our government. Bud's testimony, along with that of Professor Brougham and his internal documents from the GGG, show a direct connection between the unique financial interests, both domestic and foreign, to the political process and the workings of our government. There are the two European bankers, Jean Paul Valance and Claude Schmidt, who will testify and present documents showing evidence of foreign sources being directly involved in our elections and government. Plus, don't forget Samantha's former friend, Congressman Buck Phillips, who will testify he was approached directly by those foreign financial interests."

"I recognize that those witnesses and their testimony do, in a sense, support the fact the foreign financial interests they mention have been able to influence the political process," said A.T. "This has brought us to the point where the DOJ has been directly affected through the political process. Unfortunately, that has resulted in some wrong people being placed into positions of power within the DOJ. As you may have guessed, this has allowed them to undermine the true purpose of the DOJ and ultimately, the grand jury and the FBI."

"Although I can see how you might interpret it that way," said the Senator. "I'm looking at a much bigger picture. It is true the outside financial interests have played a part in allowing the DOJ to become more of a political animal than it has ever been before. However, before we go there, we need to get a handle on the political process itself and just how that political process is unduly influenced by big money both from within the U.S. and from foreign interests. For that reason, the first efforts at reform must be made relative to what the 'Citizens United' case has done in allowing large financial interests to essentially try to buy elections and place political operatives within departments of government, including the DOJ.

"Once again..," insisted the Senator, "You've got to trust me on this. I believe the best order is for the reform to 'Citizens United' to go first and then the matter of grand jury, DOJ, and FBI reform."

"But that could take forever. In the interim, we could lose our position as it now stands with all of the witnesses that are lined up in great order for the reform issue of the DOJ, FBI, and grand jury."

"From my read of the current political situation, I have to move with the 'Citizens United' issue. Consider the fact that you have done a great service in regard to the possibility of campaign finance reform."

"What do you mean?" asked A.T. "The whole purpose of my being a part of the investigation was for the purpose of oversight and reform to the grand jury, the DOJ, and the FBI."

"Well, I've thought about that," said the Senator. "To take this in front of the subcommittee for reform or oversight to the grand jury or the DOJ or the FBI would be seriously problematic and not politically expedient for us, at this time. I've been able to place together a coalition within the committee that will use the evidence in a manner benefiting both the Republicans and the Democrats in terms of campaign contributions in such a way that a significant change, including a Constitutional Amendment, if necessary, can take place. There are quite a number of moderate Republicans who are seriously concerned about their political party being taken over by radical and reactionary factions. I've got to strike while the iron is hot in regard to campaign reform. If I don't, I will likely lose the opportunity. There may be some change of heart, especially since the Republican side of the aisle has some very significant contributors who will try to eliminate Republican moderates. You know this! I can't wait on the 'Citizens United' issue, but I can wait on the issue of reform to the DOJ and grand jury. For me to include grand jury reform or any type of oversight as to the DOJ or the FBI would destroy the coalition I now have regarding campaign reform."

For over the next half-hour, A.T. and the Senator argued about whether A.T.'s proposal should be placed in front of the subcommittee. As expected, the Senator, who had the power to make the decision, won out and all A.T. could do for the moment was to agree to go along with the methodology of the Senator.

* *

Once the breakfast meeting was over, A.T. went directly to the meeting room where the witnesses had started to gather. Trying to be as cordial as possible, he went around the room for the purpose of visiting with each witness individually before he took the lectern to make the presentation. After familiarizing himself with the witnesses, he was compelled to conduct the meeting and present the evidence established for the Senator's subcommittee. It was a troubling time for A.T. since he was forced to listen to the evidence, most of which he had obtained. He knew the evidence would be used for a purpose quite different than he had envisioned.

After presenting the 'Minutes of Testimony' on an overhead projector system, as well as reading the minutes aloud, A.T. requested that the main lights for the room be activated. He asked if any of the witnesses, who were present for the presentation, had any suggested changes or comments. No one stepped forward with any suggested changes, except the Senator who personally presented a single typed page pertaining to an additional witness. To A.T.'s stunned surprise, he found he was about to read the 'Minutes of Testimony' of Samantha Nguyen-Henderson. He instinctively looked up to scan the room, and spied her wide smile as she stood at the back door. A.T. shook his head and then read the additional item he had been handed.

The new 'Minutes' read: "Samantha Nguyen-Plantagenet-Henderson, if called to testify, will state for the past several years, she has been working as an independent investigator for two agencies, the Knights of Malta and an organization known as the GGG. She will testify she was directed to perform an investigation into the channeling of large sums of money by certain individuals and large corporations contributing to various U.S.-based corporations, which were instrumental in funding political activity. She will further testify the agencies that had hired her were concerned the various parties she was assigned to investigate were purposely attempting to fund dissident organizations and various entities that had a stated purpose of disrupting both the American political environment and the governing process of the country.

Ms. Henderson will further testify that her employers had been active in the funding process for what was believed to be altruistic organizations that did not take specific political positions. Accordingly, these altruistic organizations would not involve themselves in the government process. She will also testify that her employers feared the newly-discovered entities and individuals contributing to political candidates and political party enterprises were doing so in order to promote a specific political agenda and they were not following the law in the process. Ms. Henderson will testify that in addition to the financial documents, she will be able to provide a clear connection between those questioned funding sources and their efforts to infiltrate the DOJ, FBI, and the Executive Branch of government, including the Department of Defense, the FTC, the SEC, and the FCC.

Ms. Henderson will additionally testify that she will be able to demonstrate from documents made available to her that these funding entities are specifically expecting to overthrow and/or eliminate various aspects of the United States government. Her testimony will include a description and detailed schematic of an enterprise described to her as a cauldron of deceit and will include the names of the individuals involved and the corporations they have set up in an attempt to accomplish their ends. She will testify as to all other material facts and circumstances known to her about this matter."

* *

Upon finishing the proposed testimony of the additional witness and while A.T. gathered the witnesses together for a final review, no one at the W Hotel realized a meeting of another kind was taking place at a large law office only a matter of blocks away. It wasn't the first time Lee Mattson found it necessary to purposely schedule a meeting with his dear friend, Osborne Leeds, while the Senator was "otherwise" occupied. In the private area of Osborne's office for the prearranged meeting, Lee thought to himself: *I believe I have been quite efficient and masterful in my channeling critical information to LESTER and to Osborne. When Osborne and I came up with the idea of LESTER and when I tied him to this law firm, I knew all along we would have the best of both worlds with my working on the inside of government and his working on the outside in a shielded and structured environment. Now, even our large financial contributors have to realize the idea of LESTER was ingenious. I deserve as much credit as anyone for what we have been able to accomplish.*

Abruptly, during Lee's reminiscing about the formation of LESTER, Osborne's secretary came to the small conference room where Lee was waiting and guided him across the hall into the large conference room adjacent to Osborne's law office. When Lee entered the room, he was greeted by Osborne who was waiting with two other individuals. The large bald individual Lee immediately recognized as Victor Salensky; however, the small emaciated man was someone whom Lee had never seen before. After Osborne and Lee shook hands, Osborne offered an introduction.

"Lee, of course you know Victor, but I don't believe you have met Leslie," said Osborne. "Leslie, I'd like to introduce you to Lee

Mattson; he is one of our key people on the Hill. Lee, I'd like you to meet our newest member. This is Leslie Winthrop, who is handling our affairs in the upper Midwest. Leslie, in fact, is the individual who has been providing us with routine information, including the whereabouts and movements of A.T. Van Doren. I've called Leslie and Victor in today because I wanted the four of us to discuss the information we have just learned about A.T. and the GGG member, Samantha Henderson. These two men, along with 'Squeaky' and 'Big John,' will be traveling to New York tomorrow since we have learned A.T. and Samantha Henderson will be attending a secret meeting of the GGG. Leslie's job will be to tail A.T. from a distance, and I have met privately with Victor, along with 'Squeaky' and 'Big John,' in regard to what exactly they will be doing while Leslie is reporting on A.T."

"Nice to meet you, Leslie," said Lee. "Now, Leslie, I presume you realize my presence here is strictly confidential and that, if ever asked, you will have to disavow you ever met me here."

"Yes, sir," answered Leslie with a beaming smile on his face. "I have been instructed to be totally discrete and to make sure no one sees me.'"

"Very good," smiled Lee. "Before we get started with a discussion about A.T. and Samantha Henderson's trip to New York, I thought I should give you a copy of the 'Minutes of Testimony' the Senator is intending to present to his subcommittee. Please devote special attention to the addendum including the unexpected testimony of Miss Henderson. It presents a very serious problem for LESTER. It includes the purported testimony of Orville Felthaus. I want to give you part of what I have been able to copy from the investigation being done by A.T. It isn't complete; however, it is all I could get my hands on and copied before today. I will try to get more of the investigation to you as soon as possible."

CHAPTER 26
A FIERY CAULDRON

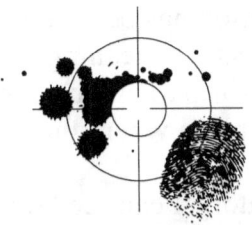

While Osborne Leeds, Victor Salensky and Lee Mattson were finishing their meeting at the large law firm, the meeting at the W Hotel had also concluded. A.T. gathered his paperwork and left the lectern. While walking towards the back of the room, he observed Blaine, Julian, and Samantha visiting near the entrance. It was his intention to thank each of them personally and then retire for the day. He noticed Professor Brougham and Gerald were talking together not far from the other three. He needed to speak with them, but he wanted that conversation to be a private one. He noticed the Senator was standing alone at the back door with a large smile on his face. The Senator caught A.T.'s eye and motioned with a movement of his head to the space to his right in such a way that A.T. understood the Senator wanted to speak with him.

His plan was to speak with Gerald and Professor Brougham first and then join Blaine, Julian, and Samantha; however, after noticing the Senator's nod, he decided he should first go to the Senator and then later confer with the others when he could. All of the other participants were milling around in small groups, apparently discussing what they had heard and what they expected would happen once the Senator had set up the official subcommittee hearings. Other than the addition of Samantha to the list, there were no changes or substitutions.

Giving first consideration to the Senator, A.T. went to the doorway where the Senator, still with a broad smile, was waiting for him. The Senator extended his hand and exclaimed, "Nice job, A.T. I thought the entire presentation, or at least the part I heard, came off quite well. I believe the subcommittee will be quite pleased, and we will be able to get on with a major reform regarding the manner of political contributions. If need be, we might have the necessary support to bring about a powerful change, even if it means a Constitutional amendment to alter the course of the 'Citizens United' case."

"Don't forget," A.T. reminded the Senator, "my underlying purpose of the investigation has been to bring about some reform to the grand jury process so meaningful oversight is in place. Plus, we can't forget as a part of the process, some additional oversight needs to be in place where the activities of the DOJ and FBI are concerned."

"Well," said the Senator, "I can see how you might be enthused about such a possibility; however, any reform to the grand jury, the DOJ, or the FBI will need to be placed on hold for some time until we have the subcommittee proceed with meaningful reform to the campaign contribution issue and meaningful regulations that will counter 'Citizens United.' As we discussed earlier today, you will just need to be patient about your desire to have some type of reform in terms of the grand jury, the DOJ or the FBI. Those matters will simply have to wait."

"But, Senator," asserted A.T., "I thought we had an agreement that if I worked with you on this investigation, the evidence gathered would be presented to your subcommittee in reference to grand jury reform and oversight relative to the DOJ and FBI, once the Minutes of Testimony' were completed and ready. It would certainly appear such is the case."

"Such is the case, A.T.," acknowledged the Senator. "However, first things first. The subcommittee must first consider the 'Minutes of Testimony' as they relate to campaign contributions and the efforts by certain individuals and entities to place financial contributions above the principal of 'one person-one vote.' At a later time, the subcommittee will take up the matter of grand jury reform and oversight. Regarding new oversight in terms of the DOJ and the

FBI, you have to remember that there are already systems in place for such oversight."

"Not nearly enough to suit me," responded A.T. At that point the two men shook hands and parted.

The matter was now in the hands of the Senator and his staff, except for a couple remaining tasks. Once those were completed, a new meeting with the Senator would need to take place. A.T. was hoping to withdraw from the investigation, except for the addition of a few refinements he would be making over the next couple of weeks in regard to the DOJ and the matter of oversight relative to the federal grand jury process. However, first he needed to address the two remaining items on his agenda - the promised meeting with the professor and Gerald as well as meeting with Samantha's benefactors. He thought he would first set up the meeting with the professor. Out of the corner of his eye, A.T. could see Samantha anxiously waiting for him to confer with her. He decided she could wait. What he needed most of all were the new documents the professor and Gerald had promised.

"That was a good presentation," said Gerald. "I was impressed that you found no need to go into any detail relative to the GGG or the Vatican or the Knights of Malta."

"There was no need to do so," exclaimed A.T. "As far as I'm concerned, they could still be a part of the general investigation since I personally see little difference between them and the private companies or individuals covered by the Minutes of Testimony. The money laundering, the illegal transfers of funds, the failure to report the offshore earnings, the orchestration of acts to cause the violent overthrow of the government, the improper and illegal political appointments to positions of trust, the misuse of the government offices, the abuse of the executive branch of government, the improper privatization of government functions, the profiteering through the privatization of government duties, and the use of public funds to illegally alter the voting electorate are all separate items to be addressed by the Senator's committee. To me there seems to be little difference between the acts orchestrated by the lunatic fringe and the acts by the GGG," said A.T.

He continued pushing the point, "I realize the GGG is interested in the Senator's office doing a full investigation on the 'fringe' operatives; however, I see no reason to exclude your superiors at the GGG. I know it is not up to me, so I will leave that matter to the Senator and his committee. My interest will now be directed to doing what I can in order to see some form of oversight takes place whenever a federal grand jury is convened for any purpose. A change to the system, especially the grand jury process, is drastically needed and necessary in order to assure the protection of individual rights as was originally intended."

"That's a noble thought!" exclaimed Gerald. "I'm beginning to think you are one of those individuals who decides to ride a white horse around while you commence chasing windmills and rainbows."

"If you think any attempt to correct a flawed system abused by an isolated group of people who have attained some positions of power in the DOJ and the FBI is foolhardy, then you need to consider what will continue to happen if the system is not changed," warned A.T.

"Well, I think it is just fine for you to confine your work and investigation to that worthy endeavor and leave all of the other matters up to the Senator and his committee. Plus, I am very confident once the Senator assembles all the facts and figures, he and his committee will find the irregularities and illegal acts occurring in regard to monetary contributions as related to the illegal reframing of the government are exclusively generated by the 'fringe' interest groups, along with the individual supporters behind them. I believe he will also find the GGG, the Vatican, and the Knights of Malta are his best allies in ferreting out those illegal efforts and acts that have been the hallmark of 'fringe' activity over the course of the last forty years or so. Having said that, let us now visit about the final set of documents we have agreed to provide through Professor Brougham who is with me now for the purpose of explaining the details. We tried to give these directly to the Senator and one of his staff members, but the Senator insisted the material be provided to you for your analysis and report to him. So, shall we find a place to sit down and review the items?"

While pointing to the nearby wall A.T. suggested, "Let's move over to the wall and grab a couple of chairs, so we can review the documents. By the way, how are you, professor? Where is Gretchen?"

"Hello, A.T. I'm just fine. Gretchen is out in the hall waiting for me," commented the professor as the three of them walked to the nearby wall where they situated themselves in a cluster of chairs that had been a part of the configuration for the meeting.

"I'm glad to hear you are doing well," said A.T. "Now, you're going to provide additional documents for the investigation. Is that correct?"

"Yes," answered the professor handing a new bundle of envelopes to A.T. "I didn't want to provide these materials to you earlier because I wasn't sure if they would be a part of the investigation or what the Senator needed for his committee. Plus, Father Gerald and others advised me to hold on to these materials until after this morning's review of the testimony was provided."

"Why would that be? In other words, if these documents you just handed me were important, it would seem they should have been supplied before today in order for them to be incorporated into the investigation as a part of the Senator's committee review," urged A.T.

"These documents are different from what I previously provided," explained Professor Brougham.

"Would you be kind enough to explain that to me?" asked A.T.

"Certainly," answered the professor, looking about the room in an apparent effort to be certain no one else was watching or listening. "At a point directly before I decided to part with the GGG, I had been approached by a group of people who were trying to become a part of the GGG. The people who approached me said they were 'free-lance' contractors who had been hired by a collection of people who wanted to join the GGG. I believe they call themselves LESTER. They were aware of the fact I had worked for the GGG because they had seen me during some of the preliminary meetings with GGG members who were assessing the appeal these folks were making to become a part of the GGG. I had been introduced to them at that meeting as one of the economists for the GGG, and in the process of their being considered for membership, they were required to disclose certain information about themselves and their companies. It was because of my introduction to them and the fact they were told to disclose the information to me that they continued a dialogue on a confidential basis. I was even asked to sign a 'Confidential Non-Disclosure,' which I did."

"So, wouldn't it be a breach of the disclosure for you to be providing the information you just handed me, and wouldn't it be a breach of the disclosure for you to be speaking to me about such matters?" asked A.T.

"It is a breach of the non-disclosure; however, I have been directed by the GGG to purposely violate that disclosure since my failure to do so might possibly make me complicit in being a part of certain acts by LESTER that I believe are illegal under the law. Frankly, the GGG has informed me they will stand by me as long as I follow their instructions and make this material available to you. Otherwise, the GGG has told me they will turn the information over to you and the Senator and indicate in the process that I have withheld the information that directly impacts the investigation and would make me an accessory to a crime if I do not make this disclosure. Some time ago the GGG had me transfer the LESTER inquiry over to Ms. Henderson, whom I believe you have met," explained the professor.

"You see," interrupted Gerald, "We, at the GGG, are showing our good faith and honorable intentions by directing the professor to bring these matters to your attention. We are really on the same side as you. The GGG has done nothing wrong and is willing to be sure the information the professor has brought forth will be out in the open relative to the very same people you have been investigating. We are the 'good guys,' and you need to know that."

"Nice speech," commented A.T. "However, I am not convinced the GGG is the altruistic entity you are attempting to portray. I have told you it will be up to the Senator as to how he and his committee handle the GGG. Once I have fulfilled my investigative duties, which are now about complete with the exception of being introduced to the benefactors behind Samantha, I will focus only on the needed reform to the federal grand jury system that is far overdue."

"The point we at the GGG are trying to make by providing the material the professor is handing you is simply one to demonstrate the GGG is exercising good faith in proving there is a marked difference between the GGG and the people and companies who were trying to gain membership and who are the subject of the materials you now hold."

"I hear what you are saying," responded A.T. "Please understand I have no idea where the Senator's continued investigation or committee meetings will go from here. Once I finish reviewing the material I just received and prepare a report for the Senator, and once I meet with Samantha's benefactors and add that to my report, my work will be exclusively focused on grand jury reform. So, if you have issues with how the Senator and his committee handle matters from here on out, permit me to suggest you set up a meeting with him."

"That's already been worked out," said Gerald. "A confidential audience between the Senator and some of our key people at GGG has been arranged. But first, it was necessary for us to get this information to you because it needs to be a part of your report to the Senator. Now, what's this business about your meeting with Samantha's benefactors?"

"Samantha stated her benefactors wanted to meet with me about my investigation, and I understood there would be some new information coming from her in regard to the investigation," answered A.T.

"I really doubt it; however, if Samantha told you her benefactors wanted to meet you, then I am equally interested since they are the same people at the GGG who direct me. I will be interested in that meeting and its purpose," noted Gerald.

"Tell Samantha that," said A.T. while starting to look through the new documents the professor handed to him. "What am I looking for in these documents, professor?"

"In a nutshell," explained Professor Brougham, "these documents were provided as a part of the due diligence I performed regarding several very wealthy individuals, some of their companies, and a number of their programs. They wanted to be a part of the GGG, which may well be one of the most powerful consortiums in the world. As it turns out, they were refused membership in the GGG for several reasons. First of all, the GGG does not accept applications for membership. It is a group that gains its membership by invitation only. Secondly, the membership of the GGG is typically made up of entities in existence for many decades and, most generally, generations. There hasn't been a new member accepted since shortly after World War II. Most of the members have held their seats, or I should say their entities have held their seats, for so long you would have to go back hundreds of years in quite a number of membership cases. Thirdly, the individuals who contacted me about membership on behalf of LESTER wanted to be a part of the GGG for their own reasons, including matters never a part of the GGG principles. I turned my due diligence of LESTER over to the GGG quite a while back, and I believe that is when Ms. Henderson took over the investigation of LESTER."

"Can you explain that more particularly?" asked A.T.

"Certainly," answered the professor. "The LESTER group is comprised of some individuals who have a practice of funding a number of companies which are essentially lobbying organizations and special interest groups that focus on a particular political agenda. A good share of the money that goes into their organizations is used for the 'signing bonuses,' benefits, and salaries of people who either are or have been in government positions. When the people in government positions such as congressmen, senators, Executive Office officials, and even members of the Justice Department provide certain services while in office, they are later remembered by receiving positions, or as it is called in the industry, a 'well-upholstered' chair,' in lobbying groups or other corporations, sometimes significant positions in well-known companies, after they leave the government."

"What exactly are you telling me?" inquired A.T.

"Bluntly," answered the professor, "they are receiving the 'bribe' they were promised while they were in a government position. In other words, by public officials providing services while working in the government, they are remembered later and upon leaving office by receiving a signing bonus; other benefits such as homes, positions, titles, vehicles, and a number of other items; plus, a generous salary for a set number of years in an association with one of the corporations of the petitioning groups, lobbying entities, or other organizations. Once such individuals receive their 'well-upholstered chair,' they are in a position that prevents them from complaining, and they become a part of the organization thereby preventing any disloyalty. There is almost always a patriotic title to the company or group where they are given a position so at least publically, it appears as though they are continuing to do something for the public good."

"Did you earlier say individuals within the Justice Department were included in this process?" asked A.T.

"Without a shadow of a doubt," responded the professor. "Also, I might say such positions have been made available to former FBI agents and officials, as well as a large number of people who have left the DOJ. There are a number of very large law firms with an international footprint that are a part of the petitioning group. Security firms and large law firms, particularly those with worldwide connections, are a part of the programs offered by the people and their interconnected companies, whom I mentioned, that petitioned for membership with the GGG. One particular individual might be of special interest to you. Do you know Osborne Leeds?"

"If I am not mistaken, our paths may have crossed years ago when I was involved in Republican politics. But I haven't seen him for a very long time," commented A.T.

"No doubt he remembers you, but we'll talk about that at another time," interrupted Gerald. "Throughout history, people have always been bought and sold, but this new wrinkle about rewarding them after they have performed is hard to prove as a 'bribe,' unless you have the information we have just given you. There are the names of the wealthy individuals involved, along with their lobbying groups, their corporations, and the names of a number of individuals who provided those promises to quite a group of former and some current government employees."

"There is even a list of some of the people who have been promised a 'well-upholstered chair' after their term of service with the government," said Professor Brougham. "Here, I'm talking about people who are currently with the government in one capacity or another. I have handed you the evidence I believe you will need to prove the 'bribing' of public officials is going on with a new wrinkle."

"And, I might add," said Gerald, "it does not include our people at the GGG. We do not and have not done anything like this in our history."

"Forgive me if I find that hard to believe," commented A.T.

"Forgiving is a part of my profession as a priest," smiled Gerald. "Look as much as you want and be as diligent as you can in your investigation, but you will not find any evidence of the GGG or the Vatican or the Knights of Malta engaging in such activity. These groups are clean and mean to stay that way. However, we do not appreciate being tied to the groups that do engage in such acts, and that reason is precisely why we are here with this evidence for you to take to the Senator."

"I still think these documents should have been provided earlier as a part of the testimony," said A.T.

"Think about it," insisted Gerald. "If this information had been exposed before this moment in time, it is very likely your entire investigation and the matters just reviewed over the last couple of hours would have been relegated to a dark place in a remotely obscure file folder and would most likely never see the light of day. All of your work would have been in vain, and nothing would move forward."

"What makes it different by presenting this to me now?" A.T. inquired.

"Your Senator friend is no fool," stated Gerald. "He will know better than to include this new and most damning information in what both sides of the aisle presently agree to pursue. There is enough information, as you have presented it, to bring about an immediate inquiry by the Senate subcommittee. Both sides of the aisle will agree to that. Once the inquiry by the Senate Judiciary Committee is underway with the materials already presented, the new information we have just given you will be hard to turn down. This is especially true if it becomes public knowledge through witnesses, such as the professor and possibly Mr. Felthaus, as they testify before the Senator's committee. It will prove most interesting for them to volunteer this new information during their testimony. The Senate Judiciary Committee will then have to consider this new information as it becomes a part of the record. At that point, the 'cat is out of the bag,' as they say. There will be no turning back. The Senate's committee will have no choice but to look into the matter we have just described, along with the evidence we now provide. Since that should answer your question, we trust you are smart enough to convey this material to the Senator in confidence and as a second tier effort of material to be reviewed after the testimony read today has been presented and processed by the committee. That is, assuming you feel you can completely trust the Senator. We're giving you one more reason to think long and hard about when you will provide this information to the Senator."

"What if I choose not to take this to the Senator?" asked A.T.

"That's up to you. But we think you will," answered Gerald. "You are too much of a 'Boy Scout,' and besides, we have a backup plan in place. Nevertheless, timing on this matter is critical; therefore, you need to think carefully about when you provide this information to the Senator."

"You have a backup plan?" A.T. questioned.

"Indeed," smiled Gerald. "In fact, she has become a dear friend of yours, as I understand it."

"I'm sorry, but you have me at a total loss. What dear friend?"

"You always like to play games, don't you? That dear friend is none other than your recent partner at social events. I understand you and Samantha have become quite close these days."

"You, sir, are misinformed," said A.T. "How exactly does she become your backup plan?"

"You yourself informed me she is about to introduce you to some of her benefactors. Now, knowing that, it all makes sense to me. I had been in the dark as to who the GGG was using to communicate directly to the Senator. Now, I know. It is your friend, Samantha. She is apparently far more involved in this entire matter than I realized," observed Gerald.

"What exactly do you mean by that?" asked A.T.

"Isn't it obvious? Samantha has been the party behind the scene who has been assigned by the GGG to be sure the Senator got all the information he needed for his investigation. You, on the other hand, were the party who was being used by the Senator to connect and compile the information into the reports the Senator needed," explained Gerald.

"I don't believe that," said A.T. "I have had a very long-term relationship with the Senator, and we have worked together in the past. I would think he would have told me there was another avenue of information, especially if that avenue was coming through Samantha."

"Why would the Senator tell you that?" asked Gerald. "It is a fairly well-educated guess that some information had come to the Senator through another source like Samantha, but, being a cautious man, the Senator contacted you to expand your investigation into other matters because he trusts you. Isn't it a fair presumption the Senator had you doing the investigation in order to verify what had been brought to him by the GGG through Samantha?"

"That does make sense to me now," noted A.T "As I look back on the investigation, at nearly every phase of my work, Samantha always seemed to pop up. In fact, her 'Minutes of Testimony' was handed to me at the last minute while I was at the lectern. Plus, I see she is waiting in the back of the room for me. She had informed me that she has been instructed to introduce me to her benefactors."

"Well, now you know. Samantha is a very key person to what is happening and the reason the Senator has expanded the investigation through you," explained Gerald.

"That's too bad. Now I am wondering if I can trust her at all and whether I should even agree to meet her benefactors," commented A.T.

"You should be flattered. You should feel good about yourself in that the Senator trusted you with such an investigation. The real question is whether you can trust the Senator, not Samantha. It should be somewhat apparent to you that she is trying to lay everything out for you without being too obvious," noted Gerald. "Plus, you should consider yourself very fortunate the GGG has assigned Samantha to help you behind the scenes. Although she and I do not always agree, she is one of the most trusted field agents the GGG has. There is no doubt you have been accorded a great honor by even being invited to meet her benefactors, who are members of the GGG. I must urge you to go to the meeting. I must see if I can get into that meeting. I believe her benefactors at the GGG will be able to convince you that you will need to discuss this new information with the Senator, in case you were to decide otherwise. If you decline to cooperate and provide this new information, I'm sure Samantha has been instructed to present it directly to the Senator. Certainly, you had to be a bit surprised she was included in the 'Minutes of Testimony.'"

"It's very true. I was surprised she was belatedly included as a part of the 'minutes.' Just so you know, I will consider just how and when to relay the information the professor gave me after the reading of the 'minutes;' however, what the Senator does with this information will be entirely up to him. My focus will be upon grand jury reform, and that's it."

"Don't be hasty. At least wait to see what the Senator says about submitting this new material after the professor and Mr. Felthaus are called as witnesses. Also, please wait until you have met Samantha's benefactors," begged Gerald. "Let this play itself out. I assure you that you will not be disappointed. Now the time is getting late, and I believe Samantha is waiting to speak with you," concluded Gerald while nodding in the direction of Samantha, who by now was standing alone at the door obviously waiting.

At that point, the professor and Gerald departed for the door with Gerald nodding to Samantha while passing her. She had started walking toward A.T., who observed the professor hugging Gretchen at the doorway while Gerald waited. As Samantha approached, A.T. wasn't sure what he would do. At times during the investigation, he felt he had been manipulated into a deeper position than he had wanted. Now, he was sure he had been manipulated, and he wondered how he had allowed himself to get so involved in the entire matter. He purposely made a promise to himself that he would end his role in any further investigation once he had met with Samantha's benefactors at the GGG and submitted his report to the Senator. It was apparent Samantha enjoyed the kind of intrigue that was taking place, but he did not.

He waited until Samantha walked to his location, which was now near the center of the room. All of the individuals from the meeting had left, and besides A.T. and Samantha, the room was empty except for some hotel personnel who were busy breaking down the stage, lectern, and central table area. Most of the chairs and tables used by the attendees had already been removed. Once Samantha reached A.T., he remained silent. Although he began to feel a degree of trust in her, he had mixed feelings because it was now apparent she had been more deeply involved in the events that had become a part of the investigation. Looking at her in an attempt to assess her from a new prospective, she smiled and shook her head.

"So, do you finally get it?" she asked.

"What do you mean?" A.T. responded.

"I've been trying to tell you all along that I have been on your side, and my benefactors at the GGG have been trying to help you and the Senator as much as possible," said Samantha.

"Frankly, I'm pleased you are a witness for the Senator's committee," insisted A.T. "However, I am a bit distressed so much has been going on behind the scenes. It is now apparent you and the GGG have been doing what you could to assist the Senator, while doing your best to divert any attention away from the GGG itself. I realize I may sound ungrateful for the behind-the-scenes help, but I cannot help feeling I've been used to a significant degree. As I reflect back on many of the events of the investigation, I see you have had a considerable amount of influence on the direction of the investigation. What I am unsure of at this stage is whether your involvement and the involvement of the GGG have been for the better good of the entire matter or if the GGG has simply found a way of keeping the Senator's attention diverted from the GGG itself."

"You know, A.T.," said Samantha, placing her hands on her hips as if she were about to scold a ten-year-old, "you are perhaps the most untrusting individual I have ever met. By nature, you are either totally incapable of trusting anyone or is it impossible for someone with your background to allow yourself the ability to trust someone who is doing her best to help you."

"You may be right. It's probably my background and training that I find it difficult to trust people who say they are trying to help me...or -"

"Or, perhaps," interrupted Samantha, "it is because of what happened to you when you were wrongfully charged. Maybe that's why you cannot allow yourself to trust anyone. You weren't always this way, were you?"

"Perhaps," answered A.T., "in fact, now that you mention it, I won't even take a call if I don't recognize the phone number on the Caller-ID. I've become quite suspicious of most people's objectives and intentions these past few years. So much has been tied to politics recently that I've come to believe there is probably some improper motive behind the acts of most people, especially if they have been a part of the political arena in one respect or another."

"What you really need," insisted Samantha "is to bury those thoughts and forget about them. What you need to do is to mentally take all of your cares and concerns and place them in an imaginary box and imagine further the box has burned with all those cares and concerns totally obliterated. Perhaps then you can get back to leading a normal life."

"That sounds like one of the acts of the 'Bohemian Club,' and I'm not a part of that sort of thinking."

"Then, you need a diversion that will relax you completely in order to get your mind off matters that have plagued you and your life over the last several years. Why don't you and I go to the hotel bar and have a few drinks?" urged Samantha.

"Perhaps we could have a cocktail. In fact, it is well past the lunch hour, and it wouldn't be a bad idea to get something to eat," said A.T.

"Yes, I could use something to eat to go with a nice relaxing cocktail. You know, it is so unfortunate it always has to be business with you. I've decided you chose to lead a boring life...and here I thought you were still a Republican," said Samantha while they walked toward the nearby restaurant. Once they were seated in a private location, they placed their orders, including a glass of wine for Samantha and an 'Irish Coffee' for A.T.

"Now, what about the supposed meeting with your benefactors, or was that an empty promise?" asked A.T.

"Well, that's right, A.T., let's get right down to business," answered Samantha. "Since you refuse to take at least a moment to relax, permit me to inform you that I have already booked the two of us on an early flight into New York tomorrow morning. That being the case, you may want to cancel any plans you have made for the next two days."

"Isn't that a bit presumptive?" inquired A.T., remembering how the next couple days opened up since the Senator had moved the meeting with the two former agents to the day before. He doubted Samantha was aware of that fact, so he said, "Actually, I have completed all my necessary meetings here; therefore, an early flight into New York will work. I trust we will be back in the evening because I had hoped to have dinner tomorrow evening with Allen and his family here in Washington."

"Sorry, but you will need to cancel that dinner engagement because I have made reservations for us in New York, as well." She then smiled while noticing the troubled look on A.T.'s face. She tilted her head, gave him a squinted look, and continued, "Don't worry; we are booked into separate rooms, although they are right next to each other in case we need to confer. Our return flight to Washington is set for two days from now. It is my understanding members of the GGG may wish to meet with you privately after the main meeting with the committee, and that is why I took the liberty to book your stay in New York for part of two days. Perhaps you don't realize it, but you have been accorded a very rare opportunity to not only meet with the GGG committee itself but to also have a private audience with some of its members. I had to pull some strings to get all of this accomplished, so you can thank me after you have had your meetings."

"I hope you realize I do have other matters scheduled that I will have to try to change an I should-"

"Well, get on the phone and change them."

"I think I will do that after we finish lunch," said A.T. who really didn't have much to change at all. "By the way, exactly where are we booked in New York. I may wish to pass that information along?"

"I'm not sure I should tell you," smiled Samantha while watching the strained look on A.T.'s face. "All right, we're booked at the 'Yale Club.' I hope that will suit you."

"Don't you have to be a member? I don't have a membership, and I don't want to be a 'club crasher,'" said A.T.

"Relax," said Samantha. "I have a membership there, and so does the GGG. You are registered as a guest, and I believe you will find the accommodations to be quite comfortable."

"I'm sure they will be. Thank you." It did seem the meeting with the GGG was falling into place at the right time, so A.T. could finish his work on the East Coast in both New York and Washington D.C. and get back home to the Twin Cities. Once back there, his work would then focus upon federal grand jury reform, which was the original purpose of the investigation. He then inquired, "Have you taken any other liberties with my schedule or otherwise?"

"Not yet," said Samantha. "However, I haven't planned for the entire time we will be in New York together. I'm creative. I'll think about it."

"Be careful of what you think and plan," said A.T. "It's a dangerous world out there."

"Don't worry, A.T., I'll protect you like I did in Paris and again in La Jolla. By the way, did you see anything more of 'Big John' and 'Squeaky' after I removed the tracking module from your rental car?"

"I haven't seen them since the meeting I had with them in the hotel coffee shop, but I did encounter a guy in a BMW who started tailing me after I dropped you at your condo."

"I warned you there is always a third one. Those guys always work in threes. How far did he tail you?" asked Samantha.

"I'm rather confident I gave him the slip on the way up to Newport Beach. I haven't seen him since."

"Don't be surprised if he, along with 'Big John' and 'Squeaky,' shows up again. They are obviously very interested in your investigation, and I'm confident they are trying their best to get their hands on whatever you have. I was actually surprised none of them showed up here. It's probably because the Senator kept changing the meeting location, and that's why none of us knew where today's event would be held until the very last minute."

"The Senator is pretty crafty. I even recall his moving rather quickly to collar your Congressman friend at the time of our encounter on the steps of the Lincoln Memorial."

"That was a really bad day for me, but in actuality, that encounter is what led to my being a part of the 'Minutes of Testimony' presented today. A few days after that Lincoln Memorial event, the Congressman called me," said Samantha.

"Is that when you recorded the message with the Senator?" asked A.T.

"It was one of the calls from the Congressman, yes," answered Samantha. "Actually, I thought it was to get back together, but instead, it was an introduction to your Senator friend. On the one hand, I was disappointed the news from the Congressman wasn't a plea to get back together, but the fact the two of us have gone separate ways is probably a good thing. Plus, I was intrigued with what the Senator was doing and realized it was an opportunity for the GGG to clear the air and an opportunity for me to provide some vital information about the group called LESTER. I thought you would be surprised that I was included in the 'Minutes of Testimony' reviewed today."

"I was," admitted A.T. "Gerald told me I shouldn't have been surprised since you have played a critical role in targeting the folks that are the subject matter of the Senator's expanded investigation."

"Gerald has a big mouth," said Samantha extending her hand with the tape. "Here's the tape I promised. Personal matters have been deleted. Use it only if and when you absolutely have to. This is the proof I promised. Now in regard to Gerald, he thinks he knows more than he really does. I was the one who was asked by the GGG to check on the LESTER people who thought they could simply apply for membership with the GGG. After Professor Brougham did his initial due diligence, the file was given to me. I am the one who has been hot on their trail, and I am the one who exposed the FBI agents who were tailing you and attempting to get the documents from you in Paris. Those two agents, if you don't know by now, were a part of the same LESTER group that petitioned for membership with the GGG. There are some very rich and powerful people who crave more wealth and power. That's where LESTER's interests fit in. They want control of the government, and they will do anything to get that control. In my opinion, some of them have already positioned themselves to take control of the Republican Party. They haven't done it yet, and I, for one, am going to do everything within my power to see that the full control of the Republican Party by those bozos never occurs. As you know by now, I am very committed to seeing that the Republican Party gets back to what it once was. Frankly, A.T., I'm surprised that as a Republican, you are not more outraged about what has happened to the Party. In case you haven't figured it out, it's the same people who have tried to control the Republican Party that went after you."

"Really, Samantha," said A.T. while placing the tape into his pants pocket. "It sounds as though this has become a personal vendetta for you. Are you sure you're not getting too involved...

even more so than I? What tripped your trigger so much? Surely, it isn't your benefactors at the GGG. It strikes me as though there is something more to your anger. What is it?"

"I will just say when my brother ran for office, the 'lunatic fringe' did everything they could to defeat him, and they were supposed to be fellow Republicans. The 'fringe' that has taken over the Party will do what they can in order to defeat their own Party members, if they feel those members of the Party do not march to the same social agenda that stokes the interest of the 'fringe.' By now, they know I am one of their enemies."

"Maybe the tail in California was directed more at you than at me," said A.T. while looking sternly at Samantha.

"That's possible, but I doubt it. I have been on their list for some time. It now appears they are blaming me for the fact the GGG would not invite LESTER into their age-old network. I'm sure the 'fringe' would love to see me compromised."

"In that case, permit me to suggest we exercise some real caution during our time here in Washington and more particularly while we are in New York," offered A.T.

"Don't worry, I will protect you both here and in New York," reassured Samantha. "I have your back and others, who are independent contractors for the GGG, have my back. So, don't worry, I am confident everything will go well and without a hitch."

"Perhaps I should have Allen go with us, or better yet, why don't I call a former FBI agent friend of mine who worked security out of the New York office for quite a number of years," insisted A.T. "If I remember correctly, he lives just across the line in New Jersey. We are good friends, and I'm sure he would help, especially with the connections he has with the various law enforcement offices in the area."

"Let me assure you there will be no need for that. Now, let me tell you about the first meeting with the GGG in New York," said Samantha as the waiter brought their order. While the two of them ate their meals and enjoyed a second round of beverages, Samantha laid out the procedures for the meetings at the GGG office in Manhattan. Once the meals and instructions were finished, Samantha gave A.T. his e-ticket and a copy of the 'Yale Club' reservation, with the promise the two of them would meet early at the W Hotel coffee shop for breakfast, directly before their departure for New York.

* *

In the taxi on the way to the airport, A.T. noticed Samantha was once again wearing the expensive perfume she had worn at the restaurant in Paris and at the Republican fundraiser in California. He thought to himself that the meeting with Samantha's benefactors must be of some importance because she seemed to wear the same perfume for special occasions. If his memory served him well, he also recognized her coat and the hat that had reminded him of a Russian-styled hat. For whatever reason, he thought the Russian-styled hat look seemed to match her personality.

A.T. had put on the new suit Adam had acquired for him. As Adam had instructed, A.T. opened a phone line to an additional cell phone he had brought along. The tiny cell phone was placed inside a hidden compartment in the base of the leather suitcase that had also been especially designed for the trip to the GGG. The cell phone was used to call a pre-designated phone that recorded everything captured by the video system.

During their brief, uneventful flight, Samantha and A.T. engaged in light conversation. Once they landed at La Guardia, they were met by a friend of Samantha's, who told them the GGG wanted to be sure they were checked in at the "Yale Club" and ready for the meeting later that afternoon at the GGG office.

Once at the entrance to the club, Samantha and her friend stepped away to discuss a private matter. At that point A.T. took a moment to call his old friend, Rick Helms, a former FBI agent who had retired from the FBI New York City Field Office. Rick and his family lived across the Hudson River and up in the northern part of New Jersey outside the town of Wanaque. A.T. informed Rick that he was in the city for a visit, and just in case he needed some assistance getting around, he would give Rick a call. He also was hopeful the two of them could spend some time together getting reacquainted. A.T. said he would call Rick the moment he was free and available to meet..

The Yale Club was impressive. At its stone façade and entry there was a full complement of efficient doormen. The 'club' had an air of old European aristocracy that included marble flooring and walls. Inside the doors to the main entrance was a large lobby with the front desk a short distance to the right. Straight ahead and across the central area, appointed with comfortable looking sofas and chairs, apparently arranged for small group discussions, was the busy Yale cloak room. The activity was likely due to a series of meetings that were listed on the scheduling easel. Around the large open lobby were paintings of some of the 'club's' more notable founders, members, and officers. To the far right and near the check in desk was an elevator bank behind large marble pillars. There were several gatherings of people most notably to the left of the entry. The people in attendance seemed to be having a jovial time although their apparent enthusiasm was a bit muted as one would expect in such a forum. Also of immediate notice was the business attire of the people who were present throughout the lobby.

When A.T. and Samantha checked in, she informed him the GGG office was only a matter of blocks from the "Yale Club," which was across the street from Grand Central Station. After locating their rooms, they walked to the building in Manhattan that housed the GGG office.

The main floor of the building hosted a bank, a brokerage firm, a parking garage entry, a gift shop, and a coffee emporium. They went through the main entrance where a security guard at the elevators inquired about their floor. After signing the guard's log, the guard directed them to the proper elevator bank.

Samantha pushed the appropriate button for the desired floor, and the elevator ascended. When the doors opened and they began to exit the elevator, A.T. observed a cavernous empty space. It looked as though the floor had not been in use for some time. Debris littered the floor, wall partitions had been partly demolished, and the ceiling tile hung loosely, while electrical cabling dangled from the ceiling. The place was dusty and didn't appear as though it had been occupied for a very long time.

A.T. looked about the vacant space and seemingly devastated floor and grew tense. Apprehensively, he turned to Samantha and asked, "What's going on? Where are we? Is this some kind of joke or -"

"Remain calm," said Samantha. "This is a bit of a diversion. There is no danger. You are perfectly safe. We had to be sure we were not followed. Plus, this really is one of our floors. It is simply undergoing some remodeling." She turned to her associate, who was a large, muscular, young man in his late twenties, and said, "Daniel, please remain here in order to be sure no one has followed us to this floor. A.T., you need to follow me."

At that point, Samantha led A.T. around the elevator bank to what appeared to be a stairwell. Next to the stairwell was another elevator. She pressed in a code on the control pad, and in a few moments, the doors opened to a plush elevator. She motioned for A.T. to follow her. After the two of them entered the elevator, she pushed an elevator button with a "B-3" designation. The button lit up, and the elevator proceeded to drop, following a downward path at considerable speed.

When the elevator stopped and the doors opened, there was virtually no sound. The elevator opened onto a large beige-colored marble floor in a semicircular area that contained no furniture. The width of the room seemed to match at least half the distance of the width of the building as it presented a vast and arched opening with large double doors placed exactly in the center of the room. The doors were shielded under the huge sweeping archway that began at one end of the room at the base where the wall met the floor and then gradually curved upward toward the ceiling to the center of the room where it continued downward in the opposite direction in a similar fashion to a point where the wall and the floor met again on the opposite side.

Recessed about four feet under the center of the sweeping archway were the double doors. On each side of the doors was a refined mahogany system of woodworking that served to accentuate the solitary double doorway in the middle of the room. Several ultramodern metal sculptures were positioned just outside the large archway on each side of the room. In addition to the overhead can lights, there was some indirect red and white lighting positioned under the archway throughout, with a focus toward the center of the sweeping arch. He looked to his right and smiled at Samantha. He shook his head as he thought she might well have been leading him into a fiery cauldron and perhaps to the entrance of Hades.

They approached the doors, and A.T. found himself hoping the mini-video system in his suit coat was operational. A.T. mentally reviewed an imaginary checklist for the activation of the system. Suddenly there was the sound of an unseen door closing in the area where the archway met the floor to his left. Turning, A.T. saw a figure approach from the shadows. When the figure came into the vicinity of the red and white lights, he recognized Gerald, who presented himself in a dark blue business suit and a broad smile. A.T. expected Gerald to take on some demonic appearance under the lighting, but to his surprise, the lighting instead seemed to accentuate Gerald's complexion in a healthy sort of way.

Knowing he had probably caught A.T. and perhaps Samantha off guard, Gerald extended his hand in a welcoming fashion and said, "I'm so pleased to see the two of you have had a safe journey. I have been asked to come forth to extend a proper greeting, and of course, to advise that you almost made it through the elevator body scans without issue."

Gerald looked at Samantha and said, "I must say you look your best, as usual. Although I am a priest, I must confess it is always a treat when I'm able to observe the scan of your image, Samantha."

"Once a pig, always a pig, Gerald," Samantha retorted. "Come on, A.T., let's go in before this pervert completely forgets he's supposed to be a priest."

"Not so fast," said Gerald stepping between the two of them and the doorway while extending an open plastic tub. "Apparently, Samantha, your dear friend, A.T., is carrying some type of signaling device. I don't quite know what it is, but it is obviously something that triggered the system. First, permit me to receive the cell phones each of you has on your person. Samantha, as you know, I will need to temporarily confiscate your handbag. Please deposit the phone and purse into this tub. A.T., I will need to frisk you, but first, please remove your suit coat."

"What is going on here? First, the diversion to the upper floor, and now, I'm taken to a subterranean hold of some sort. Additionally, you're asking me to remove my suit coat?"

"Relax," urged Gerald. "The main floor that normally provides the office space for the GGG is being remodeled; therefore, you have been brought down into what is our remote meeting and storage area. I believe you will find it to be a pleasant environment. However, the GGG does not approve of any individual bringing any electronic equipment into its meetings, and apparently, something has been detected in your suit coat. So, please comply and remove the coat. It will be returned to you when you leave."

Satisfying the request, A.T. realized that he was not going to be able to take the integrated video system past the doors. He followed the instructions provided by Gerald, and his compliance included the release of his suit coat, along with his iPhone and the contents of his pockets. A.T. deposited all of his pocket contents, his iPhone, his suit coat, his belt, and shoes in a tub that Gerald provided, Then A.T. was asked to walk back into the elevator, where he was apparently scanned again. He heard a voice come from the direction where

Gerald had entered the room. The voice said, "He looks clean; let him pass."

At that point, Gerald motioned for A.T. and Samantha to follow him as he led them through the large double doors. A.T. immediately noticed a gathering of unusual characters.

Before him was a man with a large bulbous head, who seemed to look straight through A. T. Next there was a man with a thin face with deep creases along each side of his mouth running upward along his nose. He had similar deep creases in his forehead, as well as under his eyes, with matching 'crow's feet' at the end of each eye. The next guy's face seemed to express a permanent and benevolent smile. He had dark bushy eyebrows and thick silver hair. The next man had dark hair combed straight back in a rather outdated style. Next, there was the balding guy with strips of thin hair streaked back over his bald head. His full beard was neatly trimmed, and his glasses seemed at least two sizes too small for his face. The man next to him had to have been from the Far East and had the most proportionate face of them all. His glasses were thin-framed with very thick lenses. To his left was a man whose glasses had extraordinary large oval lenses; with his thick grey hair and mustache, he had a Mediterranean look about him and was possibly from Greece or Italy. Then there stood a younger-looking clean-shaven man who seemed to have the attention of the others. He was probably in his late forties or early fifties and quite trim-looking compared to the others. Next to him was a lady of about the same age. She was also serious looking and seemed to constantly stare at A.T.

Some of the participants were present through large flat-paneled video conferencing systems positioned directly above chairs where they would normally be seated.

Each of the people at the table greeted Samantha by name, and most of them seemed quite pleased to see her. They allowed Samantha to return their greetings and requested that she introduce A.T. After Samantha provided a very brief introduction to A.T., the young-looking, clean-shaven man urged Samantha and A.T. to take a seat directly behind the portion of the large oval-shaped conference table in front of them near the others who were either physically present or present by video for the meeting.

The large conference table which seemed to consume most of the enormous conference room had an opening in its center. A.T. noticed there were flat panel computer screens positioned on the table in front of the seat or video monitor of each participant in such a manner that each of the meeting attendees could review items that might be routinely placed before each of the table monitors for individual review. A screensaver with an image of the earth in rotation against the dark universe revolved on the monitors. The image appeared to have been taken from a satellite.

Samantha sat down in one of the rich leather chairs in front of her. She motioned for A.T. to sit directly to her left. A.T. sat down and noticed that Gerald didn't leave but sat next to him on his left. The vacant chairs they chose were nearest the doors where they had entered the room.

To Gerald's left, there were two vacant seats and then a lectern positioned at the apex of the oval table on the left. Once Samantha, A.T., and Gerald were comfortably seated, the young-looking man walked around the table past Samantha, A.T., and Gerald. The younger man positioned himself at the lectern. Organizing some paperwork, it became apparent this man would be conducting the meeting.

The man cleared his throat and said, "Let us begin the GGG proceedings with a moment of silence as we contemplate our purpose and the reason why we are here. In this moment of silence, let us also remember we are a part of the cosmic consciousness for which the fiery cauldron burns. We are destined as guardians and leaders of the road ahead. Permit me to say, '*carpe diem.*'"

After he made that statement, the members situated around the table responded in Latin, "*ambulo viam.*" Then, the room became silent.

CHAPTER 27
ONE FOR THE ROAD

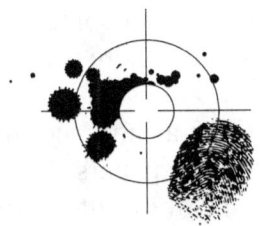

That was it. That did it for A.T. He thought: *Enough of this nonsense. It is clearly time for me to leave; this display is definitely 'one for the road.'* As the moment of silence began, A.T. rose up from his chair to leave. Under no circumstances had he contemplated this very strange set of events nor did he want to be any part of it.

He thought: *This is getting too weird. I don't care what road these people think they are traveling. They are bona fide and should all be committed. I don't want this sort of thing being a part of a perfectly good investigation. My original investigation was specific and had a genuine focus in regard to the Department of Justice. That's where I will refocus my investigation, here and now.*

After he had risen from his chair and started to turn to leave, Gerald grabbed his arm and pulled him back down to his seat. Gerald shook his head at A.T. and emphatically pointed to the table and whispered, "Sit down now! What will they think?"

A.T. sat down and wondered: *I don't care what they think, and I certainly don't care what Gerald thinks. They mean nothing to me. The Senator was wrong in asking me to meet with the GGG. In accommodating the Senator, this investigation has made too many turns, delving into the world of finance, paramilitary groups, infighting throughout the Republican Party, efforts to unduly influence the political process, and the people who have become known to be 'tea party' activists. Now, it seems to involve some seriously disturbed people. I need to get out of here as soon as possible. After all, what could this strange combination of people offer that would be in any way helpful? It could taint what has already been accomplished. My best bet is to get the hell out of here. Of course, first, I'll need to get my belongings from that tub that Gerald had.*

Once again he began to rise from his chair, but Gerald again pulled him back down to his seat. Gerald shook his head at A.T. and said, "Don't do that again!" If those present saw the incident, and it was impossible for them not to see it, they paid no heed and continued with their silence as they contemplated the "road" ahead. A.T. decided to sit, but as soon as there was a chance, he was heading for the door.

After what A.T. perceived as an uncomfortable period of time, the man at the lectern raised the papers he was holding and clapped them on the lectern as if he were attempting to straighten them. That seemed to be a signal for the procedures to begin. For some unknown reason, A.T. decided to listen to what the man was about to say. At that point, the man with the bulbous head to the left of the lectern asked in a strong, deep voice, "For what purpose or endeavor has this meeting of this worldly order been assembled?"

Being a bit taken aback by the fact this group was going to proceed with its meeting and a question had come from one of the participants, A.T. began to feel trapped. However, before again taking any action to leave, he decided not to excuse himself just yet nor ask Gerald for his belongings. He didn't want to be completely rude. The man at the lectern said, "An audience has been requested, Sir Reginald."

Once again the man to the left of the lectern spoke, asking, "An audience by whom? The GGG is a private enterprise and may not be addressed by any non-member, unless the proposed speaker is a "Head of State" or unless there is a war emergency. Time is a valued commodity, and trifling matters need not be considered. Therefore, my recommendation is this matter be immediately referred to the Office of Administration. Do you wish to entertain a motion to adjourn? If you do, I will so move."

A.T. thought: *Fine, I should be able to leave soon without having to make a scene.*

But just then, he heard, "No, Sire," from the man at the lectern. "Today's meeting has been properly approved and is the result of a petition by a committee member. The petition I mention is before us on behalf of a descendant of a former committee lord."

"Explain the petition," insisted the man to the left of the lectern as he folded his arms across his chest.

"Today's petition comes directly from Lady Benson. She has petitioned for this meeting on behalf of our beloved Samantha Nguyen-Henderson, whose great-great-grandfather was a former Lord of the Predecessor to this entity. Please remember, Lord Françoise Toulouse of Montpellier."

At that point, the lady at the other end of the table who had kept staring at A.T. exclaimed, "Hear, hear, Samantha." Apparently, she was the person known as Lady Benson. After she made her exclamation, most of the members present responded with a "Hear, hear!" That is, except for the dark-haired man sitting directly across the table from A.T., who instead uttered what sounded like a disapproving guttural attempt to clear his throat.

All attention seemed to focus back to the man at the lectern, who said, "I will begin the meeting with a synopsis of the facts. As this committee knows, an irregular application for membership to the GGG was made by an outside entity composed of a number of investment bankers, as well as some individuals who have attained a considerable amount of wealth through businesses that include the energy industry; a private marketing enterprise, now worldwide; a large private security group, also worldwide; a worldwide media conglomerate; a religious enterprise with multiple financial holdings; and a large law firm with a world presence.

"This conglomerate is known as LESTER. The history of LESTER is several decades old. A couple young Republican Party activists from the late 1960s and early 1970s were behind the effort to bring these varied parties of interest together to form LESTER. Those individuals, who today are in or past their 60s, are still active and hold key advisory positions with this entity. Ultimately, the varied interests that I have mentioned were brought together by these political activists to form the LESTER coalition. LESTER is an acronym for 'Legislative Enterprise of Study to End Restrictions.'

"This group, LESTER, was loosely organized in 1968 and was formalized in 1972. It was the 'brain child' of certain neo-conservatives in the United States during the presidential term of

Richard M. Nixon. The individuals about whom I am speaking met at several of the infamous CREEP meetings. They joined together and conducted their own private meetings while the CREEP meetings continued. As the GGG is aware, CREEP was an acronym for Committee to Re-elect the President. It functioned primarily in the late 60s and early 70s. However, there is evidence it is still a functioning organization of sorts but under a different name. In front of each of you is my report supplemented by the detailed investigative findings of Ms. Nguyen-Henderson. Included in the report are dossiers of the men who formed LESTER, as well as dossiers of current members of LESTER.

"To the founders of this group, it was believed that a media entity, a legislative group, and a political organization needed to be tightly formed in order to promote certain beliefs to the public. They felt such activity could be best processed through the Republican Party. To that end, LESTER was formed. That association has evolved and today supplies information, direction, funding, and guidance to what is popularly known as the 'tea party movement.' The investigation reveals it now has formalized subgroups or organizations in each of the fifty states.

"One of LESTER's first exercises was to involve the then sitting president, Richard Nixon, in certain activities designed to discredit certain political candidates and individuals who were considered to be 'political enemies.' Our investigation of this group has revealed that the individuals who helped form LESTER were instrumental in secretly releasing information tying the Nixon administration to the Daniel Ellsberg matter. We also know once they found such an activity, which they call 'the proactive approach,' to be successful in bringing down a sitting president, they have used the same method to discredit their political enemies through individuals who they have planted in various departments of the United States government including the Department of Justice.

"Our investigation also disclosed those at LESTER who felt President Nixon had deviated from certain precepts of conservative thinking. That conglomerate believed that Nixon was detrimental to its cause. In other words, it believed Nixon had to go. The investigative report we have states, through its members, LESTER believed that Nixon had gotten too far off track and could not be properly controlled. Essentially, the investigation shows Nixon was 'done in,' if you will, by some of his own people, as well as through his acquiescing to considerable illegal activity.

"It was at a point in time, between 1968 and 1972, the founders of LESTER felt it was important for its members to require candidates for public office to sign pledges and for those candidates to sign specific commitments to the consortium. That exercise has become more pronounced. Routinely, overt attempts are made to get public officials to sign pledges by which the officials agree to follow specific principals and guidelines on everything from reducing government involvement in various areas, promoting certain religious precepts and taxes, anti-union measures, etc. Today, from LESTER's perspective, it has become necessary for candidates to pledge they will agree to follow a specific agenda and show fidelity to the various causes of that group. This is the way LESTER has operated ever since the mid-seventies. A very significant number of Republican officeholders at both the state and national level are members and remain as members under the threat LESTER will find candidates within the Republican ranks, or Democratic ranks in the case of the few Democrats that have signed pledges, to run against any officeholder who does not operate within the guidelines set forth by LESTER. Today, there are only a small handful of Democrats who have agreed to sign such pledges, while a very significant number of Republicans have done so."

The man at the lectern continued, "The investigation also reveals that over time LESTER has orchestrated the 'take over' of the Republican Party and has effectively done so, or at least 'stalemated' it, through some interesting alliances in the process. The alliances include many people who are Libertarians, social conservatives, racists, militants, separatists, non-federalists, anti-unionists, tax protestors, Federal Reserve abolitionists, legal reformists, and large conservative business interests. As might be expected, the individuals who make up the membership of LESTER have their own views of history and political science. I might add such views are significantly at variance with generally accepted historical facts.

"Next, permit me to mention that before the individuals representing LESTER submitted their application to join the GGG, they did their homework. They not only found out about the GGG, but their research about the predecessors to the GGG was accurate. It was apparent LESTER was frighteningly aware of our past, our activities, and our membership."

"They should have known we do not and have not accepted any applications for membership," interrupted the man with the large bulbous head as he unfolded his arms and placed both hands on the table.

"That was explained to them by Samantha," answered the man at the lectern. "Nevertheless, the people at LESTER insisted she personally deliver a statement of their reasons as to why they felt LESTER should be allowed to be a part of the GGG. Samantha delivered those materials to our office, and she was commissioned to conduct an investigation, which she did. Samantha reported LESTER and its philosophies were at significant variance with the philosophies of the GGG."

"How were their philosophies different?" asked the man with the slicked back hair.

"In sum, according to the report and the investigation, at the core of the LESTER philosophy is the reasoning that only those who control wealth and hold the reigns of political power are destined to lead. The group believes the masses do not have the proper understanding of world economics or government to be a part of the decision-making process.

"Although LESTER espouses democracy, in reality, it does not subscribe to the theory every person should be granted the same rights to make political decisions. It essentially believes less government is better, and the average person should leave the governing process to those who know how to use the resources of the world for the betterment of mankind. In actuality, it does not believe a large middle class is of much merit, and having a strong middle class essentially makes the average person too complacent and content. It also believes people could be put to better use as long as they have daily needs they should pursue on a routine basis. LESTER is completely opposed to any form of social program, and it is against taxation in virtually any form. It is the belief of LESTER that the taxing process used by countries throughout the world is a device to take from the rich and give to the poor, who are unappreciative of benefits. LESTER believes most often citizens, especially in the United States, are too lazy to survive, unless they have either social programs, or they are directed on a daily basis to perform their designated tasks."

"How absurd!" laughed the man with the large round glasses and the thick grey hair. "They are espousing slavery. The GGG

524

has worked many years to move mankind away from the bonds of slavery. As the GGG evolved, it realized the masses must be given the basic elements for livelihood and incentives to move their lives forward. People are better citizens when their needs are met and when they have an incentive to improve themselves and their families. Our GGG predecessors worked hard to help create the notion of forward thinking by allowing everyone the right to present new ideas, inventions, innovations, and the like. In fact, as everyone here realizes, the predecessors to the GGG helped carve out a system in the United States that would follow such an example."

"Plus, this LESTER group must have at least some realization of the fact that a country does not operate without some form of taxation or other revenue-generating enterprise," inserted the man with the small eyeglasses and the thin strips of hair combed back over his balding head. "Apparently, they have never heard, 'Give unto Caesar what is Caesar's and unto –'"

"Yes, yes, yes," interrupted the first man next to the lectern. "It is a preposterous notion such a group could attempt to come to us about membership in the first place. How did that ever develop?"

"Our Samantha was approached directly by a United States congressman," answered the man at the lectern.

Everyone in the room looked at Samantha. She then looked to the man at the lectern who nodded to her, acknowledging she should proceed.

"The group known as LESTER has had a relationship with the congressman who made his pledges to them," answered Samantha. "The congressman knew I had done some investigative work for the GGG; yet, he didn't really know the purpose of the GGG. He thought the GGG was a benevolent organization working with major banks in the funding of worldwide needs; he knew nothing more. Pursuant to my oath, I never told him anything more. He apparently learned more from others, and I don't know who that would be. That was how it came about.

"The congressman asked me, on behalf of LESTER, if I would approach the GGG. Subsequently, the contacts between LESTER and me were done through two individuals named Harry Johnson and Brent Wilson. I believe Professor Brougham did the initial due diligence on them and the matter was turned over to me. Johnson and Wilson are independent contractors and think of themselves as soldiers for a better America. It may be fair to say they march to their own drummer and hire out to help promote what they believe are righteous causes. They've been around for decades and have done odd jobs since Vietnam.

"The two of them were involved with Oliver North back in the Iran-Contra days. They never were implicated and generally hire out to fringe interests for a price. They liked the fact I had been born of American-Vietnamese parents. It was their supposition that, like many people from Vietnam who settled in Orange County, California, I was of a similar conservative philosophy. They would often set up meetings with me, and a couple of them took place at the congressman's office. I told them the GGG did not accept members. However, they insisted they were influential in the political arena, through the media, and in the world of finance. As you will note in their petition, they claim they control significant aspects of politics, the media, and wealth in the United States. My investigative report details these matters. They wanted to be heard."

"As I recall," said the man sitting to the left of the lectern, "LESTER's membership application was rejected. So, why are we spending valuable time on this today?"

"LESTER is under investigation by a United States Senator, and Mr. Van Doren here has been conducting that investigation for the Senator and his subcommittee," interjected the man at the lectern.

"Is that a concern of ours?" asked the man to the left of the lectern. "Can't you tell the subcommittee to have a fine investigation and if we can help, by all means -"

"The answer to both of your questions is yes," answered the man at the lectern. "Yes, it is a concern of ours, and yes, we can tell the Senator's committee to have a fine investigation with our help."

"What do you mean by your answer to Sir Reginald that the Senator's investigation is or should be a concern of ours?" inquired the Asian-looking man at the far end of the table.

"Apparently, Mr. Van Doren, who is now sitting here before you, believes certain laws have been broken, and the GGG might be as guilty as LESTER in the violation of those laws. Do I have that correct?" asked the man at the lectern who turned directly to A.T.

A.T. sat silently with his arms crossed in front of him. The man at the lectern said to A.T., "We would very much appreciate a response, Mr. Van Doren."

"If you expect a detailed response from me, please understand I am not here to answer your questions or anyone else's questions about my investigation," responded A.T. leaning forward in his chair. "With all due respect, I was invited here, as I understand it, for the purpose of meeting the benefactors of Samantha Nguyen-Henderson and not for the purpose of discussing or defending some investigative work I am conducting for a United States Senator. This committee should know," continued A.T., while looking about the room in a deliberate fashion at each of the GGG members who were present either physically or by video, "the nature of my investigation is confidential. However, I will tell you I do have some serious concerns about the conduct of the GGG and more particularly of certain segments of the GGG, in addition to some individuals whom I have just learned are a part of an organization you are calling LESTER. In the event you have an interest in my reports to the Senator, permit me to suggest you contact his office."

"Rest easy, Mr. Van Doren," said the man with his dark hair combed straight back, "We are not here for the purpose of engaging in a form of inquisition. Isn't that right, Gerald?" he asked while smiling and nodding at Gerald in the chair next to A.T.

"I've tried to tell Mr. Van Doren we no longer engage in any of the techniques used during the Inquisition, your eminence," commented Gerald as he smiled, apparently amused at his own effort at humor while he nodded to the man, whom A.T. surmised was Gerald's superior and perhaps the Bishop himself.

"If we may, gentlemen, I would like to get us back to the topic at hand. Also, with the presumption that the committee will allow me, I would like to assure Mr. Van Doren we are not here to solicit information from him. We know without a doubt that, as I am sure Mr. Van Doren will soon realize, the GGG is without fault or blame of any kind and stands with a crystal clear record in terms of all U.S. laws," inserted the man at the lectern. He looked directly at A.T. and said, "We wanted to meet you because we have become fully aware of your investigation, as well as its details. Plus, we wanted to share some vital information about some of the individuals who make up the LESTER group. In fact, we would like to bring to your attention some critical information both you and your Senator friend will want to know about some of the people who are influencing the direction of LESTER." He scanned the individuals at the table and with a sweeping gesture of his hand, turned again to A.T. and said, "This group of people, known as the GGG, believe it is their civic duty to bring certain facts to your attention with the belief that these new facts being provided will aid you in the remainder of your investigation."

"That was my understanding and the reason why I am here," answered A.T. "Subsequent to the Senator's directive that I expand my investigation into matters beyond the Department of Justice, it was my impression this group, known as the GGG, was going to provide information that would assist me in connecting the various parties and aspects investigated. Those parties and aspects to which I am making reference would, at least from my perspective, include the following: foreign funding and bank accounts being used to illegally influence U.S. politics, a connection between various paramilitary groups operating within the country, large corporate financial interests, an entity that is supposedly a qualified tax exempt religious organization improperly funding political enterprise in the United States, illegal political contributions, sophisticated offers to elected officials that would constitute bribes in violation of the law due to the promises of future enrichment, and a direct connection between these various matters and a specified group of individuals the GGG would identify for me with the underlying proof of wrongdoing. That is what I understand. Am I correct?"

"You are," answered the man with the bulbous head next to the lectern. "But I am curious how you became so involved in a most intricate investigation that has brought you to our doorstep."

"The investigation I began over two years ago relative to certain irregularities at the Department of Justice and the FBI became known to several other individuals, including an investigative reporter friend of mine and a United States Senator with whom I had worked on a project years earlier. Those two individuals were aware of what I had been investigating. They both contacted me and advised me that the two of them had also been privy to certain information they believed had a connection to my investigation. After a visit with the two of them at the Senator's office, I was directed by the Senator to expand my investigation. That investigation led me in several different directions that initially did not seem to be connected. However, as the investigation progressed, I could see the connections. I then understood why the Senator wanted me to investigate those additional matters. It is apparent the people whom you have identified as members of a group called LESTER are the same people whom I have found to be at the core of the different segments of the investigation. When Samantha told me this GGG committee, which she identified as her benefactors, wanted to meet me, I contacted the Senator. He suggested I attend this meeting, so here I am."

"What do you hope to learn from us?" asked the Asian-looking man at the far end of the table.

"I don't know the answer to that," answered A.T. "Samantha told me the GGG had information that could tie the various segments of my investigation together with real evidence. That is why I am here."

"Yet, as I understand it, it is your belief the GGG is similar to LESTER and that the GGG might be somehow exposed in a criminal sense," continued the Asian-looking man.

"I didn't say that exactly," responded A.T. "However, I can't help but be a bit suspicious of any entity that operates secretly while it purports to somehow be helpful to the governing process of the United States."

"Have you any evidence of wrongdoing by the GGG?" asked the man next to the lectern.

"I can't say that I do," answered A.T. "However, such a matter is not for me to determine but for the Senator and his committee once all of the evidence is before them. What I do know, I cannot and will not reveal. I am not at liberty to do so. Again, permit me to suggest if you are interested in learning of such matters, you need to contact the Senator and discuss the matters with him."

"What do you know about LESTER?" asked the Asian-looking man at the end of the table.

"It wasn't until recently that I heard of the name LESTER," said A.T. "If the members of LESTER are the same people who seem to be at the apex of my investigation, I will need evidence. Perhaps that is why the Senator encouraged me to meet with you."

"I suspect it is," said the Asian-looking man. "As I understand our efforts for today, you will be given certain detailed information providing we are satisfied about two things."

"What are those two things?" asked A.T.

"First of all, we need to know you feel assured that LESTER is nothing like the GGG in any respect. Secondly, we want to address just how you are involved in this matter," insisted the man directly to the left of the lectern.

"Permit me to say I am doubtful you will be able to convince me today that the GGG and LESTER are indistinguishable from each other, unless you plan to provide documentation," said A.T.

"We will provide documentation," stated the Asian-looking man. "If I may, Mr. Chairman," he said while nodding to the man at the lectern. The man nodded affirmatively back. The Asian-looking man continued addressing A.T., "Today, we will provide all the documentation you need in order for you to serve as a special, closed courier so you may deliver the material, which is strictly confidential, directly to the Senator. However, first we will expect an explanation as to how you became so involved. Now, before you answer that, let me just say you will soon learn from the documents we provide that the GGG and its predecessors have done a great deal for this country since the time it was founded. You will also learn that LESTER and its supporters nearly caused the economic collapse of the United States government in the summer of 2011, later to a lesser degree in December of 2011 and even as recently as October of 2013 due to its misplaced philosophical stand on the debt ceiling, wage tax withholding amounts, and in general, the U.S. economy. What it and its members did, including those commonly called the 'tea party' in your country, was to nearly create a catastrophic economic collapse worldwide. The GGG worked feverishly to avoid such an event. Unfortunately, we were compelled to expose our position to several parties whom we would not normally address and ..."

"Although I know those events had a very serious impact upon the Chinese government, its relationship to the U.S., and your business interests in Hong Kong, Chang," interrupted the man to the left of the lectern, "do you feel any additional explanation is really necessary? Doesn't the report cover that issue as well as other matters?"

"It does," said the Asian-looking man at the far end of the table. "Perhaps I have said enough for now. We will let the report speak for itself. This may then be an appropriate time for Mr. Van Doren to provide an explanation of his involvement in the investigation."

"Yes, it is. Please provide some information about your involvement, Mr. Van Doren. It is a bit of a formality we require in order for the GGG to be fully comfortable before the materials for the Senator are imparted to you," urged the man at the lectern.

"It is a matter of my being wrongfully charged with an offense I did not commit," answered A.T. "After much consternation and once the facts became fully evident, including the fact my client and I had been victims, the matter was dismissed."

"Let me tell you what we know," said the man left of the lectern. "Although some of your suspicions might have traction, it is our belief the reason you were included was more directly due to the fact you are an attorney, a former prosecutor, and a former FBI agent. That kind of profile makes for good press coverage. The DOJ and the FBI under President George W. Bush, at the time you were charged, were simply looking for people with high profiles that would make media news."

He continued, "They were already loaded with exculpatory evidence exonerating you. They didn't need more. The GGG investigation also shows they felt all along they would be able to intimidate you into some kind of plea deal because you would be facing the unabridged power and financial strength of the federal government. You surprised them by fighting them; most people would have 'caved in'. You have provided some interesting reasons as to why you might have been targeted. However, it is our understanding it was simply a matter of your having the kind of credentials that would give the DOJ and the FBI good press. They had no regard for your reputation or your well-being. Perhaps you need to recognize that and get on with your life."

"No thanks," responded A.T. "I don't operate that way. If something is done wrong, I won't stop until those responsible are held accountable. Now, forgive me if I am being rude, but will you grant me the promised information?"

"In regard to the promised information, the answer is 'yes,'" inserted the man to the left of the lectern. "Except for your earlier attempt to leave, you have been attentive during these proceedings of ours, and we recognize some of what we do may seem a bit outdated or unusual. However, we are bound by some tradition in this group. You have provided an explanation that, based on their reports to us, matches what Samantha and Gerald have learned about you. We believe you are being truthful; however, we have to be sure that if we commit certain information to you, it will be delivered directly to the Senator and to no one else. That means you will agree to not copy the information we provide. Will you agree to such conditions if we entrust you with certain information?"

"If the conditions you set forth are that any information you provide be delivered directly to the Senator without copy, I can assure you I will do so," answered A.T. "However, I would like to at least be able to review the information so I may be satisfied it is appropriate for me to deliver. I will also want to be able to use any of the information that might be helpful to me in regard to my personal investigation."

"That is agreeable," responded the man sitting to the left of the lectern. "However, if you do find something in the materials helpful for your personal investigation, we would ask you agree to have access to such information only if the Senator agrees to provide that information to you. Is that acceptable?"

"It is," stated A.T., knowing if there were something in the materials that would aid him in regard to his case against the DOJ or the FBI, the Senator would willingly allow him to have it.

"Well, then," said the man at the lectern, "may I provide the information to Mr. Van Doren?"

"You may," answered the man next to the lectern. "First, however, you may want to instruct Mr. Van Doren as to how the information will be conveyed and how he will be required to deliver it."

"Exactly," responded the man at the lectern while holding up a USB thumb drive with a fabric lanyard attached to it. While holding the lanyard in A.T.'s direction, he said, "This thumb or flash drive contains the information promised. You will be permitted to review the contents while the GGG committee takes a recess in a few minutes. Once you have had the opportunity to review the contents and you are confident you will serve as a courier in taking this information to the Senator, we will reconvene."

"Wait," said the man with the dark hair sitting across from A.T. "You should tell him how this thumb drive is to be carried and delivered."

While many of the GGG participants chuckled, the man at the lectern cleared his throat and said, "Yes, Mr. Van Doren, you will need to agree to carry this item to the Senator in a unique way. Let me warn you the reason for it being carried for delivery in the fashion I am about to describe is simply because we want you to be constantly aware of the importance and urgency of its delivery directly to the Senator. More importantly, we want it to be delivered in a fashion that ensures it will not be detected by the majority of screening devices currently in use."

"All right," said A.T. looking suspiciously at the GGG committee. "How do you want me to transport it?"

"I will instruct you in a moment, but first you need to know there are coded passwords to memorize in order to have access to the information. Personally tell these passwords to the Senator and no one else. Is that understood?" asked the man at the lectern.

"It is understood," answered A.T.

"All right then," said the man at the lectern. "The first password that is case sensitive is: uppercase 'G,' lowercase 'd,' uppercase 'G,' lowercase 'q,' uppercase 'G,' lowercase 'h,' then the number '8,' followed by the number '5,' and then the number '3.' Don't worry about memorizing them now; I will give you another run at it before you leave. The second password is the Senator's last name followed by the number '8,' then the uppercase letter 'Y,' followed by the lowercase letter 'u,' then number '9.' Before you leave, I will again provide these codes. Is that acceptable?"

"It is," answered A.T. "I believe I already have a good idea of both passwords and think I have already memorized them. When it comes to numbers or letters, I have been blessed with near photographic memory. It doesn't always work for me, but in this case, it was easy."

"Very good," remarked the man at the lectern. "We'll see later just how good that memory is. Now, let me tell you just how you will carry this thumb drive. The lanyard is large enough and adjustable so it can fit around your waist. You will wear it under your undershorts and will conceal the thumb drive in and under your private parts. You will need to be wearing it before you are permitted to leave. To be sure you are wearing it appropriately, Gerald will accompany you to the men's facility when you are ready to appropriately conceal it."

"Really! I never expected such a request. I don't understand why I just can't place it in my pocket, especially since it requires two codes to access," commented A.T. "This is something I will need to think about. If you don't mind my saying so, this is one of the strangest, no, correct that, this IS the strangest request anyone has ever made of me."

"Sorry," said the man at the lectern, "but we must insist it be done this way in order to assure the device will not be detected by anyone or anything. It may seem embarrassing and out of the ordinary, but we must insist for security reasons. We don't even want the risk of the wrong people seeing the contents. In fact, we don't want anyone other than the Senator seeing the contents, with the exception of your review of it here today. I hope you will understand our special request in this regard."

"It is absurd, but subject to what I see when I am permitted to access the thumb drive, I will reserve my decision, if you don't mind," answered A.T.

"All right, the committee will adjourn while you are permitted to view the contents," said the man at the lectern presenting the device to A.T. When A.T. gave him a skeptical look, the man said, "Don't worry, no one else has worn it, and it is clean. You can handle the device. Here it is. You may have access to the computer in front of you while the committee is at recess. If you can remember the passwords, you may begin your review."

While the committee members were adjourned, A.T. took the device and connected it to the computer in front of him. He had no trouble remembering the passwords when he opened the drive. In reviewing the contents, he was astounded at the detail of the investigation Samantha had done in regard to the group known as LESTER.

Included in her reports were documents that demonstrated an orchestrated tie between specific financial interests, a large paramilitary group, several large industrialists, a large marketing group, and organizations that involved "tea party" members throughout the country. It was also apparent LESTER had arranged for beneficial positions in various committees and parts of industry for people who had previously served as public officials at nearly every level of government. There were even attachments of letters, emails, and recorded conversations where promises of a "comfortable" or "well-upholstered" chair would be waiting for certain politicians once they left office.

The evidence demonstrated LESTER and its affiliates had positioned a large number of individuals at the DOJ and even within the FBI, with the specific names of particular individuals being mentioned. Samantha's investigation revealed how LESTER and its affiliates were preparing for the future use of violence and private militias in the event of public discord. There was ample evidence showing how foreign financial interests from both Europe and South America were tied to LESTER and its activities. Many foreign bank accounts of LESTER and its affiliates were identified, and it appeared to A.T. that the handiwork of Professor Brougham was involved in revealing these accounts.

A.T. was overwhelmed with what he was seeing on the thumb drive. He thought even if a fraction of the contents were true, the Senator would be more than interested. There was no doubt if the contents were true, it would add some final touches to the Senator's investigation, and specific individuals who held government positions, both elected and appointed, would be exposed. Based upon what A.T. saw, it was evident Samantha was going to be a critical witness for the Senator. She even mentioned in her included report that she had been intimidated by "Big John" and "Squeaky," who were documented to be independent contractors. From the reports he saw, it appeared as though the two of them operated well beyond the realm of the directives they had received from LESTER. After taking nearly two hours to review the material, A.T. came away with the impression Samantha Nguyen-Henderson was one hell of an investigator. There was no doubt about it; she was good. Not only was her investigation revealing, it was also well-documented and extremely detailed.

After completing his review of the materials and research, A.T. told Gerald who was standing nearby as a sentry that he was satisfied with the material, and he would agree to take the material back to the Senator.

A.T. could feel the rush of excitement in knowing that he was about to be entrusted with some earth-shattering information that would peel the shell off the LESTER organization and most of its affiliates. He was pleased to note there were specific individuals and organizations identified. He couldn't believe how integrated certain financially powerful individuals had expanded their reach into offices within the United States government, including the Department of Justice, the FBI, and the judiciary, along with particular paramilitary groups, political action committees, the Republican Party, and other wealthy individuals. Just seeing how well-organized and influential LESTER had become was frightening. Critical evidence relating to the "well-upholstered" chairs was the sort of material the Senator could get his teeth into, and it would be difficult for his committee members, regardless of their party affiliation, to ignore. Specific cases of bribery were documented in a detailed fashion from what A.T. was seeing on the thumb drive device. Now more than ever, he could understand the suspicions of the Senator, and he could see why the Senator wanted the investigation expanded into realms A.T. had dismissed as senseless diversions from his original investigation.

A.T. removed the thumb drive and handed it to Gerald. He told Gerald he had finished his review, and he would agree to transfer the device and its contents to the Senator with the understanding the GGG would provide the necessary witnesses, including Samantha, Gerald, Professor Brougham, and others who had been identified on the device. Gerald told A.T. he would assemble the GGG members.

The GGG was reconvened with all the individuals reclaiming their respective seats or monitors. The younger man immediately went back to the lectern and asked for A.T. to either affirm he would take an oath to securely deliver the flash drive to the Senator under the terms outlined or relinquish the item back to the speaker. A.T. explained he would agree to deliver the flash drive personally to the Senator, and he would agree to the manner of delivery explained earlier; however, it would not be in the form of any oath. The GGG indicated A.T.'s word would be sufficient. While the GGG remained in session, A.T. went with Gerald to the men's room in order to secure the item as previously detailed. Although the placement of the flash drive was uncomfortable, it was tolerable enough for him to walk with a fairly normal gait. It was amazing how it was designed to fit in a manner that seemed to become a part of his underwear. It was his guess the GGG had delivered items in such a manner on other occasions and knew it was extremely unlikely such inert items would be detected even through full body scans.

Upon their return to the GGG conference room, A.T. was given final instructions and informed Samantha would remain with him as an escort on a late flight to Washington that had already been booked for the two of them. As a precautionary matter, A.T. was asked to stand in the elevator for a body scan before he and Samantha were permitted to leave the building. After the final scan and after being brought back before the GGG for final instructions, A.T. and Samantha were dismissed. The GGG continued with its meeting, presumably to discuss other matters.

Gerald returned all their personal items and escorted Samantha and A.T. back to the elevator where they were joined by the muscular young man whom Samantha had earlier instructed to remain on the upper floor. At that point, the young man, Gerald, Samantha, and A.T. took the elevator back up to the original floor that appeared to be under construction. On the way up in the elevator, Gerald handed A.T. a package containing flight confirmation and instructions. After arriving on the upper floor, the four of them then walked to the main elevator bank. The young man and Gerald remained on that floor, while Samantha and A.T. took one of the main elevators down to the lobby where they had entered earlier in the day.

A.T. and Samantha left the elevator and walked toward the revolving doors to the street. A.T. felt somewhat relieved. It was the beginning of the afternoon rush hour, and although there were people coming and going in every conceivable direction, the two of them hardly noticed the noise, the people, or the traffic. Although they each had top coats, neither of them had dressed for the unexpected cold or the newly falling snow. They began walking back several blocks toward the restaurant where they had met earlier and were oblivious to the daily routine of pandemonium around them.

* *

When they neared the restaurant, A.T. suggested that they warm themselves with a cup of coffee. Samantha agreed but insisted instead upon a hot chocolate or two. After being seated in a booth, they placed a food order since neither of them had eaten since breakfast. Then A.T. excused himself for a restroom break. In the restroom, he made sure there was no one else present. He took out his iPhone and called his friend, Rick Helms. He informed Rick that he had been in a meeting of a sensitive nature, and he would be on a late flight back to Washington D.C. Unfortunately, he would not be able to meet with Rick on this particular trip but would try to be in touch with him the next time he came to New York. Former agent Helms gave A.T. his private cell number and told A.T. to call him on that number the next time he was in town.

A.T. made sure the flash drive was in place and checked to see whether the video device was still in place. He was pleased to see that the device that Adam had engineered for his suit coat was in place and operational. It was a relief to know no one at the GGG had attempted to tamper with it. A.T. returned to the table to find Samantha waiting, along with the food that had been delivered.

"I thought we were supposed to get new travel arrangements from the GGG before we left," said Samantha. "Did Gerald give you the information?"

"Yes," answered A.T. "He gave me copies of the e-tickets just as we were on the elevator from the sub-basement to the upper floor. Here, let me give you your copy just in case we get separated."

"Oh, we won't get separated," commented Samantha. "My job is to see that you get safely back to D.C. It does ruin my plans since I had expected to have you to myself this evening."

"What do you mean by that?" asked A.T. while placing his empty cup back onto its saucer.

"I guess you must be feeling like your guard is a bit down while you are in my presence."

"Don't be silly, I –" A.T. started to say as he noticed that the waiter approaching their booth was losing control of the small glass coffee urn he was carrying. The urn broke and shattered right next to the table with glass particles and coffee flying in every direction. Both Samantha and A.T. ducked, and the waiter threw up his hands and began to apologize.

Since both Samantha and A.T. had reacted as they did, and moved to regain their upright positions in the booth, Samantha rose slightly and looked around the restaurant in a rather crouched posture. When she did not observe anyone other than the waiter and seemed satisfied there was no danger, she sat back down and said first to the waiter, then to A.T., "Sorry to have overreacted, but after - ; I seem to have gotten a bit jumpy."

The waiter apologized again. A.T., who was also looking around the restaurant, said to the waiter who had started to clean up the mess, "It's really okay. I've never seen an urn shatter like that before." Once the waiter was out of earshot, A.T. said, "I'm the one who should be jumpy since I'm the one carrying the flash drive. Should we be concerned?"

"I don't think so," exclaimed Samantha. "The shattered urn sounded like a gunshot to me, so I overreacted. I'm sorry, but it is my job to get you back to Washington in a safe and sound condition. Since the GGG views your immediate return to Washington D.C. as a matter of the highest importance and because I'm responsible for you, I may be a bit over-sensitive."

"Perhaps we need to pay our tab and get back over to the Yale Club to check out since we must fly out yet today," commented A.T.

At that point, A.T. quickly got into his coat. Then he carefully removed Samantha's coat from the hook at the booth and helped her put it on. He could sense she was still shaking. A.T. carefully stepped over the shattered mess that the waiter was continuing to clear. He then aided Samantha in a maneuver around the debris on the floor. The two of them proceeded to the counter where A.T. paid the bill.

Once outside, he stopped a moment to look at Samantha, who still seemed a bit shaken. He asked, "Are you all right? Are you sensing something went wrong at the GGG meeting?" asked A.T.

"No," said Samantha. "The meeting went well, as far as I could tell. In fact, I thought it went quite well. I just don't know -"

"Is there anything I can do?" asked A.T.

"I don't think so," said Samantha while situating her black Russian-styled fur-trimmed hat over the top of her head. "Let's just head back to the Yale Club and get our things, okay."

"Sure," said A.T. The two of them began to walk toward the club.

CHAPTER 28
THE SHATTERED URN

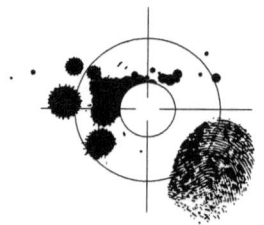

Walking toward the Yale Club, they noticed that the newly-fallen snow made each step a bit tricky. Samantha placed her arm through A.T.'s and drew herself close, presumably to stabilize herself, while they moved with the flow of the other pedestrians. For a full block they walked without any discussion, until they came to a stoplight and waited for the "walk" signal. Samantha asked, "You don't think I'm crazy, do you?"

"Do you want an honest answer?" laughed A.T. "I have to admit I have thought exactly that on several occasions, and it certainly didn't help having to sit through that bizarre ceremony we just experienced."

"That's not what I had hoped to hear from you. I had hoped by now you would have felt comfortable around me, and I thought you would at least trust me," said Sam pulling herself closer to A.T.

"This may sound ridiculous," said A.T., "however, I believe I am starting to feel somewhat comfortable around you, and that's in spite of today's weird events. I guess I do feel I could trust you to some degree. I'm not exactly sure why. Perhaps that's a mistake I am making. In actuality, I should have never agreed to be a courier for you and the GGG, but since I have, I must confess at least in some strange way, I have learned to trust you. Is that what you wanted to hear?"

"Not exactly, but, I guess that will do," commented Sam lowering her head and pressing hard against him. While the snow continued to fall on her hat and face, she looked up at him, blinking through the flakes and said, "You know, I have always been strong and almost exclusively self-reliant. I think it was because my father was so strong, and I always idolized him. Maybe that's why people don't feel close to me, and maybe that's why people have trouble trusting me. Maybe I'm too strong a person."

"That's not it, Sam," said A.T. "It's what you do for a living. There is no doubt in my mind that your work is at the core of the feeling you have about others trusting you. You have to admit that in your line of work, assuming what I know is factual, people are not inclined to trust you, and you are no more inclined to trust them. I believe that is the nature of the work you seem to enjoy while you travel the world as an agent for either the GGG or whoever else might hire you. You must have realized that at some point in time before today."

"No, I don't think before today I even thought about it. Maybe I need to do something different with my life," commented Sam. "Sometimes I question whether I've made the right decisions. Perhaps I'm a bit weary."

"You probably just need some rest," noted A.T. "Even though the flight back to Washington is not that long, it's possible for you to get some rest on the plane. Plus, once we are back at the W Hotel, you can go to your room and get a good rest."

"But I don't feel like I want to rest," insisted Sam, who abruptly changed the subject and asked, "Have you ever thought about how different your life would have been if you had made other choices?"

"Everyone has moments when they have those thoughts. You're no different, Sam. It's natural. I can't imagine anyone who hasn't wondered about the choices he or she has made in life. Making the choices we do at the time we make them is what makes us who we are," said A.T. Once they were again able to move forward, A.T. was bumped by several other pedestrians. He felt the New York pedestrians were annoyed that he had not moved forward to cross the street fast enough. Of course, they had a point since he had been looking long and hard at Samantha. The two of them had gotten to know each other fairly well over the past few months.

Her new behavior seemed out of the ordinary. At least by now he felt Samantha was not a participant in any "fringe" group as he had originally believed. Nevertheless, there were times like the one they had just experienced when he wondered if she were more aware or involved in matters that had not been disclosed to him.

He wanted so badly to trust her. The simple truth was that he had started to feel sorry for her. Perhaps she had grown on him. He knew that the feelings he had for her were those of a friend and not of any romantic nature. However, the fact he was beginning to care about her was a dilemma that made him uncomfortable. The two of them seemed to be getting to the point where they were beginning to sense what the other was thinking before the other would speak or act. That too was an uncomfortable feeling for A.T. This was one of those moments. They had stopped to wait for another "walk" signal when she broke her grasp and moved ahead of him.

She stood directly in front of him, looked up at him, and placed one hand on each of his shoulders. The snow continued to fall sticking to her hair, hat, and eyelashes. She stared directly into his eyes and said, "Damn it, A.T.! I am a good person, and I have been trying to do the right thing. If I weren't convinced that the GGG was doing the right thing, I would tell you. That's why I asked about trusting me. Haven't I been helping you all these past months? Haven't I placed myself at risk by simply helping you? Haven't I given you names, dates, places, accounts, and other details? What do you want me to do to prove I am acting properly? I've been foolish enough to offer my friendship to you so many times I can't count them. I just don't know what more you want from me."

At that moment, several people seemed to bump into them at once with one of them shouting, "Get off the sidewalk; you're stopping everyone, you know. Don't be so damn rude!"

"I'm sorry," said A.T. to those around them, while grabbing Sam's arm to escort her across the street. He looked at Sam and said, "I'm sorry, Sam, but sticking exclusively to business, let me tell you I had some serious apprehension about meeting with the GGG. After seeing the upper floor empty, and then having to go to a subterranean conference room and being exposed to a strange environment, strange people, and even stranger procedures, you have to admit I have had good reason to be paranoid. When I get paranoid about something, it is hard for me to trust people. So, let me tell you that I feel I've been as trusting as I can possibly be in regard to my relationship with you. I believe that says a lot about your character, and that is why I do feel I can trust you in spite of what you do and what I've seen. I hope that explains my feelings well enough to you."

"If you are still paranoid, I hope it's not because of me," she said.

He lied and said, "No, it's not about you."

"Fine! Then let's get back to the Yale Club where it is warm. When we get there, I would like to go up to the restaurant on the 22nd floor and have something warm to drink. We can talk there, and then we can pack for the airport," urged Sam.

"Okay. When we get back, I'll get you more hot chocolate," said A.T. "And let's remember to keep our relationship completely professional."

At that point, an unknown gentleman who had been walking alongside the two of them, apparently couldn't contain himself any longer, smiled, and said, "By all means, keep it professional and pay this attractive lady."

Not missing a beat, Sam said to the strange man, "Why thank you for looking out for me, sir. However, my friend here has been such a good customer for all of these years, I just thought I would be his without charge from here on. What do you think?"

The man turned to A.T. and said, "Go for it, man. She's a doll!"

Sam looked at A.T., who was shaking his head, and she jokingly said, "Why do you suppose he said that?"

"You didn't need to say what you did," answered A.T. "You're obviously tired and not making any sense," said A.T. as he tried to quicken their pace across another street.

They were partly through the crosswalk of the intersection when the light was just changing, with the pedestrian light indicating the number of seconds left for them to cross. When Samantha stepped ahead of A.T. in the crosswalk, urging him along, a van turned sharply in front of them, appearing to run the light from the opposite direction. A.T. instinctively reached out across Samantha's body to stop her. Fortunately, the van slid, and A.T. was able to keep Samantha from stepping in front of it.

"Oh! You're my hero!" proclaimed Samantha.

"Stop it, Sam! I was lucky to see the van in the first place."

"You were like a guardian angel just then."

"No. Our guardian angels were, and have been, working overtime as it is," said A.T. attempting to steer the conversation.

"You know, I never told you this, but that was my code name with the GGG. I was called 'the guardian angel,' considering that on several occasions, I was able to prevent some disastrous results because I found flaws in various plans to be set in motion."

"If anyone would find a flaw in their operations, it would be you since you seem to be detail-oriented… at least when it comes to matters that do not involve the heart."

"So, you do think I am better than…Wait, what do you mean matters that do not involve the heart? I can prove to you how worthy I am in that regard. Soon, I expect to prove that to you."

"No. There will not be any more discussions on that topic. I guess I was thinking about you and your Congressman friend. Forgive me for that."

"I don't know if I can. We'll see."

Continuing to cross the street, A.T. said, "So, they called you 'the guardian angel?'"

She grabbed his bicep with both hands, moving close to him so that as they walked across the street, they moved as if they were a single person. She then answered, "Yes. That was my signal. Some called me 'the guardian' and others called me 'the angel.' I didn't object because I really liked both monikers. There is more I can and will tell you but not tonight -"

At that moment, A.T. started to stumble, and for whatever reason, he started to see flashing in his eyes. It was probably the excitement of the near miss by the van. Sometimes when he was under extreme stress or had been researching for a long while, he would see flashing in his eyes. His ophthalmologist had told him when that happened, he was having a migraine. He never actually had any headaches to go with the flashing; nevertheless, he took the good doctor at his word. It must have been a migraine he was experiencing.

Now there was something more than just the flashing. A deafening crack followed by a whoosh of air and the inhaling of a rasping breath brought A.T. to attention. Samantha jerked his arm. Startled, he turned to face her, her penetrating gaze and furrowed brow before him. A deep grey spot inches above the bridge of her nose transfixed A.T. Blood began streaming from the wound. The upper part of her forehead was distorted. She was collapsing onto A.T.'s side while he fell to the street with her. This couldn't be happening! Everything seemed to be moving in slow motion.

A.T. exclaimed, "My dear God! What just happened? Sam! Sam! Are you… What have they done? Help! Will somebody please help?"

A.T. and Samantha were both on the ground; and now A.T. felt the throbbing in his head. This time, he did have a headache to go with the flashing in his eyes. Samantha gasped again for a breath and fell still. Her eyes stared straight ahead with no sign of life. A.T. closed her eyes and then tried to position her as comfortably as he thought possible. Although in a dazed condition, he tried to stand up. No one seemed to be interested, and no one offered to help.

People continued to walk by. The traffic just kept moving and honking as if it were just another day in New York City. Finally, a well-dressed man in a business suit and a lady who claimed to be a nurse bent down to help. Soon, there were two men dressed in white paramedic coats. A.T. noticed they were dressed casually under the white coats. Where did they come from? Somehow, they seemed familiar.

He managed to ask them what they were doing. They said they had brought an emergency vehicle. A. T. thought to himself: *An emergency vehicle? How would they know? Sam was in no condition to… It was too late.* Another man started to protect them from the traffic.

A.T. was having trouble getting up. The flashing in his eyes seemed to be getting worse. He looked at the people helping and wondered how an ambulance had come so fast. He was sure that he recognized the two men, one large and one short. He wondered: *What the hell are the two of you doing here?* A. T. was not sure whether he was speaking aloud or just thinking to himself. It didn't matter because he passed out when they began to move him from the street to the ambulance.

* *

Positioned on a bed near a window, a groggy A.T. squinted at the bright lights and the white walls. The man in the bed to his right was visiting with a man in a suit who was sitting on a chair next to the bed. The two of them were discussing documents that the man in the chair was placing back into a briefcase. The pastel pictures above the dresser opposite the two beds offered the only color in what A.T. surmised was a hospital room. To the left of the bed where A.T. was lying, a bald man seemed to be adjusting the window drapes. The man looked familiar to A.T.

A.T. was certain the man was the same person whom he had seen weeks ago in the BMW on I-5 in California. The man started to smile at A.T. then abruptly looked at the door where another man, who appeared to be a doctor, looked into the room and inquired, "Who are you, and what are you doing here?"

"I'm new on staff here and –" the bald man started to say when the incoming doctor cut him off.

The doctor said, "Oh, no, you're not. I am the head psychiatrist on this floor, and I don't know you. Get out here in the hall, and come to the nurse's station with me immediately."

"You go on ahead," said the bald man standing at the window, "I've got some business to finish with my patient and -"

"No," insisted the man, who had identified himself as the head psychiatrist. "You will come with me now." He then looked at A.T. and inquired, "Who are you, and what are you doing in this room? Never mind. Just stay right there, and I will deal with you when I return." The psychiatrist in the doorway looked at the bald man and again ordered him to come out.

At that point, the man with the dark suit who was sitting on the chair next to the bed near the door rose and motioned to the man in the bed next to A.T. and said, "Let's go down to the lounge, Frederick. It seems as though these folks have other business that doesn't pertain to us. We can discuss the matters that you need to sign in the lounge."

"That's all right with me," laughed the man who was sitting on the other bed. At that point, he rose and left with the man who had been sitting in the chair. The psychiatrist allowed the two of them to pass, and motioned for the bald man to come with him.

After everyone had left, A.T. got out of bed and noticed he was still clothed in his shirt, pants, and socks. His belt and tie were gone. His slip-on shoes were at the foot of the dresser, and his suit coat had been neatly placed on the top of the dresser.

It seemed likely the man who had been in the bed next to his was a patient who had been visiting with his attorney before the two of them left. A.T. noticed a briefcase had been left on the bed next to him.

Once they had left, A.T. started to move toward his coat and realized he would have to move slowly because he was continuing to experience the headache that had begun earlier. Sitting on the edge of his bed, he reached across to the other bed and pulled the briefcase close to him. Examining the contents, he was convinced that the man who had been in the chair was the attorney for the man in the other bed. The paperwork in the briefcase confirmed his suspicions. The paperwork was for a voluntary committal for the man in the next bed. A.T. recognized the paperwork as he had often seen similar pleadings during his practice of law in the Twin Cities.

Aware that his senses were coming back, A.T. cautiously began to stand. He reached in his shirt pocket where he normally kept his phone, but it was gone. He patted down the pockets of his pants and found they were empty; his shirt was no longer tucked into his pants. The pockets of his pants were actually inside out, and his wallet, keys, change, and cell phone had all been taken. The pen he kept in his shirt pocket was gone, along with the napkin on which Samantha had written her phone number. He noticed his topcoat near the dresser in the room, and it looked as if someone had rifled through it.

While he tucked in his shirt, he felt a discomfort near his private parts. He then realized that the device the GGG had given him was still in place. Obviously, the GGG knew what they were doing in demanding the method of transporting the flash drive. While making a final adjustment to his shirt and pants, he felt grateful the flash drive and its contents had not been discovered.

He walked over to the dresser and slipped on his shoes. He grabbed his suit coat, which he immediately put on. Noticing the lapel pin camera was still in place, A.T. hoped the implanted video system had been working from the time he left the GGG meeting. However, he would have no way of knowing until he got out of this psychiatric ward and back to the Yale Club. He needed to call the police and report what had happened. It was imperative that he stay calm and think of a plan to get out.

Before A.T. went into the hallway, he picked up and partially shut but did not latch the briefcase that had been left on the other bed.

Since A.T. had his suit coat on, he buttoned it so the absence of a belt could not be noticed. Once he had the briefcase in hand, he slowly walked through the doorway. He looked up the hallway and noticed the psychiatrist and the bald man, along with a security officer, were having a discussion at the nurse's desk.

The discussion seemed animated, so A.T. continued to observe while standing by the door to the room in which he had found himself. He tried to listen to the conversation, but the fact that he still had a headache prevented him from hearing exactly what was said. After a couple of minutes, he watched while the apparent psychiatrist and the security guard escorted the bald man out the door near the nurse's station. He also heard the buzzing sound of the door release when the three men left the nurse's station to the corridor on the outside.

After waiting another minute, A.T. approached the nurse's station. A male nurse on the other side of the desk asked A.T., "Just where do you think you are going?"

"I'm leaving," responded A.T. "The work for my client is finished. I will need to get back to my office. My client needed to review some consent documents, but we have to make some changes, so I will need to get these revisions over to my office and then come back to -"

"What?" asked the male nurse. "Aren't you the patient they brought in last night?"

"No," exclaimed A.T. "I'm the attorney who came in earlier to -"

At that point, an older male nurse came up and asked, "What's going on here?"

The younger male nurse at the desk said, "He wants to leave, and I'm trying to tell him patients are not permitted to leave without the doctor's consent or without a court order. He claims to be an attorney and -"

The older male nurse then said, "I am the one who let the attorney for Mr. Wells in earlier. With the disturbance we just encountered, security is now with the doctor, and I don't need another problem on this floor. I especially don't want more problems from an attorney. Let's see, I -"

Before anyone else could say anything, A.T. set the briefcase on the nurse's counter and removed the paperwork inside, and said, "Here, let me show you the paperwork I was discussing with Mr. Wells. For example, here is the Amended Petition for Voluntary Submission and -"

"Go ahead and put your papers away," said the older nurse. "I'm sorry for any inconvenience. We're all a bit jumpy, especially since we just had someone who got in here claiming to be a member of the staff. None of us had ever seen that guy before."

A.T. cut him off, and in a most indignant voice, he said, "You had me concerned there for a minute. I was worried that you were going to keep me in here, and I would miss a court appearance later this afternoon. Now, if you will please let me pass." At that, the door release buzzed, and A.T. closed the briefcase and walked out of the ward. He felt fortunate that the bluff worked. He was lucky the attorney who had been in the room earlier had been wearing a suit similar to his own.

In the hospital corridor, A.T. tried to walk as steadily and quickly as he could in order to convey a purposeful gait. The headache was still there, but it wasn't as bad as it had been. The corridor was empty, and he could see that at the far end, there was another nurse's station. He thought: *So far, so good. I need to take my time, so I don't appear to be in too big a hurry. I've got to find an elevator bank and locate an exit. Once I'm out of here, I need to find out where I am and get focused.* The events on the street came back to him while he walked down the hallway. He wondered: *Could this all really be happening? Why am I here? Did I really see what happened to Sam? Was she really shot? What happened to her? Why? Who?*

Progressing down the hall, he noticed most of the offices on either side were empty and closed. There was very little activity anywhere. On the wall clock straight ahead, the time was 8:43. He inferred it must be 8:43 in the morning. It was his guess he had been brought to the hospital sometime overnight since it was late afternoon when he and Samantha left to collect their belongings for the scheduled flight to Washington. That was one flight that was long gone.

About halfway down the hall to the nurse's station, he saw an off-setting hallway. Once at the intersection of the two hallways, he peered around the corner and saw an elevator bank. After he got to the elevator, he pushed the "down" button and waited. Soon an elevator stopped, and he noted it was going down. Fortunately, there was no one on the elevator. Since he had represented clients who had been in mental wards, he knew if he had been in a hospital ward for dangerous patients, he would have been in hospital apparel rather than his own suit. At least he was grateful for that. He was even more grateful for the set of circumstances that allowed for an attorney to be in conference with a patient next to him.

Once he reached the lower level that indicated "lobby," he left the elevator and noted how busy the hospital was. There were doctors, nurses, patients, visitors, and service personnel everywhere he looked. He saw a sign to his right where the elevators exited into a junction of hallways. One sign at a "T" intersection indicated the lobby was to the left and emergency was to the right. He needed to decide whether he should simply walk out through the lobby or try to locate Samantha. He needed to find out what they had done with her. Plus, he needed to make some calls. No doubt that would be difficult because he no longer had his cell phone nor did he have funds for a pay phone.

First things first. He went to the reception desk at the center of the lobby and placed the briefcase on the counter and waited while one of the receptionists finished giving directions to an elderly couple who were attempting to locate the room of a relative. When a receptionist looked in his direction, A.T. said, "Miss, I found this briefcase. Surely, someone will be missing it, and I was wondering if I might leave it with you?"

"Sir, there is a 'lost and found' office down the first hallway on the opposite side of the lobby."

"I really don't have time to deliver it to them. Would you be able to find someone to take it there?" asked A.T. "I am here following up on an emergency. Where would I go to check on an admission arriving at the emergency room?"

"Since it's an emergency," said the young receptionist, "leave the briefcase on the counter. I will need to have security check it before they take it to the 'lost and found.' Now, what is the name of the patient whom you are seeking regarding the emergency?"

A.T. was silent for a moment, then said, "Thank you. I'm sure the owner of the briefcase will appreciate that. The person who I am trying to find should have been brought to the emergency room."

"I understand that, sir," said the receptionist. "I will need the person's name."

"Oh, excuse me," responded A.T. "Her name is Samantha Nguyen-Henderson. The last name is H-e-n-d-e-r-s-o-n. She has an 'o' and not an 'e' at the end of her name."

After scanning the hospital's directory, the receptionist said, "I don't see anyone by that name listed. Perhaps she may not yet have been booked by the emergency staff. If you will just go back the way you came and follow the hallway to its end instead of turning at the elevator bank, you should end up directly in the emergency room area. You might inquire with them."

"Thank you," said A.T. turning and heading directly toward the emergency area. Although he had planned to leave by the front door, he decided that it would look odd if he did not follow the directions that the receptionist had provided. Walking away, he could hear the receptionist call security with a request that they come for the briefcase. A.T. knew that he would need to move as swiftly as possible because he didn't need to be questioned by some security guard until he was sure of where he was and what exactly was happening.

Continuing to walk down the hallway, he encountered an office labeled "Security." A man in plain clothes with a "security" label on his coat pocket was coming out of the office just as A.T. was passing by the door to the room. From a glimpse inside the room, A.T. noticed a number of people questioning someone who could not be seen from the hall. The man who was leaving the security office nodded to A.T., who then asked if he was heading the right way for "emergency." The man said yes and pointed to the end of the hall at the opposite end from the reception area. A.T. couldn't very well go into the security office, so he thought he would see if there was another room where he could momentarily disappear.

At the next intersection, there was a hallway that seemed to end with a single door. He thought it might be locked, so he decided to continue down the hall in front of him. A few doors down toward the emergency area, A.T. spotted a room labeled "Building Maintenance." He thought maybe he could begin a conversation with anyone within the custodial office under the excuse of complaining about the condition of a hospital room on an upper floor. Perhaps that would buy him some time.

Upon entering the "Building Maintenance" office, he noticed it was empty. There was no one at the main desk. He called out, but no one responded. He noticed a phone on the desk and a number of boxes, presumably with supplies. With all that had happened, A.T. needed to get word out to the Senator and others. Since he was without his phone, and there was an open phone on the desk in front of him, this was his chance to call the Senator, Allen, and Rick Helms. He needed to let them know about what had happened to Samantha and him.

Given the fact he had no identifying material on his person, the sooner he could get some help, the better. First, he tried the Senator's private number. There was no answer at the Senator's private number; however, A.T. did not want to leave a message.

Next, he tried Allen's number, but all he got was Allen's voicemail. Thankfully, A.T, remembered Rick's cell number.

"Hello," Rick answered.

"Hello, Rick. This is A.T. "Can you talk? I need your help."

"Yes, what's up," asked Rick? "I didn't expect to hear from you until your next trip into the 'Big Apple.' I'd be happy to help. What's wrong?"

"Unfortunately, I was forced to stay over. There has been an emergency, and I have found myself in the middle of it," answered A.T.

"What kind of emergency?" asked Rick.

"Someone I had been with has been shot and apparently, I've been mugged because I don't have any identification left on me," said A.T.

"Are you all right?" asked Rick.

"Yes, I'm fine," answered A.T. "However, I need some help getting around. I will need some transportation. Can you help me?"

"Sure," said Rick. "Did you see who mugged you? Are you still in Manhattan? The other day when you called, I thought you were in Manhattan. Do you need medical help? Is anyone around who can help? Tell me if there is anything I can do before I head out to find you. By the way, where are you, exactly? You've called the police, right? They should be able to help. Where are you? I'll head on over," inquired Rick.

"I'm in a hospital. I'm not sure which hospital. Let me see..." said A.T. while he looked around the room for some idea of his location and the hospital name. He again noticed the boxes on the desk. He saw the address on the boxes and said, "I believe I am in St. Joseph's Regional Hospital in Patterson, New Jersey. I think that's correct."

"You mean, you don't know?" asked Rick.

"I'm pretty sure this is St. Joseph's Hospital from what I'm seeing. I was unconscious for a while, so I didn't know where I was, but I'm pretty sure that is where I am," said A.T.

"How in the world did you get there?" asked Rick. "Never mind; I'll find out when I get there. I'm not really that far from you. If you're at St. Joseph's, I can get there in about twenty to twenty-five minutes, if the traffic is decent. Meanwhile, I trust you are talking to the doctors and police. Can you tell me your room?"

At that moment, A.T. heard someone coming in the door. He said into the phone, "Rick, please get here as soon as you can. Thanks."

He hung up the phone while the man entering the "Maintenance Office" stood in the doorway with a stunned look on his face.

The man at the door, dressed in business casual, asked, "What are you doing in here? Where is Jeanette? What are you doing at that desk?" The man stepped forward and ran into a cylindrical-shaped dumpster. The man again asked A.T., "What are you doing in here, and who gave you permission to use our phone?"

"Sorry," said A.T. "I was looking for someone in order to file a complaint about the room my cousin is in on the third floor. Would you be the proper person who can address my complaint?"

"If you have a complaint, you need to file it at the nurse's station on, what did you say, the third floor? We can go up there together, but first, where is Jeanette?" asked the man.

"I don't know who Jeanette is," answered A.T. "No one was here when I came in. I called out to see if anyone would answer, but no one did, so -"

"So, you decided to use our phone," noted the man. "I certainly hope you weren't making any long distance calls."

"No, I didn't make any long distance calls. At least, I don't think the call was long distance," insisted A.T., although he couldn't remember whether the call to Rick Helms was long distance. At that point, a woman, approximately forty years of age, came through the door directly behind the man talking to A.T. The man turned to her, and in the process, moved the mobile dumpster out of her way. The dumpster rolled closer to A.T., who suddenly thought he smelled something quite familiar. He sniffed the air, and noticed the familiar odor was coming from the dumpster.

"Where were you, Jeanette?" asked the man while A.T. began examining the contents of the dumpster.

"Sorry, Mr. Jensen, but I needed a restroom break, and no one else was here," said Jeanette. "Both Rob and Tommy went next door to 'Security' to help out. Apparently, there was a man impersonating a doctor up on the psych ward, and security needed some help. I think that…"

"Wait a minute! Did you say something about a man impersonating a doctor? I might be able to help –" A.T. started to say as he continued to look and smell into the dumpster and stopped dead in his tracks. In the dumpster he saw only some plastic and a black fuzzy-looking object. He reached down and pulled the plastic back revealing a hat. He pulled out a woman's black Russian-styled hat that gave off the same scent as the perfume Samantha wore.

While A.T. continued to smell the object, the man named Mr. Jensen asked, "What in the hell are you doing with that garbage? Who are you, and why are you in here?"

"I recognize this hat," said A.T. "I know it may seem strange, but I think this hat might belong to the lady I was with when -"

"That's garbage that we discharge in the big dumpsters and large incinerators out back. Put that back! Apparently, one of the guys didn't get this completely emptied," said Mr. Jensen. "If that hat belonged to your lady friend, it is my guess she 'tossed it,' or it wouldn't be in the garbage."

"I seriously don't think so," said A.T. "We need to find out what happened to the lady -"

"I have no idea where your lady friend is, but that trash should have gone into the incinerator," said Mr. Jensen. He turned to Jeanette and asked, "Whose dumpster is that, and why is it in here?"

"That was Tommy's dumpster," said Jeanette. "He was in here earlier after dumping the contents into the incinerator out back. After he got in here, he noticed some of the debris got stuck in the bottom, and he was going to take it back out when Charlie came over from security and said they needed some help and -"

"Where would the person who owns this hat be?" asked A.T.

"What are you talking about? This dumpster, according to the number on the outside, belongs in the emergency area, and is assigned to Tommy. It's for non-toxic paper and cloth items marked for incineration," said Mr. Jensen. "You said earlier you knew something about the doctor? If that is the case, you need to come with me and go next door. And please drop that rag back into the dumpster." Mr. Jensen turned to Jeanette and said, "I'll send Tommy back, and when he gets here, have him empty the dumpster, along with that rag this gentleman has latched onto."

"I'll go with you, but this is not a rag. It is a Russian-styled hat, and if I am not mistaken, it has a lot to do with your fake doctor," insisted A.T., keeping the item. "Before we go to security, I'd like to see where this dumpster gets emptied, and if it's in an incinerator, we better see if" -

"Oh, no!" said Mr. Jensen. "You're going to come with me to security, and we are not going to engage in any more dumpster diving. By the way, what did you say your name was?"

"I didn't," said A.T. following Mr. Jensen.

Entering the hallway and turning back toward the reception area, they looked ahead and saw the same plainclothesman that earlier had given instructions to A.T. for the emergency area. He was walking toward them.

Once the security man saw A.T., he said, "There you are. I need to talk to you about the briefcase you dropped off at the main reception area. Where did you find this man, Lance? He apparently dropped off the briefcase I am carrying at the main reception area and then disappeared," the security man told Mr. Jensen. "I ran it through a scanner and see that it just contains some paperwork, so the case is ok."

"He was in my office, Charlie. He was using the phone, and then he started digging through the trash. That item in his hand was in the dumpster," answered Mr. Jensen.

"What the hell is that?" Charlie asked A.T. as he pointed to the hat in A.T.'s hand.

"If I'm not mistaken," said A.T. "this is a hat that belonged to a lady friend of mine. It is my guess the two of us were brought to your hospital in the same ambulance and -"

"Brought here in an ambulance?" asked Charlie. "You don't look hurt. What's wrong with you, and what is wrong with your lady friend?"

"I passed out, and she was shot," answered A.T.

"She was shot? Well, then she must be in 'Emergency.' Did you shoot her? What are you doing running around the hospital? Have you been checked in? Look, you'd better come with me. My office is right across this hallway and -" said Charlie as A.T. interrupted him.

"No. I didn't shoot her," interjected A.T. "If I had shot her, I wouldn't be standing around here. I need to find out what happened to her, and I am concerned as to why her hat would be in a dumpster."

"Perhaps the medics in 'Emergency' decided to destroy some of her clothing if it was ruined," said Charlie.

"Wouldn't they want to keep it as evidence?" asked A.T.

"Only if she didn't survive the gunshot," said Charlie.

"She didn't," said A.T. "I saw her die right in front of me while we were on the street in New York. And, that's another thing. Why would they transfer us all the way out here to Patterson, New Jersey? She was shot in Manhattan. I don't know why we were brought here."

"If what you say is true, that's a mystery to me, as well," said Charlie while leading A.T. and Mr. Jensen to the security office. "Tell me about the shooting and how you came to be involved."

"It is complicated and difficult to explain, but first we need to find her," answered A.T. "What do they do with someone who has been shot?"

Charlie opened the door to the "Security" office and said, "In this city, we call the police and have them order an autopsy if your lady friend was shot and died as a result of her wounds. Our policy requires that she be held in the ER area until the coroner gets here, and then she would be transferred to the city morgue, if she died."

"I think in that case, you need to let me go to the ER area so I can identify her," said A.T., who then entered the "Security" office, looked up, and pointed to a bald man sitting behind a glass window where the psychiatrist from the psychiatric ward and two other men were talking. A.T. exclaimed, "It's him. What in the hell is he doing in here?"

"Don't get so excited. Do you know him? We'll soon see if he knows you. Have a seat over there," said Charlie as he pointed to one of the chairs in the reception room area. "That guy claims he is a psychiatrist and that he checked one of his patients into the ward upstairs. We are trying to check out his story and his paperwork."

"He's no psychiatrist," exclaimed A.T. when he began to sit down with some difficulty due to the flash device that was still in place. While trying to sit, he said, "I believe he is the guy who may have shot Samantha. Where are the other two?"

"What the hell are you talking about? What other two?" asked Charlie. Before A.T. could answer, Charlie turned to the security office secretary and said, "Alicia get the ER on the phone and find out if they have had any possible homicides or any record of anyone being shot."

At that point, the people in the interview room turned to focus on the animated discussion between A.T. and Charlie. The bald man got up from his chair at the conference room table, turned, and looked through the glass window directly at A.T. Although the discussion from within the room could not be heard, in a matter of minutes, everyone in the room emptied into the security office reception area where Charlie and Mr. Jensen were standing by the chair in which A.T. was sitting uncomfortably.

The first one out the door into the reception area was the bald man who pointed to A.T. and said, "That's him. That's my patient. He's escaped. You need to restrain him. He's dangerous. Do something now!" At that point, Charlie held his hand toward A.T. indicating he should remain seated.

A.T. stood up, looked around Charlie, and exclaimed, "That man is no psychiatrist. He is a contract hit man. He's working with two other guys, a little guy and a large one. Both of them are older and have been following me, as well as Samantha. It's my guess this man is the person who killed Samantha while the other two were in the ambulance."

Not missing a beat, the bald man moved toward A.T. and said, "Watch him. I told you, he's dangerous. He's also delusional. Let's get him back up to the psych ward."

"I want everyone to calm down," said Charlie, who pointed to A.T. and said, "You sit back down before I have you restrained. Fred, Rob, Tommy, escort our supposed psychiatrist back into the interview room, and be sure that he sits down and doesn't move." He shook his head at A.T. and said, "I've seen some strange things in my twenty-five years in this office and as a police officer before that, but this is one of the strangest cases I have ever seen." Turning toward the hospital psychiatrist, who had brought the bald man down to security, Charlie said, "Dr. Farnsworth, please stay with your 'guest psychiatrist' while I try to sort this out. Keep questioning him to see what, if anything, he knows about psychiatry." He turned to his secretary who was seated behind her desk and asked, "Alicia, did you call the police earlier when I asked regarding our supposed guest psychiatrist?"

"I did," said Alicia. "They said they were sending someone out. I'm still checking with the California hospital where he claims to be a resident psychiatrist. So far, they have not gotten back to me."

"Keep checking," said Charlie. "What about the ER? Did they have anyone who came in with a gunshot wound?"

"No, sir," was the answer from Alicia. "They said they haven't had any reported gunshot wounds for over two weeks."

"Did you hear that?" asked Charlie while looking down at A.T. who was patiently sitting on the chair. "Now, let's get some facts straight. Just who are you, and who is this Samantha whom you keep mentioning?"

"My name is A.T. Van Doren," answered A.T. "I'm an attorney from St. Paul, Minnesota. I am a former FBI agent and a former prosecutor. I've been engaged in an investigation for a United States Senator and -"

"I told you he was delusional," interrupted the bald man who was listening through the open door to the interview room. "We need to get him back up to the psych ward and have him sedated."

"You'd like that, wouldn't you?" said A.T. "What did you do with Samantha?"

The bald man shrugged his shoulders, looked at Charlie, and said, "I have no idea what he is talking about, and I have no idea who this Samantha might be. This guy is dangerous, delusional, and will -"

"This is her hat," exclaimed A.T. "Now, where is she?"

"I'll ask the questions," said Charlie as he turned to Dr. Farnsworth and said, "Shut that door for now, and see what your alleged doctor friend knows about psychiatry. I'll be back in there as soon as the police arrive. Charlie turned to Mr. Jensen and asked, "Where did he get that hat?"

"He got it out of the garbage dumpster. I saw him dig it out myself," answered Mr. Jensen.

"Let me see the hat," said Charlie putting his hand out to A.T., who handed him the hat. Charlie examined the Russian-styled hat and said to A.T., "This could be any lady's hat. What's so unusual about this particular hat? What makes you think it belongs to your friend, Samantha, who apparently must still be among the living since the ER just told us there had been no admissions with any gunshot wounds?"

"This hat has a very distinct trace of a perfume I've noticed only on Samantha," A.T. responded. "I saw the bullet wound to the center of her forehead, so I know she has been shot. She was bleeding, and while we were both lying on the street in Manhattan, I tried to get a pulse, and there was none. That's when I started to lose consciousness. We need to find her. I'm sure the bald man in there is involved. If my guess is correct, he is also a suspect in an attempted murder at Dulles International in Washington D.C. His two accomplices, whom I can positively identify, were placing my friend, Samantha, into an ambulance when I passed out. She's got to be somewhere, and I would suspect she is somewhere at this hospital, if she came in the same ambulance. Unless, of course, they dropped her body somewhere else -"

"Do you expect me to believe this story?" asked Charlie. "I've tried to grant you as much leeway as possible, but your story just doesn't make sense. I believe we will need to have Dr. Farnsworth and some members of his staff get you upstairs to his ward until we can sort this out. Under the circumstances, I think I should defer to him in listening to your story before I have the time to personally interview you. Besides, this is a big hospital, and I would have no idea where to look for your lady friend, even if she were here."

"Would you at least be willing to check out my story and sources while I sit here in your office?" asked A.T. "In the meantime, isn't there some way this hospital could be checked for Samantha? She is about five feet eight inches tall. I have no idea of her weight; however, she is slender and attractive. She is of American-French-Vietnamese ancestry. She was wearing a beige topcoat with that hat and an off-white business suit. She was carrying a small red handbag, and she was wearing red shoes with some type of heel. Oh, and she was wearing a perfume of the same scent you can smell on that hat. I would be willing to help find her."

"Sorry," said Charlie. "I'm not about to have you wandering about this hospital. As I said, it's a big place. What do you have in mind? That we try to smell our way through the hospital?" He put the hat to his nose and said, "Your nose must be a lot better than mine. I can hardly smell the perfume on this hat. Besides, I would have no way of knowing where to start looking for your friend, Samantha."

"What about in the area of the incinerator?" suggested A.T. "That's where the one custodian had apparently been with the dumpster that contained Samantha's hat. What do you have to lose? If she was murdered, and I'm sure she was, then you've got the suspect in your interrogation room, and you have me as a witness. If her body gets incinerated, then you've allowed them to destroy the body and the evidence."

"You're a convincing fellow, aren't you? Or, perhaps you actually believe this story you're telling me," smiled Charlie. "Now, you may be totally nuts as the man in the other room has said. On the other hand, according to Dr. Farnsworth, your bald friend in the conference room seems to have been impersonating a psychiatrist, and so far we are unable to verify his story as well. Personally, I could see it wouldn't be hard to impersonate a psychiatrist, at least judging from the behavior of some of them around here. So, I don't know just who to believe or what to believe.

"But let me tell you what we're going to do. I'm going to have Reggie come up here from the front of the ER. He's big and fit. I assure you that you will not want to mess with him. He generally doesn't trust people to begin with. He's going to sit with you while you sit over there in the chair by Alicia's desk and tell her your life's story with contact information, references, your doctor's name, and any other vital information you can remember. You will behave, and the moment you don't, Reggie will have instructions to have you sedated and taken to Dr. Farnsworth's ward." Charlie turned to Alicia and said, "Get Reggie over here immediately. Mr. what's his name, Van Dorn or whatever, will give you all of his vital information."

"The name is Van Doren, A.T. Van Doren, D-O-R-E-N," interrupted A.T.

"Fine, just tell Alicia here," said Charlie who motioned for A.T. to come over and sit in the chair near Alicia's desk.

While Alicia got on the phone, apparently to call for Reggie, A.T. got up to walk to the chair near the desk. When he did, he felt one more plea to Charlie might be in order, so he asked, "What about Samantha? We really should look for her. Even if you don't believe me, wouldn't it be wise to at least check around to see if she might have been brought here. What about asking the bald guy? If I were investigating this matter, I would -"

"You're not investigating this matter," said Charlie, his face turning bright red. "I'll handle my own office, if you don't mind. I'll have you know as long as I have been in charge of security at this hospital, we have never had a reportable incident. It's going to stay that way. As soon as the police get here, I'll have one of them join my assistant, Fred, who is still talking to your friend in the conference room. I will have the two of them search the hospital for your lady, Samantha, and I'll have them start in the area of the incinerators. The incinerators are only fired upon a scheduled routine, and this is done by Mr. Jensen or his designee. They are only fired pursuant to state regulations. I don't know about his schedule or the regulations, but I'll check with him. Hopefully, that search will satisfy you.

"Now, in actuality, I doubt they will find anything, but I want you to know I didn't like the looks of the guy who claims to be your psychiatrist from the moment Farnsworth brought him in. So far none of his story checks out. Maybe your story won't either. First, we need some of your identifying information. We'll soon see. Don't think for a moment you're getting any 'free pass.' I'm usually a good judge of character, and I can get a good sense of people by just sizing them up. So far, you're in the neutral zone, and the bald guy isn't, but that could change. Both of your stories are hard to buy;

however, I'm going to check out your concern. Now, does that make you feel better?"

"Yes, thanks," said A.T. "What if they've incinerated Samantha? That would be a very bad situation and -"

"That's why the search will begin there," interrupted Charlie, who shook his head and said, "I have no idea why I'm even doing this. Perhaps it's because I once had a case when I was a detective where several suspects tried to burn the evidence and a body in a car. In that case, the police department didn't get the information in time, and we were not able to stop them from destroying the evidence or the body. However, due to forensics, we ultimately did identify the body from what was left. Unfortunately, we never did catch the bastards. That's probably the only reason I'm agreeing to have a search of the hospital grounds starting with the incinerators."

When Charlie finished the statement, two uniformed officers walked through the door accompanied by a very large man who was wearing a hospital security uniform. It was A.T.'s presumption that the big guy was Reggie. Charlie instructed Reggie and one of the uniformed officers to remain with A.T. and motioned through the glass of the interview room for Fred to come out. The bald man remained with Dr. Farnsworth and the other two hospital staff members, Rob and Tommy.

Once Fred came out of the room, Charlie said, "Fred, I want you and Officer Miles to conduct a search for a possible missing woman. Start in the area of the incinerators since our friend here thinks she has been murdered and that someone brought her body here to the hospital. He believes this hat I'm holding belonged to her. Since this hat was in one of the hospital dumpsters that came back from the incinerators, that's where you'll start. If the alleged psychiatrist in the other room had something to do with her murder, presuming she exists and was murdered, and if he tried to hide her body or place it in the incinerators or anywhere else in this hospital, I want her found. After the two of you finish checking the incinerators, I want you to check again with ER to determine if and when an ambulance from Manhattan may have stopped. Then check the hospital records for a Samantha -" Charlie turned to A.T. and asked, "What's this Samantha's full name?"

"Her name is Samantha Nguyen-Henderson. She is of American-French-Vietnamese ancestry. She is at least five feet, eight or nine inches tall. She has dark hair, is attractive, and was wearing an off-white suit. She had been wearing red shoes and had a red handbag. She is in her early forties but looks a good bit younger," answered A.T.

"All right," said Charlie. "Reggie will stay here with Mr. Van Doren. Fred, you and Officer Miles get started on a search and do it fast, but do it thoroughly. If you find anything, call me on your radio immediately." He turned to Reggie and said, "Stay with Mr. Van Doren, and be sure he provides Alicia with all his background information and have him show you any identification he has on his person. Oh, and one more thing, put this hat in an evidence bag and see that it is properly marked with a new file number and date."

"I don't have any identifying information on me," answered A.T. while squirming uncomfortably in his chair. "…they took everything from me when they put me in the ambulance."

"Oh, boy," said Charlie. "This is getting more interesting by the minute. Since you don't have any identifying items on you, you had better give us some contact information with some names of credible individuals who can vouch for you, or you're headed to either the ward upstairs or the police station." He looked at Reggie and said, "This guy doesn't leave this room under any circumstances."

At that point, Charlie escorted his assistant, Fred, and the uniformed officer out the door of the security office. Next, he came back to where A.T. was sitting, waved his finger at A.T., and said, "No funny business. Is that understood?" He turned to go to the interview room.

"It is," said A.T. "By the way, I've noticed there is a coffee pot behind Alicia's desk. Since I haven't eaten or had anything to drink for quite a while, would it be possible for me to have a cup of coffee?"

"Sure," said Charlie opening the door to leave the interview room. "Help him out, if you would, Alicia."

At that point, Alicia went to the credenza behind the counter and said, "I can get some coffee for you, but this might be quite strong. How do you like it?"

"I'll take it black, and I really don't care if it is the final percolation," said A.T.

CHAPTER 29
FINAL PERCOLATION

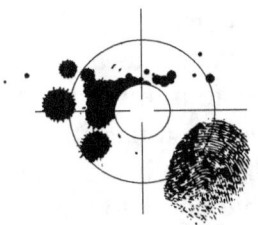

With Reggie standing over him, A.T. sipped a cup of coffee from what Alicia called "the final percolation" while he provided his background and contact information, including the names of his family, law partners, the Senator, Lee, Allen's son, and their phone numbers. He suddenly noticed through the glass of the interview room that Charlie had become quite animated while talking on his hand-held radio. Apparently, he had gotten a call while he continued his interview of the bald man. Within an instant, A.T. saw Charlie get out of his chair and point his finger toward the bald man; he appeared to be providing instructions to Dr. Farnsworth. After he said something to them, Charlie rapidly left the interview room and rushed past A.T. and out the door of the security office.

"What's going on?" asked A.T.

"Don't know," said Reggie. "Just stay in your seat and tell Alicia what she needs to know."

A.T. continued to supply his background information, including the fact he had been conducting an investigation for a United States Senator. He provided an explanation of what had happened in Manhattan before he lost consciousness. He omitted telling Alicia where exactly he found himself in the hospital and just how he managed to escape from the psych ward. He felt fortunate that neither the bald man nor Dr. Farnsworth had mentioned anything to Charlie or other members of his staff about A.T.'s being in Dr. Farnsworth's ward earlier in the day. Perhaps they had presumed as much, or perhaps they were so preoccupied with the bald man's supposed credentials as an itinerant psychiatrist, they forgot to ask.

Less than a minute after Charlie left, he was back at the door. He motioned for A.T. to come and said, "I think you had better come with me. Reggie, you come too."

"Why?" asked A.T. "What's going on?"

"They may have found your friend, Samantha. Let's go!"

A.T. bolted from his chair and followed Charlie, with Reggie in tow. Charlie led them down the hallway that intersected with the main hallway. When they reached the door at the end, Charlie used a key to open the door leading to a stairwell. The three of them proceeded down the stairs to a lower level and exited the building through a door that opened to a parking ramp. They went through the parking ramp until they came to a double set of opened doors. Moving through the double doors to the outside, they went down a set of stairs to an area enclosed by mesh fencing with metal strips woven throughout in a manner that made it impossible to see what was on the other side. After pushing their way through the gate, they unexpectedly halted; two large incinerators loomed over a body on the ground. Fred and the uniformed officer noticed Charlie, A.T., and Reggie. They stopped, looked up, and shook their heads.

Charlie immediately led A.T. and Reggie to the spot where the men stood by the body. He suddenly stopped, turned to look at A.T., and said, "I'm going to ask you to see if you can identify the person who has been found. I don't want you to panic. It's not pretty. Please try to stay as calm as possible, and whatever you do, I don't want you to touch the body. Is that understood?"

A.T. felt his heart pumping as he answered, "I will try."

"Again, I ask you to refrain from touching anything and to stay calm," cautioned Charlie.

"Understood," said A.T. stepping forward to where Fred and the uniformed officer had placed the covered body. When A.T. approached, the uniformed officer drew back the sheet. There was no doubt that it was Samantha. Her color seemed to be a light shade of white-purple, and although it looked as though someone had attempted to wipe the blood from her forehead, it was plain to see that a bullet had pierced her skull about an inch above the bridge of her nose. The small Maltese Cross tattooed below her left eye was less distinguishable than normal due to the fact her skin had darkened. Her clothing was in disarray and smudged, apparently with the residue from the incinerator.

A.T. knelt down near the body with one knee on the ground. He looked down at the still figure that was once a vibrant person.

While continuing to kneel near Samantha's body, A.T. either began to hear or his mind began to replay the *Addio, fiorito asil* from the opera *Madame Butterfly.* Somehow, the sad and compelling melody seemed appropriate to him as he bid farewell to Samantha, who had really been like a flowery refuge to him over the past months. At that moment, A.T. felt certain her gentle face would haunt him forever. He was sufficiently overwrought that he wasn't sure if he were actually hearing Placido Domingo singing or if his mind were simply recounting the melodious variation for its private audience. It was as if it were Samantha, in her usual direct way, tugging at him to let him know she was aware of his thoughts. The music stopped abruptly when Charlie put his hand on A.T.'s shoulder and asked, "Are you all right?"

A.T. slowly rose from the body, turned to Charlie, and confidently said, "It's Samantha." Having noticed A.T.'s demeanor while he examined the body, Charlie replied, "Look, I'm sorry you have to go through this. It's always difficult when you lose someone who is close. That's especially true under these types of circumstances. I notice your eye is twitching. That's probably a natural reaction of your emotional state at this time. I take it that you're definitely sure it's your friend, Samantha?"

"I'm certain," answered A.T. "If you get close enough, you will notice the perfume matches that of the hat. Also, directly below her left eye, you will see a small permanent tattoo. It is a Maltese Cross and represented her desire to maintain a mark of her membership in a particular society. At least that is what she told me months ago when we first met."

Charlie bent over the body to examine the tattoo. He took a moment to look at her; then he stood. He instructed Fred to get a gurney out for removal of the body back to the hospital and to then call the medical examiner. While Fred went to his radio, Charlie turned to A.T. and said, "You will need to give us a statement. I will have a detective from homicide come over immediately. Did you provide your basics and background to Alicia?"

"I did. Now what about –" A.T. started to ask when he was interrupted by sudden shouting in the direction of the parking ramp. They were stunned to see Tommy, one of Mr. Jensen's custodians, running toward them.

At first, they were unable to hear what he was saying. Once he got closer and came into the fenced area, Tommy, who was gasping for breath, said, "Dr. Warton has escaped."

"Who?" Charlie asked.

"The bald guy has escaped," repeated Tommy between breaths. "He pushed Dr. Farnsworth's chair around, hit Mr. Jensen as he got up, and ran out of the interview room right past Alicia. I was on the other side of the table; I tried to chase him, but he was too fast. The last I saw him he was heading toward the ER."

"Let's go, Fred! You too Reggie," instructed Charlie who took off running. He yelled back at uniformed Officer Mills and said, "Wait there until the gurney comes. In the meantime, before the body is moved, get some photographs. I want pictures of everything, including the body, the incinerator, the general location…everything. After you take the photos, I want you to come to the ER. Van Doren, you stay put."

"No," said A.T. running after Charlie, Fred and Reggie. It was difficult for him to keep up because running became somewhat problematic considering the flash drive was still attached to his body. However, A.T. was determined to be a part of bringing the man who had shot Samantha to justice. Pain or no pain, he was going to do his best to run as fast as he could. "I can help," A.T. continued. "If it's the man I think it is, he may be heading to a BMW. If it's the same car he was in a few weeks ago, it's a dark blue BMW with a light blue round emblem on the upper part of the front doors."

Charlie turned back over his shoulder and asked, "How do you know that? Never mind, come on!"

The four of them ran as fast as they could toward the ER. In reversing their path, they went by the security office, and A.T. noticed the only people remaining there were Alicia and Dr. Farnsworth. He surmised the uniformed officer and Rob, the other member of the security team, had gone after the bald man who had identified himself as a Dr. Warton. A.T. hurriedly followed Charlie, Fred and Reggie to the ER. When they arrived, they were told that the uniformed officer and Rob had run out of the main ER door chasing a bald man in the direction of the west parking ramp.

Rounding the corner to the parking ramp, they followed the voices they could hear and bounded up the down ramp. Once on the first level, they could see what the commotion was about. On the floor of the ramp in the middle of parked cars on either side, the bald man, the alleged Dr. Warton, was being restrained by three people - the uniformed officer, Rob Lindsey, and none other than Rick Helms. The uniformed officer was in the process of cuffing the bald man when Rick Helms looked up and said, "Well, A.T.! It doesn't surprise me to see that you'd be involved in this chase somehow." Rick looked at Charlie and said, "Charlie Beecher, you old son-of-a-gun. Here I am retired, and I'm still doing your work for you."

"Well, I'll be, Rick!" exclaimed Charlie. "What brings you to my domain on this very disruptive day?"

"I got a call from my old friend, A.T.," said Rick. "I see the two of you have met. I came down in response to a call from A.T. that sounded rather urgent, and I guess it was, given what I'm seeing. I had just gotten out of my car when I noticed this bald guy running from a police officer and this other gentleman. I figured they needed some help, so I grabbed the guy while he was running. It took three of us to get him down."

"Thanks," said Charlie. "The officer you helped, Officer Robbins, came here today to assist us on a number of matters." At that point, Charlie turned to A.T. and asked Rick, "Do you know this man, Mr. Van Doren?"

"I sure do," answered Rick. "A.T., as we know him, and I were in the FBI together many years ago. He left early to become a prosecutor and then to practice law up in the Twin Cities. We've known each other for nearly thirty years."

Charlie looked at A.T. and said, "Well, Mr. Van Doren, it's beginning to look like you were telling us the truth all along." Charlie looked at Officer Robbins and said, "We'll help you keep this alleged Dr. Warton under control until your department can get a unit out here. Why don't we get this guy back to my office?"

"Wait," asserted A.T. "While we're here, shouldn't we get a look at this guy's car?" A.T. looked at Dr. Warton and asked, "Where were you headed? Where's your car?"

"Screw you, bastard," said the bald man. "I'm not telling you anything."

"What's your real name?" asked Charlie.

"If I told you, I'd have to kill you," said the bald man.

"That's not the right answer," said Fred shoving the bald man forward.

"Fred," said Charlie, "you and Officer Robbins take this character, who is obviously not Dr. Warton, down to my office. Reggie, I want you to go with them just in case they need some additional muscle." Charlie then turned to A.T. and said, "Did you say that you might know what kind of car this impersonator might have been trying to find?"

"I think I do," said A.T. "I'll know it if it's the same vehicle that he was using when I saw him out in California several weeks ago. If it's the same car, it's a dark blue BMW with a light blue emblem on the front part of the driver's door, and the same emblem is on the opposite side passenger door."

"If you don't mind, how about you, Rick, and I check the lot over to see if we can find such a vehicle," insisted Charlie.

For the next ten minutes, the three of them searched the parking garage and found the blue BMW parked in an obscure corner of the third floor. Consistent with what A.T. had mentioned, the car had a light blue emblem in the upper corner of the front door on both the driver's side and the passenger's side. A.T. observed that the car had Florida plates and wondered if firearms might be found in the blue BMW.

A.T.'s speculation on the firearms was confirmed later in the day when the police sought and received a search warrant. When the car was examined, several firearms were found, along with a computer, various disguises, clothing of all kind, and A.T.'s billfold, iPhone, keys, and other personal items. The police detectives allowed Charlie to examine the car, along with A.T. and Rick Helms, as long as they wore the necessary surgical gloves. When the trunk was opened, two assault rifles were found under a hidden floor panel. The main detective examined the sleeker of the two firearms. Turning, he said, "If I'm not mistaken, this is a 'sniper special,' otherwise known as a 7.62 x 51 M40."

That's close, but no cigar," interjected Rick Helms. "It's a 7.62 x 51 all right, but it's an M40A3. That's another version."

"How do you know that?" asked Charlie.

"I was trained on numerous weapons while working in the Bureau as part of a swat team," answered Rick. "I was also a qualifier for the U.S. Olympic team many years ago. I definitely know the difference is slight. In this case, I would say the bolt action is the 'give away.'"

"Whatever the case," said A.T. "I'll bet if you do some ballistic tests on those sniper rifles and compare them to the bullet that killed Samantha, you'll get a match."

"That's exactly what we will do," explained the lead detective. "We've already had a chance to confer with the medical examiner, and he has confirmed death by gunshot. He is also gathering additional information and told me he would be finished with the examination yet this evening. Tell me, A.T., do you have information relative to next of kin?"

"I don't personally, but a good friend of mine is close to the family," responded A.T. At that point he was determined to call Blaine in order to explain what happened. Blaine, who was still in Washington D.C., could contact Samantha's brother in California. "Let me call my friend and see if he can get one of Samantha's family members to call as soon as possible."

"The sooner you can do that, the better," commented the detective.

While the detectives continued their search of the car, they placed A.T.'s billfold and other items in a separate evidence bag. A.T. asked, "Would it be all right if I could have my billfold, ID, and other items?"

"Not without a court order," answered the principal detective.

"In that case," asked A.T. "How soon before that could be accomplished?"

"It will probably take days or even weeks since everything here will have to be processed," answered the detective. "We will need to take a statement from you, and the sooner we do that, the better it will be for you."

"That's not what I wanted to hear," commented A.T. "Those are my identifying personal items; plus, my credit cards and cash are in there. I won't be able to function in any way without those items. I've got to settle up my hotel bill; I must return to Washington D.C. and then back home to St. Paul. After I purchase a plane ticket from Kennedy to D.C., I will need identification no matter where I go."

"Why don't you come to the police station with me so we can confirm your identity? Then we will see if we can get a special order from the court for the release of your items. No doubt we can make copies of the items, if that will satisfy the judge. I'll make no promises, but once we get to my office, I can get the wheels in motion for the possible release of your items. While that is taking place, I will want to get a sworn statement from you and the more detailed, the better."

* *

With little choice in the matter, A.T. consented and was taken to the police department detective division by Rick, who agreed to stay with A.T. until matters could be resolved. Rick also agreed to take A.T. back to the Yale Club in Manhattan after A.T. was finished at the police station. A.T. bid farewell to Charlie and the members of his staff, who turned out to be more helpful than hostile once they confirmed A.T.'s identity and were able to confirm with the Senator's office that A.T. was conducting an investigation on the Senator's behalf. It was well into the evening when A.T. learned his personal items had been released by the court. He had to plead long and hard in order for a release of his iPhone; however, the judge, who had been called back to his chambers for the matter, agreed to release the phone after receiving a personal call from the Senator.

Once A.T. got his iPhone back, he made a call to Allen to advise him of the developments in New York and New Jersey. The two of them added Allen's son, Eric, in a conference call in order to suggest that Eric contact the Patterson police. Both A.T. and Allen felt sure it was more than likely the bald man in custody in Patterson was the same man who had made an attempt upon the life of Mr. Felthaus. As it turned out, according to the Florida vehicle registration, the bald man was Gilbert Gleason; however, it was likely the name was an alias. Efforts would continue to determine his actual identity.

A.T. told Allen as soon as he got a flight booked to Washington, he would again call Allen in order for them to meet back at the W Hotel. He also mentioned that he would need to meet with the Senator as soon as he was back in the nation's capital.

Once A.T. finished his call with Allen, he contacted the Senator on his private line to advise the Senator that he was transporting some vital information from the GGG. The Senator was pleased but was immediately saddened when A.T. mentioned what had happened to Samantha. He asked the Senator if he would convey the fact that Samantha had been shot to her former friend, the Congressman. Next, A.T. called Blaine, who was still in D.C. He told Blaine what had happened to Samantha and requested that Blaine contact

Samantha's brother with the tragic news, along with information on the hospital in Patterson so Samantha's brother could make appropriate arrangements. A call to Jacci followed, with a less than detailed explanation of the side trip to New York. A.T. told Jacci he would travel to Washington for a few days, and then he would return to the Twin Cities. After making the calls, A.T. joined Rick Helms for the trip back to Manhattan.

During the first part of the trip to Manhattan, A.T. detailed the situation regarding Samantha and how it was that A.T. had met her. He explained to his old friend the nature of the investigation he had been conducting over the course of the last couple years. He also brought Rick up to date on the incident that precipitated A.T.'s involvement in the first place.

While A.T. and Rick traveled to Manhattan, A.T. couldn't help but wonder if he had been experiencing a nightmare similar to those he had dreamed after he had been wrongfully charged and taken into custody a few years earlier. He certainly didn't want to experience anything like that again. He thought to himself: *As soon as this is over and I get back home, I'm definitely going to retire. Jacci and I will take off and travel.* Then he thought: *Of course, I will need to continue my quest of getting some meaningful reform in regard to the federal grand jury system. It cannot be allowed to continue the way it is today. Far too many people have been the victims of a bad system administered by an abundance of unethical prosecutors. There has to be some kind of oversight, and the sooner, the better. Plus, I need to get rid of this uncomfortable flash drive device.*

"Are you all right?" asked Rick while managing the traffic along Interstate 80 on the way to Manhattan while watching A.T. fidget in his seat.

"I'm fine," answered A.T. "I just need to get back to the Yale Club and get some rest before I fly out tomorrow. Please let me buy dinner for you. The food at the Yale Club is excellent. Again, thanks so much for coming to my rescue. Who knows, if you hadn't come along when you did, the bald guy might have gotten away. You did a great service, Rick. You helped catch a cold-blooded killer. I'm confident once the authorities in Washington D.C. get to comparing notes with the detectives in Patterson, they'll find it's the same guy that tried to murder George Felthaus in Washington." After that comment, A.T. decided to change the subject and visit with Rick about his retirement. The time passed quicker than expected and before they knew it, Rick, who declined the dinner invitation, pulled up to the entrance of the Yale Club. A.T. thanked Rick once again as the two shook hands. A.T. closed the car door, turned, and entered the Club.

* *

Once in his room, A.T. decided to order room service since Rick had declined his offer of dinner. After ordering his food, A.T. removed the flash drive that had been placed on his person. He marveled at the fact that no one had bothered to do a very thorough search of him either when his billfold and phone were taken or when he had been admitted into the hospital psych ward. While thinking about it, he decided to double-check the contents to be certain the flash drive had not been damaged and contained the information he remembered. He fired up his laptop that had been left in his room at the Yale Club and checked the flash drive.

The content of the drive was as he remembered it. This little device was going to give the Senator the kind of information he needed in order to tie certain offshore and foreign funding to specific politicians, as well as to individuals at the DOJ and the Bureau, to paramilitary groups, to media interests, to particular industrialists, and even to some supposed religious leaders. Reviewing the contents of the flash drive, he recognized that Samantha and the GGG had delivered in aces. Now it was up to him to get it delivered to the Senator.

Then A.T. called Blaine to find out whether he had been able to reach Samantha's brother. Blaine confirmed that he had and that he would be available to meet with A.T. in Washington. At that time he hoped to have details regarding any arrangements that had been made for Samantha.

After speaking with Blaine, A.T. received a call from Lee, the Senator's aide. Lee said he had spoken to the Senator and explained that he would be setting up a second meeting with A.T., Blaine, Julian, Bud, and Allen to follow directly after the meeting with the Senator. Lee did not provide details but stated the second meeting would be necessary in order to coordinate any future efforts.

A.T. decided to check out the video recording device. He found the device had operated continuously for over a day, except for the time A.T. had to relinquish his coat during the meeting with the

GGG. Remarkably, the device had worked as planned with the open phone line to a set recording system back in St. Paul. A.T. called Adam, and between the two of them, they were able to access the system. They found that more of his conversations of the past day and a half had been recorded than they originally believed possible. Both were very pleased as it occurred to A.T. it would be a good idea for the device to be activated during the upcoming meeting with the Senator, just in case the Senator would try to conveniently forget any new promise.

While skipping through the recordings, he was surprised to hear faint conversations taking place even while he was in the psych ward of the hospital. He made a note to review the entire body of recordings upon his return to the Twin Cities. With the assistance of Adam, he was able to reset the device for potentially an entirely new set of recordings. If it were still good, he would continue to use the system until he returned to St. Paul.

A.T. realized he was getting very tired. However, before he rested, he decided to stop at the front desk in order to verify the checkout time and to see if there had been any messages that had not been forwarded to his room and recorded on the room phone system. With the coat video device reset and ready for a new test, he set out for the front desk. He left his room with the flash drive now in his pocket and went to the elevator bank for the trip to the lobby.

When A.T. stopped at the front desk to inquire about the checkout time, he was told two men who were looking for him had stopped twice during the day. That was puzzling. Apparently the two men had been asking as recently as ten minutes earlier. A.T. looked around the lobby. Over to the left, he saw quite a number of people gathering beneath the mounted pictures of the former distinguished Yale Club members. None of the people gathered beneath the pictures looked familiar. Considering the formal dress of the group, it appeared as though the gathering was for an event in the ballroom at the Club.

A.T. continued to scan the lobby and glanced at small groups of people in the coat check area, the sitting area where there were clusters of stuffed chairs surrounding coffee tables, and the area with the elevator banks. However, he saw no one he recognized. Finally, he turned and thanked the young lady at the desk and headed in the direction of the elevators.

When he pushed the "up" button at the elevator bank, he heard someone behind him call out. It was a familiar voice and not one he expected to hear so soon. Turning to look in the direction of the voice, on the other side of the barrier between the two columns he observed a large man and a small man heading in his direction. Feeling his anger grow, he walked past the column to his left in order to face the two individuals, whom he suspected were going to be a part of more bad news.

He reminded himself to hold his temper. In addition to the fact that the Yale Club was a very exclusive organization where one expected to see well-heeled individuals smoking cigars and nipping brandy near a fireplace, it had strict policies relative to patron conduct. Excessive noise was not permitted; everyone was required to be properly attired at all times; cell phones could not be used in common areas; smoking was prohibited; discussions were expected to be conducted in a quiet voice; also, it was understood that such rules and others would be strictly enforced. Keeping that in mind, A.T. acted as though he was in court and had just received news of devastating evidence against a client. He would keep his "cool," no matter what happened.

Approaching the two men, whom he now considered to be public enemy number one and public enemy number two, he did his best to smile and act like nothing was wrong, especially since his real desire was to administer his own form of justice. The fact they were on the scene immediately after Sam was shot was more than coincidental. He needed to see if he could get them to admit to being a part of what had happened. This was going to require some academy award-type acting. The two men waited by a grouping of stuffed chairs while A.T. cautiously approached. He shook each of their sweaty hands and afterward wiped his hand off on his trousers. A.T. couldn't hold back, so he quietly said, "Why gentlemen, it was my sincerest hope the next time I saw either of you, it would be when you were wearing something with a vivid orange tint to it."

"It's nice to see you too, Mr. Smart Ass," mumbled "Big John" motioning for A.T. to sit down in one of the stuffed chairs.

After waiting for both "Big John" and "Squeaky" to sit down, A.T. took a seat across the coffee table from them and asked, "Isn't it a bit of a risk for the two of you to be out wandering around? I would think that you would be in hiding or making plans to leave the country."

"Why on earth would we even consider doing such a thing?" commented 'Big John.' "We have nothing to be worried about. Why would anyone be looking for the two of us? It would seem you should be the one with concern."

"Actually, I expected the two of you would be worried that sooner or later someone would step forward to implicate both of you in the disastrous loss of a certain young lady," said A.T. in an accusatory tone. "On the other hand, why would I ever need to have concern?"

"Perhaps you should be concerned about your own safety," began Big John. "Maybe you should be concerned about your apparent ties to the GGG. We know you either have been given some information from them, or you are to receive some information from them. When we had the opportunity to examine your belongings during the ambulance ride and at the hospital, we couldn't find anything. We performed a thorough search, including the removal of everything in your pockets, shirt, coat, pants, and shoes. We looked through everything, but we didn't find certain information we are sure you either have or will be receiving. Therefore, is it fair to presume you will be trying to pick up some information?"

A.T. asked, "Why would you possibly be searching me, and what did you ever hope to find? You two are expecting me to have some particular information, and I presume that is the sole reason I am still alive."

"Stop being smart," exclaimed Big John. "It is the information we want. We think it would be in your best interest if you would convey that information in order to avoid any further involvement in something that doesn't concern you and is well beyond your level of understanding," explained Big John. "As far as a certain young lady is concerned, we have reason to believe she has simply disappeared from the face of the earth."

"What do you mean she has disappeared from the face of the earth?" asked A.T. since it was obvious they were unaware of her body being located in one of the hospital incinerators.

"She is gone, evaporated, and never to be seen again," interjected Squeaky. "Samantha Nguyen-Henderson, if that is who you are referring to, is gone. It is safe to say not only has she expired, but in biblical parlance one might say, 'remember man, thou art from dust and unto dust thou shall return,'" stated Squeaky while Big John turned to scowl at Squeaky.

"Yes, I am talking about Samantha Nguyen-Henderson. What have you done with her?" asked A.T.

"Let's just say she will never be seen again," answered Big John. "She will no longer be a problem for anyone, and as Squeaky has said, she has evaporated. You really liked her, didn't you? What kind of relationship did the two of you have, exactly? Well, it doesn't matter. Perhaps it would be best if you were to put aside any memories of her and divorce yourself from the investigation that you have been pursuing."

"It is none of your business what type of relationship I had with her. I realize she is gone, and that is something that will forever haunt me. However, before we discuss my investigation," said A.T. "At least tell me why she was murdered and just how the two of you were involved. What did she ever do to the two of you?"

"She was a smartass bitch," smiled Squeaky, obviously trying to provoke A.T. "She did her best to ruin an opportunity for us to bring a group of true Americans into a strategic partnership with the GGG. She cost us dearly, and as a result, we lost the confidence of a long-standing client, to say nothing of a handsome fee the client had agreed to pay us if we secured its membership in the GGG. Furthermore -"

"Let's just say she met with an unfortunate and untimely end due to her meddling in matters well beyond her level of interest," interrupted Big John.

"I saw what happened. Did the two of you forget I am a witness?" asked A.T.

"You were a witness to what? Tell us exactly what you believe you saw," urged Big John.

"I saw her drop before my eyes. I saw the wound, and I heard the crack. Then within seconds, the two of you appeared dressed as medics and with an ambulance. It doesn't take a genius to tie the evidence of involvement to the two of you," said A.T. raising his voice.

Big John smiled and waved his hands in a downward fashion in order to try to get A.T. to remain calm. He asked, "Isn't this quite an exclusive club? I understand they have rules about disorderly behavior. Perhaps they will remove you from the premises if you become unruly. How is it that you are allowed to be lodged in such a fine place anyway?"

"Actually, I should go to the front desk and ask the staff to call the police."

"Really," laughed Big John. "What would you tell them? Would you tell them the two of us were paramedics who happened to come upon one of the many traffic accidents in Manhattan during rush hour? Would you tell them that these two paramedics assisted you and a young lady and then took you to a hospital? Would you have them investigate us for being good Samaritans? What exactly would you tell them?"

A.T. sat back in his chair and took a deep breath reminding himself to play this out without showing any emotion. He asked, "Why was she murdered? Who is the guy who shot her?"

"What makes you think we would possibly know the answers to such questions?" inquired Big John.

"For starters," answered A.T., "Squeaky already said the two of you believed Samantha had stood in the way of some entity that was going to pay you a commission for attaining membership in the GGG."

"What Squeaky here meant to say was that we were hired to provide a proper submission for possible membership into the GGG by an entity that employed our services. When membership was denied, we were quite certain your friend, Samantha, had somehow maligned the entity that hired us. We think she did it purposely because she didn't care for the two of us," said Big John.

A.T. pushed on by asking, "What was so important about a membership in the GGG? More importantly, what was the entity seeking membership, if I may ask?"

"I'm sure you would have never heard of the entity, so it wouldn't matter," interjected Squeaky.

"If you're talking about LESTER," said A.T., trying to further stimulate a response, "I can understand why even the GGG wouldn't want those nuts as members."

"They're not nuts. They are very loyal patriots," responded Squeaky. "For your information, LESTER and other similar groups will soon be positioned to move this country back to its underlying principles. As you should at least have presumed by now, they and other like-minded individuals and groups control a major political party, as well as parts of the government. They have power and are gaining more power each day. Neither you nor your Democratic Senator friend will be able to do anything to stop them. They have the power, and they know how to use it."

"So, why would they want to have Samantha murdered?" asked A.T., who sensed he was getting at least Squeaky riled.

"What LESTER does or doesn't do is none of your business," said Squeaky.

"It is obvious that either LESTER or the two of you were involved in Samantha's murder. At least for my own edification, tell me, and I will willingly tell you about my investigation and what the GGG told me," pleaded A.T.

"If you want us to admit we had something to do with her murder, why not. You're never going to tell anyone. The dangerous way you live will settle that matter on its own," said Squeaky.

"Are you threatening me?" asked A.T.

"Of course not," said Squeaky. "No one would ever believe you. It is your word against the two of us. There is no body, and there is no proof of any crime. As far as anyone knows, you just had a bad dream. Besides, she needed to go. She was causing more harm than good. Her life was a small price to pay. There is no turning that clock back. She had caused enough grief. With her gone, many people will benefit, and the government of this country will be better off. There is no 'corpus.' There's no body, Mr. Lawyer. Additionally, Mr. Lawyer, there is no 'corpus delecti.' There is no proof of a crime."

"We've told you more than you need to know. Besides, what made you think we had anything to do with her disappearance or departure?" asked Big John.

"It was too obvious," answered A.T. "Before I passed out, I saw her react to the gunfire and fall to the ground with her face shattered. The two of you appeared out of nowhere and happened to be in an ambulance that took Samantha and me from a busy downtown street in Manhattan. The evidence is significant against the two of you. Now, why don't you tell me the name of the man who pulled the trigger?"

"Everything you say is nothing more than circumstantial evidence," said Big John.

"Circumstantial evidence can be used to convict," insisted A.T.

"But in the case of murder, you will at least need evidence of a murder. It could be easily argued your friend, Samantha, simply disappeared as she would often do in performing her investigative assignments for the GGG. I doubt the GGG is going to step forward and admit that one of their secret investigators, whom they paid handsomely, has been murdered," casually remarked Big John. "Do you suppose the GGG is going to voluntarily come forward and discuss their relationship with Samantha Nguyen-Henderson or what they do or how they do it or what kind of organization they operate or anything else for that matter? No, Mr. Van Doren, you are on your own in this matter. We could openly admit to you that we were a part of eliminating your friend, Samantha, and there is nothing you can do about it. You are alone on this. You will look like a fool. No body, no crime, and no witness, other than you, and we know your credibility is worthless."

"I must differ with you on all accounts," said A.T. "Someday the two of you will pay for this crime."

"Cut the crap, A.T.," insisted Big John, "Let's get to the point about your investigation and exactly what the GGG plans and what exactly they have either given you or plan to give you that might be significant in regard to the entity we've mentioned too much. We have already been more than patient with you, and if we didn't think you could be helpful by coming to your senses, we wouldn't be wasting our time with you.

"So, are you going to give me the name and contact information of the 'shooter' in exchange for that information?" asked A.T. "If not, I see no reason for me to provide you with any information. Yes, you are wasting your time if you think I would turn any information over to you."

"Everything has its price, and everyone has a good reason to cooperate," said Squeaky. "Surely, your life is worth something."

"So, you are threatening me," insisted A.T.

"No, no," interrupted Big John, "He's not threatening you. We just want to know what it will take to get you to provide the information we seek."

"All right," said A.T. "You give me the name of the 'shooter,' and I'll tell you where the meeting is to take place."

"We'll tell you his name when you give us the information you expect to receive or have received from the GGG," insisted Big John. "Now, try, for your own sake, to cooperate."

"What if I told you I had a meeting planned for tomorrow at 11:30 a.m. at Grand Central Station across the street from here," said A.T. who expected to be long gone and back in Washington D.C. by that time. "Tell you what. I'll go to my meeting and see you back here at noon."

"No chance," cautioned Big John. "We'll be at Grand Central, and we will meet with you there directly after you receive whatever package you get at that time."

"Why?" asked A.T. "Is the 'shooter' going to try to pick me off?"

"No, there will be no need for that. Plus, we want the information, and in the process, who knows, you may decide to help us more after that. We'll see you tomorrow at 11:30 directly after you receive the information from your friends at the GGG. Until then," said Big John while he stood and smiled.

After A.T. watched the two miserable excuses of mankind saunter to the entrance of the club, he went to the front door to be sure they had departed in a cab. Once satisfied they were gone for the night, he returned to his room. Back in his room, he called Adam, for assistance in accessing and downloading the video conversation that he had just finished with Big John and Squeaky. The system worked without a flaw. He now had what he believed were confessions by both Big John and Squeaky.

A.T. requested that Adam overnight a copy of the video to Eric, the Senator, and the detective bureau in Patterson. He organized his materials for the early departure to the airport the next morning. Now he needed to get the GGG flash drive into the hands of his friend, the Senator. Once that was done, he would be free to resume his quest to do whatever he could to reform the federal grand jury system while claiming to be retired. He was looking forward to a "unique retirement" since he and Jacci would now be able to travel, while he still had something meaningful to do with his life.

* *

Following a sleepless night, he departed from the Yale Club in order to make the early flight into Washington D.C. After Allen met him at the airport, they stopped for breakfast, and A.T. shared the series of events from the last couple of days. He mentioned the help that Rick Helms, also a friend of Allen's, had provided. After breakfast, the two of them traveled directly to the Senator's office. When they arrived, although the Senator was at his office, he was engaged with other matters; therefore, A.T. provided the Senator's principal aide, Lee Mattson, a vague rendition of what had happened to Samantha. He then discussed his encounter with 'Big John' and 'Squeaky.'

When the Senator was finally free, A.T. insisted he meet privately with the Senator. First, the Senator expressed his sympathy regarding the loss of Samantha Nguyen-Henderson. He asked if A.T. would supply her family information in order for the Senator to send a letter to the family expressing his sympathy and acknowledge her service to the United States. The Senator said he wanted to let the family know that Samantha had provided a real service in regard to her earlier testimony and efforts to cooperate with a Senate investigation.

The Senator inquired as to whether A.T. had been successful in regard to the meeting that Samantha had arranged with the GGG. A.T. acknowledged he had, and at that point, he presented the GGG flash drive which A.T. had transferred earlier to his shirt pocket. Having verified that the flash drive was free of any virus, the Senator's docked the drive into his main computer, the passwords were applied, and the Senator personally began to review the information.

After nearly twenty minutes had passed with the Senator skipping through the device and reviewing sections of the contents on the drive, the Senator finally looked up from the computer and said, "Nice job, A.T. This information is going to blow the lid off. It is just what we need in order to tie the other information from the investigation to foreign interests and the movement of money from offshore accounts into the political process here in the United States. Not only will this benefit what we will be presenting to the subcommittee in conjunction with the other information from your investigation, but this should be exactly what we need in order to convince those on the other side of the aisle of the viability of the proposed Constitutional Amendment relative to ending the corporate and foreign interests funding of our political process. I would say your job is done, and we can now move forward with the committee hearings."

"What about the help I will need in reference to my continued quest to address the shortcomings of the federal grand jury system, along with issues at the DOJ and the FBI?" asked A.T. when he activated the lapel video system. "With all due respect, Senator, I believe you made a promise to me that you and your subcommittee would seriously examine the need for immediate changes to the grand jury system, along with meaningful oversight in terms of that system, as well as the DOJ and the FBI."

"Are you back on that old matter, A.T.?" asked the Senator. "I would have thought with the loss of Samantha, along with this new information, you would be willing to wait. A lot has been accomplished so far and there are bigger fish to fry, if you don't mind my saying so. Changing the system of contributions to political campaigns and the help you have provided in that regard is a tremendous service to your country and the protections of individual voting rights without large financial influence. You should be overjoyed for what you've accomplished."

"It doesn't seem as though I've accomplished what I set out to change if I'm asked to stop," A.T. responded.

"What needs to happen," began the Senator, "is for you to relax a little and kick back. A.T., I believe I can get you to do that. Perhaps you have been too involved in the investigation and maybe, just maybe, you have lost your compass a bit. I did extend an invitation to both you and Jacci for a bit of a fundraiser scheduled for this coming weekend. In fact, perhaps Jacci may have mentioned the event to you since I told her about it during a call we had.

"She did mention it, Senator," admitted A.T. "However, after discussing it with her, we've decided to pass on the invitation. Unfortunately, she had already made a scheduled commitment to be in an equestrian event for this weekend, and I am just not in the mood for any political activities."

"Forgive me for saying so again, but you need to relax a bit. Perhaps, getting back into the political world might be just what you need in order to get your mind off of the investigation that seems to have taken over your life," noted the Senator.

"Both Jacci and I wish to thank you for the thoughtful invitation; however, I made a decision years ago to get out of the political world, and I have no intention of getting back into it," said A.T.

"The fundraiser this weekend might be just the thing that could get you to change your mind," interjected the Senator. "I was hoping you and Jacci could join us. You would be our special guests at the event, and I would be delighted to introduce you to a number of very influential people who should hear your story. I think they might be able to get you to see things a bit more from a political perspective and reacquaint you with the political process you were once a part of. It might bring back some of the old political interest you once had. As you well know, it is the world of politics that, in reality, gets things accomplished."

"Again, no thanks," pleaded A.T. "The investigation has taken its toll and with what has happened to Samantha, I need to get home and clear my head. Attending a political fundraiser is the last thing I would want to do at this time."

"Just remember," exclaimed the Senator, "opportunities like the one I am offering you don't come along every day, and perhaps you could consider it a payback from me for the help you provided on the investigation. Far more can get done through private discussions at the quiet political table than even a presentation to a Senate subcommittee. Who knows, you might even find some sympathetic politicians who could help in your quest."

"I'm not interested in a 'payback,' exclaimed A.T. "I'm interested in your fulfilling your promise to get the matter of oversight relative to a grand jury and the DOJ in front of the subcommittee. It was always my understanding that the investigation I was doing was for those purposes."

"The investigation had a dual purpose," exclaimed the Senator. "I never hid from you that I was interested in the investigation being used in my efforts to overturn the 'Citizens United' case. You are not naive; you realize the political process is how and where things happen. I believe once that political 'fire' is rekindled within you and Jacci, you will both realize how much can be accomplished. I believe some of the people whom you will meet at the fundraiser will be able to help you personally. In the process, you may realize that across the board reform to the system would not be necessary."

"Again, no thanks," said A.T.

"Well, I would once again ask that you reconsider," urged the Senator. "If the folks you meet can help you in cleansing the record for you and helping you personally, why would you care about any reform to the system? The people whom you would meet can help you in many ways. You need to remember the system that is in place has evolved into what it is for good reason. For example, when it comes to the grand jury, one of the major powers held by a prosecutor is his ability to 'direct' the grand jury the way the prosecutor sees fit. We have both been prosecutors before, as have some of the people whom you will meet at the fundraiser. In order for the prosecutor to hold the proper power, he needs to be able to direct the grand jury. I'm sure the people who you will meet at the fundraiser will help convince you of this, since it seems as though you have forgotten what it is like to hold the power of indictment in one's hands. Plus, and without spelling it out in gross terms, the people whom you would meet could help you in many significant ways."

"Thank you for the thought, Senator," said A.T. "However, I have no interest in once again getting involved in the world of politics, and I don't want personal help 'in many ways.' Additionally, I don't think, given the circumstances of the investigation, it would be appropriate for me or anyone else to try to 'back door' the issue of oversight that is needed for grand jury reform by 'helping myself' through the political process and obtaining some personal benefit from it through political connections. The type of oversight needed must be the sort of thing that is presented in a full-faced manner before a proper legislative body. I'm not interested in some kind of special consideration for my own purposes."

"Can't you just let the oversight issue go for now?"

"No, I can't let it go," said A.T. "All I ever asked was for the evidence I've been gathering to be submitted to the subcommittee, and I was certain I had a promise from you that such would be the case. I also recall it was your promise that induced me to expand the investigation into many additional matters that happened to coincide with your interests in curtailing campaign spending. I believe we are at the point where some efforts should be made to get the relevant evidence before the subcommittee on the judicial reform I have requested and that was promised."

"Sorry, A.T.," responded the Senator. "I cannot do that right now. Perhaps as you refine your investigation on the grand jury matter, I would reconsider taking the matter before the subcommittee."

"The investigation is virtually complete. It needs to get before the subcommittee while the evidence is still fresh and the witnesses are available," urged A.T. "For the many years we have known each other, Senator, I don't ever remember you not following through on a promise, at least any that was made to me in what I perceived was good faith. Grand jury reform and DOJ reform is needed now. It needs to be done while everything is fresh and ready for presentation. We have already lost a key witness in Samantha; we don't need to risk additional delays or losses."

"Damn it, A.T.," exclaimed the Senator, "don't be so obstinate. In time I will try to fulfill the promise I made to you regarding the reforms you seek. I've even offered a political solution for you. However, at this point in time, I must use all of my efforts to reform the system now allowing unbridled campaign contributions to influence elections in place of 'one person one vote.' I can't do that and also use my efforts and office to bring about grand jury and DOJ reform. Please give me a break. We have been friends too long for this to come between us. Try to understand my position."

"I have tried to understand your position, and I realize there is only so much time in a day; however, it seems to me since so much of the evidence is the same on the issues of campaign contributions and the need for oversight and reform, both items could be presented in tandem thereby eliminating a lot of duplicitous efforts," explained A.T.

"Please," begged the Senator, "let me do this first, and I will hold good to my promise; I will provide the help you will require. However, you will need to formalize any and all requests in writing. Additionally, I will need to discuss the copies of the materials that you and Bud insisted be held by four different parties in the media. I will want that material held until further notice from my office, especially given the new events involving the material you have just supplied. Lee will set up a meeting with you for tomorrow, and he will provide you with the final instructions and mandate from my office," ordered the Senator. "Finally, under no circumstances will the two issues be presented in tandem. I have trouble enough with all that is going on for members of the committee to follow a single issue at a time."

A.T. said, "I thought I would have unlimited access to the information so far as my investigation of the DOJ and the FBI is concerned. I intend to proceed with my efforts to see that there is some meaningful oversight as to those particular agencies and any others that have been continuing to abuse the grand jury process. I thought I had your word on that, Senator. Plus, I would want to be able to disclose certain parts of the investigation to outside law enforcement agencies that will be prosecuting the individuals who murdered Samantha."

"Listen, A.T.," explained the Senator, "I have to maintain complete and strict control over the entire investigation, including any work you have done. That is also true of anything Bud has done. I will personally discuss this with Bud. As far as your efforts to get teeth into some form of oversight in regard to the DOJ and the FBI, let me assure you I will work with you on that matter. I would think you would want it that way because it will ultimately require some form of legislation or Congressional or judicial oversight. That would be best done in cooperation with my office. Therefore, you will absolutely clear anything and everything with me, and you will receive written consent from me before you are authorized to release anything."

A.T. interjected, "But it is my investigation, and I don't want all of that work to be for naught. Besides -"

"Just relax, A.T.," said the Senator. "I will not deny you the work you have done; however, it will need to be cleared and coordinated through my office in every respect. Is that understood?"

"It is; however, what if the timing is such that the investigation will need to be used in order to force the DOJ and the FBI from continuing in the way they have?" asked A.T. "By that, I mean without due regard for the rights of many innocent people."

"In the short term, this will also be handled by my office," answered the Senator. "I've already spoken to my friend who is a Deputy Director, and he will be working with me on a regular basis to sort out the problems within the Bureau. In regard to the DOJ, you have to admit the current administration has done a significant number of things already to stop the problems that previously existed. In both the case of the Bureau and the DOJ, you have to remember the changes you want cannot be instituted overnight. Let me assure you changes are being made and you will be invited to be a part of those changes. Some changes will be structural and others may come about as a result of personnel changes that might occur from one administration to the next. The structural changes will take longer and will take time that we do not have at the present. I will also have hearings on the issue. Please keep in mind we cannot be working at cross purposes. Therefore, anything you would want to do with the results of the investigation you have been a part of will need to be cleared either through Lee or through me directly. Is that understood? If not, I will require that all documents, including all copies, be immediately turned over to me."

"It's understood," said A.T. reluctantly. "What about the murder case? What about Samantha? She cannot be forgotten. She played an important role in getting the information we have. Much of her information and key parts of the investigation will be crucial for the various law enforcement agencies, including the police in Patterson, New Jersey, in solidifying their case against the 'shooter,' whom I believe you will find is the same guy who tried to murder Mr. Felthaus. Also, there is significant evidence against 'Squeaky' Brent Wilson, and 'Big John' Harry Johnson, including a videotape of the two of them confessing their involvement in Samantha's murder. We really cannot -"

"Don't worry," the Senator responded. "The video confessions you obtained and any other relevant information will be used as evidence in the murder case and that would include anything that might be considered exculpatory. I'm sure the Patterson police and any other law enforcement agency would be very happy to have the assistance of a United States Senator. Plus, they will have you as a witness. However, as to any other reason beyond the murder case, do I have your word you will clear all other matters either directly with me or through Lee?"

A.T. hesitated, got up from his chair, walked over to the window, and reluctantly said, "It's agreed, but I must say I am very disappointed it has to be this way."

With that, the meeting with the Senator came to an end with A.T. and the Senator joining Lee and Allen directly outside the Senator's private office. When A.T. and Allen were escorted out into the reception area, Lee instructed the two of them to meet him at Arlington National Cemetery the next morning at 6:30 a.m. in the parking lot of the Custis-Lee Mansion, now known as Arlington House. Lee asked that both A.T. and Allen be prompt because he would have a busy day. He wanted to spend some time discussing the investigation and, as he put it, "going forward." Lee stated in addition to the presence of A.T. and Allen, Bud, Julian, and Blaine would also be needed.

CHAPTER 30
ELUSIVE VAPORS

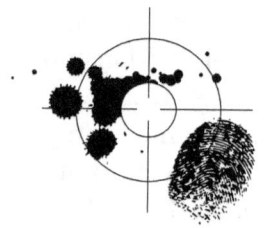

By 6:30 a.m. the next morning, A.T. was where he was supposed to be in the parking area near the Custis-Lee Mansion at Arlington National Cemetery. From inside the rented car, he looked out over the grounds before him and observed the eerie and elusive vapors rising from the surface of the cemetery. The cup of coffee A.T. held in front of him was also emitting vapors, but at least the coffee had a calming aroma. Samantha's death was still troubling him. Her life, like the vapors rising from the ground before him, seemed somehow to be slipping away as only memories of that somewhat remarkable and elusive lady remained. And now, he was worried about Allen. Allen didn't show up for breakfast, and A.T. was unable to reach him by phone. A.T. also tried Allen's family in Washington D.C. and was unable to get any response. Therefore, A.T. went to the designated meeting place by himself with the hopes their messages had crossed and he would meet Allen there; however, there was no Allen, so A.T. waited alone.

Other than a few security guards and vehicles likely belonging to cemetery staff, A.T. was the only individual there to observe the fog rising from the turf. Within less than ten minutes, Lee arrived with Bud Hawthorne. They parked their car directly next to A.T.'s rental and got out. Lee and Bud walked over and slipped inside the back seat of the rented vehicle. The first thing Lee mentioned when he got into the car was that Allen would not be joining them.

"Why not and how do you know this?" asked A.T, turning and facing the two new passengers. "I've been trying to reach Allen."

"It turns out we got a call at the Senator's office to inform us very early this morning that Allen had to make for a hasty departure back to the Twin Cities. Apparently his lady friend, Cynthia Brownell, has disappeared. From what I understand, a close friend of Miss Brownell had access to her home and when she repeatedly called for Miss Brownell, there was no answer. The friend went to the house and found it had been broken into and Miss Brownell was missing."

"What!" exclaimed A.T. "That is bizarre. As I recall, she lives in a very fashionable area of Minneapolis. They never have break-ins there. It is a gated community. I wonder why Allen didn't call me. The two of us are good friends, and I would expect he would have at least called. That is most unusual and -"

"Apparently he was unable to reach you, so he called the Senator's office and left a message to let me know he would not be at the meeting this morning. He said I should tell you once I saw you today since he had to fly out on short notice," informed Lee. "As a normal practice, I check all of the voicemails for the Senator and my own voicemails each morning before I begin the day. It is part of the job I perform for the Senator. I'm sorry to be the one to tell you the bad news about Allen's friend, Cynthia."

"I still can't believe Allen didn't leave a message of some sort for me," said A.T. "That is most unusual. Maybe, I should give him another call."

"I wouldn't do that," said Lee. "No doubt Allen has enough on his mind and most likely he is currently in flight on his way to the Twin Cities. He wouldn't be able to respond to your call anyway." Despite Lee's admonition, A.T. again phoned Allen and left a message for him to call.

A.T., Lee, and Bud engaged in subdued conversation while they waited. After another ten minutes, Blaine and Julian drove up to join them. Upon their arrival, the three men got out of A.T.'s rental and went over to greet Blaine and Julian. At that point, Julian broke down as A.T. mentioned the loss of Samantha. Lee, who had an inquisitive look on his face, began to lead the group up to the Custis-Lee Mansion.

Walking up to the main entrance, A.T. turned to Blaine and Julian to ask, "Do either of you know anything about Sam's funeral arrangements?"

"We do," answered Julian who was still sobbing. "After our meeting here today, let's talk privately, and I will tell you what I know. Details won't be known for a few days, but since I have been asked to help the family, I will send you an email with the details. Is that okay?"

"It is," said A.T. "By the way, when all of this is over, what do the two of you plan to do? I thought that the three of us would meet and -"

"There is going to be a funeral?" inquired Lee. "I thought Samantha had simply disappeared. How can you have a funeral for someone who is just missing? I always thought there had to be a body, and in this case there isn't a -"

"What are you talking about?" asked A.T. noting from Lee's comment something was amiss. "Samantha's body has been recovered, and it is being prepared for delivery back to her family in California, if that hasn't happened already."

"I didn't know that," said Lee displaying a very perplexed look on his face. "When I heard there had been no trace of her, I simply presumed she had disappeared from the face of the earth."

"What exactly had you heard?" asked A.T.

"Simply that she had been…, I mean…that there was no trace of her and she was gone," stammered Lee.

"Who in the world told you that?" inquired A.T.

"It must have been the Senator," answered Lee.

After hearing Lee's response, A.T. thought to himself: *That's very odd. I personally told the Senator that Samantha had been murdered and her body had been recovered near an incinerator at the hospital in Patterson.* In order to divert further discussion about any details, A.T. purposely changed the subject and reasserted his question to Blaine and Julian, "What do the two of you plan on doing after Sam's funeral?"

Julian and Blaine looked at each other a bit nervously, then with Julian nodding to Blaine, he said, "We are starting a new political organization."

"Are you serious?" asked A.T. "I guess I don't understand."

"No doubt you'll remember the fundraiser we had out in San Diego a number of weeks ago," said Blaine.

"Sure," said A.T.

"Well, a number of us from that event have been meeting and have decided to start a political organization that will be known as 'RHINO.' It is an acronym for 'Republican Hope In a New Organization.' So many of the 'lunatic fringe' of the Republican Party already call us 'RINO,' which they cleverly think means 'Republicans in Name Only.' So, we decided we would capitalize on the idea and set up 'RHINO,' the correct spelling, and attempt to reorganize the Republican Party from within."

"Neither Blaine nor I believe we are a part of the current make-up of the Republican Party," asserted Julian while she patted her eyes with a handkerchief Blaine had provided. "The two of us, along with quite a number of Republicans throughout the United States, have decided we need to take the Party back, and we have some fairly extensive membership lists that will allow our new organization, RHINO, to do just that."

"We feel we have been totally disenfranchised by the extreme factions within the Republican Party that have taken over," added Blaine.

"Well," inserted A.T. "there are factions."

"Yes, indeed," said Blaine. "There is the faction of fanatic and extreme religious nuts who aren't even close to any of the mainstream religions. You know the ones who believe in the creationist theories and that man simply popped onto the scene along with the dinosaurs. They have taken up quite a position within the Party. I don't belong with them. Neither does Julian or the others we represent. There is the group that call themselves 'tea party' activists, who in reality have absolutely no idea historically what the tea party of December 16, 1773, was all about. Most of them think it was to eliminate taxes altogether instead of a cry of 'no taxation without representation.' Plus, the 'tea party' people of today think the event that captured the name in Boston over two centuries ago happened in 1776. There is no way we can relate to that group. Next, there is the Libertarian faction that has presented a totally distorted and misunderstood view of the Constitution. Needless to say, we cannot relate to any of them."

"Don't forget the group that believes the woman's role is to remain barefoot and pregnant, no matter how any pregnancy comes about," interrupted Julian. "We cannot relate to that crazy faction within the Republican Party. Those people want to treat women as property and there is no other way of assessing it."

"Also, don't forget the somewhat-related Party dissidents who subscribe to the precepts of the Ku Klux Klan – you know – the 'cluckers,' as they are more frequently called," added Blaine. "We can't relate to them in any way."

"They are just like the neo-Nazis that have also taken up a position within the Party," inserted Julian.

"Related to the neo-Nazis are the 'separatists,' the 'anarchists,' and the 'paramilitary nuts' who are just hoping for some kind of rebellion simply so they can get out and shoot somebody or anybody they don't like," added Blaine. "We cannot relate to those characters who Teddy Roosevelt called the 'Lunatic Fringe.'"

"Don't forget the very wealthy individuals who actually believe that, as the 'privileged' who have attained a position of financial standing, they have earned the right to rule over everyone else,'" said Julian.

"Now that you have identified various 'fringe thinking' factions making up today's Republican Party, don't you realize the Republican Party has essentially become a political party of dissidents and social extremists?" asked A.T. "It hardly seems the Republican Party is worth saving. Why don't you simply start your own political party?"

"Because, damn it," exclaimed Blaine, "the Republican Party has a lot of good people who have been pushed aside by these extremists. Now it's time we let them know you don't need to have extreme views to be a Republican and most Republicans are not as crazy as these fringe groups. There are so many mainstream Republicans who have had enough and are willing to reclaim the Party. That's the movement we have started, and it is our intent to take the Republican Party back."

"That sounds like a monumental task," said A.T. "I wish you luck."

At that point, Blaine looked at Lee and asked, "Why are we meeting here, and where are we going?"

"I thought this would be an appropriate place," answered Lee.

"Why, exactly?" inquired Bud.

"From the recent news I am hearing, let's regard it as a tribute to Samantha," answered Lee, who was obviously a bit shaken. After taking a moment to regain his composure, Lee continued, "Also, it will enable us to have a very private conversation at the Custis-Lee Mansion where I've arranged for a private self-guided tour. A friend of mine works here. It will enable us to speak confidentially and frankly about what lies ahead."

"A tribute to Samantha is appropriate, but why here?" asked Blaine.

"This cemetery," answered Lee, "is where so many valiant and patriotic Americans have been laid to rest, so I thought we could meet here to think about their great efforts, along with the efforts that others, people like Samantha, will make in the future.

"Perhaps none of you, except for A.T., are aware of the information that Samantha was instrumental in providing to the Senator. Through her introduction of A.T. to the GGG, the Senator now has the information he believes will enable his committee to conduct an inquiry as to the way financial contributions will be made to political campaigns in the future. One item that has been gaining support from both sides of the aisle is the proposed Constitutional Amendment relating to eliminating financial political contributions by corporate interests. That has stirred the nerves of some powerful organizations, as well as individuals.

"It would seem," continued Lee, "after Samantha's efforts, along with those of A.T., were able to draw so much attention, many of the people in Congress who were opposed to campaign reform seem to be changing their minds. Since each of you has been quite involved, I simply wanted to take some time to caution you about going forward. Perhaps because the 'Citizens United' case pronouncement by the Supreme Court has been a pet concern of the Senator and due to recent pronouncements by certain political candidates that corporations are people too, making significant changes to election funding is now a priority for some politicians on both sides of the aisle, particularly the Senator. The age-old myth and recognition that a corporation was entitled to some of the same rights as individuals under the law that related to conducting business, entering contracts, suing and being sued, and so forth, were never meant to include any rights when it came to the election process.

"Finally," added Lee, "the Senator believes it will now be possible to curtail the future promises of what have been termed 'well-upholstered' chairs to sitting elected officials. The Senator feels the proposed changes to the law will make it a criminal offense for promises and salaries of reward to be made by individuals and corporations to sitting government officials for when they retire from government service. And that will apply for several years after retirement. For decades now, and perhaps much longer, as rewards for providing a friendly ear and a vote on specific issues, people and corporations have promised positions of power and prestige, coupled with large salaries, for helpful office holders once they retire. Just so each of you knows, there are power brokers with a lot of money behind the scenes who will oppose such efforts of reform. I wanted to privately warn each of you in the event the Senator's committee proceeds with the hearings, if you testify, those powerful parties will take notice."

"Are you cautioning us not to testify?" asked A.T. "That would seem to run contrary to what the Senator has asked us to do."

"Not at all," exclaimed Lee. "I just thought that by bringing you to this location for a private discussion with no chance of recording our conversation, my concerns might have the impact of demonstrating how serious a matter this is in the eyes of some very powerful people."

"You are definitely scaring me," asserted Julian.

"I view it as a part of my job simply to inform each of you as to just how serious a matter this has come to be," said Lee. "Simply stated, there are parties who get hyper-sensitive whenever they sense someone is trying to upset a process that has been in place a long time -"

"Why don't you give us an example of the types of parties you are referring to?" questioned A.T.

"I'm sure most of you have never heard of them. However, I do believe A.T. may have come across a couple of such groups in the course of his investigation," exclaimed Lee while smiling at A.T. "In fact, A.T. can probably give you the details of a private meeting he had with two individuals at the Yale Club in New York, where the two groups under investigation were discussed in some detail."

"Why don't you be more specific, Lee?" insisted A.T.

"Wasn't your friend, Samantha, involved in a group called the GGG, and didn't you have an animated encounter with a couple of former investigators while at the Yale Club in New York regarding another group called LESTER?" asked Lee.

"The name LESTER has surfaced during my investigation and I did speak to a couple of old acquaintances," answered A.T. "However, Bud, Blaine and Julian don't have anything to do with that part of the investigation, so why are you trying to frighten them?"

"I'm not trying to frighten anyone and besides..." said Lee, "I think ..."

"I've known Samantha for many years, and I can tell you straight out she wouldn't have anything to do with the kinds of organizations you mentioned," interjected Julian. "I would have known if she had been a part of a GGG organization or a LESTER group."

"Same with me," joined in Blaine. "Samantha and her family have been involved in Republican politics for about as long as I have, and I have known everything about Samantha and her family. I can assure you she would not have been a part of some sinister political group of any kind."

"She wasn't," asserted A.T. "I can verify Samantha was not a part of something sinister. Do you mind if I speak to you privately, Lee?" requested A.T. firmly grasping the fabric on Lee's coat.

"But, of course," responded Lee as he and A.T. walked out of hearing distance from the others. During the walk, A.T., who had worn the video recording suit, activated the device.

When the two of them reached a considerable distance from the others, A.T. looked directly at Lee and asked, "What the hell is going on, Lee? Whose side are you on? Does the Senator know about this unique little meeting we are having? What kind of double play is this? Is there any purpose to this meeting other than to scare Julian, Blaine, and Bud?"

"Whatever do you mean?" asked Lee with a perverse smile on his face.

"You know perfectly well what I mean. It seems to me you are doing everything you can to discourage Bud, Blaine, and Julian from being a part of any testimony before the committee. So, may I presume you intend to have similar meetings with other witnesses?" asserted A.T.

"I'm sure you have mistaken what I have said and my intentions. I consider it a part of my job to be sure certain witnesses will stand up under pressure," noted Lee.

"That's a crock," exclaimed A.T. "There is something not right, and it seems to me you are in the middle of it. You are trying your best to undermine any effort the Senator might be making to bring about changes to the political process. I believe I will need to mention this incident and your behavior to the Senator."

"Go ahead," insisted Lee. "I've worked for the Senator for over twenty years. He has total confidence in me. I can assure you he would take my word before yours any day. He trusts me implicitly. Your credibility is questionable, and you would have no evidence that could possibly convince the Senator I have done anything that would undermine his efforts. Plus, I'm sure it will seem to the Senator that you are so upset that your pet project regarding oversight and the grand jury is now off the table that you would do anything to get your little project back on the table."

"Not so fast," insisted A.T. "The Senator has also known me for a very long time, and he would never think I would undermine his efforts. Plus, I am still hopeful the Senator will reconsider and get the matter about grand jury oversight before the subcommittee. On the other hand, there is quite a bit of evidence I already can piece together indicating that you may not be working exclusively for or with the Senator but for other individuals who harbor a totally different agenda."

"Oh, really," exclaimed Lee. "Why don't you give me one example?"

"How about several?" insisted A.T. "First, it strikes me as more than obvious that you have purposely brought three key witnesses out to a cemetery setting in order to scare the daylights out of them about testifying. Second, it makes no sense that you are the one to bring forth apparent news that Cynthia Brownell has disappeared and Allen called you instead of me in order to advise that he has flown back to the Twin Cities. Unless something strange is going on, and maybe you called Allen instead of his calling you and told him he didn't need to call me, Allen would have called to inform me himself. Third, is the fact you seemed surprised that Samantha's body was located. You did seem to know she had disappeared. It couldn't have been the Senator who told you she had disappeared because if the Senator had told you about Samantha, he would have told you she had been murdered and her body had been found. No, it was someone other than the Senator that had to have told you Samantha was gone with no trace of a body. It is also obvious you haven't visited with the Senator since he learned of her death. Fourth, there is no way you could have known I met with two individuals at the Yale Club in New York unless those two individuals, 'Squeaky' and 'Big John,' have spoken to you about that meeting. Fifth, how would you know about the investigation possibly involving LESTER unless 'Squeaky' or 'Big John' or an individual by the name of Osborne Leeds had been in conversation with you about LESTER, since that was never openly discussed? I want to know what exactly you are up to before this goes any further."

"You are confused, A.T.," insisted Lee. "I may have called Allen just to check on whether he would be here this morning, and perhaps I had heard about his lady friend, Cynthia, from someone at the Senator's office."

"That's bullshit, and you know it," exclaimed A.T. "You probably heard it from your attorney friend, Osborne Leeds."

"Who," asked Lee? "I'm sorry, but I don't know anyone by the name of Osborne Leeds."

"That's really strange," noted A.T. "because the other day when the Senator and I were reviewing the 'minutes of testimony,' I asked if you would be joining us, and he told me you couldn't because you had to meet with your attorney, Osborne Leeds."

"You really think you're onto something, don't you?" asked Lee.

"After talking with you just now, I'm convinced of it," commented A.T. "You have exposed yourself, and it is apparent you are involved with quite a different agenda than that of the Senator. Just who are you working with, Lee, and just what are you and Osborne Leeds up to?"

"I'm doing my job and nothing else," answered Lee.

"The question is what job and for whom," commented A.T.

"This is not the time or place for this discussion," said Lee. "It's apparent the two of us will need to have our own discussion after the meeting here today. Since you are so concerned about my scaring the others, permit me to suggest we save what has been just said between us for a private and later discussion. I would suggest we go ahead with my planned tour of the Custis-Lee Mansion, and afterward the two of us will arrange for a private discussion. For the sake of your friends, I suggest you pretend nothing unusual has happened during our talk."

"I will agree to do that so long as you keep the three of them out of whatever events unfold from here forward," insisted A.T.

"That's agreed," said Lee while leading the two of them back to where everyone else was standing. Then in a very cheerful voice he said, "Thank you all for excusing us. A.T. and I had some private matters to discuss about the investigation. Now, please allow me to provide you with a personally guided tour of the mansion."

"As I said," continued Lee, "I wanted to let you know what the Senator intends to do in moving forward with the information that has been received as a result of the investigation and what each of you has provided."

"Why don't you get right to the point and tell us?" asked A.T.

"All right," answered Lee. "The Senator intends to join a number of other members of the Senate in sponsoring a Constitutional Amendment that will regulate the funding of campaigns. It will directly address the issues raised by the 'Citizens United' case. From the draft I have seen, the amendment will prohibit any and all corporation contributions to any candidate that runs for public office on the federal level. It will prohibit the 'political action committee' completely.

"It will prohibit any and all 'offshore' contributions by any party, regardless of the amount and regardless of who is making the contribution. Additionally, the draft prohibits any form of future rewards, benefits, positions, salaries, or other financial arrangements between an elected official and any party that promises anything remotely resembling what has been termed a 'well-upholstered chair.' That prohibition will have at least a three year future window of application and will allow for the investigation of any former elected official, as well as high ranking officials such as deputy officials, who take positions with any entity that conducts business in any fashion with the United States government. The Senator is quite excited about this, especially with the new evidence he has received from the GGG through A.T. and the efforts of Samantha."

"That's really a step forward, and I applaud the Senator's efforts. I am glad the investigation has been fruitful in such regard," commented Bud. "But what is going to happen to the work I did and the additional investigative work A.T. did? The unification of the paramilitary groups, in my view, is more than a danger; it is a clear and present danger. Plus, the undue and extraordinary placement of people with specific religious thinking into government positions, from my research at least, creates an additional danger and problem as far as the Constitution is concerned. These are two issues and areas where there are some very serious problems the Senator needs to address. In fact, he promised he would address these two issues."

"You've got to separate the two issues you're addressing, Bud," said Lee. "The paramilitary groups have always been an issue –"

"It's more of a problem today, and I believe it is at the point of presenting a 'clear and present' danger to the government of this country," interjected Bud.

"You're right, Bud," said Lee, "at least in reference to the paramilitary groups. They have always been a danger to this country. It is a violation of the Constitution for there to be private militias, and that has been regulated and controlled in the past by the government. Furthermore, the Senator recognizes that the problem has grown and is now a greater problem than ever before in the United States. Since that is the case, the Senator has instructed me to tell you he will be conducting separate hearings on the current status of the paramilitary organizations. However, those hearings will not take place immediately. The Senator believes more must be done. In that regard, he wants you to visit with me privately either before or directly after an upcoming fundraiser for the Senator. I understand you and the Senator have certain family ties. Regardless, he believes your investigative reporting on the issue should continue with possibly an article or two that you might wish to publish at a later time."

Lee continued, "As for the concern you have relative to the religious groups that have been infiltrating various branches of government, including the Executive Branch through the DOJ, I felt I should specifically instruct you that he will not be conducting any hearings on the subject. His concern is the separation of church and state coupled with the rights of religious freedom. Should you decide to continue your investigation on that issue, you will need to do it on your own and without the Senator's help. The Senator will not be involved in any way, shape, or form in regard to that matter, and I hope this is the end of that matter. If you don't believe me, please feel free to talk to him privately, but he was quite adamant when he instructed me to tell you there would be no Senate hearing that would involve him relative to any religious group. So don't say I didn't forewarn you."

"So, will any continued investigation by me be sanctioned by the Senator?" asked A.T.

"We will see about that. The Senator has expressed interest in working at some point in the future with you on the issue of grand jury reform and oversight. He was hopeful you would see the wisdom in this decision."

"I guess I expected much more, especially based upon what the investigation has shown," commented A.T.

"Permit me to suggest you call him," urged Lee. "Oh, and when you do, I would caution you to limit your discussion to that point only. I don't think either of us would want the Senator to become agitated."

"Are you suggesting such a discussion will need to happen privately between us before I call the Senator?" asked A.T.

"Most assuredly that is the case," insisted Lee.

"Understood," noted A.T.

"What about the two of us," Blaine asked. "Julian and I have not been involved in the investigation, so why did you invite us?"

"For the simple reason that the two of you have been privy to key information in several respects," answered Lee. "In your case, Blaine, you have been entrusted with a portion of the documents relating to this investigation. Those are the documents A.T. provided with the approval of the Senator. Additionally, both you and Julian have been good friends with both A.T. and Samantha. There is no doubt you have either heard or seen some very confidential information that, under no circumstances, can anything be released to the media or to anyone else without the expressed consent of the Senator. Do you understand this and how important it is for the body of the investigation to be held in the strictest of confidence? In addition, do you understand there are statutes that prohibit the unauthorized release of certain aspects of the investigation that were obtained in the course of a Senate inquiry?"

"I fully understand," said Blaine. "I have no intention of revealing the information that I have or know."

"That's good to hear," said Lee. "Just so you know, many of the details that have come into your possession might be the sort of thing certain individuals might try to obtain forcibly; therefore, the Senator wanted to be sure the two of you were aware of that possible danger. He wanted to be sure the information was safely locked away in regard to printed material. Also, any knowledge each of you has in your relationship with either Samantha or A.T. needs to be safeguarded and never disclosed or discussed. In fact, from here on, it would be a good idea for you to share that information with me only."

"That's not a good idea," exclaimed A.T. "The original instruction from the Senator was that the investigation was not to be shared with anyone without his approval and not yours. I believe each witness should stand by that commitment unless the Senator otherwise advises."

"Of course," answered Blaine. "I believe it would be best for me to keep the information totally confidential until I hear from the Senator."

"Very well," interrupted Lee scowling at A.T.

"What about you, Julian?" asked Lee as he looked directly at her. "We know you are writing a book, and we want to be sure none of this knowledge finds its way into a book or other publication. We also want to be sure you don't discuss the investigation with others. Your own safety may be at stake. Do you understand, Julian, and do I have your word you will not reveal any of the information you have learned as a result of what A.T. and Samantha may have told you?"

"You have my word; I will not release anything from the investigation without the Senator's okay," responded Julian. "Why would my safety be at stake?"

"Perhaps I should have mentioned it sooner, and this is important for all of you to know," said Lee. "A.T. is aware of a man who was involved in an attempted murder at the Dulles International Airport. Who knows, he might even be the same man who caused Samantha's disappearance."

"Well," exclaimed Julian, "that's interesting news. Blaine and I will want to tell Samantha's family, especially if it turns out to be the same man." She turned to A.T. and said, "By the way, I forgot to tell you the funeral will be in San Bernardino. I will email all of the details to you, A.T. I know you will want to attend the service, but I won't know the details until I get back to San Diego."

"Thanks," said A.T. "I will want to attend the funeral. That's appreciated."

The five of them left the Mansion and headed back to the parking lot. Blaine and Julian departed together, and Bud was asked by Lee to wait by their car while Lee had a private word with A.T.

* *

When Lee approached A.T. at the side of his car, A.T. was already calling the Senator on his private line. Nearing A.T., Lee could hear a portion of the conversation. "That's right, Senator," said A.T. "It is my firm belief Lee is the cause of information being leaked from your office; furthermore, I believe Lee is working directly with some of the people we have under investigation -"

"Stop it," exclaimed Lee as he tried to take the phone from A.T. "Here, let me talk to the Senator -"

"What?" asked A.T. into the phone. "Lee is standing right here, and he is trying to have me give him the phone, no doubt for the purpose of setting forth some type of excuse. Yes, I have proof of what I am saying -"

After some discussion by the Senator, including the scheduling of a private meeting with A.T., the Senator asked if A.T. would hand the phone to Lee, which A.T. did.

"A.T. is getting paranoid, Senator," urged Lee while he took the phone from A.T. "He is now jumping to conclusions…No sir, he has absolutely no proof of any such thing…You know of my total loyalty….You know I would never do anything of the kind… It is my firm belief A.T. is disappointed he did not get his way with the results of the investigation and is now somehow blaming me that the subcommittee will not be taking up the issue of grand jury oversight…Not at all…My meeting with Osborne Leeds was for personal estate planning and nothing more…All other matters that A.T. has mentioned, I'm sure were a part of the discussions between you and me regarding the investigation. Sure, I will give you back to A.T."

"Right, Senator," said A.T. "I will go there immediately. Bye!"

"Where are you going?" asked Lee. "Are you meeting with the Senator? If you try to screw up what is in place and going on, I will do everything I can to be sure you never get anything in front of the subcommittee. More than that, I am confident your friends, 'Squeaky,' 'Big John,' and your new friendly psychiatrist, Victor Salensky, will be more than ready to deal with any efforts you take from this point forward."

"You've just admitted your involvement with what happened to Samantha in that threat you just made," exclaimed A.T. "The only way you would know that the hit man, Salensky, was portraying a psychiatrist would be a result of your direct involvement."

"You will never convince the Senator of anything. Let me assure you that you will need to watch your back now more than ever," asserted Lee. "Anything you do from this point forward will be monitored 24/7, and you better be sure you have the kind of protection that disappeared when your friend, Samantha, departed."

"That's quite a series of admissions," said A.T. "Is there anything more you would like to confess at this time?"

"You can go to hell!" exclaimed Lee. "There is way too much at stake! Believe me when I tell you that you are in over your head beyond your wildest dreams. There are very rich and powerful people involved, and they are a part of an exclusive club. You are not a member, and I can assure you that you never will be. You have just marked yourself as a primary target. Not only will I refute anything you tell the Senator, but there are others who are a number of pay grades above you who will be there to convince the Senator that you are standing out in the cold."

"We'll see," said A.T. while getting into his car. He drove off, heading to the location where the Senator asked to meet.

* *

The meeting with the Senator took longer than anticipated. During the span of over three hours, A.T. was able to provide the Senator with copies of the videotapes he had made of his Yale Club meeting with 'Squeaky' and 'Big John,' along with the video he had just made of his exchange with Lee. The Senator, who was baffled at what Lee had been doing and the evidence that A.T. presented, explained that he would listen to Lee and act as if nothing out of the ordinary had happened. Additionally, the Senator assured A.T. that he would contact his close friend, the Associate Director of the FBI, and have an investigation done on Lee because of various statutes. Lee's duties and functions would be limited, and the Senator would send Lee out of the country on a fact-finding mission while office procedures were changed and the FBI investigation of Lee got under way. The Senator explained that although he appreciated what A.T. had done in exposing Lee, the Senator's mind had not changed in regard to any presentation of grand jury oversight to the subcommittee. That matter would simply have to wait, and A.T. would need to live with that decision. With nothing more to keep his attention in Washington D.C., A.T. was more than thrilled to get on a plane and fly back to the Twin Cities.

When A.T. returned to the Twin Cities and greeted Jacci at the airport, the two of them headed out to one of their favorite restaurants for a quiet evening meal. While Jacci drove to the restaurant, A.T. activated his iPhone and noted he had a number of emails. The two emails that caught his immediate attention included one from Julian who, as agreed, informed him that the funeral for Samantha would be held on Wednesday at Saint Joseph's Catholic Church at Big Bear Lake, northeast of San Bernardino. Immediately, A.T. mentioned to Jacci that he would make travel plans for the two of them to fly out to the West Coast on Tuesday of the upcoming week.

Before A.T. got on the phone to book airline and hotel reservations, he decided to access the second email that he felt was noteworthy. It was an email from Gerald, who wrote of the details of Samantha's funeral. Gerald made special note of the fact he would not only be in attendance at Samantha's funeral but he would also be one of the guest priests who had been asked to participate in the Mass. Gerald also stated it was imperative that he and A.T. plan to visit after the ceremony at the gravesite and before the reception since Gerald had some critically important information to convey.

Next, A.T. telephoned Allen, who immediately answered the phone. As it turned out, it was true Cynthia Brownell had turned up missing and her home had been ransacked. Allen explained he had gotten the call from Lee in the early morning of the scheduled meeting at the National Cemetery. The police had become involved before Allen had returned to the Twin Cities. Allen expressed fear that something dreadful might have happened to Cynthia, especially since her home had been significantly damaged by someone who was apparently looking for something. A.T. needed to see his friend immediately.

Upon arriving at Allen's home, A.T. and Jacci did their best to console Allen and learn what they could about Cynthia's disappearance. The entire matter was very troubling, and A.T. discussed with Allen the possibility that whoever was involved in the disappearance of Cynthia might be the same individuals who were involved in Samantha's death. A.T. brought Allen up to speed on the recent events involving the Senator's aide, Lee. Upon leaving Allen at his residence, A.T. and Jacci had a quiet evening together.

Pleased that Jacci would be able to attend Samantha's funeral with him, A.T. scheduled their flight to southern California. Years earlier when A.T. had been involved in politics, Jacci met Blaine, Angel, Julian, and Bernie. So it was going to be a bit of a reunion of old political friends. Typical of Blaine, he had made hotel reservations and had picked up the tab for everyone that was to be a part of the meeting, including A.T. and Jacci. Although the circumstances were unfortunate in regard to Samantha's funeral, everyone was looking forward to getting reacquainted after so many years had passed.

* *

While A.T. and Jacci were driving to Big Bear Lake, Jacci accessed an email reminder from Gerald that had been sent to

A.T.'s iPhone. Gerald was reminding A.T. that it was important for them to meet directly after the ceremony at the cemetery. Gerald said he would approach A.T. when he felt the timing was right. It was during the drive that A.T. explained to Jacci exactly how his investigation and Samantha's investigation crossed paths. A.T. recounted his discussion with the Senator and explained how disappointed he was with the Senator. Jacci was quick to remind A.T. that she had warned him about the Senator and again stressed that even though the Senator may have promised to help in the future in regard to A.T.'s desire to bring about some oversight to the grand jury process, it wasn't worth holding one's breath in terms of any expectation the Senator would ever make good on his promise.

The more A.T. gave it some thought, the more he realized Jacci was probably right. It was becoming more apparent A.T. would need to seek out some alternative if he ever wanted to get the results of his investigation in front of the Senator's subcommittee or any other government entity that could do something worthwhile with the work that A.T. and Samantha had accomplished. He still was without a solution to the problem.

"Why don't we put the entire investigation out of our minds for now as we pay our respects to Samantha," urged Jacci.

"You're right," responded A.T. "Nothing can be accomplished by reliving the past and the hardships of the investigation," responded A.T. "In fact, we should start planning some time off and perhaps a bit of a vacation."

"Great idea," said Jacci. "Let's plan to go someplace far away where we can relax and put this entire matter behind us."

"Perfect idea," noted A.T. "Let's find a place where no one knows us and where no one can find us."

"I'll pick up some brochures when we return to the Twin Cities," suggested Jacci.

"I'll go along with that, and now no further talk of the investigation," said A.T. smiling.

* *

After checking into their room and freshening up, Jacci and A.T. decided they would go to the church a bit early. This would give them time to pay their respects to Samantha's family before the

Mass. Once at the church, they discovered that Samantha's family had been called back to a conference with the priest, so they entered a room that had been set up for the visitation. The only other person they noticed was none other than Father Gerald. Father Gerald acted very formal and when A.T. began to ask a question, Gerald said, "Not now and not here. We will speak at the cemetery after the gravesite service." With that comment Gerald turned and left while A.T. and Jacci remained for a while longer before going into the main part of the church for the Requiem Mass.

Fortunately for A.T. and Jacci, they were able to find seating in the church as the pews filled beyond capacity, and the side aisles and back of the church had standing room only. It was apparent Samantha had been an extremely popular and well-loved person. Not unlike any other Requiem Mass, the liturgy was very long. When the congregation passed through the doors at the conclusion of the Mass, everyone was handed a map providing detailed directions to the cemetery. With Jacci providing directions from the map, A.T. was able to locate the cemetery. Since it took a while to park the car, the two of them found the graveside service was already underway when they arrived.

While walking to the gravesite, A.T. did a double-take when he noticed a group of men off in the distance who had gathered around what appeared to be a maintenance shed. He was certain he saw two men whose faces seemed familiar. That did not seem possible since one was Victor Salensky and the other was Leslie Winthrop. It did not seem likely either of them would be at the cemetery. And there was virtually no chance they would know each other.

Although A.T. had been informed by both Allen and Eric that Salensky had escaped, the chances of his being at the cemetery seemed totally inconceivable. A.T. had been very careful not to tell Jacci or anyone else that he had been informed Salensky had escaped. Allen also advised that it was believed someone had aided Salensky in his escape.

Troubled about worrying Jacci, A.T. decided to not mention anything until he was absolutely certain the men he saw were Salensky and Winthrop. However, when A.T. looked back at the location, the men he thought he saw were no longer there. Nevertheless, he decided he would keep a sharp eye out just in case he happened to see the men again.

When A.T. and Jacci quietly walked up to the gravesite, A.T. again did a double-take. Only this time what he saw was even more of a shock. He could feel his heart stop, and he hesitated to move forward. Jacci turned to him with a concerned look and whispered, "Are you okay?"

Regaining his composure, A.T. whispered back, "Yes, I'll be okay, but you won't believe what I thought I just saw."

"What?" asked Jacci.

"I'll tell you later when we are alone," whispered A.T. when reaching the gravesite. What A.T. thought he had seen was the ghost of Samantha! He didn't think he'd really seen a ghost but a nun that looked exactly like Samantha. The young nun was at the end of a group of nuns who were near the front of a large group of people gathered under the tent-like structure at the site. A.T. strained to look again, but the people in front of him blocked his view. It was difficult for him to concentrate on what was being said by none other than Father Gerald. Gerald continued to deliver his gravesite eulogy, and A.T. continued to try to get a better view of the young nun without appearing too obvious. At moments he could see her face; when he did, he felt certain he was looking at Samantha. In fact, memories of Samantha on the steps of the Lincoln Memorial with tears streaming down her cheeks came back as a vivid reminder of her face. It wasn't her. He knew better. That couldn't be. He saw her get shot and die in front of him. He identified the body at the hospital incinerator.

Whatever was said by Father Gerald or anyone else may have been heard by others, but to A.T. the memories of the past few years played themselves out in his mind. While his mind was replaying the events of the past days in Washington, including his confrontation with the Senator and the confrontation with Lee, A.T. was nudged by Jacci who smiled at him and said, "Everyone is leaving. Are you sure you are okay?"

"Yes, yes, I'm okay," responded A.T. smiling back at her. At that moment, the nuns approached the area where A.T. and Jacci were standing.

The young nun, the one who looked like Samantha, stopped directly in front of A.T. and attempted to smile at A.T. and Jacci. Straining to smile, she extended her hand to A.T., offering him a thick eight and a half by eleven inch envelope. A.T. couldn't stop staring at the young lady, who said, "Hi! My name is Sister Amanda; they call me Nan. As you might have guessed from my appearance, I am Samantha's younger sister."

Feeling stunned, A.T. finally stammered a greeting to the young nun and said, "Hello Sister Nan; I'm A.T. and this is my wife, Jacci."

Jacci hugged the young nun and said, "Sister Nan, we are so sorry about the loss of your sister. Since I met Samantha once at the airport in Minneapolis, I really didn't know her; however, A.T. has told me so many wonderful things about her. I'm sure she will be missed by so many people."

"Thank you for your kind words," Sister Nan responded. A.T. opened the envelope and pulled out a stack of papers including a surveillance photo, apparently taken by Samantha showing the Senator's aide, Lee, at a table in a restaurant with none other than Osborne Leeds, the principal spokesperson of LESTER.

"Not here and not now," insisted Sister Nan.

"I understand," responded A.T. returning the photo and other documents to the envelope.

"When it is convenient before you leave the area, perhaps you might be kind enough to call me," urged Sister Nan. "My number is in the envelope I just gave you. Samantha left something more, and I will want to deliver it to you personally. It cannot be here or now. It will take time for all of us to understand what has happened. But for now, I must go with my sisters. We will meet again, and then we can talk. We will speak privately; however, Jacci, you are more than welcome to be present when we speak."

With that final comment, Sister Nan turned and left A.T. and Jacci standing alone but not for long. Within moments they were joined by Father Gerald, who had silently positioned himself behind. When A.T. turned around and saw Gerald, he almost lost his composure, perhaps due to the pious pose of Gerald, which seemed a bit out of place as far as A.T. was concerned. But A.T. had learned to prepare for nearly anything, so he extended his hand to greet Gerald. Shaking Gerald's hand, A.T. said, "Father Gerald, this is my wife, Jacci. Jacci, this is Father Gerald who has also been working on an investigation relative to the case."

"It is finally nice to place the face with the voice. Nice to meet you in person," said Jacci.

With some obvious surprise, A.T. said, "Have the two of you spoken before?"

"We have on a couple of occasions when Father Gerald telephoned the house," said Jacci. "Father Gerald has already informed me that he has been working on similar matters to yours; however, he never did explain any details. But he did tell me enough for the two of us to share some mutual concerns we had about you and the type of pressure the investigation was having on you."

"Forgive me, but this comes as a bit of a surprise," said A.T.

"No, perhaps you should forgive me," interjected Gerald. "I have taken the liberty to inform Jacci of exactly who I am and how it is that I have become involved in an investigation that involves some of the same facts and circumstances that have been a part of your investigation. Despite what you may think, A.T., I really have had some genuine concerns for you."

"What type of concerns?" asked A.T.

"There are many," responded Gerald. "I was worried about how hard you have been driving yourself. There are issues about the completion of your investigation. There is a matter regarding your relationship with the Senator. Plus, since Samantha's untimely death, I have had some serious concerns about your safety. Forgive me, but I may have expressed some of these issues to Jacci. Here it is that I, a priest, am asking for your forgiveness."

"With no disrespect, 'Father' Gerald," said A.T., "I can handle myself quite well. I have learned, including most recently, I am better off if I do things myself and not trust others who make a claim to be helping me."

"A.T.," scolded Jacci, "at least be polite. I genuinely believe Father Gerald is really trying to be helpful. Think about it; he has no reason to not be helpful. You do need to be more trusting, if I may say so."

"My being trusting has not been very beneficial to me so far," said A.T.

"If you are talking about the Senator, I can fully understand," inserted Gerald.

"It is true that I trusted the Senator, and look what happened," commented A.T. "Sorry, but you probably don't know what I'm talking about, Gerald. Why should you?"

"I know very well what you are talking about," responded Gerald noticing A.T. look at Jacci. "No, she didn't say anything to me. But I have sources, and I know all about your conversations with the Senator and -"

"How would you know about my conversations with the Senator," asked A.T. "unless you have spies in his office too?"

"Quite confidentially," said Gerald, "I do. Lee Mattson is my former college roommate, and we are, to this day, very old friends.

That information is exclusively for the two of you and no one else. Lee is loyal to the Senator and wouldn't do anything to breach that trust. However, I do not work for the Senator, and I believe I have a way for us to see that the Senator reconsiders his decision -"

"From what I now know and from what I have recently learned," interrupted A.T., "I have very good reason to believe under no circumstances can your friend, Lee, be trusted. I can show you from my investigation that he is working against the Senator's interests, and it is your former college roommate, Lee, who has been leaking information about the investigation all along to members of the LESTER group."

"You can't possibly be serious," commented Gerald. "I've known Lee for many years, and I am fully aware of most of his life activities. I am quite certain he would not work against the Senator's interests or be a part of anything inappropriate. I certainly cannot see his being involved with an organization like LESTER."

"You are dead wrong," asserted A.T. "You don't know him as well as you might think. For example, I can let you hear a video recording I have in which your friend, Lee, admits his involvement with LESTER. I can also prove to you that Lee has been meeting with one of the principals of LESTER, namely Osborne Leeds. I have just received a copy of a photo of your friend, Lee, in a meeting at a restaurant with none other than Osborne Leeds, the head of LESTER."

"I must see the evidence," said Gerald.

"I have the evidence, including the photo I just mentioned and a copy of the video conversation I made a few days ago where Lee admits and details his involvement with LESTER and his relationship with Osborne.

"If that is the case, let me see it," insisted Gerald. "If we are going to trust each other going forward, let's put the cards on the table."

"Here's the photo I just received, and I will send you the video," said A.T. He then allowed Father Gerald to see the photo he had just received from Sister Nan. While Gerald examined the photo, A.T. explained the happenings at the Custis-Lee Mansion at Arlington Cemetery.

After A.T. detailed the events from days earlier and Lee's admissions, Gerald returned the photo, and walked around for several minutes in the immediate area as if deep in thought. He paused, turned back toward A.T. and Jacci, and said, "Now that I think about it, there have been instances where I thought I had imparted strictly confidential information to Lee, and later I found out that other parties had learned of what I had told Lee in confidence. The fact that Lee may have been double dealing all along is troubling to me. However, it does make some sense."

"I will also show you more evidence," offered A.T.

"This is taking me a bit off-guard," admitted Gerald. "The photo is proof they know each other, and if your tape reflects what you just told me, then the two of us will need to collaborate. I have an idea as to how we must proceed from this point forward. However, we will need to bury the hatchet and agree to work with each other."

"Here we go," commented A.T. "I have a feeling we are going to hear a real plan. What do you plan to do? Blackmail both Lee and the Senator?"

"I wouldn't call it blackmail," smiled Gerald. "It seems to me the Senator was trying to invite you into a bit of a compromise situation by having you attend a fundraiser from what I was told. It would be very embarrassing for the Senator if there was evidence he was trying to do such a thing. Plus, if Lee was complicit in terms of activities with LESTER, it would appear Lee might have crossed more than one line and may have violated several statutes; therefore, Lee would be subject to prosecution."

"In terms of the Senator, exactly what evidence are you speaking of," asked A.T., "and in regard to Lee, why would you want to work toward discrediting him?"

"There is quite a bit of evidence the Senator might not want to have as part of a record," explained Gerald. "For example, I believe Samantha had a recording where her former Congressman friend spoke of the Senator trying to use the relationship between Samantha and the Congressman as leverage. I also understand either that same recording or another recording from Samantha's answering machine reflects a statement by the Senator that he was using you to complete work for his purpose, but he did not have any intention of fulfilling his promise to you about grand jury reform being considered by his subcommittee. Now, finally as to Lee, even though we are former college roommates and friends, perhaps I owe him one, especially if he has been crossing a line."

"How do you know about Samantha's recordings?" asked A.T.

"Just think about it, A.T., even though Samantha and I had our differences, we had a mutual respect for each other. In fact, it might be said we had a sort of love-hate relationship -"

"Love-hate relationship," asserted A.T.

"Not in the sense of a romantic couple but as co-workers who both believed in what they did for a living. I didn't volunteer to be a part of Samantha's funeral. I was asked to be a part of it in Samantha's Last Will and Testament. This may be hard for you to realize, but she and I were still friends, even though we may have been a bit of competitors, as well. Neither of us had many people whom we could trust, so we were forced to trust each other. That's how I know about the recordings. At least those recordings and your testimony from the meeting you had with the Senator might well be enough for the Senator to reconsider getting your investigation in front of the subcommittee for a genuine review. Naturally, the idea of reconsideration by the Senator will need to be approached delicately. If you were to have a frank discussion with the Senator while someone else happened to anonymously drop-ship the tapes I've mentioned to the Senator, he might just want to reconsider," urged Gerald.

"I'm not going to be a part of any threats to the Senator or anyone else," responded A.T.

"You won't have to be," said Gerald.

"What do you mean?" asked A.T.

"What If I told you there was an overly ambitious young prosecutor in New York who wanted to endear himself to his voting constituents and at the same time gain favor with certain members of Congress who are interested in some judicial reform that just happens to include changes encompassing grand jury oversight? What if I told you this young prosecutor was looking for a high profile case that could aid him in the eye of the public?"

"If you are asking me to set up the Senator," interrupted A.T., "I won't agree to do that."

"Nothing of the sort," said Gerald. "There are two things the young prosecutor would get. First, there would be a high profile murder case. Let's say the murder case of the individual who we know murdered Samantha."

"Good luck with that," said A.T. "If you are talking about Victor Salensky, if I'm not mistaken, he is still at large. In fact, I was a bit jumpy about coming here today after I got an email from Allen's son, Eric, about Salensky's escape. Plus, I thought I saw him here at the cemetery."

"You did," said Gerald. "Some of my associates tailed him here since we felt there was a good chance he might be here. Oftentimes, as sick as it sounds, many of these types of ego-centered hit men will actually attend the funerals of the people they have murdered. As it turns out, he was no different. Additionally, we had a very good hunch he would be following you after he escaped. You were going to be his next target whether commissioned or not. You were some unfinished business he felt he needed to resolve. In other words, he had you marked."

"Are you saying your people were tailing him and he is planning for me to be his next mark? So, I've been the bait?" asked A.T.

"Better than that," commented Gerald. "Our people, in conjunction with some local authorities, whom we trust implicitly, have just taken Victor into custody. He was carrying a weapon, plus a silencer that undoubtedly fit the firearm. Let me assure you he won't escape this time. Immediately after the service I was told another man was also taken into custody. The man was a sort of emaciated guy by the name of Leslie, who claims he had no knowledge that Victor was carrying a weapon. Yes, you were the bait in a sense. It was simply due to your tying Victor to Samantha's death."

"So, how does all of this help the young prosecutor you have mentioned, and how does it get the Senator to change his mind?" asked A.T.

"It's a bit complicated, but let me explain," answered Gerald. "The young prosecutor makes a deal with Victor in exchange for his plea of guilty and for Victor identifying the people who have been hiring him to perform their dirty work. Victor will do life instead of the death penalty. For your information, New York still technically has the death penalty, although it hasn't been used since 1963 when Eddie Mays was executed at Sing Sing. Since that time, capital punishment has been declared unconstitutional, but then former Governor Pataki signed a law that once again allowed for capital punishment. However, that was declared unconstitutional, and former Governor Patterson signed an order that disestablished the penalty. The matter is still controversial enough that some prosecutors, including the Senator's young prosecutor friend, still argue in favor of such a penalty. Therefore, the young prosecutor gets some immediate attention; plus, it will give him cause to stand on the soap box relative to a pet project of his, which ironically is grand jury reform. You should like that. Additionally, and quite fortunately, the young prosecutor is a protégé of the Senator. You are a key witness for the prosecutor in nailing Victor. I suspect you will also be a key witness in bringing 'Squeaky' and 'Big John' to justice, especially since you have a video recording of their confessions from a recording device you used -"

"How do you know about that?" interrupted A.T.

"Did I mention that Lee Mattson, the Senator's aide, and I are dear friends," commented Gerald.

"You did," responded A.T. "What about Lee Mattson? How does he fit into the plan, and just how am I going to get the grand jury reform issue back in front of the Senator?"

"First things first. In a minute I will come to the issue of Lee Mattson. In regard to the matter of grand jury reform, you won't need to be the one to ask," answered Gerald. "The young prosecutor has grand jury reform as a pet project of his, and he will be the one to beg the Senator, his mentor, for it. The only problem is the young prosecutor wants more power for the prosecutor rather than less -"

"How nice," interrupted A.T. "That's the opposite of what I want."

"Indeed it is," smiled Gerald. "However, you have the evidence that can demonstrate the need for oversight and not greater power to the prosecutor. So once the Senator's subcommittee is convened, your evidence will get presented, and the Senator and his committee will be compelled to look at reform and oversight rather than an expansion of powers. That will place the Senator in a position to then tell his new protégé essentially what he told you. More particularly, there is nothing he can do since the matter will be out of his hands and in the hands of the subcommittee. Then and because of the Senator attempting to please his young protégé, you will get your shot at reform while the young prosecutor will be like you are now, on the sidelines. And as an added bonus, a New York detective will be charged for his efforts in helping Victor Salensky escape. Don't thank me now, but this will all be made possible by your friends at the GGG."

"So, as I understand it," said A.T., "the young prosecutor gets a major and high profile murder case against Victor Salensky in front of the public that will result in a plea deal, as well as my evidence and testimony against 'Squeaky' and 'Big John' before the grand jury. Salensky gets life instead of the death penalty. The detective gets charged, and the young prosecutor also gets at least a chance to get in front of the Senator's subcommittee since the Senator will grant him the favor because of their relationship. 'Squeaky' and 'Big John' will get indicted."

"Right!" exclaimed Father Gerald. "The Senator can favor his young protégé by opening a subcommittee hearing relative to grand jury reform. Next, the young prosecutor will think the effort to open a subcommittee hearing is to expand the power of a prosecutor. Meanwhile you get a chance to present your evidence and investigation before the same subcommittee of the Senator where the issues of reform and oversight get presented. The Senator can save face with his young protégé; plus, the Senator still has his subcommittee conduct a hearing on campaign finance reform."

"If those facts are understood correctly by me, I still have two questions," said A.T. "What happens to Lee, and what does Gerald get?"

"Lee will have to face the consequences of his own acts. He will, no doubt, agree to testify against the people at LESTER. In exchange, he will probably get a suspended sentence of some sort, unless he is more involved than we realize at this point in time. It's not what I get but what the GGG gets," commented Gerald. "The evidence against the group called LESTER and their ties to Osborne Leeds, 'Squeaky,' 'Big John,' and Victor will be presented to the Senator and to the young prosecutor in New York. They, in turn, will be able to show the public how they are cleaning up one of the most corrupt groups of people to come along as they forge ahead with the prosecutions and campaign reform. And not least of all, your wife, Jacci, gets you back safe and sound."

"Are you sure that there isn't something in it for Gerald, excuse me, Father Gerald?" asked A.T.

"Well, maybe just a bit of ego satisfaction and the fact that, at least in my own mind, I will be able to put to rest to some degree a minor and age-old issue between Lee and me. If Lee is implicated with LESTER as your evidence would indicate, then someone will need to console Lee's wife, who was my college sweetheart before she fell in love with Lee, who, as I mentioned, was my roommate. That's perhaps what finally drove me into the priesthood. Don't get me wrong," insisted Gerald, "the priesthood has been very good to me, and I have absolutely no interest in any form of personal relationship with her now; nevertheless, it might be a gratifying position for me to be in. It might be interesting for her to find out she picked the wrong guy. Now that I said that, I suppose I will have to add it to my next confession. However, facts are facts, and we must all face the truth sooner or later."

"It looks like you and the GGG have planned this well," commented A.T. "The only person who has lost it all has been Samantha. What a price she has had to pay."

The three of them bowed their heads, silently shook hands, and walked their separate ways with A.T. and Jacci heading to their rental car and Gerald disappearing back toward the gravesite.

Walking away, A.T. couldn't help but wonder exactly what, in addition to a phone number and photograph, was in the large envelope he had been handed by Sister Nan.

NOVEL CHARACTERS:

None of the characters that are portrayed in this novel, except for publicly known figures, are real. Although many of the events portrayed in this fictional account are based upon actual occurrences, the characters in this novel are imaginary and are not intended to be real people. All of the names of the individual characters created for this novel are fictitious, including but not limited to the following:

S.A. (Special Agent) Mark Coffee is a Special Agent with the FBI who participates in the arrest and transfer of A.T. Van Doren.

S.A. (Special Agent) William Stern is a Special Agent with the FBI who joins S.A. Coffee to serve the arrest warrant on A.T. Van Doren.

Judge Rice is the federal judge who issues the arrest warrant of A.T. Van Doren and instructs S.A. Coffee and S.A. Stern to take Mr. Van Doren to a county jail facility.

Milford Dunreath is the United States Attorney who authorized the arrest of A.T.

A.T. Van Doren, (A.T.), a former FBI agent and former prosecutor, is charged with a criminal offense he did not commit. When he conducts a counter-investigation, he finds that individuals from his political past have used their positions within the DOJ and the FBI to attempt to discredit him. He exposes an intricate web of political deceit and intrigue.

Jacci Van Doren, the wife of A.T. Van Doren, unwittingly gets drawn into assisting her husband in determining that "things are seldom as they seem" when she helps sort through the deceptive interests of former political allies.

George Lipke is a supposed coconspirator with A.T.; however, he is not known to A.T. and has never had any relationship with A.T.

Pat Merrick, like Lipke, is a supposed coconspirator with A.T.; however, he is not known to A.T. and has never had any relationship with A.T.

W.J. Perry, like Lipke, is a supposed coconspirator with A.T.; however, he is not known to A.T. and has never had any relationship with A.T.

Darrel Simpson, like Lipke, is a supposed coconspirator with A.T.; however, he is not known to A.T. and has never had any relationship with A.T.

Lester Gee, like Lipke, is a supposed coconspirator with A.T.; however, he is not known to A.T. and has never had any relationship with A.T.

Albert Cherry, like Lipke, is a supposed coconspirator with A.T.; however, he is not known to A.T. and has never had any relationship with A.T.

Ralph Nester, like Lipke, is a supposed coconspirator with A.T.; however, A.T. was actually conducting an investigative due diligence on Nester.

Julian Tilson-Gould is an old political friend of A.T. from years earlier when both of them worked in Republican politics. As a result of her political activities, she ended up working in the White House for nearly eight years.

Blaine Jeffers is also an old political friend of A.T. who worked on various political campaigns with him many years earlier.

Blaine is also a very trusted friend who shares many of the same philosophies with A.T.

Angel McCoy-Jeffers, the wife of Blaine Jeffers, is also a former political friend whose father was active in the Republican Party in the state of California.

Leslie Winthrop was an old political acquaintance of A.T. and took over A.T.'s position with the Republican Party when A.T. decided to abandon any further active participation in Republican Party politics.

Dotty Winthrop is the devoted wife of Leslie Winthrop.

Osborne Leeds, a former assistant United States Attorney, now in the private practice of law in Washington D.C., is a principal in the operations and organization of a group known as LESTER.

Victor Salensky, a former military specialist, holds an independent contractor status with LESTER through his relationship with Osborne Leeds.

Aaron Farmer, a former DOJ attorney who was brought onto the LESTER committee by Osborne Leeds. Currently, Mr. Farmer is one of the clerks for a justice on the United States Supreme Court, as well as performing particular duties for LESTER.

The United States Senator, whose name remains undisclosed for the novel, became a good friend of A.T. when the two of them worked on a case of political corruption years earlier while A.T. worked for a former state prosecutor. The Senator and A.T. team up in this investigation as well.

Bud Hawthorne is a political operative who has worked for both Republicans and Democrats. After working for several months in the office of the Vice President while Dick Cheney held the office, Bud left and began working as a freelance investigative reporter. He is related to the Senator and previously worked with A.T. years ago on a political corruption case.

Robert Wellington is a former Navy Seal who, after tours of duty in both Iraq and Afghanistan, brings a matter to the attention of the Senator and Bud Hawthorne. He joins A.T. in part of the investigation.

James Robbins, currently an engineer and the son of a deceased urologist from Cincinnati who was a friend of the Senator. Because of his knowledge of Kentucky, he is able to assist A.T., the Senator, and Robert in conducting a part of the investigation.

Rosey (fictional name for Ruth [last name unknown]), is a good friend of James Robbins and is helpful relative to the identities of certain individuals under investigation.

Professor Charles Brougham is a former adjunct economics professor who began working with the Good Government Group (GGG) but decided to leave under unique circumstances, taking with him some key Accounting documents that become a part of the investigation.

Billy Simonson is an informant for Bud Hawthorne and provides some inside information relative to certain paramilitary groups operating in the U.S. and particularly in the Houston area.

Allen Rodriquez Aranda is a good friend of A.T. Van Doren and assists him in his investigative efforts. Allen Aranda is also a former U.S. Marshall and was a former desk supervisor of Interpol in Paris, France, during an exchange operation with the U.S. Marshall Service.

Jean Paul Valance is a French banker who is a personal friend of Bud Hawthorne. When Mr. Valance is made aware of certain international banking irregularities, he contacts Bud with information that is conveyed to A.T. Van Doren for his investigation.

Rene LePonte is a member of the Paris police department. Years earlier he and Allen Aranda became friends while both worked for INTERPOL. Allen introduces A.T. Van Doren to Mr. LePonte while A.T.'s investigation takes place in Europe.

Michelle LePonte, the wife of Rene LePonte, is also a friend of Allen Aranda and is introduced to A.T.

Jacques Bouline, a police officer with the Paris police department, works for Rene LePonte and is introduced to A.T. and Allen Aranda in order to assist them while the investigation continues in France and Switzerland.

Claude Schmidt, a Swiss banker, is introduced to A.T. and Allen by Jean Paul Valance during the investigation that is conducted in Europe. Mr. Schmidt provides crucial information about certain offshore and questionable banking practices that are used by certain U.S. companies and individuals.

Cynthia Brownell, the lady friend of Allen Aranda, is an employee of a major news network and becomes involved in the investigation when she agrees to exchange information that she has with A.T.

'Squeaky' Brent Wilson, an aging investigator with a political agenda who hires himself out as an independent contractor for an entity known as LESTER. His job is to perform certain assignments on behalf of large corporate interests and the interests of LESTER.

'Big John' Harry Johnson, an aging investigator with a political agenda who works with 'Squeaky' Wilson, hires himself out as an independent contractor for an entity known as LESTER. His job is to perform certain assignments on behalf of large corporate interests and the interests of LESTER.

Will Blake, a mentor of A.T. Van Doren, agrees to assist A.T. in his investigation and in the process agrees to "hold" certain documentary evidence that is used in the investigation.

Marjorie Blake, wife of Will Blake, assists her husband in the safekeeping of critical investigative matters and evidence.

Del Hudson, a former FBI agent and confidant of A.T. Van Doren and Will Blake, is considered as one of the individuals designated to "hold" critical evidence for A.T. and the Senator.

Bob Billings, a court reporter friend of A.T., who gets officially involved in the investigation as a certified court reporter, travels with A.T. in order to take official statements of various witnesses.

Gerald Peterson, who initially appears to be a nemesis of A.T., begins to play a significant role in the investigation at every opportunity. Assigned with a particular task while conducting his own investigation, he attempts to team up with A.T. in order to direct the investigation as his benefactors require.

Samantha Nguyen-Plantagenet-Henderson is a very attractive and mysterious lady, who continues to "pop-up," in the oddest places, while A.T. conducts his investigation. A.T. learns that Samantha has her own agenda as she attempts to fulfill her assignment on behalf of an entity known as GGG.

Sunny, mother-in-law to A.T., does her part to aid her daughter, Jacci, and her son-in-law, A.T.

Lee Mattson, who works for the Senator, has a significant involvement on behalf of the Senator's office, as well as, a hidden relationship with LESTER.

Lisa Nadler is one of the aides to the United States Senator and an old friend of A.T. Van Doren.

Samuel Bernstein is one of the aides to the United States Senator and an old friend of A.T. Van Doren.

Fr. Albert Wendling, a Catholic priest and old friend of A.T., is used in name only by Gerald Peterson in order to attempt to convince A.T. to join forces with Gerald Peterson in continuing the investigation.

Wilbert Edison (a/k/a Norvell Emerson) is a current FBI agent who is engaged in activities that are not known by the FBI. Those activities involve the dissemination of information from FBI files not authorized as Edison conducts investigative work for a subversive political group existing within the DOJ and the FBI.

George Tarkanian (a/k/a George Teller, a/k/a George Kowalski) is a current FBI agent who is engaged in activities unknown by the FBI. Those activities involve the dissemination of information from FBI files not authorized as Tarkanian conducts investigative work for a subversive political group existing within the DOJ and the FBI.

New Vista Mesa is a shell company set up by Edison and Tarkanian in order to attempt to "set up" political enemies.

Adam Van Doren, son of A.T. and Jacci Van Doren and law associate in A.T.'s law firm, is the principal of a high tech company that develops various and useable "tools" for surveillance and recordation for investigative purposes.

Rachael Van Doren is a daughter of A.T. and Jacci Van Doren.

Renee' Van Doren is a daughter of A.T. and Jacci Van Doren.

Remington is A.T.'s pet dog.

George Orville Felthaus, a former DOJ attorney, becomes a key witness for A.T. and the Senator in the investigation.

Eric Aranda, the son of Allen Aranda, is a Washington D.C. detective who gets involved in the investigation.

Gretchen Locksley, an employee of the GGG, develops a relationship with Professor Brougham that, by design, brings professor Brougham into tighter control of the GGG.

Lon Jeffers is the son of Blaine and Angel Jeffers.

Grayson Jeffers is the son of Blaine and Angel Jeffers.

Blake Jeffers is the son of Blaine and Angel Jeffers.

Bernie Gould, the husband to Julian Tilson-Gould, is an activist in the Republican Party of California and a friend of A.T., the Jeffers, and other political activists.

Congressman Buck Phillips, friend of Samantha Nguyen-Henderson, becomes an unwitting witness for the Senator and the investigation that is being submitted to a Senate subcommittee.

S.A. Richard (Rick) Helms, a retired FBI agent and friend of A.T., assists A.T. near the end of the investigation as significant issues develop.

Daniel Frank is a New York employee of the GGG.

GGG Group, also known as the Good Government Group, is an international organization that has existed for many years and it boasts that it has influenced many governments in a "positive" way over the years. Its membership is from various locations across the globe and is dominated through European influence.

LESTER committee, otherwise known as the Legislative Enterprise and Study To End Restrictions. It was founded by a number of very wealthy individuals, along with a number of former members of the Department of Justice.

Lord Francoise Toulouse was a former member and Master/Lord of the GGG. His great granddaughter, Samantha Nguyen-Henderson, has contracted to perform specific investigative tasks for the GGG.

GGG Member Sir Reginald is the current Master & Lord of the GGG.

GGG Member Chang is a member of the GGG from the Far East.

Jeanette Joens is a secretary to Lance Jensen, Director of Maintenance, at Patterson General Hospital.

Lance Jensen is currently Director of Maintenance at Patterson General Hospital.

Rob Lindsey currently heads the custodial crew at Patterson General where he works for Lance James.

Tommy Gardner currently works for Rob Lindsey as a custodian at Patterson General.

Charles Beecher currently is the Director of Security at Patterson General Hospital. He was a former detective with the Patterson Police Department.

Fred Sullinger is the Assistant Director of Security at Patterson General.

Reggie Stanton is a very large and muscular member of the security department at Patterson General where he works for Charles Beecher.

Dr. William Farnsworth is the Head of Psychiatry at Patterson General.

Alicia Gardner is the secretary to Charles Beecher in the security department at Patterson General.

Officer Terry Mills is a member of the Patterson Police Department.

Officer Aaron Robbins is a member of the Patterson Police Department.

Dr. Warton is in actuality **Victor Salensky** who works for Osborne Leeds and the LESTER committee.

Sister Nan is a Catholic Nun who is the actual sister to Samantha Nguyen-Henderson.

EPILOGUE:

The events that are portrayed in this novel include a mixture of actual occurrences, historic political activity, and some fictional interactions that have been combined in order to bring key elements of the story line together. Efforts to alter the operations of the United States government in order to serve a hidden political agenda, including the infiltration of the Department of Justice (DOJ) and the Federal Bureau of Investigation (FBI) have been taking place for several decades. The methodologies described in the novel, including the questionable "proactive approach," are often used by the DOJ and the FBI to "trap" particular parties. As a result, it is often an innocent individual, actually the victim of a crime, who is recklessly coupled in an indictment with targeted and known criminals by overzealous prosecutors and careless FBI agents who have lost their ethical compass. There is an aggressive practice and belief by certain DOJ prosecutors and FBI agents that by including victims in an indictment, the victim will say or do about anything as a "friendly" witness instead of confronting the financial strength and power of the federal government.

As it now stands, the federal grand jury system is out of balance and has often become simply a rubber stamp facility for whatever fancies the mind of a politically ambitious prosecutor. Today, there is no oversight to the grand jury system in the United States; consequently, it has been seriously abused.

The power manifested in both the DOJ and the FBI cannot be overlooked as certain individuals within those agencies have positioned themselves to bring about their own political objectives. Although most attorneys within the DOJ and most agents operating within the FBI are honest and dedicated individuals, there are political operatives who have infiltrated both agencies in order to see that certain political and/or personal agendas take place. Ties between some very well-funded private entities and individuals have been linked to individuals within these government agencies. Unfortunately, those entities and individuals are determined to use both the DOJ and the FBI as their personal instruments of supposed enforcement in their efforts to promote and carry out their private political objectives.

Once a person has been falsely accused through an indictment and once those false accusations have been publicized, it is virtually impossible to remove the stigma and public perception that remains. Sadly, that is true regardless of whether the case against an accused is dismissed or if there is an acquittal. The most difficult task is finding the strength and heart to forgive those who have acted so recklessly or maliciously to have brought such charges in the first place. It is true that "to forgive is divine"; but we humans are far from divine. It is the belief of this author that a novel on the subject serves a greater purpose than a stilted effort to forgive.

The motivating force behind this novel was what has been perceived as reckless and outrageous conduct by certain employees within the Department of Justice (DOJ) and the Federal Bureau of Investigation (FBI), who rendered an indictment that was ultimately dismissed against this author. In actuality, the author, a former FBI agent and former prosecutor, was conducting a due diligence investigation on various venture funding operatives who had secured significant funds (nearly $500,000) from a corporation represented by the author. The author had filed an official complaint with one FBI Field Office relative to a venture funding source with direct connections to other venture sources that were the subject of the due diligence being conducted by the author. This FBI Field Office properly determined that the author and his company had been victims of criminal activity and even recovered some funds. In so doing, this FBI Field Office and its agents performed admirably and properly.

Meanwhile, other FBI agents and DOJ attorneys, who were operating a task force through a second FBI Field Office, deviated from enumerated guidelines, including those in the FBI Manual and the Undercover Operations Manual when they failed to check the FBI indices as one of the first required actions regarding any investigation. When later confronted, they admitted that they had failed to check the indices relative to the author. Had they done so they would have determined that the author, who was a former FBI agent, had been a complaining victim and had been conducting a due diligence on the very people whom the task force was allegedly investigating. Unfortunately, it was because of the author's due diligence that his name became familiar to a defendant in another matter (a supposed informant) who sought to plea bargain with the DOJ and FBI. Informants will often say and do anything in order to lessen a sentence they may be facing.

Ultimately, numerous invitations were extended by the task force to the author inviting him to attend meetings set up by the task force. All invitations were refused except the one where the task force represented that a company it operated was interested in providing venture funding to the author's client/company. At that single meeting the author was introduced to parties who he did not know and with whom he had no dealings. The task force completely missed the fact that the author and his company had been determined by another FBI Field Office to be the victims of criminal activity by the very venture funding people who introduced the author to one of the individuals the task force was attempting to trap. That individual was acquitted in the case. Before that individual was tried and acquitted, his attorney contacted the author's attorney to see if the author would be willing to testify as a witness. When this was reported to the prosecutor through legal counsel, the prosecutor in the case advised in an email to the author's attorney that if the author testified, he might face a re-indictment. Obviously this was an example of a federal prosecutor's attempt to intimidate a witness who had been dismissed from the case.

After the indictment, once it had been determined that certain exculpatory evidence had been withheld and that audio tapes had been altered with portions of conversations missing, the author began a counter investigation. The counter investigation revealed many surprises including the fact that certain political contacts and outside motivations were involved. When this novel was drafted, it originally included over one hundred and seventy pages of supporting documentation that were to be included as "End Notes"; however, the addition of that material would have made the book far too long. It was decided to save the "End Notes" for a separate endeavor.

ACKNOWLEDGMENTS:

Although it is not possible for this author to set forth the names of the many individuals who provided moral support and legal counsel for the author or to those who assisted with efforts to complete this novel, particular individuals deserve special recognition. In alphabetical order those individuals are as follows:

Marty Berry, the quintessential English teacher, whose editing skills and patience with the changing story line were invaluable. Her assistance is most deeply appreciated since a readable novel would not have been possible without her editing efforts.

Attorney Patrick DeLong, who, along with his law firm of Wicker, Smith, O'Hara, McCoy & Ford, P.A., made remarkable efforts in pursuit of a case on behalf of the author and his company to recover funds paid to a venture funding source that made unfounded claims of having ties to the Federal Reserve. I am also indebted to him for his referral to Attorney John Early.

Attorney John Early, whose unparalleled good legal counsel made it possible for the Department of Justice to see that it had made a mistake and needed to dismiss the case against this author. Mr. Early's extraordinary knowledge of federal criminal procedure, his research skills, and his ability to craft concise legal briefs on key legal issues are without peer. I will be forever indebted to him.

Attorney Jerald Kinnamon, whose careful evaluation of the facts and his ability to assess the law that related to various defenses was particularly helpful. Without his assistance, the entire body of defenses would not have been fully assessed. I will be forever indebted to him.

Attorney Jon Kinnamon, whose ability to assess and explain the various legal concepts set forth in the numerous cases that related to outrageous government conduct was essential. His dogged

ACKNOWLEDGMENTS:

determination to sort out those legal concepts as they related to particular defenses was critical. I will be forever indebted to him.

Attorney Mark Meyer, whose extraordinary patience and steady legal abilities were vital to many aspects of the case in formulating appropriate responses to government pleadings. His appearance in the local federal court and his willingness to be present during a troubling time were of immeasurable value. I will be forever indebted to him.

Bette Tropek Miller, who added the burden of editing this novel to her busy schedule of teaching college English classes. Professor Miller's editing skills and untold patience through the constant review of the written material proved to be helpful, essential, and necessary. Without her editing assistance, this novel would not have been possible. Her help is deeply appreciated.

Heather Pundt, who knew that the truth would prevail.

Jennifer Pundt, who knew that the truth would prevail.

Joyce Pundt, who has provided unfaltering support, stability, dignity, and grace throughout this entire ordeal that have been essential to my well-being. Her patience, deliberate evaluation of the novel, and the assistance in the editing process is far more appreciated than anyone would realize.

Attorney Vince Pundt, whose daily support, legal research, and constant good counsel have been without flaw, and were necessary for my maintaining direction throughout a life-altering ordeal. In addition to his legal research, his technical knowledge of electronic media and the ability to research that media for necessary information have been flawless in my attempts to clear my name.

Attorney Les Stokke, whose legal advice, research, support, appearances at hearings, including travel to California, and his good legal counsel have been critical and essential to my case and well-being. His efforts to assist me in clearing my name are also appreciated. I will be forever indebted to him.

Attorney Larry Thorson, whose professional advice and personal support, including his travel to California, in assistance with efforts to clear my name, have been most appreciated. I will be forever indebted to him.

Investigative Reporter Joseph Trento, whose knowledge of writing and publishing has been crucial. The experience that he was willing to share from his many publications, including his award winning efforts, was essential to this work being completed. He has been more than supportive and essential to this work.

Undisclosed sources have been most helpful in bringing forth the facts and details about the many government officials, along with insight into the operations of the Department of Justice and the Federal Bureau of Investigation. Needless to say, those efforts are deeply appreciated.

Additionally, I am grateful for the support that was provided by numerous individuals to whom my gratitude cannot be overstated. Included within that body of people are the following: Retired Judge, the Honorable Robert Ford; former U.S. Marshalls, Roger Aerghica and Dennis Blome; former FBI agents, Dick Heft, Bernie Brown, and John Schweibert; former law partners, Phil Klinger and Mike Sheehey; former DCI agent, Mike Marlin; Father George and Reverend Bill Harnish; friends, John Leland, Bill Cubbage, Carol Cubbage, Jerry Chaffee, Jim Kemp, Charlie Weepie, Mary Harker, Amy Fischel; and neighbors, Dr. Wayne Alberts and Dan Meyer. There are many more, and for their support I am very grateful, as well.

Finally, what has happened to me has happened to others and I would love to hear those stories. In such instances, please feel free to drop me a note at: Three Tree Ridge Publishing, Ltd., 330 First Street S.E., Cedar Rapids, Iowa 52401.

www.ingramcontent.com/pod-product-compliance
Lightning Source LLC
Chambersburg PA
CBHW071329020726
47502CB00001B/23